1969

A BRIEF AND BEAUTIFUL TRIP BACK

FIRST EDITION PUBLISHED JANUARY 2019

Cover design by Dazz Media

Library of Congress Cataloging-in-Publication Data has been applied for.

ISBN 978-0-578-48779-3

10 9 8 7 6 5 4 3 2 1

Acknowledgements

To IT: the Truth and those who search for it.

To my Creator: whatever force there is that has blessed me with the opportunity to share this story and has lit that spark of inspiration that has turned into a mighty flame, continually stoked and fanned by the Universal Mind.

To my mom: you were the first person I shared this story with and your enthusiasm, excitement, and open communication aided the writing of this novel more than you could ever know.

To my dad: for providing me with a solid foundation to build on and a childhood from which the inherent ideas for this novel have sprung. For your stories and your support, thank you.

To my fourth grade teacher, Mrs. Treglia: for nurturing that flame and encouraging it to burn bright.

To George: for recommending *The Electric Kool-Aid Acid Test* to me. This story in its current form would never have been conceived—let alone written—without you.

To Goosedove: for sending me in the right direction.

To Anderson: for being there. For your love and for your mind, a million thanks. I love you.

In Commemoration

"We're all one. The deeper I got into it the more I realized that there was a different force working. The only mistake we ever made as a force was thinking for a while that we were going to win. We developed vested interests in the victory to come and began to parcel off into little groups. And all of a sudden we're all jumping up and down in front of it until nobody can see it clear anymore. If we never made this mistake we would have been way ahead and this is sort of why I am retiring from the ranks. It's something about what we're doing that we are meant to lose."

—Ken Kesey [Swashbuckler] (September 17, 1935-November 10, 2001)

"Today a young man on acid realized that all matter is merely energy condensed to a slow vibration—that we are all one consciousness experiencing itself subjectively—there's no such thing as death, life is only a dream, and we are the imagination of ourselves."

—Bill Hicks (December 16, 1961-February 26, 1994)

"It's a funny thing, but when you're dealing with your information second-hand, it all gets very distorted. You produce a very strange version of the thing that inspired you."

—Pete Brown

1969

A BRIEF AND BEAUTIFUL TRIP BACK

∞

SEA GUDINSKI

PART I

…It was hot in Fresno.

I might venture to remind you… So hot, in fact, that even the window air conditioning unit in my mother's garage could not keep the sweat from beading on our foreheads. It feels to me like a very long time ago, but I remember it as clearly as if it were yesterday…

I sat on a wooden barstool and gazed out the dirty window, one hand on the pane, the other twirling a drumstick around my fingers. The sweltering June air outside hung motionless and thick, and the air inside was without much improvement. Cars passed slowly on 7th Street that day. I lifted a towel off of the barstool, wiped my face, and swiveled the chair back around, away from the window. The scene that I witnessed was typical of a Sunday afternoon: our band was gathered in my garage, rehearsing for an upcoming gig. In those days, we mainly hung out and rehearsed at Marty's, but that afternoon, the heat had driven us back to my place.

We had been practicing for about an hour already and were taking a smoke break. Marty popped a lit Marlboro between his lips and riffed off the beginning of the Stones' *Satisfaction* on his brand new red Gibson. He leaned against a barstool, one foot on the gray cement floor and one balanced on the footrest. He wore baggy denim jeans with the knees torn out, a dark blue sweatshirt with the sleeves cut off, and his dirty Converse sneaker tapped on the floor as he kept time without me on the kit. His head was cocked to the left, listening closely as he played, and a string of white puka shells encircled his neck. His eyes were closed, and his greasy black hair, parted neatly in the middle, fell in front of his eyes and curled behind his ears in the back. His expression was thoughtful and intent, all of his staunch virility was channeled into the task at hand. He played perfectly; every note was clear and defined and timed impeccably—the result of countless hours of dedicated practice. He did the song justice, it was the type of playing Keith Richards would be proud of.

Shania stood alongside Marty in front of the air conditioner while she tied her long ochre hair back into a ponytail. She was dressed in a sleeveless white lace outfit, which looked outstanding on her sporty build and against her olive skin. Her dark, amiable eyes were wide open as she watched Marty play, and her lips moved slightly as she silently recited the lyrics that she knew by heart.

Leanne was perched next to her on the third barstool, her delicate shoulders hunched over as she tuned her signature teal Les Paul bass. Her hair—fire-engine red in color at that time—reached to the middle of her back; it had been combed to one side and flat-ironed within an inch of its life. The color contrasted drastically against her pallid skin, and her piercing green eyes gazed out from underneath her red bangs which were so long that they almost reached the bridge of her nose. A cigarette was balanced between her lips, and I watched as she inhaled once, twice, and then blew the smoke out through her nostrils. She waved her hand sharply in front of her face to clear the cloud that had formed, enough to reveal the shiny black ring that hung from her nose. She was dressed in a black Led Zeppelin t-shirt, a checkered flannel, black jeans, and a pair of Dr. Martens. Despite the heat, Leanne never adjusted her wardrobe, even while the rest of us were practically stripping.

Behind Leanne, Jeff squatted down next to the cooler, popped the cap off a Coors, and wiped his hands on his khaki cut-offs before downing half of it and letting out an unnecessarily loud belch. He stood up, grinned, and tipped the bottle in my direction. His brown hair was cut in a vertical stripe down the length of his head—which he usually wore spiked up in a Mohawk but today had been combed flat—and beads of perspiration ran down his face and bare chest. I held up my hands and caught the beer that he chucked in my direction, then spun the barstool back around to face the window.

My daydreams always begin with a drumbeat: slow, concise—like a heartbeat manifesting the imagery I conjure up into the realm of reality. At first, that is all I hear—my drumbeat—and then quickly, quietly, the rest of the band starts to fade in. It begins with Marty and Jeff on their guitars—heavy and dynamic—and Leanne on bass—melodic and contemplative—and finally, Shania's voice emerges out of the brew—strong and powerful—orchestrating my reverie.

Initially, I can only hear, but as the song ends and I strike the final beat, the scene in front of me is transformed so that my reverie encompasses my entire visual field. From behind my drum kit, I can see Jeff, Marty, and Shania standing in front of me, the three of them facing out into a sprawling audience. This is nothing like the abject handful of leftover hippies that used to come and watch us perform at The Joint on Friday and Saturday nights; from the elevated stage I can see that the club is packed from wall to wall, and they are all cheering, loudly chanting: *'Encore! Encore!'* A haze of smoke and incense swirls above them in the mystique darkness and settles around us on the stage. The room smells like weed and booze and stale tobacco, and on the second floor of the club, a line of go-go cages are occupied by several scantily-clad female dancers. The audience turns away from them and crowds around the stage instead. Jeff arches his back and pumps his fist in the air, and Marty throws both his arms up, palms out, and backs away from the mic, shouting something that is drowned out by the audience's applause. Shania places the microphone back in the stand, takes a corner of her dress in each hand, and curtsies for the insatiable crowd. I turn to my right and shoot Leanne a grin—this, indeed, is satisfaction.

"Rhiannon…"

My eyes snapped open, and I spun around. Marty stood there with his hand on my shoulder and his guitar strap around his neck. I shook my head to reorient myself with reality, then hopped off the barstool with my sticks in hand and took a seat behind my drum kit as dignified as possible.

A smirk slid across Marty's face, "You're a chronic dreamer, Rhiannon," he said, shaking his head.

"Are we gonna run through that one again?" I asked in an attempt to gauge how long I'd been absent from the conversation.

Marty shrugged and glanced at Jeff, who polished off his beer and dropped the empty bottle back into the cooler, "I think that sounded pretty tight, it's your call, man."

I reached down under my stool to grab a smoke, expecting to hear Jeff's reply, but instead what I heard was the sound of the heavy wooden door from the kitchen swinging open suddenly and slamming against the railing at the top of the stairs. A feeling of dread and impending doom rushed through me, and I glanced up as my mother stepped into the room.

She was wearing freshly starched church clothes and had a white cardigan draped over one arm. Her wardrobe alone, never mind the rest of her, was enough to get me to start sweating again. Her blue eyes bulged wide behind her wire-rimmed glasses in apparent disbelief at what she was seeing. She wore a permanent scowl on her face, and her lips were pursed tight as if she was not sure where to begin. Boy, was I in for it now.

"Rhiannon Karlson! What in God's name do you think you're doing?!" her voice shook and her face grew increasingly red as she surveyed the scene. The five of us exchanged various frustrated glances—she wasn't supposed to be home for at least another hour.

She stared at me, her face twisted and distorted, searching for an explanation and an answer. I provided neither and stared back defiantly.

"Rhiannon, I leave the house for a few hours on a Sunday morning and what do you do? Not only do you bring the devil's music into this house, but these dirty louts as well! You should be in church!" she hollered, gesturing to indicate Leanne and Marty who, like the rest of us, had begun to pack up their instruments at lightning speed.

This wasn't the first time my mother had barged in on one of our rehearsals, and we all knew that the best course of action was to leave the fire zone as quickly as possible. As everybody else scrambled to gather their things, I stayed silent as my mother continued her verbal barrage, her voice raising with each syllable. She had a loud, nasally voice which was especially irritating when she was angry with me, and in those days that was just about all of the time. Her tone of voice was critical and condescending—not to mention obnoxious. I had long grown used to these types of encounters. She was easily incited by the pettiest of ordeals; however, as of late, the bulk of our disputes were in regard to my musical career. She didn't much object to my drumming—in fact, she even acknowledged my talent—however, when it came to us and our band, she seemed to become increasingly disgruntled.

It didn't take long for us to disperse. With guitar cases and amps in tow, Shania, Jeff, and Leanne ran out the side door. A wave of oppressive heat from outside passed over the room and for a moment, so did a wave of nausea.

Marty was the last one out the door, "Good luck," he called back

4

with a sneer directed toward my mother.

I rested my elbows on my knees and hung my head between my legs until the nausea passed. With the slam of the door my mother had gone silent, and now she just eyed me with a look of complete and utter disappointment on her face—which pissed me off even more than her screeching.

"Rhiannon—"

"What?" I snapped back.

She recoiled, "You need to learn how to control your attitude!"

"What fucking attitude?! You're the one who barged in here in the middle of our rehearsal!"

"You know you're not allowed to rehearse here! And don't use that language with me, girl, I'll wash your mouth out with soap!"

"I'd like to see you try!" I retorted.

"I know who it is you learn these antics from, those no-good friends of yours, that's who!"

"There's nothing wrong with my friends, Mom, I've known them since high school!"

"I didn't approve of them then, and they're only worse now!" she yelled.

"What the hell is wrong with my friends?"

"They look like thugs, they all need an attitude adjustment, and that kid with the black hair—"

"Marty?"

"Whatever. He's on dope, Rhiannon. And that girl with the ugly perm and that ring in her face—what a fake. They're deceiving you, Rhiannon!"

"He's not on dope, Mom!"

"Don't tell me he's not on dope, I know an addict when I see one! And this house smells disgusting—like cigarettes! They're bad influences, Rhiannon. You'll be out at a party or a gig and they'll offer you something… You won't even think twice! Jesus—"

"Would you shut up already?" I screamed back, finally losing my cool. "I don't give a damn what you think! You don't know anything about me, and you don't know anything about them either! Why don't you just leave me alone?!"

She shut up, but only for long enough to allow another searing breath to enter her lungs and reload another cartridge of verbal ammunition, "You haven't been the same since you graduated high school—you've been belligerent, rebellious, and disrespectful. You wouldn't be this way if you went to college instead of listening to and playing that obscene rock music day in and day out—it fills your head with lies and disturbs your spirit with illusions of grandeur. You think you're going to make it big and be a star and before you know it you're alone in an alley blue in the face with a needle in your arm, a crowd of junkies waiting around for you to die so they can strip you down and steal your fix!"

If I wasn't so angry, I would've laughed. As if she knew the first thing about being a performer—what a joke! "I think you're jealous," I shot back. "I think you're jealous of me because you never had any talent and never made it anywhere in life, divorced Dad and got stuck with me! I think you envy the fact that I have a chance to achieve my dreams and have satisfaction! I don't think you ever had any dreams or any talents at all—besides busting my ass all the time!"

She was substantially taken aback, "Well, look at you, knowing just about everything about your mother's life. For your information, I lived plenty of years before you were born. I've had many dreams—some of which I've seen achieved—and I have talents just as well as you do!"

"Yeah," I muttered under my breath, "you're a professional buzzkill."

"What was that?" she hissed.

"Nothing," I muttered before standing up and hopping off my bench, skirting around some of the equipment that had been left behind, and slamming the door behind me loud enough to rattle the hinges.

The heat hit me like a solid object, and the air was so thick it felt like I was walking through soup, but even the weather wasn't as oppressive as being in the same room as my mother. As I squinted through the waves of heat that rolled up the block, I saw that Marty's black, four-door pickup truck was idling at the corner, and I ran to it. When I reached it, I yanked open the back door and was immediately hit with a blast of revitalizing cold air from the A/C.

Marty glanced at me in the rearview mirror, "That couldn't have gone well," he said.

I shook my head and sank back into his gray interior, and Jeff switched on the radio as Marty shifted the truck into drive and slowly accelerated up the road.

This wasn't the first time I'd walked out on my mother during an argument, and it sure as hell would not be the last. If I didn't think my mother would notify every precinct in the state of California, I

6

would've moved out long ago; Marty and Jeff had been offering to take me in for years.

As far as any of us knew, Marty's father was some kind of a journalist, and since he traveled often for his work, was almost never home, so Marty had basically lived on his own since he'd started high school—I envied him more than I could ever tell you. Jeff moved out of his parents' house the summer before senior year and had gotten a two bedroom apartment with his older brother downtown—and had been offering me his couch on just about a weekly basis since. I mean, my mother wasn't such a bad mother, I guess. She fed me three times a day, went clothes shopping at Kmart once a month, made sure I went to class all 180 days of the school year, and didn't let me out of her sight until I was about fifteen. She was one of those parents that were overprotective to the point of obsession—I even checked my underwear every so often to make sure she hadn't sewn in GPS trackers. But it wasn't just that she was afraid something awful would happen to me—as mothers often are—instead, it seemed to be some groundless paranoia that I would go out for a night with my friends and come back a few hours later a raving drug addict or something of the sort. As a teenager and a musician, I smoked and drank—we all did. Those were things that just kind of came with the territory, but I stayed away from anything heavier than weed for the most part. It isn't as if I wasn't curious—I definitely was—but fear of what my mother would do if she found out and general apprehension kept my curiosity at bay.

As I sat there in Marty's truck, I felt uneasy, as if a pair of eyes were drilling into the back of my skull and trying to watch the movie reel spin as these thoughts raced through my mind. I glanced out the back window, and I could see my mother standing out on the sidewalk. Her arms were crossed in front of her chest, and her face was drawn down in that same old familiar scowl that was her default expression. I couldn't have been more relieved when Marty hung a left and drove out of sight. She was perpetually miserable, and therefore, couldn't help but make everyone else around her miserable as well. It didn't matter how good your day had been going, she could ruin it with just one word or even a single disapproving glance—that was her greatest talent. I crossed my own arms in front of my chest and wished I could just disappear. I figured now that we couldn't play, we'd kill the rest of the afternoon driving around in the truck, or else go back to Jeff's apartment and finish off that cooler full of Coors. I didn't care very much either way. I fished a lighter out of my pocket, lit a cigarette, inhaled deeply, and closed my eyes.

"What did you say to her?" Marty asked.

My head lolled to the side, and my eyes met his in the rearview mirror, "I told her the only talent she ever had was busting my ass."

A sly grin slid across his face. Marty always got a real kick out of any comebacks I dished out; he too hated my mother. In fact, hate is a kind word when used to describe the way Marty felt about adults and authority figures in general—especially the parental variety. "I hope you're ready to get your ass beat when you go home," he told me.

"I'm not going home," I replied. "I'm staying at my dad's tonight."

****

Everyone who has ever known me knows that my father is a very interesting man. He's lived over in Madera ever since 1983, in the basement of a house owned by Jack Hartford, his old deadhead buddy from back in the day. Jack and his wife Marie got married that year, and it seems to be around that time when my father decided it was a good idea to kick coke and thereafter acquired a penchant for smoking mushrooms and hasn't quite been able to get it together since—or so the story goes. Anyhow, one of the main reasons old George has been living with Jack for so long—besides being unable to keep any kind of a job—is because of his trips.

By the time I was old enough to remember, George had long since given up smoking mushrooms; however, after Jerry died, George would randomly disappear for weeks on end. The first few times we were worried, but it wasn't long before we realized that when he would hear the date or a recollection of the past it would set him off, and he would hop on a bus or a train or on the back of one of his buddies' motorcycles and set off to where some Dead concert had been held years before. We recognized the pattern fairly quickly, but no matter how many times we told him the that the Dead no longer performed and it was the year 2000, he still up and went at least a couple times a year. He's certifiably nuts, it's impossible to deny, but it's a kind of harmless insanity—unlike that of Meredith who I long suspected might send me away to a nunnery as soon as I turned eighteen. Meredith and George were as likely a pair as Joe McCarthy and General Mao, and the question of how the two of them had ever gotten together was an unsolvable mystery, making me the eighth wonder of the world.

The morning after the tiff with my mother, I sat at Jack and Marie Hartford's kitchen table with George. It was a Monday. Jack was at work and Marie was out grocery shopping, so George and I had ascended from the basement to scrounge up some breakfast. I poured myself a bowl of cornflakes and orange soda and made George a scrambled egg doused in syrup, his favorite.

It's no question that we were an amusing sight seated together at the table like that. Anyone who knows both George and me claims that we look exactly alike. George is about 5'8" with a slight build and long, brown hair the same color and texture as mine. He has a thin, angular face, and deep blue eyes, traits that I noticeably share as well. However, George also has a pretty long goatee and smells like he hasn't showered in a week, so I've never been entirely sure if this observation should be taken as a compliment or not.

That morning, I had on one of Jack's old double XL Rasta Baja sweatshirts which I'd found in the drier and came down to my knees. George, on the other hand, was dressed in a denim work-shirt and a pair of Levi's from yesterday, and his hair was pulled back into a ponytail. I gave him credit, George always made an effort to look presentable whenever I visited; however, he never changed or washed over the course of my visit either, so he always looked a little wrinkled and scruffy. There was an ashtray on the table between us, and we both smoked over breakfast. I alternated between spoonfuls of cornflakes and puffs on a Marlboro, and I watched George do the same.

George hadn't lit my first cigarette for me—that had been Marty—but he didn't tell me to quit once he knew I had started; I guess he figured that would have been hypocritical. All in all, he was a good father, as surprising as that seems. He was supportive, loving, and he gave me everything, even though he had almost nothing of himself to give. He had even given me my first car—a white 1970 Galaxie convertible with gorgeous red leather seats, the entirety of his possessions that were worth anything at all—the day I had turned seventeen in March of last year. My mother nearly had a conniption when I drove up in that car, and that first night I was terrified that she would key it or smash the windows—or worst of all, roll the top down in the rain. Now don't get me wrong, my mother has never been prone to violence, but she hated George, and I'm sure driving up in his thirty-year-old antique car didn't exactly make her feel all warm and fuzzy inside. Sometimes I feel real bad for my mother.

Many of the times I ended up at my dad's were nights after I'd had a fight with my mother or was otherwise exhausted by her. Sometimes, I crashed there after gigs if we were performing in the area, but that was rare, so all in all, I was at George's about three or four times a week. Considering the circumstances, a common tenant of most of our conversations was how much I hated my mother. I'm sure I sounded a bit like a broken record, but I knew George didn't mind; he only owned one record, *Let It Bleed* by the Rolling Stones, and he listened to that nightly. He wasn't much of a conversationalist, but he was a good listener and always had some sort of advice for me.

The conversation that morning started just that way. I swirled the few remaining soggy cornflakes around in the soda at the bottom of the bowl with my spoon and dropped my cigarette butt into the ashtray.

"You know, I really can't stand it when she screws with my music," I complained, starting in on my rant. "If it wasn't for her, we'd be out in L.A. by now or performing up in San Francisco. We've been at this for five years—since ninth grade when we got together as a band! Hell, we've been playing the house at The Joint alone for over two years! We're doing just fine there, but it's time to move on. There's a good scene for cover bands like ours in San Francisco, but she'll never let me go…God, I hate her! You know how she is. She came in yelling that rock and roll was the devil's music and that we all should be in church—what year does she think it is anyhow, 1950? I'll bet your parents didn't even tell you that. I haven't been to church in years and haven't missed it neither, but she's been harassing me ever since I stopped going, telling me I have to confess my sins and come back to Jesus and shit. She's mad, I swear! I'll have to be married before she lets me move out, and it's not like she approves of any of the guys I go out with anyhow. I'm eighteen, and she still treats me as if I am a child! She thinks I'm entirely incapable of doing anything for myself."

"Plenty of good things come to those who wait, with or without the want. Good things will come faster to those who wait and who do not want," George replied thoughtfully.

"We just need a lucky break. A talent scout from a record label up in San Francisco is coming to watch us perform at The Joint tonight. If they want to sign us, I'm going; I don't care how much of a fight she puts up. I don't give a crap about getting famous, but getting signed is my only chance to ever get out of Fresno. That's the way it is for all of us; none of us are smart enough to get into college—except for maybe Shania. Besides, I want to have the same experience as all the musicians I've been listening to since I've been a little kid. The Airplane got their start in San Francisco as well as Janis and Big Brother, Santana, the Dead…it's the only place I've ever really wanted to go, besides Woodstock, of course."

George nodded slowly, tilted his head to the side, and closed his eyes as if he was trying to remember something that had long since faded back into the foggy recesses of his memory, "I lived in San Francisco in the seventies, I think. What a trip. It's a wild city—unreal! It's like a time warp, man, you think you're just gonna go up for the weekend, and before you know it, it's years later and you feel as if you've just rolled in. Rhiannon, you'd love it. It's the hub of a culture, and the weed never runs out. Old S.F. ain't just a city, it's a lifestyle, man."

"It's just so frustrating!" I fumed. "All I've ever wanted to do is play music! It's the only thing I'm good at. I love what I do, and I know I'll be an even better musician when I'm on the right scene and she's out of my hair. Once I get away from Meredith, I can go anywhere!"

"Life is wild," George interjected. "You gotta keep a balance and learn how to hold onto that balance through life as the circumstances around you change—no matter where you are." He stood up from the table on one leg, dish in hand. He stayed that way for a moment, then wobbled and grabbed onto the back on the chair for support. "I'm still working on mine!" he laughed before dropping the dish into the sink with a clatter. I watched him curiously as he lit another cigarette and leaned against the counter, staring at me silently and intently, "It'll all be copasetic," he said.

"You really think so?" I asked, partly dubious and partly excited. "Do you think we could ever make it to L.A? Think we'll ever play at the Whisky?" I paused, "I really want to drop acid in San Francisco, just to see what it was like, you know, relive history?"

George laughed again, "Take your foot off the gas, little girl, you gotta go slow around the turns. Life is just a ride—and it's a round trip at that. What we are experiencing now isn't what's real or valuable— this world is nothing but a shadow cast upon a smokescreen. I've shuffled the deck more times than I can remember, been put through the rinse cycle a couple times too—I like to think I learned a few things from it all. You're a smart kid, Rhiannon, whatever you decide to do, you'll be just fine. Unlike Meredith, I'm not worried—I'm confident in you, you have a chance in life, Kid."

I pushed my chair away from the table, dropped my bowl into the sink, and hugged him, "Thanks, Dad." I glanced at the clock that hung on the wall, it was quarter after noon, "I gotta to get going," I told him.

George was still smoking in the kitchen by the time I'd gotten cleaned up. I hugged him once more before I left, and he walked me to the door and watched as I got into my car, "Love ya, Kid, you're gonna ace this thing!"

I grinned, started the engine, and shifted into reverse.

"You'll play like Bonzo!" he called after me, excited. "Rock on!" he yelled, pumping his fist in the air.

I shook my head with a smile and honked the horn as I peeled out of the driveway.

12

It only takes about forty-five minutes to drive from George's house to mine depending on what kind of traffic there is on the freeway. That Monday afternoon, the drive only took a half hour, and I pulled into my driveway around one-thirty. My mother's tan station wagon was nowhere to be seen. I was never religious by any stretch of the imagination, but I uttered a quick word of thanks to any angel that might have been hanging around before hopping out of my convertible and unlocking the garage door.

I climbed the steps, yanked open the door to the kitchen, and stepped into the house. It was dark and cool inside—a stark contrast to the relentless California sun. The A/C was blasting, and it felt wonderful. I walked over to the refrigerator, browsed for a moment, then pulled out a carton of leftover Chinese food. As I stood in front of the open refrigerator and ate, I realized just how quiet it was—how blissfully quiet. There was no one yelling at me to stop spending so much on take-out or to change out of my ripped jeans, no one telling me to take out the garbage or to turn off the garbage on the stereo. I locked all the doors in the house in order to keep it that way, then retreated back into the garage. Now that I had gotten over the initial delight of my mother's absence, I had to admit that it was far *too* quiet for my taste. I never could gain any appeal for silence; I did not like the sound of nothing.

The story is as follows: like many children, from the time I'd learned to walk, I would sometimes sing or hum when I was bored, but making noise with my hands had always suited me far better. I would bang on the table, the walls, or anything else that would stand still long enough with pens, silverware, sticks—just about anything I could get my chubby little toddler hands on. Needless to say, it drove both of my parents crazy, and at the age of four, my father noticed that when I would bang or tap, I would repeat patterns over and over again. One day, he brought me upstairs to Jack and Marie's and took all the pots and pans out of the cabinets, arranged them in front of me, gave me two long-handled wooden spoons, and let me go at it. From that point onward, I was hooked. Whenever I visited him, I'd ask to do this, and he'd stand back watching, amused and entertained. When I was eight, Jack and Marie bought me my first drum set, and after months of persuading, I was allowed to bring it back to Meredith's. I certainly wasn't a prodigy, but at the age of ten, George started bringing me to coffeehouses to sit in for one or two songs anytime there was a live show. That's where I got my start. I did a pretty damn good job with any traditional rock and roll, except when I was ten I fucked up a whole lot more when I played in front of a live crowd. For me, it was the audience factor that took the most getting used to.

As I reminisced about these things, I walked over to the CD player on the floor behind my drum kit, turned on the dial, and out came a blast of *Rock and Roll* from *Zeppelin IV*. Since there was no one home, I turned up the volume until the floor vibrated slightly beneath my feet and sat down behind my drum kit. I picked up my sticks, fell into time with the beat of the song, and went at it.

Bonzo has always been one of my greatest idols, and my principal goal in life for a very long time was to master every song he had ever recorded—something I was sure would keep me busy for quite a while. I would spend days playing the same song over and over again until I'd just about worn out the rewind button on the stereo. If anything, it was probably the persistence I had always shown toward my trade that had kept my mother at bay all these years—especially when the volume of equipment started to consume most of our garage, various funny-looking teenagers began appearing every so often for rehearsals there before she forbid it, and those couple of times the neighbors called the authorities because they thought they were experiencing seismic tremors. However, even being allowed to practice at home without a band had its downsides. My mother was eternally nagging me about the 'impure lyrics' and 'sexual innuendos' of the music I listened to—which was why on rare occasions such as this when I had the house all to myself, I practically went mad. That afternoon, as the rhythmic pulsing of rock music poured from my speakers and sweat poured from my brow, I played like Bonzo to an empty house.

I played for almost an hour, and by the time I had showered, dressed, and packed up my drum kit, it was five o'clock, and Marty and Jeff had called to tell me that they were on their way. In a hurry, I loaded my equipment into the backseat of my car and set off for The Joint. By the time I arrived there, the parking lot was already crammed full of cars. All week, local bands that frequented our humble venue had been auditioning for an A&R guy from Track Records who'd come down from the City in search of fresh talent, and people had flocked from all over to soak up the live music. Because we were the house band, we were booked for the preferred time, happy hour—which at The Joint ran from six to nine on weekdays. It was because of this clever marketing, as well as a strategic location, that brought so much business into the little dive.

I remember it now with such pleasant fondness—that little, round, windowless building constructed of asymmetrical wooden slats painted brown or black depending on which side you were standing on and plastered along the outside by posters and advertisements put up by performing bands or local attendees looking to make a buck. It was the biggest eyesore for miles around and built just beyond the intersection of South and Emory on the way into town. Many more new and better-maintained bars and coffeehouses could be found along South Street, but there was something about the classic air and dusty ambiance of the place that appealed to Californians and made The Joint the favorite local watering hole of aged hippies, those at the tail end of their midlife crisis, and grungy, stoned teenagers like us who'd decided to make their living playing classic rock—and what fun we had there!

That evening, a large, rectangular poster hung discernibly on the front door, printed in towering powder-blue bubble letters that screamed: '*The Descendants Performing Tonight @ 7:00*,' and decorated with cute anime-style caricatures of us playing cartoon instruments. Leanne had drawn it up by hand, as she did all our posters in those days. Considering most of the advertisements there were just simple messages scrawled in indelible ink on the cardboard of broken boxes, ours was quite striking.

We always unloaded our equipment around back where there was a loading dock for deliveries and four rickety, wooden steps that led up to the back door and the bandstand. Marty had parked next to a pile of pallets, and I parked next to him. I was heaving my bass drum out of the back of my car when Jeff banged on the door and Juan Pablo, The Joint's effervescent manager, appeared in the doorway and waved hello.

Juan Pablo, who looked like a little Mexican Groucho Marx and always insisted people call him by his full name, is one of the most inexplicable characters I have ever met—and that's saying a lot. He was as animated and cartoonish as the characters that Leanne drew on our posters. He had this huge, goofy-looking mustache that he stroked excessively so that it curled up at the edges and a sense of fashion that outdid the likes of Freddie Mercury. The man shamelessly wore some of the most outrageous outfits I have ever seen in my life, and I swear thrift stores across the state set aside entire racks of their ugliest, most unsellable shit just for him. The outfit he had on that day consisted of a gray, short-sleeve dress shirt covered in yellow rubber ducks with

Nirvana-style x-ed out eyes, layered atop a pair of blue, striped hemp shorts, and complete with Birkenstocks and Kelly green suspenders. He grinned at the three of us from under his mustache, his hands planted firmly on his hips, "Howdy, y'all!" he called.

The boys and I looked at each other and smiled. You couldn't help but smile when you were in the presence of Juan Pablo, he was just too absurd.

"Hey boss," Marty grinned, and Jeff high-fived him as he passed by. I picked up two of my cases and called out my own greeting before continuing on to the bandstand, but Juan Pablo stopped me at the door.

"Rhiannon," he spoke in his heavy accent, "tu mama been blowing up de phone for de last half hour, she mus' have call half a dozen time already!"

I was both relieved and dismayed. I had only left the house half an hour ago, so I must have just missed her. She may have even seen me pull out. "What does she want?" I asked.

"Puta won't tell me!" Juan Pablo exclaimed. "She just call, ask for ju, then hang up! Das all!"

I sighed. *This might be the most important gig of my life thus far,* I thought. *I haven't even been here five minutes yet and she's already finding a way to preoccupy me with her relentless hovering.*

There was no way in hell I was going to call her back—that was just asking to get chewed out. I was already tense, and getting screamed at for god-knows-what that soon before going out there wouldn't much help my nerves. "If she calls again, just tell her I'm playing and can't come to the phone, she should stop eventually," I told him.

"If I can get a word in, ay, señora locisima!"

"Tell me about it," I agreed.

"House is packed tonight!" Marty exclaimed, walking back from the bandstand with Jeff close behind him. "Which one is our guy?"

Juan Pablo spun around and stuck his head out between the floor-grazing gold curtains that were The Joint's garish centerpiece, "Mister in the red shirt, black hair, beard, thirty-somethin', right out of a little label on California Street, San Francisco called Track Records."

The three of us copied his stance. The man he described was sitting on the left side of the house at one of the many high top tables that surrounded the bandstand. He looked bored, as if he had been sitting there all day and hadn't yet seen anything that impressed him.

"You could have just told us he was the guy who looks like he has a stick up his ass, goddamn!" Jeff exclaimed.

16

"Tough crowd," Marty contributed.

"You know it," Juan Pablo agreed. "Man don't even buy a beer, been sitting dere all day."

My stomach began to churn, and I checked the clock on the back wall twice—we still had half an hour. As I turned away from the curtain and finished carrying my equipment up to the bandstand, my hands were clammy, and I could feel my heart hammering away in my chest.

Shania and Leanne showed up just as I dropped my last two drum cases at the rear of the bandstand. I wiped a bead of sweat from my forehead and looked around: Shania and Marty had already begun to wire us up, and Leanne and Jeff were getting the last of the equipment out of Shania's station wagon. The talent scout from the record label wasn't even watching us. While my brain was doing somersaults as I imagined all the ways in which we had already disappointed him, someone came up from behind me and tapped me on the shoulder. It was Leanne.

"Everything OK?" she asked me. "You're all worked up."

I nodded, then hopped down off the bandstand and made a beeline for the bar; I wanted a beer.

One of the best things about The Joint was that they didn't ask any questions above their pay level, but I carried my fake I.D. on me at all times anyhow. The bar was off to the right of the bandstand and encircled by barstools, all of which were occupied. There were two bartenders behind the counter, and they both wore brown polos emblazoned with The Joint's insignia: a bright green marijuana leaf. My mother would have an aneurysm.

"What's on tap tonight?" I asked.

"Bud, straight up," answered the bartender closest to me. He was bald, wore a goatee, and had one ear pierced.

"Put it on my tab."

He handed me the chilled mug still frosty with ice. I leaned against the bar and guzzled half the glass in one gulp.

"Big night for you guys tonight, eh?" he asked, amused.

"I'd say," I replied.

I drained the rest of that glass, left it on the bar, and with a fresh beer in hand, headed back over to the bandstand to start setting up. I began unzipping all my cases and pulled out my bass drum and all my traps. The Joint didn't have its own drum set; therefore, every day I had to set up and break down my kit and lug it to and from my house. Because of this, I could just about put it together in my sleep. Daily set up has always been like a ritual to me, and I can devote so little attention to the process that most of the time I am thinking about almost anything else. That night, my hands worked independently of my mind, and I watched them as they flitted about grasping hardware and fitting it together—creating a functional whole out of the many pieces provided.

In this state, I was swallowed by my thoughts—my inner ponderings, my worries, preoccupations, dreams—so much so that I began to have this strange inkling that I was, in fact, sleeping—that in reality I was completely detached, completely unaware of what was actually going on in my life. It was as strange a feeling as it was an unprecedented one. I glanced toward my second empty mug and blamed it on the beer. I began to question what I had felt in an attempt to analyze it, to provide some explanation, but at the same time, Marty plugged in and riffed off the first few chords of the night. My mind was flooded with music, and I finished my set up in lightning speed, those feelings of uneasiness all but forgotten.

We struck up at seven o'clock sharp with a scale by Shania and a riff by Marty. All the heads in the place turned toward us; two dozen pairs of ears tuned in for the ride. Our setlist had been compiled earlier in the week, and we opened with The Who's *Long Live Rock*.

The lack of attention I devote to my set up is the exact opposite of the quality of attention I devote to my playing. When I hear the music start, whether it's Marty on guitar or that of the whole band, it draws me in—it absorbs every inch of my consciousness in a way that enchants my senses. The music becomes my physicality, the beat of my drum becomes my heartbeat.

I do not believe there will come a day when I discover something I love more than a steady, driving, rock and roll beat. To play it is the most powerful feeling in the world: my right hand dropping eighth notes on the high-hat, my left on the snare—coming together on counts two and four—stomping the bass pedal with my right foot on counts one and three, and working the hi-hat with my left. I can play it all night long, song after song—there's nothing like it, it makes the world go round.

I love to see the crowd really getting into it and drinking to our groove. My favorite trick is to start real slow and gradually begin to play faster and faster; that always gets them going, especially when we're all in it together. After all, every part of a band is essential to making the music, each person is a piece of the soul.

As we finished up the first song of that set, with a steady beat we rolled right into the next—*I Love Rock N' Roll* by Joan Jett and the Blackhearts. I grinned as exhilaration, adrenaline, and alcohol rushed through my veins. There's a whole lot of adrenaline in performing. You move and play a whole lot faster when there is more adrenaline, more people, and more energy—it's the best drug in the world, and it's a whole lot better when the audience is in it with you. A good night in rock and roll is when your name gets out, but a great night in rock and roll is one when you can't stop playing. We may not have been famous, but we'd closed up The Joint at two and three in the morning more times than I could count.

As Leanne began the third song of that night with a few bass chords, I could feel my body responding to my most recent drink. My senses were cool and my insides, warm. I was no longer worried about my mother or the talent scout sitting out there watching us; I was entirely content to just play and simply surrender to what may be.

We played almost nonstop for the rest of that hour, and that show was likely one of the best The Joint had ever seen. When we were in time and in tune together, we sounded like a locomotive at full throttle, and the music that flowed out from the speakers hit you like a wall of sound. This same quality was mirrored in the cheer that rose up from the crowd once the music stopped and we struck that final chord. I remember laying my sticks across my snare and looking up from my kit and out into the audience: they clapped and whistled, and a few even stood up—Track Records talent scout included. I was elated; I felt as if I was walking on those fluffy, white clouds that appear in a sunny sky in the early morning hours. I was soaring.

Once the applause died down, an extremely drunk bearded man seated at one of the closest high-top tables began slurring his wishes to buy us all whiskeys and did not cease until Juan Pablo sauntered over to us with a dishtowel thrown over his shoulder and a tray of shots in his hand. We left our instruments in their respective places and walked to the edge of the bandstand. We toasted to our show, drank our whiskey, and returned the empty glasses to Juan Pablo's tray. Before we could even turn around, the drunk bearded man's drunk bearded compadre ordered a second round for the band, and Juan Pablo returned with a fresh tray. Shania went back to the mic to announce our thirty-minute break, and the rest of us hopped down off the bandstand and proceeded to disperse into and mingle with the crowd. I headed toward the back corner of The Joint where Juan Pablo was leaning across the bar hitting on a long-legged, red-haired woman who was completely out of his league.

"Ahh Rhiannon!" he exclaimed when he saw me, pausing his conversation with the woman and handing me a topped off beer mug. "Drink, drink!"

I took the glass from him, had a swig, licked the foam off my lips, and pulled a wad of crumpled singles from my jeans.

Juan Pablo held out his hand and declined my offer to pay, "Free. From Señor Track Records over dere."

I whirled around and saw that Shania was sitting at his table. I began to feel optimistic about our future with Track Records; not many people could turn down a contract if Shania was included.

I took a seat at the bar next to the redhead and finished my beer. I was surprised by how many people approached me to tell me how much they enjoyed our set and as the night progressed, how many middle-aged men wanted to buy me drinks. By the time our break was over, I was feeling pretty tipsy. Shania, Leanne, and Marty headed back to the stage for an acoustic set, and I ordered another beer and sat back to watch. They opened with *Going to California*—one of my favorites from Led Zeppelin. Marty and Leanne harmonized on guitar while Shania belted out the lyrics. She was beautiful; with a face like Joan Baez and a voice like Stevie Nicks, Shania was irresistible.

Jeff wandered over at some point and lit up smokes for the both of us. Much to his dismay, the redhead next to me whom both he and Juan Pablo were trying to score was much less than interested and left after a couple of minutes. Deflated, he took her seat, and between the two of us, we smoked half a pack and filled the counter in front of us with empty mugs while we watched the set. I was feeling real good, and they sounded real good. I glanced over to where the Track Records talent scout had been sitting and saw that he had left for the night. I remember thinking that I wanted to go back up there and play, and before I knew what had happened, that's exactly where I was.

I don't quite remember how I got there, but pretty soon I was back on the bandstand behind my drum set, playing the hell out of some song.

God, I don't think anything I've ever played has sounded this good! I thought triumphantly, *I wish that talent scout could hear this, he'd call up his boss right now, wake him right up out of bed to come and see us play! Shit, I'll be surprised if the whole goddamn bar doesn't buy us beers after this set!*

Shania hit the chorus, and I opened up into a solo that probably made Keith Moon roll over in his grave. I came back in out of the ride in perfect time with Leanne and Marty on guitar, and with a sauced grin of utter delight, I glanced up at my bandmates. Immediately, I was taken aback by what I saw.

Shania and Marty met my eyes with a look of sheer horror spread across their faces. Suddenly, it was if I had just removed a pair of earplugs and could now hear as they did. I was completely off the beat, and the song sounded choppy and awkward as they attempted to compensate for my drunken playing. My elation had turned to desperation, and my positivity had become stark paranoia. As hard as I tried, I could not get back on the beat. Every time I thought I had it, my playing was just a little too fast or a little too slow. A sense of stillness and detachment rolled over me; everything seemed just a little bit less immediate, less intense, and just a little further away. Just when I thought that I'd come back in on time, I was half a count ahead or behind where I needed to be. Leanne signaled for me to stop playing, and I watched helplessly as she and Marty finished up the song. I looked out into the faces of the crowd to gauge just how bad my playing had been, but I couldn't see them. They all began to meld together as the entire room itself began to spin and waves of squalid drunkenness swept over me. I stood up and backed away from my kit, stumbled off behind the golden curtain, and was sick backstage.

The only other memory I've retained from that night is a quick flash of pavement and the sickening smell of bile as Marty carried me to Shania's car and Leanne held a brown paper bag in front of my face. He sat me up in the back of the station wagon next to Jeff, and Leanne stuffed the paper bag between my knees.

"Watch her," Shania instructed Jeff.

Jeff looked up at her with bloodshot eyes and a well-oiled expression on his face, "Yo, Shania, I'm as drunk as a skunk. I'll watch 'er but I ain't sure if she's goin' anywheres."

She slammed the door, and I met Jeff's expression, "I'll never drink again," I moaned before heaving into the bag Leanne had left.

Jeff patted my back, "Yeah, yeah, that's what we all say."

****

The next thing I remember is waking up in the morning with a splitting headache and the world's worst hangover.

I was in Shania's room, tucked between Shania's purple sheets, and completely alone. I checked the clock that hung on the wall in front of me; it was almost one in the afternoon. The purple curtains had been drawn to prevent the afternoon sunlight from streaming into the room, but even so, I couldn't look in the direction of the windows without an increase in the pounding behind my eyes. I threw the covers off me, swung my legs over the side of the bed, and sat up; I was in my underwear. I yawned—my mouth felt like it belonged to a five-thousand-year-old mummy. I had almost no recollection at all of anything that had happened the previous night after we'd left The Joint; however, the garbage can beside the bed provided the first clue to what fun I'd had. My stomach churned, and I looked away. A piece of paper and a bottle of aspirin on the nearby dresser caught my attention. I stood up, stretched, and shuffled over to it.

The note read:

Rhiannon,

Take two aspirin when you wake up. The coffee is already in the filter, just hit the green button to brew. Your clothes are in the wash, so take something of mine to wear. We went to the mall. Marty's home, you can call him to pick you up. Feel better!

—S&L

I unscrewed the cap to the bottle, popped two of the little pink pills in my mouth, and swallowed. A mirror hung on the wall in front of the dresser, and as I stood there in front of it, my disheveled reflection stared back at me. My eyeliner had run and was smudged and sooty beneath my bloodshot eyes. My hair had been tied back into some ridiculous bun by one of the girls and protruded about a foot from my head in all directions. I felt like I wanted to crawl back into the bed and sleep for a month. Disregarding that option, I dug into the drawer beneath the mirror and pulled out an old, green Roosevelt High sweatshirt and a pair of cotton shorts and headed for the bathroom. I stayed in the shower for almost an hour, allowing the steam to aid my sore muscles and aching head. However, when the hot water began to run out, I decided that it is impossible to wash away a hangover. I reset the dials, dried off, and changed into Shania's sweats before walking into the kitchen and turning on the coffeepot. As the comforting drip of the russet liquid began to fill the pot, I dialed Marty. The phone rang twice, and he picked up on the third.

"Yo."

"Marty? It's Rhiannon."

"What's up? How are you feeling? You were fucking wasted last night, it was crazy!"

"I feel like someone was working over my head with a jackhammer all night," I moaned.

Marty laughed, "As if! I'm sure, it's been a while since I've seen you that fucked up."

"I literally have no idea what happened after the acoustics."

"I'm not surprised," he said. "Jeff told me that when you were at the bar with him, you started hitting on Juan Pablo and the bartenders. Then the scout left, and you jumped up on stage and started playing all by yourself, so we all plugged back in and went with it. You were having a good time," he laughed. "Then after about fifteen minutes you started trying to play just about the hardest shit you knew, and it was just plain awful. After that, you couldn't even keep a beat. We tried to get you to stop playing, but then you ran backstage and started puking."

My cheeks burned red with humiliation, "That is so embarrassing!"

"Ah, don't worry about it, by that time mostly everybody had filtered out, and the ones that were left were pretty comatose. Anyway, the boss didn't think you'd be feeling too good today, so he gave us the night off."

"No kidding," I groaned. "My car is still at The Joint, can you drive me there to pick it up?"

"Yeah, I'll be there in fifteen."

"Thanks," I said and hung up the phone. The coffeepot beeped to announce that it was ready, and I poured it black into the biggest thermos I could find. I took a sip, then went about cleaning the house. I washed the sheets, tidied up the bathroom, took out the garbage, and threw my own clothes in the drier. As I was finishing up, Marty sounded his horn outside. I slipped on my ratty, Converse sneakers, grabbed my coffee, and locked the door behind me. I squinted as the bright rays of sunlight struck my eyes like a million tiny, painful daggers and practically ran to Marty's truck.

He took one glance at me before reaching into the glove box and pulling out a pair of sunglasses, "I hope you feel better than you look," he remarked.

I shook my head, "Thanks," I scoffed as I took the sunglasses from him.

"Your mother's car wasn't in the driveway when I passed your house," he remarked in an attempt to lift my spirits.

"God knows she's probably out looking for me," I muttered as I pulled my first smoke of the day out of the pack on the seat. "You're so lucky your father's never home."

"I guess," Marty replied, keeping his eyes fixed on the road. "We don't get along neither. My whole life he's barely ever been home—he's always away for work. When I was a kid, he always wanted to take me with him, but I didn't like tagging along, so he shoved me off on my aunt. We're nothing alike at all. I don't think he's got all fifty-two cards in his deck—like mentally, you know? Some of the things he says sometimes I can't tell if he's a genius or a madman. He reminds me of your dad, sometimes."

"At least he's not on your case all the time like Meredith. She's obsessive, compulsive and manic. If anyone belongs in the nuthouse, it's her, not George. Did I tell you she thinks you're hooked on dope?"

Marty cracked a humorous half-smile, "No, you didn't."

"Seriously, I think she's the one who's on something. We've never once celebrated Christmas because according to her it's a secular holiday for American consumerists, and she spoiled Santa Claus for me when I was three. Same thing with the Easter Bunny—and don't even get me started on what she thinks about Halloween. Sometimes I wish I had different parents, or at least a different mother. I wish I could just forget every memory I have of her and only remember the ones I have of you guys and George—or just erase my entire childhood altogether."

"Well, at least you had George," Marty said. "I never had anybody, and I could tell my aunt didn't really want me around, you know?"

The two of us fell silent. Marty stopped at a red light and popped a tape into the cassette deck. He kept the volume low in order to aid my aching head, but when I heard what tune it was, I turned the volume up myself. It was an album by the band America. The first song on that tape was *A Horse With No Name*; it was one of my favorites, and I knew it well. I leaned back on the seat, closed my eyes, puffed away on a smoke, and listened. The first verse of the song was acoustic, and the lyrics went like this:

On the first part of the journey,
I was looking at all the life.

24

There were plants and birds and rocks and things,
There was sand and hills and rings.
The first thing I met was a fly with a buzz
And a sky with no clouds.
The heat was hot, and the ground was dry,
But the air was full of sound.
I've been through the desert on a horse with no name,
It felt good to be out of the rain.
In the desert, you can remember your name,
'Cause there ain't no one for to give you no pain.
After two days in the desert sun,
My skin began to turn red.
After three days in the desert fun,
I was looking at a river bed,
And the story it told of a river that flowed
Made me sad to think it was dead.
After nine days I let the horse run free,
'Cause the desert had turned to sea.
There were plants and birds and rocks and things,
There was sand and hills and rings.
The ocean is a desert with its life underground
And a perfect disguise above.
Under the cities lies a heart made of ground
But the humans will give no love.

As I listlessly bobbed my head to the music and watched the summer scenery pass by behind the window glass, I felt almost as if I was once removed from reality—exactly how I liked it. I did not like this here, this now. I wished that I could be somewhere else, anywhere else—the Mojave, for that matter, or Woodstock.

"You know, Marty, I think I was born in the wrong time," I said, opening one eye and glancing over at him while he was driving.

"You and me both, Rhiannon. The only difference is that I live in this reality and you live behind your eyes."

"I just can't stand the way things are nowadays. Nobody speaks their mind anymore, nobody's got a clue. At least back in the day people had some kind of an idea of what was wrong with the world and had their own notions about how they were going to fix it. Nowadays everybody's just another cog in the machine, another brick in the wall. They protest nothing and complain about everything. Everybody just acts like they're a victim and that nothing they do is at fault."

Marty shrugged, "That's just the way things are. Besides, there's not much that's controversial anymore. There's no Vietnam War or civil rights marches or Watergate Scandal."

"Columbine? Government corruption? Bad milk? Kurt Cobain? You don't think those are big enough controversies? Gas is $1.50 a gallon, I'd protest that!"

"Bad things are always happening, Rhiannon, you can't protest everything."

"See, you're the perfect example. Just because certain things are happening, it doesn't mean that they *should* be happening! Back then, people actually had opinions, and if they didn't agree with something, they said something. That's what their music was. The music that we play is what the artists back then wrote because they wanted to get a message across, make people understand something about their time that they understood themselves. Those are the things that they believed, the things that *I* believe. The problem with today is that people have forgotten what revolution is, they've forgotten about the way the world used to be."

"I know that's what it is," Marty replied, "and that's why it's so good, why people still want to hear it. I mean, can you imagine people still listening to NSYNC in thirty years?" he trailed off. "I guess you'll just have to keep playing music then. What else can you do? As much as you hate the way the world is now, you can't live in the past. It's not like you can go back in time."

"I can't do anything but play music, Marty. Playing music is the only thing I know how to do, the only thing I *want* to do. Sometimes it's the only thing that's real to me. I wish I could be free, like Woodstock free," I wished, staring off into the distance. "Half a million people, no cops, three days of rain, and yet—peace. There is nothing more inspiring to me than that. If they didn't have something right going for them, then I don't know who does…"

Marty started to answer me, but I cut him off.

"I feel like I'm swimming in an ocean and I can barely keep my head above the water, you know? It's like the damn song," I gestured toward the tape deck, "I wanna go out into the desert where there's nobody who knows me, and nobody here can find me. I wanna know who I am, I wanna find myself. I can't do that in Fresno with my mother breathing down my neck. Just once I want to be able to walk into my own house and not feel like I'm under scrutiny. Just once I want to be able to go out and play a gig and not feel like I need to constantly look over my shoulder. Just once I want to be in a place where I feel like I really belong..."

"We'll all get out of here soon enough," he assured me, "then we'll be out in San Francisco. Not much has changed there in the last thirty years, you'll be in heaven."

I turned and stared out the window, frustrated. I knew that Marty was just trying to make me feel better, but I felt like he was missing something. And it wasn't only him, it was our whole generation. To me it seemed like collectively, there was something that had been lost; like we were all stumbling around in the dark looking for something we couldn't specify, and every time we got close to it, it moved further and further out of our reach.

"I wish I could just go back for one night," I spoke to any force out there in the universe that might be listening. "Just one night..." I turned to Marty, "Don't you?"

He nodded, "We've all wanted to be somewhere else in time. I'd sell my soul to the devil to watch Jimi Hendrix play *The Star Spangled Banner* at Woodstock. I know exactly how you feel."

We fell silent again. Marty stopped at a red light and rewound the cassette. When the light turned green, he hit play, and *A Horse with No Name* started over again from the beginning.

"It's funny the way time is," I remarked, "...merciless."

When Marty dropped me off in the parking lot of The Joint, my car was the only one still there. I patted the shiny, white hood, then yanked open the door and sat in the driver's seat as the relentless summer sun beat down on me. The backs of my legs burned where they made contact with the seat, and I winced. The air was hot and heavy and thick, and I struggled to breathe comfortably. I raised my eyes to the sky and squinted at the sun, but it was only a moment before the dull thumping behind my eyes rose to a crescendo, and I was forced to wrench my gaze away. There was not a cloud in sight, and it had been far too long since it had rained. Sweat broke out across every inch of my skin, and I pressed my shower-wet hair against the back of my neck. I lifted my key out from under the rubber floor mat and inserted it into the ignition; it was time to go home and face the music.

When I walked through my front door twenty minutes later, my mother was standing at the kitchen counter, flipping through some magazine. When she heard the door slam behind me, she spun around, cleared the kitchen floor in about three steps, and stood a few inches from my face.

"Rhiannon Karlson, where in God's name have you been for two whole days?! How many times do I have to tell you about your curfew and how you're supposed to call me every two hours?! I phoned that coffeehouse of yours probably a dozen times, and you didn't even have enough common courtesy to call me back once! You have no respect!" her voice shook, she was livid.

I was not in the mood to argue with her. My head was pounding, and I felt nauseous again, "I am eighteen years old, Mom, I am a legal adult. I don't have a curfew. I had a job last night, it ran late."

She scoffed at me and rolled her eyes, "Yes, Rhiannon, I'm sure you were playing until two o'clock this afternoon," she said sarcastically, checking the gaudy gold watch that hung from her wrist.

"I spent the night at Shania's," I explained.

"Well, it's reassuring for me to know that my daughter is now spending her nights with gutter trash."

"What the fuck, Mom! Why do you have such a problem with my friends?!"

"You must watch what company you keep, Rhiannon," she warned, wagging her finger at me. "You have potential, but they will pull you down. Peer pressure, Rhiannon, is a terrible thing. You may have all the best intentions, but they don't. You won't even know it when you get caught up in it." She shook her head as if I was the biggest disappointment of her life.

"They're good musicians, Mom," I insisted. "We have a good thing going. We'd be even more successful by now if you didn't have me on a leash! You destroy our potential! It's your fault we haven't gotten any further than we have!"

"What do you even want to do with your life, Rhiannon, since you've got it all figured out?" she asked, exasperated.

"Live it!"

"By going out every night and partying and playing that desensitizing music?"

"Rock and roll, Mom?" I cried. "This is what *you* grew up with! I'm not playing rap or punk or heavy metal, but rock and roll and you have a problem with it! God almighty! I wish I could've grown up with rock and roll, I wish I could've been there. You were, and you don't even know enough about it to appreciate it for what it was! This is just one more of the many reasons I wish I lived with Dad, not you."

"I know exactly what it was," she protested, "and your father is an addict. He fried his brains and ravaged his body with drugs and what does he do? He brings you into that culture. You can't be a hippie, Rhiannon, no matter how hard you try. He's so stupid. All that...all that shit was dead and gone years ago! People are finally starting to recover from it all. It was a sickness; that whole generation was sick! They caused all the problems we have today: AIDS and venereal diseases, this war on drugs, the moral decay of our society..." she trailed off. "I tried to do a good job with you, and you would've turned out just fine if it wasn't for your father!"

"Leave him out of it!" I cried, defending him. "Besides, I don't want to think about what I'd be like without George. He's the only reason I'm anything other than a carbon copy of your sorry self. And what's so bad about it all, anyhow? A lot of great people and great ideas came out of *your* generation. The only reason it all died out was because of people like you who weren't open to it!"

"It was the *DRUGS*, Rhiannon!" she hissed. "You are so naïve. All those people you worship were high! That's how the devil gets in you, he disguises himself as something great and fun and unparalleled and then you're trapped! That's evil! It's all evil!"

"You should have been a preacher, Mom."

"Don't talk back to me with that snarky attitude of yours! I'll—"

I didn't stick around to listen to her threat. Instead, I turned my back on her and slammed my bedroom door. She was hopeless, absolutely hopeless. She didn't stop, either, and continued to bang on the door with the palm of her hand as she shouted at the top of her lungs. I ignored her. Her voice continued to drone on until I plugged in the stereo, at which time she was promptly silenced.

I hid in my room until about seven-thirty that night. My mother had gone out somewhere for the evening, and in her absence, I quickly changed into a pair of jeans and a t-shirt, hopped in my car, and took off for The Joint. Before I left, I idled awhile in the kitchen and made myself a Hot Pocket. While I was waiting for it to finish heating in the microwave, I glanced at the magazine my mother had left open on the counter when she'd started screaming at me earlier. It was a brochure for a rehab facility. I chucked it in the garbage can, then leaned back and laughed incredulously. I didn't think my life could get any more absurd.

The parking lot at The Joint was bustling when I arrived, so I looped the building once, in search of a spot. Around back where another local band was offloading equipment, I noticed Shania and Marty parked side by side, so I pulled into an empty space next to them. There was a boombox in the bed of Marty's truck playing something by Ten Years After, his all-time favorite band. A pink and orange sunset blazed on the horizon, and the heat of the day had begun to ebb with the sunlight. Everybody was gathered around Shania's station wagon. The hatch was open, and Shania and Leanne sat inside. Marty leaned against the rear fender smoking a cigarette, and Jeff was on his feet talking a mile a minute, excited as hell. I walked over, and Jeff interrupted his story in order to greet me before continuing.

"Where was I?" he said. "Oh yeah, remember my brother's friend Dave? The one who left for New Mexico just about two years ago?"

I remembered him. He was every stoner's best friend in high school. He knew where to get any drug imaginable and was remarkably negotiable when it came to the price. Every pothead in Fresno mourned when he skipped out.

Jeff's next sentence retracted me from my memories. "He called me this morning to tell me that he's coming up here in a few days and bringing with him some, uh, interesting merchandise," he said, raising one eyebrow suggestively.

"Oh yeah?" Marty inquired. "What's he got?"

"He told me he's been calling in some favors lately and has just about everything under the sun! He's got weed of course, and I heard he got his hands on a batch of pure ecstasy from Dallas. He said he'll have some salvia and magic mushrooms too, I forget what they're called."

"Psilocybin," Shania answered from the back of the station wagon where she and Leanne were rolling spliffs for the five of us.

Marty shot Jeff a grin, "We're gonna trip balls!"

"Fucking A," Jeff replied excitedly as he leaned over into Marty's truck to skip a track on the CD.

I thought about what it would be like for the five of us to spend a night together tripping on some illegal psychoactive substance. I knew that Jeff, as well as Marty, had done ecstasy before, and he'd told me that it had been cool as hell; that he had felt more aware and happier while he was high, that there had been no boundaries in-between people, and that sex had never felt so good. I was interested to say the very least. I couldn't deny that I wanted to know what was beyond that which I was capable of thinking and imagining in my everyday life.

I still have some cash left over from our last few jobs, I'd thought to myself, *maybe I'll buy a few hits of ecstasy and hold onto them for a while...I don't need to take them right away. I'll wait a while until I can get away from my mother. Maybe Track Records will give us a call and tell us to ride up to San Francisco—I'll take it up there. Or maybe I shouldn't, you never know with street drugs...you never know after all...*

As nervous excitement regarding all these new opportunities began to crowd my mind, I crawled into the back of the station wagon to think. Spread out in front of me on the floor was a mess of rolling papers, tobacco, and weed contained within their respective plastic baggies. Off to one side was a pile of spliffs which steadily increased as the contents of the bags dwindled. I picked one up and rolled it between my fingers; it was almost a perfect circle—Shania's work. She could roll a cigarette better than just about anybody because she never smoked store-boughts—"too many chemicals," she said. I stuck the spliff between my lips and breathed in the sweet aroma of fresh tobacco and the familiar earthy scent of good weed. Shania handed me a lighter, and I sparked it up. The dry herb sizzled as it burned, and I inhaled a lungful.

I leaned back on the wheel well, and after a few more hits, the ceaseless flow of cerebral noise ricocheting around the inside of my skull began to quiet. I started to feel that same sense of numbness and detachment as I had the night before, but this time around it was pleasant—a weed high is more fluid than drunkenness. The streetlights seemed to burn brighter, and our laughs sounded almost musical. Everybody else grabbed from the pile, and I watched them through drooping eyelids as they smoked. Jeff turned the stereo up louder, and Ten Years After resonated throughout the parking lot. I stared out the rear hatch past the parked cars and tree branches as darkness spread like a blanket across the sky and battled the sun for its nightly supremacy over the Earth. A slight grin broke out on my face, and I giggled. For once, I was at peace with my world, aware of my surroundings, and content with my life all at the same time.

I like smoking weed for the same reason as I like sitting at the back of the bandstand when I play the drums—they both give me a feeling of being outside reality. I prefer to be on the outside looking in, not on the inside looking out—I think they call that objectivity.

"Hey Rhiannon," Marty called, poking his head inside the station wagon, "if you had your own strain of weed, what would you call it?"

I thought about it for a moment, "It Don't Stop," I replied.

"What don't stop?" he asked. "The high?" That just about knocked him out, "It's like you smoke one joint and you're high forever! Imagine that?" He giggled, "It's like you sell it to somebody and they come back asking when they're gonna come down and you're like, 'Nah man, this shit's *permanent*!' Imagine that? Or you get pulled over and the cop asks if you're blazed..." He put on his best drawl, "*W'ell officer, technically, I haven't smoked in about two weeks...Hehehe!"*

That was all it took; we were cutting up. Leanne, Shania, and I rolled around the inside of the station wagon holding our stomachs from laughing so hard. It wasn't even that funny, but once we all started going, we fed off of one another's laughter until tears streamed down our faces and we each had to look away from one another in order to regain our composure.

"Nah," Jeff commented after we had gotten the last of the giggles out, "I think eventually I'd just get paranoid and go screaming into the night."

"Well, what do we have here?" an unsettling, brassy voice sounded from behind us. "Dirty white trash!"

The five of us spun around in shocked surprise. Kyle Cochran, Roosevelt High's resident asshole and ringleader of the jocks, stood there before us. He was dressed in a pair of designer jeans that probably would have cost us a whole night's pay and his green and gold Varsity jacket. Behind him, three more of his crew-cut cronies stood in front of the baby blue Corvette that his CEO daddy had bought for him off the showroom floor junior year. It had been the only thing anyone in high school talked about for probably half that semester: Kyle Cochran and his cool car. What a jerk. Cochran and his minions harassed us all through high school, shoving us into lockers and otherwise humiliating and demeaning us—not so much us girls, but Marty and Jeff and anybody who looked like us.

What I could never understand was how the preppies—who dressed like they were attending an eternal office party with their pleated pants and oxfords—could evade the wrath of the jocks while the five of us—clad in washed out denim jeans, probably the same sneakers we wore on the first day of high school, and baggy t-shirts displaying band names or some obscene slogan—were the object of their bullying. OK, so the jocks had their fancy cars and football scholarships, but they didn't have much of anything else. Like, come on, how much talent do you need to catch a ball and run? Besides, by the time they turned thirty they'd be out of a job, and by the time they were forty, they'd probably be bloated alcoholics with back problems and alimony payments. I sure as hell didn't want to be like them; I just wanted them to leave us alone, and it always amazed me how rotten the bunch of them could be to people who'd never done a thing to them in their lives.

However, one thing we had that they didn't was our attitudes. While we may have harbored a bit of cynicism or maybe even a touch of apathy, we kept to ourselves and enjoyed our purposeful isolation—there was a reason we didn't want to be associated with the likes of them. They were the ones who sought us out—always looking to start trouble just because they thought that their money and popularity made them better than us. I think that's what pissed me off the most about them. Actually, no—correction—the fact that their inexplicable ax to grind persisted even after high school was what pissed me off the most about them.

"Well, what do you know," Jeff said sarcastically, every trace of his former enthusiasm absent from his voice, "it's Kyle Cockroach and the Backdoor Boys."

Cochran stepped a few feet closer until he was right under Jeff's nose, and the other three filed into position around the station wagon. Shania, Leanne, and I climbed out through the passenger-side door and stood behind the boys. I was close enough to Cochran to smell his goddamn aftershave—it smelled like Jack Daniels. And it wasn't just him—they all reeked of Jack. They were drunk; drunk and dangerous.

"Alla you gotta get outta here and go take a goddamn shower, dirty, no-good punks," he slurred, turning toward his cohorts. "Do you have any idea what kind of drugs are probably in that car? Mikey, your father's the chief of police, ain't he? We should give him a call!"

The kid Mikey and the other two nodded in contempt and joined in a shower of their own obscenities and retorts.

"'*Just Say No*,' eh, Nancy?" Jeff remarked. "Damn Uncle's got you so you don't know your ear from your asshole!"

"Just look at them," Cochran addressed his minions. "The whole lot of them are probably high as a kite!"

Marty stepped out of Jeff's shadow, "Enough about us. Tell me this, Cochran, what kind of pompous, conceited asshole wears his Varsity jacket a whole year after graduation?"

He grit his teeth, "You think I'm dressed funny? Why don't you come here and let me help you take off that necklace so you don't look like such a faggot, eh?" Without any warning at all, he lunged at Marty and got behind him, holding his arms back in a full nelson. Marty's eyes flew open in a panic as he tried to break the hold, but he didn't have a chance. Cochran had played quarterback on the football team since freshman year, and he had biceps the size of softballs. Mikey and the other two rushed toward Jeff, and I stood by, blitzed and helpless.

A split second before the fists began to fly, Shania stepped between Jeff and his assailants. "No!" she screeched, holding her arms outstretched between them. "No fighting!"

The three of them hesitated, and Shania turned toward Cochran who hadn't flinched, "I said no fighting!" she repeated, this time accompanied by a swift, hard kick between Cochran's legs. It was a direct hit. He instantly doubled up in pain and released Marty, falling forward onto his knees on the dusty pavement, his hands flying toward his crotch. Marty stumbled away and went to sit in the back of the station wagon, tenderly examining his neck and shoulders as he glared coldly at Cochran on the ground.

"That's what you get, you rat bastard," Jeff told him, spitting in his direction.

Shocked and without direction from their leader, the three candy-asses backed off and exchanged nervous glances between themselves. Cochran cussed us out as he struggled up from the ground, and we flipped them off and waved as they made it for their car.

"Fuck," Marty spat after they drove off. "Leave it to them to spoil a perfectly good evening. Let's blow this joint. I wanna get outta here." He was pretty bummed out; we all were.

"Your place?" Shania asked.

Marty nodded. "Hey, I owe you one," he said, thanking her with a kiss on the cheek before reaching into the bed of his truck and ejecting the CD that had been playing. "Hey Rhiannon, I think this is yours."

He threw the case in my direction, and I caught it. My initials were scrawled in indelible ink on one side. The name of the album was *A Space in Time*. It was recorded in 1971, I think. I stuck it in my glove box.

We all pulled into Marty's driveway about twenty minutes later. I took a peek into my own driveway as I passed it, and to my relief, I saw that it was empty; Meredith wasn't home yet. The five of us filed through Marty's unlocked front door and immediately scattered throughout the house. In his father's absence, Marty had full reign of the house and everything in it, except for his father's bedroom, the last room on the left at the end of the hall. That being the case, the place looked like an advertisement for a fungus convention, and the longer his father was gone for, the worse it got. Upon entering that evening, you could tell that Marty had been the only one home for a while. Empty pizza boxes, beer bottles, and take-out containers cluttered the kitchen counter and the floor in the living room. Wires and instruments took up one corner of the room, and the other contained a television set situated in front of a table with three legs and a gray couch with

34

torn upholstery. The whole place smelled like stale cigarettes and dirty socks and was stuffier than a sweatshop, but I was still substantially more comfortable there than I was in my own home.

The first thing I did when I walked inside was light up a smoke. Jeff made a beeline for the fridge in the kitchen, Marty disappeared into his room, Shania turned on the television set, and Leanne crashed on the couch. I followed the girls into the living room and lifted a clogged ashtray off the table before taking a seat next to Leanne. A few minutes later, Jeff returned from the kitchen and handed us all beers, and Marty emerged from his room with a cordless telephone in one hand and a second bag of weed in the other. He chucked the bag at Shania who cleared off the three-legged coffee table and began to roll, while he sat down on the arm of the couch and ordered us four whole pies from Emilio's Deep-Dish Pizza.

I slid down from the couch and sat cross-legged on the floor in front of the coffee table and helped Shania roll with a can of Coors in my lap and a Marlboro protruding from the corner of my mouth. The five of us situated ourselves in what was more or less a circular formation and passed around the bones while Leanne and the boys took turns battling one another in *Final Fantasy* on the PlayStation. We were totally ripped and ravenous by the time the pizza delivery man came, and Marty threw him a fifty dollar bill, even though the order was less than $40.

Considering Marty's laxity with cash, I couldn't help but imagine that his father was holding some serious dough, but Marty hardly ever spoke of him, and when he did, it was very equivocally. I had met him a time or two before, years ago. I remembered him as a tall man with a shaved head and kind, dark eyes. He reminded me a bit of Marlon Brando, with a thin face and a squared off jaw. He seemed nice enough, and I never could quite understand why Marty resented him so much.

I thought about these things for about a minute and a half, until my train of thought was completely derailed and I was drawn into a conversation between Shania and Jeff:

"I really hate those yellow-bellied sons of bitches," Jeff slurred between slugs of beer and mouthfuls of pizza. "What I don't understand is why they bother with us. I can't stand them neither, but you don't see me goin' over into their business and causing a scene, drunk as I am. That's what I don't understand..."

"They're jealous," Shania explained to him, shaking her pointer finger shamefully at no one in particular. "They ain't got no business of their own to mind, so they mind ours for us."

"Nah, nah, that ain't it," Marty interjected. "They're afraid of us because we smoke and get stoned sometimes—that makes us dangerous drug users. We spend our time playing music they don't like and dress in different clothes and that makes us freaks."

Shania shook her head back and forth like a pendulum, "This world would be a much more beautiful place if everybody didn't care so much about what other people did with their bodies and their time. Can't everybody just live their own lives? High school is like Hollywood, and everybody shits on the couple people who aren't afraid to be themselves. Nothing ever changes; it's an endless cycle that not even graduation can stop. I feel like society is one big soap opera, and as for the parts we play, status is denoted by appearance, most definitely," she sniveled. "It sucks knowing the only reason people like you is because you're pretty."

She spoke from experience. To say that high school had been an unpleasant ordeal for all of us would be an understatement. Jesus, even the band kids wouldn't talk to us—all of us, except for Shania, that is. Shania had been extremely popular all through high school and had had a hell of a time trying to get everybody else to lay off of us.

"I think it's something in their brains, like a gene or something that automatically makes them assholes," Jeff replied.

"Assholes will be assholes," Leanne shrugged simply.

"It's ignorance," I spoke, feeling a strange sensation of enlightenment resulting from the conversation, "and ignorance is responsible for some of the most serious problems in this world. Ignorance and indifference; nobody cares to understand anyone because they're all too busy trying to get everyone else to understand them."

"That's why we have wars," Shania chimed in, "everybody believes in something different, and they all think they're right."

"I feel like we're all at war with one another constantly. Everybody is always threatening each other and competing with each other, and everybody wants to be better than everybody else. Why can't we all just help one another achieve our goals rather than trampling them underfoot?" I contributed.

"That's just not the way the world is," Shania replied sadly.

We all stared at each other silently through half-mast eyes. Save for being uneducated, obscene, and ill-mannered, I didn't think that we were any less entitled to our inquiries than the scientists and politicians that pondered the same things.

"Do you think we'll ever get to be someplace where everybody is just like us?" Leanne asked.

"Would that make us normal then?" Jeff inquired, turning his beer bottle upside down to make sure that it was indeed empty.

"Nah, we'll never be normal, but it would make assholes like Cochran the minority," Marty pointed out as he munched absently on cheese puffs that he'd found in a bag under the couch.

"I hope I live to see the day our world looks like that," I spoke.

"If not, Slab City is only a couple hours' drive from here," Jeff grinned. "A bunch of anarchists and freaks out in the desert, no cops, no laws—what could be better?"

Nothing, I thought to myself as I sprinkled cheese puffs on my pizza and laid back to watch the TV.

"Ah, we don't need Slab City," Shania declared excitedly. "We *will* get a callback from Track Records, I can *feel* it!"

"Nah, that's all the pot you smoked," Jeff countered, jabbing her in the ribs with his elbow.

The phone rang then, startling all of us. Marty checked the clock on the rear wall; it was after midnight. We all exchanged confused glances. All four of us that would place a call to Marty this late at night were sitting there in the room with him. Plus, there was a second problem—we could hear the phone ringing *somewhere* in the room, but none of us could find it. We all set about searching, and Leanne pulled it from in-between the couch cushions just as it clicked over to voicemail.

Marty furrowed his brow, "If it's important, they'll leave a message."

The four of us followed him into his room where the cordless receiver sat on his bedside table. It beeped, and a deep, masculine voice spoke through the tinny speakers, casting such an eerie effect on the caller that I shivered.

"This is Fresno P.D.," the metallic voice spoke. "There has been a missing person reported within city limits. The subject is an eighteen-year-old female named Rhiannon Karlson. She has long brown hair, blue eyes, and was last seen wearing a green sweat-suit. Also missing is the subject's white antique convertible. The subject is a suspected runaway, and there is a high chance that she is intoxicated and a hazard to both herself and others. If you have any information regarding the whereabouts of this person or her vehicle, please contact the authorities immediately."

The message cut out, and I felt the floor jerk beneath my feet. My butt landed on Marty's step, and my hands flew to my forehead. Paranoia began to course through my veins along with every emotion one could name: fear, anger, confusion, dread, and most especially desperation. My mother's nerve was becoming too much to fathom. The stares of eight red, concerned eyeballs bore down at me, growing longer and longer as the tick of the clock became louder and louder.

Marty broke the silence with a string of curses directed toward Meredith, and then reached out toward me with both hands and helped me to my feet.

"I cannot believe her!" I cried, exasperated. "Jesus H. Christ, what a—" I began to cuss her out myself. I could only imagine the whole town listening to that message on their answering machines in the morning. I could only imagine all the cops out patrolling the city that night who had just heard that on their radio receivers and were going to be on the lookout for me. I could only imagine one of Marty's night owl neighbors peering out their kitchen window and thinking to themselves, *Say, that looks like an old, white convertible,* right before they rung for the police.

I turned and flew from the steps into the bathroom at the end of the hall. I tore through the medicine cabinet above the sink and found a bottle of eye drops. I poured an absurd amount into each eye in hopes that they wouldn't be as red as the rest of my face by the time I made it back across the street to where my mother would be waiting like a vulture for what she knew was my imminent return.

I called out a hasty goodbye and slammed the door behind me. Even in the dead of night, the air was thick and stagnant; it clung to my skin, and not even the slightest of breezes arrived to shake its suffocating embrace. It was a heat so hot it made me feel as if my soul was parched. I stared up at the cloudless, starless, smoggy sky and begged desperately for a thunderstorm, but nothing changed; even the atmosphere was mocking me. I jammed my key into the ignition, shifted into reverse and backed into the street, past two houses, and safely into my own driveway. I considered backing right into my mother's station wagon in spite, but I didn't want to scratch my paint.

I dropped my keys into the pocket of my jeans and made it for the door. I expected to walk into the kitchen and be met by my mother's wrath, but to my overwhelming surprise, the room was empty, and the house was quiet. I didn't hang around to see if that would change. I shut myself up in my room and threw open both windows—it was almost as stuffy inside as it was at Marty's; my mother had shut off the A/C. I plopped myself down on my bed and kicked off my sneakers and socks, emptied my pockets, and changed into a pair of cotton shorts and an old blue tank top, but my efforts were futile; I was far too frustrated and angry to get comfortable. Silently, I crept to the door and opened it a crack before scurrying down the hall to the bathroom and locking the door behind me. I turned the shower dial to the coldest setting and stepped into the stream of water. A shudder passed through me, and I lifted my head and looked up, opening my eyes and letting the icy liquid sting my face. Water droplets gathered in my eyelashes and created gray marbled patterns before my vision while hot tears fell from my kaleidoscope eyes as I cried in vain for rain.

****

1969

****

The next morning, I was awoken by the shrill tone of the ringing telephone. I did not remember much from the previous night after getting home, not getting out of the shower or even getting into bed. Disoriented, somewhat delirious, and still slightly on edge from the last time I'd heard a phone ring, I stumbled out from under the covers. Half-asleep, I fumbled around my cluttered dresser before finally locating the cordless phone and mumbling a few indiscernible words into the receiver.

The voice on the other end of the line spoke quickly and excitedly to me: "Rhiannon! Rhiannon! It's Marty, you're not going to believe it!"

"Lay it on me," I mumbled, bracing myself against the dresser in case he said something like *"The entire Fresno police fleet is converging on your driveway right now!"*

"We got a callback!" he burst out, unable to contain his excitement. "I got a call from Track Records! They want to meet with us up in San Francisco!"

The fog that had settled over my brain instantly lifted, "No fucking way! When?" I asked him.

"Eight o'clock on the 9th! That's tomorrow night! He wants to meet us at The Fillmore! Can you believe it? The Fillmore!"

"No way!" I cried as tears of joy welled up in my eyes. "Tomorrow at The Fillmore in goddamn San Francisco! It's happening, isn't it Marty? We're really gonna get outta here!"

"Come over, I'll tell you more later. I'm calling everybody up. We gotta start getting everything together."

"And bug out tomorrow afternoon," I added.

"How was Meredith last night?" he asked finally. "Did she give you a hard time?"

"I didn't even see the witch," I replied, still surprised by that fact. "I wonder what she's going to do when I tell her tomorrow I'm leaving for San Francisco!"

By the time I hung up the phone, my heart had swelled to double its size inside my chest, and I felt as if I had the wings of Mercury on my feet. I couldn't believe it—this could be our lucky break! I was so full of hope, encouragement, and relief that it seemed unreal; I even

40

pinched my cheek to assure myself that I was awake and not dreaming. I couldn't wait to call up George; he would be so happy for me! I imagined him grinning from ear to ear as I told him the news, displaying every one of his nicotine-yellowed teeth and shaking his head from side to side in overwhelming pride as he sent me off, yelling *"Rock on!"* as I drove away.

With this image in mind and a grin of my own apparent on my face, I swung open my bedroom door and found myself nose to nose with my mother. Not only did my wings disappear and my feet return to the ground, I felt like sinking through the floor. I started to back up and close the door again, but she stepped forward and jammed her finger into my chest.

"Did I hear you correctly?" she spoke, completely enraged. I could tell that she was gearing up for a full-blown mêlée. Her face was getting redder by the second, and I was sure that pretty soon smoke would start curling out from her ears. I figured I really couldn't get in much more trouble than I was in already, so I answered her question truthfully.

"Damn right you did! A record label wants to sign my band. Tomorrow afternoon I'm cutting out of his hellhole, and good luck stopping me!"

"Don't you use that tone with me, Rhiannon, and don't you tell me what you think you're going to do! San Francisco, Rhiannon? Do you know how many crazy people, homeless people, homosexuals, and perverts are in San Francisco? How many drugs? Bad drugs, Rhiannon; cocaine, pills, heroin… Do you know that eighty percent of heroin users are under the age of twenty-six? Twenty-six, Rhiannon, you're only eighteen! And you think you're going with those no-good friends of yours, don't you? They'll lure you in, you'll just want to try it, and then you'll be addicted to drugs! You'll come crawling back here in six months begging for money so that you can feed your habit! You know what I'll do? I'll put you away. No, I won't allow you to go! No daughter of mine is going to ruin her life by trying to be some kind of hippie musician up in San Francisco!"

"It's just like any other city!" I cried. "We live twenty minutes from a city for God's sake! And I'm not going to get hooked on drugs! What the hell is your problem? If you trusted me, you'd let me go!"

"Trust a teenager?" she blurted out. "What do you think, I'm stupid?"

"If you thought you did a good job raising me, you wouldn't have any trouble at all letting me go! In fact, you'd be happy to!" I accused her. "If you weren't feeling guilty about the shitty parenting job you did, you wouldn't be calling the goddamn cops on me, would you? Or listening to my conversations outside my bedroom door! How long have you even been standing there anyway?"

"You're out of control, Rhiannon! Since you won't obey me, you'll obey the law—you can't disrespect the police the way I allow you to disrespect me!"

"You don't understand me! You don't know anything about me!" I screamed. "You don't know what it's like to be a teenager, and you don't let me live my life! You only want me to like the things that you like and do the things that you do! You don't want me to be my own person, you don't even like me!"

"Rhiannon, Hollywood and fame are evil! I'm trying to stop you from making a very big mistake."

"I don't want to be mainstream, I don't want to be famous, I just want to play music! Unlike you, I want to do something with my life! I want to perform, I want to do what I love and travel the country, see the things I've always wanted to see, do the things I've always wanted to do, and most of all, get away from you!" I shouldered past her and stomped out the front door, leaving it wide open behind me so that she could see me walk right across the road and straight through Marty's front door, all without even the slightest glance behind me.

As soon as I got on the other side of the door, I groped around until I found the deadbolt and crouched down to peer out the stained glass window. Frankly, I was terrified that she would follow me, start yelling and banging on Marty's door and make enough of a scene to wake the rest of the neighborhood—after all, it wouldn't be the first time. Suddenly, I began to feel very foolish. I was still wearing my pajamas, I still looked a wreck from the previous night, and I didn't even have shoes on. I surveyed 7th Street through the warped, red and purple glass until I was positive she was not coming, and then called out Marty's name and began to tear apart the house in search of a cigarette. I found one in no time at all, scrounged up a lighter, sat down on the couch, inhaled deeply, closed my eyes, and sighed.

When I reopened my eyes, Marty was standing there, still dressed in his jeans and t-shirt from the night before.

"Well, good morning, stranger!" he greeted me good-naturedly. "Jesus, Rhiannon, when I said come over, I didn't mean you had to sprint here! I know you're excited and all, but you at least could've put on shoes first!"

42

"Meredith," I explained, inhaling another lungful of smoke.

"What, she gave you a hard time over last night?"

I exhaled. I could feel a buzz starting to come on. "Nah. Cat's out of the bag," I answered him. "She knows we're leaving tomorrow. She fucking eavesdropped on our goddamn conversation! She stood outside my bedroom door and called me on it as soon as I hung up the phone."

Marty shook his head and scratched his chin where a cluster of coarse, dark hairs had broken through the skin, "Need to shave," he commented mindlessly. "But seriously, Rhiannon, it's time for you to get the hell out of here. If she follows us up there or something ridiculous, you can press charges for stalking and obsession. You are eighteen, you know."

I rolled my eyes and ground my cigarette butt into the ashtray, then looked around for more. Marty pulled a brand new pack of 100s from his back pocket, threw the cellophane wrapper on the floor, and smacked the pack against his hand a few times before tossing it to me.

"I'd just gotten back from 7-Eleven when the A&R guy called. Leanne crashed here last night, and we were out of smokes. I thought you'd be needing these," he explained.

"Thank you," I replied gratefully. "The fact that you guys are all a year older makes my life a hell of a lot easier."

"Anything for our little Rhiannon," he grinned playfully, swaggering over to me and mussing up my hair.

"If there's one thing I can thank Meredith for, it's putting me in school a year early. If she hadn't, we probably wouldn't have been friends."

I opened the pack, tore off the silver paper, and inhaled the sweet aroma. In those days, there were few things in life I loved more than a brand new pack of cigarettes. I shook the pack, pinched a filter between my fingers, and placed it between my lips before offering one to Marty. He sat down next to me, and we both lit up.

"You know the only reason I started smoking these things was because of her?" I asked him.

Marty nodded slowly, "I remember, I was there. You came over here all aggravated and frustrated because of something she'd said to you, and I had some, so I gave you one. That was what, freshman year?"

I nodded and took another drag, "Yup. Sometimes I think the only reason I'm a rebel is because of my mother. She never smoked, so I smoked. She never drank, so I drank. She wanted me to dress in pink and bows, so I went out and bought black eyeliner and blue jeans. I've defied her at every turn—sometimes for no other reason than the fact that I don't want to be like her."

Marty nodded, and I continued; I felt as if the words were just tumbling out of me like clouds of smoke, "It's hard to understand somebody when they don't talk to you. I don't even think my mother is capable of starting a conversation unless her blood pressure is 140/90. I've been with her almost every single day since I was born, and yet I know almost nothing about her life. George used to tell me all kinds of things about his: about living up in Washington in the sixties when he was our age, about all the Dead shows he went to in the seventies, about all the drugs he took in-between..." I trailed off. "It's hard to get along with somebody you don't know anything about and who doesn't talk to you, especially when they don't listen to you, either. I think that's why the music we play is so important. Rock and roll speaks for me; once I started playing the drums, I stopped taking her shit. I felt like suddenly I had the power to make people listen to what I wanted to say."

Marty started nodding more vigorously now, "Yeah, yeah," he replied excitedly. "That's exactly how I feel—except the difference is my father never stopped talking long enough to hear what I had to say, and whenever he did, he was always correcting me. He's just so idealistic, we're just too...*different*."

Leanne entered the room then. She was wrapped in a bath towel, and water dripped from her damp, red hair, "Greetings, earthlings," she called from the doorway. Her voice was chipper, and her eyes were bright. She looked to be just about the happiest I'd ever seen her. "I just called my grandmother and told her the news," she announced. "Quite honestly, I think it's the first time anyone's been proud of me for anything."

Her enthusiasm was contagious, and I cracked a smile. All of us complained about our parents for some reason or another, but Leanne was a foster kid. She'd been living with her biological grandmother for the last two years, but before that had been bounced around like a ping-pong ball between broken families and temporary homes. She'd had a harder childhood than any of us, and yet was the most talented bassist I'd ever played with. If any of us deserved this, it was her.

"It doesn't even feel like it's actually happening," Marty admitted. "It's like you dream about something for so long and then when it finally comes true, it's almost impossible to believe."

"You know it!" Leanne smiled, displaying the mouthful of sharp,

44

white teeth she usually kept hidden behind her black lipstick. "Hey Rhiannon, I have some extra clothes if you want to change out of your PJs."

I stood up and followed her into Marty's guest room where there was a pile of clean clothes in a laundry basket in the corner. I dug through it and found a pair of her Levi's and a t-shirt that probably belonged to one of the boys. I cleaned myself up in the bathroom and changed. I was coming back down the hallway when the front door swung open, and Shania and Jeff stepped into the house.

"WHOO!" Jeff yelled, charging into the hall. "Look at us musicians! Shania and I just swung by my parents' house. When I moved out, they told me I'd get nowhere in life and be a drunken bum like my daddy. Well, guess who was wrong!" He sprinted into the living room and tackled Marty on the couch, and the two of them wrestled one another to the floor.

"And what else," Shania prodded him, amused.

Jeff looked up from where he was working Marty over with fake blows to the head, "Oh yeah, Dave called me this morning from L.A, he'll be here sometime this afternoon. Our last night in this town will be a bang, that's for sure!"

"And tomorrow night we'll be at The Fillmore," Leanne added. "Fuckin' A."

"What else did the guy from Track Records say, Marty?" Shania asked. "You said you'd tell us when we were all together."

Marty furrowed his brow as he recalled his conversation from earlier that morning, "Well, the scout who saw us the other night at The Joint wants to speak to us in person about signing a deal memo and recording with them. He's the one who called me up. His name is Dev—as in Devon—Dev Marshall. He told me he's bringing somebody with him who may be interested in managing us. He asked if it would be possible for us to make the trek up to San Francisco to see him, and he told me that he had three gigs at a bar downtown lined up for us as a favor to make the trip worth it. He said the only thing needed to secure them was his word of mouth—do you know how influential this guy has got to be?! I said yes—of course—how fucking awesome is that?! We have to pay for a motel, but we'll be pulling in twice what we make now, and if he's pleased, we'll have a record deal in the works! He said that as soon as we sign, he'll get us in the studio and we can lay down about a dozen of our best tracks and market it as a debut classic rock cover album—they'll pay us an advance and everything!"

"Sounds like a solid deal to me," Shania replied. "My parents told me they'd give us $500 cash for gas and food until we get on our feet. That should carry us for a week at least, plus whatever we make."

We all looked around at one another; the energy in the room was electric. We were buzzing; high on good fortune and anticipation, and it didn't take long before all thoughts of my mother had vanished. We spent the rest of that afternoon speculating and spit-balling; envisioning all the things we hoped this opportunity would bring us. We chattered on about the Whisky and The Fillmore and how we hoped to play there and make a name for ourselves in the cities where our idols once performed, and Marty gushed about how he dreamed of meeting Clapton and collaborating with him. Jeff told him his chances were about as slim as mine were of meeting Bonzo, but when he let it slip that he wanted to make it with Dolores O'Riordan, we all agreed that Marty's fantasies were far more realistic. Even Shania and Leanne contributed some secret aspirations, each becoming more and more outrageous as the day progressed.

I didn't care much for the absurd. I knew that I'd probably never get the chance to interact with the remaining members of some of my favorite bands such as the Dead or the Airplane, and I knew that I'd never get to watch Janis or Hendrix or Led Zeppelin perform. I knew that most of the San Francisco hotspots had been demolished or were no longer in operation: The Avalon had lost its lease in '68, and Bill Graham's Fillmore West was now a car dealership. Even The Matrix—one of the most important venues in rock history—had closed its doors in 1972. I knew these things as well as anyone, but still, in my mind, it all came to life. I imagined walking the streets of that revolutionary city in the midst of a countercultural movement that continued to shake the world thirty years later. I imagined the shops, the people, the sounds—it was therapeutic, but at the same time, eternally disappointing. Hope came by way of the legacy contained in the history, in the music, and in the memories of those who had lived it. For me, it was simply the prospect, the possibility that I might get the chance to perform on the same stages as the greats I held in higher esteem than any other that motivated me. Just the fact that I would soon be walking through the doors of The Fillmore—a club I'm sure ghosts of hippies past continued to patronize—was sufficient enough to satisfy me.

Collectively, we decided that our goal as a band was to recapture the essence, to recreate the experience in order to share it with those who appreciated it. In San Francisco and places like it, there was quite a market for that sort of entertainment. Once we made moves to get the hell out of Fresno, it would be easy—gaining traction was the hardest part. No longer would we be the house band at a stagnant, backroad dive—a frustrated, talented group of young musicians lacking the means and opportunity to become anything more. The prospect of being able to afford to leave town in and of itself was exhilarating.

As the hours passed and the sun rose higher in the sky, the temperature in Marty's house began to soar once more. To combat the heat, we sat in front of the broken air conditioner and drank cold cokes, smoked cigarettes, and shared a quart of ice cream from the freezer. It was about four in the afternoon when Jeff checked the clock.

"It's getting late," he commented, "Dave should be rolling in soon. Does everybody have cash for when he gets here?"

"Oh shit," I gasped. "No. I have to go back across the street and get my wallet." I stood up and glanced down at my bare feet. *I might as well put on shoes while I'm at it*, I thought. *I really hope Meredith's not home.*

My hopes were dashed as soon as I stepped out onto the sidewalk. My mother's station wagon was parked in the driveway, and right next to it was Jack Hartford's forest green Pontiac. I felt my stomach drop into my feet—there wasn't a snowball's chance in hell that anything good, right, or constructive was going on inside those walls. I sprinted across the street and into the garage. Even from the other side of the kitchen door, I could hear my mother's nasally, angry voice.

"She's throwing her life away and you're encouraging her! You promised me that you would help me raise her, but what have you done for me all these years? Craft my daughter into an unruly, disrespectful, ornery teenager—that's what you've done for me! You've never once paid child support; I paid all the bills! I've put in all the work, and what have you done? Given her false views about a lifestyle that she does not and cannot understand? Taught her to hate me? You're nothing but a deadbeat burnout! *I* was the one who always had to discipline her! *I* was the one who had to help her with her schoolwork! *I* was the one who had to drive her places! *I* was the one who had to make sure she didn't do anything stupid, and *I* was the one who had to pick up after her when she did! Me, George, me!"

"Now, Meredith, you've heard her play," George answered. His voice sounded apprehensive, worried almost. I knew he didn't much like being around Meredith, and it had probably been years since they'd seen each other. "You know how talented she is. The only way she'd be throwing her life away is if she stays here in this town. I never gave her false views about anything. I never taught her to hate you. I let her make her own decisions and grow up to be her own person. I may not be the best parent, but I support her like a parent should."

"Bullshit, it's your fault she turned out the way she did," Meredith snapped back, "and I'm not blind, I can see that she's talented. There's a praise band at my church, for years they've needed a drummer. There she'd be able to play music and remain in a healthy environment at the same time. It'd give her a sense of purpose, of faith. Maybe then she'd go to college and make something of her life and forget all about this awful phase. If only she started going to church again and got away from those rotten friends of hers—and you."

George paused, "You mustn't've thought there was too much wrong with me eighteen years ago," he murmured in a helpless sort of way. "I don't understand, you didn't even want to have her. If it weren't for me, that little girl wouldn't have even been born."

"OK, so I never wanted a child, but she's still my daughter! I don't want her to go out into the world and try to become some kind of hippie rock and roll star. It's not going to work, George, she's going to get hurt, and I've invested far too much in her to let her waste it all on some stupid dream!"

A shock like someone had punched me struck me deep inside my chest. A sharp pang of hurt and resentment coursed through me, and I backed away from the door and left the garage before I could hear anymore. I stood outside around the corner of the house as my brain tried to make sense of what my ears had just heard. Their angry voices rang inside my head, crashing and echoing about inside my skull. *I need a cigarette*, I thought desperately, *I need a cigarette, I need a cigarette...*

As I started to head back across the street, I noticed that Dave's gray Honda was parked in Marty's driveway, and I tried as hard as I could to compose myself. I let myself back into the house quietly and went searching for a cigarette. Everybody was gathered in the living room, so I snuck into the kitchen and bummed one off of whoever had left their pack out on the counter. I leaned against the refrigerator and breathed in the sweet smoke.

"Rhiannon?" I glanced to my left and Leanne was standing there. "I thought I heard you come in. Everything cool?"

"Yeah, of course," I lied.

"You gotta come see what Dave brought," she replied, reaching

48

into the fridge to grab a can of soda. "You know I pretty much stick to weed and E, but he's got more drugs than Pablo Escobar."

I followed her back into the living room so as not to seem weird. As much as I tried to push it out of my mind, I kept mulling over what I had just heard—I couldn't help it. It's not as if what Meredith said had particularly surprised me, but I never thought that I would ever hear my speculations confirmed, at least not like that.

Everybody was crouched around the three-legged coffee table sorting through various bags of illicit substances. Once he noticed me standing there, Dave stood up to greet me and shook my hand—his skin was smooth and soft. He was taller than all of us at about 6'2" and had dark brown hair that grew to his chin. He had a deep desert tan and was wearing sun-bleached denim and a faded green t-shirt. His round, hazel eyes were serene and comforting, and upon meeting them, I became instantly calm.

"You're Rhiannon, right?" he asked—he had this slow, soothing voice. "I remember you."

I nodded, "Hello."

"Here, come out to my car, I'll show you what I've got. I already took care of your friends." He began walking past me out the door before I had a chance to tell him that I didn't have any cash, so I just followed him outside.

I stepped out into the heat of the day once more and squinted against the glare of the sun to see if Jack's car was still in my driveway—it wasn't. I turned away and tried to forget about the conflict and the animosity and watched instead as Dave unlocked his trunk. I peered inside, and when I did, I couldn't believe my eyes. The entire trunk was filled with an assortment of colored plastic baggies.

"There's good old California-grown weed and hash in the green bags, ecstasy in the blue bags, red is for psilocybin mushrooms, yellow has salvia, I've got some speed and coke if you can find a purple bag, and those wads of tin foil are Mexican black tar…if you're into that," he stepped back. "Help yourself."

I stared back at him with wide eyes, "You better hope you never get pulled over, man!"

Dave laughed, "Man, have I heard that before!"

Dumbfounded, I turned and surveyed the heap of baggies. I had a whole host of mind-altering, life-changing substances at my fingertips. My hands trembled as I picked through a couple of the baggies. Inside, I could see various dried plant materials, pills, blotter squares, white powder—every kind of drug I could imagine—and yet

I couldn't buy even one.

"I don't have any cash," I confessed, stepping away from the car, "I'm sorry."

Dave gazed back at me, his content expression unchanged, "Well, that's alright. Here, I have something special for you."

I watched as he reached forward into his trunk and from behind the wheel well retrieved a single pink baggie. He handed it to me, and I took it from him. I inhaled a sharp breath and began to examine the gift. Inside the baggie were two elongated crystals and a tiny silver pipe.

He must have realized how confused I was because he answered my question before I even had a chance to ask it. "This is the most powerful psychedelic known to mankind," he told me. "There is enough in there for two trips. It's a short trip, usually twenty minutes or less, but it is the most incredible and fulfilling experience you will ever have in your life. To get the most out of it, you must not be afraid. You must be willing to accept what you are experiencing and know that it is your mind that is creating it. I prefer to smoke mine in a quiet, dark room in a place that I know is safe. Remember, all this drug will do is intensify your expectations, so make sure to take it when you're in a good state of mind and being."

I looked down at the baggie in my hands. I could almost feel a sort of supernatural energy emanating from it. "T-thank you," I stammered, stuffing the baggie into my pocket.

Dave smiled, "Anytime."

The CCR was blasting over the stereo when we re-entered the house. During the time the two of us had been outside, everybody else had gotten down to business. They had moved both mattresses from Marty's bunk bed into the living room and removed all the cushions from the couch and arranged them in a circle on the floor with the coffee table in the middle. Some of the baggies on the coffee table had been opened, and I watched as Shania, Marty, Leanne, and Jeff popped two tablets of ecstasy in their mouths and washed them down with a swig of beer from a bottle they passed around. I considered smoking my crystals but decided against it. Since my mother knew where I was, I knew that I'd better be home early and sober, before she called the cops and had us all busted. Dave stood up, lowered the shades, and fiddled around with the stereo. The CCR died down, and a track by The Doors began to seep through the speakers. Dave returned to his seat and started to munch on a piece of dried mushroom, and Leanne began packing a pipe with herb and hash oil.

I watched them for a good while. Leanne offered me a hit from her pipe, but I declined and opted for a cigarette instead. The six of us talked for a while, sparingly. Once we finished remembering old times and catching up on the last few years, Dave and I got into a conversation about literature. I think it started when I began to tell him about San Francisco and the offer we had gotten. He asked me how much I knew about the history of the music scene there. I told him I knew quite a bit, and we started talking about The Grateful Dead. I told him about how much of a fanatic George was, but we really hit it off after he mentioned the name Kesey. I know a lot about Ken Kesey.

I'd always loved to read, and whatever I read usually had some bearing on hippie culture. I'd read Kerouac and Ginsberg, Huxley and Hesse, but by far my favorite book had been *The Electric Kool-Aid Acid Test*. I'd discovered it on Jack's bookshelf when I was a kid and was immediately hooked. It was written by a man named Tom Wolfe about Ken Kesey and his wild life. Kesey was a household name in literature after the publication of *One Flew Over the Cuckoo's Nest* and an LSD freak before anyone else in California knew what that was. He'd driven across the country in a psychedelically painted bus to meet Timothy Leary in New York, introduced LSD to San Francisco in a series of acid tests, helped make The Grateful Dead famous, skipped the country and fled to Mexico when the heat was on, and then returned to watch it all culminate and die out. I'd read all of his books and any publication written about him. I felt that if there was any one single, vital cultural figure that history overlooked, it was him. I was a self-proclaimed Kesey-freak, and I told Dave all about it. He soaked it up, listening intently to every word I said and nodding fervently on occasion. He told me about Burroughs, Brautigan, Ferlinghetti, McClure—beatnik names I'd heard but scarcely read. We talked of *On The Road, Siddhartha*, and *The Doors of Perception* while everyone else reclined on their mattresses giggling and pointing at the TV.

It was about eight-thirty when things really started to kick in, for everybody except me. I was as sober as ever, my lips clamped tightly around a Marlboro—I'd probably smoked two packs since this morning. When I realized that I was the only one in the room who could still tell you what the room actually looked like, I started to feel a bit uncomfortable and unwelcome. I was sullen and my heart was heavy while everyone else was at peace and having a good time. I wished for nothing more than to trip along with them, to escape the confines of my mind, to escape this here and now. With a wave of my hand I sent them on their way and wished them well wherever they ended up, then I walked home once again, more confused and troubled than I'd ever felt before.

Once I made it back across the street, I dawdled awhile in my driveway in an effort to postpone any unpleasant encounter that might take place. I kicked a few stones off the pavement and back under the neighbor's shrubs, then sat awhile in my car. I hid the pink baggie Dave had given me in my glove box and threw in a lighter and a half-empty pack of cigarettes. I reclined awhile, looking up at the sky. It was a peculiar night; there was not a cloud in sight, and a slight wind stirred around me. The stars were abnormally bright. Although it was early in the evening, it was quiet. No dogs barked, and no cars passed—even the crickets were silent. I felt as if the night itself was holding its breath.

Several minutes passed. Eventually, I succumbed to boredom and tried to sneak into the house. The key word there is *tried*. Just as I closed the door behind me and stepped inside, I turned to see my mother walking out from the kitchen straight toward me. In her tightly clenched fist, she held a bag of weed. *My* bag of weed. I thought about turning around and walking right back out the door for all the good it would do, but I ignored that and every other bit of common sense and self-preservation that my mind offered. The adrenaline was pumping, and every one of my neurons was screaming at me to get the hell out of there, but I stood my ground. This is what it had come down to—a showdown. It was me against her; I was ready.

"What the hell is this?" Meredith growled, holding the bag up to my face. It was green and sticky, and it smelled great. It was a whole ounce that had probably cost me around $300, and I was *not* going to let her take it.

"Mine!" I replied, grabbing for the bag. "That was in *MY* room in *MY* dresser under *MY* clothes! What right do you have going into my room and rifling through my shit? Don't touch my shit! Give me that!"

She pulled it away, and I stumbled forward, "This is my house, and you live under my roof! I pay the bills; therefore, I can touch anything I damn well please! You mean to tell me this is *yours*?!" she spat accusingly, her eyes wide.

"Give it to me!" I screamed, lunging again. "Fuck off!"

She ran straight into the bathroom. Dismay and alarm coursed through me. I charged after her and banged on the door as hard as I could. I pulled on the doorknob, but she had locked it. After a few moments, I heard the toilet flush. I saw red.

Meredith reopened the door, empty bag in hand. "Now, Rhiannon, we are going to sit down and discuss this," her voice trembled in an attempt to regain her composure.

I exploded, "Sit down and talk about it?! You just flushed my fucking weed!"

She wasn't calm for long, "*Your* weed, Rhiannon?! I can't believe it, my daughter's a pot-smoker! A drug user! I've been housing an addict! I've always suspected, but I was never sure! My God, you probably smoke cigarettes and drink too, and Lord knows what else you've done!"

There was no point in holding back now, "You know what? You're right! I've been smoking since I've been thirteen and drinking since the year after. And you know what? I'm not even a virgin! I lost it behind the dugout to Scotty Jordan when I was in tenth grade!" I was on a roll, I couldn't even control the words that were spilling from my mouth; my tongue had possessed me, "Wanna see something else?" I pulled up my shirt to reveal the peace sign tattoo on my hip. I wish I could've taken a picture of her face. "I got this little beauty at a convention when I was seventeen, and I used my *fake ID* to buy it! You'd love to know the things I've done and the places I've gone without your permission! Unfortunately, I'm still here—just about the only thing I haven't done yet is run away! I won't be here for much longer though, oh no, this is the last night you'll see me. And then you'll be free of me—snoop through anything you damn well please!"

"That's why you want to go out to San Francisco! I know why you're going: to go stand on the corner of Capp Street and pay for your habits you little crack-whore!"

"Crack-whore!" I cried in disbelief. "You're the one who got knocked up by some stoned hippie!"

"What did you say to me?!" she threatened, storming closer.

"You heard me," I cried, turning away as hot tears sprang onto my cheeks, "I wish I was never born!"

"You better not walk out that door, Rhiannon!"

I walked out the door, and I slammed it behind me too. The tears were flowing now, and I couldn't let her see them. I jumped into my car, jammed the key into the ignition, slammed it into reverse, screeched to a halt, grinded the gears as I shifted into first, and sped away, tires squealing and all. I have to admit it was pretty dramatic, but I was so upset I couldn't care less.

1969

As soon as I made it out to the main road, I floored it. I had no idea where I was going, and I could barely see the road ahead of me through all the tears. All I knew was that I needed to get away, far, far away, and I couldn't wait until tomorrow. I needed a sanctuary, but I had nowhere to run to. A stream of tears fell upon my steering wheel, and my eyes burned. At once, bright lights appeared before me. I hoped that it was a trailer truck that had come to claim my life, but it wasn't. It was The Joint, made to shine like a beacon by the line of cars waiting to leave the parking lot. I whipped the car around, flew past them, and parked in one of the rear spaces, a good distance away from anyone else. I shut off the engine, switched off the lights, and sat there alone in the night and cried. I rocked back and forth in my seat, banging my head gently against the steering wheel. I needed to escape.

Escape...

The idea struck me at once, and I used the collar of my shirt to wipe my face as I reached forward into my glove box to retrieve the little pink baggie. I took out the tiny, silver pipe and examined it. It was intricately decorated with carved designs and motifs; however, it was so old that the illustrations had been rubbed smooth from years of use and the colors faded. I wondered where he had gotten it and who had used it before me—what trips they had taken. I removed one of the crystals from the bag and placed it in the bowl at the end of the pipe, then I stuck the end of the pipe between my lips. I clutched my lighter tightly in my hand and sparked a flame. There was no turning back now.

The first thing I noticed that wasn't quite right was the smoke coming out from the pipe. It was thick and gray, and it curled and drifted—floating upward as smoke should—but when I blinked and my eyes were closed, the image seemed to remain. I could still see the smoke swirling, gray and blurry against the darkness on the inside of my eyelids—or at least I thought. I reopened my eyes and took another hit from the pipe, it sure was different than smoking pot. I closed my eyes again, and this time the blur of smoke was even clearer. Gradually, it grew brighter and brighter and became more easily distinguished. I could see shadows of strange patterns in colors like a film negative. They were barely there, flitting around and flickering dimly when I closed my eyes. I could feel my heartbeat pounding in my head and the blood rushing in my ears. It echoed around me, becoming louder and louder until I was struck with fear that someone else would hear it and I would be discovered. I glanced around me at my surroundings, paranoid and apprehensive. Everything seemed to be slowly disintegrating—as if it was made up of television snow—as if all that was around me was some kind of a projection and had never really existed at all.

I sat, catatonic, and watched in frozen terror as the static became more and more severe until it affected not only my vision but my hearing as well. The thumping of my heart seemed to grow slower as if an eternity passed in-between beats, and all of a sudden, it was replaced by an alarming high-pitched whine. All around me, reality fell away and was replaced by this static, this encroaching state of formlessness—as if all was dissolving—as if soon my own body would be reduced to nothing more than an insignificant bit of cosmic dust.

In overwhelming horror, I stole a quick glance at the radio clock; not a minute had passed since I first lit the pipe. It all came on so quickly, so rapidly, and so intensely. No single sensation remained for any more than a moment, and before long, I could no longer accurately judge what a moment was at all. Frantic, I turned my eyes to the sky. The stars suspended above the Earth were no longer cold and distant, but close enough to touch. They were not the same stars I saw earlier, they were different—alive. And the moon, the crescent moon was small and green. There was no time for me to try and understand what I was seeing—there was no time at all! Just when I imagined that it could not possibly become any stranger, or at least any more terrifying, I felt this sudden sensation of being grabbed, and a bony, celestial hand wrapped its fingers around my spine and hurdled me headfirst out into that sky. Panic struck me like a stake to the heart. *How in the world will I survive the fall?* I thought, but logic no longer applied in any of its great capacities. I was suspended in this space—below me, there was no Earth, no evidence at all of Fresno, of my car, or of The Joint. I was no longer present in that world; I was somewhere else entirely.

I looked down at my body and saw that upon my arms were strapped numerous golden watches, and as I stared, one by one, they began to crumble and fall away in sequence as gears and numbers rained from my wrists. It was then that I began to feel like my entire reality had shifted into reverse. It was if God had just stepped on the gas pedal of the universe. There was this sensation of rapid backward motion, continually increasing in speed. Not only was I moving, but all that was around me was moving as well. Glyphs and geometric patterns manifested in space and flew past me. I felt as if all these things were coming toward me in as much as I felt that they were moving away. All that I saw was inexplicable; at every moment I was experiencing something new and even more alien. I attempted to focus on one illusion at a time in an attempt to try and determine if I was really seeing what I thought I was seeing, but each time I attempted to zero in on a particular manifestation, it changed yet again. I felt like I was going stark raving mad. I'd never heard of a drug like this before; maybe he'd given me poison or some new kind of compound. Maybe I'd fried my brains and would be doomed to bear for eternity the cacophony of this insane world—if it didn't kill me first. My head was pounding so violently I felt as if it were about to explode, and shortly after these few thoughts, I lost the ability to think. I was helpless except to bear witness and experience what was now before me.

My entire environment was transitory and soon seemed to be moving at such a great speed that it was imperceptible that any faster motion could possibly be achieved. The sensation was relentless; however, and as greater speeds were in fact reached, the void I was in seemed to become elastic and flexible. Space and time were not separate, they were the same, and as I was propelled backward into the infinite, the continual increase of speed became such that it seemed to skip in chunks or blocks, and contained within those increments were whole worlds. Flashes of light, color, and rapid mechanical motif emanated from a central point before me. Visions manifested themselves as sounds, and sensation was saturated in color. I began to feel my body—along with my surroundings—stretch out and become elongated. My arms and legs extended further than my bones and ligaments would ever allow, and horror pulsed through me as my physicality transformed—bending, twisting, and lengthening until my being was nothing more than a bowl of cosmic Jell-O. This did not remain, however, for as the recessive propulsions began to slow, my form began to fold in on itself. I began to feel my body become compacted as if I was being crushed and squeezed through the eye of a needle. All that was around me packed in closer and denser, the hallucinations moving ever nearer, as a fantastic culmination of sense and form inundated me.

These sensations, innumerable and terrifying, were simultaneous—until finally, it all stopped. All sense of movement and of transformation ended as suddenly as it had begun, and I was suspended in an eternal moment far away, on the very tip of the mind's final antipode. Before me, existed eternity—in silence, frozen—glittering in every unnamed hue. And I—an impartial observer—saw all entombed in a single moment, shrouded in unbelievable mystery, in such incommunicable perfection that there was no possible way I could obtain any comprehension of any of it—and yet just as I felt I was about to grasp it, in all its fullness and entirety, it disappeared; just out of my reach. In an instant, it was there, and in an instant, it was gone—and I along with it. Every molecule, every sense of myself had disappeared. I was no longer a human, an animal—and any sense of form, living or nonliving, had been suspended.

You have never experienced Nothing. In waking life, there is always some source of stimulation. Even when you are sleeping, you are breathing, and your heart is beating. True nothingness is not only a lack of stimulation, it is also a lack of sense. Nothingness is not dark, it is not cold, and it is not even silent—in fact, it cannot be explained in words because such words do not exist. It is absent from every experience you will ever have, and so different from such, that it cannot even be imagined.

The nothingness I experienced was again momentary—it was almost as if the Cosmos blinked. When sense and sensation did return, it was the most intense feeling I had ever felt; it was titanic. In waves, the molecules of my being were sent forth, in many pieces but still one consciousness—mine. Existence exploded from non-existence. It was as if reality itself had folded inside out, and not only was I experiencing it to the greatest degree, I was also watching it transpire. I was, but I also was not.

In such vivid undulations did whole worlds and universes around me spring forth, and as I gazed toward each, entire lifetimes passed before me. Creatures and beings so outlandish and bizarre, so absurd but yet so real passed in and out of my field of vision. They were spectacularly diverse, and a select few even seemed remotely human. However, all of them shared a similar nature: they were still and tranquil, so silent that their very essence hummed a single monotone. I became aware of the fact that they, though formless and ephemeral, were even more real than I. Language abounded in foreign tongues, vignettes communicated without moving a muscle, understood purely and exactly through a simple gaze. Their eyes were alive and magnetic—as if they held the secrets of existence within their depths. They weren't looking at you, they were looking through you, and their eyes didn't just focus on one thing, they focused on all things at once. I was captivated and curious, and I did stare, through virgin eyes, at the figures manifested there. It was then that I completed my passing in that world, through the eyes of the one without form.

In apparent consequence of that action, I was immersed in the sensation of a separate world—one of searing pain, not only physical but emotional, as if my consciousness itself was being torn and broken apart. I was greatly afflicted by a sense of such deep hurt that it felt as if an unfathomable heaviness was upon me. There was a renewal of that encompassing sense of fear, doubt, and resounding uncertainty. I felt that same sense of carrying motion, of universal propulsion, but this time all was rushing forward—all, including myself. The speed and intensity of the trip were again gradual and cumulative; however, this time I was aware of a certain sense of dreadful imminence—as if rather than being suspended, I was indeed traveling toward something. And arrive I did at that something, in an impact so violent and unprecedented that it resulted in infinite nothingness. This time, I knew beyond a shadow of a doubt that I was dead.

PART II

I do not know for how long it was that I experienced Nothing; for how long I experienced that which can be remembered by no mind but mine. There was no fear, just the reality of raw existence. Jubilation, freedom in exit—without a body, only soul.

—And then, there before me was a gently glowing light, a great orb at the center of my vision. It was fuzzy and dim and vibrated at such a high frequency that it created a soft buzzing. The longer this orb maintained its position within my focus, the louder the buzzing it created became. This was alarming and maddening and insomuch inexplicable. *How could I see if I had no eyes or listen if I had no ears?*

This paradoxical realization seemed to jolt me into a state of semi-awareness, and the indeterminable hum that I was hearing began to meld into another sound, one that invoked both comfort and confusion. It was the sound of voices echoing soft and sweet all around me as if they were spoken from very far away—the voices of angels. I tried to remember what I had been taught in catechism as a kid. I really didn't claim to believe in anything after debunking Catholicism; I didn't seek an alternate path, I didn't even entertain the notion. An all-powerful God? It was a laughable thought—until now. They spoke in a familiar tongue, their voices inquisitive and full of astute wonder. I listened as they marveled over me, amazed at what I heard.

"I wonder where she's from."

"She looks as if she has traveled far."

"Look how beautiful she is."

"Look at her hair!"

"How peaceful she looks… I wonder why she's come here."

"I wonder who she is…"

I began to regret my decision to so quickly discount religion. I figured if the angels didn't know my name, I didn't have a chance in hell of ending up in heaven—if there was such a place.

"Well damn, maybe if she wakes up we should ask her for a lift. It'll take us all day to walk to Richmond, and we ain't got enough bread for the bus."

A stimulating rush passed through me as if I was reentering my body. *Cursing, bus-riding angels? I must still be tripping*, I thought. I opened my eyes and watched in stunned amazement as reality began to cumulate before me. In pieces, fragmented like shards of cut glass, matter and energy manifested, dazzling and circling, and out of the disarray, emerged a city.

At once, I was overwhelmed by an astonishing wave of cognitive dissonance. The sounds of blaring car horns, sirens and noon-tolling bells, and the whipping wind rushed past my ears. The smell of Middle Eastern cooking and the salty ocean breeze filled my nostrils, and I could feel beads of cold, damp perspiration beginning to form on my bare arms. The repetitive flashing of neon lights and storefront signs transfixed my eyes and bounced and reflected off the shiny, metallic green paint of a trolley car that passed by as it rolled along iron tracks embedded deep in the pavement—disarray had ensued once more.

After the initial sense of helpless awe had passed, as well as jubilation at the fact that I was very much alive, I was struck by the paralyzing realization that I was someplace else entirely. For as far as I could see, brightly colored shops and apartment houses lined the streets, and above my head, trolley cables and telephone wires swung in the early morning breeze. I was still sitting in my car, parked haphazardly on the side of a road in front of a large brick building. My eyes spun in their sockets as I attempted to take in every inch of the incredible panorama set before me. I was atop an enormous hill of some kind, and below me, where the city rooftops seemed to fade right into the water and all roads dropped straight off into the bay, a single russet peak rose out of the fog—the Golden Gate Bridge. My jaw dropped into my lap—I was in San Francisco.

Did I drive last night? I demanded my stubborn cerebrum to no avail. *It's over 200 miles to San Francisco…that's a three-hour drive! In my condition, I would've totaled the car trying to get out of the parking lot, let alone on the highway…*

"Look! Her eyes are open!" a delighted voice called, rocking me from my troubling thoughts. I spun around in my seat to find the source of the 'angels' conversation and instantly found myself face to face with four hippies—two men and two women. 'Hippie' was the

60

way in which I first perceived them because frankly, there was just no other way to describe them. The girl who had most recently spoken leaned on her elbows against my car door, her chin resting on her knuckles, inches from mine. She wore a white, airy peasant blouse layered atop a green hemp dress embroidered with occult symbols that grazed the straps of her leather sandals. Around her neck were many strands of glass beads, an ivory elephant, and several carved wooden peace signs. She wore a pair of sunglasses like John Lennon's that she pushed back into her long blonde hair to reveal a pair of dazzling sapphire eyes.

"So," she inquired with a grin, "what brings a gal like you to the big city?"

I was far too stunned to form words. My jaw twitched around a bit as I tried to stammer out one lousy sentence, but the man behind her beat me to it.

"Looks like she's loaded, Mary. She probably doesn't even know you're talking to her. See if you can get her eyes to focus, bring her back," he leaned over her shoulder and snapped his fingers once, sharply, in front of my face. "Ask her if she knows what her name is." He was short but stocky, with muscular arms and a round, protruding gut and looked to be in his early twenties. He was dressed in denim bellbottoms and a nonmatching denim work-shirt, over which he wore a thin leather vest. He had dark, curly hair that fell past his shoulders in greasy ringlets and a full beard that concealed his mouth. He looked like someone you wouldn't want to mess with, but his narrow eyes were gentle and kind, and his voice was calm and assured.

The girl Mary reached out toward me, bracelets and amulets dangling from her thin wrists. She placed one hand on either side of my head and spoke to me in long, drawn-out syllables, "What—is—yo-ur—na-me?"

"R-r-Rhiannon," I stuttered, finally finding my voice. "I'm sorry, but I don't seem to remember how I've gotten here...I don't seem to remember anything at all."

"Ahh it's cool, happens to the best of us," the other kid said good-naturedly from where he leaned cross-legged against my car smoking a cigarette. He spoke with a heavy Brooklyn accent and looked substantially younger than the former, with a round face and bright ginger hair that protruded in equal distance all around his head like a fluffy, red cotton ball. He had about a six or seven day's beard and looked like he hadn't showered in quite a while. He had a thin leather strap tied around his neck, half concealed by the collar of his paisley shirt. Around his waist was a fringe belt holding up a pair of Levi's with the cuffs half tucked into a pair of combat boots. "I've got it, I'll quiz you," he announced. "If you can tell me the date and the name of the man who sits up in the big house and runs this godforsaken country, then you remember more than me."

I looked over my shoulder at the fourth member of the group that had gathered around me. She was standing in the back seat of my convertible, her dirty huaraches on my red leather interior. She wore dark harem pants and a heavy camel's hair coat that she had wrapped around her body like a sari. Her hair was cut just above her shoulders, and she was towheaded, despite her bronze skin. A crown of daisies adorned the top of her skull, and clutched in her right hand was a sparkling faeries wand with a gold star on one end. She looked like a fortune teller from a foreign land, a strange mystic, a gypsy goddess. Suddenly, as if obeying some unspoken command, she ceased swaying in the breeze and knelt down on the seat, met my eyes with pupils the size of nickels, and tapped me on the shoulder with her wand, "Good luck," she spoke in a foreign accent I could not place.

I blinked in confusion and turned back toward the ginger kid. Having stood up to his full height, skinny and tall, he hovered over me, awaiting the answer to his question.

I steadied my shaking voice and answered him verily, "Today is June 9th, 2000 and the president is Bill Clinton, that horny bastard."

The three that were somewhat coherent exchanged various stifled, humored glances.

"Far out!" the red-haired kid marveled, grinning at me. "Well, the results are in…"

The blonde, Mary, took the opportunity to build suspense by enacting a drumroll on my dashboard.

"…you've officially fried your marbles!"

I furrowed my brow in confusion, "How's that?"

"Well, I can't tell you the date—it's June something or other—but it's certainly not the year 2000, and as far as I know, Dick Nixon's still in charge of this here Establishment."

I gaped at him as if he had just sprouted two more heads, which in all honesty wouldn't have been any stranger than what I was currently facing. *I must still be tripping*, I thought. *Don't panic, Rhiannon. This is all an illusion, it's all inside my own mind. It sure seems like it's been longer than twenty minutes though, and this is nothing at all like what I was experiencing before…*

"Wh-what year did you say it was?" I asked in complete and utter disbelief.

"Why, it's 1969! June 1969."

I fell silent then. I didn't have anything else to say. The wheels of my mind spun furiously but remained hopelessly stuck in the mud. *It's some kind of a gag*, I thought. *Leanne, Marty and them—they must be pulling a joke on me! They were just as stoned as I was last night. They probably watched what went down at my mother's house and followed me. They probably had Shania drive me up here and hired these clowns to screw with me when I came to. Yeah, that's definitely what happened—they're probably in that building across the way laughing their asses off!"*

I hopped out of my car and stood on the sidewalk with my hands on my hips, "Leanne! Jeff! I know you guys are out there," I called across the street. "The joke's up! Ha! Ha! Ha! Very funny! Shania! Marty! I know you're here somewhere!"

Save for the sounds of the city, there was no answer. Across the street, two bums on the corner lifted their heads and looked around, but other than that, I received no reply. The silence spoke volumes. I watched as a black vintage Buick fresh off the assembly line passed slowly by me, followed by a red Chevy and a Studebaker. I turned back to my own car, dumbfounded. The red-haired kid was sitting behind the wheel, and Mary was riding shotgun.

The curly-haired twenty-something greeted me with a friendly smile from the back seat, "Since you can't find your friends and you don't know how or why you're here, I guess you should stick with us then." He extended a hand toward me to help me climb in next to him.

I was still speechless. The red-haired kid gazed at me through the rearview mirror, "Don't take me for a square, the future trip is cool and all," he began to chant, "Clinton, Clinton, he's our man, if he can't do it no one can! I was just trying to help you get it together, you know, keep you in touch with reality, man."

"Aw fuck, man, what is reality anyhow? If she likes to think it's the year 2000, that's groovy. It's her trip," Mary replied from the front seat. "Where did Faye go? Faye!" she called.

The sorceress looked up from where she was wishing good luck to the trash can along with every other inanimate object on the sidewalk and drifted over to the car. As soon as we were generally settled, the red-haired kid fired up the engine and pulled out onto the road.

"Man, this is one mean machine," the curly-haired twenty-something remarked. "New too, ain't she?"

New?! I gaped. *You've got to be kidding me! It's thirty years old and in goddamn perfect condition and you've got your stinky asses all over it!* I considered freaking out on them, kicking them all out at the next light and gunning it, but it seemed like a senseless plan. I had nowhere to go, and besides, I still didn't even have on shoes! I figured it was better to just go with it and stick with these freaks, at least until the trip ended or I came up with a better idea. At least I knew that they wouldn't put me up in some kind of a nuthouse—they were even madder than I!

"She's a '70 Galaxie," I replied finally to the long-haired kid's question. "Everything's stock, right down to the air in the tires. I replaced the radio though."

He sighed, "She's a beauty."

"Thanks. Say," I asked, leaning forward between the flower child and the red cotton ball, "mind telling me where we're driving to?"

"Oh, I do hope you don't mind!" the girl Mary replied, appearing to have just realized their conceivably disastrous faux pas. "I need to be in Richmond this afternoon to see my mother, she's very sick."

I was instantly reminded of Meredith. Surely, she'd sent out numerous amber alerts by now, and the police would be searching; however, if what the red cotton ball said was indeed true, there was no possible way I would ever be found—unless, of course, Fresno P.D. had a time machine at their disposal. I did not understand any of it, in fact, I didn't even know if any of it had the potential to be understood, but in spite of it all, I felt as if I had been relieved of a heavy burden. I might have been lost in time and stuck in the past, but never in my life had I felt so incredibly free.

Exhilaration passed through me in affirmations never before conceived. I stood up in the back of my car with my arms outstretched as the red cotton ball rocketed down the city streets, past the panhandlers and peripatetic travelers that lined the avenues and adorned the Victorian storefronts. I watched them go by and felt my heart swell until I thought it was due to burst from happiness. I had found myself in a dream, a vacuum, a cone of reality I was sure would cease to exist at any moment purely because of the vast absurdity of it all. The wind whipped through my hair as we cruised along, rising and falling up and down the rolling San Francisco hills—I felt like I was flying.

However, mid-flight, just as we crossed over Masonic Street, the curly-haired hippie reached up to give a quick, sharp tug on my arm, pulling me back down to the seat. "Big Brother," he explained before I could protest, pointing out a sleek black and white police car as it passed in the opposite direction. So, I sat, sandwiched between the good luck fairy and the twenty-something in what was agonizing silence until:

"What the fuck are your names?" I burst out with an added chuckle thrown in to complement the absurdity of the situation.

"My name is Mary Jane Greene," the girl Mary replied, turning around in her seat, "and this here is The Spaceman—best goddamn barterer you'll ever meet." She gestured toward the red cotton ball and he, in turn, offered up his right hand over his shoulder for me to shake.

"I'm Billy Smith," the curly-haired twenty-something smiled, extending a hand toward me.

"—Known mostly around these parts as Billygoat," Mary Jane Greene interjected, tugging playfully on his beard. "And then there's Faye of course," she smiled, acknowledging the presence of the gypsy, who in turn tapped me on the head with her wand and wished me good luck.

"We also call her Alice the Acid Queen," Mary Jane giggled, reaching out to hand her the piece of candy she had pulled from her dress pocket.

"So which is it?" I asked, slated by confusion.

"Which is what?"

"Is her name Faye or is it Alice?"

"Neither, actually," Mary explained. "She never told us her real name, so Billy started calling her Faye. The nickname Alice came about later, but by that time she'd gotten so used to answering to the name Faye we felt bad changing it again."

It was after that I decided not to ask any more questions for a while.

We remained on the same tree-lined road they had found me on for the majority of the ride, but I saw the City ebb, flow, and change in the architecture of the neighborhoods we passed through. From the professional buildings and modern facilities where we had met, the scenery had changed to feature mainly brick construction and stucco homes—practical living spaces constructed atop single car garages. They were built so close together that it almost looked as if the entire block was made up of just one eclectically decorated structure.

Mary's mother lived on 30th Avenue, the first turn we took off of Geary, the road on which we had been traveling. Now, San Francisco is infamous for its hills; however, I never quite understood how massive they really are until The Spaceman turned onto 30th Avenue—which I later learned was considered a minor brake check compared to a gear-grinder like Hyde Street or Filbert. It seemed like the pavement rolled right on into the sky like a ramp to the heavens; just when you thought that you had finally reached the top of the hill, you came to a cross-street and continued on, the peak nowhere in sight. I could see now why The Spaceman had so readily taken the wheel from me—I could only imagine how many accidents per day were caused by stalled tourists.

We drove on 30th for about a block or two and then took a sharp left into the empty driveway of a blue Victorian with bay windows at the very bottom of the hill. The house was the color of a robin's egg and set far back from the road. The windows were thin and rectangular, and a long concrete staircase led up to the front door.

"Home sweet home," Mary Jane sighed, glancing back at me and rolling her eyes sarcastically. "I grew up on Haight Street, on the corner of Haight and Webster. About four years ago, my father decided to pack up and move down here when things got too *radical*," she swung her legs over the door and hopped out of the car.

"Now if anyone's a square, it's that man," The Spaceman added.

"He's a *banker* for Christssake!" Mary Jane cried, exasperated, wrinkling her nose as if she smelled something bad. "I'm the daughter of a capitalist!"

I nodded empathetically.

"Say, Rhiannon, looks like you could use a pair of shoes. Are you a size 7?"

"As a matter of fact, I am," I replied, surprised.

"So am I," she said. "Come with me, I think I have just the pair you need."

The Spaceman left the car idling, and I followed Mary Jane up the steps and into the house. A striking crystal chandelier hung above a neatly polished dining room table in the parlor upon entry, and a single hallway led to the other side of the home. It was a charming little flat with freshly shampooed carpets and walls painted a deep chestnut color. She left me to look around and darted down the hallway into the first of a succession of identical bedrooms. I trailed my finger along the immaculate, dust-free furniture before lifting a framed photo off of the nearest end table. The photo was a family portrait, featuring a much younger Mary Jane, a clean-shaven youth who looked to be about my age, and an older man in a tweed suit and coke-bottle eyeglasses standing next to what I imagined Marilyn Monroe would have looked like if she ever made forty.

"I must have been about seventeen there," Mary Jane said, coming

66

up behind me. "That was taken right down the street from my old house, in Golden Gate Park, right before we moved. My mother was wearing her favorite dress there," she sighed. "Oh how she loved that dress!"

The dress was pleated and blue and had buttons on the collar; it looked like a dress that Meredith liked to wear anytime she went out someplace fancy. "She doesn't wear it anymore?" I asked.

"Oh no," Mary Jane remarked, "it'd be far too big. She's been bedridden for almost a year now, she's very sick."

"Well, what's wrong with her?"

"Right around the time we moved out here to Richmond, she started getting these mad migraines. The doctors gave her medicine and told her she'd be fine, but then she started forgetting things and becoming confused. She wrecked our car and started calling us by the wrong names, walking into things and losing her balance. Pretty soon she couldn't even work anymore—she was a piano teacher, you see. Then she started getting moody—crying all day or throwing fits that just made no sense at all. She went to go see a neurologist at the university, and he said she had an inoperable brain tumor—that means they can't do surgery. When she started having seizures, the doctors said it would be best if she just stayed in bed." She spoke to me of these things as casually as you would recount a night out on the town with friends, as if she didn't fully understand the gravity of what she was saying.

I eyed her quizzically, but she just smiled back at me pleasantly, holding a pair of boots in her outstretched hand. I took them from her and laced them on. They were high-cut OD green army boots with a canvas pocket on the outside of each and surprisingly, were quite a comfortable fit.

"So, your mother, she won't get better?" I asked as I threaded the shoelaces through the eyelets.

Mary shook her head and gazed out the window at the street, "No," she replied, "but the doctors gave her three months to live six months ago, goddamn quacks. It's 'cause I'm the one taking care of her. I probably would've left San Francisco by now, but my mom kinda keeps me here."

Well, don't we have something in common, I thought to myself. "What about your father?" I asked.

"I don't like the way he treats her," she answered, "like she's some kind of mental-defective or something. He'd rather have her put away. Besides, all he does is give her these pills that the doctors prescribed, and those just make her worse. She's been much better ever since I decided to start my own treatment."

"And what's that?"

An amused glimmer sparkled in her eyes as she reached into her satchel and pulled out a single chocolate chip cookie.

"You give her cookies?" I asked, incredulous.

She smiled slyly, "Not just any cookies," she admitted, "they're baked with Mary Jane Greene's special recipe."

"And that helps?"

"Sure it does," she smiled. "She remembers our names now and isn't so depressed and frustrated anymore. Her seizures are fewer and further between, and she's off the pain meds. She even sings sometimes like she used to…here, why don't you come and meet her?"

She didn't wait for my response. Instead, she took my hand and led me into the last bedroom on the right at the end of the hall. Inside, once a beautiful blonde like her daughter, Mary's mother sat upright in a hospital bed, propped up against pillows. She had disheveled, graying hair that hung in tangled clumps around her misshapen skull. Her chalk-white skin was stretched tight and leathery across her cheekbones and lips and down her thin neck and scrawny arms. She wore a faded yellow housedress and stared blank and unmoving at the television set which prattled endlessly on, throwing Technicolor pictures upon the walls. Her delicate hands were folded neatly on her lap, her bony fingers intertwined. Now appearances may deceive, but at a glance, my first impression was that she was already dead. And what scared the ever-living hell out of me was as soon as such a thought entered my mind, it seemed, she turned her head and met my gaze with her crazed blue eyes. We were frozen there for a moment until she began to work her jaw like a cat and choke out fragments of words, syllables at a time.

"Oh, why-y m-my M-ma-a…"

Mary Jane rushed over to her and hugged her, enveloping her in the folds of her dress before pulling away and beginning to fret over her, "Why Mother, what did you do to your hair? This is the same dress you were wearing yesterday! When's the last time Dad fed you? Here, have a snack." She unwrapped the cookie and placed it in her mother's hand, then turned toward me as she began to nibble on one corner, "Don't be shy, Rhiannon, introduce yourself."

Astonished and generally bewildered were two ways of describing how I felt—not just about the situation, but about my entire life at that point. I could already feel all sense of logic and rationale pouring out of my ears. Mary and her mother were both staring at me, so I introduced myself to the poor woman.

"R-rhiann-on?" she repeated after I had done so, "L-like th-the witch?"

"Ma! That's rude! You're supposed to introduce yourself to my friend!"

"I'm An-i-stasia."

"Your name is Sophia, Mom."

"Don't fib, M-Mary."

"Did you have breakfast?"

"C-Carl b-b-brought i-it."

"Who's Carl?"

"The b-bu-utler."

"We don't have a butler, Mom."

"Uncle M-Mark was he-ere f-for d-di-dinner."

"Uncle Mark died when I was a baby, Mom."

"We had P-porterhouses."

The exchange went on accordingly for a bit as I watched, speechless and dumbfounded. There was a newspaper lying on the bedside table, so I lifted it up and read the headlines. It was this morning's edition of the *San Francisco Chronicle*, dated Monday, June 9th, 1969—just as The Spaceman had said. *There's no way that I'm not high*, I thought. *This is all just too weird to be real. It's just not possible...*

Thoughts swarmed around the inside of my mind like angry bees as I wandered out of the room and back over to the window in the parlor. I looked outside expecting to see my other three acquaintances waiting in my car, but to my shock and disbelief, I saw that they were gone. My car was no longer parked in the driveway, and there was no trace of them anywhere on the street. They had split!

"Mary!" I screamed, and she rushed back into the room, alarmed.

"What! What's wrong?"

"Billy and The Spaceman and Faye, they took my car! They're gone!"

She stared at me, surprised, as if she couldn't understand why I was so upset. "They'll be back," she replied calmly.

"When? Did you know that they were going to leave?"

Mary Jane shook her head, "In a few hours, probably. I have to take care of my mom. They'll be back to pick us up. Take it easy, Rhiannon."

It was all just too much to bear at once, and suddenly, I began to feel overwhelmed, as if the walls were closing in around me. If this were really true, it would mean that I was completely alone, and in that instant, the world began to creep back in. I had no clue what was going on, and now I didn't even have my car! I had no money, one set of clothes, and not only was I a stranger in this city, every soul I knew hadn't been born yet! I could try to find my father, but he wouldn't know me, he was only a teenager! The revelations that befell me were so strange that they were incomprehensible and so illogical that it became impossible to truly consider this as my reality. A sense of draining exhaustion passed over me, and I swayed on my feet. Mary reached out and steadied me.

"Are you OK?" she asked me, her blue eyes wide.

"I'm a runaway," I confessed, which was partly true. "I've been driving all night, I smoked this stuff, and now everything is all just so strange...I can't understand any of it, and I'm just having a tough time..."

Mary patted my shoulder empathetically, "I'm hip to how you're feeling, we've all been there. You look wiped out. If you wanna crash, there's a pad set up in the basement; my father never goes in there, and it's quiet and private. You can shower if you like as well. Make yourself at home, take what you need—what's mine is yours."

With that, the faintest glimmer of relief began to quiet my raging mind. Mary pointed the way to the bathroom, and I stripped down to the skin, peeling off the clothes I had picked up at Marty's the day before and letting the water dissolve some of my anxiety and fear. Twenty minutes later, I emerged wrapped in a towel and discovered a neatly folded pile of clothes that Mary had left outside the bathroom door. There was a pair of black harem pants like Faye's, a white peasant blouse, and two nonmatching tube socks. Once I'd showered and dressed, I was markedly more comfortable than I had been, so I rolled my dirty clothes into a bundle and per Mary's directions, took the door off the parlor down the stairs and into the basement.

The basement was fairly empty. There was an unused desk in one corner, a few cardboard boxes in another, and a red couch at the center of the room positioned in front of a dusty coffee table. There were no windows in the room, but a screen door leading outside let in the afternoon light and drove away my claustrophobia. I laid down on the couch and sank into the cushions. Immediately, I was overcome by drowsiness, and I knew that the refuge of sleep was upon me. The last thing I remember was staring at the clogged ashtray that sat on the table in front of me and wondering absently if Mary had any cigarettes. I thought about walking back upstairs to ask her, but before long, the room became increasingly fuzzy and I drifted off to sleep convinced that when I awoke this would all turn out to be some kind of an absurd lucid dream.

When I reopened my eyes, I was immediately blindsided by what I saw. For a few seconds, I was still in disbelief—I even think I rubbed my eyes to make sure that I was seeing correctly—but the sight of my own bedroom was unmistakable. I shot straight up in bed and hugged my pillows. I took in every sight: my cluttered blue rug, the tattered plastic blinds that hung over the windows, the enormous Zeppelin poster that was plastered to my ceiling—I was home!

I breathed an initial sigh of relief to be somewhere safe and familiar, but after a few moments, that same process of recalibration started up again. *How had I gotten home from the parking lot of The Joint? Had Meredith seen me come inside? Was it morning yet—time to leave for San Francisco?*

San Francisco…

What was that crazy trip? How much of it had been a dream? How much had been real? I didn't know what to think, but as I looked around, I began to feel extremely melancholy. For once in my life, my dream had come true; I had been somewhere else, visited another space in time: the sixties, San Francisco—it had all seemed so real—*it was real*. I knew that my soul had traveled that night; maybe not all the way to San Francisco, but it had definitely gone *somewhere*—and that somewhere was real; chaotic, terrifying, but real—and now, I was back here, grounded in reality once more. I'd missed it, my only chance. I'd been so caught up in trying to understand and rationalize that I'd missed the experience—the here and now of then—and now, here I was, back home again.

And yet, as I sat there tucked between the tousled comforters, listening to my clock prostrate on the wall as it announced each second with an affirmative tick, staring at my bedroom door, and considering the uncertainty present on the other side, it was this reality that seemed unreal. Or, if not so much wholly unreal, untrue.

I flung the covers off me and marched across the room to my mirror. When I looked into its depths, I was not greeted by my reflection, but instead by a juxtaposition of the empty room behind me. My eyes fell to my hands; they were still there, just as present and physical as they ever had been, but yet in the mirror, they were invisible. In the midst of this paradox, a sound knock was placed upon my bedroom door, and a sound voice followed: "Rhiannon? Rhiannon?" —It was Meredith.

I was not struck by fear or apprehension or uneasiness, but instead by a deep sadness. The place I had been—though confusing, though absurd and even frightening—had been beautiful. I sighed, ceded my tortured soul to reality, and reached toward the door handle, closing my eyes as I did so. The next time I opened them, I was back on Mary's couch.

I blinked several times and mystified, sat up and looked around the room. I rubbed my eyes and pinched my cheeks, but since I had just been dreaming that I was awake, I was still unsure as to whether I was actually awake or not. The room looked the same as it had before I'd drifted off to sleep, and I was still dressed in Mary's clothes. I would have imagined that such a discovery should've moved me back to discord—with questions, uncertainty, and fear—however, my mind was quiet, as if strangely satisfied.

It was then and there that I vowed to sacrifice all counts of certainty and rationale for the sake of pure experience. It was there I traded logic for absurdity, understanding for existence, and discordance for peace. The next breath I took was earth-shattering, and when I stood up from that couch, for the second time in my life, I felt as if my feet didn't even touch the floor. I was positively elated, and this time, absent was the inevitable paranoia that went along with the knowledge that at any moment Meredith could be right around the corner. This time when I sighed, it was out of relief. The absence that had so terrified me before was now overwhelmingly comforting. I remembered riding in Marty's truck one dystopic afternoon no more than a couple days earlier, listening longingly to a song by America and wishing that I could be somewhere else, wishing that I could escape the time I was born into and hoping that was what it would take for me to discover myself. I wished Marty could see me now.

I stretched my arms out on either side of me and inhaled another deep breath. With wakefulness came increased awareness, and as I looked around the room, I took in every detail; my mind was like a sponge. Now, not only did I see the boxes in the corner, I saw the labels 'Silver,' 'China,' and 'Sophia's Quilts.' I no longer perceived the desk alongside the wall as void and empty; instead, I now saw yellowing sheet music scattered across its surface and a black fountain pen that acted as a paperweight. The afternoon sunlight streamed in through the screen door, illuminating the dust and bathing the entire room in a smoky yellow light. And sunlight was not the only thing that drifted in through the door—the voices of the hippies and the smell of my two favorite kinds of smoke accompanied it. I wandered over to the door but did not open it; instead, I leaned up against the wall and listened awhile to their conversation.

"Man, what are we gonna do?"—that was The Spaceman's voice— "Jules left us high and dry, man, we're hard up!"

"Well, we gotta get a drummer or we'll lose the gig. When is it anyhow?" Mary's voice spoke.

"Next week sometime." My ears perked up, it was a man's voice I heard, but not that of The Spaceman or Billy.

"Well, fuck, we can't bail on Bill Graham! It was goddamn hard enough landing that gig! He'll never hire us again! We're not serious about playing gigs like Santana or Steve Miller," The Spaceman said.

"That don't mean we can't be, man, we were serious 'til Jules freaked out and booked. We gotta earn bread some way," the unknown man protested.

"Chill out, man, I know half a dozen cats who'll play drums for one night. I'm sure Space could scrounge up Spence Dryden or Jack Pinney, ain't that right, Space?" Billy's voice resounded

"Sure is," The Spaceman/Space replied.

"No, we need somebody *solid*," the man's voice complained, "not some one-night sit-in. If we wanna get big, we need a drummer we can count on!"

I made my entrance then and stepped out from behind the screen door to the bottom of a set of concrete stairs leading up from the basement. My acquaintances dotted the steps like canaries on a perch with the exception of the new arrival whom I had not yet been introduced to. From the first glance, I was struck by the sheer presence of this man. Mary, Billy, Space, and Faye could be described in a variety of terms ranging from hip and beautiful to freaky and strange, but if anyone could ever accurately be described as tall, dark, and handsome, it was this kid. He was just above average height and well-proportioned, and he leaned against the concrete stairwell coolly smoking a cigarette. His thumbs were hitched in the belt loops of his Levi's, and on his feet he wore a pair of black shit-kickers with cleats that clacked against the floor when he shifted positions. He was wearing a black leather motorcycle jacket the same color as his goatee and wavy shoulder-length hair. His dark, cotton t-shirt stretched tight over the lean, sinewy muscles of his chest and stomach, and around his neck was tied a red bandana. His eyes were steely gray and serious, and they looked me over with the same curious intrigue as mine did him. He was a few years older than me, maybe twenty-two or twenty-three—and tough. Physically he was an Adonis, but his eyes were shifty and mysterious and told me that there was far more to this virile specimen than appearances had to offer.

After we had performed sufficient examinations of one another, my eyes met his. "I play the drums," I said.

"*You* play the drums?" he asked, the tone of his voice wavering somewhere between surprise and disbelief.

"Yes, I do."

He raised one eyebrow, "I'm Bobby," he replied. "Who are you?"

"She's Rhiannon," Mary Jane interjected. "We found her this morning; she owns the Ford. She's a runaway—a head like us."

Bobby unhitched his thumb from his belt loop and held his hand out, "Gimme some skin."

You don't have to ask twice, I thought to myself before shaking his hand. His palm was smooth, but his fingertips were rough and calloused. "You play guitar," I commented. It was a statement, not a question.

He raised his eyebrow again, "You say you're a drummer, eh?"

I nodded.

"Can you play like Moon?" he asked.

"Sometimes," I kidded.

"Like Baker?"

"On a good day."

He cracked a smile, "Let's see."

Before I knew what had happened, the six of us were packed into my car: three in the back, Bobby in the driver's seat, Mary riding shotgun, and me in the middle. I was about to ask where we were going when the car roared to life, and Bobby swung out from the driveway and continued down 30th Avenue in the opposite direction from whence we had come.

As soon as we were back on the road, I was once again overwhelmed by the exquisite panorama that the City had to offer. One of them handed me a joint, so I settled in and watched the hills roll by. The afternoon sun had burned off the morning's fog, but a cold wind, augmented by Bobby's lead foot, rushed through my hair and the thin fabric of my shirt and pants. I shivered—San Francisco weather sure was different than Fresno's.

A BRIEF AND BEAUTIFUL TRIP BACK

The weather wasn't the only thing that was different. Fresno was dull and green, a flattened suburbia with aluminum siding and white picket fences. San Francisco was a prism; a rainbow jungle of brightly painted stucco, Victorians, and classic cars that looked like it had been caught up in a whirlwind and dropped on the side of a mountain. The scenery alone did not provide many clues that I had entered into another time, but the cars were something else entirely. There were '67 Camaros and '64 Mustangs, Volkswagen vans and minibusses of all sizes and colors. Some were shiny and new, and others had chipped paint and rusty fenders as regular features. Some were psychedelically painted, dressed with Day-Glo in mock replica of Kesey's bus Furthur, or covered by bumper stickers and protest slogans. When we reached the end of 30th and turned onto a street called Fulton, we passed a camper van the same color as Mary's house with an enormous pot leaf painted on the hood and the words *Legalize Marijuana* quotated, capitalized, and underlined along the side. Marty had been right—I was in heaven.

We continued along Fulton Street for a while, where the single-family stucco homes began to transform into apartment buildings with fire escapes that scaled their exteriors and bus stops that waited outside their front doors. Single-car garages were tucked neatly under dining room windows, below which were planters with flowerpots that were taken inside each night to avoid the chill. Along the right side of the road, where redwood trees and other assorted foliage ascended into the sky, groups of flower children pedaled by on bikes and walked along on foot, their flowing lengths of golden hair streaming out behind them in the afternoon breeze. They carried guitar cases and carpet bags, dressed in quilts and fringe, and were trailed by dogs that strolled leisurely beside them. As we neared the top of the hill, a pack of motorcycles emerged from over the rise, their engines gleaming and snarling. Their riders were clad in leather jackets, their colors proudly displayed via shoulder patches and saddlebags. Bobby touched two fingers to his forehead in a subtle greeting, then stepped on the accelerator, and in turn, the City passed by indiscriminately, masked by a blur of color and the cool rushing of the wind past my ears.

After several miles, we took a right off Fulton onto Stanyan, where shops with upstairs apartments lined the street. The buildings were bigger now, and the road was wider. There were more cars and more people. As we continued on down the street, I began to hear music and the rhythmic beating of tribal drums. I looked all around, but I could not see where it was coming from, and with each block we passed, it grew louder and louder, until finally we came to a cross street, and Bobby put on the blinker. We couldn't turn right because all along the right side of the road was the sprawling and verdant Golden Gate Park, so as we turned left, I looked up at the street sign. It read Haight Street.

I knew all about Haight Street. Hell, everybody knew about Haight Street—it was the megalith, the cultural epicenter, the very neighborhood where it had all begun. Excitement climbed into me, and as we turned onto the Haight, my mouth fell open. It was a sight like none I had ever witnessed before. There was literally a haze that hung over the street, a cloud that gathered between the open windows of the apartments and the steady plumes that wafted up from the sidewalk. The buildings were wildly decorated with spiraling mandalas and Wes Wilson psychedelia hung up in shop windows or posted in alleyways. An electric symphony poured from record players and stereo systems out into the lively streets. I heard strains of the CCR mingling with Jim Morrison's low, husky drawl, and from the innards of a bookstore echoed the mellow tones of Ravi Shankar on sitar becoming entangled with the passionate chanting of mantras ringing from the upstairs lounge of a smoke shop. The music washed out over the crowded sidewalks, over the squatters and the tourists and into every passing car—encapsulating every man, woman, and child in the Haight's siren song.

Hippies spilled from the vibrantly painted Victorians out onto the streets. They gathered in small groups, camped in storefronts, and congregated in open doorways, hunched over their guitars and beatnik novels, smoking cigarettes and all kinds of things, sinking down comfortably into their mountains of blankets, grime, and hair. Although one would imagine that such a place would be full of great chaos and confusion, the exact opposite was true.

They greeted the travelers with an incredible display, as if they'd gotten all dolled up just for the occasion. Every face was painted with stars and swirls and hundreds of designs yet to be named. Circlets of daisies and wildflowers adorned the crown of every skull. Ankle bells chimed as their wearers journeyed, offering peaceful greetings, well wishes, and homemade trinkets—protest buttons, strings of beads, and pint jars of body paint. It was a picturesque glimpse into an exilic society. They were different, once-removed from the world, and anyone could tell that was just how they liked it. They wanted to be different, they wanted to be separate, and I understood! They knew they had something different going for them that straight society didn't. At that moment I saw a collective vision of a new society presented to me not through theory, speculation, or wishful thinking, but through action—they brought it to life. They weren't communicating by picketing or protesting—although every so often you'd see one or two hippies brandishing a sign inscribed with the modernly cliché requests of *'Love Not War'* and *'Bring Our Troops Home Now'*—but for the most part they were peaceful and kept to themselves and each other. They were providing the straight world with a demonstration, truly an experiment in living—and everywhere I looked it was growing.

I was so intrigued, so captivated by the world into which I had stepped, that I didn't even notice that we had stopped moving until my acquaintances began exiting the car. We were parked in front of a big, white Victorian with wooden bay windows and clapboard siding, along with other traditional architectural embellishments. It was an impressive structure—assertive, grand, old, and professional-looking—it even had plaster cherubs on each corner of the roof.

"Where are we?" I marveled, taking the hand Bobby offered to help me out of the car.

"This is the Trips Center," he said with a smile, displaying a set of pearly whites, "and we are The Day Trippers."

I didn't understand what he meant, and I didn't get a chance to ask either, because I was swept up in a flurry of movement and emotion, carried up the stairs by a rush of excitement, and when the enormous oak-panel door swung open—inscribed with the words *Peace to All Who Enter Here*—I was left standing in a room I couldn't begin to describe even if I stood there all day. Tapestries and wall hangings encased the spherical space with an ineffable display of tribal, archaic design, and dozens of ornate oriental rugs covered the floor. The smoke of burning incense rose from painted clay pots that dotted the room, and the flames of scented candles gently flickered from inside glass canisters atop the wooden end tables that were strewn around the space. Various nonmatching pieces of furniture were gathered in a circle in the center of the room, and an antique china cabinet stood in the far corner. Blankets and assorted articles of clothing were draped across the couches and chairs, and a bearskin rug covered the floor in the center of the circle. On the walls hung abstract paintings and posters, and the doors on either side of the room had been removed from their hinges and replaced by strings of beads that swayed gently in the breeze from the open window. Over the windows too hung strands of glass crystals off of which sunlight reflected, sending out rays of diffraction that cut through the smoky haze. Directly to my left, just inside the door, was the largest private record collection I have ever seen. There were albums everywhere: stacked in piles on the floor, lined up two rows deep on shelves, and leaned up against the Hi-Fi console. I could see three or four speakers mounted on the walls around the room, and from them, Traffic's *Dear Mr. Fantasy* played softly.

The more I looked, the more I saw. Each corner of the room contained a million different things in a million different colors and shapes and patterns, but yet seemed to vibrate at a frequency so tranquil it approached stillness. There was a sense of deep calm and harmony that was present in that place, and it was so intense and pervading that any discordant emotions I was feeling were immediately diffused and replaced by a feeling of quiet and abiding peace. I looked up in wonder and found that a single blue spiral representative of Van Gogh's *Starry Night* had been painted on the ceiling, lightening in hue and tone as it carried on toward its revolving white center. Despite being as high as I was, I imagined that even those who were sober would become transfixed upon that spot and feel as if they were being sucked up into the infinite. That painting did more than create an illusion, and I was convinced that the room was not confined within those walls, but in fact transcended its inhabitants to galaxies and universes similar to the one I'd journeyed through to get there. It was a portal; the eye of God.

I was soaring at around 30,000 feet when Mary Jane put her hand on my shoulder and began to guide me out of the room I had become fixated upon. The portal closed and turned back into a painting, and I was led out of the room in a procession through the first doorway on the left. The room we entered was far different than the first. The walls and floor of what I assumed had originally been a garage in function had been freshly painted a radical, blinding white. Dozens of record covers dotted the walls and ceiling, and a string of speakers had been mounted around the room.

There was an array of different instruments scattered throughout. There were guitars—both electric and acoustic—mounted in stands and leaned up against the wall. There were wires and amps crisscrossed haphazardly across the floor running to everything from keyboards and basses to a few combinations of instruments I didn't have the faintest idea how to play and looked more to me like medieval torture devices than anything that made music. There was a black Harley chopper half covered by a sheet near the garage door parked next to a yellow floral couch that somebody had sawed in two, and standing against the wall in the middle of the room was a record player, silent at the moment as I admired this strange and breathtaking sight.

Just when I thought that I'd seen it all, I saw that there in the corner, right at the bottom of the steps, sat the most beautiful drum set I had ever laid eyes on. It had all the bells and whistles my kit back home didn't have and was painted an attractive shade of blue that glittered when bathed by the fluorescent lights fixed in the ceiling. I stood there speechless with my mouth gaping as Bobby, Billy, and Space picked up guitars, and Mary started hooking up microphones—the gypsy Faye had disappeared elsewhere in the house. I watched them for a while, then sat down on the bench and started playing around while the rest of them set up.

"What is this place?" I asked again, still blindsided by awe. I couldn't even fathom what the rest of the house looked like.

"The Trips Center," Bobby answered simply, for the second time, "and—"

"And you are The Day Trippers," I finished. "So what? You guys are a band?"

The group of them nodded.

"So, you any good? You gig around?"

Billy shrugged and adjusted the strap on the bass around his neck, "Here and there. Enough to pay the Man. We just jam mostly."

Bobby cut in, "What songs do you know?" he asked, striking a match and lighting a cigarette.

I didn't answer him, my eyes were on that boag. It didn't take very long for him to catch on and toss me the pack, and just in time too—any longer and I would've started salivating. I couldn't remember the last time I'd smoked, and my head was aching for a buzz.

"I'll tell you what," he said, amused, as I sat there gulping down lungfuls of smoke, "we're gonna play a song. You just give me a nice, steady beat, and play along if you know it."

I nodded, and Bobby and the rest of them turned toward me in a semi-circle.

"What are we gonna play, Bobby?" Mary Jane asked.

He didn't answer her; instead, he made a slight gesture with his hand—like some kind of a cue that they all instantly understood—and then looked toward me.

I laid a beat, and just like that, they all struck up.

There was no way I could have ever been prepared for the power and sheer volume that erupted in that garage. Confined in such a small space with only one window and a couple 50-watt amps, initially, I felt as if my ears had been blown right off the sides of my head. It was so loud and so sudden that I lost the beat, and it took a couple seconds for me to regroup; however, by the end of that first riff, I knew full well what song they were playing. It was Steppenwolf's *Born to Be Wild*; a song I had played hundreds of times—probably even more than they had—and I was excited to show off. It had been years since I'd played with anyone other than The Descendants, and we knew one another inside and out. We'd already uncovered all of one another's strengths, weaknesses, and idiosyncrasies. It had taken years, but we were all on the same level. We all knew what one another was capable of; we had our own habits, our own cues, and we were experts at keeping it alive onstage when one of us got too drunk or too high. For the purposes of a performing band, it was an integral advantage, but sometimes playing the same old stuff with the same old people got a bit boring. There were no surprises anymore; for the most part we always knew what to expect, and for the most part, we were always right.

One might imagine that being here with this clearly well-established band of musicians would make me nervous and uncomfortable. I was well aware that they were testing me, but my nerves had never been calmer. Instead, I was eager. I was excited. I knew that I was plenty good at what I did, and I wanted to establish a positive rapport with these people. I wanted nothing more than to have the opportunity to play with them, to get to know them—their quirks and cues and idiosyncrasies. I wanted to get on their level, so I put everything into that song. I played all the breaks clean and smooth, and for the most part, they stayed with me. The five of us played surprisingly tight, and the first chance I got, I broke out into a ride. Falling back in together that first time was horribly choppy, but Billy kept with me, and one by one the rest of them found the groove, and we finished the tune out strong.

Even when the room was silent my ears continued to ring. I felt as if somebody had just lit a stick of dynamite next to my head. It didn't help that the garage was so small we were practically standing on top of each other while we played—I was convinced I'd be hearing feedback in my sleep that night. I could only imagine what their neighbors had to say.

Mary holstered her mic in its stand and shot me a grin and a wink, "She's pretty good ain't she, Bobby?"

"Damn right she is," he replied. "I think you'll do just fine here."

An enormous grin spread across my face, "Well, thanks," I obliged. "You're quite talented yourself...I mean, you all are."

"I'd say, that's why we call him Mr. Heavy Metal Thunder," Mary announced from where she sat atop the motorcycle on the far side of the room where she had dragged the entire microphone stand, "Bobby really digs Steppenwolf."

"I'm hip," I replied, using a bit of their lingo. "How about Clapton? Can you play like Eric Clapton?"

"Name a tune, baby, any tune," he insisted, accepting my challenge.

"*Sunshine of Your Love*?"

"You know that one, don't you Mary?" Mr. Heavy Metal Thunder inquired.

"Of course I do," she answered.

And with that, Bobby riffed off the first few chords and we all struck up—except for Space who plunked down on the couch and rolled a smoke to be circulated around.

The rest of the afternoon passed just that way. We played for hours—two or three at least—but I couldn't be sure, there wasn't a clock or a watch to be found anywhere in that room. For the most part, we just jammed, with a Cream chorus or a Zeppelin instrumental thrown in for good measure. The five of us played tight; however, the more hours that passed and the more we smoked, the less structure our jam session maintained. Billy and I stayed together, keeping the rest of them in steady time and collaborating when we thought we could. At some point, Space put down his guitar and started screwing around with the sound equipment and hooked up some kind of a lag so that the wall speakers broadcasted what we played a second or two after we played it.

We weren't trying to sound great, although we didn't sound bad. We were just playing around and having a good time, learning about each other and grooving on one another. It didn't take long for me to realize that this band was nothing at all like The Descendants. In our band, we all possessed roughly the same level of skill and could more or less match one another solo for solo and lick for lick, whereas in this group it was easy to recognize that Bobby was by far the strongest force. His guitar led the band; it guided us along and left us each a chance to solo but always prevailed in the end. His fingerwork was intricate and flawless, and he knew the riffs he played as well as if he had composed them himself.

Out of them all, it seemed Billy had been playing with him the longest. During the few short hours I was able to observe that afternoon, I became aware of a sense of silent communication that existed between all the members of that band, but between the two of them especially. They navigated changes and constructed arrangements that would have been difficult even with verbal cues. It was truly humbling and magnificent to watch. Billy's bass was the source of balance in the band. He kept Bobby from moving too far ahead of us and playing off the hook and stayed in sync with me. His sound was lyrical and sophisticated, as if he had learned to play guitar first.

Space—like Bobby—strummed guitar; however, while Bobby was focused and concentrated on his playing, Space was his capricious polar opposite. He was wired and erratic, playing with the band for a song or two, then wandering over to the other side of the room to mess around with the sound equipment or to have a smoke. He always had something in his hands or his hands in something—whether it was a guitar pick or a jumble of electrical wires—and he never stopped moving! He walked from one side of the garage to the other so many times it was dizzying, and sometimes it was exhausting just watching him. However, there was no denying that he was an incredible guitarist. He played mostly rhythm, but it depended on the song— sometimes he'd accompany Bobby, and other times he would lock in with Billy and me. Although the whereabouts of his mind could not be determined at any particular time, he seemed to possess a natural ability that influenced his playing, despite the fact that he was undoubtedly speeding.

And then there was Mary. Despite Bobby's prodigious displays, Mary Jane was the real key to The Day Trippers' sound. She had this soft, Californian drawl that was sultry and enticing; a cross somewhere between Grace Slick and Janis Joplin. I could tell that she was aiming for more of a Janis-like effect, but her voice was just not raspy enough or powerful enough to sing the blues. Nevertheless, she had her own unique sound, which in some ways surpassed both of them. She could sing just as the lyrics were originally written, or tune into the melody of any one of our instruments and vocalize entirely wordlessly, completely changing the effect her voice invoked. Despite the boys' musical prowess, it was Mary's input within the band that elevated The Day Trippers to truly psychedelic proportions.

Everything about them was so exceptional and so remarkable, and as time went on, the more of a spectacle they became. By the end of that afternoon, I was superbly gassed. Heavy was drenched in sweat from playing so rapidly and intensely. Space had stripped down to his boxers, dragged the soundboard out into the center of the room, and had started messing around with the effects levels and frequencies. Mary Jane was half-potted and perched atop the arm of the couch, dramatically reciting the words to an Allen Ginsberg poem while we jammed, "*I saw the best minds of my generation destroyed by Madness. Starving, hysterical, naked; dragging themselves through the Negro streets at dawn looking for an angry fix...* " Billygoat had pulled a stool up next to mine and was attempting to lock in with me while I tried as hard as I could to keep a steady beat and simultaneously hold back a mounting tide of laughter. Finally, when I couldn't hold it in anymore, I erupted into a giggling fit which seemed to be contagious, and one by one, the rest of the band digressed into a spell of hysterics.

After considerable time, once the laughter had ceased and we'd commenced to looking around at one another through our rosy eyes, Bobby decided to break the silence.

"Damn, man!" he exclaimed. "What's a guy gotta do for a butt around here? I haven't had a smoke in ages!"

"We're all out," Space replied as he checked and rechecked the empty packs scattered around the room.

We sat there awhile, exchanging various disappointed glances until—"Heyyy, I think I have some in my car!" I remembered suddenly, jumping up from the bench.

In an instant, enormous, goofy smiles spread across all of the stoned faces in the room. Bobby let out an excited yell and threw open the garage door, consequently framing the most magnificent sunset I'd ever seen grace the skies. Wide-eyed and speechless, I stepped over the mountains of equipment and walked slowly out the door and toward the road. The sun had set the violet sky ablaze, and ruddy pink clouds billowed out from the star's fiery center and caught in the upper branches of the ancient tree that stood at the edge of the park before me. Through the lenses of Mary's sunglasses, I watched the daylight culminate and begin its nightly descent below the horizon. When I turned and looked down the street, I saw that the Haight had been bathed in a crimson spotlight as the sun sank behind the buildings and cast its dusky neon shadows upon the city's inhabitants.

I was so entranced and captivated by the sight that I clean forgot why in hell I was even standing out there until a man walked by smoking a cigarette and the familiar scent jogged my memory. Once I got to my car, it didn't take me long to find what I was looking for; however, while I was rooting through my glove box, it dawned on me that I was clueless as to the whereabouts of both the pipe and the psychedelic crystals that had landed me in this situation in the first place. I dug through the glove box and checked underneath CD and cassette cases and empty packs of cigarettes. I looked around on the floor and along the sides of the back seats to no avail. I slid my hand in-between the folds of leather interior, behind the pedals, and inside the cup holders, and just as I heard Mary's voice call to me from inside, my fingers closed around the little pink baggie lodged underneath the driver's seat.

"Yo Rhiannon, are you hungry?"

"You have food?!" I cried as I hurried to stuff the baggie inside a cassette case. Honestly, I couldn't even remember the last time I'd eaten. My stomach began to growl in protest, and I hurried inside.

Upon reentering the Trips Center, I was again mesmerized by the pulsing of etheric energy that emanated from every inch of the place. For the second time, I stopped and stood to admire my surroundings. My eyes drifted around the room from the lush tapestries that created the semblance of a courtesan's chambers to the arrangement of various cerebral paintings tacked to the plaster walls and the thin ribbons of incense that wafted up into the dank air. The effect the combination created was ineffable, purely and positively. The words it would take to describe the feeling I felt have not yet been uttered, not yet inscribed into any dictionary in the world. They only existed there—in that world that was the Trips Center—and within the surreptitious minds of those who lived within its walls.

I stood there for what felt like an eternity, thinking about words. I thought about how in the beginning, about a hundred thousand years ago, we humans sat around in caves sharpening sticks and grunting at one another until whether through the course of necessity or divine intervention, the spark of language was instilled in man. I imagined that this, in turn, solved a whole wealth of problems—there were words for food and sex and Saber-tooth tiger where there hadn't been before, which eliminated a great deal of confusion, I'm sure. Sounds gave value to the material world, and primitive mental ponderings became community interest. Soon there were words assigned to abstract concepts: birth, death, and God in heaven—thus philosophy ceased to exist solely within the minds of men. At that moment, it seems, the phenomenon known as difference in opinion was born. It is less likely, though possible, to debate the quality and existence of a rock than that of the origin of the species. Therefore, it is through language that silence was shattered, that the divine heart of man was divided. It was through deception that man was made to leave the garden and through anger borne of disparity that the first blood was shed. It is through language that truth becomes untruth and worth is allotted to that which cannot be seen except through the eyes of experience. It is through language that perception becomes narrowed and controlled. For I do not perceive happiness or sadness, freedom or anger, beauty or hatred in the same manner in which you do, and yet all around the world there exists definitions set in stone, preconceptions carved into generations, walls erected around the expression of what is and what is not.

It is in this way that connotation serves a necessary evil. For I would describe the room in which I stood as incomparably beautiful. Though messy, cluttered, and collected from the excrement of straight homes and the varied inventory of secondhand stores, the contents of the room weren't what defined its condition—it was the feeling they invoked. Though disorganized by ordinary standards, I felt as if I'd never seen anything so harmonious. It was lawless—yet set in perfect order. There exists no words to describe such a contrast. To be immersed in this feeling and experience that which was unable to be communicated via vocal medium made me feel entirely alone, and yet at the same time connected to all those who had come there before me. This paradox, this lack of words, awakened something primeval deep within me. Was it inspiration? Enlightenment? Or simply hunger?— For I would have stood and pondered this all day, but the enticing smell of something delicious drew me from my thoughts and into the kitchen.

I left my revelations in the living room and walked past the door to the garage and into a long, rectangular kitchen that ran the length of the house. The floor was covered with speckled green, white, and blue tiles that stood out against the pale yellow cabinets that Space and Billy were rummaging amongst in hopes of finding a satisfying morsel. Directly in front of me stood my objective: the refrigerator— which Mary was holding open and currently contained nothing more than a few cans of Coca-Cola, a half-empty bottle of ketchup, and Bobby's entire upper body. It seemed food was in high demand and short supply in the Trips Center. In an effort to parlay their enthusiasm, I handed out the cigarettes I'd found in my car, and we all lit up. I was just about to slide the pack back into my pocket when a woman's voice from behind startled me.

"You got one more of those?" she asked.

I whirled around. Another woman whom I'd failed to notice before stood at the stove to the right of the doorway. She had a wooden spoon in her hand and stirred a pot of rice and beans that was cooking on the burner. She was short and Indian and wore a purple patterned dress that grazed the tops of her carved leather cowboy boots. Her skin was soft, sun-kissed Californian and she had long, dark, curly hair that reached to the middle of her back. She was pneumatic and voluptuous, but her face was as round as a child's. She turned toward me and pointed to my cigarette with a smile.

"U-uhh yeah," I stuttered as I pulled the last of my smokes from the pack and handed it to her. She lit it using the flame from the stove, then wiped her hands on the apron that was tied around her waist and began to serve the meal onto plates which had been stacked up on the countertop. She passed one plate to each of us in rotation, starting with me.

"My name is Melinda," she said, handing me a fork. She had a thick Punjabi accent but spoke English clearly and without difficulty, "We've all been waiting for you, Rhiannon."

Before I could say anything in reply, she disappeared out the back door next to the refrigerator, and I wondered absentmindedly to myself in-between spoonfuls just how many other people there were in the house that I didn't know about yet.

As I ate, my eyes drifted to the small, round kitchen table in the left-hand corner of the room where Faye sat smoking a water pipe. A wooden photo border hung on the white-washed wall above her head, framing the painted outline of a circle. Its simplicity caught my attention. *In all seriousness, why would anyone go through the trouble to frame a painting of a circle?* I thought to myself.

Faye caught me staring, stopped smoking her pipe, and blew a smoke ring into the air. "Ouroboros," she spoke, followed by a sentence in a language I did not understand. Her sagacious eyes met my perplexed ones for a moment, and then she hopped off the barstool and exited the room, painting in hand, "Ouroboros."

I turned to Mary for an explanation, but instead was greeted by another question, "Hey Rhiannon, have you ever been to The Matrix?"

I shook my head, "No."

"Let's hit the scene tonight," Space suggested. "Whaddya say?"

****

A BRIEF AND BEAUTIFUL TRIP BACK

****

Before I knew any different, we'd left the Trips Center, and I'd found myself standing with the group of them on a street corner, waiting for the lights to change. I can't tell you how we got there, but I'm fairly sure we hadn't walked. It was sufficiently colder now, and as the wind whipped through my hair, the chill of that Pacific evening nipped at the back of my neck. The sun had just about completed its descent below the horizon, and the darkened city streets shined in electric phosphorescence from the storefront signs that lined the sidewalks like neon night watchmen. All the winos and junkies had crawled out from the recesses of their daytime respite into clear view of the city to get drunk and high off the San Francisco nightlife. All of the straights had cleared out at ten-to-eight and scurried hastily home to their little white picket fence worlds to escape the onslaught of the flower children who terrorized the town with their long, greasy, unwashed hair and week-worn Levi's and pranced about in bare feet and crazed costume, scoring lids of grass and an invariably good time.

All this, while somewhere in the country, their mothers slaved about in the kitchen over their gourmet crock-pot soup and honey-dinner's-almost-ready meatloaf that would be served just after sundown to the fathers of this nation's youth, who were snoring softly in their La-Z-Boys with their ties pulled loose, parked for the night before the family boob tube, endlessly spewing propaganda into the nation's pulpy subconscious. And all this, while right there in the City, Junior and Sissy, just thirteen years old, stole wide-mouthed glances out their parents' station wagon windows at their brothers and sisters, cousins and fun-uncles who'd dropped out of straight life without a kiss goodbye. Their stares hovered over the City day after day, hour upon hour: '*Why does that man have such long hair?*' '*What* is *that funny smell?*' their youthful innocence remarked; more and more curious each day...

Mary took my hand and led me across the street as I dreamed, looking up into the night and remembering the future. Trolley car cables stretched across the sky like an enormous net which kept all the good vibes inside and recycled them, allowing them to build and grow stronger and stronger.

I held Mary's hand until we reached our objective: a crappy little dive with a disproportionate following—The Matrix. I recognized the place from the stories George would tell me of a windowless little hole in the wall, the front door of which was pushed back two or three feet from the surrounding buildings. There was a cabinet to the right of the door where handbills and psychedelic posters were hung up, customarily flanked by one or two heads who were always hanging around and checking the listings. Just inside the door, there was a bar that served pizza and beer, and a few barstools and cocktail tables were strewn about. The ceilings were low and so was the lighting, and there was a small dance floor in the back situated in front of a stage that was only built up about a foot or two off the ground. As you continued further in, the place seemed to open up indefinitely, that is, the ceiling was pushed up about another ten feet or so higher than it was at the entrance. This created quite a disorienting effect, seeing as how all the smoke in the room accumulated in that area so that you couldn't actually see the ceiling at all, and I found myself standing in the center of the dance floor, staring upward into the billowing gray mass, struck by such a sense of wonder that one would imagine I had set my eyes instead upon the Pillars of Creation.

In the entire place there couldn't have been more than fifty people, but to me, it seemed like there were a hundred on the dance floor alone. There were people drinking, smoking, dancing, loving, swaying back and forth to the rhythm of their own consciousness... And the music! A band of four played onstage: two guitarists collaborated, and a young Negro drummer kept time while a woman dressed in a long, white wedding gown sang, filling the room with a fantastic gentle melody. There were cries of glee and glory, and the audience grooved on every note.

From somewhere in the darkness, a film projector cast the image of some kind of colored, fluorescent, gelatinous mass upon the wall, and it was writhing, exploding, imploding, expanding, contracting, behind, in front of the band...and we were all moving *with* it. Before I knew it, I was dancing, mirroring the images that flashed across the screen like lightning across the sky. This was nothing like the 1990s. There was no one standing stone-faced in the corner, no sullen, detracted display of trodden, dismal humanity. Nobody was 'cool,' everybody was 'cool'! There was no hierarchy, and everybody was smiling. For me, everything seemed to coalesce in a way it never had before. Everything seemed fluid, malleable, changeable—finality seemed to be a very abstract concept.

However, thirst did persist.

After quite a while, I released the hands of two others I was grasping as a group of us danced in a circle to the beat of the music. The guitarist on the left, a bearded freak in a purple smoking jacket, had lit out on a solo in B minor and it sent me flying! I had never been one for dancing, having preferred that spot in the corner instead with a cigarette in my hand and a grimace on my face; 'cool' in my time, perfectly miserable by the standards of this day. There was something about the atmosphere—be it the sound or the echo, the lights or the contact high—that stirred my soul and set me moving, and I skipped, shook, and shimmied from the dance floor all the way over to the bar.

"I'll have whatever's on tap," I announced to the bartender—a short, pink little man with Moroccan beads braided into his beard.

"Pabst OK?"

"Pabst'll be just fine."

"That'll be seventy-five cents," he said, setting the full glass down in front of me.

It was only after I patted down my pockets that I realized I had nothing: not a crumpled up dollar bill, car keys, or even a half-smoked roach—I was flat broke.

"I-I'm sorry," I stammered, flustered, as I looked around the room to find the table where my companions were sitting, "I-I just remembered that I don't have any money on me."

"Put it on my tab, Larry," came the calm voice of the woman seated on the barstool beside me.

"Thank you," I told her, surprised and grateful.

She turned toward me with a smile, felicity radiant in her dark, benevolent eyes. Her face was full, and her features were kind. She had mousy brown hair that fell just past her shoulders, and an aura about her of welcoming and mysterious influence. She looked far too familiar for it to be a coincidence.

Stunned and astonished, I hurried over to my companions' table near the wall and leaned in close as I pulled up a chair and spoke in a low voice bursting with excitement, "Grace Slick of the Jefferson Airplane just bought me a beer!"

The group of them were clearly unimpressed because apart from a few high smiles, the extent of their collective reaction was when Mary lifted her head in surprise and asked, "Oh, Grace is here?" before casually waving to the singer seated at the bar.

"Do you mean to tell me you *know* her?" I whispered incredulously.

They all looked around at one another and nodded.

"Sure we do," Mary replied. "We knew Grace when she was just starting out, years before she was as big as she is today."

I stared blankly back at her in a daze, and she took this as an invitation to continue.

"In fact, we know all the musicians on the San Francisco scene: Janis, Jerry, Pete Albin, Dino Valenti...all them cats. We were some of the first people to come here to The Matrix after Marty Balin took it over. Jefferson Airplane was just getting their thing together then, they were the house band. That was back in '65. We were what? Eighteen, nineteen...Bobby?"

"I was eighteen in '64; you'd just turned eighteen in April," he answered her. "We really shouldn't have even gotten in, seeing as how they served brew and all, but we knew Marty. That's what me, Mary and Jules would do almost every night—go to the ballrooms and the dance clubs, listen to the music, and be a part of the new scene. First it was Longshoremen's Hall and the Acid Tests, then it was the Avalon with Big Brother and Janis Joplin playing the house and The Matrix with the Airplane, The Fillmore and The Carousel each with about four or five bands playing every night. All this that's happening now started in those ballrooms; that's where you first started to see it."

"See what?" I asked.

"That things were changing, that something different was happening—something big. We'd always known about the whole beatnik scene down in North Beach, but we were probably about fifteen or sixteen when we realized it was changing faces, seventeen or eighteen when we realized it was growing, and closer to nineteen or twenty when we realized it wasn't going to stop. See, at first, the Heat was all over the scene. We technically weren't even allowed to dance at The Matrix because they needed some kind of a special permit or something, but once it started happening, there was no stopping it. People were getting closer to one another. This is a pretty big city, but everybody who's been on the scene for as long as we have knows one another, and all of us knew that when we went out to the clubs that we were contributing to something bigger than ourselves, bigger than this city even. It started out with just a couple of kids trying to have a good time, but it's become so much more. Us and a whole bunch of other cats like us began to realize that there are ways of living better than the way our parents were doing it—but you know where that's at."

I nodded in agreement.

"Then in '67, there was the Summer of Love. It seemed like just about the whole damn country showed up in Golden Gate Park for those couple of months. What a zoo that was—there were just so many people around. But everybody got together to help one another out in '67 when they needed it. Everything was free: free stores, free clinics, Diggers in the Park...I think we went for a whole month without spending ten dollars, that was unreal—remember that Billy? You were living with us then, weren't you?"

Billy laughed heartily, "You know it! Rhiannon, you wanna know how I came to be friends with these maniacs?"

I nodded, intrigued.

"Now '67 was clearly when the whole thing exploded out into the open, but I think '66 was truly the greatest time to be on the scene. You see, I grew up around La Honda, so I knew about the whole Kesey-Prankster trip that was going on. I was about twenty-two at the time, and I used to ride down to his place and smoke grass and drop acid whenever there was any kind of a happening. I met a couple people and saw a couple things that made me realize that I didn't want to go back and live with my folks anymore, so I hitched a ride down to Frisco. I spent some of my time hanging around Kesey's warehouse, but I was a little young for their scene, so I took up living with a friend of mine who was renting a place on Page Street.

"It was a real good scene; pure, if you know what I mean—the bowl of M&M's before everybody's got their hands in it. I went to a couple of the Acid Tests, and I went to the last one, around the end of '66— Kesey called it the Acid Test Graduation. I was hip to it, but there were a lot of people on the scene who weren't and who were trying to stop it. Now, Kesey's bag went a little like this: he's always wanted to break the ice, he's a trailblazer. He lets an idea sit around just long enough for you to get hip to it and then," Billy snapped his fingers, "he blows past it and starts in on something else. *'Moving Further'* is what he called it. Now all the cats here were just getting turned on to acid and peyote and mushrooms and all that, and all of a sudden, here's our knight in shining armor standing there on the front page of the newspaper telling everybody it was time to pick up and move on again. Now I dug him; I'd been around long enough to realize that he didn't mean to stop taking it. What he was saying was, 'Man, now look here, we've had our year of kicks, we know what this stuff's all about, and now it's time to start using it responsibly'—not the Tim Leary League of Spiritual Discovery thing, but there is something to be said for moderation."

"Ahh go home, get a job," Bobby interrupted, exhaling an

enormous lungful of smoke. "Drugs are gonna change the world."

"Now listen here, man," Billy replied patiently, "I didn't say they ain't gonna. Acid and grass *can* change the world, but in order to do that, you gotta turn people on, and once you turn somebody on, you're responsible for them for the rest of your life and theirs—karmically, you know? He didn't want a bunch of kids running around the City blindly tripping without any kind of guidance, and since there was a handful that'd already fried their marbles and he was like the shaman on the whole scene, I guess he decided it was time to show 'em one of the better directions to go in. You dig?"

I nodded. I remembered reading about the Acid Test Graduation in *The Electric Kool-Aid Acid Test*. Somehow though, Billy's version seemed much more real, not in the amount of truth it contained—for the stories paralleled one another—but real in that Billy's story wasn't read from the pages of a book, but instead told to me first hand, complete with a compatible setting. It was my childhood fairy tale brought to life.

"So," Billy continued, polishing off his beer and brushing the pizza crumbs out of his beard, "I went to the Acid Test Graduation. First it was going to be at Winterland, but somebody must've jumped ship at the end there because the Pranksters ended up having it at their warehouse on Harriet Street. It was supposed to be an acid test graduation, but a lot of the heads there were dropping acid. A lot of people didn't trust Kesey anymore; they thought he sold out to the pigs to get out on bail. Most people showed up just to see if he would go through with his stated intentions of telling all the heads to go '*beyond acid*.' It really wasn't like any of the other acid tests. Sure, it looked the part—the Pranksters had worked hard cleaning up the ol' rat shack and rigging it with all kinds of lights and speakers—but the vibes were all wrong. There were a whole lot of reporters there from the radio, television, newspapers…it was too *public*. Plus, The Grateful Dead weren't there to jam, neither. The whole thing was a real bummer. Kesey had been away too long, and the Movement had grown in his absence. It was bigger than he was, and his sphere of influence was far too small to make any kind of real difference. I had taken acid that night, and I bailed after the pigs showed up. They didn't break it up or bust anybody, they just kinda walked around like they were checking up on us or something, man, making sure we weren't doing anything they didn't like. It was the only truly bad scene I've ever experienced in Frisco. Man, what a pisser."

I stared back at him after he'd finished recounting his memory, my eyebrows knit together, confused, "So...how did you meet Bobby and everybody?" I asked.

Billy reclined in his chair, "Man, you dig, that's exactly the point—I don't know! One minute I'm leaving the Graduation downtown, and the next thing I know I'm sitting on a hill in Golden Gate Park tripping on LSD—stoned out of my gourd with a group of heads, playing this old guitar painted with green Day-Glo. There were three of 'em: Mary, Bobby, and Jules. We were all laying back in the grass, just jamming. I don't remember speaking a word to them...not one word. There was no communication at all; it was just...*understanding*. It's Jules I remember most of all. He had this little Indian water drum, man, blow your freakin' mind, man, the sounds that thing made. We were tight, Jules and I. That was one mother of a good time. I can't even explain it to you, Rhiannon. Magic happens in that park, unspeakable magic.

"Anyhow, after that night we didn't see each other again until the Be-In in the Park in January of '67. I was just sitting there in the midst of the multitudes listening to Leary talking about turning on, tuning in, and dropping out when over the roar of rock n' roll music and bursts of Hindu chanting I began to hear the beating of this little Indian water drum, and I looked to my right and there was that same little group of heads, Velvet Hammer and all—that's what we called Jules. You see, after I found out that they played music together, there was no getting rid of me, and they were happy to accommodate—I was the bass player they didn't have. I crashed at the Trips Center most nights, and after the whole Summer of Love thing started up and I made Faye my old lady, my buddy ended up moving down to San Gregorio, and the Trips Center became my pad full-time."

"That's wild..." I replied. I was loving every second of Billy's nostalgic musings, hanging onto every word and imagining each scene in vivid Technicolor. "How'd you meet Faye?" I asked, gesturing to indicate the girl to my left who was holding her empty beer bottle up toward the lights on the ceiling and gazing through it like a kaleidoscope.

"Well, like I told you about magic..." Billy, Mary, and Bobby exchanged an amused grin. "During the Summer of Love, all kinds of people showed up in the Park—every kind you could possibly imagine, from every nook, cranny, and radical organization in America—and they all had the same fantasy: they were all looking for something *different*. They came seeking a world away from the world; a world of peace, love, brotherhood—and LSD, of course—and many of them who showed up were amazed to find so many people who were just like them: *different.* The thing is, when you get a whole bunch of people gathered together wanting to be different, you're also gonna get all the people who are already living differently in the bag as well.

"Well, early one morning we were walking through the Park—coming down, you know—and there was this gypsy caravan parked right next to Alvord Lake at the end of Haight Street. It looked like someone had taken their back porch and put wheels on it, then painted the whole thing with this ornate blue and green mandala," Billy laughed. "I'm not so sure that's how it actually looked, but that's how it looked to me. They'd staked a clothesline in the ground and had hung their colorful dresses and skirts and pantaloons out to dry. There was an old man sitting outside in a rocking chair smoking a pipe, and what he was smoking, well, it smelled sweet to us, so we parked ourselves at the edge of the lake too and we were all groovin' on it—how we were the only ones in the whole goddamn world: me, Bobby, Mary, Jules, and this old gypsy man smoking his pipe at five-thirty in the god-blessed morning—Christ, what a trip!"

He paused to shake his head and share a glance with Bobby and Mary, all of their eyes glowing with ineffable memories and love, "So we're sitting out there, carrying on, watching the sun commence to fighting its way through the fog over the lake when all of a sudden I see this girl—this woman—come out from the lake! Now I'm thinking to myself, *Woah now, Billygoat, you're more zonked than you thought you were!* We'd been there for quite some time, and we'd have noticed if there was somebody in that lake, so I looked at my friends there, and they were seeing the same thing! At first, I thought it was some kind of LSD-merging-consciousness-trip but nah she-she was really there! She passed right by us as if she hadn't even seen us—like some kind of otherworldly denizen—and you know, I swear, her clothes weren't even wet!"

"She was white as a ghost," Mary interjected, "or a vestal virgin."

"If so, Billy fixed that in a timely fashion, eh Billygoat?" Bobby added suggestively.

Billy's cheeks flushed pink as Faye began stroking his beard and whispering inaudibly into his ear, "So anyhow, she disappeared into the wagon, and we watched her go, thinking we'd seen the last of her, but she reappeared after a minute or so, walked right up to me and handed me—you'll never believe this—a jar of butter. After that, she just kind of hung around and started following us everywhere. I called her Faye 'cause that was the name of Kesey's old lady, and she's been around ever since."

"Butter?!" I repeated. "You're making all this up, you're putting me on!"

Billy wrapped his arms around his mistress gleefully, "I don't have that good of an imagination."

"Does she play in the band?" I inquired skeptically.

"Helen Keller had a better ear for music than she does," Mary answered comically. "She's more of a mascot, an emblem of the Aquarian age. But make no mistake, she's made her contributions—I don't know what we'd be like without her. We've grown quite fond of her, to say the least."

"Yeah," Billy chimed in, gesturing toward Space, "she discovered our Spaceman here!"

"Discovered is a real nice word, man," he replied sarcastically. "That crazy chick scared the shit outta me!"

The rest of the group responded with sporadic nostalgic laughter.

"OK, so, Rhiannon, I bailed outta Brooklyn about a month after the Be-In. I was like seventeen, and I'd heard all about what was going on out in San Francisco on the radio and on television, and I'd had it up to here with New York City," he held his hand about a foot above his head. "What a drag! Anyway, they'd kicked me outta my fourth boarding school in three years, so I told the preppies to stick it in their pocket protectors, said see ya later to my baby sister, and split."

"He's the real-life Holden Caulfield, man," Bobby interrupted.

"Yeah, man, except I'm not sex-obsessed and neurotic," Space replied, pretending to twitch in his seat. "Anyhow, I didn't have enough bread for the train, so I jumped in the back of my friend's El Camino, and we rode out to Pennsylvania. He told me he had a friend in a pickup group who needed a guitarist for some gigs, so I played with them a couple times, then headed out further and ended up working as a roadie in Chicago for another band. I wanted to get to San Francisco before the Summer of Love, but I guess the Universe had other plans for me because no matter where I was, I ended up staying there far longer than I had planned. It should've taken me a week to get to California—two at most—but I left New York in March and rode into the Haight on September 23rd—the day of the fall equinox—in the back of a fruit truck, at two in the morning, in the rain. I was bummed out, wiped out, and hard up, so I walked along the street until I found the first comfortable-looking doorway, propped myself up, and nodded off.

"Next thing I know, some crazy chick throws open the door, damn near sends me flying, scares the shit outta me, then sits down and starts dumping everything in my sack out on the front steps. So I start yelling at her, right, and she just looks at me and without a word goes back inside and closes the door. So I'm like, shit, man, I came out here to get *away* from the bullshit, to keep my own space, you know, and this is the first person I meet on the West Coast? So I'm picking all my shit up off the steps, swearing up and down, right man? And the damn door opens again, and I think it's the chick again, and I'm ready to jump her shit, right? But it's some dude in this Japanese gi offering me a cup of coffee in one hand and a number in the other—that was Jules—and I decided that it wasn't such a bad place to be after all."

I shook my head as a bewildered smile spread across my face. It sounded as if he was recalling an epic he had read out of some novel rather than a story taken from the pages of his own life, "Unreal, man."

"So how about you, what's your story?" Mary asked.

Immediately, all five smiling faces turned toward me, their eyes bright with piqued interest.

"Me?" I responded.

"Yeah! You've heard all about us now, and all we know about you is that we found you zonked out of your gourd this morning double-parked on Sutter Street. Where are you from, anyhow?"

"Fresno," I replied simply, unsure of what else to say. I was unaware of the facts themselves—let alone how to explain them—and they didn't press me. Instead, Mary screwed up her face in reply.

"Ah man, no offense, but Fresno is square."

"None taken," I replied, holding up my hands, "that's why I left."

Given the approval to do so, Mary continued to insult my hometown, "...full of right-wing sell-outs, rednecks, and Ken dolls."

"The proverbial pen for every free, long-haired head in California," I added.

"Where white, well-bred shaggies are persecuted like Negros!"

"Down with Darwinism, up with Prohibition!"

"No room for the farm kids, they save it all for the sleaze!"

"The sleaze that drinks their tax dollars by day and sleeps with the suits by night!"

"I like you," Mary Jane grinned, and I grinned back.

"So, you learned how to play the drums in Fresno?" Billy asked, lighting up a number and taking a few hits before passing it to me.

"My dad taught me," I replied. "He's an old hip—...progressive."

"I'm hip," he nodded. "A peacenik, huh? One of them guys who didn't fight in the Second World War?"

96

I shook my head.

"Sounds like a very groovy dude."

"He is."

"How about your mother?"

I rolled my eyes, "She hates everything about me: my hair, my clothes, my music, my mind—hassles me constantly. She never wanted a kid; she got knocked up. That's why I ran away; I'd had enough."

"Right on, man, me too," Space spoke up.

"Sounds like my father," Mary commented.

Billy shrugged, "Like I always say, never trust anybody over thirty."

Bobby eyed me sympathetically, "Must be hard to lump it."

"Well, how did your parents respond to you lighting out to San Francisco?" I asked him.

"My parents are dead," he replied, his expression unchanged. "They were immigrants, real into the whole American Dream trip. They were tenant farmers in Armenia and dreamers at that. They wanted the whole American experience: wealth, liberty, justice—you know the rap. Jingoism and prostitution is what it really is, although writers tend to put it in more poetic terms. We moved to S.F. from Idaho when I was seven, from a horse farm to the Tenderloin slums. My father got a job as a butcher, and my mother worked in the telegraph office. They saved up some dough, and by the time I was twelve, we'd moved into the house on Haight Street. The area was always cheap with the college a couple blocks away and everything, but they thought they were hot shit because they bought the biggest pad on the street. A couple years later in '63 they bought an Oldsmobile. You know what they did with that car?"

I shook my head.

"Crashed it right into a goddamn trolley at forty miles an hour. That's what the American Dream'll do to you—work you to the bone and then kill you before you see your first social security check."

"My God, that's terrible! How old were you then?"

Bobby shrugged, "Seventeen," he replied. "I remember the day it happened. My brother, Jules, Mary, and I trashed the whole house. We tore it apart from floor to ceiling—everything. Then after some time went by, we got to work making it new again. My brother painted the whole place, we wired up the garage so we could jam, and we even planted a garden in the lot around back. The garden was Jules' idea; he wanted us to be self-sufficient, like a little communal family—

especially since we were only busking in the Park with my guitar case open on the ground in front of us at that time—you don't earn much bread that way."

"This Jules seems like a real cool guy," I observed.

"Oh man, he is. Jules and I go way back. He's like my brother from another mother," Bobby replied.

"Those drums in the Trips Center, those were his, right?"

The group of them nodded.

"Was he any good?"

"Man, he was the best goddamn drummer I've ever jammed with, and I've played with a lot of cats," Billy exclaimed. "He was one of those heads who played better high than straight, and there ain't a lot of those kind. He was way out there, like the George Shearing of percussion! Man, he could've made it big."

"Well, where's he at now?" I asked.

They all fell silent.

"Last I heard he was heading for the border," Mary answered finally.

"He hadn't been the same since he ate some White Lightning about a month ago. He'd just gotten a draft card in the mail, and he had a bad trip and wigged out," Bobby explained. "He kept telling me that his fingers were burning him, that he could see monsters in the mirrors and pigs behind every door. He sat in the corner for hours with his tongue sticking out between his teeth because he thought it was a snake he was going to swallow and wouldn't let any of us near him."

"It didn't get any better afterward either," Space added, "he just got paranoid about everything. He barely went outside, and when he did, he thought everybody was after him—pigs and narcs of course—but also the neighbors and the guys at the farmer's market, cats he'd known for years!"

"Yeah, he kept saying things about how he needed to get out of the City because 'the high-rises were choking the life from the sun' and how he quit playing gigs because he 'couldn't go on as a mirror any longer.' I tried to understand him, I really did, but he was really rattled. One morning he just up and left—packed a bag, said goodbye, and split for Mexico," Mary said.

"He needed to," Billy replied.

"The hell he did!" Bobby disagreed. "All he needed was to cool off for a while!"

Billy held up his hands, "Alright, man, alright! Stay cool! Everybody's gotta do their own thing, right? He'll be back. And we don't gotta worry about who's gonna play those drums for us, 'cause Rhiannon is staying with us for a while now."

I nodded my shared sentiment.

"Yeah, yeah, you're right, man," Bobby apologized. "It was just, you know, so sudden. And Rhiannon, I'm real glad you came along when you did. It wouldn't be too difficult to bag another drummer, but you've got some serious chops. It's real cool you decided to stay in the City," he met my eyes, "…real cool."

"Thanks," I replied, flattered.

"You see," Bobby explained, "one day The Day Trippers are gonna be as big as the Stones, but considering the rate we were going, I figured we'd be the old guys on the scene before we got the ball really rolling."

"You wanna be famous, huh?" I inquired jokingly.

"Damn straight! There's no reason we shouldn't be! We've been playing together for years, and you're better than half the drummers on the scene right now."

"Here's the way I see it," Mary explained, "we gig around a little bit and get ourselves a bite from a record company and sign on. We cut one real groovy album, and then we don't gotta worry about scoring bread all the time, and we can just play and live the good life."

"The best thing about fame is that you have a captive audience," Bobby added. "I want to have a following, I want people to know my name, you know?"

"Dreams…" Faye spoke with an endearing smile radiant upon her face.

Billy laughed, "Man, she's right, we can't hope to be headliners as a jam band."

"What about The Grateful Dead, then?" Space pointed out. "All you need are a few good tunes, man, a few good riffs and a few good lyrics…that's all you need, man."

Bobby shrugged, "My brother's the only one of us who can pen songs. I'm a musician, not a poet."

"Didn't you say he was coming up to the City?" Mary asked.

"Yeah, soon too—or at least that's what he told me when he called last, anyway. You never can tell with him; he's like the wind. But he's in California; he was down around Santa Cruz as of a week ago…"

The hours passed like water through a sieve as the conversations continued. Before we knew it, the club was closing, and we were one of the last tables out. The chill of the midnight air cut through my thin clothes, and I found myself wishing for a heavier jacket. The cold didn't last long, however. Upon walking outside, we ran into a friend of my acquaintances who was leaving a bar down the street, and the whole group of us jumped into the back of his red VW microbus, turned the heat and radio on full blast and sped off toward the Haight. Jimi Hendrix's *Purple Haze* poured from the custom-rigged speakers, buried somewhere in the folds of paisley curtains and psychedelic tie-dye that hung from every inch of the bus's interior. Most of the city had already turned in hours ago, but all along the Haight, some houses remained aglow. Music still filled the streets, though quieter and more tranquil than before. A few heads were still out and about, and others had commenced to hunkering down on park benches or in door jambs to wait out the night. Whether it was the nature of the evening, the sudden change of atmosphere, the quantity of weed we had smoked, or a combination of all three, I could see that the gentle fog of sleep had begun to envelop each of us in succession. Even I was lulled by the Sandman's enticing whispers of a soft pillow and a comfortable place to end the night.

We arrived back at the Trips Center sometime in the very early morning, although the exact hour was unobtainable—it seemed like there wasn't a clock in the whole city. When we pulled up outside, the house was dark and quiet. The front door wasn't locked, so we walked right in. Immediately upon entering the front room, Bobby plunked down in one of the padded chairs and was asleep within a minute. Space was the second to go. He sat down on a pile of blankets on the floor and pulled off his boots and his shirt and placed both items on a chair before stretching out, turning on a handheld transistor radio he'd pulled from under his pillow, and retiring to never-never-land. Faye and Billy entered last and after shutting the front door, ran up the stairs on the far side of the room to embark on a love trip upstairs. In short, it didn't take long for Mary Jane and me to find ourselves to be the only waking occupants of the room.

"Are you hungry?" she asked, turning toward me.

"Starving," I replied.

Mary Jane led me into the kitchen and lit a candle, "Do you like apples?" she inquired, choosing one from a bowl of fruit on the counter.

I nodded, and she tossed it to me before taking one for herself and picking up the candle to carry with us into the living room. She seated herself on the bearskin rug, tied back her hair, wrapped herself in a blanket, and began munching away on the apple. "You can crash on the couch if you want," she told me in-between mouthfuls.

I laid down on the couch, found myself a pillow and a blanket, and stared up at the blue spiral painted on the ceiling. All was peaceful, all was quiet—save for Bobby's soft snores, the crunching of apples, and the telltale thumping coming from upstairs. Many bizarre thoughts passed through my mind as I laid there.

I thought about my life as I'd known it—an uneventful, ordinary, somewhat dreary and mediocre existence largely confined within Fresno's conservative city limits. I thought about The Descendants and the poignant fact that I had left them on what was supposed to be the last night we would be seen under the unflattering perspective of our parents and peers, the fact that it was the first time in all our lives that a foreseeable future somewhere other than Fresno existed within reach outside of a daydream. I couldn't imagine that it'd been a thought in any of their minds that their star drummer would disappear in the night; that when they awoke, I would be gone—departed to reaches unknown. I wondered if the same amount of time had passed for them as it had for me. I wondered when it was that they had discovered I was missing. What had they thought? What had they done? I wondered if they had gone up to San Francisco anyway, how long it would take for them to find another drummer, and what life for them would be like without me…what my life would be like without them.

I thought about George sitting in the Hartford's basement, listening to *Let It Bleed* and eating scrambled eggs. I yearned to tell him of the things I had experienced, to have him listen to me just once more and offer his timeless advice. I began to feel bad about having left so suddenly, then laughed at how silly that sounded—as if I had planned on leaving at all! In all actuality, George would be ecstatic if he knew of the miracle that had taken place. He wouldn't be worried about me when I failed to show—he'd *know*. The longer I was gone for, the surer he'd become that I'd finally ended up exactly where I'd always wanted to be—in San Francisco and out of my mother's reach. My mother…

I thought about Meredith—her smothering, over-protective angst and our daily disputes, all the dread and anger she caused me—how I loathed her…and yet, how far away it all seemed now.

I now walked amongst the legions of victims of the inexplicable, standing somewhere in-between John Salter Jr. and the Blessed Mother. Questions without answers and notions lacking confirmation whirled about inside my mind. Once more, I looked around the darkened room before letting my gaze travel toward the painted ceiling, beyond which the thumping had ceased and been replaced by deafening silence. The spiral caught my attention all over again, and I let out an enormous sigh. I locked my eyes on that spiral, and it seemed to carry me away from my corporeal confusions and my theoretical worries and instead toward a vivid inclination to dream, to question, and to wonder.

"Is this reality?" I asked Mary after several minutes of silence.

"That depends on what 'this' is," she answered. "Reality is existence as you perceive it. Subjective reality is reality substantiated by your perceptions of the world. Objective reality—ultimate reality—is reality on a universal scale."

"Have you ever felt that reality has…changed for you in some way? That the things you remember as real and the things you are experiencing now are so far removed from one another that it seems impossible that they could both be true? How can you tell what's real and what's delusion?"

"I'm hip. Everything is indeed real, but not always as we perceive it. Once you've seen through the veil of the physical realm, you have the potential to observe, understand, and emulate everything in the universe," came her reply.

"So you've seen through this 'physical realm'?"

Though I could not see her, I could tell that she was nodding; I could *feel* it. "There are other planes of reality that we have just begun to explore, whole planes of existence and possibility that aren't physical and cannot be explained, so there really is no definite, explicable reality."

"So us talking right now, is this reality?"

She smiled, "If it isn't, it sure is a wonderful dream."

"If it were a dream we would have to wake up at some point, wouldn't we? Or if it was a trip, wouldn't we have to come down?" I insisted.

"Only if time itself is real. Is time real, Rhiannon?"

"I used to think so…"

I wished I could have asked her more questions, but she'd drifted off to sleep. As for me, I continued to stare up at the spiral and the suggested void beyond. I thought about the things that Mary had said about the existence of reality. For all intents and purposes, objectively at least, this wasn't the past anymore, this was the present. Everything that was happening around me was happening in the moment and for the first time.

I thought about Grace Slick at The Matrix buying me a drink, radiant and youthful—thirty years old at most. If Grace Slick was twenty-something, that meant all the other musicians on the scene were also twenty-something. Janis Joplin, Jim Morrison, and Jimi Hendrix didn't die until they were twenty-seven years old. That meant I was cohabiting the planet with the same music gods I had idolized and sought to emulate my entire life thus far. Somewhere in the country and probably not too far away at that, Janis, Jerry, Bonzo, and so many others were not only alive, they were in their prime! I thought about all the great music that simply didn't exist yet: *Stairway to Heaven, Imagine, Layla*—the list went on and on. Led Zeppelin had only released their first album last year, The Beatles were still a super-group, and Clapton was still playing with Cream. Elton John and Santana were virtual unknowns, and Arlo Guthrie had only been arrested for littering three Thanksgivings ago.

I thought about the friends and family I had grown up with; half of them had not been born, and my parents were my age! I was not a thought in their minds, a figment of their wildest dreams, a bothersome eyelash in my mother's eye. Likewise, there was no record of my birth in the Fresno town hall, I did not have a social security card, a birth certificate, or even a valid license. I—like the music—simply did not exist.

1969

****

When I awoke in the morning, the scene remained virtually unchanged. Bobby was still fast asleep in the chair, Space's radio still hummed indistinctly from under his pillow, and Mary was still curled up on the bearskin rug in the middle of the floor. I flung the blankets off me, padded over to the front window, and peered outside through the hanging strands of glass beads. Though the sunlight had just begun to break through the morning's fog, the streets were already full of excitement. Cars passed in both directions, although the majority of the traffic was headed west into the center of the Haight. The sidewalks were markedly less crowded than yesterday, although a costumed cluster passed leisurely by the Trips Center, headed by a long-haired man in a white tunic playing a flute.

I turned away from the window after a while and began to wander about the house. I walked across to the opposite side of the living room where there was a second entrance to the kitchen and the staircase that led to the second floor of the house. Across from the staircase was a darkened study behind two closed glass doors. I peered inside and could see several bookshelves lined up against the rear wall. A collection of paint cans stood in one corner along with a variety of other artist paraphernalia, and some blank canvases were strewn across the large burgundy desk in the other corner. I thought about Bobby's brother, the artist, and how talented he was; how much of a visionary he had to be to be able to paint so beautifully and eloquently. Although I had never met him, his presence in the house was so strong that I felt as if I already had.

After leaving the study, I climbed the stairs in search of a bathroom. When I reached the top of the steps, I was greeted by yet another incredible mural; this time of an enormous lion's head whose open mouth framed a window. I peered into the great lion's gullet and out over the neighbors' rooftops, pastel in the morning haze. The lion's mane spread out from his head in all directions, melting into soft golden spirals traced by lines of blue and gray that eventually became clouds and elaborate chains of snowcapped mountains. These illustrations were spread across all the walls and doors of the hallway, melding and changing into different and more complex detail as they went on.

104

A BRIEF AND BEAUTIFUL TRIP BACK

There were seven doors off of the upstairs hallway, three of which were bedrooms, two of which were occupied. The only unoccupied bedroom was to the right of the stairs at the end of the hallway. I peeked inside. The walls, floor, and ceiling were all painted wonderfully psychedelic. From sheepshead mandalas and dramatic reproductions of acid rock posters to abstract characterizations and classic tribal imagery, the room had just about every color and design I could fathom, and even some that I couldn't. I was beginning to become convinced that Bobby's brother was a reincarnation of Hieronymus Bosch.

The other rooms were markedly less dramatic. The first door to the left off the hallway was a simple closet filled with towels and other typical closet things. It could have easily been a closet in any straight house, except for the few suspicious-looking bags of potting soil stacked on the floor. Directly at the top of the stairs, to the left of the lion's head window, was a small room without a door on it—instead, earth-tone Indian tapestries were hung across the entrance. Inside, the room was virtually empty, save for a rectangular mat in the center of the floor, a small, wooden incense burner, and a Buddha statue in the corner. The room was painted seven different colors, divided into seven different stripes. From floor to ceiling they were: red, orange, yellow, green, blue, indigo, and violet. The ceiling was painted a bright white, and the floor, a deep red. The adjacent room was completely white: ceiling, walls, rug—everything—and it was totally empty, except for a single retractable attic staircase, thematically painted white.

Directly across the hall was the object of my prying, and thankfully, this room had a door. I went about my business, splashed my face with cold water, and looked in a mirror for the first time in over twenty-four hours. Between my boho getup, red eyes, and unkempt hair, I didn't look at all different from any of the freaks out there on the Haight. If Meredith could see me now, she'd most likely disown me immediately and without question. George, on the other hand, would probably flash back to the Dead show at Winterland in 1973—a story I had heard seventeen-thousand times, the most-repeated line of which was 'There was hair *everywhere*, man!' Personally, I kind of liked the look, but regardless, I decided a nice, hot shower was in order before I began another unpredictable, surrealistic day in Haight-Ashbury, San Francisco. I pulled back the shower curtain to inspect the facilities and found myself staring up at two six-foot-high pot plants, planted where else but in the tub. I figured showers weren't a common occurrence at the Trips Center. Now I understood why the entire place reeked like the Tijuana customs.

Smiling to myself, I walked back down the stairs, poured myself a glass of water from the faucet in the kitchen and let myself out the back door and into the garden Bobby had told me about the night before. The area was the same width as the house and enclosed by a wire fence. A few assorted fruit trees grew against the rear of the fence, and bean plants were entangled just about everywhere else along the perimeter. Tomatoes, peppers, carrots, potatoes, and several other varieties of vegetables grew amongst the weeds and grass in fairly straight rows, and some berry bushes were planted at the base of the trees on the far side of the garden. Little yellow wildflowers grew interspersed throughout the entire yard in small patches like sporadic bursts of gilded sunshine, and right there in the center of it all, a man lay spread-eagled in the grass, wearing nothing but a mess of blonde curls and a pair of khaki cutoffs. His eyes were closed while his head bobbed back and forth and his lips twitched—the outward manifestation of the electric concerto firing and exploding inside his mind.

I watched him for a moment, full of curiosity and intrigue. As I did, I began to recall my own psychedelic experience. I remembered the suddenness, the striking fear, the inability to comprehend, the disintegration of my world, and the deadly imminence. But I also remembered the brilliance, the unspeakable perfection, the creatures I'd seen, the incredible speed, and the sense of Nothingness. Like in a flashback, I remembered every detail. I wondered what it was that he was experiencing and how different his experience was from mine. I smiled as I watched him smile, bathed in the morning sun like a spotlight, and a strange urge moved me closer. I stood up from the step, walked further out into the garden, and seated myself amongst the heads of lettuce.

A few moments later, I moved even closer until I was near enough to reach out and touch his hard, bronze body. However, I refrained and walked to the opposite end of the garden and stood in the shade of the fruit trees. I surveyed their bounty: dozens of sun-ripened apples, figs, and pears hung only a foot above my head. My stomach growled, and I reached up to pluck one of the apples off of the lowest overhanging branch.

"The fair child picks an apple from the tree of life..." the man spoke.

I was so startled by the voice that I jumped up and spun around,

106

apple in hand. I expected the source of this voice to be standing right behind me, but he had not moved from his place in the grass, and his eyes were still closed.

"...the tree from which Spirit has sprung," he continued. "She is woman, she is Eve. She has found herself the maiden of Eden. Bite the apple, Child, and you shall bear witness to the birth of the universe."

Astonished yet curious, I stepped carefully over the rows of vegetables until I reached his side. Even as I did, his eyes remained closed.

"How did you know I was there?" I whispered.

"Just because my eyes are closed, it does not mean I cannot see. I see you in my mind, you are a part of my trip."

"Who are you?"

"God."

"You're God?"

He didn't answer, he just kept on as he had been, bobbing his head and running his hands through the grass.

I looked down at him and then down at the apple. My stomach continued its protest, so I bit into it, chewed a few times, and swallowed. I half expected something incredible to happen, but nothing did.

"Rhiannon!"

The sound of Mary's voice brought me back to reality, and for the first time, I realized exactly where I was. I was standing in the center of the garden with an acidhead tripping at my feet and a half-eaten apple in my hand, waiting for my surroundings to erupt into some spectacular zenith of psychedelic proportions with every bite. I felt extremely silly.

Mary beckoned me over, and I navigated my way through the garden and up to the step where she was standing. "I see you've met God," she smiled humorously.

I nodded.

"I was looking for you. Bobby was afraid you'd slid out on us."

"Oh no," I replied hurriedly, "I was just looking around."

"That's what I told him," she replied casually, holding the door for me as we walked back into the house. "Are you hungry?"

"Not anymore," I replied through a mouthful of apple.

"How's your head?"

"What do you mean?" I asked, puzzled.

"Now, now, Rhiannon, you can't forget to feed your head, not here."

107

1969

She took me by the hand and led me through the house, which was now bustling with activity. It seemed like every head on the Haight had crawled out from the woodwork and gathered in the living room of the Trips Center. I counted eleven all together: the five who had found me, the woman Melinda whom I'd met in the kitchen, and five I had never seen before. They were seated all over the living room; all over the couches and chairs and on the floor in some kind of a lopsided circle. Mary Jane seated herself on the rug in-between Faye and another girl, and I moved in next to her.

"G'mornin', Rhiannon," Space called to me from across the circle where he and Bobby were rolling numbers.

"Good morning!" I called back.

A chorus of *'good mornings'* erupted all around the circle, and somebody got up and put *Sgt. Pepper* on the record player—track four on the B-side, to be exact. I closed my eyes and listened to the music and its parallel there in the room. I listened to their laughs and the sounds of their voices, the ones I knew and the ones I didn't. I listened to their jovial joking and their good-humored, good-spirited, early-morning esoteric chatter.

I opened my eyes as the songs changed, and again, I found the spiral staring back at me. The tone of the gathering changed with the music, from cheerful to a sort of tender sentimentality in reminiscence of a story we'd all been told about a man we'd all met at one time or another.

"*I read the news today, oh boy,*" Mary sang, next to me, "*about a lucky man who made the grave. And though the news was rather sad, I just had to laugh, I saw the photograph...*"

A man a few faces down the line began to copy the sound of the maracas, singing, "*shuka-shuka-shuka.*"

"*He blew his mind out in a car,*" the girl next to me continued. "*He didn't notice that the lights had changed.*"

Billy came in periodically with the bass part, "*bum-bum-bum-bum,*" and I did my best to imitate the drums, "*ba-da, shup-da, da-da.*"

Another girl close by me giggled in delight and picked up the next line, "*A crowd of people stood and stared; they'd seen his face before, nobody was really sure if he was from the House of Lords.*"

The song continued all around the circle. Nobody knew who was going to sing the next lyric, but somebody always did.

Bobby finished rolling his number, lit it, and sent it around—after which Space handed him his guitar and he began to play and sing while grinning right at me, "*I'd love to tururururn youououou*

108

onnnnn..." He reached behind him then, pulled out this little Indian water drum, and tossed it to me as the song rose to its anticlimax. "Go!" he urged me.

He continued to play, effortlessly and faultlessly, and I joined in, beating out rhythms I knew by heart. My playing seemed to catch the attention of the circle, and they all began to clap and sing along, "*Found my way upstairs and had a smoke, and somebody spoke, and I went into a dream, ahhh-ah-ahhh-ah-ahh-ah-ah-ah-ah...*"

As the end of the song approached, the two numbers that had been passed from around the other side of the circle both found their way to me at the same time. I rolled the drum across the circle over to Billy, and he struck the final beat as I inhaled that sweet smoke, one joint in each corner of my mouth. The circle fell silent in a kind of stoned reverence as that final chord faded slowly away. We all listened intently—and I most especially—to every little undertone of the note, so much so that I could even hear doors creaking and windows opening; the heartbeat of a generation, all contained within that final E major.

"See, Ouroboros," I heard Faye say in the moment of silence before the conversations started up again.

"Rhiannon," Mary spoke quietly, nudging me out of my musings. "Humphrey Bogart…"

"Huh?"

She gestured to indicate the two joints I was holding.

"Oh!" I responded, noticing for the first time that I was still holding on to them.

She smiled, amused, "How's your head?" she asked again.

I smiled back at her. There was a feeling of numbness in my jaw and oneness in my mind, "Groovy."

"Hey, Rhiannon," Space called, getting up from the circle with Bobby, "we're gonna go score some acid, wanna come along?"

I shook my head, "Actually, I was thinking about going down to the Haight and looking around and seeing what's what and maybe buying another shirt or something. But, uh, I don't have any cash, do you think anybody could lend me a few bucks?"

"Don't sweat it," Mary Jane cut in. "Look," she said, pointing to a bowl next to a pile of albums on one of the shelves. It was filled with spare change and crumpled green bills. "Take what you need."

"Thanks!" I replied in surprise. "Thanks a lot!"

"Don't mention it," she replied with a smile before heading out the back door with Bobby and Space.

1969

Walking through the Haight was like being on the inside of a prism. There were people and posters, vibrant colors and elaborate architecture, and cars of all makes and models passing up and down the street. There were trollies crammed full of freaks, heads camped in stairwells, and hippies loitering in storefronts and gathered on street corners. There were legions of backpackers, knapsackers, bums, and trash-baggers. There were freaks with the Jesus Christ hair and the tunics and turbans, ankle bells and beads, amulets and cigarettes. There were girls in mod skirts and high boots with Twiggy-style haircuts standing alongside men wearing braids and flowers. There were mime troupes and minstrel shows performing for free for the general populous out on the streets of San Francisco, weaving in and out of the traffic-stopped cars, their feet bare on the gray, gum-covered sidewalks. And the music—there was always music—it drifted from the open doors of the head shops and cafes where inside, aspiring writers and side-street philosophers sat with their paperback copies of *Walden* and *All and Everything* discussing the use of defoliants in Vietnam and civil disobedience over a cup of coffee and a number. Then, of course, there were the gawking straights, the street vendors selling stares, crying: 'What has become of our children?':::: LSD—an entire generation gone down the rabbit hole. And despite the illegality of it and everything else, there was a sign in a shop window right out front for everybody to see, proclaiming:

Trips For Free!

I stopped at this store after seeing the sign, and after peering through the windows, I decided it looked promising enough and ducked inside. The store was a little bohemian boutique. It was small, dark, and intimate, but it had just about anything you could ever want or need: racks of secondhand clothes, blankets, baskets, tables full of jewelry, and shelves of books in every condition ranging from brand new to time-ravaged-cover-torn-off-carried-across-the-country-with-chapter-four-missing. At the back of the store, there were handmade ceramic pots and hand-sewn quilts, tapestries, incense, and statues of Buddha, amongst other things. There were people all around: browsers like myself sifting through the jumble and those who I assumed worked there. One girl attempted to organize some of the shelves which held painted plates and cups, and another sat at the front counter, partially hidden from view behind bouquets of artificial flowers and a colorful array of

110

other merchandise. In the rear corner of the store, behind a rack of costume hats, a blonde couple sat, collaborating on a pair of whimsically painted acoustic guitars. Their gentle music rose like smoke into the rafters where several gray-bellied pigeons were perched amongst antique chandeliers and hanging stained-glass lamps.

I spent most of the day in that store and walked out several hours later after buying two shirts, a pair of Levi's, a lumpy woolen sweater, three pairs of socks, a few strings of Indian beads, and a rucksack to hold it all in slung over my shoulder. I had spent eight dollars.

As I stepped out onto Haight Street for the second time that day, I began to recall a conversation I'd had with George not too long ago, when he'd told me of his time in San Francisco, calling it 'the hub of a culture', and 'not just a city, but a lifestyle.' Looking around, I realized that old George had never been more right. Every one of those radical, counterculture kids all across the country weren't just living the hippie lifestyle, they were living the San Francisco lifestyle. I may have been lost in time and stuck in the past, but I had found myself in the center of the universe. Right then and there I realized *this was where it had all started; right here and right now!*

—And it was still forming. It had begun, but it was still beginning. People hadn't turned sour yet, they hadn't turned cold. They hadn't forgotten yet, they hadn't had time. *This* was the time, and it was happening; it had been happening for quite some time now, and it would continue to happen for a while longer. Yet somehow, many of the things I'd revered my whole life hadn't occurred yet: the Moratorium March on Washington, the Isle of Wight Festival in 1970, *Led Zeppelin IV, Abbey Road*, Woodstock! To imagine a time before those things so central to my knowledge had come into existence was surreal, and to live it was unbelievable—just the thought itself made my life seem extremely convoluted and strange. I strolled along the street with these things in my head, pondering them repeatedly and turning them over and over in my mind, trying to make sense of this thing that had happened to me. No answers came, and I was left with the simple conclusion that life just doesn't make sense sometimes.

"Rhiannon! Hey, Rhiannon!" I jerked my head up out of my thoughts and searched the faces on the sidewalk around me to find the source of the voice, but none of them looked familiar.

"Rhiannon! Yo, Rhiannon! Over here!" I shot a glance through the traffic, and there, walking parallel to me on the opposite side of the street was the group of hooligans who had adopted me: Billy, Bobby, Mary, Faye, and Space with his hands cupped around his mouth, calling to me. I waved to them, and they waved back.

"We're going to the Park, wanna come along?"

I cupped my hands around my own mouth and called back, "Sure!" then I raced down to the next cross street and met them at the corner.

"Heyy-y Kid!" Billy greeted me.

"Hey," I responded, out of breath.

"Where's the fire?" he asked. "We ain't gonna book. Actually, we're gonna stop at this sweet shop here, want anything?"

I checked my pockets; I still had a few dollars left, so I followed them inside and bought a pack of smokes at the counter. As I paid, Billy came up behind me with two ice cream sandwiches in hand, "Have you ever had an IT'S-IT?" he asked me.

I shook my head, tore open the pack of smokes and stuck one behind my ear before shoving the rest of the pack in my rucksack.

"Here," he said, handing me one of the frozen treats as we walked out of the store and continued on down the street.

I took a bite, "Crazy good!" I exclaimed. The IT'S-IT was two chocolate-covered oatmeal-raisin cookies with vanilla ice cream sandwiched in-between them. The only thing I'd eaten the whole day was that apple this morning, and damn was I hungry! I could've eaten five more if I'd had the money. I looked over at Billy and saw that he'd scarfed down his as well.

"If you want pure San Francisco, that's it," he said, licking the chocolate from the corners of his mouth. "I think those things are half the reason I stayed, can't get em' no place else," he laughed.

I lit up a cigarette, I was really beginning to love this place.

"So, Rhiannon, have you been introduced to *IT* yet?" Billy asked as we shared a cigarette on the way to the Park.

The first thing I thought of was Stephen King's *It*, the book that had scared me shitless in the seventh grade, but I was pretty sure that wasn't what he was referencing.

"What is? What's it?" I asked, confused.

"*IT* is."

"I don't understand," I replied, truly lost.

"If you'd like me to put it poetically, *IT* is the ultimate Truth that has always remained the ultimate mystery to mankind."

I paused to think about that for a moment, "So *IT*'s like the nature

112

of consciousness?" I replied slowly. "The constructs of reality discovered, proven once and for all? God and religion? Heaven and hell?"

"Yes, yes, the nature of consciousness, the constructs of reality, God, true religion, awareness without perception..." he went on zealously, " *IT*'s that epiphany that never quite materializes, that mysterious woman you chase in those dreams where you wake up just before you get to see her face. *IT* is the essence of the unknown: the edge of the universe, the bottom of the ocean, life after death, life before life—*IT* is everything—but more importantly, everything in relation to everything else. You dig?"

"Right on, man, but *IT* is also nothing," Mary cut in before I could answer. "*IT* is form, but *IT* is also entirely formless. *IT* exists within everything but takes up no space. *IT* is the ultimate paradox, and yet, really, *IT* is very obvious."

"I-I think I see what you're saying," I replied, feeling a strange sense of familiarity with the topic, and yet at the same time not truly understanding a word they said, "but I think I've gotten so much of what *IT*'s not, that I don't quite know what *IT* is."

"You'd know if you knew. You have to experience *IT* before you can understand *IT*. *IT*'s not something you can read in a book or watch on television or have explained to you. It's one thing to grasp the concept, but it is another thing altogether to be *IT*—to embody that paradox, to see exactly where in the universe you fit, to understand exactly what it is that you are, what everything is." Mary stared down the street, unblinking, as she said this as if she was seeing something other than I and remembering an experience far too great to describe.

"What if you experience *IT* and you find you are disappointed by where you fit in, by what you are?"

Mary turned to me with an amused smile on her face, as if she had taken what I'd said to be extremely funny, "Oh Rhiannon, I wouldn't be worried about that."

"How do I experience *IT*?" I asked her.

"There are many different ways. After all, all roads lead home—some are just longer than others," Mary answered cryptically.

Billy translated, "Just experiencing, truly experiencing and digging life teaches you to dig *IT*."

I turned this over in my mind for a while as we walked, contemplating the foreign concept of *IT*. When put into words, the notion's essence seemed elusive; the words they strung together in an effort to untangle the idea seemed to nullify it all together. However, somewhere deep within me, somewhere past the range of verbal explanation, a tiny ember glowed; an instinctual urge that'd laid dormant for years had been awakened. An intrinsic knowledge, something ancient and something intuitive that existed inside had been stirred up by their questioning, and now it gnawed at me. It was the most complex of all human desires: the desire to understand—to unlock the secrets of our own existence, to solve the mystery that is ourselves, to know the Truth—ultimate, irrefutable Truth—and hold it in our own hands. I knew even then that I was standing right there on the edge of it—at the dawn of a new day—and I wholeheartedly embraced and awaited the journey that was ahead of me.

The six of us walked into Golden Gate Park just as the sun began to set, and as the evening crept toward the twilight hour, the strangest cast of characters began to emerge, set against the most inconspicuous of backgrounds. Amongst the meadows, nestled between rolling hills full of brightly colored flowers that shivered in the gentle breeze, there were laughing hippies chasing Frisbees, hillside prophets, and Diggers handing out bowls of soup to the scratch-less sect who pranced about under the trees flying kites and seeking the miraculous in a couple hundred micrograms. I saw a red-haired goddess with diamonds in her eyes and men in masks of ancient Greek tragedy reenacting *The Odyssey* as a group of children followed the flutist from this morning up the hill to where people danced to the sounds of his song—and Ulysses and the Pied Piper greeted one another with a kiss. There were groups of yogis clad in fluorescent vests and social circles hooking down acid orange juice and nibbling on questionable chocolate chip cookies. There were hand-tooled boots and granny-glasses, naked ladies nursing babies, flags and patches, bells and processions, headdresses, beads, drums, sweat, and that customary cloud of smoke that drifted amongst the treetops—all bathed in the sweet orange sunset glow of excitement.

I followed Mary and the others over to one of the drum circles situated under a cluster of trees near the edge of an open field. They greeted the four or five heads who were there, shook hands and exchanged embraces, then sat down, filling in all the gaps around the circle. I seated myself in the grass between Mary and a kid of Middle-Eastern descent who was introduced to me as Avi.

As soon as my ass hit the ground, there was a joint in my hand.

"I could get real used to this treatment," I exclaimed, taking a

114

drag and passing it to Mary.

The circle laughed. In the center, apart from somebody's fringe satchel stuffed with weed, there was a basket full of musical instruments: maracas and tambourines, finger bells and wooden castanets. I leaned forward to inspect it, and Faye took a tambourine then scurried away to sit behind Billy.

"Here, Rhiannon, is this what you're looking for?" I glanced up from the basket and saw that Bobby was holding the little Indian water drum in his hands with a smile, and I took it from him gratefully.

"Looks like we're gonna have some kinda powwow tonight!" the kid next to Bobby exclaimed. He, like the first, was of Middle-Eastern descent and wore a pair of gold harem pants and an open vest with a round mirror on a leather strap in the center of his bare chest. He sat cross-legged with a tamboura in his lap. Next to him, The Spaceman—who'd tied his red afro back into a bun—tuned his guitar expertly by ear.

"You know," Avi said as he handed me what was now barely more than a roach, "we come here to this park every night to jam and see who'll come and join us, and these here cats," he gestured to indicate the group I had arrived with, "are my favorite."

"Awww, ain't he the sweetest?" Mary exclaimed, leaning across me to give him a peck on the cheek.

Billy laughed, "That's real cool, Brother," he said with a smile as he pulled a tiny purple mandolin out of the knapsack he had been carrying. "What's happening?

"Well, we were just discussing the weather," Avi replied. "Tomorrow Uranus will enter the constellation of Libra for the first time in eighty-four years. It looks like a lot of beautiful things are going to be happening."

"What kind of beautiful things?" Mary Jane asked.

"Communes, mostly," the kid next to Bobby explained. "Unconventional marriages, unexpected changes in laws—grass and LSD will be legal before the next decade is over, for sure. All the things we've been doing and the way we've been living is gonna start to catch on over there in Middle America. By the time Vietnam is over, it'll be known as the last war—world peace is coming on, I can feel it in the vibrations," he leaned back with arms open and eyes closed, the orange sunlight exploding from the mirror on his chest like some kind of divine link with the universe.

"What do you think about world peace, Rhiannon?"

I hesitated, distracted from Mary's question by the beams of refraction being sent off by the mirror. "Uh, well, I don't know quite what to say about world peace," I replied slowly, recalling the things I knew of the future: Israel and the Middle East, the Gulf War, the current dwindling situation in the Balkans and every news report I'd listened to since I'd been able to understand the concept of war, "but I think it has something to do with working together, forgiving each other, and helping one another out. I think it has something to do with love."

"Right on, baby, right on," Avi praised me, clapping his hands together. "You've got to be one with the universe, man, because you *ARE* one with the universe. Everything else is a game, and games separate."

"A-fuckin-men," Bobby exclaimed, plucking away at the mandolin.

"God bless the Aquarian Age," Billy added with a salute before laying back in the grass with Faye and a cigarette.

"What are you, anyway?" Mary Jane asked me, abruptly.

"What do you mean?" I answered back, startled.

"I'll bet she's a Pisces," Bobby said.

"I am," I replied in surprise. "March 2nd. How'd you know?"

"You've got the eyes," he answered. "Beautiful, translucent blue—like the bay."

I blushed, then asked quickly, "What sign are you?"

"Scorpio, November 22nd, 1946."

"Scorpio and Pisces go well together," Mary added, clearly playing matchmaker, "they're both water signs."

"I don't know very much about astrology," I confessed. "Sometimes I used to read the horoscopes in the paper, but I never really believed in it."

"Well, of course not," Mary exclaimed. "Astrology is not a belief at all, it's an awareness. Just like your DNA is your material blueprint, your astrology chart is your physical, mental, and emotional blueprint. You see, Space here is a Gemini—he's dualistic and ever restless. Billy is a Capricorn—he's reserved and resilient, our father figure. And Faye, Faye's an Aquarius, no doubt, she's unusual and unconventional, full-blooded Bohemian—an old soul. There's nothing to believe, it's all right there in front of you, you dig?"

I nodded, she'd piqued my interest, "What are you?" I asked.

"I'm a Taurus."

116

"She's stubborn as a bull!" Bobby replied affirmatively. "But she has a kind soul."

"So it's more of a science than a religion?" I ventured.

"Oh, absolutely," Avi replied. "It is the science of the heavens. Don't forget, astrology is nearly as old as the human race itself— people have always looked up."

"Then why isn't it something everybody knows about, that they teach in schools and such?" I asked.

"Big Brother knows it works, but they don't want the rest of us to," the kid with the mirror and the tamboura explained. "It's a powerful thing to know."

"What was that thing you were talking about before? Uranus in Libra and the Aquarian Age…what does that mean?"

"Well, look here," he took a stick and scratched the symbols for the twelve signs into the dirt between us in order. "Every two thousand years or so, our solar system is subjected to a different 'age,' each accompanied by the attributes of whatever zodiac sign it is associated with. For the last two thousand years, we have been in the age of Pisces, the keyword of which is *I believe*. It has been an era of blind faith, religious persecution, sorrow, and suffering. Pisces is the sign of the martyr, and if you know anything about Christianity you can see that reflected clearly in the stories of Jesus, the grandest martyr of the last two millennia. But now, the age of Pisces is drawing to a close, and we are nearing the dawn of the Age of Aquarius. Rather than blind faith, this time will be a time of the awakening of inner knowing, and our generation is the first wave. We will usher in an age where belief is paired with science and technology and where tolerance, acceptance and Universal Brotherhood replace persecution. There will be all sorts of experiments in living differently, and the whole world as we know it is going to change; it will be reborn, into Aquarius." As he finished his speech, he leaned back again, assuming the same position as before and allowing the weakening strains of daylight to reflect off the mirror and back out into the sky.

"I'm still a bit confused," I admitted. "What does that have to do with what you were talking about? About communes and world peace?"

"Here, look," Avi leaned forward to where his friend had drawn the zodiac, and above the existing symbols, he drew ten more. "These are the ten planets. Each planet rules one or more of the signs. All the planets move through the zodiac at a different rate; the moon takes approximately twenty-eight days to do so—one month—while Uranus takes eighty-four years. As the planets move, different things happen depending on the planet and what zodiac sign it is in. The transits of Uranus are of utmost importance now because Uranus is the ruling planet of Aquarius. You dig?"

"I think so," I hesitated. "It seems mad complicated."

"It's not, really," Avi insisted. "It's very logical, it just takes some time to get hip to it. You see, up there in space, Uranus is the only planet that spins sideways and backwards. It is a celestial rebel—literally eccentric—an individual, a revolutionary, just as Aquarians are; just as *we* are."

I nodded, "It's actually very cool," I admitted, hoping that he'd tell me more.

"You're a Pisces. That means your ruling planet is Neptune—god of the seas. You're probably a very good swimmer, are you not?"

I nodded, "I am."

"And you are a musician also, that's very Piscean. Neptune is the dreamer, the prophet, the magician and the mystic. It also rules alcohol and drugs like LSD, you know that feeling when you're wasted and you feel like you're on a rocking ship?"

Bobby laughed and nodded, "We all know *that* feeling. Hey Rhiannon, have you ever taken LSD before?"

I shook my head, "No," I replied, "I never got the chance. I used psychedelics only one time, the night before you found me in my car."

"Oh yeah," Mary nodded, as if she'd already forgotten how we'd met. "What was it you took? STP? LSA? Mushrooms?"

"I don't know," I confessed. "It was a crystal I smoked."

Everyone in the circle exchanged hesitant glances.

"I've never heard of anything like that before," Bobby answered finally, "and I've done just about everything there is to do. That'd be a new one."

I shrugged, "Some pusher my friends know gave it to me for free. It was a real strange trip." I went on and attempted to explain—in all the inferior words language had to offer—the things I had experienced that night—leaving out, of course, the part where I woke up afterward thirty years in the past.

"Wow, that's real far out, man," Bobby replied after I'd finished my poor explanation. "Acid ain't like that—speedy—like you said. It's like...the tides. Here, we're going to drop some if you like..." he reached into his shirt pocket and extended his hand out toward me. In

118

his palm were about ten blotter tabs, each with a whimsical pattern imprinted on them.

I took one and turned it over in my hand, examining it, "How much?"

"350 micrograms," he answered. "Good for a first-timer."

"How do I…"

"Like this," Bobby instructed; I opened my mouth, and he tucked the little square under my tongue.

My heart was racing from nervous excitement, beating so loudly I was surprised Avi next to me couldn't hear it. The acid I took had no taste and no smell, and I remembered once somebody had told me that's how you can tell if it's pure. I began to have a very good feeling.

After I had taken my dose, everyone else took a tab from Bobby's hand and placed it under their tongue, except for two members of the original circle and Billy, who opened the leather satchel and began rolling a number for himself and whoever wanted to share.

"How long will it take?" I asked. I could feel my heartbeat fluttering away in my chest, my senses alert and ready, waiting impatiently for something to happen.

"About an hour, usually," Avi replied, sensing how tense I was. "Now, I've dropped acid many, many times, and I've never had a bad trip. I've taken strange trips, enlightening trips—even scary trips— but I've never had a bad trip. But just in case, there's this downer called Thorazine," Avi pulled a little capsule out of the side pocket of the satchel to show me. "If for some reason you feel like you're starting to have a bad trip, take this. But you'll have no reason to, we're all right here with you. You just gotta listen to Leary, man: '*turn on, tune in, and drop out*'—just relax and go with it. There's been a first time for everybody…"

The circle nodded, and Mary wrapped her arm around my shoulders reassuringly, "It's normal to be nervous your first time."

"Rhiannon, have you ever heard the story of Albert Hoffmann?" Bobby asked me.

I shook my head, "No," I replied. "Who's he?"

"Alright," Bobby began, and the whole circle quieted, as if this were some kind of a ritual tale, "so it's 1943 in Basel, Switzerland, and there's this young, successful chemist who's closing up his lab for the night. You see, he's working on synthesizing a compound to cure migraine headaches, and he accidentally gets a couple drops of the compound he created on his hand, but he doesn't think much of it until he gets home. By then, he's feeling kinda weird—restless, you know, and dizzy, like he's drunk. But it wasn't bad, just strange, so he lays down, draws the curtains, and closes his eyes and starts to see all these pictures and colors and shapes playing against the inside of his eyelids, and he's thinking to himself, man, this is wild—but it's *groovy* too! What is this shit? Sure enough, that compound was lysergic acid diethylamide—LSD! So he goes back to his laboratory a couple days later, and he takes the stuff—the first bona fide acid trip! He thinks he's only taking a small dose, a couple drops of the stuff, but before he knows it, he's stoned out of his gourd on pure Sandoz LSD! So he gets his assistant to bike home with him, and he's someplace else by this time, thinking that he went and poisoned himself with this shit! Now that is one mother of a first time—that poor bastard had a right to be scared, huh, Rhiannon? Haha!—And it all took off from there!"

I smiled bashfully.

"—blast off toward deep space, never to return the same again!" Space added.

"Believe it or not, they were using it for medical experiments for over a dozen years," Billy commented.

I nodded, "Yeah," I replied, "they used to hold clinical trials at hospitals and places like that to try and find a cure for schizophrenia. They'd pay people to volunteer. That's where Kesey first took it."

"That's right," Billy remarked with a smile. "This chick's got her facts straight!"

"LSD is just like anything else, its use is more or less contained until they make it illegal, and then it's everywhere. During the summer of '67 you couldn't walk down a street in all of San Francisco without seeing somebody tripping outside," Avi said.

"The thing is," Billy began, lowering his voice to a hushed whisper, "word got out to the System, and the Feds started doing experiments on their own. Forget everything you've heard about the government being the holy grail of clean-cut, anti-drug all-Americans; Big Brother's got their hands in more pies than Space when he's got the chucks. The CIA got involved and started using it during interrogations on prisoners of war and testing it out on soldiers in secret, just like they used to give speed to pilots in the second World War to keep 'em awake and fighting. You see, Uncle Sam has a rap for making messes and leaving the general public to clean up after 'im. When the war was over, he had a bunch of shell-shocked speed freaks who didn't know Methadrine from a baby

120

aspirin—no wonder so many of 'em knocked themselves off.

"Anyhow, after the Feds got wind of what Leary and Alpert were doing on the East Coast and what was going on in San Francisco, they started piping it out into the public. They wanted the Norman Rockwells of America to take acid and see what happened. We're doing their bidding right now. This whole thing is a great big social experiment! We're sitting inside the biggest test tube ever constructed! However, they didn't bank on where it would take us. They didn't place bets on this," he raised his arms to indicate the park and beyond that, the whole city. "Now we're starting to scare them because we're on to them, we threaten the power of their Establishment. LSD didn't turn us into lab rabbits, but into free-thinking individuals! Their poison has turned into the sweetest antidote, and their opiate has begun to cause them great anxiety. What they've forgotten is that good always prevails, even when they try to use it to perpetuate their evildoings. They've fucked themselves real good this time; they've started a revolution, and nothing can stop us now! LSD is a gateway; the key to the universe!"

"Yeah, revolution!" Bobby shouted, breaking out into a tune on the mandolin.

"They've fucked themselves!" the kid next to him grinned, harmonizing with him on the tamboura.

"To the universe!" Mary cried out, picking up a pair of castanets from the basket in the center of the circle.

"And beyond!" Avi added.

They went back and forth, rapping off one another.

"Beyond the planets!"

"Beyond the stars!"

"Out of sight! Into the mind!"

"Beyond the night, beyond the day!"

"Beyond where the night turns into day!"

"—and where the day turns into night!"

"—and the night turns into infinity!"

"Beyond the beyond!"

"And beyond that, too!"

"Ouroboros!" Faye cried, dancing around inside the circle and shaking her tambourine. "Ouroboros!"

I started beating along on that little Indian water drum as the circle erupted into song. Seconds turned into minutes, and minutes began to feel like hours. As time rolled on and we continued to play, sitting around together in that city from the past, making music with instruments as old as humanity itself, I began to feel as if I were a caveman who had discovered fire for the first time.

I was standing somewhere at the very reaches of civilization, where the lines between man and wilderness, antiquity and modern revolution, and reality and fantasy were becoming increasingly blurred. Blurred also were the lines of physicality, the forces dividing man from man and mind from mind—for as we played, the need for me to think ceased. My hands moved of their own volition, stayed in time and in tune, and as I leaned back and closed my eyes, I could feel the energies rising.

And as I sat there with eyes closed and senses open, a small red dot—a light so dim and fleeting I questioned whether or not it was really there—existed a mere moment in the very corner of my visual field; and just as I fixed my attention upon it—it disappeared. I opened my eyes, and when I did, I saw that everyone in the circle had assumed the same position as I: cross-legged and reclined back with eyes closed, playing their instruments in a state known as *No Mind...*

When I closed my eyes again and returned to that same state, I was simply astounded by what I saw. Each time I beat on the drum, great orbs of color impacted the inside of my eyelids. They were gently glowing, ebbing and flowing—colors I'd never seen before, colors I couldn't imagine—fantastic, vivid colors—and at every moment, a different hue appeared. They never repeated, they were *infinite*.

"It's starting!" I whispered, my voice cracking with excitement. Mary picked up my right hand and held it in hers, and Avi did the same on my left. *I'm with you*, the silent gesture screamed, *we all are!*

Dizzy from anticipation and from the drug, I laid back in the grass. The visions were coming without my beating on the drum now, and what began merely as pulsating colors had evolved into intricate patterns—patterns like I'd never seen before, patterns I can't describe. It was like a kaleidoscope had opened up inside my mind; as if the blackness behind my eyes suddenly contained dimension and space and all those patterns started merging into one another. They opened up into all kinds of different shapes: circles and cylinders, octagons and trapezoids, and shapes that have no names and forms beyond that which I can explain.

As the speed and intensity of the visions increased, the physical manifestations of the drug increased as well. Inside my skull, I felt pressure, as if someone was pushing down with their thumbs on my closed eyelids. I felt as if there was a slight electric current rushing through my body, just under my skin. It flowed from my head to my toes and out through my fingertips into the bodies of Mary and Avi, and from their bodies, it returned to mine. Transfixed with awe and filled with a sense of acute restlessness, I sat up and opened my eyes once more. Looking down at my body, I could *see* my pulse, my heart beating away in my chest, bulging under my skin—skin that had become translucent. I could see *into* myself—my muscles and ligaments, every tendon and tissue, my internal organs—lungs and stomach, intestines and liver—my veins engorged with blood, filling my body with life energy. I traced their path with my eyes down my torso and into my toes, up again and into my heart, and then out once more through my arms and into the tips of my fingers—and it didn't stop there. In fact, my body was not the only body that had become diaphanous—the same blood that flowed through my veins flowed through the rest of the circle. Where my hands held the hands of Mary and Avi, the flow of blood did not stop; rather, it continued uninhibited throughout all of us. I could *see* the blood flowing through our veins, and along with blood, life energy the same color as the tip of a flame.

—And in regard to color, all that I saw was bathed in hues far more bright and intense than I had ever seen before. My eyesight was sharper and clearer than I had ever known it to be, and everything around me—the ground, the trees, the people—seemed to emanate a kind of light, a light that came from within—the light of life. Everything around me was *ALIVE!*

As the experience of the drug continued to heighten and I became aware of these things—things that had been invisible to me before—a dimension of consciousness that had ceased to exist prior started to emerge. I began to feel the urge to be strangely candid and entirely out-front, in order to bare my soul to the same extent as my body.

"T-There was something else," I stammered out loud. I hadn't realized quite how difficult it would be to talk; each time a syllable dropped from my tongue, the inside of my head echoed like feedback from an amplifier, "about my trip."

The dilated stares and attentive silence of the circle invited me to continue.

"When I said I thought it was the year 2000, I wasn't tripping. I really am from the future," I announced, anxiously awaiting their replies.

From around the circle, a few blissful grins and humored laughter greeted my revelation. I even giggled myself hearing for the first time how ridiculous I sounded…but it was *true*! I was being totally honest and out-front, and they thought that I was just high, that I was still playing *games*!

The guy across from me, a member of the original circle who'd been sitting under a blue cotton blanket this whole time, suddenly lifted his head and began to speak to me. "That's very groovy," he said. "I too am not of this era. I am Vishnu. I have wandered ever since the Brahman sang the world into existence. I do not believe we have previously met in time."

As he said this, the blanket that cloaked him began to melt into his body, and his entire form turned a deep shade of blue from a pigment exuded from his skin. I watched, disturbed and fixated, as out from his blue shoulders grew two more arms that swayed at his sides.

OK, this is beginning to get a little weird now, I thought to myself, feeling my heart hammering away in my chest, harder than before. *He is not menacing,* I told myself, *I should not be afraid.*

However, he was not the only one transforming.

Next to Vishnu, Space, who held one of his blue hands, began to morph and change as well. His skin became increasingly pallid while the ruddy color in his cheeks and the splash of freckles across his face began to run together and converge on the tip of his nose. His bright red hairline receded, the strap of leather around his neck became a fabric collar, and his wide-lipped grin and acid eyes grew startlingly crimson, and suddenly he was...*Pennywise!*

I was floored. Fear is not a comprehensive word, and this feeling was magnified exponentially as they began to laugh. What started out as stoned giggles broke out all around the circle, but this time I did not laugh with them. They were all looking at me, their eyes fixed on my reflection; they were laughing *at* me! They thought what I'd said was funny! They were *passing judgment* on me! As this realization hit me and I came onto the truth, their laughs became cackles, savage and guttural, and their smiles became wide and predatory; with teeth that grew long and sharp like porcelain knives and protruded from their gums, dripping saliva—they could *smell* my fear.

In terror, I looked from one evil, diabolical face to another; each maintaining only the faintest trace of their former identities. All of their initial personas had melted away, revealing their true moldy selves, oozing yellow dragon pus from every cloying pore. Their expressions closed in tighter; everywhere I looked, there they were: hanging disembodied before my eyes like ghouls, screeching while raw blood dripped from their fangs. Their faces vibrated and fibrillated before my very eyes—eyes I was too horrified to close—juxtaposed against one another. The same image duplicated, triplicated, multiplied increasingly as their features became molten: four goggling eyes melted into boiling flesh, and witches' noses emerged from mouths wide with malicious intent.

I choked out a gasp and dropped the hands of Mary and Avi and at the same time scuttled backward. The barrage of faces ceased, and instead, I saw blood and golden ichor come squirting out of Avi and Mary Jane's disengaged wrists onto the dirt at my feet. I watched as they glanced down, saw it spilling out, and subsequently took one another's hands, mending the leak and restoring the flow. In doing so, two things occurred: they stopped the liquid from spurting all over the ground and shut me out. I was excluded; I was *the Other*. I was no longer *us*, I was separate; I was *I*, and I was alone.

The previous wave of terror, which had not receded for very long, welled up inside me again and I scurried away from the circle and seated myself under a tree a few hundred yards away. I hugged my knees close to my chest and peeked over my shoulder back at the group of them; the glow of their menacing red eyes followed me. I quickly turned away to conceal myself on the other side of the tree.

It'll be OK, I reassured myself, *I just need to get away. I'm tripping, remember? It's all in my mind. I've got to relax, it's really OK...but no! That was real! I didn't imagine it, they were real! Maybe if I close my eyes they'll go away. Yes, maybe if I close my eyes...*

Behind my eyelids, however, a whole other reality was manifesting.

The first thing I saw was a dwarf—a little old man with an enormous white mustache dressed in a sackcloth tunic. He passed by me without even scarcely acknowledging my existence and was followed shortly by a band of imps. They gamboled about as they scampered past under the mushrooms that rose from the ground and towered above me as did the tallest of trees. Atop one of the red, spotted caps, a character was perched. He was half man and half beast and had the mouthpiece of a trumpet clamped between his lips. So extraordinary was this world that I blinked to confirm its validity— and as I did so, everything inside came spilling out.

When I opened my eyes, I realized that there was no change whatsoever between the world inside my mind and the one that existed in front of my face. At my feet was a gold earthen path, winding up the hill and through the trees of the forest that loomed before me. All around me, the wind that blew in the fog and the mist began to stir. I sat there watching, feeling, listening...

1969

I seemed to hear more now, and what I heard was quite often extraaudionary, that is, inaudible to the human ear: the snapping of branches deep in the wood, the cries of birds circling so high in the sky that they were hardly visible, the creaking of wooden cart wheels rolling over pebbles in their paths long departed from my view down the road, the trumpet music drifting down to earth from atop the soaring mushroom…whole conversations, even. But as I listened, they began to ebb, as if their participants were moving further and further away from me. I listened intently, trying to catch the words they were saying. I followed them by the sounds of their voices, those of men talking and gesticulating somewhere further down the road.

I rose from my seat beneath the tree, which by this time had grown infinitely higher into the sky and changed so drastically in shape and form that if I had moved previously, I in no way would have been able to tell that it was the same tree. Before I carried on along the golden path, I stole a glance behind me toward the circle I'd abandoned and was relieved to see that they'd dispersed.

I carried on behind the men, walking along the road in pursuit of the unknown. My eyes were wide as an entirely new world—in every way different from the one I'd once known—appeared before me. It seemed to be the final resting place of every myth and legend that no longer captured the hearts of humanity and in turn was sent there, to a world buried somewhere deep within. It was wild; there were parades of half-human hybrids tossing rings and waving flags. I saw Abraxas and Ra accompanied by legions of Pegasus and satyrs with Dracaena and the Minotaur taking up the rear along with so many variations thereof I knew they couldn't be named. I even shook hands with the Valkyrie. I took up following them along the golden trail, a path that seemed to lead in many different directions at once. In the distance, dragons circled the stone towers of a medieval castle, bellowing their primeval cries that echoed throughout the antediluvian night.

Sitting on the wayside, a court jester blew sulfur bubbles from the valves of a reed flute, inside which were little furry creatures—not entirely mouse nor man—sniggling as little furry creatures do, as their transparent chariots carried them toward the heavens. Behind him, dryads and faeries played at the edge of the wood, darting in and out of the iridescent bushes and other such polychromatic foliage. They ceased their frolicking as the parade passed by, and rather than continue their game, they rushed out to the front of the line. I watched nearby as they led the procession in their march across the drawbridge and into the belly of the castle. I stood by the side of the road as they disappeared and the drawbridge was raised on chains drawn by masked men in armor on the other side of the moat, a sword and a poleax resting at each of their sides. After the massive door had been sealed shut, the bell in the tower began to toll, and each time the knell rang out over the kingdom, I was met by a great profusion of color and light. By the time the ringing subsided, dusk had fallen, and silence arose.

The piercing silence endured for what felt like quite a substantial spell, but my ability to judge the passing of time had been compromised immensely so I cannot venture an accurate guess as to its duration. Anxious to find some form of excitement to break the unsettling silence, I started off down the path again. I did not travel far at all before I began to hear voices a second time. At first, they were not immediate but carrying, as if their source was still quite a ways off. Assured of this, I hurried past the countryside scenery, the cottages and gardens nestled in the hills surrounding the castle, and deeper into the darkening wood.

I walked for what felt like *hours*, still following those mysterious voices, and before I knew it, I'd come to the end of the road. It ended in a blind alley, enclosed by a grove of great and ancient oaks. As soon as I stopped to look around, the voices rallied with unprecedented force. I heard voices, not only of the men—men I had not seen but had followed nonetheless—but voices that sounded feral and carnivorous and one of a child. I heard voices that faded as they grew louder; disembodied voices that drew me in. I tried to cry out, but I was choked by fear. I swiveled my head from side to side, swinging my arms in an attempt to stop the noise, beating at the air to no avail. And just when I thought the situation could not escalate any further, I began to hear a set of dreadfully familiar voices and cackling, screeching laughter that carried with it a deep pang of fundamental loneliness and such a striking sense of panic I thought I'd die right there. It had been a trap!

You see, there are forces of the Darkland just as there are those of the light—those that prey on the weak and strive to break down the strong; those that thrive on disbelief and those that vulnerability makes great. In teams, they rally around the deepening spiral that is a bad trip, and fear makes them grow hands.

Paranoia and adrenaline like I'd never felt before in my life coursed through my veins, and I began to run. I ran until I felt my lungs were due to burst out of my chest, and all the while, those voices surrounded me. No matter how fast I ran, it seemed like they were right there behind me, chasing me, but at the same time, I couldn't tell if I was actually running toward them rather than running away. No matter which direction I went in, they followed me, and they brought with them horrors in visions and ideas unfathomable. I tried to look back to see how far I'd come, but the darkness had enveloped me; I couldn't even see more than a few feet in front of my face.

As I continued to run as hard and fast as I had been, it became increasingly hard to breathe. It seemed the air around me had become thick and soupy, and my nose and throat had become a numb liquid. I gasped for air and stopped and bent over, my hands on my knees. *Oh God*, I thought. *Oh GOD, make it stop! Oh make it stop, I need to get out of here—oh my God! I can't breathe! I'm going to die! I'm going to DIE!*

—There was something about those words—though uttered silently to myself as those demonic shrieks drew ever closer, growing stronger as my fear heightened and my sanity deteriorated—that awakened some sort of survival instinct, a surge of level-headedness, however brief, that I never knew I possessed.

I've got to FOCUS, I urged myself, feeling that I was rapidly losing ground. *I've got to calm down. I've got to make sure what I think is going on here is really going on. Listen,* I chided myself, *I'm breathing. I can hear myself breathing.*

—That much was true. I could hear breathing. It was labored, heavy, and it sounded like it was coming from behind me...like it belonged to someone else...

All traces of level-headedness expended, I spun around to confront my invisible pursuers. As I looked about me, shadow creatures and other such surreptitious inhabitants of my mind began to emerge and animate my surroundings. The trees of the wood surrounding me began to morph and change, and faces began to grow out of the gray bark so that they exhibited the likeness of the terrible faces of the circle: red eyes and dripping fangs—and won't this horrid *laughing* ever stop? Trembling in terror, I backed up as the grotesque creatures started to close in, nearer and nearer. I tried to run, but in the darkness and shocked confusion I began bumping up against them on all sides, and the drool from their greasy fangs and wide mouths splashed onto my skin and burned me like hot oil. I felt as if I was being smothered. This dark energy—not an illusion created by the drug, but as real as you and I—was creeping into me. This was it, this was how I would meet my demise—death at the hands of demons.

I opened my mouth to scream a final scream, hoping that maybe one insane angel might take pity on me and save me from the horror, from the evil that was dragging me down and tearing my consciousness apart. "I believe in God!" I cried, and when I did, the force engulfing me trembled. "I believe in God!" I cried again, and a strain of light appeared. "I believe in God, I believe in God! Yes, I believe in God!" I yelled at the top of my lungs over and over again.

Each time I did, the forces of evil wavered. In one final, desperate attempt, I broke out at last from the forest and stumbled away incoherently. Even though the voices had begun to recede with the tree line, confusion still reigned, and convulsing, I fell upon my hands and knees at the feet of a tall, dark figure.

He turned slowly, for he did not seem startled or disconcerted by my sudden appearance. He was tall and thin and had straight, silky, black hair that reached to the small of his back and was almost as long as mine. Serenely, he gazed down at me; he reminded me of someone I'd seen in a movie once. He had a dark goatee and wore dungarees, a cotton t-shirt, and an open denim work shirt. His features were young and almost feminine—save for a handsomely chiseled jaw—but his eyes were a thousand years old. Although I was still swathed by fear, nameless and unfathomable, I knew that this man did not mean to cause me harm. I was assured of this by his presence alone, for his aura was one of deep calm.

From where I knelt looking up at him, I opened my mouth to explain myself, but rather what came out sounded something like this: "Help me! Oh, you've *got* to help me! *Please* help me! Make them stop—the voices—this *noise*! They're after me, they're all after me! They're going to kill me! They're going to take me to hell! You've got to help me, make it stop! Just make it *stop* already! I need to get back, I need to come *back*! I *need* that Thorazine, have you got Thorazine? I don't want to die! I don't want to die! I don't want to *die*!"

I continued in hysterics as he listened calmly to my frenzied babbling. He stared down at me unalarmed and still entirely composed. He took my hands and helped me stand. Although the outline of his face was rapidly melting into the darkness behind him—interrupted only by the lantern at his side—I could read his expression clearly. He listened intently to every crazed word I spoke. He did not dismiss me as a lunatic, rather he gave me his total attention. He allowed himself to become absorbed in my lament. And the most inexplicable part of it was that I knew that he knew! I knew that he completely understood the predicament I was in before he ever uttered a word. He knew all about the acid, about the deafening noise echoing away inside my head, about the crippling paranoia, about how I was pulling away from the trip—away from *IT*—in the wake of my fear because of the wholesome veracity that becomes startlingly apparent and cannot be avoided whenever the doors of perception are opened.

He clasped his hands firmly yet gently on my shoulders. When he spoke to me, his voice rang out as if it were broadcast from every inch of my surroundings, and I was standing right there in the center of it all to receive his message. Just by the sound of his voice alone—full of calm and certainty, lacking any form of judgment or skepticism—I could feel myself ascending back toward a more inhabitable realm.

"When it is not quiet, you must be able to make quiet," he spoke. His accent was impossible to place; he sounded as if he had previously lived at every corner of the Earth, yet hailed from nowhere in particular at all. "If you can overcome your fears, you can take your hallucinations wherever you want."

"But...but I feel like there is a screen between here and there and I'm just trying to get back, back into my body...and there is this immense pulling sensation, like a tugging to only one side, you know, and I need to hold on because if I let go..."

"That's right, that's right," he reassured me, "just let go and float; go with it and don't fight it and you *will* return—you must *know* that you will return—when the trip ends."

"But...but it just doesn't make any sense! Nothing is real, everything is changing! I'm scared; there are things here that want to hurt me and..."

"Peace, peace! Nothing is going to hurt you, only yourself. Those are just the ego games that you've been trapped in for so long. What you must understand is that there is always order. Even when there seems to be only chaos, there is always order, rationale, MEANING. If one looks beyond the transitory, beyond what one only senses as change, then real Truth will emerge. You must have order before there is DISorder. Where there is disorder, there is cause, effect, and karma. It is like a wheel," he drew a circle in the air with his finger, and the image lingered before my all-seeing eyes, "one turn is all it takes for order to prevail. Where there is chaos, there is the potential for cosmos."

Cosmos...

As I turned my wide eyes upward and stared into his dark ones, I found the universe. Unblinking, they drew me in like a portal to another dimension, like the spiral at the Trips Center. Galaxies burst in and out of existence and comets with tails the length of the Golden Gate Bridge flew by. I reached out and held in my hands planets and stars and let them run through my fingers like grains of sand. Great celestial tendrils grew and split off from one another like vast cosmic neurons. Like time and the river, this space was infinity.

As I saw and experienced these things that were in nature and content so far removed from the hallucinations earlier, affirmations of truth—this time much more easily swallowed—began to make themselves clear in my mind. As I surrendered myself to the astounding and wordless beauty and what could only be described as divine perfection that I was witnessing, I received a burst of transcendent energy and physically jerked backward. The prophet held me steady and greeted me with a smile as I blinked and parted my eyes from his. I could see his face once more, but the universe continued its transformation all around us, filling this once spectral forest with the bright light and ephemeral imagery of the infinite.

His smile alone communicated all that needed to be understood.

"Here, come with me," he spoke, "there is something you need to see."

He took my hand in his and led me along a path I could not distinguish, for I was lost in the intersubjectivity of the cosmos.

We stopped when we reached the place of which he spoke, and with the point of a finger, he directed my attention to a spot beneath a great oak, the place from which I'd come. The band of Day Trippers and their Middle Eastern counterparts were still gathered as they had been before, though the circle itself had disbanded and its members scattered beneath the tree. They were no longer clad in horrific masks from the world over, but instead looked peaceful, serene, and quite beautiful.

"These are your friends?" he asked, already perfectly aware of the answer.

"Who are you?" I marveled, studying his face as multi-colored meteors deflected off his forehead and nose.

"Aladdin," he replied, and as he did so, he too began to transform—this time not in a way that was fearful, rather in one that revealed his true and divinely intended form, without the mortal games of judgment and paranoia, doubt and fear. As the universe exploded around us, I watched as his garments were transformed from secondhand rags to the thobe and ghutra of Arabic royalty, sewn from golden thread with richness and precision. Beside him, the lantern that had guided us to our destination began to stretch and compress until it no longer contained a bulb and filament, but instead was shaped like a genie's lamp and emitted light entirely of its own faculty. I was overcome by a sense of tender awe, as if I were in the presence of a highly revered individual.

"Won't you stay?" I entreated him, glancing sideways over at the congregation under the tree.

"I will stay for as long as you need me," he answered.

Reassured of his company, I made my way over to my stoned consorts.

"Hey-y Rhiannon! There you are!" Mary exclaimed, tapping Bobby on the shoulder to get his attention. "There she is! We were wondering where you'd split to!"

"I-I got lost."

"Why'd you leave us?" Bobby asked.

"I-I was afraid," I admitted, determined to be entirely out-front with them.

"Oh Rhiannon, there's nothing to be afraid of," Mary replied, rushing forward and grasping my hands. Instantly upon contact, the appearance of our skin changed again to the transparency of before, and I could feel as well as see the prana begin to circulate between our bodies. She was *welcoming me back*!

We remained that way for a while, grooving on the flow of energy that we shared.

"How'd you find your way back here?" Bobby asked.

"A man...he-he brought me back. A magical man."

"A magical man?" Mary echoed.

"Yes, look, he's right over there." I pointed to the tree under which I'd once hidden from them, the place where Aladdin stood—but he was gone, and I was unsure if he had ever really been there at all...

"That's real beautiful, Rhiannon, real beautiful."

"There's some real stuff happening," I told them, "some real wild things..."

Mary smiled at me and Bobby put his hand on my shoulder, and together, the two of them led me over to the base of the tree. I laid back in the grass with Bobby and Mary and watched the rest of them let it all hang out. Avi had climbed out onto one of the limbs of the tree above us with the little purple mandolin and was vigorously pinging and twanging along to his inner melody. Periodically, he would throw the instrument down to Billy who was lying in the grass directly beneath him, after which Billy too would take up the instrument and begin to play in some kind of exaggerated and satirical call and response. The Spaceman and Vishnu—who was still blue and had six limbs while Space looked far less like Pennywise and more like Bozo—were prancing around the tree, Space beating on Jules' little Indian water drum while Vishnu followed behind him with two pairs of finger bells bleating out "*Hare Krishna, Hare Krishna, Rama Rama Hare Krishna!*" The kid with the tamboura sat a little ways off from me playing his instrument with his eyes closed and full of deep concentration. Although all three groups of them played separately with no intentions of harmonizing, the music they made sounded as if it were produced by the most beautiful synchrony.

In the midst of it all, Faye danced wildly as if she was practicing some kind of ancient ritual. Man, was she zonked! She had put the tambourine around her neck and shed her gauze blouse so that her bare breasts swung freely in the midnight breeze. Faye was so chaotic, unpredictable, and spontaneous that she was hypnotizing. She was like a radio antenna or a divining rod. Time seemed to bend and slow around her. The more she moved, the more everything else slowed down. And the more she moved, the more clearly I could tell that her body was made out of…feathers…and she danced like some kind of exotic bird of paradise, like a gypsy queen on the deck of a traveling show, performing for all those seated in the hills of the natural world around me: the young urchins following the mime troupe, and the yogi circles gleaming Day-Glo phosphorescence.

For me, all of this was set against the background of the exploding universe, as if by double exposure. Each reality could be seen and experienced just as clearly as the other, leading me to understand that they were not separate, but one and the same, both ever-changing, cycling, growing, breathing, and living eternally in the present moment—NOW!

"Mary," I whispered, enraptured, "look…" I opened my mouth in a vain attempt to try and explain to her what I was experiencing. Without success, I laid there with my mouth open as if it were on hinges.

"Rhiannon," she whispered, "look…at this leaf…"

I sat up. Mary laid next to me on her stomach, clutching a single verdant leaf between her fingers and staring at it as if it were the Holy Grail.

"…inside this leaf are a million leaves. Inside this leaf are all the leaves that have come before. Millions of years of evolution for this one leaf…"

I could see the outline of the leaf plainly, sharp and defined against the lines in her liquid face which shined like a golden pool of light. As she said these things, I was filled with the wonder, beauty, and ecstasy of life. The leaf took on a meaning entirely of its own, and it too was filled with divine significance. It too had a specific place in the universe, and without it, the universe could not exist; it would break apart into the fractal images of, of—Dave and The Descendants and the crystals he'd given me. Whatever they were, theirs was an experience of disintegration, while LSD was their antithesis, evoking visions of fluidity and complete and utter connection. For when I looked at Mary beside me, I could see that her skin had become eternal. Her body flowed into the grass, the grass into the tree, the tree into the expanse of land itself, the land into the night sky, and the night sky...the night sky rolled over us like a blanket, a blanket made entirely of Mary's skin; enveloping the globe and wrapping the world in a midnight effusion of color—living colors bright and corporal and as real a presence as I.

The notions that accompanied the things that I saw were impermeable in as much as they were all-pervading, and their effect was momentous within me. I was but one very small part of one very large universe. Others could enter my dwelling place, but I could not be taken from it—even when I found myself in the back of Avi's minibus with the rest of them, wheeling down Haight Street away from Golden Gate Park. Finding myself closest to one of the windows, I peered outside to where the Haightian nightlife had reached its apex. The strangest of realities mixed with the strangest of surreal visions and what resulted was inexplicably beautiful. In the midst of the startling artificial glare and the melodic whistles of passing cars, there was a man in a buckskin shirt with fringe, sunglasses, and a ten-gallon hat standing on the porch of a historic Victorian painted purple, where inside a party was roaring. He just stood there facing the street with his head thrown back, laughing hysterically as if at that moment he had just realized the absurdity, comic relief, and satirical truth that walked the streets before him and filled his mind and his world. It was as if he were seeing exactly as I was, and the only sane reaction to the madness of it all was to laugh. As I passed by him in a van of unknown origin, on a street without name, I too began to laugh uncontrollably with inconceivable euphoric bliss.

The city lights rolled through the windows of the van in a wave as the single-family homes grew into gleaming high rises and the head shops gave way to supermarkets, neon martini bars, and car dealerships. Everything was deeply saturated in the richest of colors.

Buildings constructed of brick and concrete—materials that usually have no natural light of their own—became significantly brighter and glowed, cast in some kind of single color negative. Ominous, looming, luminous, the collection of buildings before me began to fly apart and become disjointed and irregular, reconnecting at impossible angles and all leaning slightly to the left. The van came screeching to a halt, and as I looked out the windshield, I could see that the traffic light was an enormous eye, red and unblinking. And behind that eye, I could see pipes, wires and mechanical mechanisms that pumped, gargled, and clanked—driving life into the dead gray metallic shafts and otherwise inanimate city structures.

Whoever was driving hit the gas, and downtown San Francisco flew by in a hallucinogenic blur. Everything was distorted in rapidly changing motion, but at the same time, there was harmony—gleeful, blissful harmony. However, I couldn't look for too long. The lights began to hurt my eyes, and it was *too much*. I retreated away from the window and rode the rest of the way hidden under a blanket I'd found on the floor.

When at last the van stopped, we all climbed out the back. When we did so, we found ourselves standing atop the tallest hill in all of San Francisco. Fearlessly, we walked to the very edge of the cliff and looked down at the City: the sparkling, glowing, mesmerizing City. It seemed as if the entire world below me was made up of stage props and tiny little dollhouses, and the people—like a colony of ants on a hillside—were microscopic and insignificant. Meanwhile, above them, far from their nightly respite, we were the lords of all the Earth—not through power or position, but rather perspective. We all stood around groking at the thing until I spoke the emblematic words we were all turned onto, but nobody opted to speak aloud: "Now that's a hill!"

The utterance of this simple conviction sparked a whole host of awe-laden observations.

"Down there someone is sleeping in bed and his wife is snoring…" Billy spoke.

"Someone else has been up all night speedballing…" Bobby replied.

"Someone is laughing," Mary added.

"And someone is crying," Avi countered.

"More than one is smiling," the kid with the tamboura answered.

"Smoking grass!" "Reading a book!" The rest of us took turns chiming in: "Listening to records." "Dreaming." "Skinny dipping."

"Tripping!" "Making love." "Working late." "Cooking dinner." "Giving birth." "Being born." "Dying." "Praying." "Writing a letter." "Losing a tooth..."

And the unspoken significance of all these things? —They were all happening at the same time, NOW!

"Talking on the phone." "Playing chess." "Looking at the stars..."
Looking at the stars...

I turned my eyes upward. The stars hung up in the sky, twinkling in all their familiar, enigmatic majesty, brighter than I'd ever seen them, just out of reach of my outstretched hands. With my eyes trained on their beauty, I stepped to the edge of the precipice. From the northernmost corner of the panorama set before me, a trembling orb seemed to fall from its place in the heavens and come drifting down toward the mountain. As it came closer, I realized that it was not an orb at all, but a chariot set ablaze in a striking myriad of colors. Before I knew any different, it transformed again in an instant, and Lady Justice stood before me.

She was inhuman in every sense of the word. Rather, she was exotic, epicene, and godlike. Her skin, lips, and eyes rippled in every golden hue, and her garments flowed out from her body in waves, enveloping the ground around me. From each hand hung one dish of the scales, and the bar laid across her shoulders like an oxen's yoke. What was understood from these visions, passed by osmosis from the Mind at Large to me, was that this was Libra, and I was standing trial before the Universe.

When she addressed me, she needed not open her mouth to do so; instead, the messages she communicated were transmitted directly into my mind: "Do you promise to bear witness to the Truth, the whole Truth, and nothing but the Truth?"

I nodded, spellbound.

"You are here now, with and a part of the universe," she telegraphed to me. "Once you have come here, to a state of transcendent awareness, you can no longer allow yourself to be caught up in the games, in the practice of muddling your mind with concerns regarding mundane life as the one and only serious existence—as is the nature of your past..."

She extended her arm out over the chasm and scenes from my life flashed before me, suspended in the air in the form of spinning pictures. As I watched these things unfold, I began to experience this overwhelming sense of déjà vu as a reaction to the shapes and colors

136

presented to me. Suddenly reminiscent of my past, they triggered emotions and memories normally latent and trivial, but as of now possessed such incredible importance I considered them central to my very being.

"You must act without an investment in self-interest, with total love, and without playing your paranoid games..." her voice resounded around the gorge, echoing about me in wordless synesthesia, "...the game of self and I and my, you and yours, them and theirs—it's all an illusion. You must act in accordance with what you are: a part of everything else! In acknowledging the truth in this, you must accept that all actions committed in the hope of personal gain are fruitless, and in acting for yourself alone you forego your place in the collectively conscious universe. You must be aware of everything that is happening now and become one with it. In doing so, it too will become yours—!"

As the vision rose to a crescendo and reached its climax, it disintegrated into a million golden flakes that poured out over all that I could see, beginning a reverberation that stretched on toward infinity; and for the briefest of eternities—*Kairos* in Keseyspeak—everything in the universe was mine!

****

1969

****

In the days immediately following my acid trip, I saw the world in an entirely new light. Even when I was completely sober, a sensation of vast connectivity and increased awareness remained. I felt as if I'd awoken from a deep sleep that had blurred my senses for years. What I'd gained from my experience was a deep-seated appreciation for the little things in life and a sincere respect and love of all life: from the lowliest insect to the most beautiful rose, from the bums who lived on Harriet Street to my friends who'd taken me in. The world around me was fresh and new and free of many of the confusions that had plagued me earlier. I was no longer hesitant to step from the darkness into the light for fear of judgment, rather, I reveled in it; for the honesty required in being out-front brought me closer to the Universal Mind, closer to *IT*. Not only had I been granted a more complete understanding of the world in which I was an inhabitant, but also the goings-on inside my own mind; and the linchpin to this succession of revelations was the ability to accept the fact that I really knew very little after all.

Out of all the aftereffects I experienced, the most significant that remained was that I was *happy*. From the very moment I awoke in the morning, I was at peace with my surroundings. The details of my situation that had so troubled me lost their priority and importance. Although from time to time, when the hype of my day-to-day existence faltered and I was left alone with the silence of my thoughts, the question of my existence in that world nagged at me. Some nights I stayed awake, conscious of the all-too-plausible fact that if I closed my eyes and drifted off to sleep, when I opened them again, that same transcendent reality might not be there to greet me. Therefore, I lived each moment as if it were fleeting, as if at any moment I might find myself back in my own world. However, it doesn't take long to drop out in San Francisco, and it did not require much time at all for me to adjust to the life I'd found myself living. In fact, the stranger the situation became, the less strange it all seemed, and it was because of this paradox that in no time at all, I felt as if I had been living this way forever.

In the mornings, we would all gather in the living room of the Trips Center and 'wake and bake' as we called it in the nineties. There was

138

always a group of half a dozen or more heads hanging around smoking grass and listening to the newest music, and every day there was always somebody running through the front door of the Trips Center holding a record above their heads and yelling "You've got to check this out, man!" In this way, the Trips Center was like a revolving door. None of the doors or windows were ever locked, and still, there was always food in the fridge and bread in the bowl near the stereo. Despite the sheer volume traipsing in and out every day, the ones who took, took only what they needed and left the rest for whoever came after them, and if they were holding a little extra, they gave some back. It was truly a beautiful system they had worked out, and the most beautiful part of all was that it was an entirely unspoken process. It was not expected insomuch as it was not mandatory; in fact, it was not altogether conscious either. That was just the way things were on the Haight—*natural*!

At the Trips Center, the daily stream of visitors began very early in the morning, and despite how unusual it was for me, more often than not I found myself awake at that hour. Gathered in one of the upper rooms, there was always a small group of about three or four of us performing Hatha Yoga—an activity I'd taken to participating in on the days I was up with the sunrise—the practice of which is all about balance, focus, rejuvenation and capturing the breath.

Back in Fresno, before all of this, I used to think that meditation was a sham, something practiced only by the religious devout— Hindus and Buddhists and Catholic monks—boy, was I mistaken. In fact, out of all the lessons and values I've taken from my experiences on the Haight, meditation might be the most important. I initially encountered the practice on one of the first days I was living in the Trips Center, when I was up early and heard a sound like none I'd ever heard before coming from upstairs. It was a loud and reverberating sound that was followed by utter silence, and one that repeated itself several times—a resonant OM powerful enough to shake the beams of the house. I followed the sound upstairs and into the room with the painted stripes and the incense burner. Half a dozen people were in there, seated on mats with eyes closed. In awe I watched as together they inhaled—taking almost half a minute to do so—and in exhaling, produced an OM that rolled over the room like a wave and was so deep and powerful that it was dubious to accept that it was the product of human voices. I sat down on an open mat among them that morning, and for every morning that's followed, I've found myself in that same position. Meditation is moving past the cerebral noise, and I sure had a whole lot more of it when I first arrived there on the scene.

Early morning on the Haight was probably the only time it was closest to quiet. There was always music drifting down the streets, but the thick morning fog seemed to muffle its sound and make the whole neighborhood appear like a sleepy small town. Even though the shops on the avenue didn't open until about ten or eleven o'clock and the vast majority of residents had only turned in a few hours ago, there were always people walking about. There were the men in the marketplace unloading fruit and vegetables from an old rack body truck across the way, Jon from next door dragging his overflowing trash cans out to the corner, and the cyclists making their way down to the wharf.

I loved this scene that greeted me most mornings because it made me think. It inspired me to ponder many different things, but most of all, it made me contemplate the nature of the Haight itself: its magic, its character, its penetrating magnetism and essence of freedom, beauty and self-expression. The conclusion I came to after many mornings of this was that once you spent a good deal of time on the Haight, you began to feel as if you were a part of it; and that sense of connection wasn't only with the neighborhood, but with the people. It didn't matter whether it was in the marketplace, in the Park, in the alleyways, or in the ballrooms—everybody seemed to vibrate along the same frequency. Everybody you talked to, everybody you interacted with was there for the same reasons and looking for the same things. We were all spiritual pioneers, cultural researchers in a practical setting, soul searchers and urban shamans alike, and yet we all came from many different places and countless different backgrounds. It was this remarkable diversity that its inhabitants hailed from that contributed most of all to the Haight's tolerance and its distinction. You were on the Haight, but at the same time, the Haight was within you. It substantiated every urge you had: the urge to dance, to sing, to create, to smile, to give, to love, and it carried on with you when you left. Which was why, I learned, so many people came back…

It was probably about a week after my first acid trip that Bobby's brother finally made it to the Trips Center. I had been sitting in the study, reclining in a high-backed chair with my feet up on one of the bookshelves reading some Hindu text called *The Upanishads*, relaxing after a morning's jam session, and listening to Crosby, Stills & Nash's self-titled debut album as it played over the speakers from the living room. The study of the Trips Center was the unofficial library of

Haight-Ashbury and another popular spot for heads passing through. It was filled from floor to ceiling with books along one wall and smelled like fresh paint and lacquer. On a typical day, a dozen or more people would visit its shelves. Many were regulars, and others were friends of friends who'd come to browse, give, take, and exchange literary works. On more than one occasion, I'd struck up some of the most interesting and thought-provoking conversations with complete strangers over the book that either they or I were reading, so I didn't think anything of it when I heard a vaguely familiar voice behind me comment on my book, as if they had been reading over my shoulder: "Ah *The Upanishads*, now there is a selection well worth reading."

I spun around in my chair to confirm the source of the voice, and when I saw the face of the man who had spoken to me, my jaw just about hit the floor. He was tall and thin, wore a goatee, and his long black hair was combed neatly back. He wore paint-splattered dungarees, a red t-shirt, and he had a denim work shirt slung over his shoulder. When I looked into his eyes, I saw that they were a thousand years old.

"Aladdin..." I whispered.

At first, I couldn't believe what I was seeing; I thought that my eyes were deceiving me. I had about a million questions, and as it turned out, I didn't need to ask any of them.

"I'm Bobby's brother," he stated without any further prompting, as if that explained everything. "Call me Al."

"*You're* Bobby's brother?" I gaped. "All this is *yours*?!" I cried in disbelief, gesturing to indicate the Trips Center walls and the pile of artist paraphernalia in the corner.

He nodded slightly, in a self-effacing sort of way

"You're amazing!" I went on. "Incredible! Fantastic! Visionary!"

He continued to nod, "Thank you, thank you, but all of my paintings are inspired. I am just a conduit, a tool—a means of expression, if you will. The paintings themselves come from Beyond, from the Collective Unconscious. It's all a matter of knowing how to plug in; if you've got a closed circuit, the bulb will light up, you know? It's a potential everyone is capable of..."

From that point onward, I became incredibly drawn to Al Black. However, it was a purely platonic sort of attraction, an intellectual kind of romance—I was simply in love with his mind. Almost immediately, I became determined to learn all I could from him. It was a kind of thirst for knowledge and perspective that exceeded every urge I had ever encountered throughout my academic career, and a driving interest that incited me to retain and ponder every word he uttered, adding every little morsel to my repertoire. Every parable, late-night musing, and general observation became to me like the words spoken by an oracle. And from very early on, I knew that the feeling was mutual. The communication that existed between us was one of little words, though discussion flourished rather often. The minor nuances of language and comprehension were never necessary, and complicated explanations became somewhat obsolete. If reassurance of an understanding were ever questionable, all I ever had to do was look into his eyes, and without fail, I always seemed to find my answer there.

Although I found it increasingly important to learn from Al with every passing day, I was never in a rush to do so. Time was a resource there always seemed to be an excess of at the Trips Center, and although the days rolled on, time never felt like it was passing. I knew that it was, yet there was never any kind of anticipation or impetus. It was like being in a state of suspended animation, and it was incredibly beautiful. The focus was always now, the instance always here. There was no schedule and no agenda. We played music, we were groovy, people liked us, they talked about us, and they knew who we were when we passed on the street, but there was never anything commercial to it. There were no expectations.

Following the day we met in the library, Al seemed to be a permanent fixture at the Trips Center, and his unprecedented arrival had a profound effect on The Day Trippers' dynamics. In addition to being a prodigy in the visual arts, Al proved to be a musical genius as well. He played the keyboard as well as if he had come out from the womb with one. Once Al's Vox Continental organ *Connie* had been dragged out from the corner and dusted, The Day Trippers' jam sessions became longer and more frequent. More often than not, they ran long into the night. The best nights were the ones when we weren't working; when we could get real high and hole up in the Trips Center and play until daybreak, or those nights when we came back from a gig just in time for breakfast and woke up again in time for dinner. There was just something about the music that was addicting. When the seven of us got together, the effect was electric, and every new night of grass, tunes, and good vibes surpassed the one before. It was impossible to quit. Only when we were practically passed out on our instruments did we finally turn in. However, one good thing about being in a band is that our time doesn't run the same way it does for other people. It didn't matter if we'd gone to bed at daybreak, we didn't have to play a gig until late that night, so we were never rushed, and there was always plenty of time for everything we wanted to do.

After Al arrived, we started playing gigs just about every evening. There were a few dives and coffeehouses around the City where we played regularly, but none that held more than two dozen people at a time, and seldom was there any more than fifteen front of house on a given night. Regardless, the company was groovy, and whenever we played, it was a blast. The pay wasn't great, but it was sufficient, and those early gigs really gave us a chance to get it together as a band.

One of the things the acid had affected most dramatically was my ability to play the drums. My creativity had been enhanced significantly, and I was far more organized in my thoughts than I'd ever been before—and just in time, too. More so than The Descendants, playing with The Day Trippers was a stimulating challenge.

Our jam sessions were like a stream of consciousness: nothing was rehearsed, and everything was spontaneous. Order and structure had no place there. The beats we used to count, they had in their brains, and I was forced to learn the art of silent conversation. Luckily, I was a quick study. The hallucinogens seemed to enhance my sense of rhythm and timing, melody and groove; however, they affected none of those as much as they did my intuition.

There were rarely any words spoken during our jam sessions, and physical cues only got you so far. Therefore, what The Day Trippers had and I quickly adopted, was instrumental to the cohesion and flow of our jam sessions. The only way I can describe it is telepathy, although it wasn't that we heard each other's voices in our heads as much as it was a meeting of the minds. Implicit impressions and subliminal cues allowed all of us to ascertain who would play when and where our musical dialogue would wander next. Some of them had it more readily than others. Bobby and Al seemed to be the most proficient. They could collaborate and construct elaborate improvisations that would have been difficult even after composition and rehearsal. If I'd thought that Bobby and Billy were in sync, then it was undeniable that the connection that existed between the brothers Bobby and Aladdin defied all measures of time and distance. Both of them were no more than five years older than me, and yet if any record producer or talent scout listened to the arrangements they performed, they'd be signed within minutes and revered as an overnight sensation.

Often there were times when it was difficult to play behind them because the effect their combined talent induced was one of such awe that all I wanted to do was sit and watch in idle wonder.

Bobby especially was well-suited to life as a performer. As the lead guitarist and front-man, he was fully aware of the effect his music had. Even at the coffeehouses and the Trips Center, his heady charisma leaked out and completely captured everyone in the room. Bobby, more than any of us in the band, seemed to possess an innate ability to turn heads. His style was not quite unpredictable and not overdramatic, but still curious enough to maintain an active excitement. He could be feeling and expressing any emotion fathomable and it would carry over into the audience like a wave spilling out of him everything he wanted them to feel.

More than any other band on the scene at that time, The Day Trippers were known for their improvisations. The vast majority of what we played was conjured on the spot, a byproduct of the moment. We let whatever energy the atmosphere provided set the tone for the night, and rather than play specific songs rehearsed beforehand, we played what was in the air, what was on our minds, and whatever the audience was putting out. Whenever we did play your traditional two minute and fifty-second rock song, whether it was covered or original, it was always followed by at least twenty minutes of strict improv. There wasn't always a message or meaning; it wasn't all in understanding the music. Because it was spontaneous, inspired by the present moment, sometimes it didn't seem to make any sense at all. But for us and anyone else who was turned on to it, it was easily understood because we had each played a part in both its creation and simultaneous experience.

Our music may have been spontaneous, but it wasn't chaotic. When we were just jamming, one of us would start playing any way we wanted to at all, and the rest would follow, each of us invested in our own individual composition. However, it was when those original compositions began to overlap and knit together of their own accord that nothing less than pure musical mysticism was unleashed onstage. Every show was so charged, so full of energy and emotion that it was almost tangible.

This is the way it was the night The Day Trippers played the Fillmore West. It couldn't have been more than a week after Al arrived at the Trips Center that we were packing up the trunk of my car with equipment and heading south on Van Ness toward the infamous venue. Space, through his connections with other performers, had landed us a gig there as part of Bill Graham's Tuesday night sessions. Even as I drove there behind the wheel of my own car, I still didn't wholly believe it. The entire time I sat there I kept recalling to myself the story George had told me about the time he'd gone there on one of his Deadhead trips around '95, and that after he'd arrived, he'd been greeted by a parking lot full of brand new Hondas for sale. Despite the obvious absence of the venue, having been slighted by confusion, he'd gone inside anyhow. I wasn't familiar with the details of whatever exchange had taken place, but it ended up with a sales associate buying him lunch and a bus ticket back to Madera.

As it turns out, when I pulled up alongside the building situated on that corner, I too was surrounded by cars. However, rather than rows of Hondas, they consisted almost entirely of old clunkers, Volkswagen vans, and minibusses—a good portion of which were wildly painted in screaming psychedelia. As much as logic dictated otherwise at times, there was no denying where I was: it was a Tuesday afternoon, and I was crawling down Van Ness at the height of lunch hour traffic with Al in my passenger seat and Space in the back, hardly visible beneath the throngs of equipment we'd piled in on top of him.

"I've got to see about getting us some kind of a bus," he mumbled.

"How much would that cost?" I asked, glancing at him in my rear view mirror.

A cloud of smoke billowed out from where his shock of bright red curls emerged from between my snare drum and one of Bobby's amps, "Nothing, if you work the right kind of deal. I haven't yet come upon a situation that couldn't be solved besides with bread."

"How?" I asked skeptically.

"Currency is a very loose term," he replied with a toothy grin, "especially here on the Haight."

Here on the Haight...

A week before, his words would've sounded strange and foreign, but now, although it was still a recent affirmation, it no longer shocked me to hear it; rather, it instilled a sense of wonder. I was Rhiannon Karlson, and I lived at 1216 Haight Street. It's what I said when I introduced myself: "Hi, my name is Rhiannon, I live on the Haight, I play drums for The Day Trippers."

I always marveled at myself when I said it, like it was some prideful achievement I'd spent my entire life working toward.

Which—in a way—was completely true and similar to the feeling I experienced when I walked through the doors of the Fillmore West for the first time.

We were some of the first ones there. Really, the place was just about empty, except for a few sound guys mulling about. The ballroom itself was huge. Wood panel flooring ran the entire length of the building, and at either end of the great room, basketball hoops were fixed on the molding. The walls were covered with a psychedelic display of rock posters advertising previous dances and functions, and various t-shirts were tacked up amongst them, bearing slogans such as *'I'm Not Just Another Usher'* and *'Save Tibet.'* A large stage was erected against the rear wall, and off to the side at the bar, bartenders replaced stacks of glasses and bottles of liquor in anticipation for that night's customers.

Upon entering the building, as I trailed behind Space and Al and gazed up at the light fixtures in the ceiling and the spinning color projection wheels mounted on the balcony railing, we were approached by a man I recognized immediately as Bill Graham. He was a relatively short man with a round, broad, clean-shaven European face and wavy, dark hair. He wore a dress shirt with the top three buttons open and a loosened tie. His attire resembled that of a businessman after long hours of paper pushing at the office, and his air was that of an executive. His mannerisms were brisk and austere, yet dealings with him remained completely comfortable. He greeted the three of us in sequence with a handshake, beginning with Al, with whom it seemed he was quite friendly.

"Day Trippers, right?" he inquired knowingly, in an accent that proved he hailed, most assuredly, from New York. "You must be Space, who I spoke to on the phone."

Space nodded, "That's me! What's the good word, my man?"

"Two hundred and ten," he answered. "That's how many tickets we've sold for tonight."

"Groovy, groovy," Space replied, "that'd be our biggest crowd yet! That's a lot of people come to watch us jam."

"Well, I have to say for a local unknown, you come quite highly regarded. Before I decided to hire you, I had about three different groups dropping your name around my desk. Marty Balin was telling me 'any band with Al Black is bound to put on some kind of a show.'"

"—my unofficial publicity agent," Al laughed.

"—and I kept telling him I know, I know!" Graham continued. "I remember seeing you play a couple nights at Winterland with the

146

bunch of them a while back. I wanted to hire you then, and you turned me down, what changed?"

"Ah, well, that was just a temporary kinda thing. Marty and those guys were just sort of helping me get on my feet. I was never officially billed with them or anything. I've spent the last few months painting down around New Mexico and before that, Lake Wissota. The Day Trippers is my brother's band, and I like to play with them whenever I find myself in the City."

"Well, it's a good thing you're finally getting the chance to play here. Say, doors is at seven, and you're opening for Cold Blood. If you want to start bringing your equipment in, we're setting the lights up right now. If you have any questions about sound, Frank's upstairs working it all out—he's the one with the glasses and the ponytail— just ask him. If you need me for anything, I'll be in and out of my office."

"Groovy, groovy," Space nodded, stroking his goatee. "You see, I was thinking of linking three main speakers, all in the front. We can run keys and lead into the first one 'cause Al and Bobby like to do a lot of collab, and we can have Mary coming through loud and clear on the second…"

The two of them walked off immersed in conversation, leaving Al and me to the task of unloading. We'd parked streetside, and as we lugged our gear back through the lobby, I watched as a bouncer brought in a huge tub of apples and placed it on a table in the very center of the room. A sign was hung on the front: *Have One.* I lingered there for a moment, then plucked one from the pile, shined it on my shirtsleeve and took a bite.

Billy and Faye arrived shortly after us in Avi's van which we'd borrowed for the night to move equipment back and forth from the Trips Center. We took our time setting up, becoming acquainted with the place as we did. Set up at the Fillmore West proved to be a strange animal for me. Despite the novelty of the situation, it was the most normal I'd felt since my arrival. There was no series of actions I was more thoroughly accustomed to than preparing for a show—and this place actually had clocks. We'd arrived around three-thirty and were running sound checks by five.

Throughout the afternoon, an astounding variety of popular local musicians dropped in. I met Grace Slick a second time—this time formally—along with Jorma Kaukonen and Marty Balin. As I set up my kit in the back, assembled my traps and cymbals and screwed on lugs, I listened to the three of them kibitzing with Al, filling one another in on the time they'd spent outside of San Francisco. I listened to Al recount his time in the desert and his stories of living out of the back of a '38 Studebaker coupe eating cactus and selling his paintings for bread, and then to the three members of Jefferson Airplane as they told him about the gigs their band had been playing, the places they'd been, records they'd cut, and the people they'd met. I was a fly on the wall while Jefferson Airplane—*The* Jefferson Airplane—prime movers of psychedelic rock and main faces of the San Francisco scene engaged in casual conversation with my friends.

But that's just how it was in San Francisco. These were their stomping grounds, and the natives drew absolutely no distinction between them. The members of this band and others like them were simply people who'd grown up a part of this scene, and everybody in the Bay Area was used to seeing them around. Nobody batted an eye except for the outsiders—and as having defined myself as an outsider in several regards, my reaction to the events that followed was humorously typical.

I'd been tuning my drum heads when I heard another deeper, smiling voice join the conversation. When I heard it, my blood froze in my veins, my heart skipped a beat, and the cigarette I was smoking fell right out of my mouth. A chill passed through me as if I'd just heard the voice of a ghost long dead and all but forgotten—Jerry Garcia. I peered out from behind my bass drum, and there he was in all his glory: glasses, beard, rosy cheeks, and matching eyes—the great papa bear of San Francisco rock n' roll.

I was tempted to rush forward and blurt out everything I wanted to say to the man, but I had to compose myself first. Once I was reasonably sure I wouldn't start crying when he looked at me, I joined the cluster of them over by the edge of the stage. I introduced myself in a shaking voice, complimented him about a dozen times, and told him how much my father loved his music. As much as I tried not to show it, I was so starstruck I could have fainted and so noticeably amped up he suggested we all smoke to mellow out. I wasn't the only one—seeing as how Space was eternally wired—and since we were just about finished with our setup, we all reclined around the stage, and Jerry Garcia produced a fat joint from his shirt pocket.

It was in this manner that I ended up blowing grass with the man whose name is synonymous with the 1960s. As I took my first toke from that joint, it occurred to me that he was completely unaware that in ten, twenty, even thirty years people would still listen to and revere his music; that decades from now, even after he'd passed away, some

148

of the kids that attended his shows in 1969 would still be following the band around like pilgrims endlessly pursuing an ever-yielding mecca.

Since by this time it was obvious that I was a recent resident of the City, as a fellow musician, Jerry took some time becoming professionally acquainted with me. I told him a thing or two about my past, and for the first time since I'd arrived, I spoke of The Descendants. He reciprocated, telling me all about his days growing up in the Excelsior and Menlo Park and about how he'd fallen into the rock scene in the first place. While we continued to converse, the satellite members of our discussion drifted away until we were the only two left. And I stood right there in the middle of Bill-freaking-Graham's Fillmore West and had a conversation with the man. We talked like old chums, and when the conversation started to dwindle, he produced a second joint, and we enjoyed that one together as well, after which I returned to setting up for that night's gig, and he split to go score some takeout.

The only thing I could think about thereafter was George. In speaking with his idol—Jerry Garcia, a man who basically served as God for George—I felt close to him for the very first time since I'd arrived there. Though it was strange not seeing my old friends every day, since I'd become acquainted almost immediately with another group of peers that functioned very much in the same fashion, the transition had not taken nearly as long as the realization that my father was now absent from my life. He was alive, surely, although not in any vaguely recognizable form. That being so, as impossible as it seemed, I promised myself that one day I would communicate to him in some way that I—Rhiannon, his daughter—had smoked grass with the lead singer of The Grateful Dead.

And what dank grass it was. By the time Bobby and Mary rode up on his chopper at quarter after six and we finished running sound checks, I was smiling like a little kid on Christmas, and my eyes were as red as the spotlights that bathed the venue. When we struck up, I knew I was very high. However, despite the fact that our band had been together for less than a month and we were playing a ballroom for the first time, nobody was worried that we were going to play a bum show. After all those nighttime sessions at the Trips Center, where I'd witnessed what we were capable of as a force—as a group where everybody backed everybody else—I knew beyond a shadow of a doubt that this was going to be one killer performance.

Al had this one song that we'd been rehearsing, Dawn Train, and that's what we opened with. It was a relatively easy song, opening and closing with a flamadiddle on the snare and a bossa-nova cross-stick pattern through the verses. Obviously, Al and Bobby did most of the showing off during that first number, but I had a chance to solo toward the end, so I took them and the audience for a ride on the crash for a while and then climbed all over the kit. When that song was over, we were greeted by a full round of applause, and seeing as we'd gotten their attention, we rolled almost immediately into a tune madly popular those last few weeks, *Somethin's Comin' On* by Joe Cocker.

Truly, there couldn't have been a more appropriate song, for most assuredly, we all knew that there was something coming on. From the moment the music started, there seemed to exist a kind of cosmic energy that pulsated and reverberated around the venue from the crowd to us, and from us, back to the crowd. I have always felt a kind of ethereality in performing—a sort of feeling felt no place else, an experience exclusive to the exposition of musicality. There is this singular oneness, this sense of unity with the sound and my instrument that is unparalleled. After all, music is energy, and in making music, you are indeed transforming and regenerating energy—sending it forth to be received by others. And the scope of this process was amplified greatly at the Fillmore West. Rather than just another coffeehouse gig, a performance like this where everybody was synched in truly became liberation in hearing.

At a venue of this caliber, the drugs served to bring both the player and the listener into the music. The music we created became their environment, and they became the inhabitants. At the Fillmore West, just like everywhere else in San Francisco, there existed a distinct and powerful magic that had the ability to shift perception. After you had some THC coursing through your system and a guitar riff or two ringing in your ears, the Fillmore West seemed to take on the air of an outdoor arena or an enchanted forest. The lights that washed out over the crowd in the otherwise mystique darkness became like different colored stars, and microphones grew about the stage like scores of silver mushrooms.

For the crowd, this combination of set and setting resulted in an overwhelming loss of all inhibitions. Out there on the dance floor they were gesticulating, writhing, gyrating, clapping, hopping from foot to foot—simply moving; men and women together. There was no uncomfortable, suppressed sexual tension. The ballroom was not full of cavalierist gentlemen, and the classic country club courtship did not apply. A man and woman might dance together the entire night and part without ever having said a word to one another and the satisfaction remained the same. It was just like it had been at The Matrix: loose and comfortable; a population of kids just looking to have a good time and let it all hang out. What was amazing wasn't so much that I was like them, but that they were like me. It seemed some fundamental values continued to persist even through time—such as the quest for Truth, the beauty of a good time, and simple out-front-ness that, though crude, had never been so pure. You wouldn't know it from their faces or their movements, but they were all looking for something—the same something—and an exchange of words to be assured of this was not necessary, for before a word was even said, their eyes spoke volumes.

For us too, the spirit of the Fillmore West invoked transformation. The experience of playing a ballroom forever dwarfed the predictability of playing a coffeehouse—as it well should. In a ballroom, there is more of everything: more people, more speakers, more room, and more freedom. The biggest difference, it seemed, when it came down to the nature of performing itself, was the size of the stage. Within fifteen minutes of playing the Fillmore West, I was struck by a great and irrevocable love of big stages. Unlike a platform raised a foot above the dance floor, the stage at the Fillmore West provided us with enough room so that there did not have to be a predetermined configuration, and unlike the confines of the Trips Center garage, it granted Mary Jane and the guitarists the liberty to move about in any way that pleased them.

In the midst of a burning solo, Bobby moved right over to me from across the stage, and as he did so, it began to look like he wasn't even holding his guitar anymore. It had become as much a part of him as his arms or legs, and he commanded it as such—with total control. Clad in his leather pants with his long hair and square jaw, head thrown back and eyes closed, he was like the Jim Morrison of electric guitar. In this way, Bobby mirrored Jim's essence; he completely captured Jim's mysterious enchantment, prodigious talent, and sensual prowess. However, unlike Jim, who in the early days played with his back to the audience, Bobby played most assuredly with his face to the crowd. To them, he was a superhero up there on the stage, a kind of Übermensch who had come to deliver this whole race of freaks and hairies, fags, fairies and cultural revolutionaries to an Elysium of their own creation. To me, under the lights, he looked like a god.

1969

We played two sets that night, from seven to eight-thirty. Rather than take a collective break, we spent the middle hour rotating in and out—an instrumental gave Mary a chance to go grab a drink, and a long solo by Al and Bobby gave me the opportunity to use the bathroom. Eventually, we each got fifteen minutes or so to chill out and watch the show ourselves, except for Space, who played straight through, and Bobby, who never left the stage although he took his break.

After our set was over, we broke down our equipment and dissolved into the crowd to dance, rap, and mingle while Cold Blood—a fellow San Francisco group—struck up. After their set, we watched Moby Grape do the same. It was past midnight by the time we started back to the Trips Center, and as soon as I left the interior of the Fillmore West, the same sensation of timelessness that I had felt before washed over me again, and along with it came a strikingly unusual sense of relief. I pondered this in silence as my friends laughed and joked around me. I was about to climb into my car with a mess of tangled black wires and various effects pedals riding shotgun when Bobby's voice rang out in the night.

"Brother, you drive Rhiannon's car back to the Trips Center," he requested of Al from where he straddled his hog. "Rhiannon, you come with me."

I tossed Al my keys then walked over to Bobby. He gestured for me to climb onto the bike behind him.

"I've never ridden a motorcycle before," I confessed. "I don't know how. I'll just drive my car back, I can make room for Al."

"Aw, come on, it's nothing," he insisted. "Here, sit."

I sat.

"Just keep holding on tight to me, and you'll be fine," he instructed, wrapping my arms around his waist. "Just keep holding on."

I blushed, but I did as he said.

Space, behind the wheel of Avi's van, pulled out onto the street first, followed by Al in my car, and lastly by Bobby and me. The frigid night air cut through my clothes like a knife and stung my face. I wrapped my arms tighter around his waist and buried my face in his shoulder as I listened to the rumble of the engine echo and crash against the walls of the towering buildings that lined the streets, rattling the bedposts and rocking the cradles inside every home we passed by.

We traveled that way in a convoy for quite a while, until we reached the intersection of Haight and Masonic. Space and Al bore right to head back to the Trips Center, but Bobby turned left and headed toward the Park.

"Where are we going?" I yelled above the roar of the motor.

Bobby lifted one gloved hand off the handlebar and pointed down the street. We rode for about three blocks or so, then pulled off to the side of the road when we reached an alleyway stretching from Haight to Page in-between two head shops. Bobby cut the motor, dismounted, and gestured for me to follow him. I wasn't afraid; not nearly as afraid as I should've been, having found myself in an alley at three in the morning with an unfamiliar man on the radical side of town. But the alley was vacant, and I trailed closely behind him until we came to a dim floodlight illuminating a service door on the side of one of the stores. Under the scarce glow sat a mulatto street peddler. He was dressed in purple rags and seated on a crate, his table of wares spread before him and a benign smile spread across his face as Bobby and I approached.

"What's happenin', Heavy?" the peddler spoke, extending a hand for Bobby to shake.

"Gig at the Fillmore West tonight," Bobby replied. "We played real good tonight," he turned toward me, "real good."

"I heard, groovy," the peddler replied before turning toward me himself. "You must be new on the Haight," he spoke, "I don't think we've met. Are you Bobby's chick?"

"I'm Rhiannon," I answered, ignoring his question regarding the nature of my relationship with Bobby. "I've been here a few weeks now."

"Call me Doobie," he replied. "Now, what can I do for you two?"

"I'm thinking a little bit of sunshine to brighten up this chilly evening, wouldn't you say? Maybe twenty hits?"

"Twenty hits of double barrel sunshine, coming right up," Doobie smiled as he lifted the lid of his traveling stand. Inside was a wooden tray with several compartments containing articles of every sort, ranging from eyeglass repair kits and sticks of gum to matches and a few little bottles of Doctor Good's snake oil.

"Really, Doobie, tell me," Bobby inquired, "do people really buy any of that shit?"

Doobie cracked a smile and chuckled, "Man, you'd be surprised how many people take me for a square." As he said this, he lifted the corner of the wooden tray to expose a second, identical tray beneath it, this one filled with an array of articles of a different sort. I watched as Doobie pulled a baggie from his jacket pocket and filled it with twenty round, barrel-shaped pills. With a quick sleight of hand, the two of them exchanged the baggie for a roll of bills and shook hands.

"Peace out, man," Bobby said as they did so.

"Same to you, man, it's always a pleasure."

"I'll be seeing you."

Once we'd emerged from the darkness of the alley back out onto the street and remounted the chopper, I asked him: "He never gets busted having all that shit like that?"

Bobby shook his head, "Never. Narcs don't see him. It's just so obvious what he really is, so maddeningly apparent and right there in front of your face that it becomes impossible to see him as anything other than what he's not. He's so out-front about it, pushing right there in the street like that, that he becomes invisible. Everybody who ain't his customers thinks he's a simple street peddler. Bums come to him to scrounge up thread and gloves, and it keeps the pigs at bay. It's fuckin' incredible. The man's a legend in Haight-Ashbury, but he's got karma on his side."

"How's that?"

"For as long as I've known him, there's been certain things that he won't sell you. He don't look it, but he calls himself a connoisseur. All his dope is clean. He won't sell you anything heads got busted over, and he don't touch goofballs, bennies, speed, or junk—even when he knows the guy down the street who does is making twice the profit. It don't matter how much you hassle him, he won't sell it. He says that kind of dope will bring you too many hassles, and he's right—I know."

"Yeah?" I asked curiously.

Bobby's eyes shifted, and he stared off into the distance, "Boy, do I know."

I was waiting for him to elaborate, but he shifted his gaze away and jammed the key in the ignition. I assumed the same position as before as we sped away from the curb and back toward the Trips Center, but this time I held on just a little bit tighter, my body just a little bit closer in hopes that proximity would bridge the disparity in our memories.

Back at the Trips Center, the nocturnal festivities were in full swing. In the living room, a substantial group had assembled in a game of charades, as I gathered when Bobby and I walked in to find Mary standing atop the couch with one foot on the arm and the side of her hand on her forehead, peering intently around the room.

"You're 1492; Columbus in search of America," Bobby sighed as he closed the door behind him.

Mary's arms slapped her sides in disappointment, "Oh come on!" she exclaimed, stomping in feigned anger. "Why'd you tell?! You weren't even playing this round!"

"You've been using the same two mimes since we've been ten years old," Bobby laughed. "That one and Uncle Sam." He put his hand on his hip, furrowed his brows, and pointed his finger at her.

"Arrgh! You spoiled my next one!" she flung the ribbon of fabric she had wrapped around her head at him and plopped down on the couch, her arms crossed in a fake pout.

"Bah, Columbus!" Billy spat from where he reclined on his side on the floor. "Columbus didn't discover America, he raped Indians! That's uncool, Mary."

"It's no matter," Bobby said dismissively. "This game is always more interesting when you've got some el-es-dee running through the ol' veins, eh?" He sifted through his pocket and tossed the baggie across the room to Mary.

"Yippie!" she cried before sliding off the couch and beginning to hand out hits to those seated on the floor.

"Are you going to drop, Rhiannon?" Mary asked me from where she sat near my feet.

I looked around at the warmth, safety, and fullness of the Trips Center—at the dim candlelight, trails of incense, and the eclectic group of heads scattered around the room. I took note of the smiles that adorned each and every one of their faces, although not necessarily directed at me. Rather, they smiled simply out of content as they blissfully swallowed their enlightenment and toked away at late-night humor—laughing mildly at rubber crutch jokes and Bobby's wild tales. I considered my previous experiences and smiling to myself, held out my hands to receive the sacrament delivered by the radiant girl kneeling before me.

After I'd taken my hit, I plopped myself down on the couch that Mary Jane had vacated. I lit a cigarette and reclined back as I kicked off my shoes and listened to the sounds of the Trips Center stirring. The cluster near the door had abandoned their game following Bobby's interference, and instead, they gathered around him as he leaned back casually against the coffee table and recounted a memory that someone had incited.

"It was the night we watched The Beatles play Cow Palace," he was saying, "We were in some crazy antique car, and we were riding it up and down the freeway. I don't even know whose car it was—Jules would remember—anyhow, we'd all pushed off and were so high we couldn't see. Whoever was driving was up on black beauties and the rest of us on china white. It was only three of us that I remember: Jules riding shotgun and me in the backseat sick on junk and knee-deep in greasy takeout wrappers, bouncing around on those ancient shocks, knocking into empty bottles of Jack and puking. And this madman driver, he runs the damn thing right into the median and floors it 'til it won't go no more. So we coasted over to the shoulder, got out, and kicked the shit out of it—knocked in the windows, busted the whole thing up, and just left it there. That's just about all I remember, besides riding sick in the back of a Greyhound. Bus drivers just love junkies," he chuckled and shook his head. "But that was back in my wild days…"

From my spot on the couch opposite him, I was absorbed in his tale. No matter where he was or what he was doing, Bobby always wore this shroud of mystery that at the same time both compelled and appalled me. The more secrets he assumed to possess, the stronger my drive to unleash them became. I wanted to know him: the darkness of his past, the dirt of his wild days, the sharpest pang of hurt he held within his heart—and his dark, shifty eyes simply lured me in further. Just when I thought that he wasn't watching, that he hadn't noticed my ogling gaze leering at him from across the room or the stage or wherever we were, he would turn toward me and meet my eyes with the faintest of smirks evident on his face, inviting me to the challenge. And at that moment, as he leaned against the coffee table with clouds of incense billowing up around him in the dim light of the Trips Center, he appeared more cloaked in furtive intrigue than I'd ever seen him before.

I was so captivated, in fact, that I failed to notice that Al had approached me until he was seated next to me on the couch, offering me a bowl of vegetarian chili from his outstretched hand. I accepted it gratefully.

"Thank God for Melinda," I replied with a laugh. "It takes a saint to feed a house full of hungry hippies with insatiable munchies."

A thin-lipped, good-natured smile slid across his face, "You're very new on this scene, aren't you, Rhiannon?"

I nodded, spooning a portion of chili into my mouth.

"Where are you from?" he asked.

"Fresno…I ran away," I answered.

"That's right, Mary told me you were a runaway. She told me they found you loaded, high on some kind of future trip up in Pacific Heights."

156

I shook my head and laughed to myself, "It seems like she told that story to just about everybody. I'm gonna have to start introducing myself as Rhiannon from the new Millennium."

Rather than laugh at my bad joke, to my great surprise, he met my eyes with composure and asked me in a very grave tone: "Is there any truth to that at all?"

I'm not quite sure what came over me then, but before I knew it, I was remembering the experience to him. For the second time, I tried in vain to explain the drug and its effect: how I'd gotten high in one city and came down in another without an explanation—how I'd regressed thirty years in the span of twenty minutes. I scrambled for words that lacked sufficiency and stumbled over unilateral adjectives absent of substance. I choked on morose synonyms and drew comparisons to inferior examples that in no way accurately conveyed or objectified my experience. "Really, I can't explain it to you. There ain't words, you dig? Besides…as for how I've arrived here, I don't understand it myself," I finished finally, looking down regretfully into my chili. "You must think I'm crazy."

Al placed a hand on my shoulder, "Listen, Rhiannon, I've traveled the country; I have passed through every one of the contiguous states dozens of times. I've ridden with, slept with, talked with, played with, and sat down to eat with thousands of individuals. I've met men and women claiming to be Buddha, Gandhi, Caesar, Cleopatra, Joan of Arc, Martians, Venusians, and God himself…" Al gestured across the room to where God was tripping through en route to the kitchen, "and Rhiannon, you are the sanest one I've met yet. It takes a very honest and humble soul to admit that they do not know something."

A smile appeared at the edges of my lips, "Well, that's certainly a relief to hear."

"The drug you took was DMT," he replied with certainty. "I've taken it before, and the experience as you describe it sounds very similar to my own. But Rhiannon, there's no drug that causes time travel. Not physically, not permanently, anyhow."

"It did for me!" I insisted. "I'm not from this time."

"And I believe you…what I mean is that I don't think it was the drug. There are all kinds of phenomenon that are unexplained, such as that of Amelia Earhart or Barbara Follett and those stories you hear of amnesiacs showing up on the streets without a past or proof of their very existence. If all the tales like those are true, it would seem that time travel occurs more often than we think—and maybe it does. After all, I'm the last person to discount the possibility of something existing outside my realm of understanding. But if you don't understand the mechanics of your displacement, I don't suppose that there's anyone who does. But rather than by the influence of the drug itself, it seems you've become the subject of an extraordinarily outlandish coincidence."

I nodded slowly, "I suppose so; but having been left up to the will of chance, what a place to end up in, what a time!"

Al beamed back at me, excitedly, "So tell me, what's it like, I mean, for an outsider? What's it like to know, to really know? To know what's going to happen tomorrow and the next day while the rest of us are simply guessing?"

I shifted somewhat uncomfortably under his expectant gaze, "I mean, I know some things, the big things—the things that'll happen in the news—but as for my own life, I'm just as clueless as you, if not more so. If anything, I'd like to understand what happened to me, to know why I'm here."

Al laughed, "Wouldn't we all?"

"The problem is, I can't seem to put it to bed. You see, I've always been kind of an anti-realist, a notorious daydreamer. I may have grown up in the future, but I've always felt as if I should've been born a part of the past. I've lived inside my head for eighteen years. My friends called me a hippie and a surrealist, and all this time I've been entirely content with viewing esoteric subject matter as just that, through the eyes of theory and speculation—a matter of contemplation when I was feeling existential. But this particular situation has opened up a whole other can of worms. All those concepts that have always seemed so far away and fleeting are the reason I am here today. The world I inhabited inside my head is right here before my eyes, and here I am—all of me. I'm not complaining—don't get me wrong—I love it here, this is where I've always wanted to be; I just want to be able to understand how it's possible."

Al nodded, his dark eyebrows knit together as he deeply considered what I'd said. "I don't suppose the experience of DMT at the same time helped any, especially as a first time trip. DMT kind of blows you out of the water. You find there exists no comfort zone, complacency becomes impossible, and if you're not prepared, it is downright terrifying. It seems that for both you and I, the end result has been the same: if the answers you seek aren't revealed to you through the experience of the drug or otherwise, it inspires you to go looking for them."

I shook my head with a laugh, "I'd say, what an experience! What

158

I learned from that drug and acid is that there is a greater truth out there, greater than my mind can accurately perceive. I'm starting to question everything now, I don't even know what reality to believe in anymore—here I am and left to wonder!

"For example: talking with you right now—this seems real, but for what it's worth, I could just as easily be remembering a past life or having a very vivid dream. Or maybe I'm still tripping on DMT or whatever the hell—maybe this whole thing is just some kind of deep and convoluted illusion. Or if I really did travel through time, do I no longer exist in the world from which I've come? Have I simply disappeared like Amelia Earhart? Is time there still passing, or has it stopped entirely? Are there two of me—present Rhiannon and future Rhiannon? Is the Rhiannon that inhabits the time I am familiar with doing something altogether different than I am now? Am I just visiting another incarnation of myself? Did I just step into a parallel universe? If so, that would mean that all realities are happening at the same time..."

As both of us paused in an attempt to tackle the stellium of questions I'd just asked, I realized the truth inherent in what I'd said. *Funny,* I thought to myself, *all realities happening at the same time? That sounds a whole lot like what I experienced at Twin Peaks the last time I dropped acid. That's not too far out; why, if every person were their own universe but still remained a part of the same cosmic identity, then really, we are all just bits of consciousness becoming aware of one another—and therefore, becoming aware of ourselves...*

"In my years of psychedelic escapades, I have traveled through space and time," Al began. "I have lived, I have died, and I have been reborn. I have been torn apart, and I have been put back together. I have seen entire civilizations, whole worlds created and destroyed—disintegrated, with me solely responsible for rebuilding them—all in the span of a few hours. How does one explain that? It's all in the mind! Consider dreaming, perhaps; I've read that every night you dream a dozen or more times. A dream may seem to span hours, even days, and yet, only lasts mere seconds. And if you think about it, globally it is regarded as perfectly normal to lay down and tune out the world for six or eight hours and, in a sense, step into another reality. And if you don't, you go mad or die! How's that?"

"It's all in the mind," I repeated.

"So then, which reality is more real?" he asked rhetorically.

"Does time exist?" I countered, citing the question that Mary Jane had once asked me.

159

1969

Al exhaled a long breath, "Maybe it does, and maybe it doesn't. Maybe it only exists inside us, maybe it's something that we create. If time exists, what follows naturally is that there was once a beginning and that someday there will be an end. If it doesn't, it means that everything is and always has been; that all of existence is cyclical, without beginning or end. Processes like aging seem to confirm the notion that time does in fact exist, but couldn't that same process and others like it be carried out by factors that we do not yet have the means or luxury to understand?"

"The sixty-four-thousand-dollar question," I replied.

Al shook his head in a way that made him appear somewhat disenchanted with the human race, "We are born confined to the limits and conditions of our reality and have adapted accordingly for centuries, millennia, but in all that time only a small percentage, such a small, minute percentage has ever been skeptical of it. Most of us just accept our realities as they appear to us, and as they are explained to us as children. How many people do you know, back where you come from, who ever considered the non-existence of time?"

I shook my head, "Not a soul."

Al stared up at his painted spiral on the ceiling, "I have never ceased to ask questions. The notion of whether or not time exists and other such inquiries have followed me wherever I go. They are the mysteries I see reflected in every waking moment..." He proceeded to drill me, "What the hell is perception anyway? Am I looking out at the world, or is the world looking in at me? Who am I, for that matter, and where did I come from? Did all life on Earth evolve out of some kind of primordial soup? Did we come from outer space? How did the nonliving become living? Or were we put here? Were we an accident or the result of some form of intelligent design? Were we created, or did we create ourselves? Is this the ultimate reality? —I would suppose not—and if it isn't, what is? Is life just a short series of dreams? Are we born into a dream? Does death bring awareness?"

My head was spinning. No fragment or complete, coherent thought stuck in my mind. Everything seemed indefinite, indeterminate, unclear, and ill-defined. However, there was something about his last question that brought me back to middle school CCD, to memories of a room full of eighth graders reciting excerpts from holy texts under halogen lights in the church basement.

"There's a Bible passage I remember," I recalled without the characteristic cynicism usually present in my voice whenever I spoke of religious ideas, "something like, *'at the moment of death you will*

160

know the truth, and the truth will set you free.'"

Al beamed with satisfaction at my ability to keep up with the conversation, "Ah that old paradox; so it is that when you die, you are dead only to this world. Once you are no longer a part of it, you are finally able to understand it. Death is a state of pure objectivity where you are free from the cycles of subjective reality..."

"That seems to speak to the nature of the soul, does it not?" he asked suddenly, completely changing the direction of our conversation. "To the existence of an immaterial, nonphysical, intangible component of the human form—something entirely separate."

At that, he lost me, "What do you mean?" I asked.

"Look at it this way," he clarified, "how old are you?"

"Eighteen."

"So where were you twenty years ago?"

I paused, "I don't know. Non-existent, I guess."

"Well, your soul didn't just go '*poof*' and appear out of thin air when your parents got it on. Einstein says, '*energy cannot be created nor destroyed, it can only be changed from one form to another.*' It's a principle of reality—our reality, anyway. So you had to be somewhere, even if you were un-manifest."

"I suppose so," I agreed. "Where do you think the soul is in the body, anyway?"

Al drummed his fingers on his chin, "Some say the eyes are the windows to the soul, others say it pervades us entirely, and there are even some who assume it does not exist at all, and that what we think of as a soul is simply a level of consciousness. But I say, since the soul is not an object but a force, it really cannot be physically within us because the soul exists yet does not take up any space."

"But when we die, our souls leave our bodies," I pointed out, "so if what you're saying is true, then our soul must simultaneously be a part of and apart from us."

Al smiled, "That's the mystery of existence, isn't it beautiful? All we can claim to know of the nature of the soul is that it is the only part of the human form that is real, like really real. It is the only component of our otherwise mechanical carbon bodies that cannot be explained without acknowledging something bigger than ourselves. When we die, our bodies—just like any other matter—are recycled back into the Earth, but the soul is separate from that fate. It is the only element of the human experience that transcends time and space."

"Except for me," I noted, my humor resting somewhere between jest and awe, "I've traveled through space and time, both body and soul."

Al rubbed his goatee thoughtfully, "The miraculous event of body and soul defying the confines of both space and time, breaking every natural law that seems to exist? Sounds like the story of Christ."

I considered his inference as I stared off toward the place across the room where The Day Trippers had hung the crucifix in succession with the wheel of dharma and a brass OM. *Maybe Jesus was a time traveler like me*, I wondered.

As the acid came on, I felt calm, serene, and clear-minded, as if the sweet whisper of Truth had breathed a breath of inspiration into me, and I was overcome by a sense of certain wonder, "What if we all use our minds to create reality as we know it and perceive it the way we do because we are societally conditioned to remain in total subconscious agreement with this view of reality? So, when that groupthink quality is surpassed, wouldn't we all have the ability to perceive things separately and create our own worlds? What if we really are all connected somehow and what we are looking at is a projection of ourselves? That would explain why there is such widespread belief in a monotheistic god—because really we are all one..."

"That would mean that all life is an allegory then," Al responded, "of the impossible struggle of humanity, tasked with rejoining that universal link composed of all energy, all thought, and all being...all wars emerging from the disorder that exists without it and love as an example of the harmony that exists with it...worldwide despair functioning as the desperate cry of the Absolute explained away by human rationalization, with fields like philosophy and religion providing a glimpse into what *IT* really is. All life could simply be a projection, depicting our futile attempt to reestablish a universal awareness of here and now..."

"Of the eternity that is contained within the passing of a single moment..." I whispered.

A fluttery feeling erupted in my chest, and I felt like the words I spoke couldn't tumble out from my mouth fast enough—the experience of presque vu. "I don't think time exists after all," I speculated with solid assurance as the etheric fogs of the Trips Center enveloped me. "Maybe at every moment we are being born, at every moment we are living, and at every moment we are dying. Maybe time exists only as a measurement of reality as we can perceive it, but in actuality, existence is a singularity—all one."

Al bobbed his head up and down repeatedly in agreement, "Right on, right on! But Rhiannon, what seekers like us must always remember is that it is the here and now that is of utmost importance. Sometimes by harboring uncertainty and tenacity, you sacrifice the present moment. Question we must, but we also must be mindful of the lessons present in the here and now. At the end of the day, we must always remember to yield to the fact that everything happens for a reason and that one day, everything we question will make sense, whether it be in this lifetime or the next. You've got to be able to question and at the same time surrender yourself to the moment. You only get this moment once, so let it be!"

"Here and now, huh," I repeated. "That seems to be a new kind of existence for me lately, but still now and again I find myself troubled. What if I were to ask where and when exactly is 'here and now?'"

"Well, just think of it," Al replied, his characteristic benevolence spread across his face in a smile, "if you are truly here and now, you are Nowhere!" As he said this, he reached across me to take my empty bowl back to the kitchen, and suddenly there were many of him, all performing the same action, superimposed upon one another. But it was only for a moment, only for a—*FLASH*—and at that, he left me alone with the vastness of my mind and the lingering image of his bright eyes that hung in the air for a few moments before dispersing.

'If you are truly here and now, you are Nowhere...'

His words continued to ring in my ears as a ripple of calmness and well-being lapped at the shores of my mesencephalon. A radiant smile spread across my face, and I laid back and stretched out on the couch. Above me, the spiral began to move and change. Slowly, it rotated inward and outward, ascending out through the ceiling and descending into the room, expanding, contracting, and spinning in all directions at once. It was as mesmerizing as it was intoxicating; for inside myself, I too began to experience feelings of motion. I felt as if my insides were being shaken loose and stirred together in some kind of pulpy intestinal stew. The feeling was not as unpleasant as it sounds described, but it was so strange, and the notion of which was so uncomfortable that I sought to resolve the sensation. I stood and climbed the stairs to the bathroom, and once the churning of my insides had not quite ceased but lessened, I turned to face the mirror.

As I righted myself before the sink and the cold water from the tap ran over my hands, I admired the reflection that stared back at me. I gazed into the depths of my own enormous eyes, peering uninhibited into the shiny darkness. As I continued to look, a kind of hypnotism ensued, and I was sucked into the blackness like a vortex. Into the abyss my senses were cast, and there they remained. I was transported through a transcendental universe of solar sparks and living colors as numbers, figures, and glyphs soared through the infinite space that exists inside and winked at me as they passed. It was as if I was inside the echoes of my own thoughts, romping around a universe of my own creation, full of infinite possibilities and unimaginable manifestation, all without ever leaving the Trips Center bathroom.

When I finally opened the door and stepped into the hallway after god knows how long, I felt the effects of the drug really starting to intensify. By this time, the sensation was familiar. In many ways, this experience was similar to my previous one; however, the content was entirely different. In contrast to my last trip, this one contained far less visual experience and was more of a concrete awareness. Although the photo effects were present and ample, this trip felt very personal and comforting. I did not feel as if I was losing touch with reality; instead, I felt as if my experience of this current reality was being immeasurably heightened.

From where I stood in the hallway, I could see that before me on the wall hung an embroidered tapestry in the shape of a mandala. To me, it appeared three-dimensional and spun slowly, and I allowed myself to be drawn into it for a time. There was truth and magic inherent in its immemorial design, and the longer I allowed myself to be consumed by it, pearls of knowledge hand-sewn by _IT_ became blissfully apparent. I really began to appreciate tapestries and mandalas after that; I never looked at them the same way again. Rather than merely a thing of beauty, I saw in them their transformative potential. In a mandala—as in anything—as you move further from the center you find an increase in entropy, less purity, less peace. You find Truth, the Absolute, while traveling to the center of everything.

The tapestries were not the only things that were illuminating. All around me, the walls spoke in resounding reverberation of the memories they held, and on the floor, the grungy, remnant carpeting began to shine like marble tile beneath my feet. The soft, orange glow from beneath me drifted up the stairs calm and serene and carried with it the sounds of smiling laughter. As I walked down the hallway—which proceeded to become longer and longer upon the settling of each step—I observed that the lights in all the rooms had been put out, except for a violet emanation that crept down the chamber and drew me in like a moth to a flame. I followed it and found that the room into which I had entered was illuminated by a single black light. The room was empty, but all around me, I felt an effusion, a soothing and peaceful presence that invited me to stay. I seated myself on the bamboo mat which was rolled out in the center of the crimson ocean that engulfed my feet. Before me, a candle flickered, and as I fixed my eyes upon it, its flame became a million different colors. Flashing, it looked like it was on a page popping out of a book. All around me, little oval glows drifted in the thickening air, and when I closed my eyes, the image of them remained. Inside and outside, the same world existed, yet different were they from one another. And within my own mind, source and reflection merged—spirit merged with substance, and spoke of the most perfect and beautiful quintessence.

Simultaneously, as these truths revealed themselves to me, a feeling similar in effect to floating persisted. I had become so still that my physical connection to the earth no longer seemed firm. The form of my body was stretched, and I grew taller and taller until it seemed like I would hit my head on the ceiling. However, although the distance between floor and ceiling did not change, the space between the two increased dramatically.

Inside myself also, rumblings abounded. Up and down my spine, bone boiled and skin fissured, fire leaped from the floor and rushed throughout my body, burning a path up my back and building inside my skull before bursting out through the top of my head. The pressure that had accumulated lessened, and the energy flowed through me freely. It was an enlightening sensation. I no longer felt blocked; instead, I felt akin to my surroundings. It was at this moment that a different sensation began. The feeling was similar to that which I endured during my previous trip when in the throes of fear, feelings of separation thrived. However, rather than pulling away from the trip, this time I was pulling away from myself. I felt as if I was hovering just above my body and coming apart from myself. Affirmations I'd been aware of my entire life began to elude me: the sound of my name was cold and metallic, and my intrinsic identity seemed a hollow persona. It was as if I was standing on the edge of an epiphany, on the furthest outcrop of nirvana. There was no such thing as an individual, I was a part of something larger, something inconceivably bigger than myself—but before I could become immersed in the deluge, before I could understand the cosmic truths that orbited my awareness, before I could let *IT* in…

I had to *let go*.

And I did—and there was a certain sense of elation, a kind of rising…

But only for a moment—for as soon as I clamored for it back, as soon as I attempted to re-grasp, to reaffirm the safety of myself, that transcendent awareness had disappeared.

In a flash, I descended back to my previous state of awareness. For more than a few moments, I was disoriented. I had to make an effort to remember where and who I was, but once those questions were answered, I saw clearly. I had been on the threshold of ultimate Truth and bailed, but rather than disappointment in my own inadequacies, thankfulness for the experience and an improved sense of perception were the immediate result. Everything hummed at a higher frequency, both around me and within myself. The room I occupied—a reflection of the shades and mirrors inside my mind—was illuminated twice as bright. I was nine feet tall.

Silly, silly Rhiannon, I chided myself, *why are you running away? You belong to the Universal Mind anyway, you only perceive that you are separate.*

I rose from my respite with gently shaking legs as revelations tumbled forth in waves. Perspectives shifted, ever-changing. The matter of my existence was as convoluted as ever, and yet, befell me in perfect, simplistic harmony. It was all right there before me, without theoretical argument, without imposed ego sentiments, senseless games, or ignorant dismissal. My mind itself had been cracked open, and what flowed inside was the peace that resided all around me. The peace had always been there, I just hadn't previously made myself available to receive it; I'd yet to let go. It wasn't something I could've happened upon by philosophizing or petition; rather, it was something that was available only through unconditional surrender. Inner peace isn't a feeling, it's a presence as real as you and me and found only within the moment.

There is no scene as groovy as the present. In the midst of my euphoria, I started downstairs, coaxed by the thudding of a dozen hearts, nestled within a dozen warm bodies—my own heart beating in time. I had never before felt such sheer ecstasy at being alive! I laid myself down on the floor in an empty place and joined hands with those around me. Together, we gathered in the center of the living room under the dim starlight that shone from the galaxy that whirled above us. None of us spoke, but it was not quiet. When I listened, the sounds I heard did not come from one direction in particular; rather, they seemed to emanate from everything in the room: the chair, the couch, the stopped record player—they all emitted sound. All around me, this state of ephemeral permanence, ubiquity, and godliness persisted. Even the glass table, the glass table itself was God, brimming full of sacred magnificence. And the smoke, the smoke from the incense burners was pure divinity, God even before it was lit as intercession with itself. And the walls, the walls were God—God was in the walls. God was all around me like luminiferous aether.

There was one moment in the midst of all that grooving and groking and revelation when I felt a sudden compulsion to stand up, like eyes on the back of my head, like unspoken words. And sure enough, as I did, there was Mary dressed in a covering of blue scales over by the record player, thumbing through albums and beckoning me over to her with a glance. I stepped toward her, and the floor shifted, creaked, and moaned to accommodate my exaggerated form. I lumbered over, and the house lurched again. She handed me a stack of perspectives, and I took them from her. My hands, I saw, were in rare form. My skin had been turned inside out; tendons bulged like ulcers, and my finger was made up of letters—everything that I was taught it should be called. Less the gore, I was unalarmed. Instead, I was surprised and delighted, for these sights carried with them an unwitting consequence of humor, and I laughed at the notion of my disfigured flesh—*I am not my body.*

Each individual album offered a trip of its own. There was motion in still pictures, and the previously inanimate figures on each cover came alive and moved. Monsters and ghouls were hiding in Ten Years After's record sleeve. Shrieks and whistles escaped from between its covers, and the jelly worm peapods writhing around inside invoked nothing but fear…but no fear came.

"This one's a bad trip," I told Mary, who in turn swatted it away with a broom, and the jelly worm peapods went wai-i-iling away into the depths of the springy foam insulation that poured out from a tear in the Trips Center wall, and we went back to browsing.

A black fog-like grease that rolled like a shadow over a sundial came pouring out from Country Joe's *Tonight I'm Singing Just For You* which told an unending tale of repeated heartbreak, loss, and unsuitable psychic mixing. "Not this one, either," I advised, "it's a bummer."

In the end, the only one that remained was none other than *Tommy*; the greatest tale ever told about a blind, deaf and dumb boy who wasn't really blind, deaf and dumb at all, and after being mistreated and abused, finds God in an analog mix of colors, wires, sound, and motion—none of which he can perceive—but the vibrations… It took the vibrations, the Acid Queen, and one good mirror for him to really see. And Sally Simpson? Well, that's another story.

Speaking of the Acid Queen, she left me breathless. Poised and erect she stood before me, radiating a glowing golden aura like the Virgin at Guadalupe. Every shape and edge of her body was sharply defined, and the colors were outstanding! With a sigh, she sunk into the surfeit of pillows beneath her, and she emerged the one, the only, the beautiful Faye, Queen of Mystery. Every molecule of her being spoke directly to my soul, inviting me to seek and find. After all, there's no use in entertaining that which is already known. To hell with it! Go forth with uncertainty and your search will bring you to some bright and beautiful, not to mention some dark and dank places. Like Mrs. Walker says, '*Sickness will surely take the mind where minds can't usually go.*' And while Faye's condition couldn't exactly be defined as madness, per se—after all, aren't we all mad in Wonderland?—her proverbial sickness—rejection of the human condition—caused her to reach heights the rest of us would never know.

And as for *Tommy*, like the rest of us, *Tommy* was tripping out. As the record spun and pinwheel illustrations colored the inside of my eyelids, the corrugated sounds that reached my ears conjured images of a story I was unfamiliar with. Even though I'd listened to the album dozens of times before, this time was different. Like in a dream, mirages flashed into existence, and new, preconceived realities popped up, ready for experience without question, each as genuine and unprecedented as this world and the next. I remained rapt in each one for what felt like days, but the notion of time as it passes in this reality was thrown out altogether. There was no cognizance of any kind of concrete time, and time in as much as it could be perceived slowed down and extended.

There was this one hallucination in particular that began as the sounds of the *Overture* slid past me, creating a suffusion of red, blue, and green against my visual cortex. And as I blinked my eyes closed, that suffusion became a vast expanse of pebbles and stones of all colors and sizes that stretched from horizon to horizon. A jungle canopy of unfathomable height loomed in the distance, and beyond that, the sky gave passage to the infinite.

There I was amongst the pebbles, a god in comparison—superior in every way. And yet there were still those things incomprehensible in magnitude. After all, I was just a simple inhabitant of my own indiscriminate pebble—for if the tops of the trees are to Earth what moss is to a stone, then we along with all of humanity are mere bacterium, invisible. Our world really is just a pebble in a vast quarry, and the distance from one planet to another—billions of miles—can be thought of as condensed into the space between one adjacent pebble and the next.

It was as if I was both witnessing and a part of the universe at the same time. With eyes closed and mind wide open, in the time it took to blink, in the time it took for ash to fall from the butt of a cigarette to the clay dish below, I'd become aware of an entirely new perception of my relation to the universe and my place in and of it all. These concepts and truths were conveyed and understood effortlessly—without trial, without circumstance, without that period of internalization—it was instant understanding.

As these revelations filled my mind, I was not only there in that reality experiencing and relishing in those things, I was right there in the Trips Center, watching the patterns oscillating across the Rorschach carpet and the mandalas sliding up the walls. I was in two places at once; I was watching myself. The causation in one world was the effect in the other. And whenever I opened my eyes, the room drifted in and out of focus, interrupted by pulses of blue and neon pallid purple, and other colors you can only see inside the Trips Center.

As the night progressed on toward morning, I wandered around the darkened Trips Center pulling shades to keep out the painful rays of sunlight. I felt like I was stepping deeper and deeper into a world I never knew existed—a world many of us don't know exists—a world right here around us every day of our lives. As I descended the stairs, Bobby beckoned to me—after which I found myself along with the rest of The Day Trippers chasing sounds around a still room with one window. Together we jammed, listened to one another improvise, and watched the vibrations reverberating about the room manifest right there all around us like we were peering through the lens of a million oscilloscopes. We were all in sync, in tune—not only in sound but in thought and projection. When we were all high like that, all on the same level, and all jamming, we functioned like independent parts of a single being, and the inspiration flowed through us like we were of one mind. Playing with them was like honing in on a wavelength.

The most important facet of what acid does is provide you with a free consciousness in the most literal and far out sense of the word, and nowhere is that more evident than in music. The seven of us wouldn't talk for hours; we never needed to. For the first time since I'd been playing with them, I became truly initiated into that telepathic-type communication that existed amongst the members of The Day Trippers—that same ability I'd observed the very first time I'd watched them play. Now I was a part of it too, and it all went up from there.

We played for what must have been hours; until the acid began to wear off and all through the aftereffects, the whole time truly feeling the music. And when we finally stopped jamming, there wasn't silence; instead, there was this dull ringing, like a bell. And you didn't have to be high to feel the energies rising.

A BRIEF AND BEAUTIFUL TRIP BACK

****

By the time the Fourth of July rolled around, Space—in typical Haight-Ashbury fashion—had stayed true to his promise and hustled up a van for us—a green Volkswagen Type 2 microbus, to be specific. We found it parked out front one morning with Space around back, crouched down with his head inside the engine compartment checking fluids and making repairs. All in all, the van was a sweet score. It was three years old and had something in the neighborhood of 40,000 miles on it. According to Space, the guy he'd gotten it from had been living on the road since he bought it new in '66. Its previous owners had installed a metal rack on the roof which we used to cart amps and instruments to and from gigs, and with the exception of the front bench seat, all the other seats had been removed. There was enough room inside for the seven of us to sit comfortably along with any instruments, mics, wires, converters, inverters, mixers, monitors, and speakers that didn't fit on the roof. I thought about what Space had said the night we played the Fillmore West—how he'd never come across a situation in which he needed to use money—and wondered how he'd acquired the van. Later in the week, I discovered that one of the two pot plants growing in the tub was missing.

The first ride we took in the van—which was almost instantly coined the Trips Mobile—was that same day, down to China Beach. In the mold of Kesey and the Pranksters, Independence Day was the biggest holiday of the year for us Day Trippers. We were completely decked out from head to toe in American regalia. We painted stars on our foreheads and stripes down our arms, we wrapped ourselves in Old Glory, and Space parodied Uncle Sam in a red, white, and blue top hat and tailored suit he got from the thrift shop up the road.

As we drove down to the beach and made our way to the shore, people stared even more so than usual that day because now in addition to being freaks and communists in their eyes, we were also anarchists and traitors.

—And while we may very well have been all of those things, we saw ourselves as more patriotic all-Americans than the squares who stood gawking, shaking their fists and wagging their heads at us. After all, our founders were dreamers and our forefathers were revolutionaries. We saw ourselves as the descendants of political dissidents, adventurers, and pioneers and we were inclined to keep their tradition. America had this rebel thing going before anybody else, and though our ancestors had kept it going for a while, we felt that as of late, that resolute spirit had begun to waver. We were never meant to conform; we were never meant to settle, and every once in a while a generation comes along to shake things up a bit and say in so many words: *If you support an Establishment that perpetrates actions that violate your basic human rights, you are actually more reprehensible than they are. You may fly the flag and vote and say your prayers, but in the end it's worthless because it's a crock; you are merely going through the motions. The Establishment's game is one of position and power, and it's not moral. You know how the old narrative goes: if there's a system put in place that isn't working, sweep it out of existence, start all over again, and build off of a foundation that works.*

We saw the foundation that worked as going back to the garden and living the way we felt we were supposed to be living: in harmony with one another, regardless of race or sex or creed. That's what the Message was, that's what we were trying to communicate, and for those who were willing to listen, that's what we did. For everyone else, we were right up there in front of their faces, obscene, colorful, and loathsome every day of their lives until they were.

It was a beautiful, clear day when we got out on the beach, a rarity for San Francisco. All the fog had blown out, and we could see the Golden Gate Bridge hovering above Sausalito in the distance. The seven of us hoofed it along the shore, joking around and cutting up. Long walks and short sentences abounded on the beaches of San Francisco that day.

"Hey, did you guys hear about that groovy festival happening down near Atlanta?" Space asked. "I heard about 100,000 people showed. Jon and Cassandra and a bunch of guys from the head shop up the street drove down."

"Who's playing?" Billy asked.

"Joe Cocker, the CCR, Janis, Zeppelin, Spirit…"

"Man, why didn't we go to that?" Bobby asked, surprised that this was the first he should be hearing about something so big.

"Damn," Mary added. "Bummer, that's a killer lineup!"

"I know a couple of queers down in Atlanta on 10th street—that seems to be the hip neighborhood now—we could've crashed with them," Al added.

"Well, now that we have the Trips Mobile, we can go anywhere," Mary Jane pointed out.

Space nodded, "I'll see if I can bag us some tickets to the next festival I hear about."

"I heard rumors there is going to be some kind of happening up in Seattle this summer," Mary Jane suggested, "maybe we can go to that."

Of late, I'd become so absorbed in living in the moment that I'd often forget where it was that I'd come from, but every so often I'd remember something about the future, and once more realize exactly where I was. This was one of those times.

"There's going to be one in Upstate New York too," I added.

"When?" Mary asked.

"For four days in August. We need to go!"

"Where in New York?" Al inquired.

"A town called White Lake."

"Is there a venue there, or a park?"

"It's a dairy farm up in Hicksville."

"Well, where are they going to put all the people?" Mary asked.

"In the fields."

They all took a moment to look around at one another. "Sounds groovy," was the unanimous reply, with the exception of Faye who answered back, "*Rama Rama.*"

It seemed to be a most ironic situation—me telling hippies about Woodstock—and as this and other free-flowing revelations marked me, the magic ether of the Trips Center seemed to roll right over me like fog off the bay. We were all toking up and pretty high, and they were chattering away about festivals and camp-outs and love-ins when I dropped a doozy on them:

"How do we know we really exist?"

My eyes were transfixed on the water when I asked this. It was bay water, so it wasn't exactly the cleanest—but how it shone! Then again, everything shines when you're smoking hashish. Faye had brought along a satchel, inside which was a small block of black Afghan hash and a free-standing wooden pipe about the size of my hand. It had a long, thin mouthpiece with a bowl the size of a silver dollar on the end of it, and she and I were hitting that thing like mad. We had a tendency to leave all the drugs with Faye most of the time, the reason being that with Faye there was no paranoia; she drew no distinction between cops and straights and heads. For her, all human interaction was pretty much the same.

"How do we know we really exist?" Billy echoed after a moment.

1969

"Not because of physical manifestation," Mary pointed out right away, as Faye passed her the pipe. "Our thoughts exist, and our ideas exist."

"And our dreams," Space contributed.

"And our souls," Billy added.

"—and all those things are real."

"But the question isn't reality," I clarified. I felt as if I was honing in on a fuzzy, unclear truth drifting out there somewhere in the Pacific, "because we already know there are many realities, the question is actual existence."

"You don't know what existence is?" Bobby asked, sounding sort of incredulous. "I'll tell you what existence is—it's all about experience: going, doing, being. That's what existence is."

"What do you mean?" I asked, puzzled.

"Explain yourself, man!" Space demanded, pointing a piece of driftwood at him with a bullshit scowl spread across his face in that kind of friendly aggression that accompanies camaraderie.

"It's like this: if you haven't gone somewhere or done something in this lifetime, it doesn't exist inside you yet, and even though you may know about it, you can't understand it. That's why you've got to experience everything once," Bobby elaborated.

"I say existence is anything we can become aware of," Billy suggested, "If we can become aware of something, it must exist. And if we can imagine something, it also must exist. Therefore, everything must exist, even if it doesn't."

"Exactly, man!" Space exclaimed, clapping him on the back.

"But that only works inside our reality," I honed in closer. "If you couldn't use any of your senses, how would someone communicate to you that you or they really exist?"

Silence ensued.

One or two of them opened their mouths slightly to begin a reply, but in consequence closed them again after realizing they lacked any kind of evidential knowledge in this matter.

"You've got me," Billy admitted.

Al, who'd been quietly pondering this whole time, spoke up after we'd all gone silent, "Existence *is* the mystery. It is infinite and it is ubiquitous. There is nothing before and nothing after. It's impossible to know because it's impossible to conceive of, but we can become aware—at least in part—of what existence is, and that's *IT*."

We all pretty much stayed silent after that with the exception of a chorus of, "Whoa, man!" and "Far out!" of which I was a part.

174

We walked along the beach for quite a while until we came to a cove, at which point we all began to drift off in our own separate directions. Space pulled out a Frisbee he'd brought along and started tossing it to Mary Jane and Billy who ran after it and dove for it over rocks and into sand dunes. Al disappeared into one of the crevices of the cliff with a canvas and a set of paints he had wrapped up under his jacket, and Faye began playing what looked like a game of red light green light with herself. I hung back to watch, as did Bobby, who came up behind me, put his hand on my shoulder, and offered me a light.

"Come on, let's go watch the submarine races," he said to me before leading the way out to one of the rock jetties further along the beach. The tide was very low, and several treasures stuck out in the sand—sea glass, mostly. I collected a couple things in my pockets and examined them once we'd climbed up on the rock.

"What've you got there," Bobby asked, leaning in to look at my finds. I handed him some of the better pieces. There were a few really nice ones, sharp bits of broken bottles and jars smoothed and faded by years of tumbling through the waves—there was something very teaching about the concept. It seemed the longer I stayed there and the more I smoked, the more I began to find moral education in the slightest of circumstances and casual nuances of everyday life—I figured a couple more months with The Day Trippers and I'd be a regular existentialist.

I was really grooving over the things I'd found, but a biting gust of wind off the shoals jerked me from my thoughts.

"Damn, it's cold!" I exclaimed, rubbing my arms. "I'll tell you one thing, the weather in Fresno is nothing like the weather here."

"Here," Bobby replied, shrugging off his jacket and handing it to me.

I thanked him and pulled it on; the fabric inside was warm from his body. "Are you sure you're not going to be cold?" I asked.

"Nah," he replied, lighting up a cigarette, "I only wear that cuz I gotta be cool."

I laughed and looked away from him and back at the beach where our friends gamboled about. The Frisbee game continued, only now Faye had joined in as well, and Al had just about concealed himself within the crevice of the rock—only the very top of his easel stuck out.

"Your brother's a real trip, ain't he?" I said, turning back to Bobby.

"Yeah, he is," Bobby replied, "Al is a nomad. He's like pure energy—he's only stable in a state of entropy, he's not stable when he's standing still. When he does, it almost seems like he's about to blow apart at any moment—just completely break up and go off in all directions at the same time. He fits in much better with the Exis than he does with us rock n' roll types. He'd rather spend the night munching on peyote and laying out under the stars than playing a gig."

"It seems like he gets on well with you guys," I said. "Nobody hassles him, and his keyboard really makes the band."

"Well that's only 'cause he's been with us forever. Here, I'll give you an example: at fifteen, not too long after our parents bought it, Al lit out for New York City as an enterprising artist—painter and musician. He lasted about four months out there, then slinked back onto the Haight one day after declining three apprenticeships because he didn't like the scene. He's real eccentric."

My eyes widened, "Wow," I replied in surprise, "that's incredible!"

"Pfft, yeah, the kid's a fucking genius. Mary's mother used to give us piano lessons when we were kids; I dropped that after a few months and bought myself a guitar, but Al stuck with it and he got real good, real fast. It wasn't a year before he was even better than Sophia, and when we first started gigging, Christ! You should've seen us! It was just me, Al, Mary, and Jules. We didn't have a bass player, so Al figured he'd just play two instruments at once: a '66 Fender Rhodes piano bass we'd just about scraped together enough bread to buy with his left hand and his Vox organ with his right. And he did it with no trouble at all! He's always been naturally ambidextrous, able to write and paint with both hands at the same time. Really, it was kind of weird, and when you were high, his hands seemed like two totally separate organisms."

With that, Bobby began waving his hands around wildly and tickling me. I swatted him away playfully with a laugh and gazed out again at the bay. "It's really beautiful, isn't it?" I asked. The water out there seemed brighter than usual, the sky was bluer, and the smog, less smoggy.

"Yes, you are," he replied.

I tried to hide the fact that I was badly blushing, "No, seriously," I insisted, "look at it all!"

Bobby sighed, "What *do* you see out there?"

"I don't know. A lot, I guess, but at the same time, nothing at all. When you look at the horizon, you can't tell where Earth stops and where heaven starts…"

"It sure does have that effect," he agreed. "I used to come out here

176

a lot, actually. On days like today when the water is clear, the sky seems to melt right into the bay."

All was quiet for a moment except for the lapping of the water against the rock, and the bell of a buoy somewhere in the distance.

"It's sort of surreal to think about the sky," I commented, "Every time you've ever looked up in your entire life, you've seen the same sky, and yet it's always different."

"It's like the river—that part in *Siddartha*—or like this ocean, for that matter."

"You've read that book?" I remarked, surprised.

"No, but I had Al explain it to me."

"Why not just read it yourself?" I asked.

"Reading is bullshit," Bobby declared. "When you read, you're completely out of the now, out of the moment, out of sync—you're inside someone else's moment exactly the way they want you to be; it's mind control."

"When you don't like your now, your moment, you tend to read a lot," I answered, defending my literary habits.

"Or you shoot junk."

"You shoot junk?" I asked innocently as if I hadn't heard his story back at the Trips Center the other night.

"Sometimes."

"Why? I mean, why junk?"

When I asked this, Bobby's eyes seemed to glaze over in a kind of blissful recollection, "I tried it once, and everything…everything else just went away. But when you start using a lot of it, it gets real expensive, you know? Shooting heroin is like dancing, except your partner is leading you in directions you have no control over. It's almost romantic at first, but then you get so caught up in the motion, in the spins and the steps and the way it makes you feel, that before you know it you're off the floor and off your feet."

I nodded silently.

"I used to be hooked, but not anymore—though it took me a while to cool off and get it together. Now I mostly just smoke opium, but I can bang anytime I want and I'm not hooked, I can stop whenever I feel like it."

"What's it like?" I asked, feeling as if I was reaching out to take hold of some forbidden fruit. "To shoot it?"

"Before a shot, there's always this moment of anticipation—like before a kiss—when you hold your breath, close your eyes, relax all your muscles, and just wait for that…"

Well, I waited alright, but what came next wasn't more words, but a feeling, because at that moment, he leaned right in and kissed me! I wasn't sure if he'd done it just to make a point or what, but he didn't seem to have a problem with it when I kissed him back, and in no time at all, we were really mugging out on that rock.

I have to say, there really is something about kissing a Scorpio that really is...something. He was imbued with this kind of underlying passion, this kind of private intrigue that changed making out from a display of romantic affection to a kind of search. There was the rush of course—that initial sensation that feels like you've just had twenty gallons of cold water dumped over your head—and then there was that period of testing the water and feeling around for boundaries. But with him, there were no boundaries, and there was this powerful sense of urgency—not urgent as in fast, but as in slow and deliberate and steadily intensifying—as if in the time it took to breathe, either he or I would disappear. I hadn't realized it before, but both of us had been seeking something, some kind of completion, and I found it in that moment. In his kiss and in his touch I was whole, as well as entirely and invariably *in the now*.

We stayed out there for a long time until the tide began to come back in and we soaked our socks and shoes getting back to shore. By then, the rest of our friends had gotten a small bonfire going, and we all huddled together around it as we passed that pipe back and forth. After night had fallen, we watched the fireworks shoot up out of the darkness and explode over the bay, over the bridge, and over the hills of Sausalito—hanging there huge and vibrant in that eternal sky, booming and echoing off of the cliffs, and then fizzling out and falling away into the ocean, to be carried away by the eternal tide.

A BRIEF AND BEAUTIFUL TRIP BACK

****

For The Day Trippers and the rest of the Haight, the holiday festivities didn't end with the fireworks; in fact, they stretched out over a whole week. There was something about the celebration of being an American—a resistor, a rebel, a revolutionary—that really fueled the whole counterculture thing. We were proud to be Americans, but not in the conventional sense. For us, patriotism didn't equal xenophobia. We were proud of what being American made us; we were proud of the responsibility that came with the title, the responsibility not to take anybody's shit—parliament or no parliament, president or no president, king or no king.

So, on one of the days following that Friday the 4th, after smoking a whole lot of grass one morning, The Day Trippers and I decided to pull all of our equipment out of the garage and into the driveway and play in the street. The air that day had a kind of jubilant, radical feel to it, especially after we found out from the flock of doves living next door that all those rumors about pulling out in Vietnam seemed to be true. So, we ran our cables out as far as they would reach and docked our mics out by the sidewalk—enacting our own little corner of revolution. We stacked our amps on and around my car and struck up in the heat of the noonday sun.

A crowd gathered almost immediately. Many people who had been walking along the street stopped to watch and listen, and more emerged from the bushes in the park across the way. Wherever there was music, there were hippies, and wherever there were hippies, more hippies appeared. Gaily they danced and hunkered down in the grass to listen as we played.

Throughout that afternoon, we played a fine cross-section of songs about revolution, unity, and the Movement for the beautiful people who'd showed up in our front yard. Billy and Bobby on acoustic guitar, Al and I playing percussion, and Mary's vocals washing out over the hazy summer Haight put our typically mediocre Dylan covers to shame, and our rendition of Country Joe's *I-Feel-Like-I'm-Fixin-To-Die Rag* got almost all of the bystanders on their feet and clapping. We did everything from *Masters of War* and *For What It's Worth* to *Alice's Restaurant*, which Mary had spent the majority of last year committing to memory.

Personally, I found it to be quite an enlightening sort of day. My favorite cover was our impromptu version of *Get Together*, ad-libbed in the style of the Youngbloods, with fifteen minutes or so of improv interspersed between the three lyrical verses. The last of those improvisations was a solo of mine. The lyrics Mary had been singing and the truth in them had gotten me so fired up that my hands just flew! As she was belting out, *"C'mon people now, smile on your brother, everybody get together, try and love one another right now!"* inside my head I was screaming: *In hating one another we're working against the powers that be! We all want the same things, so let's GET TOGETHER! Let's become something greater! We've got to get out of ourselves and into one another!*—and that passion just poured out all over my kit.

And boy, was that crowd grooving on it! My motivation for playing music had never been political, although the music I played had always carried with it strictly liberal connotations. Quite frankly, it couldn't be helped. The music of that era was born out of foreign and domestic turmoil, even though its overall message can be applied to strife in any space in time. Behaviorally, I'd always been a resistor against the expectations of any conventional system, but I'd never been an outright protester. In my own time, I was out of touch with current events, and in 1969 I would've been considered somewhat a part of the silent majority. I'd always been an advocate for peace, but that moment was the first time in my entire life that I'd ever taken action. I, like everybody else, had become swept along with the issues of the day. That time wasn't anywhere near perfect, and nobody really knew what was going on—but then again, what time is, and who ever does? However, the efforts to combat the hatred, the war, and the games—starting at the source, the people—despite their trials and errors, was perfect. Revolution is never achieved by an ideology, but by a vision, a need for motion—and damn were they moving: dancing and gyrating, huge, obscene, loud, and radical:::: REVOLUTION!

And the funny thing was, everybody looked toward America—that global pillar of democracy, economy, and freedom—despite the insanity, despite the corruption, and despite the instability. All over the country, we were letting it all hang out, and the whole world was watching.

—Although not everyone was patriotic.

"The West is dead, and we killed it," Al had announced that evening after we'd moved our equipment back into the garage and gone for a walk in the Park.

At this point, the rest of us just groped through our pockets for the last of the day's roaches and geared ourselves up for some serious late night philosophizing before asking him what he meant by that.

"Tell us what you mean, Brother," Billy asked, pulling out a matchbook.

"Just like our ancestors murdered the Natives without a shred of regret, because of preoccupations such as material fulfillment and societal advancement on this physical plane, neglected have been countless generations of spiritual and mental needs. Attention to the requirements and growth of one's mind and collective consciousness has been sacrificed for the superficial games of everyday life."

It was one of Al's more loaded comments. Billy passed me the roach, and Al continued: "We are pridefully in love with our competitive, consumerist, stressed, scheduled-away lifestyle and naively and violently protect our freedom to pursue our own selfish games of wealth and ownership."

"Right on, man, you said it," Space replied, patting him on the back.

"So, it's up to us to set an example," Mary Jane chimed in.

"Revolution is never achieved by an ideology, but by a vision, a need for motion," I murmured, repeating the thought I'd had earlier. "The clearer the vision, the stronger the revolution."

"I'd say our vision is pretty clear," Billy replied, "and it's clear because it's close; it's about to explode out into reality. You'll see, as soon as the war ends, acid, grass, peyote and mushrooms will be legalized as sacraments. Everybody will start working together, man, and communes, man, everybody will start living in communes. The straights will start quitting their jobs; the politicians are already huffing grass in the restrooms, wait until they start doing it out on the streets. The power is in the people, man, *we* have the power. The whole world will change, man, there'll be peace after all."

I was so into what he was saying, so into the moment, that I clean forgot everything I knew of the future. As far as I was concerned, everything he was saying was as right as rain, and all I knew was that I was going to be a part of it, that force, that peaceful example that helped to change the world.

"You always see the present clear and the future clearer; it's the blurry memory past that clouds your vision," Bobby added. "All we've got to do is keep acting out-front about everything, living in the moment, and letting go of what holds us back."

Al shifted uncomfortably, "The present is never clear unless it is objective; you can't see it when you're in it."

"So what you're saying is that we can never be sure of anything ever?" Space clarified.

Al smiled, "Only the past."

Space's eyebrows knit together, "But the past is what holds us back."

"You're one hundred percent correct, Space," Al assured him, "but history lends itself to repetition. We need to be well-versed in our past in order to better our future. The lessons we don't learn will only come back to test us over and over again until we do, and that's as true for individuals as it is for whole societies."

"How can we live in the moment if we need to be constantly aware of the fuck-ups in our past?" Mary asked.

"Awareness and mental residency are two different things," Al replied. "Some people rehash their past again and again—this is wrong. Awareness is accepting our past. Once we are mindful of it, we can make strides toward transcending it. There's a balance in it, just like in anything else."

"What about what you said about being blind to the present? '*You can't see it when you're in it*'—what about that?" Space implored him.

"Deception does not lie in front of or behind you, it lies next to you. Circumstantially, we are not able to see as clearly as we might like to, but we can certainly be aware of our own actions. As for their consequences, we can only hope that they will be for the better, but the more good we do now, the more likely it is that our future will be good as well. We've just got to keep the faith, you know that," Al chided. "And that's the challenge. Life will always be there to throw a wrench in the gears when you least expect it, and then more than ever is when we've got to keep on keeping on; that's the only way it's ever going to work, you understand…"

There was something about those late night philosophizing sessions that must have really stuck with those of us living on the Haight because we were continually bringing the themes, words, and ideas of our conversations into practice in our daily lives. We'd begun to build a whole new framework of society, a society of people resolved to 'living differently,' as Al always called it. We never really considered ourselves to be 'counterculture;' we weren't the immoral freaks the straight world saw us to be. We had it together, we were turned on to the order of the universe, and there was nothing life could present to us that our arsenal of sex, drugs, rock n' roll, and stoner diplomacy couldn't combat. And the thing was, it really worked! At least it did for us. When we were truly turned on to it, affirmations would appear all over, making sense of the things we spit-balled about in our free time and giving us a glimpse into the synchronicity that exists all around us.

****

1969

****

When you got to living on the Haight, your former identity passed away, and at some point you received a new moniker that encapsulated you more accurately than the one you were given at birth. After all, living on the Haight and embracing that lifestyle was in and of itself a kind of rebirth. However, by this time I'd been there over a month and I still didn't have a new name, that is, until one night in July when we decided to go to the movies.

I'd been the first one to notice the posters and suggest going to see *Easy Rider*. I'd seen the movie before, and I was well aware of its cultural significance, so when it came out in theaters, I ragged and ragged on The Day Trippers until they scrounged up some bread and we walked a couple of blocks to the Harding Theater on the corner of Divisadero and Hayes. The Harding Theater was an old movie house, and I was really grooving on the antique vibrations of the place once we'd bought our tickets and took our seats.

I waited in anticipation for the film to begin. *Easy Rider* was one of my favorite movies, and I'd seen it many times, but that time was different. Watching it in context like that was like watching a whole other film; the screen had become the trip. This time it wasn't just a cinematic classic, a standing testament to an age since passed, but an emotional experience. I—and everyone else in the theater—connected with it, we *understood* it. It was the kind of movie that had us all frozen in our seats as the credits rolled. Everybody left that theater with a sort of silent, sullen, and shocked expression. Some were confused, asking, '*What does it all mean, Bub?*' And then there were those who couldn't believe what they'd just watched. Some were upset, and others—like Bobby—were just plain angry.

"What the fuck was that ending, man?" he cried once we'd stepped back out onto the street and he'd lit up a butt. "Why would he do that, man?"

"That's the way it is down South," Al replied, trying to lighten him up. "They're just telling it like it is, they're not trying to whitewash the truth."

"Yeah, but what kind of director writes an ending like that? What's he trying to say about us, huh?"

"Take it easy, Heavy," I said. "It ain't just a movie, it's life. That's the way real life is, and that's the way real life ends. The director didn't have a choice, you see, he's just presenting us with the facts."

"Yeah? Well, I think it sucks!" Bobby harrumphed and crossed his arms over his chest. "Everything we are and—*BOOM!*" He threw his arms up in the air in pantomime.

"*BOOM!*" Mary echoed morosely.

"Well, I'd say he's got you both swamped," Billy concluded in the calmest, most matter-of-fact tone he could muster. "You missed the part after the credits, once you two had already stormed outside, where George's ghost reappears and Hopper and Fonda rise like a couple of phoenixes out of the Louisiana dirt and ride off toward the horizon. Then the screen goes black, the camera opens up like an eye and the whole latter half turns out to be a dream Fonda had while they were copping z's back in the desert!"

Mary and Bobby stared at us, bug-eyed.

Billy and I glanced at one another, "*Swa-amp!*" we cried in unison.

"Oh you two think you're really funny, don't you?" Bobby replied.

"Now come on, really, man," Billy said, serious this time. "How did you want it to end?"

Bobby was silent for a moment, "Well, it didn't have to end like that…"

"Just think about it for a second, man," Billy entreated. "It had to've ended like that or nobody would care—there wouldn't be a message! It would just be another hip film, man, but this one—like Rhiannon said—is a little bit more."

"Yeah, Bobby," Al spoke, "I'm with Billy on this one. Don't think about the ending for just a second. It's Hopper's film, man, this guy's got our thing down righteous! He's quoting Voltaire and Joseph Addison! He's got us as free and everybody else as scared! That was the most important line in the film: '*They're not scared of you, they're scared of what you represent: freedom. But being free and talking about it is a whole different thing. Don't ever tell a man he ain't free cuz then he'll go about killing and maiming to prove to you that he is, and that's what makes him dangerous. When he sees a man that's truly free that'll make him scared*'—that's so *true*, man! And think about it, there's a reason why Hopper played the character he did. He could've been Wyatt if he wanted to, but he didn't—why? Think about that for a minute or two…"

Bobby was quiet. I couldn't tell if he had been convinced and refused to admit it, or if he was just teed off, but in any event, I decided to agree with Al and Billy.

"You gotta admit it's a real synchronous film," I commented. "Not to be a critic, but every part of it was done real purposeful, in a teaching sort of way. Even the ending wasn't really a surprise at all, there was foreshadowing all along. It's a real statement, a real sign of the times, a big hit—and you know that cat, Nicholson? The one who plays George? When they make Kesey's *Cuckoo's Nest* into a movie in a couple of years, he plays McMurphy."

Whether I'd meant to or not, I'd effectively segued the conversation away from the heavier topic for the time being, but there were no worries, *Easy Rider* received its just reviews. Within days, talk of the film blew up on the Haight. *Easy Rider* became the thing to see that summer of '69. It wasn't long after it came out that it became sort of like an anthem for us, and you could gauge a person's hipness according to whether or not they'd seen it. In a lot of ways, I really related to the movie, more than I ever had the first time I'd seen it. It deeply affected me, and Bobby as well—seeing as how *Born to Be Wild* was the theme and all—and it wasn't too long after that The Day Trippers started calling me Easy Rider.

Like any hippie moniker, a lot goes into a name. Rather than merely a form of common address, a nickname on the Haight was more like a character assessment, all wrapped up and tied into a bow within a couple of words. Just like The Spaceman or Mr. Heavy Metal Thunder, my own new name fit me well for a variety of reasons. We never really had a conversation about it, it was just another one of those unspoken unanimous agreements that we Day Trippers had. For starters, I think it had to do with my reaction to the film. Al told me later on that my disposition reminded him of Fonda's character in the movie, but Wyatt wasn't exactly a befitting name for a girl. Plus, I'd also like to think that my new name was influenced in part by my musical astuteness and the long, smooth, and flowy solos The Day Trippers coined my 'easy rides.'

But no matter the origins, from now on, both on handbills and on the street, I was no longer Rhiannon from the New Millennium, but Rhiannon, the Easy Rider. I bore little resemblance to the girl I'd been when I first arrived there, blitzed and confused in my car. My positive traits had been enriched and my regrettable ones refined. My empathy had been deepened, and my naivety expelled—and that was only the beginning...

****

A BRIEF AND BEAUTIFUL TRIP BACK

****

Every day on the Haight brought a new experience, and as time passed, I became more and more in sync with my adopted generation. I'd heard of things like the generation gap, but it's one thing to hear about something and a whole other thing entirely to experience it firsthand. It wasn't an exaggeration to say that I went days, sometimes weeks, without interacting with anyone over the age of thirty, and when I did, it was with a kind of paranoid suspicion. Some of it came naturally, but it was highly intensified by the influence of my peers. It almost seemed like anybody born before 1940 was of a different species than any of us. Generally speaking, they operated on a different wavelength. We couldn't communicate on the same level, and we were incapable of understanding one another—they just weren't hip to our groove. Sometimes this reaction surprised me. Except for my mother, nobody over thirty had personally harmed or betrayed me, but I wasn't blind to their glances as we passed on the street, and I wasn't deaf to their words, spoken to me or anyone else, and I just kept thinking of that quote from *Easy Rider*…

In a way, living on the Haight could be a little confining. When you live in the now, the daily news from the outside world isn't of much concern to you. The way we were living, all we really needed to be aware of was our immediate surroundings; all we could work to change was within them, so we didn't need ABC, NBC, KGO or KMPX. But when I did turn on the radio or the television, I began bearing witness to what the rest of the world was experiencing for the first time.

There was this one week in the middle of July when news of the space race really came to a head. Whoever you talked to, wherever you went, and whatever AM station you listened to, all you heard was 'lunar module,' 'Saturn V,' 'Kennedy Space Center,' 'Neil Armstrong' and 'Buzz Aldrin;' there was another astronaut too, but nobody ever said much about him. It seemed to be just about the biggest global event to ever take place, and for the first time in a long time, the people of America had something to concern themselves with that wasn't the war in Vietnam, Civil Rights, the death of a president, or mutually assured destruction. People all over the world were excited again, and The Day Trippers resolved that there was no way we were going to miss out.

So, on the morning of July 16th, we all jumped in the Trips Mobile and headed over to Richmond to Mary's parents' house to watch the launch since there was no TV at the Trips Center. Every couple of days or so, Mary Jane would find her way down to Richmond to take care of her mother anyway, and since most of the time a couple of us would tag along, there was nothing at all peculiar about this particular trip other than the fact that she'd woken all of us up at some ungodly hour to go and do so.

Once we got to the house, Mary corralled us all into her mother's room and closed the door behind her. Sophia looked very much the same as she had the last time I'd seen her, slouched down in her hospital bed in front of the television set which showed some news anchor equipped with a headset as he narrated the exact course of the mission that was soon to be underway. I greeted Sophia and seated myself on the floor with the rest of my friends as I watched Mary Jane empty the contents of the brown paper bag she'd brought along with her onto the nightstand. There were several small bottles of liquid, a container of brownies, and a big 20 ounce jar of white powder.

"Holy shit, Mary," I exclaimed as my eyes bulged out of their sockets. "Is that all cocaine?!"

Mary burst out laughing, "Oh, Rhiannon, it's not cocaine! It's bleach!"

"Bleach? Why?"

"Well, my mother's always been a little vain," she explained. "She doesn't understand that she's bedridden and terminally ill, and she wants her roots bleached every three weeks. There's no harm in keeping her happy."

I glanced at Sophia who was munching absently on the brownie that Mary had handed her. She was in another world entirely, and yet I watched as Mary propped her up in bed, tied a smock around her neck, and began gently combing her hair. The jostling seemed to wake Sophia up out of a daze, and she struggled to reply in a scratchy voice, "I ho-hope you b-b-bought L'Oréal M-mary. Ca-carl always b-buys L'Oréal."

Mary reassured her in a soothing tone that she had, and continued to dote on her like a child daintily beautifying a doll, or a mother cat grooming her offspring. Mary treated Sophia's ailments with such a depth of compassion and filial love that it was moving to watch. It was almost as if in this time of great need Mary was now returning all the motherly love that Sophia had once bestowed upon her. They had such a deep and beautiful bond—one I did not understand, nor could I ever. I watched the two of them interact not in envy, but in sadness. Meredith and I just never had anything in common, and if we ever did, she sure never went out of her way to enlighten me about such a pastime. I did not harbor hatred for her anymore as I once had—there was no reason to. Those feelings of recurrent hurt, rejection, and betrayal no longer churned inside me spurring anger, bitterness, and strife. She was no longer a part of my life, nor would she ever be again in the foreseeable future. And if that were not enough, I now found it impossible for me to hate her. Instead, I felt immense compassion for her. Now when I thought of her it was not with resentment, but rather with pity; pity for the ignorance that we had both allowed to rule our relationship with one another for eighteen years, the arrogance that had pushed us apart, and the emotional calamity that could've been spared as a result of our cooperation.

Now, it wasn't as if I didn't have any good memories of Meredith. She'd taken me to Disneyland when I was eight, allowed me to pursue my passion for playing music although I'd met with resistance along the way, and she'd permitted me to have a relationship with George— which was something I'd always questioned considering how much she hated him. However, the singularly most appealing memory I have of my mother is a simple one.

When I was still a young child, not more than a few years old, one night I'd awoken out of a nightmare in stark fear and began to cry, as young children often do when faced with a bad dream and subsequently with the darkness of the room in which they are awakened. I do not remember what the nightmare had been about; likewise, I do not remember how my mother had been alerted to the fact that I'd had one, but suddenly she was there, and I was in her arms. She held me and tried to soothe me to no avail, and finding that hopeless, she began to sing to me. You see, Meredith was never one for lullabies; she was the kind of mother who tucked you in at seven-thirty sharp even if it was still light out, shut the blinds, and left the door open a crack so that she could hear if you got out of bed and started to play again. But this one time when she did sing to me, it was not a lullaby in the traditional sense, but a song sung in a whisper. I do not remember the words, but I remember the sound: it was low and gravelly, and it instilled in me a feeling of unbelievable sadness. Her voice struggled and mourned; it was a song she seemed to speak intuitively. The melody was familiar, but at the same time, it sounded as if she had made it up herself—as if it was pouring out from her. As strange as it seems, in the wake of my fear, I was comforted.

Being there with Mary and her mother made me wonder about Meredith. I wondered where she was at that moment, and if she was watching the same television broadcast that was being aired and re-aired nationwide. I wondered what her life was like now, as a teenager. Without much difficulty I could imagine her in a prep school, dressed in a spiffy plaid uniform and seated at a little wooden desk in a room full of plastic clones with her short-cropped hair tied back in a bow, watching the broadcast on a 10-inch television screen that her teacher had brought from home. I chuckled when I thought of what she was missing and how much of a square she must be, and I wondered again how she could've possibly ended up with a freak like George and how and why she would have ended up with a kid like me.

I thought of these things in silence as I sat cross-legged on the rug next to Sophia's bed in a room reeking of bleach, cigarettes, and Alice B. Toklas brownies. My friends and I were pretty rapt in what we saw on the television, so except for a few side conversations, the only stimulus in the room was that of the talking head on the screen and the sloshing of bleach in the bowl on the nightstand. So, of course, I was extremely startled when from behind me I heard Mary yell, *"Faye! Don't!"* and felt the clap of wet hair against my back.

When I turned around, I found I needn't ask what'd happened; Mary's face and simple inference seemed to say it all. Faye had taken the container of bleach off the nightstand and dunked the lower half of my hair in it.

In spite of the commotion, Faye hardly seemed apologetic. In fact, she looked as if she knew exactly what she was doing. So, rather than be mad, upset, or even remotely uneasy, I shrugged my shoulders, took the towel that Mary handed me, draped it down my back, and let Faye continue on with whatever she'd decided she was going to do to me.

In thirty minutes, Mary washed it out, and by the time the last five minutes of the countdown had appeared on the television screen, my hair had dried, and what I saw when I looked into the mirror was a striking ombré style. My hair was now colored in a gradient that began with my natural brown color and ended at the tips of my hair which were now so blonde they were almost white. Really, I found it to be very beautiful.

I asked Faye why she'd done it, but I knew that I wasn't going to get an answer in the same tongue in which I'd asked. Instead, she reached down next to her and produced the dreamcatcher that she'd been weaving from a spool of leather earlier that morning. With a smile on her face, she handed it to me.

That was the thing about Faye; she was always so natural, and her emotions always flowed so freely. She was never one to be coy, deceptive, or hard to read. Faye was an open book if you took the time to understand the language she was written in. Through this gesture of hers, I realized exactly what her motivations had been; however, I still did not understand how she could have possibly known what I'd been thinking about.

Having not realized the profundity of the interaction that had just occurred between Faye and me, Billy began to answer my question for her, "Well, the cutting and dying of hair throughout history has symbolized periods of major spiritual growth and enlightenment in one's life; for example, the Indians...."

"SHHHH! LOOK!" Space cried, pointing at the television screen.

We all shut up and turned our heads: the final countdown to lift-off had begun. At five seconds to lift-off, fire and smoke started pouring out from the rocket, and an enormous plume erupted from the vessel to fill the screen. By the time the picture shifted to an alternate video camera, the rocket was already off the ground and traveling vertically into the sky. It seemed slow at first like it was just hanging in the air, but it soon developed speed and disappeared into the clouds. It was tracked by cameras onboard Air Force planes, but before long, the giant spacecraft appeared as nothing more than a tiny speck in a seemingly infinite sky; a tiny speck on its way toward a far more vast infinity where distance is measured by degrees of nothingness, the magnitude of which is impossible to comprehend.

I'd known, of course, about the Apollo 11 mission—it's launch, flight, and successful conclusion—but I'd never watched the broadcast fully, only the parts that were valued by the future, such as Neil Armstrong's iconic words, not yet spoken *'That's one small step for man and one giant leap for mankind.'* But to watch it unfold before my eyes and witness the buildup, the broadcast, and the reactions of my friends who were seeing it for the first time was in itself momentous. We didn't have anything personally invested in the mission, but there was something about the sheer magnificence of it all that was just simply maddening. The sight of it filled us with such a feeling of complete and utter awe that we all jumped up and started talking at once, with the exception of Billy who remained seated on the floor muttering something about how the only reason we were even launching a spacecraft was because of the alien technology that we'd extracted from the Fascist Nazi scientists whom we'd sheltered during the Nuremberg Trials. For the rest of us, the excitement was raw. Even Bobby, who was rarely impressed by anything that didn't concern his personal benefit, wore a broad smile on his face.

It was shortly after this outburst that we began to hear stirring elsewhere in the house: the slamming of a door, the pounding of feet, and an outraged voice. I could sense that something was very wrong even before I saw the horrified look on Mary Jane's face, and suddenly everything was in motion. The bedroom door was flung open violently by a man I recognized as Mary's father, the banker—the squarest in all the land—and boy, was he hot! His face was flushed the brightest shade of red I'd ever seen in a man, and the veins in his forehead and neck bulged as he shouted profanities and swung a brass candlestick above his head. *"Get the fuck out of my house you freaks! Go back to the slums where you belong, you dirty, homosexual perverts! And take your goddamn drugs with you!"*

With one swing he cleared the nightstand of the container of brownies, and an alarm clock took flight across the room. Wide-eyed and terrified we all scrambled to our feet and out the door as the brass candlestick left his hand and made contact with the television screen. Sparks flew out from the wound as the announcer's voice became increasingly wonky and distorted. Sophia sat straight up in bed, her eyes glazed over in confusion and fear, her mouth opened wide and askew in some kind of silent scream. I tried in a last ditch attempt to make it for the door, but he'd stepped into the room, blocking the exit. The rest of our friends had escaped downstairs, but Mary and I were left with no place to run. I cowered there in the center of the room trying to judge the size of the jump needed to clear the cellar steps in case I had to go out the window, but he paid no attention to me and lunged over to Mary who stood defiantly before him in spite of the fear I knew had to be coursing through her.

"And you!" he spat, grabbing her by the collar of her shirt and shaking her. *"If you ever set foot on this property again I'm calling the police to arrest you for trespassing! Do you hear me? You're dead to me!"*

There was a pause, a gasp, and a sharp *CRACK!*—the sound of her father's outstretched hand connecting with the soft skin of Mary's cheek. With a look of sheer disgust on his face, he threw Mary to the floor as you would throw away someone else's dirty tissue and left the room to go scream out the window at our friends in the Trips Mobile

192

who were still parked in the driveway waiting for us: *"You communists, you should all hang!"*

I knelt down on the floor next to Mary and gathered her up onto her feet. Her blue eyes were wide and void of their usual bright charm; instead, they were empty, shocked, and hurt. She was uninjured, and after a few seconds, she was the one pulling me by the arm out the door. I only paused for a moment—just outside Sophia's bedroom door—to scoop up the shattered remains of a picture frame that contained the image of a family of four standing upon a rock in Golden Gate Park, a testament to happier times that had gotten caught up in the scuffle.

For the next couple of days, Mary was completely bummed—and rightfully so. It wasn't so much the result of the falling-out she'd had with her father—according to Bobby, such an event had been anticipated for years now—but because of how he was preventing her from seeing Sophia. Despite her father's threats, Mary had gone back the following day only to find the locks changed and the spare key moved. A few days later, when she got really desperate, she found that he'd also gone around and locked all the windows.

By about the fourth or fifth day of various attempts—by the time the eagle landed on the moon—Mary had effactually given up.

"If that's the way he's going to be, then that's the way he's going to be—I've done all I can do," she affirmed decisively. "I just hope he does right by her; she's still his wife, the mother of his children. Putting her away might be easier for him now, but he'll live with the guilt for the rest of his life," she'd told me in quite the same matter-of-fact manner in which she'd first revealed to me the details of Sophia's illness.

If you talk to just about anyone who was alive in 1969 and old enough to remember July 20th, they'll be able to recount their whole day to you: where they were, what they were doing, even what they'd eaten for breakfast that morning. The events of that day have been seared into the memory of the nation—and the world—indefinitely. Like most Americans during that four day period, we tried at all times to be glued to either a television or a radio. Bars all across America—such as the one on Mission Street where we spent the majority of our time those few days— were packed from the time they opened until last call. For a couple of the nights, Space had landed us gigs there, and we'd come down in the Trips Mobile and played for comps.

'Comps for comping' was one of Space's signature selling points, which was understandable considering how most club owners jumped at the chance to have a group play free of monetary charge. Billy spent the entirety of that time drunk, going around from table to table trying to convince everyone that the mission was a sham, and they all kept buying him beers.

"I hate alcohol," he explained to us one night. "Like Jim Morrison said, *'I drink to talk to assholes.'* Brew makes you stupid and insensitive. When I get around too many drunks at once, it's bad for my health. At that point you either gotta beat 'em or join 'em, I join 'em."

Remember that old cliché that goes, *'Anybody who remembers the sixties wasn't really there?'* Well, in reality, it's only half true, because although I can't tell you where I woke up the morning of July 20th or what I ate for breakfast, I can, however, recount to you a play-by-play of everything that I experienced that night.

It was sometime toward evening when Billy, Faye, Mary, Space, Al, and I were walking down Clayton Street, a short distance from the Haight. I can't tell you why we were there, nor can I explain the feeling I felt as we watched wide-eyed as man first walked on the moon, though I am fully aware mine was an experience unlike anyone else's at that time.

We'd come upon a television repair shop, the front window of which was filled with several floor models that gleamed bright and new in the hazy, humid summer sunset, left to broadcast night and day the incredible feats of mankind. We stopped to gawk in astute wonder as fate brought us to the window just in time to witness that first small step as Neil Armstrong began to descend the ladder onto the surface of the moon.

"Look at what we can do," Al marveled, "but what have we really done? How far have we really come? We can do just about everything we've ever dreamed of doing, and yet we have learned nothing about what we really are..." At that, Al—poet eternal—pulled a notebook and pen from his pocket and began scribbling furiously into the page.

My sentiments were similar to his, yet it didn't stop me from being bowled over with awe—for different reasons, of course—but in the end, the reaction was the same. We must have stood there for quite a while with our mouths and eyes wide because we began to draw a crowd. Passersby on their way home from work began stopping and staring with us until such an audience had gathered that those who

194

wanted to walk past had to do so in the street. Billy was adamant the whole time.

"Don't believe it!" he warned. "This is just a farce! The pigs are trying to distract us from something real important going on, that's all! You'll see, just give it a few years and the truth'll come out! They're out in the Nevada basin, they're out in the desert!"

For the most part, we just ignored him, although he did make some valid points. However, his speech did convince quite a few people to leave our gathering—although whether it was due to enlightenment or aggravation, I couldn't be sure. By the time the screen split and showed Nixon talking over the telephone in the oval office with the astronauts on the moon, Billy was howling. "Laughable is what it is!" he cried. "How bone-headed stupid do they think we are? Anybody who believes this shit is a driveling moron, man! Fuck Nixon, fuck Spiro Agnew, fuck..." he ranted on until the rest of the crowd had dispersed, shaking their heads as they went.

"This is why they don't take us seriously," Al tried to explain to Billy once we were left alone once more. "I dig that you're trying to talk sense into them and make them question what they're seeing, but they don't dig your cussing at 'em, man. All they hear is profanity and none of the logic. You have to talk to them like they're children, because really that's what they are, perceptual babies."

"Any real baby's got more sense than some poor shmuck who believes this load of horse shit," Billy replied indignantly.

"Hey, political games burn my ass as much as you and the next guy, but you don't see me losing my cool over it. That's what they expect those people who can see through the wool to do; nobody's gonna believe the screaming maniac on the corner. You make an impression on them, sure, but not the right one."

"Yeah," Space added. "Hell, I just about believe you when you talk like that, and I know better. Get your head, man."

Billy rubbed his brow in frustration, "Ah well, I guess you're right, man, but I don't know..."

"Besides," Mary suggested gently, "sometimes you gotta leave a little room for good faith."

"It's not that I don't believe in things that are unproven, I just don't trust what people say. I don't trust Big Brother, I don't trust the talking heads, and I sure as hell don't trust no little blue son of a bitch who can make a phone call to the moon! How do they think he does that anyway?" he cried incredulously.

Space snickered, "He's got a real long wire, man."

Billy shook his head, exasperated.

"Just be careful," Al cautioned. "It's smart to question, but be sure you don't distrust all other people and organizations so much so that you rationalize yourself to be the only one who is correct."

Billy opened his mouth to respond, then hesitated and humbly bowed his head in Al's favor. It was in the midst of that moment when a deafening thunderclap rang out over the city, making all of us jump in fright.

"Oohoohoo!" Space chuckled, rubbing his arms. "*BO-oOM!*" he shouted back.

We all looked up. The sky was dark, and towering rainclouds cast their shadows over the sun. The clouds had been gathering since noon, but we hadn't paid them much notice until now.

"I wonder when it's going to start rai—" Mary didn't have time to finish her sentence before a spattering of raindrops hit our faces and stained our shirts. And then, within the time it took the first few drops to fall, a tempest descended from the sky. Lightning flashed and thunder raged, and instinctively, we ran the last few blocks back to Trips Center since the television shop didn't have an awning to provide us with cover. However, even if it did, it wouldn't have made much of a difference because the rain was blowing in sideways in streams and gusts so violent we could barely open our eyes to see.

By the time we made it back to the Trips Center we were soaked to the skin, and the storm continued to rage with no signs of stopping. Billy wrenched open the front door, and we poured into the living room. Winded, we flopped down on the floor, leaving puddles where we lay. We all looked around at one another and panted as we tried to catch our breaths, dizzy from the rush; a glimmer of excitement in all of our eyes. Space reached into his shirt pocket and pulled out a saturated pack of Camels with water dribbling out of one corner. With a shake of his head and a grin on his face, he chucked it in the direction of the garbage can on the other side of the room.

"You just never know in San Francisco," he remarked.

Billy reached into his own pocket and pulled out a soggy joint and dropped it along with a few waterlogged matchbooks onto the coffee table. I wrung the water out of my hair, kicked off my flooded boots, and slapped my socks onto the radiator in the corner.

"Don't squeeze it too hard," Billy joked, "there might still be a fish or two swimming around in there."

"Yours too," I shot back as he proceeded to do the same.

"Shhh! Shhh! You hear that?" Space insisted.

The rest of us looked around at one another, hearing nothing but the pattering of rain against the shutters.

"Hear what? *Together?*" Mary asked skeptically, naming the Marvin Gaye record on the turntable.

"No, that screaming. Listen hard. That's whole colonies of my bacteria drowning."

"It's about time you guys wash," Melinda scolded affably as she entered the room. "Now get back out there with a bar of soap and scrub! Shoo!"

"Oh no," Billy replied quickly as he and Space peeled off their shirts, "I don't need soap. Just the scent of my testosterone alone kills off all the germs. Besides, we're not like you girls; we don't have to loofah off the cooties." With that, the two of them began to imitate females showering by humming and shaking their hips, using their shirts in place of a washrag. Melinda took their shirts from them to hang on the banister to dry and whipped Billy in the ass with his on the way out.

"Don't go away mad, honey," Billy called after her as he and Space laughed wildly. "Just go away."

In the meantime, having watched the guys, Faye had also taken off her wet blouse and flung it over the back of the couch. This in and of itself wasn't at all alarming to me; however, when she began taking off the rest of her clothes and then stepped over to Billy on the couch and started helping him do the same, I began to get a bit uncomfortable. I looked away and occupied my attention elsewhere in the room for a while as I sifted through the mess on one of the end tables to find a cigarette to smoke. When I looked back, my eyeballs just about burned out of my skull when I saw what she was doing to him over on the couch, right there in front of everybody. In shock and embarrassment, I turned around to face Mary instead, and when I did, I saw that she and Space too had begun stripping off their wet clothes and embracing one another. I was deeply disturbed by this, partly because I knew for a fact that there was nothing at all romantic or sexual going on between her and Space, and partly because even if there was, I had no desire at all to witness it.

After a few moments more, I became the only clothed occupant of that room, seeing as how Al had already slipped away into the study to change. Finally noticing my horrified expression, Mary just smiled at me and placed her hand on the small of my back in an attempt to lead me over to the activity escalating on the far side of the room. As all the color drained out of my face and into the tips of my ears, I stuttered something about cigarettes or food or clothes or some other excuse to leave the room and bolted up the stairs as soon as I got the chance—but even from upstairs, I could still hear them. I ducked for a moment into the mandala room and snatched a few garments up off of the floor, then scurried down the hall into what we endearingly called the white room and up the ladder into the attic.

Once I'd climbed up there and been greeted by an inviting silence, I backed up and leaned against the wall, exhaling deeply and trying to expel the images of what I'd seen from the forefront of my mind. Honestly, I didn't care very much at all what the four of them were into when it came to the wild thing; however, between the shock and the suddenness of it all, I couldn't quite get behind watching it or being invited to join in. Shaking my head, I dropped the clothes I'd picked up into a pile on the floor and stripped down to my own soaked undergarments.

"Man, I never knew a bird to be so insistent," came a humored voice from across the unlit room.

With a gasp and an attempt to cover up, I stole a glance over to where the voice had come from: a set of bunk beds pressed up against the wall next to the porthole window. There, where I hadn't seen him before, Bobby laid atop the mattress as naked as I. I blushed again, this time from my head right down to the tips of my toes. This meeting was far too similar to a series of musings I'd indulged myself in recently to keep me from doing so.

He got up out of bed, walked right over to me, and slid his arm around my bare shoulders, "C'mon baby, don't tell me you've never seen a dude in his shorts before."

Oh, I've seen a dude in shorts before and less than that, I wanted to tell him, *but I've never seen you in your shorts before*!

It wasn't for the awkwardness of the situation that I blushed, but for the sheer feeling of desire that came over me as soon as I saw him, and it wasn't hard to tell in his condition that he had similar sentiments. There wasn't any need for a conversation at that point; however, once we'd started necking there in the center of the room, seeing as how he'd been able to infer from the look on my face and the sounds coming through the floor, he did pause in-between kisses to tell me one thing. "You can't judge them, you know," he whispered in my ear. "Sometimes certain kinds of physical union can lead to the experience of cosmic union. There are many ways of seeking satori."

I didn't challenge him; in fact, I didn't even answer him. I just felt this pull, some kind of magnetism, maybe, or fatal attraction—after all, what other kind is there?—and I gave myself over to him, consumed by the search, consumed by the fire of passion that burned inside him and I and threatened to overtake us unless released. Over there on the bed, he and I tussled beneath the thin sheets, embracing each other in a tangle of limbs and wild passions, shutting out all sense of the world and finding, for the briefest of moments, reflections of ourselves in one another. And at the very height of the experience, when we both felt bliss was eternal, he wrenched my face up to his and looked deep into my eyes, studying my soul with an intensity possessed by only a handful of mortals. And likewise, there was something in his eyes—not the wisdom of a thousand years, but rather a thousand crimson embers, a flame wrought by hunger, desire hewn from incomplacency, and a radical volatility that simmered and jumped with every motion.

He was most definitely a seasoned lover, and per that notion, the culmination of our rendezvous seemed to last indefinitely. Even after that last spark of lightning in his touch had faded from the surface of my skin and our parted bodies had sunk into the mattress, the air of our mingling remained.

****

In the days following our close encounter, I spent a lot of time up there in the attic of the Trips Center seeking satori. During that time, Bobby turned me on to something I hadn't previously explored: opium. It only took me a couple of days to realize that what I was looking for, I wasn't going to find in opium, but the experience nonetheless was one that was unparalleled.

"Alexander the Great once conquered the whole Middle Eastern world with opium," Bobby explained to me as I watched him pack the little bulb of the pipe with that sweet-smelling tar for the first time, "and Homer wrote about it in *The Odyssey*. During the Civil War, the soldiers called it '*God's Own Medicine*,' and unlike many other drugs, every country in the civilized world has it in one form or another."

He reached for the matchbox that rested between us on the floor and struck a light. He lit the pipe and hit it repeatedly until smoke curled from its neck. He blew an impressively large cloud out into the room, and then he passed it to me. An opium pipe is a long, wooden cylinder with a bulb about three-quarters of the way down. This one in particular was ornately decorated with poppies in bloom, stained red and purple, and about two feet long.

"Perchance to dream, my love," he said, quoting Shakespeare as I took the pipe in my hands and cupped my lips around the mouthpiece.

As soon as I had taken my first hit, it became immediately apparent to me how a drug like this could become a problem for someone like Bobby. The feeling the drug induced was in many ways not dissimilar to grass; however, opium produced both a body high as well as a head high, both of which were incredibly potent and very agreeable. Although in some ways comparable to grass, opium possessed an alluring enchantment that was all its own. I felt as if I were able to move about freely in a kind of twilight sleep, the same kind one experiences in the final moments before nodding off. By my fourth hit, I felt as if the floor was floating beneath me. My fingers and other extremities felt numb, like I had the pins and needles all over, except without the accompanying pain. In fact, there was no bad feeling at all. I was elevated to a place where any and all of life's unpleasantries could not penetrate. The chill in the room had gone out and been replaced by a feeling of closeness and intimacy with my surroundings. The smoke that passed in and out of my lungs did so in a manner slower than any I'd ever experienced before, and a feeling of suspended animation overtook me. The high was both hazy as well as remarkably sharp and clear; it felt as if I'd gone to sleep and awoken in a dream where nothing was really real and everything felt okay.

I passed whole days in this state, in a place where clouds comprised of visions buffeted the eyes of my mind and dreams laid in wait for all who arrived; where grand tales of wizards and lions and rabbit holes orated by others came alive and waltzed amongst my memories. And speaking of memories, I'd found myself so far removed from any other world I'd ever known that my own fond memories, as if from several lifetimes ago, did not even seem real anymore, but as cold and transient as a whisper in the night and as brief and beautiful as a dream.

There were several instances in which I found myself as part of a gathering in the attic, whereas the rest of The Day Trippers and other assorted visitors had heard that Bobby and I were on opium holiday and had come up from the lower floors to share. We put on The Beatles records one after the other and laid down on the mats, blissfully catatonic except to smoke…smoking grass, smoking cigarettes, smoking O…and after hours, after hours, smoking roaches, smoking butts, smoking yen pox, yen pox, yen pox…

It seems the very next thing I remember—or think or care to remember—is climbing into the back of the Trips Mobile and starting out on the road to Seattle with the rest of The Day Trippers, Melinda, Bobby, and the last of our sweet midnight oil. Once again, Space had delivered and scored us eight tickets to the festival we'd last talked about on the beach, back when this trip was still just a fantasy.

"Did you hear this setlist?" he chirped excitedly as we all settled in for the ride. "Ten Years After, The Doors, Vanilla Fudge, plus Ike and Tina Turner and Chuck Berry! —Music from when we were kids, man!"

We were all stoked for the days ahead, and the ride itself was exceedingly beautiful. We wove through the mountains and redwood forests up north, all along the coast, and right through the heart of Portland, Oregon and into Washington state. It was our longest journey yet with the Trips Mobile, and for me it was the furthest trip I'd ever taken, seeing as at that time the longest I'd been in a car at a single clip was four hours, and at the end of that ride I had a comfy Disneyland hotel waiting for me. Hell, before Seattle I'd never even been out of the state! And, as a road trip virgin, I could only speculate that eight people living out of the back of a van for a few days would be an incomparable experience—I've never been more right.

Whereas conventional road trip etiquette typically involves rotating drivers to make the trip more comfortable, Space remained the only one of us who could, or in any event, who wanted to drive. Therefore, since the speed freak was behind the wheel like our own swashbuckling Neal Cassady, we bypassed all potential stops with the exception of food and bathroom breaks, made the whole thirteen-hour drive in ten, and got up to Woodinville on the second day of the festival. The entire ride there and for the majority of the festival, Bobby and I—and in some part the rest of us—were completely zonked.

For hours, the two of us lay on the floor of the van as we continued to consume the food of the gods in vaster and vaster quantities until we were full to satiety. Pipe dreams swirled and danced inside our minds, lucidly animate, yet only bearing the slightest of resemblances to waking life. Outside the van, the scenery slid by in streaks of melded color. Hills and road, cars and sky tumbled past, running together as the blues and greens and yellows of daytime mixed in with the pinks and oranges of sunset and were stirred up in the treetops before settling hazily above the fog that was cast over the sea.

Outside, it seemed like everything was transitory; nothing was real or held any kind of significance—it was like a reel of videotape spinning by, and the only reality was us, there inside the van. It was like being inside of my own giant, impenetrable plastic bubble, from which I looked out and watched everybody else. Most of everybody else seemed so very far away, but then there were those who understood and with whom I could share the intimacy of my experience. However, even they were still outside; near enough to touch but not to feel. Nevertheless, to my surprise, every so often I'd look around and find that there were other people there in that moment with me, like Faye; Faye was almost always in the bubble. She lay there with Bobby and me and told us stories—in her own language, of course—but when she spoke, her foreign tongue evoked visions, and a violet haze slid over the world of my imaginings.

When the rays of sunlight ceased streaming in through the windows, I closed my eyes and listened to the sounds of the van: those conversations that sounded like they were a thousand miles away and much fainter—so dim and barely distinguishable that it almost seemed a part of me—the repetitive *bum-bum, bum-bum* of the old, worn tires rolling over roads patched with potholes and wet leaves, creating the quiet and eternal soundtrack of our journey as the earth leaped and plunged beneath us in swells, leaving us sailing blissfully into the night.

And what I remember most, as hazy as these memories are, is the sound of a train whistle—one that was almost musical, very long, drawn out, and whimsically extended, heightening as it faded—along with the sudden advent of tracks at sixty miles per hour, eerily splitting the night and sending us bouncing and flailing on the floor of the van.

Occasional glances out the windows—paired with a largely piecemeal memory—has led me to infer that we'd left during the daytime on the 25th and arrived under the cover of darkness in the early hours of the 26th. I remember parking somewhere and getting out and walking, wrapped in a cotton blanket and barefoot, clinging to Bobby in an attempt to avoid colliding with or falling over trees and logs in the moonlit night.

After a very long time, or so it was thus perceived, the trees began to thin out, and what emerged was a clearing, brightly lit by a scattering of campfires across the valley. For what I could see, there were people everywhere—journeying back and forth from their campsites to their cars and the makeshift latrine in the woods. Every so often, I would look around and catch a glimpse of a speaker, but they were silent. Instead, we were surrounded by the nighttime din of conversation—along with swells of laughter that rose up every so often in-between the snapping and crackling of the campfires and the flapping of bat wings just above us—hushed in an attempt not to wake the strangers sleeping only a few feet away on a neighboring blanket.

When we found a large enough spot to accommodate us, we settled in and hunkered down for the night. Right away, our neighbors greeted us and offered us cigarettes, and Bobby and I shared with Rhea, Jack, and Shelly of Vancouver, B.C. our current fantasy—the secret to happiness—the smokable brown and pulverized sister to the milk of paradise.

I awoke the next morning—or should I say afternoon—with a fine afterglow. The sun was shining over the valley, the birds were singing, the bands were playing, the people were dancing and chanting, singing and grooving, and I couldn't wait to get high. Melinda had thought to bring along some canned heat—the cooking amenity, not the rock band—and was making eggs and home fries for any and all who were hungry. So following breakfast, Bobby and I packed a bowl full of a mixture of opium and reefer and like all those 19th-century writers before us, we pushed off toward eternity; en route to Xanadu and the Promised Land.

Before long, the music was high, the sun was high, and so were we. For the great majority of the time, we sat almost motionless upon the ground, reclining back with our eyes closed, feeling the warmth of the sun on our faces and the sound of music in our ears. The rest of The Day Trippers and most of everybody else left their camps to explore the festival, whereas Bobby and I were left to man the tent. After all, when you find yourself smoking opium, you are not commonly inclined to motion exceeding that which is absolutely necessary for the preservation of the human form. So often I thought, but my thoughts were manifest in pictures that flitted about like dreams, winding their way about my mind in the same manner in which the mornings' fog envelops a city. With such euphoric joy did I respond to these images that at times I was prone to leaping into the air and rejoicing for a brief interval before laying back down again beside my grumbling lover, this being a phenomenon he did not participate in nor comprehend. While Bobby ingested opium mainly for the pleasure of the sleep that it would bring him, I continued my relationship with the drug after the first time because of its distinct allure. For when I smoked it, I felt like I was being brought closer to everything else. It was such a warm feeling; one of closeness and intimacy. I felt as if every one of those 50,000 strangers was my brother and sister, that I was not alone; that I am never alone…

If I remember nothing else from the first of those two days that we spent in Seattle, I'll remember that sky. The sky that day was so blue and so clear with a sparse dusting of clouds that passed every so often. They would come together and dance for a while, changing their form and their shape countless times before dispersing and fading away. These delighted me, and I watched them for hours until night crept in once more, coloring the sky like a rose garden and then giving way to a rich indigo. Like San Francisco, night never really came to Seattle; it was always kept as far out in the stratosphere as those ceaseless city lights could reach.

Now, there did come a time when I removed myself from the blanket and ventured out into the agglomerate, and as I did, I felt divine; as if I was alight on my feet and hovering just above the ground. The sensation was one of moving sideways through a dream, a kind of lateral experience of space and time. When I returned once more to the tent and to my sprawl, I noticed with quite a start that a long, thin, green critter had slithered up onto the blanket—a snake! But instead of fleeing in fright, I did not move a muscle and examined it instead in grotesque curiosity, only to find that it was Faye's necklace. This, of course, gave me quite a chuckle and feeling that childish inclination toward pranks bubbling up within me, I threw the jewelry across the blanket to where Mary sat with Space, and in turn, watched them jump up with a yelp as it landed between their legs. I digressed into a state of laughter; after all, the forests of Washington State aren't exactly the most pleasant place to be if you don't get on well with the creepy crawlies.

In fact, there were a whole bunch of bugs flying around in the night, some big ass bugs too: mosquitoes and beetles and moths, all of them mesmerized by the flame and the smoke from the fires. The site was swathed in darkness, but the dim orange glow that emanated from the thousands of fires all around us was suitable enough to facilitate the evening's activities. Each of the parties occupying the adjoining blankets had brought at least one board game with them, and whether it was cards or backgammon or Leela, we all shared the wealth. Together, Bobby and I—along with our neighbor, Jack—observed our companions as they partook in their speculative activities, watching them with the same degree of interest with which we attended the bugs.

My memories of Jack, to be perfectly honest, are a bit of a blur. I remember his name, but his face eludes me, and the only physical characteristic I can bring to mind is a tattoo on his leg of a Tarot card—number eleven, I think, depicting the woman and the lion. There was something else too, something that he told me as we laid there passing the pipe back and forth to one another, something along the lines of, "Oh dreamer, thou art dreamer, open thine eyes to the wonder of the world and breathe in the sweet elixir that is the velvet breath of the universe."

There was something about this particular line—maybe its tone, or by chance its deliverance—that sent me reeling, wistfully tumbling down into the infinite, down an avenue in space, time, and dream that I'd yet to traverse. And there was something else about it too, an inkling that suggested its speaker was a real space cadet—but this, of course, couldn't be confirmed nor denied, for I was just as zonked as he was.

The next day toward evening, once the heat of the day had passed and most of the great bands had already performed, Bobby and I set to packing the last of our opium into that grand pipe. We troubled over whether or not it would be enough to last us the night, for we wanted to watch the finale, the total culmination of this festival high as coons. And as we packed it in that last time knowing there'd be no more once we'd smoked this last bit, I found myself asking, *How long does it take for the fog to fade?* —Which I'd imagine is the very first precursor to addiction.

As the sun commenced to setting over the trees, Mary sat down next to me on the blanket and peered out at the stage through a pair of field glasses. She was chattering on about a whole wealth of things, and somewhere in that syllabic flood, I heard her say that she could see Jim Morrison. She handed the glasses to me, and when I looked through them, although I could hardly believe it, I saw him up there on the stage—concho belt, leather pants and all. I felt my blood run cold as I remembered that back where I came from, this man here had been dead for thirty years—or so it was widely believed. But here he was, alive as I, staggering about, smoking something, and getting his thing together before they struck up. Mesmerized, I watched him as he commanded the stage with his swaggering presence, and when his voice came pouring out through the speakers—followed by that sensory assault that was The Doors—like the flick of a switch, a wild desirous urge came over me; one that was so dark and deep and overpowering that it moved me from where I sat back into the tent where Bobby lay in wait for my imminent return.

Inside, it was dimly lit. The only light was a reflection of the fire and the sunset through the entrance flap, and from this alone I was able to distinguish the outline of his body—my dark angel, welcoming me with arms open. I went to him, and in his kiss I saw all the faces of the ages. We rolled together, our bodies intertwined and encased in light. These patterns, cast from the dying sun, moved across our skin like water. His skin and my skin were one skin, our hearts beat quick and steady with shared purpose, and the energy we made flowed out of one and into the other—our love was forever and eternal.

And the music—it echoed our passion. It drove us harder; its whip, the night's wind, cooling the sweat that glistened on our bare skin. Out there in the chill of the night amongst the stars, a Uranian quartet mingled, and out of the brew came a sound: powerful, enticing, wonderfully enthralling—under the right conditions, *Roadhouse Blues* can take you into another universe, and tonight the signs were right. And in a song like *Mystery Train*, the beating of Densmore's drums drew you in like the rhythmic pulsing of a mother's heartbeat when an unborn child is in the womb—snug, comfortable, secure. Kind—a warm whisper on a cool night—yet decadent, offensive, dirty, and sung like a Gorgon's lullaby—innocent and mad like the desires of a child. It was all so obscene—life is so obscene! It was so clean and so tight, rigid yet fluid—the art of magic, fully sustained. It was exotic, erotic, and all-consuming; a pleasure derived not from nature alone but from otherworldly ecstasy. He consumed every part of me; he was the blood in my veins and everything that was within me, of me, and springing from me.

In the midst of these crystalline entanglements—lustfully lurching—slowly and languidly, he said to me, "We're all one."

"Yes, we are," I answered, simply because it seemed to make sense, especially considering our current endeavor. However, although I *thought* I understood it, I didn't. I couldn't really understand past conjecture, even though it was something I felt like I was supposed to.

He'd started my mind going, and I went to ask for clarification. I wanted to know exactly what he knew, what he'd meant, "Bobby, I…"

"Shhhh—" He silenced me with a finger to my lips. "*One*," he emphasized.

In the end, the sound of silence was all that remained—immense, climactic, and highly anticipated; frozen in the night—the riff between call and response, the stillness that follows the final scream, that sensory shift, the one we always forget.

It could have been minutes or it could have been hours, but eventually, we reemerged out into the soft evening glow under the watchful eye of the full moon. Our friends were all there, huddled together against the bracing wind. We joined them, and they welcomed us. I began to get the feeling that we were waiting for something, but for what, I had no idea. It was then that I heard something I thought I'd never hear, not that night or ever. It was a voice, an English voice asking for a sound check. I could barely believe my ears; I felt like my eyes were deceiving me, but low and behold, they were not. I was completely stunned beyond even an utterance, beyond any sort of exclamation, because I knew who it was that voice belonged to, even if very few others did. It was my hero, my idol, gone before his time—that is, before mine. But now, here I was—a visitor of his time—and there he was in his entirety, somewhere out there in the darkness before me—Bonzo!

You can't fully appreciate a band until you've watched them perform live, and I'd always felt a tinge of guilt because of that fact. I'd always reserved a distinct fanaticism for Bonzo and his brothers, but still felt like a bit of a hypocrite when I called them my favorite. However, from that moment on, I knew I need never feel that way again.

When they struck up, it sounded like a freight train had run right off the tracks and out into the audience. It was even more of a sensory assault than the Doors; it was like a solid wall of sound. It was heavy, oh so heavy, but so intricate—so full of vigor, so full of life and lust and so fully charged with emotion. I don't think anybody could've been prepared, not even I—like I said, you can't fully appreciate a band without seeing them live, and needless to say, the crowd freaked out. After sitting there all night and watching The Doors perform— Jim weaving tales for us and leading us down into the abyss, yet never giving us everything we expected and always leaving us wanting just a little bit more—to witness a spectacle like Led Zeppelin, who gave us everything we wanted and twice over, was almost too much to bear. And with a front-man like Robert Plant, they really had the whole package: talent, chemistry, stage presence, a radical, rebellious air— the revolution was upon us!

During The Doors' set, the whole crowd had been up and about dancing, swaying, and freaking, but during Zeppelin's set, nobody moved except for the bobbing of heads and stomping of feet—it was almost as if they'd been entranced, rooted to the spot and bound by the beat of the music. I was among them—blindsided by wonder and left only to shake my head in awe of this miracle that *I*—of all people— had been, as it seemed, *chosen* to experience. And for a split second, my thoughts carried me back into my past. That same little girl her mother sang to sleep in the wake of her fear was out here in the midst of these nights—nights never to speak of their wickedness, of their wonder, of their inherent dreams—lost and found amongst these nights…

A BRIEF AND BEAUTIFUL TRIP BACK

****

The next time I awoke I was in the van, somewhere south of Seattle en route to San Francisco. I can remember fluttering my eyes open and blearily attempting to refocus on what came to be the ceiling of the van. I sat up. The van was empty except for Faye and Bobby who remained asleep, so I pushed open the rear hatch and stepped out into the daylight, completely sober and clear-minded for the first time in over a week.

We were parked on the side of a long stretch of road. To my left, lush green fields gave way to hills and mountains that reached up into the sky, and to my right, sparse rocky crags gave way to the Pacific, which roared as it crashed against the bluffs. The fog had blown out, the sun was shining, and the wind was calm and revitalizing. Out there at the edge of the cliff, my friends had gathered and were skipping and laughing. I leaned back against the fender and watched them for a while. Thinking back and remembering what I could, everything I'd recently done and everywhere I'd been felt like a dream. It was so strange and surreal. Opium was like the event of sleep; it allowed you to leave this earthly plane and reawaken somewhere that is foreign to any normal, waking state, yet more comfortable and familiar than waking life could ever be. It brings you to a place you never want to leave and is the best and greatest feeling you've ever experienced. However, in some ways, I was relieved when we ran out. It wasn't the high that was the problem, it was the kind of high. That feeling when you're both a part of but at the same time entirely apart from your surroundings—in a completely different way than grass or any hallucinogen—was what made it so desirous and so dangerous.

The sound of my name being called shook me from my thoughts and brought me back into the now. From down the road a ways, Mary was waving to me and beckoning me over. I left my blanket on the fender and went to join them, parched for human contact.

After a much-needed romp around in the fresh air, we all piled back into the van and continued south on Highway 1. Space drove, and Mary Jane and I rode shotgun. As the sun climbed higher, so did the mercury, and by the middle of the day, it was probably ninety degrees—an extreme rarity up north. By noon, the jeans I was wearing had become cutoffs, and Mary had traded in her long Indian dress for Space's paisley shirt. Space, who was always sweating from the speed anyway, was driving in his birthday suit—with the exception of his shorts and the cuttings from mine, which he'd tied around his head to keep his hair off of his forehead and neck.

Once we'd gotten down around Eureka, by popular demand from the peanut gallery in the back who'd gotten tired of singing camp songs and carving up their clothes, we abandoned the coastal highway and started heading inland in hopes of finding a cool place. Initially, we'd wanted to stop in Redwood National Park, but we'd passed it and instead agreed upon Mount Shasta. However, though we'd seen signs for it on the main road, we drove for quite a while without coming upon it, and after getting lost more than once, as the moans and groans from the back grew louder and more frequent, we decided anywhere with enough trees for shade would cut it, and somewhere toward suppertime we pulled into a national park near a place called Whiskeytown.

Trees had been the minimum requirement for stopping, and this park supplied them in abundance. Outlined against the sky, the mass of giant redwoods looked like a solid object, and as we gradually grew closer and entered into the forest, it felt as if we were moving deeper and deeper into a two-dimensional picture. The sensation it evoked was one of goose pimples and the resurrection of some underlying principle—some hidden meaning that governs all things—the implications of which, after having been deeply considered, I have never fully recovered from.

We parked near a cluster of campsites not far from a stream. It was shady and cool under the vast and ancient trees, and upon being amongst them for the first time, I couldn't help gazing up in awe; their magnificent hugeness made me feel wonderfully inferior. This glorious unperturbed wilderness was a far cry from home for us city dwellers, and it stirred something within us—or at least within me—something older than my memories and outside of myself, yet essential to my life—a sort of wonder. Goaded by curiosity, most of my friends scattered upon landing—off amongst the trails to discover the secrets this forest held. The urge inside myself to escape and do the same was teeming, but instead, I remained behind to help Melinda build a fire and begin making tonight's dinner, promising myself an exploratory walk later.

Al was the first one back. He approached the van alone, clutching a small bouquet in his fist.

"What've you got there, Al?" Melinda asked him as he came up the hill, but by the time he answered, he was near enough for us to see. In

210

his hand, he held about two dozen little mushrooms on thin stalks with nipples on their caps.

"I found them down by a stream," he announced, sounding very pleased with himself. "This is only the third time I've come across psilocybin mushrooms growing naturally in California—what a stroke of luck!"

Melinda was just as excited as he was, and she took them from his hand and began cutting them up real fine and pouring them with water into an empty soda can which she then put on the fire.

"How do you know that's what they are?" I asked as every childhood warning about eating wild mushrooms came rushing back to me at once, setting off those highly conditioned caution lights in my brain.

"I've had many experiences with them before," he explained, smiling wisely.

"Isn't it dangerous to eat wild mushrooms when you don't know what they are?" I prodded wide-eyed as Melinda sipped from the cup.

Al looked a bit perplexed, "But I do know what they are. Once you've had them, you aren't keen on forgetting what they look like anytime soon. If I weren't sure, I wouldn't have already eaten them. If they were poisonous, by now I'd be in a hell of a lot of trouble. After all, if a plant has been used for thousands of years for its psychedelic potential all over the world, it can't possibly be bad for you."

Melinda offered me the can. "Tea," she explained. "Brewing them takes the bite out."

I took the can from her. I trusted them, so I took a swig.

"…well…sort of," she added apologetically after I'd done so and she'd seen my expression.

For all the supernatural power these things possess, it may sound awful petty to demote them on the basis of taste, but believe me, it's not. All those palatable euphemisms connoisseurs use to describe foods of the least esculent sort, such as acrid or pungent, cannot be substituted to define a flavor that is most definitely and without reservation, on all counts and by all means, purely and utterly disgusting. Once my horrified brain registered that the repulsive taste accompanied a substance I was busy ingesting—one that numbed my tongue so severely I was afraid I'd killed it—it told my body to expel it at all costs. However, contrary to all good human sense, I managed to keep it down.

As the waves of nausea continued to swell, the next coherent thought I had despite them was to find the basket of cherries we'd bought along the road. After having done so, whilst I ate them in a mostly vain attempt to cleanse my palate, Al and Melinda passed the can between them, their neutral expressions belying the true and foul nature of the concoction they drank. Very infrequently, one or the other would distort their faces after they swallowed, much like the drinker of bathtub gin or corn whiskey. The rest of my friends, once they reappeared, consumed the vile vegetables in an even more inconspicuous and doubtlessly amazing manner—by simply cleaning them on their shirts and munching them like carrots, cap first.

The first threat of nausea subsided as soon as I was able to cleanse the taste and smell of the mushrooms from my senses, a feat far more easily suggested than actually accomplished. Even after eating a few dozen sweet cherries, the horrid taste still lingered for a while, until some fresh water and Melinda's hot stew promptly removed it.

Now I wasn't exactly keeping track of time or anything, but as far as I could tell, it took much longer to begin feeling the effects of the mushrooms than it did for acid. As we awaited the onset of our trips, we all sat around our makeshift camp, some of us fooling with the assortment of instruments we'd brought along while the rest of us spent this time lying about, giving our systems adequate time to digest these sacred chemicals.

Once I'd gotten my bearings and no longer felt like playing percussionist in our improvisational band, I wandered over to the van to find a cigarette. It took me quite a while, but under several piles of clothes and blankets and the tent somebody had unrolled, I found a sad, squished, half-empty pack of Lucky Strikes.

Al sat on the fender and turned around to help me, bearing a humored expression on his face, "By now you should know better than to try and find anything in The Day Trippers' sty," he condemned me affably.

"I guess I never learn," I replied sarcastically, lighting up.

"The best never do."

"Now in all seriousness, tell me something Aladdin," I asked him, "with all the acid around, why go through all the trouble to hunt up these god-awful mushrooms?"

Al chuckled, "Well, the first time I ever ate the mushrooms I was with a friend of mine down around Lake Tahoe. We'd planned on taking acid, but before we dropped we went for a walk, and down in this mucky, marshy trek, my friend got his boot stuck in the mud, and when he bent down to pull it out, he found a whole bunch of these mushrooms growing around the base of a tree. He picked them out and showed them to me and told me that they were far superior to acid and that they were what we were going to take instead. Now he was quite a few years older than me, so he had much more experience under his belt than I did when dealing with vegetation, but once we got back to our camp and washed and ate them, I thought I was going to die just from the taste alone. I even retched a bit—"

"Were you scared?"

"You bet your ass! I was real scared, but I trusted him—and it wasn't very long at all after that I realized he was right. Some of the best poetry I've ever written, I've written under the influence; not of LSD, but of psilocybin and peyote. It's not because the drugs make you smarter, but because they open you up. LSD, in some ways, can accentuate the ego, but psilocybin and peyote get your ego out of the way and make you a channel for God."

"Why do you think that is?" I asked him.

"Well, the best answer I've been able to come up with is that even though the actual LSD compounds exist by themselves in nature, the LSD that we take is man-made, and no matter how authentic the batch, it always retains that feeling. Overall, organic trips are incomparably more pure. After all, man creates in the image of his ego— imperfection. God creates in the image of himself—perfection. Anything created by God and unaffected by human hands will naturally bring you further into the Akashic records than anything made by man."

"Into the what?"

"The Akashic records—where all the material of our trips comes from."

"What do you mean?" I asked again for clarification. As it was with Al, asking him to explain something once rarely sufficed, usually it took two or three different approaches until you were left with an answer that was more or less coherent.

"Have you ever wondered where the contents of your mind go when you die?" —This was another of Al's methods; clearly, he thought the easiest way of answering one question was with another question.

"Yes," I replied.

"Well, so did the Theosophists, and what they came to figure was that all those things—all those thoughts, facts, and memories—go to a place called the astral plane and are kept there in a series of records called the Akashic."

"How do you know that's where our visions come from? How do

you know they don't come from within us?"

"Well, they do, in a way," Al admitted, "but it isn't a conscious place. How often do you experience something in your trip that you consciously remember or find to be familiar? —Not very often; therefore, it must be acknowledged that these things are hailing from a much broader memory, the memory of our souls. And since our souls are eternal and do not have hippocampi, those memories must come from someplace else—someplace inside each of us, yet common to all of us. That's what's so wonderful about it: you have this fountain of ancient knowledge overflowing, and you're completely aware that it's all coming from inside your own mind, and at the same time it's so foreign and awe-inducing that you can't help but be enlightened."

Is it any wonder my head was spinning at this point? Really, I could've used a few minutes of reflection after that, but Al just kept right on talking.

"Have you ever had a vision for your life?" he asked me dreamily.

"I guess," I answered, thinking back to my daydreams of performing at the Whisky. However, I had a feeling that what he was referring to was different than what I had imagined, "Why, have you?"

"Yes," he replied, speaking like an oracle as he recalled something visionary. "In fact, it was that first time at Lake Tahoe. I stood on the shore facing that blue, blue water, every drop just...sparkling...and I saw all the ripples coming out from the source and flowing uninterrupted to the shore, and I noticed that along the way they became less and less apparent as they died out. In this I saw reflected the lives of most people: routine, average reproductions of one another. Then I was compelled to throw a rock into the lake, and I saw that it made its own ripples that moved in the opposite direction and were stronger than the ones coming toward them. They continued outward like a shockwave for a while, and then steadily, they blended in. It was then that I decided that's what I wanted the impact of my work on humanity to be—that my art might first make waves and then eventually become a part of what is accepted and normal; moving humanity further, you might say."

"Wow," I replied, duly impressed. "That's pretty good that you can come to that conclusion all from just a stone and a lake."

"It never ceases to amaze me what the simplest things in nature can inspire."

Suddenly, a disturbing thought came to me, "If all the material of our trips comes from the Akashic records—a compilation of all the memories of all those that have come before us—doesn't that mean that nothing we envision is original? That it's always somebody else's memory?"

Al smiled gently at me, "What you've first got to realize and come to terms with is that everything you think has already been thought, and everything you consider to be new in terms of your perception has already existed for eons of years. Everything you think, do, and say has already been thought, done, and said. The only thing we can do differently is in the way that we present our knowledge and experience to others. There is nothing new about our Movement—rebellion is as old as humanity itself. As long as there has been an accepted standard of living, there have been ways of living differently. Revolution appears every so often as a push against what is considered normal, presenting itself in different modes until it sticks. The Enlightenment, Transcendentalism, Liberalism, and even the Renaissance are cut from the same cloth as our revolution. And that's another thing about psilocybin: it gives you a different perspective and sets you upon that path of difference faster and more assuredly than any other chemical aid."

After that, we just sat there in silence for a while, watching the last of the daylight streaming in through those great leaves turn to gold on the forest floor. The echoes of Al's words and their implications resounded within my brain…I hadn't even started tripping yet and my mind had already been blown. Next to me, a shiver passed through my companion. I turned toward him, anticipating another revelation, but instead, he shuffled backward in the van and began digging through the heap in search of a notebook or other unmarked scrap of paper. The utterance of, "I need to empty my head," was the only explanation he offered.

I grinned and shook my own head in amazement. *No shit*, I thought to myself. I remained there for a few minutes more, but finding that my companion had embarked upon his own intellectual trip, I decided to treat myself to that nature walk I'd promised myself earlier. Initially, all that Al and I had been discussing filled my mind like ambient noise, confusing and overwhelming, though enlightening— much like a trip itself. However, once I'd left our camp and found myself out in the midst of unperturbed nature, all of that started to subside, and I began to be filled with a sense of deep calm as I continued on my unguided trek into the evening redwoods.

As I walked, I noticed that all around me, new folds of existence were unfurling and becoming life. Life came out from life, and with each step, more and more appeared, shining in the growing darkness with its own preternatural light.

I must say, though it may've taken longer for the psilocybin to come on, when it did, it sure came on strong. It seemed only moments before I could see and observe processes normally imperceptible: watch the flowers grow, for one, and sense that things around me were happening slower—like that acorn falling from a tree that seemed to take an hour. It is impossible to list the ample scores of thoughts that entered in and out of my mind in the space of time it took to hit the ground.

This whole Earth is living, you know, all around us there is evidence of that: the low gurgle of a river, the careful approach and slow retreat of the tides—seamless, like one long breath—nature's reclamation of what is rightfully hers when an animal perishes on the forest floor. Of course, if you are keen to envision on a grander scale, there is the waltz of the continents—the sudden shift of a fault is only the almighty climax of a thousand-year cadence. And if you are to consider the more obvious contender, our sisters the Plantae, theirs are lives to be valued as much if not more than our own, not only for their beauty but for their purpose. While the daily pirouettes of the flowers to follow the sun and the endless climb of the ivy skyward via the noble trunk of some symbiotically affiliated sequoia are beautiful, it is their function that is truly breathtaking. We may never notice it, but in life, on the most mundane of bases, we are constantly taking and giving back. Every time we breathe, we are drawing in and sending forth the true elixir of life—air. But the air we exhale isn't air to breathe, it is poison, and before it can be breathed by us yet again, it must first be breathed by the plants: by the trees, the garden lilies, the algae—we survive because of plant breath. And seeing as this is such a peripheral concept, no one ever seems to thank them. But Mother Nature's got one up on us. Isn't it funny how our first breath is a breath in and our last is a breath out? There is *always* a balance, and there is no place better to see that proven than in nature.

—And how appropriate is it that the means by which I have had the occasion to become aware of these most intrinsic natures of nature is itself a plant?!

As I began to open myself up to these things, these utterly simple yet powerful and monumental truths, a passage in the forest opened itself up for me. No longer did I have to bend the ferns and the brambles to pass by, they moved away for me, and I traveled further and further on, hereafter enveloped in the sweet ecstasy of communion.

216

There are many levels of awareness, just as there are many levels to all other constituents of our universe. Once you are aware that you are aware and that your awareness is shared, you begin, or rather, take up your place in a virtuous cycle: enlightenment. And isn't it pleasing that all this humbling, revitalizing profundity comes with aesthetics?

In a variety of ways, psilocybin opens your mind, entirely unlike opium. For as many things as I learned from that plant, my favor lies with the fungi. As far as I am aware, no other organism can provide you with a crash course in ultimate empathy while you traipse through a jungle of cat-eyed flowers and dodge glowing cicadas the size of your head.

As I carried on, that everlasting principle of transience made itself known once more. The further I journeyed, the more my surroundings changed continually. In one moment, the bone-dry forest floor rippled like a shimmering lake beneath my feet, and in the next, the ground slid past, hungry, a fleet of amoebas not solid but viscous, and my feet sunk in with every step.

I must have journeyed very far, or maybe not quite far enough, because I came to a high cliff—a cliff that overlooked metropolis. I was deeply saddened by this—that the insurmountable domain of nature had been so severely encroached upon by the despotic hand of human avarice. However, as I looked closer and closer, I began to see that very same city disintegrate before my eyes. There were no more buildings, no more roads, no more cars, and everything had this soft, emanating glow. Though it was still far off from where I stood, I could see clearly—as if the distance made no difference.

As I watched, the smog-like glow began to roll back from the land, and I could see fields of dark, fresh-tilled soil covering vast tracks ahead of me, and from them grew rows and rows of small, white, identical buildings. And it did not end there; from those buildings came an even further expanse of flat, gray warehouses—a whole huge wilderness of factories, rusted and abandoned—nothing short of unauthorized occupancy. In them I could see reflected the imminence of the future and our disrespect; for the ground they stood upon was sacred—as is all ground—and ground that is mistreated and abused accumulates a repository of negative energy. We will only flourish and benefit from our pursuits once we learn to respect the land we conduct them from.

As I continued to peer out over the valley, over the industrial wasteland rotting away in the distance, chain link and barbed wire began rising up out of the ground like vast coils of brambles, covering the whole complex and completely encircling the entire area. This saddened me even more and struck me as an integral flaw in our human condition: we build up walls to keep the outside out and the inside in, and in doing so we cut ourselves off from everything except for what we are. How much easier it would be if we would remain open and let all and everything flow into and out of—right through us like the air that we breathe.

Now, the whole 'Flaws of Humanity' trip is a real bummer, and I sure as hell didn't want to bum this beautiful trip out, so I turned myself right around and marched back into the forest, leaving the sunset and the dissonance behind me. Once I was safely under the trees again, I found that Mother Nature had really turned up the lights. All of the trees, flowers, and bushes in the forest had begun to shine with their own internal light, and each glowed a phosphorescent hue that gradually changed to all the colors of the rainbow, never-ending and never repeating—kind of like a cross between those bioluminescent hadopelagic fish and a fiber optic Christmas tree.

Even though the last rays of twilight were quickly retreating into dusk, under the canopy, it was not hard at all to see. Lights abounded from every direction and were otherworldly in the darkness. All the light that I saw didn't exist in waves but in particles, not waves, but drops like rain, and every drop that fell upon me or another part of my surroundings emitted a tone like a chime until they all ran together in the sweetest song of synesthesia—it was like nighttime in Eden.

However, just like that old scientific argument, once I thought I could just about understand or gather some kind of conceptual meaning from what I was seeing, my perception changed yet again. The light that I saw no longer rained about as particles; instead, it hailed from its source in long, unbroken waves and traveled so slowly that I could see them. So amazing and hypnotizing were these visions; everything I saw, I saw in one place, but then I saw it in another—like a strobe light reflected over and over, like the tracer on the ass end of a bullet. I was completely mystified by this phenomenon; it was like an orchestra of color, an orgasm of the eyes—visual sensationalism greater than any other I'd ever experienced before.

—And it was not only what I was witnessing that elated me, but the understanding that I was a part of it. With each step I took, the ground erupted into flashes of color beneath my feet, and with every pace, the light became living color. It was no longer waves nor particles; it was both, it was neither—it was anything I wanted it to be. I raised my hands from my sides and colors began streaming through my fingers like water. They were physical and malleable, yet entirely formless—and when they dropped to the earth, they morphed into little balls like lead and rolled away from me. The entire forest floor was covered in millions, no, billions of these manifestations.

It was revolutionary, engrossing, profound, and only one infinitesimal facet of all that was happening simultaneously both within me and around me. Overwhelming is a good word, although it is not accurate. A truly appropriate word does not and cannot exist, for the laws of the infinite universe are not written in any human language. But I'll tell you what, even though entropy reigned, order remained—like the geometry I could see in the plants; and not only in the plants, in everything, including myself. We along with all matter are comprised of perfect geometric patterns—we are all living, breathing, mathematical conglomerates—both us and the trees that rose infinitely high and all the visions that echoed in me and around me.

In the light of the full moon, I saw clearer than ever before. Everything in the world was at its flashpoint, and everywhere, everything was breaking up and coming back together even weirder than before. I began to hear fractions of sound, and the quieter things sounded louder and reverberated. The cry of a hawk would warble and distort, and the croak of a toad would amplify and repeat as if on a loop, first coming from above, and then from behind, until I'd lost all sense of direction. As I wandered, suspended in that blissful reality, I realized that I had no idea where I was. I didn't have the slightest clue as to how to get back to the rest of The Day Trippers, and the further I walked in any direction, the stranger everything looked. I was not alarmed, in fact, I was oddly calm. And then, inside my head, I heard loud and clear not a voice nor a vision but some fusion of the two that told me to go to the river. Now, I didn't have a clue where the river was, and with the hallucinations coming on heavier and heavier, I couldn't tell left from right or north from south, but once I made it my fantasy to go to the river, it seemed like my feet took me there on their own accord—like they were one with the earth and knew their way alone.

And, once I'd tumbled through the pink, singing brambles on the bank, who did I find there? —Al of all people, picking his way upstream. His was a form so warped that as I came upon him, I began to laugh. He had arms and legs like Gumby and feet like Sasquatch—but it was Al all the same.

"Rhiannon! Rhiannon! Read this, read this!" he cried, thrusting a sheet of paper in my direction.

In between bursts of laughter, I answered him, "I can't read right now, Al! The letters will run right off the page! Read it to me, man!"

And so he did, his lips popping off his face as he spoke, the images he described materializing with the utterance of each word: "Nature is something personal," he began, "it is something that belongs to all of us, yet none of us at the same time. You cannot own nature, yet it is a part of all of us because all of us are a part of nature. Nature is within us and around us. To not appreciate and enjoy nature is to not appreciate and enjoy ourselves, to not care for and protect nature is to harm ourselves. In the course of our technological and societal advancements, in order to create better and more fulfilling lives, we often throw nature aside in our pursuits. We quest to conquer nature, to beat it down and replace it with our own creations, and we do not see how in doing so we selfishly limit ourselves and all future generations—after all, man's creation is ludicrous in comparison to that of the Mind at Large. We fail to appreciate that which we see around us every day of our lives; Mother Nature, the greatest of all interpretive artists.

"We cannot exist without nature. Without the sun, water, and air we could not live. Without plants and animals, we could not eat. Without nature, we could not survive. What we sometimes fail to realize is that although we cannot exist without nature, nature can very easily exist without us. It did for hundreds of millions of years before we walked the Earth, and our ancestors existed for thousands of years symbiotically alongside nature, bringing it into themselves and redistributing it out, never taking, never destroying, using only that which was necessary and leaving the rest.

"*From dust we have come, and to dust we will all return,*' a wise man once wrote. We cannot live forever, and when we die, no matter what religious or philosophical beliefs we may hold, what is certain is that our earthly carbon bodies disintegrate and once more will become one with the earth from whence we have sprung. We are all one with each other through our connection with nature. As humans, we have all come from this same Earth, and in death, we will all return.

"As impressive as man's pursuits may be, his will always be second to nature. Our lives revolve around patterns of weather, and even the most technologically and culturally advanced society can be suddenly obliterated by Kali, our Divine Mother. We are not in full control of our lives as long as the sun shines, the rivers flow, and the grass grows. So why not get back to the garden? Why not once more become one with that from which you have come? For in the eternal cycles of

220

nature, we find that which is absent from the human condition: perfection."

I quivered with delight as he orated this. It just resonated so precisely with my own trip that it brought the experience to a whole new level. "Aww man," I moaned after he'd ended his recitation. "That's outta sight, man! How do you *do* that, man, get all that down on paper and making sense like that? Huh, man?"

I took the paper and pencil from him and began to scribble upon a rock, but there were so many thoughts coming all at the same time like a barrage, each one more fantastic and enlightening than the one prior, that it was absolutely impossible to write them down. It didn't so much feel like it was my own thoughts that I possessed, rather, it was like something sliding past me—another reality, I suppose. I was so amped up, I just wanted to get everything that was within me out. I wanted to share it like Al could, but I couldn't, and the visions began to accelerate uncontrollably again, filling the whole world around me.

"Don't stop talking now," I whimpered, wishing to be bathed once more in the images hewn by Al's tongue.

He started up again, and once more my visions took the shape of his words, "I come out here to watch the trees line up and to hear the birds chirp and the sound of my footsteps loudly impacted upon the ground..." Sure enough, as he said these things, order erupted out of the fray: all the trees in the forest extended in neat rows and their branches all came to v's.

Through some metaphysical link—psychic or otherwise—I could see as he did, and upon meeting his eyes, there I saw a ring of green caterpillars walking around his pupil and down into the spongy gray folds of his cerebrum. As he spoke to me, the features of his face began to change; at once, they appeared mutable, his skin rippling like the surface of a lake. At one moment he looked like himself, at another like Thoreau, after that in the style of Gurdjieff, and in the following moment, he appeared as Hegel. Witnessing this, I began to wonder about my own appearance and stared down into the river.

When I did, I was greeted by a stranger. I—as I appeared—was not myself. I wore many different faces, but I was intrinsically the same inside. Even so, there seemed to be a disconnect—a kind of schizophrenia. I no longer identified with my body. What I saw in the reflection wasn't what was real and true, but rather a persona covering what was inside. I stumbled away from the shore, where the gentle tide lapped at my bare feet. Bobby, Mary, and everybody—they all needed to see this. But where were they? Surely there was no way to gather

221

them all here…

Come to the river! I thought, sending this message out into the universe. *Come to the river!* I thought, and I danced. As I did this, a remarkable feeling arose within me, a confidence that was not assumed but assured. Even so, I still couldn't believe my eyes when Space came bursting into the clearing through the bushes alongside me. Coincidence? It could've been when Billy and Faye emerged behind him not a minute later, but when Mary and Bobby turned up on the opposite shore mere seconds after Melinda came out from the other side of a tree directly in front of us, I knew that something extraordinary was going on. What began stirring was the obscure notion that I was no longer alone inside my own mind. It was an incorporeal sensation, somewhat like the one that possessed us when we played music, yet different in that it was all-pervading. Instead, it felt more like my consciousness was shifting, leaving my unfamiliar body and merging with those around me.

We all gathered along the edge of the water and dipped our toes in, not looking at one another, yet sharing our thoughts. Now, the body of water that flowed past us wasn't quite a river, in fact, it couldn't have been more than thirty feet across, but to us, it seemed as wide as the Amazon, as long as the Nile, and as holy as the Ganges.

"*This too I have learned from the river,*" Al spoke, quoting Hesse. "*Everything returns.*"

"Old, new, and always the same—what we have here is the Styx, come up from underground to bring us to the other side of life," Bobby said.

"Bummer, bummer," I cautioned, paying heed to my Junior High readings of *The Odyssey*.

"The Rubicon then," Space suggested. Appropriately enough, he'd tied the corners of a blanket to the sleeves of his shirt like a cape and fashioned some kind of crown out of leaves and twigs. With a branch in his hand, upright like a sword, he led our makeshift procession across to where Bobby and Mary stood. The current rushed up around our waists as we waded into the river, sweeping us off our feet. Seeing as how I was already wet and how sensually gratifying the experience of water was in that state, I stuck my head right under the surface and opened my eyes. And how that riverbed shined in the moonlight! Each rock and pebble gave off its own signature glimmer, and what was all one breath felt like eons.

I should've been born a fish; by the time I came up for air, everybody else had already climbed out and was whooping and caterwauling about, soaked from the navel down. With Bobby's help, I staggered out of the shallow water and immediately began falling all over myself like the rest of them. It wasn't because we were drunk or grossly incoherent, but because we were simply unsteady on our feet, a side effect of the psilocybin that made the equilibrium of everything feel disrupted. We still maintained that same telepathic-like communication as one by one we all sank into a half circle on the forest floor. We all gathered together, and we all drifted apart. We sat facing one another, touching each other's skin and communicating intuitively between ourselves and with nature. As unrestrained hilarity reigned, we began attempting to speak to one another, which only exacerbated the hysterics. Rather than anything even remotely resembling a conversation, what aired was completely unintelligible. Parts of sentences interspersed by laughter filled the night air and were accompanied by streams of syllables strung together that made no sense at all because we were each trying to get everything we were thinking out of our mouths at the same time.

"My body is a reverberating pinball machine refrigerator, man!" Space cried.

"Where am I?" Mary asked.

"You are here," Al replied.

"Where is here?"

"Here is near," Bobby answered.

"Near what? Near what?"

"Near the rear. I found what I was looking for at the bottom of a wicker basket in-between the laughs and the screams."

"I live in a world perpetuated by my own imagination—and so do you. We meet each other often on the battleground of reality, but really we are just visitors inside one another's mindsssss," Al declared.

The blue incandescent fogs had begun rolling in off the cliffs, and the steam from them rose, sizzled, and baked inside our menthol lozenge minds. A handful of our stoned orations really seemed to jive with the whole thing, and we grooved on it and rapped off it in the reverberating pinball machine refrigerator night.

After a series of events like this one, we abandoned the conversational route altogether and concentrated more on a deeper understanding of ourselves and the world around us, something this trip had no trouble at all providing us with. We were going deep into ourselves and exploring—tripping in nature, where there is nothing but good vibrations. We laid back in the grass and let it all in. Purple images flitted behind closed eyelids and danced and shimmered like the scales of a fish when summer sunlight reflects off the bay. I saw shapes and geometric patterns and visions that seemed to have a life and mind of their own. As I became more and more entranced by these things, they transported me to another world.

The transformations began as the hallucinations lessened. The further we journeyed into ourselves, the stranger we became, and we began to see ourselves in metamorphosis. We were projecting out from ourselves the many reflections of our countenances. The universe failed to exist as physical; rather, it appeared in symbols. I remember reaching into my pocket for a lighter, which at once turned into a bug and began crawling up my arm. It was large and blue and ghoulish, but I watched it with morbid concern, and I did not shake it from me. As if this were not enough, while we howled about like raving lunatics, completely past the point of verbal expression, the shape of our bodies began to shift to and from animals. Melinda approached the river and knelt before it, but once her knees hit the ground, her form condensed and swelled into that of a crab, her blue shell rocking from side to side as she crawled along the riverbank. Billy followed her, although not in the same manner. Instead, he stretched out upon the ground, his broad face tilted up toward the sky, waving his arms like he was wrapping a cocoon around himself, and when he emerged, his body was coiled like a Grecian beast, his head like an imperial dragon. Next to him, Faye also began to stir. However, unlike her lover, her body did not gather form; rather, she offered herself up, disintegrating with the wind's breath and retaining only traces of her former self, leaving behind nothing but mystic air.

Now I'd heard of people—psychics and the like—who through one set of skills or another, somehow had the ability to read auras—actually see the energy of others exuded all around them. Now it was I who had that ability, and those of my friends whose bodies were not busy exhibiting some foreign form were now surrounded by a glowing ring of sorts. For Al, it was green; the same as the plants, the animals, and the trees. For Mary, it was bright yellow, and the same was true for Space. However, as for Bobby, his aura was a bit of an enigma. When I first saw him he emitted blue through and through, but as I watched him carry on, the color changed and so did the feeling; and rather than uplift me, it brought me some kind of horror. As he turned toward me, I could see that even in the darkness his face shown like the sun—radiant, like the sun—but instead of purity shining through, it was a false light, ego light. From blue it changed to red, and as he moved toward me, the glow faded to gray, and a most dreadful notion accompanied his approach.

This was not long-lasting or even particularly unforeseen, but it was in the fullest sense startling, and as soon as I could get my hands on him, I led him to the river. To this suggestion, he was surprisingly adamant. I got him to look once, and when he saw his reflection, he bucked and bolted like a spooked stallion—less Übermensch and more abashed. Once I'd brought him to this point, however, what I hadn't counted on was for him to get stuck in the cycle of his own ego games, and it was at this point in the trip that Bobby began to lose his cool.

We all realized this quickly, and although dealing with psychedelic freak-outs wasn't an area I was well-versed in, my friends were experts, and all at once there was a rush of energy, and a burst of voices manifested.

"We've got to bring him back into our trip," Billy said. "Rhiannon, go and hold him, let him feel the realness of your body."

I tried, but he wasn't having any of that.

"Send him all of your good vibes, all your positive energy," Space suggested as an alternative.

Remarkably, Mary was able to get near him and talk him down a little bit, and after a few moments of forever, he began to settle down.

"Do you see those stars?" she asked him. "Look up. Do you see those stars? Good. Each one of those stars is just like each of us. Now, look at those constellations. See how beautiful they are? They could never get that way if each star remained by itself. One star may be beautiful, but a hundred, a thousand, a billion? If you feel like you are pulling away from your body, good. Let it go, just let it go... By coming into us you are only becoming more beautiful, you are not losing anything at all. In fact, you're actually gaining..."

As she said these things, her words like Al's before sent me soaring. I was coming apart from myself and moving into everything. The binds of that old, unfamiliar body were falling away, and all remnants of physical manifestation were disintegrating. The first time I felt this feeling, when I was high in my car, the sensation was terrifying, paralyzing. Now, reassured and experienced, I went with it; I trusted, I knew that I was safe. And the more I trusted, the higher my spirit soared up into the sky until I could see the world around me as if I was standing on the moon. It was like one of those flying dreams, except that I knew my soul was apart from my body—objectivity at its finest. I could see, but I did not have an eye. I was seeing with my soul, bypassing all those sensory sieves and neuropathways—that's why everything was so clear, so vividly clear. That evening, I visited whole universes separate in space but essentially the same, scattered like portals across McKenna's antipodes. I could change like the wind and go anywhere I wanted without moving a muscle; my bodily identity no longer weighed me down. I experienced thought as another dimension, and through this experience, it became evident to me that one thing cannot possibly be superior to any other because it is through the intercourse of all things that we exist.

From a perch such as this, I was not looking at things as more than they were and trying to read meaning into them, I was seeing them as they really are…and everything is not as it seems to the straight world. From this vantage point, I could truly see that all of nature and existence isn't only perfect, it is divine. God had never been more real. *IT* was no longer a principle, *IT* was a presence. It was then that I realized that not only was God there with me in that moment, but that God is everywhere…

****

The next day, we drove the last 200 miles or so down that northern coastal highway home. When I'd awoken that morning—surprisingly early considering my activities of the previous evening—I felt like the entire world had been remade. Everything I saw, I saw clearer, brighter, and sharper. I felt as if the inside of every part of myself— my mind, body, and emotions—had been sterilized and scrubbed clean. The events of everyday life no longer remained quizzical; instead, the most seemingly insignificant instances gained the potential to be understood in the minutest detail as lessons in living. I was aware of and able to enter into a new level of cosmic understanding, and I knew that all my friends felt the same.

Surprisingly, although the experience had deeply affected all of us, we very scarcely reviewed it. This was simply because we didn't need to. The experience had stamped a whole new brand of intimacy on our friendship. We still knew, to a degree, what one another was thinking and feeling. For example, when one of us was drinking from the gallon jug and another one of us was thirsty, the jug would be passed between the two without any words exchanged. And when one of us was driving and began to tire, another would be right there offering to take the wheel even before the first yawn. And as for our musical performance, the first thing we did when we arrived back home was rush into the garage and plug in. Needless to say, after only a few minutes of jamming, Space was on the phone calling up The Matrix and several other dives to see if they had a job for us that night.

We played that night and all the nights that followed, and those were some of the best gigs we ever had. We were so synched in it was purely maddening, and the inspiration flowed like water from an open faucet. At clubs like The Matrix where the sounds from inside often wafted out over the sidewalks, crosswalks, and streetwalkers, we attracted a crowd at the door more than once over that interim period between our return from Seattle and our departure upon our next adventure.

Once we got back on the Haight, it seemed like the only thing that anyone was talking about was a curious hip gathering taking place in a few weeks, all the way across the country in Upstate New York; a festival marketed with the promise of three days of peace and music

227

and referred to as an Aquarian Exposition. You didn't hear much about it on the radio, and there were only a handful of posters hanging around the Bay Area, but it sure was in the minds of the people. Why? Because that's where all the action was going to be in about three weeks. The Dead, the Airplane, Janis, and just about every other one of San Francisco's big groups were all on the setlist—and all at the same time! It was eighteen bucks a pop for all three days. Space suggested that we buy the tickets before we headed out there, but I advised him that we wouldn't be needing any. Despite how sweet the last few days on the Haight had been, we all jumped at the chance to get back on the road. The mushrooms we'd eaten in the redwoods had made us feel quite alright, but once the world gets back in, that feeling loses something. After a few days, that pure, authentic self you discovered on your trip is nowhere to be found, but inside, there always remains some vestige, and for us, it was most visible when the seven of us were alone together for extended periods of time.

The day we left, Al was the first one awake, and I, apparently, was the second. I'd found him outside mid-morning, loading equipment into the back of the Trips Mobile. With the knowledge that we had a weeks-long trip ahead of us, Al had executed the forethought to clean and strip the van of its former clutter and had started stacking our instruments and luggage in there neatly. Wordlessly, I joined in to help him. I broke down my drum kit and packed my bass, snare, cymbals, and traps, all of which—along with Al's organ, a few small amps, and the mixer—I secured to the metal rack on the roof and covered with a tarp. Together, Al and I carried a trunk down from one of the upper rooms and pushed it up against the front seats, filling it with clean clothes, blankets, towels, and canned food.

Al was completely absorbed in this process. This was the most stoked I'd seen him for anything in all the time I'd known him. His eyes were bright as he moved from task to task, and on his face, he wore the most benevolent smile. I remembered how Bobby had spoken of him on more than one occasion, '*He's like the wind,*' he had said, '*one of those types who doesn't like to stay in one place for too long.*'

"You really dig this whole trip—traveling and being out on the road—don't 'cha?" I observed, marveling at his enthusiasm.

Al just turned from what he was doing and beamed at me.

"Why?"

He shrugged, "Once I start to become familiar with my surroundings, I get bored of them."

"Did you guys move around a lot when you were kids?"

"Nah, for what I've been able to observe, in America there seems to be an innate sense of restlessness. For me, it really started up after I left the City for New York when I was about fifteen. There's a whole lot between these two coasts, and once you get a glimpse of it for the first time, you're hooked—you want to see it all."

"But that's not all it is with you," I commented, "sightseeing and the like. There's more to it than that, I can tell."

Al's thousand-year-old eyes were fixed on mine, and he spoke to me in a tone that one might use when fondly recalling memories of an old friend, "You're right. There's nothing quite like the feeling of living on the road. You can get those same sights from a coach car window or even on television, but there's something about watching it all stream past you from the back of a pickup truck or the inside of a freight car that makes it so much more raw and so much more real. For me, the open road is the most inspiring place in the entire world. Everybody is going somewhere, and you start to wonder, *which are the ones going my way? Which are the ones going away? How many will I see again, and what will happen to the ones I don't?* You really get to know people out there on the road, and that's because everybody depends on one another."

"Is it really as romantic as Steinbeck and Kerouac make it out to be?"

"Sometimes, when the stars are out and the company is groovy. And sometimes you find that no matter how hard you've tried not to, you've become Sal Paradise—a melancholy ball of sheets out there on old Route 6 in the pouring rain, going over and over again trying to remember why in the hell you're even out there in the first place, swearing up and down on every holy book and promising God that the next town you come to will be the one you settle in if only He'd bring a car your way right about now. And then, right when you're about to pack it in, what comes snarling and puttering down the road but an ancient Tin Lizzie with one headlight doing about twenty-five—which gives you just enough time to scoop up your bindle and flag 'em down. Once you jump inside and hear the sound of that rain change to pattering on the roof rather than splashing up all around you, it all comes flooding back, and you remember again just why you keep going on and on, and you wonder how you could've forgotten for even a moment…"

"Which is what, for you?"

Al produced a heavy sigh, but replied to me as a coy smile crept up the corners of his lips, "Well, Rhiannon, that answer would have to be that I'm looking for my muse."

"Haven't found her yet, have you?"

He ceased gazing past me and looked me dead in the eye, "I don't know if I ever will," he spoke. "But in all reality, there's not very much you have control over when you're out on the road, besides yourself. It is the epitome of unpredictability. You have no idea what your next meal will be or how you will get it. You don't know the next town you're going to roll into, what it's like, or how the people will be. Every day is a new adventure—you never know what you're going to do or what you're going to find. It's never boring, and even in the most barren and monotonous landscapes you have ample time to wander around the inside of your own mind."

"Sounds exhilarating and a little scary," I admitted.

Al shook his head, "The whole modality of your thinking is altered. Uncertainty, entropy, perpetual motion—they're no longer feared, in fact, they become sacred. Once you've been on the road for some time, it becomes real hard to settle down again. There's a whole cast of characters for whom these conditions make up their entire day to day lives: showmen, musicians, migrant workers, starving artists, career criminals, truck drivers, juvenile delinquents, evangelists, freedom seekers, adrenaline junkies…they blow like tumbleweeds along the interstates, pass in and out of cities, and gather around rail-yards—and they've all got the same look in their eye."

"I guess if the longest you've ever traveled for is a day to get to your destination then there's no way of knowing what that feels like," I assumed.

"No-o-o way," Al emphasized. "Every veteran traveler seems to have the same crop of stories, and they all have the same kind of face as well—one that's humbled and creased by weather and age, no matter how old they are; it's an expression you begin to wear after you've lived long enough beyond the edge. You aren't likely to find any cocky drifters—those that are have a tendency not to last very long. If you're going to survive out on the road, you've got to possess a certain degree of field expedience, and you only know you've met a true wanderer once it becomes obvious that they follow the same unspoken code as you do. The first rule of the road is that there are no rules. The second is to be nice—the Golden Rule, carried out in a very Hammurabian sort of way. There's this whole shared philosophy of the road, a collective realization that mental and physical stillness can be paralleled; that physical permanence can result in mental stagnation—kind of like a reverse psychosomatic—and that there is nothing to be learned from complacency. All these people out there on the road...every one of them is driven by some internal motivation—they're either looking for something or running from it. The longer you're out there for, the sooner you begin to realize that the roads to heaven and hell are the same, it all depends on which direction you are traveling in..."

I remained in complete awe of Al as we sat there together on the bumper of the Trips Mobile smoking that brown Mexican 'dirt' as we called it—the best Space could do that week. Behind us, the van was packed and ready for lift-off, and like proud parents we reclined back and shared a joint like a toast off the bow in commemoration of her maiden voyage across the country. I was stoked to get out there on the road with them, to blaze a trail all our own right through the heart of America like all our predecessors before us. I couldn't wait to hear the stories and acquire some of my own to tell one day.

Our road trip started out something like this:

It was about noon by the time everybody else woke up, and when they did, they were greeted by a very small motel on wheels idling out by the curb, awaiting their occupancy. It took a remarkably brief interval of time for The Day Trippers to finalize their travel plans and get all those little last minute loose ends tied up. The period of planning, projection, and wrapping up that takes the average traveler weeks to arrange took us less than an hour. Bobby didn't even know we were leaving until fifteen minutes before we split, and the only objection he held lasted only until he was able to score enough dope for the road. In all, the most urgent issues seemed to be gathering enough semi-personal sleeping bags from around the Trips Center and filling up various jugs and canteens with water. Al and Mary orchestrated this process while Space, Billy, and I rearranged what was left of our equipment in the garage so that I could pull my car inside and shut the door.

At the last possible moment, Melinda opted out of our cross-country expedition, despite my attempts to explain to her just what she would be missing. It might have been something about the ratio of 500,000 hippies to the number of porta-johns that swayed her opinion, and instead, she bid us farewell from the front step, waving to us as we drove away, never to return quite the same again.

Almost immediately following our departure—before we'd even made it to the top of Haight Street—we were no longer The Day Trippers, but The Road Trippers. We were all psyched for this adventure. Everybody was laughing and smiling, and several joints were on their way around, courtesy of Faye, who'd been rolling. Space was behind the wheel blasting The Doors, beside him, Faye and Billy sang a duet in her language, and I sat in the back with Bobby, Mary, and Al.

In his hand, Bobby held a hairbrush as you would a walkie-talkie and was shouting into it like a commo man, imitating static "—*CKAHSHTTTT!* Heavy Metal Thunder to the Spaceman, over!"

Space brought the Trips Mobile to a shuddering halt at a light and grabbed an empty soda can to answer him, "Pilot to copilot! This is The Spaceman! Recon's got two pigs at twenty clicks to the north, should we lay them a trip, affirmative? Over!"

"Stand by for affirmative!" Bobby called back.

"Arrow-wielding ace Aladdin strings his bow and aims from the cockpit…"

"Negative, negative!" Bobby yelled. "One of Aladdin's rounds has struck one of Officer Obie's doughnuts right in the jelly! Abort, abort! Here they are and coming at me! *Weeeooooooweeeooooweeeooo!*"

Al's eyes glanced up over top of the dense copy of Kahlil Gibran he was reading and met Bobby's with an amused smile.

Even though the dialogue was entirely fictional, as soon as the light turned green, Space slammed the Trips Mobile into granny gear, and she leaped forward.

"*BRRRUMM BRRUM!*" he shouted with glee as we rolled across the last intersection in San Francisco and south onto the freeway.

We all laughed and shouted along with him. We were infected with a silly kind of euphoria. We did not have a care in the world, embarked upon a voyage like the Merry Pranksters before us with nothing ahead of us short of adventure.

Around the time we were passing through Pacifica, Billy turned to Space, a note of confusion in his voice, "Hey man, why didn't you take the Bay Bridge east into Oakland? We're heading south now."

"It's not a road trip unless you ride the coast highway," Space replied.

"Do we even have any maps in here?" Billy asked.

"No."

"If we don't have any maps, how are we supposed to get to New York?" I piped up this time, realizing this was something we'd all apparently forgotten while we were packing.

Al chuckled, "We have three weeks until this festival starts, that leaves us enough time to drive wherever our hearts desire. We're gonna go whichever way *feels* right. We'll get there."

Billy laughed and shook his head, and I thought humorously about how it would be three weeks from now when Woodstock was on and we were still hopelessly lost 1000 feet in the Rockies or somewhere south of Tijuana. But I wasn't worried, like Al had said, we'd get there. Besides, worry just isn't an emotion you can feel when you are flying down Highway 1 with the sun lighting up the day and hills rising up on both sides of you, eventually giving way to staggering mountains that slope down into the sea.

Down off of the cliffside, the whitecaps crashed against the face of the rock, throwing up a fine mist of sea foam into the air which lofted out over the whole landscape. Everything was open and spacious. There were no more office buildings or high-rises or Victorians; instead of a twisted jungle of alleys and paved vertical roads that climbed into the sky, the moors that surrounded us were lush and green. The two-lane highway wound and curved its way through the hills, and around each bend there was a new scene. Everything was fresh and new and unanticipated—it was incredibly beautiful.

All along the inland shoulder, the dark earth bore endless fields of fruits and vegetables: strawberries, cherries, squashes, and other assorted produce that peeked out at the dusty roads from behind their broad, green leaves. Every few miles or so we would see vans like ours or pickup trucks parked up on the shoulder selling the mornings' bounty to passersby. You've never tasted fruit so fresh in your life—straight off the vine and into your stomach. The cherries were the best of all. They were plump and round, each one was larger than a quarter, and we scarfed down several cartons.

It took us all day to drive the 80 miles from San Francisco down to Santa Cruz. This was because every 10 miles or so we would get out to admire the view or romp around the beach, and these stops were the equivalent of stepping into a time warp. A visit planned to take only a few minutes stretched into hours before we could even think about the time. After all, it was far too nice a day to stay cooped up inside the van.

We weren't the only ones who felt that way, either—there were lots of heads out and about that day, especially down near the shore. There were several dune buggies parked around each of the rest stops, their occupants 50 feet below, paddling out into the dark blue water on surfboards. At one of these such places, a small gathering had commenced at the edge of the cliff to watch. We took the frisbee down to the beach at the bottom of the cliff and tossed it around a bit and rapped with the surfers and their onlookers. They told us that they'd driven down from northern Oregon and were heading to San Diego in search of some midsummer sun, and we told them about New York and the festival that was our current fantasy. According to them, word of Woodstock had made it to Oregon, but they felt it wasn't worth it to drive 3,000 miles across the country unless Dylan or The Beatles were going to be there. They were hard up trying to score some smoke on the road, so we bartered with them—a lid of grass for a kite they had strapped to the top of one of their buggies. We got the better end of the deal, by far. The kite was about four feet across, orange in color, and had evil eye designs on either side of it, like on the wings of an owl butterfly.

A few more miles down the road at another rest stop, some dude and his bicycle caught our attention. It was a funny-looking bicycle, and he was a funny-looking man. It had big, wide tires on it like a Harley, and he had long, red sideburns and a goatee and wore nothing but a pair of cutoffs and a bandana. He told us that he too was headed east, but not for the same reason as us; rather, he was headed that way because that was the direction from which he had come. Apparently, he'd started off biking from Montana to Maine last spring, during the winter had cycled from Jackson, Florida to Reno, and after staying around Vegas these last few months, had journeyed up the coast before deciding to head back again. Al pricked his ears up at this tale. He had been the first to approach the man—I imagine he'd recognized him as a fellow traveler. I was beginning to see what Al had meant when he'd said *'they've all got the same look in their eye.'* Al and this traveler both exuded a kind of wanderlust, a kind of starry-eyed approval of everything they touched; a sheer thankfulness for the rough tread of the road beneath their wheels—a dirty, rugged reflection of life on the skids.

A little further on toward evening we rolled into Santa Cruz. We'd been coming around the side of a very large bulge of rock with nets cast down the side of it to prevent falling shale when we were greeted by a most beautiful sight. Here, the road sloped down almost even with the surf, and dozens of people were out along the beach flying kites of all shapes, colors, and sizes. Above us, sandy cliffs towered and the sun broke through the clouds, illuminating the whole scene. Considering the bounty from our most recent barter strapped to the roof, we were compelled to stop again. We stripped down to our underwear, swam in the ocean, and took turns manning the kite, which took us a hilariously long time to get aloft. A few of the other beach dwellers were clearly frequent participants of this activity because they could make their kites do all kinds of loops and dives and tricks that we attempted to copy with very little success. It was a grand afternoon, and we stayed down by the water for what I imagine was quite a few hours, until we started to get hungry. Rather than eat what we'd packed, we decided to abandon the coastal highway and search for a diner in town, electing to save the food we had for the nights to come that we'd spend under the stars, a hundred miles from any restaurant or club.

Santa Cruz was a colorful little town in which the nightlife was booming. The clubs were packed, the sidewalks were bustling, and the roads were full of cars. All kinds of people were out and about, and the head-to-straight ratio was highly desirable. We nestled the Trips Mobile alongside the curb for the night in this one hip neighborhood, the name of which escapes me. There was an Indian head shop on one corner next to a laundromat and a quiet little dive that had attracted a somewhat larger crowd than I would've expected to see in a place of its caliber. It had a cozy, friendly, groovy vibe to it, but it lacked jive, the kind of swing San Francisco dives always had: live music. So, while we were waiting for a table to open up, since we weren't starving and had nowhere to go, we went back and grabbed a few instruments from the Trips Mobile, laid an open case out upon the ground on the corner, and proceeded to play for our dinner. However, in the time it took us to make enough to pay for seven meals, we'd attracted so much business that when we finally came inside, the manager, a head himself, fed us for free in exchange for the promise that we'd hang around until closing time.

A couple days earlier, Bobby and Space had gotten real into that Jamaican reggae stuff after picking up a few albums by Johnny Nash and The Gaylads. With Billygoat playing bass, me on the drums, and Space keeping the tempo, we could really conjure up that summery, carefree island groove which is great for walking and even better for spending an evening out on the gray concrete under the neon light California-Kingston Santa Cruz sunset, conjuring Jah with heads dancing in the city street light palm tree mists.

That's all we played that first night out on the road, and the people really seemed to dig it. Before our first contract of the night had run out, the beatnik owner of a coffee shop three blocks down invited us to come jam away the midnight hour at his place. It was already past twelve by the time we got set up, and we probably played for another three or four hours after that. There were a fair amount of Jamaican kids in this part of Santa Cruz, and they didn't seem to mind our cross-genre experimentation. Really, it was a lot of fun. I had gone through a Bob Marley phase years ago when Leanne and I had sunk our feelers into *Rastaman Vibration* and hadn't let up for about a month, so I was fluent when it came to playing that island beat. Billy, on the other hand, had a much harder time with it, but once he locked in with me, we could stay in phase forever—just as long as we didn't stop. As far as the venue went, the ship-shod tables and the big oaken bar stayed hopping most of the night while our friendly neighborhood beatnik went around filling orders wearing a huge mustached grin, so I guess it could be considered a success from all sides.

A BRIEF AND BEAUTIFUL TRIP BACK

****

The next morning I was the first one awake. Initially, I was extremely disoriented. To begin with, I didn't remember going to sleep the previous night; therefore, I hadn't expected to wake up in the back of the Trips Mobile amidst a throng of blankets and bodies. Secondly, once I realized where I was, I realized I didn't have a clue where I was. I'd assumed that we were still in Santa Cruz, parked on the street or in the general vicinity of the club where we'd played, but rather, we were stopped on the side of a highway somewhere, as if somebody had started driving late last night then gotten tired and decided to turn in instead.

That morning was incredibly gray. It wasn't dark, it wasn't rainy, it wasn't even foggy—it was just gray, and the cool morning air felt like heaven wafting through the open windows. I tried my best to wriggle out of the tangled mess in the back of the Trips Mobile without stepping on any sleeping bodies, crawled over the front seat where Space was curled up, mumbling and twitching, and proceeded to exit through the driver's side door.

The highway we were on was awfully quiet; not a car nor a soul was in sight. However, it was a peaceful quiet, and I took this time to smoke a couple of cigarettes and reminisce about last night. I smiled to myself when I thought about what we must've looked like—a group of white-as-white-can-be Californians trying to play reggae. I walked around while I smoked, shuffling the gray stones beneath my feet. I even found a flat rock up ahead which I stood upon while I did some yoga exercises.

Refreshed and full of energy for the day, I couldn't stand sleeping, so after checking that we were all present and that nobody was sleeping on the roof, I got behind the wheel and started off in the direction we'd been traveling, which I assumed was east. Space had crawled off of the front seat and back into the rear of the van to get some more shuteye, but other than he, no one else had even so much as rolled over. The Trips Mobile awoke from its nightly stupor with a tremble and a cough and a tremendous backfire. Even so, with a cursory glance backward I could tell that not one of them had so much as batted an eye. The whole group of them together could've slept through World War III.

It wasn't even a half mile before I saw the first road sign, and it was then that I actually realized where it was that we were. We were about 100 miles inland, about two hours from Santa Cruz, between San Jose and Salinas, somewhere along what I now knew was Route 152. I knew exactly where we were. We were headed for Fresno.

The dull, gray morning haze still hadn't lifted once we'd crossed into city limits. Everything was quiet. It was a Sunday for sure—cars were still parked in driveways, and there was no hustle-bustle downtown as there almost certainly was at any given time on the weekdays. Once I made it into the suburbs, where I'd lived my entire life, nothing looked familiar. Many of the street names hadn't changed, but that was just about all that remained the same. I felt as if I was passing through a place completely foreign to me, and it was the strangest of feelings.

Without even realizing the name of the street upon which I'd been traveling, I came to a fork in the road at the corner of South and Emory. Ahead of me was an empty lot overgrown with trees, shrubbery, and other untamed foliage, and as I stared at it, an insane thought came to mind. It was then that it dawned on me that this was where The Joint would stand in about twenty years. A striking sense of surreal came over me, and I threw the Trips Mobile into park. If it hadn't entirely hit me by then exactly where I was in time, it sure did now! No longer did I feel like a stranger, I felt like a savant!

"Not to brag," I spoke out loud to the others as they slept, "but I can tell you the name of the paint they'll use to stain the boards of the building that'll stand in that lot in twenty years. I can tell you how many rafters will line the ceiling and how they'll look when you've had a few too many. I can tell you the order in which the members of the band Metallica will be standing in the poster that'll hang on the coed bathroom door from 1996 'til New Year's Eve 1999 when Jeff had one too many himself and missed the bowl..."

And, I thought to myself now, *no one else in this entire city, all snug in their beds, unaware of what will happen tomorrow—let alone within the next thirty years—has any kind of a clue.* Juan Pablo himself was still just a child, living in Oaxaca with his seventeen brothers and sisters. Jeff, Marty, Leanne, and Shania weren't even twinkles in their parents' eyes yet—and neither was I.

All these phenomenal, mind-blowingly absurd yet strangely true memories—or were they premonitions—bounced and sprocketed around the inside of my mind as I passed through those eerie streets. I was just another traveler with someplace else to go; just another faceless, nameless migrant with no mind to tell.

A voice close to my ear in the near silence just about sent me out the window. "Where are we?" Mary asked with a yawn as she climbed into the front seat that Space had vacated earlier.

"Jesus, Mary!" I cried, holding my heart. "Don't do that! You scared the hell out of me!"

"Sorry," she said, her big, blue eyes apologetic. "I thought you might like some company, it's so boring driving alone."

I smiled, she was so sincere; it was impossible to be annoyed at her for any more than a couple seconds.

"So, where are we, again?" she repeated her unanswered question from earlier.

"Fresno," I told her, "my old hometown." As I said this, with a start, I realized that I'd been driving down Tulare Avenue and made a hairpin turn down 7th Street—almost taking out the stop sign in the process—before coasting to a halt right in front of my house.

Her big eyes grew even larger once I stopped, "You used to live here?" she inferred.

I nodded. The house where I'd spent the first eighteen years of my life looked almost exactly the same, except that it looked brand new, as if it had just been built.

"Your folks have got some nice cars," Mary commented, indicating the '64 Pontiac GTO parked next to the '67 Shelby Cobra and the Harley in the driveway. If there had been any prior doubt that my mother hadn't moved in yet, this was confirmation enough and then some. Two muscle cars and a motorcycle—definitely not the go-to vehicles of choice for a conservative, middle-class Christian family.

If she'd known that these people lived here before us, she probably wouldn't have bought the house, I thought to myself with a laugh. I turned away and continued on down the street; there was no more I needed to see there.

"That's my best friend Marty's house," I told her, pointing across the way as we passed by.

Mary became very excited at this, "Do you think he's home?" she asked me. "Do you think he wants to come to Woodstock with us?"

I chuckled at this, "No," I replied. "No, I don't think so."

"Oh…" she answered, and then she got real quiet. "What you told us about being—you know—from the future… Were you…serious?"

I didn't look at her; instead, I kept my eyes fixed on the road and nodded, "Completely."

"How do you think, I mean, why…" she struggled with the words.

I shrugged, "I haven't the foggiest. Other than the fact that there's clearly something I'm supposed to be doing, learning, seeing…there's got to be a reason, but I don't know what it is. That's all I've been able to sort out in over two months. I try not to pay it too much mind."

Her jaw kind of hung open like she wanted to say more, but she never did; and as I downshifted and continued on along the road, she glanced back out the rearview mirror at the home that I wouldn't see again for another thirty years.

After some time, once we'd crossed out of Fresno and started heading south on Route 99, Mary Jane and I got to rapping about Bobby.

"So," I'd asked after several miles of silence, "is all that shit Bobby says for real?"

Mary laughed out loud, "Some of it."

I cracked a smile.

"Bobby is a narcissist," she continued. "He craves attention; actually, he needs it—just as much if not more than he needs his dope—and he's a megalomaniac with an ego the size of downtown San Francisco. But he's got such a naturally crazy and outrageous life that he thinks, well, what is it to add a few more thrills? Half the time he can't even tell if what he remembers is real or fabricated anyway! So what if he tells a couple people he was backstage at Monterey or that he got into a duel with a couple of Bandidos and fought them off bare-handed? Who's going to give a shit in a day or two? Who'll even remember? It's all in good fun."

I cringed a little bit. He wasn't even two feet away behind the seat, and asleep or not, I sure wasn't brazen enough to talk that loud. "Shhh, Mar! What if he hears?"

When she answered me, she did so even louder, "Ah Bobby and I've been best friends since like third grade. There's nothing I can say to surprise him, I've said everything there is to say. We've been through everything together; our families used to be friends and all. And, he was my first."

That honestly surprised me, "Really?" I asked, turning my eyes from the road to look at her as she nodded.

"And I was his."

"I never sensed anything like that between you and Bobby at all."

Mary smiled, "There never was. It was a real long time ago. We're just really, really good friends."

A BRIEF AND BEAUTIFUL TRIP BACK

As far as reactions to the nature of Bobby and I's relationship went, the typical jealousy, animosity, gossip, and manipulation were not present. Those hang-ups that almost always go along with any physical or romantic attachment simply did not exist there, not just with The Day Trippers, but at all. Couples were fluid, and sex was as routine as sleeping or bathing or eating. For the most part, there was no such thing as exclusive relationships, and everybody knew more than they ever wanted or needed to know about everybody else's physiology and sexual preferences. Billy and Faye were really the only two I knew who confined themselves to any sort of monogamy. There was no status, no attempt to define what our relationship was, no taking bets on how long it would last—and that's what made it so good. In fact, they were so permissive that if Bobby and I wanted to make it under a blanket on the couch in the Trips Center while Faye sat across from us eating a bag of popcorn and listening to the radio, it was all copasetic. That was just how it was; and the same went for the Trips Mobile, except for sometimes, in such close quarters, it would get a little hot and sweaty, and somebody would politely ask us to turn down the enthusiasm and crack a window, as they did that Sunday afternoon.

It was almost as if they had no reaction at all except for encouragement; in fact, after Bobby and I's physical relationship changed, a whole new thread of harmony developed in our music—a kind of sensual dialogue between the keeper of the rhythm and the keeper of the beat. Music seemed to be, in the strangest way, a kind of reflection of what was going on at that time in our lives. The energy that we put in to create it was the same energy that was put out, only transformed. If good vibes were going in, it all jelled; we played in sync, the house reaction was sweet, and everybody had a groovy time. If not, there was something that needed adjustment, and normally whatever it was worked itself out. There were very few things on the Haight out of sync at that time.

Amongst the plethora of things I learned from The Day Trippers, one of the most important notions I've retained is to '*let your freak out*': the idea that you cannot expect to be accepted as you are if you don't first reveal who you really are. This seemed to be one of the more elementary principles of the Movement, and it threaded itself through all aspects of our lifestyle and our dealings with one another. It was an oasis, life without the games. For me, it was bliss. This freedom, this openness of communication, was something that I'd never experienced before in my life. Trying to have a fruitful discussion with Meredith was like trying to engage in an intellectually stimulating conversation with a rock, and talking with George was like talking with the Oracle of Delphi after a night of sake-bombs. Of course with The Descendants communication was easier; however, it was nothing like what we Day Trippers had. That kind of honesty doesn't just exist anywhere; there is a certain degree of sacrifice that must first be present, and one of the grandest manifestations of that sacrifice may have easily been personal space. It's real hard to lie to somebody or get offended by them when they know all there is to know about you and vice-versa. When you're forced to live within inches of one another for extended periods of time, you begin to become immune to one another's patterns of living. This was by far the most evident with Bobby.

Sometime around the middle of the afternoon, not too long after Mary and I'd done a Chinese fire drill at Bakersfield, Bobby himself hopped into the front seat with us.

"G'mornin'," he rasped in a voice that suggested he'd just woken up.

"Well, look who's up in time to greet the sun!" Mary replied sarcastically, initiating the first line of their daily banter.

"Whoever was there that woke up early to travel? —Besides my crazy brother, of course. After four years a junkie, you'd think I'd be immune to this sort of boredom! Don't tell me we're still in California!"

"Can't you tell from all the sunshine?" Mary joked, indicating the blanket of gray clouds that still loomed, the sun just beginning to break through around the edges.

"Man!" Bobby exclaimed, lighting up a cigarette. "Anybody want one?" he mumbled.

"I'll have one," I said.

He handed me his, then lit up another before reaching into the top pocket of his work shirt and pulling out an eyeglass case, "Time to feed the monkey."

I didn't really know what he was talking about when he said it, so I watched him with piqued interest as he opened up the eyeglass case and sifted through its contents, ultimately focusing his attention on a small triangular package which he unfolded to reveal a muddy little glob of...something. At first, I thought it was opium, and while I wasn't entirely wrong, as a testament to the last of my enduring naivety, I'll admit that I didn't realize what he intended on doing with it until he started tying up his arm with his bandana.

242

As the only child of a God-fearing, drug-hating mother, it would be entirely redundant to try to explain the level of alarm the word 'heroin' invoked. Brought up in the manner I had been, as a child, I'd assumed that everything evil, satanic, and temptatious had heroin at its roots. Since then, my convictions had lessened ever so slightly regarding the drug and its properties, but danger and heroin were still synonymous in my eyes. Now, I knew that Bobby was a banger. I'd heard his stories, I'd seen him nod—hell, I'd even smoked opium with him! But never had I ever seen him—or anyone else for that matter—inject themselves full of the drug—until now.

I tried not to let on just how much my curiosity was eating at me as my eyes remained glued to his hands no matter how strong that uncomfortable tug in my stomach became. I watched as he pushed that lump of sticky, brown gunk onto a spoon, brown and burnt from frequent use, and heated it from underneath with a Zippo—and how foul that smelled! After he was finished, he drew the sickly liquid into a syringe and flicked it twice. My eyes moved to his arm, and there I noticed something I hadn't formerly: dark lines and bruises extending vertically in both directions out from his elbow and several bloody circles the size of pencil points where the needle had been retracted. Calmly and methodically, he traced his swollen veins with his fingertip more times than it seemed he needed to, as if there was something palliative in the process that I did not understand. His hands worked quickly and expertly; this was a process he'd repeated hundreds, maybe thousands of times. He didn't talk, he didn't look around; instead, he kept his eyes down and his fingers moving rapidly, poking and prodding his forearm until he located a vein that satisfied him. Once he did, he slid the needle in and pulled back on the plunger, drawing fresh, red blood back up into the syringe. Then, with a strange quarter-smile on his face, he pressed down on the bulb, forcing the whole vile concoction into his body.

"Whoo," he breathed, extracting the needle and leaning back on the seat. His eyes were closed, his arm was still fully extended, and his works were scattered upon his lap, "good shit." After a few moments, he lit another cigarette.

My stomach churned. The sight of blood or needles had never before caused me to be squeamish, but there was something about the whole procedure that just struck me as so unseemly when considered alongside everything else. But even this I would learn to accept, although no matter how many times I saw him do it, it still made me uneasy. However, I apparently was the only one, because nobody else said anything about it except for Mary, who'd been glancing over at him as she drove.

"How much of our bread are you shooting these days?" she asked him. The way she spoke made it sound like this sort of nonchalant question, like she'd asked him what baseball team he was rooting for in this year's World Series. There was nothing even the slightest bit accusatory in her tone whatsoever.

"I've been doing a dime a day," he replied, sniffing and blinking his eyes open slowly as he began to clean up his works and return the glasses case to his breast pocket.

"A dime a day keeps the doctor away, eh?" Space joked, clapping him on the back from behind where he sat on the trunk.

"That's all?" Mary replied, sounding quite surprised. "What's this, Mr. Heavy Metal is cutting back all of a sudden?"

"I've been smoking opium, my tolerance is down. I don't want to OD."

"Hey, well, good for you man! Why don't you kick that shit altogether, huh?" Space replied, and then before Bobby had the chance to answer, he asked, "Do you guys want Chips Ahoy?"

"I love you, man," Bobby grinned, taking a handful from the blue box.

That was another thing, the food we ate back in the day was nothing like what I'd been used to eating my whole life. Everything: Chips Ahoy, Twinkies, Yodels, Fritos, Klondike Bars, Seal-Test Ice Cream—it was all just so good. Nothing was sugar-free, low-calorie, reduced-fat, whole wheat or skim. I was in the middle of an unpasteurized, white bread, high-sugar, saturated fat heaven—and I was loving every bite of it! Without Melinda to cook for us, we were stuck eating chips and cookies, candy bars and Campbell's soup heated up over the Sterno can—and I was probably the only one of us who was relishing in it. Meredith never kept any of that stuff in the house, not even when I was a kid, and by the time the nineties rolled around, the vast majority of the unhealthy ingredients in those foods had been replaced by chemical additives that ruined the taste and were probably more harmful than the sugar and fat that had been taken out. I remember George complaining about it all the time. Mostly, I just chalked it up to aging taste buds—but he was right! In fact, the quality of most things was better in the sixties—cars rode for longer, clothes were more durable, food tasted richer—even the drugs were better!

—Like the grass we smoked that day as we left civilization behind at Bakersfield and headed out into the desert. For a couple hundred miles, all there was along that awesome lonely highway were tractor trailers truckin' down from Oregon across the Mojave in high gear. There were no more mountains, no more bay fog, and everything was open and spacious—even the air felt lighter, like it too had more room to spread out. The vibrations that had been about the Trips Mobile this morning had dissipated. Bobby slept in the front seat most of the ride that afternoon, but once his fix wore off, he was up with the rest of us, bullshitting and jamming, chain-smoking and taking turns fiddling with the radio dial. Al was just plain cracked with excitement. His eyes were wild, and he was quoting *On the Road*, singing to accompany our butchered rendition of *Suite: Judy Blue Eyes* played by Bobby and Space on the mandolin and acoustic guitar and me on that little Indian water drum.

"*Home in Missoula, home in Truckee, home in Opelousas, ain't no home for me! Home in ol' Medora, home in Wounded Knee, home in Ogallala, home I'll never be!*" he sang, making up new words where the quote left off. "Home in San Francisco, home in Tijuana, home on Route 5-8, what a world to see!"

"Al! Hey, Al!" Mary called from up front, breaking up our jam session as we approached a jumble of overpasses and on-ramps. "Where does Route 15 take you? I can take either Route 15 or 66."

"Route 15?"

"Yeah!"

"If I'm not mistaken, Route 15 will take you up to Vegas."

"What about 66?"

"66 takes you east, first into Albuquerque then into Tulsa."

"We're on 15 now…you guys wanna go to Vegas?"

A whole chorus of replies erupted from all over the Trips Mobile, "Yes!" being the discernible answer.

So, we continued on along Route 15, where Al's old Route 5-8, upon coming to an end, had dumped us and all the rest of the rush hour traffic like a river tributary. On through Barstow we drove, up into the desert hills where sparse brown vegetation the same color as the sand dotted the landscape, and mounds that resembled giant anthills rose up out of the ground. We shook the last of the commuters at city limits, and then the road was quiet again; it was just us and the truckers and perhaps another van or two. Every so often, a cluster of billboards or some isolated desert flat would spring up, or maybe a drive-in or a spattering of motorhomes, but that was all. Several roads cross-cut the highway, stretching infinitely away into nothingness in both

245

directions, coming out of the clear blue and likewise leading nowhere. As the sun began to set, out there in the distance—it could've been one mile from us or it could've been ten—a freight train passed in front of the horizon, slicing that crimson desert sunset through its bulging center, causing it to bleed out mirages, heat waves, and solar radiation that washed out over the parched land and soaked into the sun-cracks as the fine-ground dust kicked up in hazy clouds and burst into invisible flames in the phantasmal atmosphere—burning itself out for the night.

Just as darkness began to fall over the desert, at a pass through some mountains, our headlights fell upon a road sign, green and curved like all the rest that proclaimed: *50 miles to Las Vegas*. Now, I'd read *Fear and Loathing* and I'd seen the movie when it came out in '98, and I'll tell you, I wasn't prepared for that kind of debauchery and excess. And apparently, neither was anyone else.

We rolled into Vegas just under the cover of darkness with Mary still at the wheel. We'd navigated our way down from the hills and the highway into the city—a palm-tree, high-rise, neon-fluorescent oasis in the middle of endless desert. The sights and sounds and smells of corporate refinement brought life to my senses, fatigued and atrophied from the heat and the road. Hundreds of cars seemed to materialize out of nowhere, blowing their horns and pumping out lungfuls of exhaust that stung my eyes—it's unbelievable, really, how fast you can forget the city. Once more, the roads were filled with traffic signals, flashing lights, and crosswalks—over which pedestrians stumbled drunk and crass as tourists descended upon this freaking crazed town like hawks.

"Man, this place is really hopping, you sure you don't want to switch?" Space asked Mary, his hands trembling; he'd been itching to move for at least the last hour.

"When I was fifteen, my color blind uncle taught me how to drive in a twenty-year-old parish truck on Filbert Street in the middle of rush hour. No kind of city driving is too hectic for me!" she replied, determined. But nonetheless, at the next traffic light, Space jumped over the seat, and Mary rejoined the rest of us in the back as he took us the rest of the way into the city.

We were in search of work, somewhere to land a gig for the night, and we found ourselves hard-up looking for it. Obviously, none of those highfalutin places on the Strip wanted a jam band like us, so we went crawling around North Vegas for a while. We stopped in at a couple divey-looking places and Space went inside to rap to the managers, but nobody really seemed to be with it too much in these parts and it was a bad scene, so we carried on. We'd rather not play at all than play for a handful of tramps and inebriates—those are bad vibrations.

We drove straight through that night, or at least I think we did. I recall waking up at one point while we were bumping along down some unpaved road, not particularly fast. I'd been sleeping in the back, and as far as I could tell, there were two other bodies in the throes with me: Bobby, who was tucked into my sleeping bag and beside him, somebody else who I assumed was Space from the periodic murmuring and jerking about; I couldn't tell if he was asleep or not. When I lifted my head, I could see the dim outline of Al's body in the darkness before me. He was hunkered down, sitting with his back against the hatch. He had all his long limbs tucked in as close as he could, fast asleep, and strangely comfortable from the look of him. From up front, I could hear the low sound of Faye's voice, hushed against the protestant squeaking of the springs and Bobby's snores. She was speaking to the driver, who from the speed and the baritone replies I assumed was Billy. "In all men's dreams, God's breath..." I heard her tell him, followed by another sentence in her own language. As I drifted back to sleep, I watched the moon—now just a sliver—as it ran alongside us outside the window in the dark, obsidian night.

Somehow, the next morning, we ended up finding ourselves back on Route 66. If I remember correctly, Billy was still driving. The Arizona sky was blue and endless and so was the road. We were in for another day of dry desert scrub, Mexican grass, and backseat coffee boiled in a percolator over the Sterno can. Space had picked up a deck of playing cards in Vegas, and I remember we managed to entertain ourselves with those for most of the trip. The only game all of us knew was war, and after several hours of that, Bobby taught us poker and hearts. We placed our bets using cigarettes and joints, and by nightfall, all our winnings had gone up in smoke.

The Sonoran desert is majorly featureless, comprised mostly of rolling hills and flat, uninterrupted ground. We drove most of the day before we saw trees again. Before that, all there was were telephone poles—the almighty outcrop of modern-day civilization—running right along the very edge of inhabitability and popping up every three hundred feet or so, bearing their burden through the desert. They were laid out in sandy valleys and nestled in the shadows of mountains or flat-top buttes that looked like a giant had been playing hop-scotch across them.

Route 66 took us straight through the desert, and then, just when we thought we'd never climb another mountain again, it took us higher. Jagged boulders and layers of compressed sediment rose up out of the shoulders and jutted out in all directions, but mainly up. They rose hundreds of feet above us, and when we gazed upward, it appeared that the sun was resting atop their peaks, casting down its brilliant golden luminesce from this rocky throne.

I remember stopping for lunch on top of one of these cliffs by way of a service road. We ate tomato sandwiches and pickles and cut into two enormous watermelons. We ate them all the way down to the rind and then proceeded to put the hollowed-out halves on our heads and run around. It was a light-hearted, silly kind of day filled with antics of various sorts.

Back in the van as Billy slept and Bobby drove, the rest of us tried very unsuccessfully to make a bong out of the leftover watermelon as Space orated a travel monologue, "If you look out the window to your left, you'll see the noonday sun at an estimated distance of ninety-three million miles. If you look to your right, under ordinary psychotropic conditions, you should be seeing an eclectic combination of prickly pines and red rocks. If you care to peer out the front windshield, you'll be able to see the chemtrails, weather-altering chemicals sprayed into the atmosphere, courtesy of your friendly United States government. If you're feeling carsick, keep your eyes on the horizon and a joint in your hand, boys, it's a rough ride out here on the long road to anywhere."

Once it seemed that the mountains would never end, the prairies began. Cattle dotted the landscape all along the side of the road, and watering holes began to emerge at the bottoms of the valleys. However, the road ran on, and besides the telephone poles, there was no indication that anyone other than us had passed this way in years. Old Route 66 had gone from a four-lane byway to a simple two-lane stretch without a shoulder and complete with hairpin turns. The pavement was so terribly worn that even at a relatively slow speed, the Trips Mobile shuddered so much that we had to postpone our poker game indefinitely, seeing as how the suits were vibrating right off the cards.

"Did you know that Route 66 was the first fully paved highway in the U.S?" Al shouted to inform us above the rattling.

"...And they haven't been back since!" Mary added.

"Actually, they're planning on bypassing this whole highway with interstate," he continued. "They're calling it Route 40."

"It's about damn time!" Bobby grumbled. "My ass hurts!"

"It's really a very melancholy thing," Al went on. "This highway was the mainline of America all through the Depression. Thousands of Okies and Arkies alike traveled through here—whole families, truckers, itinerates—the whole lot of 'em. It's so rich in history, and people are going to forget it. I myself have been up and down this road several times in my travels, and I often think of all those who have come through here before me. Once this road is gone, so will those stories be."

"That is sad," Mary agreed, "and how quickly people like to forget…"

"It's not always so," I spoke up, suddenly remembering a common feature of those diners we so often frequented back in Fresno: a black and white road sign bearing the name Route 66 nailed to the walls. "You've got to walk through the past to get to the future. There's always somebody that'll remember…"

Al and Mary met my eyes, and I soundlessly shared with them this vision of tomorrow with a smile on my lips.

A few hundred miles later, old Route 66 took us through Flagstaff. In search of gasoline and bathrooms with running water, we disembarked from the highway and found ourselves amid the throngs of city traffic once again. Once our needs were met, we took to exploring. We took a spin through downtown, where the nine to fivers were leaving their offices for the day and the bright neon signs hanging above the saloons were flickering on for the night. Everything was weathered brick and concrete archways, and the hotel Monte Vista stood on the corner.

As we crossed out of that town, we passed by a school building, outside of which teenage students were lining up. This was either some sort of afternoon summer school or a camp function, but either way it sparked… vibrations…inside the Trips Mobile.

Billy began this particular rant by making a loud and unpleasant sound at the back of his throat and a hocking a loogie out the window. "Man," he exclaimed, "if there's one thing I could never stand, it was school."

"Yeah," the rest of us agreed.

"*Especially* high school," Bobby added.

"Oh hell yeah!" Mary rolled her eyes with a nostalgic laugh. "All those stiffs in their starched blazers and pleated skirts! Then there was you, me, and Jules! Man, we stuck out like sore thumbs with our denim and t-shirts! There wasn't a day that went by that we didn't get in trouble."

"…sometimes for no other reason than showing up!" Bobby added.

"I know that," Space chimed in.

"Remember?" Bobby marveled. "We'd cut class and get smoked up under the stands, then teeter into the cafeteria and scarf down all that rancid crap they'd serve us—"

"—on those hard plastic trays!" Mary finished. "The same kind they give you in prison!"

"I was a practical joker," Space explained, "the class clown. There was always somebody finding yesterday's vanilla pudding in their desk or super glue on all their pencils! I had my own special seat in the principal's office!"

"You were one of those kids that ate paste, weren't you?" Mary asked him humorously.

"How'd you know?" he laughed.

"Lots of phonies in high school," I added, "*too* many."

"Ugh!" Bobby exclaimed empathetically, "that was the worst part! It was just a whole bunch of squares trying to act cool by talking about how they smoked Luckys and stole their fathers' beer on weekends, and I'd have two caps in my pocket, shooting up in the bathroom in-between classes! I didn't do that for very long though, I signed myself out of school and started gigging full-time junior year. I couldn't take the mentality—all those straight kids, Republicans and Conservatives, all lining up to shake their heads at me and tell me their numbskull opinions about this or that. Fuck that!"

"I couldn't take the structure," Al added, "that same old monotony day after day. I liked learning, but learning you can get anywhere— and many times you can learn far more just from living than the kind of education you get in school."

"I didn't mind the lectures, but I didn't do jack shit when it came right down to it," I said. "To be honest, I'm really not quite sure how any of us graduated. I hated school, but I commend them for trying to teach me something."

"That's just what they want you to think!" Billy was the only one of us who was not lightheartedly reminiscing. Instead, he wore a scowl on his face, and his eyebrows were knit together angrily. Obviously, this was something he felt very strongly about. "School is the highest form of social control. It's existential babysitting! They only teach you what they want you to know; they interpret history to fit their doctrines and cherry-pick literature to memorize—it's nothing short of waking hypnopaedia! They brainwash you, and what a clever way to do it! They make it mandatory to send all those young, fresh, creative minds into the meat grinder, then they dull them with tedium and repetition, narrow those wide-open perspectives, teach intolerance and bigotry, and perpetuate ignorance throughout each generation! School isn't about expanding your mind at all—it's about them figuring out how straight they can make you can see…"

"He has a point, you know," Al admitted. "Our education system is fundamentally flawed. In fact, it's practically backward! From the jump, schools present education in such an inflexible and aggressive manner that over time the very act of learning becomes abhorred and negated—therefore making mindless mass-media entertainment all the more appealing. After all, what's better than *Looney Tunes* after a long day of multiplication tables and calligraphy?"

We all silently considered his words for a moment, but it wasn't long before Mary and Bobby's reminiscences faded back into the conversation.

"Man, Bobby, do you remember learning cursive in Mrs. Connolly's class?"

"Sure I do! How could I ever forget those chalkboard slates!"

"Remember when you got a week's detention for writing obscene messages to Betty Carlisle on one of them?"

"Oh, glorious days they were!"

"You were always a flirt!"

"Remember when Jules got busted for lifting the chalk?"

"—and the teacher made him empty his pockets at the door every day?!"

"Remember that Halloween dance when we spliced another channel into the back of the speaker panel and went up on top of the school with a microphone and they *never found us?*!"

"That was just righteous, righteous!"

The two of them were in stitches. Even Billy had to smile listening to them. I leaned up against the wheel well and stared out the window at the passing landscape as I thought back on my own memories of school.

Memory—and life itself—is not dissimilar to a road trip. You can only see the scenery once, as it passes you. You can look ahead of you and get a glimpse of what's on the horizon, but in no time at all, it is already past you and out of view in your hindsight. Of course, you can turn around and see it again; you can even stay awhile and examine it, but even so, it will never be the same as it was the first time you experienced it, and eventually you will have to pick up and go again, and it will indefinitely and eternally be a part of your past. The same exists in terms of the future. You can predict what lies ahead, check a map, or call to mind stories that have been told, but you can only be certain of the form the future will take when it precedes the horizon, and even then, in the time it takes for you to move from here to there, it could change.

A BRIEF AND BEAUTIFUL TRIP BACK

****

We stopped maybe twenty miles or so outside of Flagstaff for the night. Civilization had once more receded into the distance, and now even the telephone poles were far off. It seemed like we were headed back out into the middle of nowhere, and after several hours of ceaseless motion, the decision to stop for the night was unanimous. We pulled off the highway and started heading out across the sand. We drove for another thousand feet or so until we were far enough out that we wouldn't be visible from the road by night in case the Man or some imbalanced psychopath was out crawling around. There weren't very many of either kind in these parts, but you know that old adage, *'Better safe than busted!'*

According to the signs leading up to this place and Al's best assessment, we were right on the edge of the Painted Desert, some of the emptiest and most beautiful space in America. We dragged the sleeping bags out from the back, unrolled them on the far side of the van, and lit up some joints and the Sterno. We had a couple of cans of beans and the rest of what was left of that loaf of bread, and we all sat around and jammed a bit while we ate. We had the radio playing in the Trips Mobile, but most of the FM stations out past Nevada were nothing but static, and the AM stations were playing mostly country ballads; by eight o'clock, it was almost insufferable. Bobby managed to find this one groovy station that was playing some old bop and a couple of hits from *Sinatra at the Sands*, but even that started to break up after sundown. But while the reception was good, it was real groovy and beautiful. Space had acquired a box of Cuban cigars from our stopover in Santa Cruz, and we all sat around passing a couple of them between us and listening. At one point in the evening, Bobby got up, adjusted his bandana, and began crooning into an empty can of beans:

"Angel Eyes, that old devil sent, they glow unbearably bright…"

He leaned down and extended a hand to me, so I stood up and he spun me around and we danced, shuffling around in the fine desert silt that kicked up in clouds around our feet. I was so taken by this spontaneous display of romanticism from Bobby. It was so demonstrative and forthcoming that it was almost uncharacteristic, but I guess that's what Sinatra will do to a guy. The night itself was simply enchanting. It infected you—the smell of that clean air, the vibrancy of the sunset, it got into you, into your lungs and under your skin and it did something to you—and that was all before the stars came out.

There are myths and mysteries inherent in the desert; stories petrified by the sun and frozen in time. When I looked around me, vast tracts of flat, brown land stretched in all directions, and as far as I could see, way, way out there in the distance where the horizon should have been, great pillars of mountain rose up. Darkness came quickly in those places; it approached like a solid black sheet that rolled over the land, and pretty soon, all traces of terrestrial light were gone. There were no streetlights, no cars—even the moon was on hiatus. But those stars…oh, they were just breathtaking! The sky looked like God had taken a handful of glitter and scattered it across the heavens. There were hundreds and thousands of stars—and those were just the ones you could count! Behind them, there were billions more, visible only as a golden mist. There were no clouds, and the rich blackness of space leached right on out into the earthen sky uninhibited.

This was the first time in my life that I could see the constellations. At first, all they looked like was a senseless jumble of stars, but out of that spattering, Al and Faye named them, picking them out one by one and defining them, providing the rest of us with a roadmap to the cosmos. I could see Aquila and Ursa Major and Pisces, a dim V just below the great square of Pegasus. While I laid there on my back in the desert sand under the stars with my friends, smoking, laughing, and telling stories—all while gazing in wide-eyed enchantment at the stellar wonder of creation—I began to think about something I hadn't thought about in a long time. It was a memory from a lost day many moons ago, during which I experienced a splitting headache, a conversation with Marty, and a song… As you can imagine, I smiled long into the night. Man, how I smiled.

The next morning, we picked up and shoved off around noontime. We were real hungry, so at the next town we came to, we stopped at a diner. We gorged ourselves on about three dozen pancakes between us and a carton or more of eggs. The waitress loved us, but I could tell from some of the looks that we got from the other patrons that our presence wasn't exactly welcome there. I can't say I really blame them; we had been out on the road for a couple of days now, baking under that hot desert sun, and we certainly looked the part. As gross as it may sound, it might have been the way we smelled more so than how we looked that influenced them. After all, there isn't exactly a superfluous supply of running water when you're barreling through the desert in a nine-passenger van.

Upon leaving that diner with full bellies and freshly lit cigarettes, we came across a young Indian kid hoofing it along the shoulder. He was moving at a pretty good pace, but he couldn't keep it up all day, not in that heat. So, we pulled up alongside him, and Space asked if he needed a ride:

"Hey man, where you headed?"

The man lifted up his broad, brown face at us and squinted in the bright sunlight. He answered tentatively yet matter-of-factly, as if he expected us to drive off if he told us his desired destination, "I'm trying to get to Paraje along this route here. I don't know how far it is, maybe 200 miles or so."

"Hop in, we'll take you the rest of the way."

His dark eyes lit up and opened wide as Billy brought the Trips Mobile to a halt and Mary reached over and flung open the side door. He climbed in immediately, many thanks pouring out from between his lips. He was about our age, and while he dressed like us, he couldn't have looked more native. He had long, thick, black hair like Al and carried nothing but a satchel with him on his several hundred mile journey.

He looked around the van, scanning our faces, "You all just saved me five days of walking. I expected to be out on this road for a week, I—" When his eyes met Al's he stopped and studied his face intently. "I—I know you," he said. "We crossed paths many moons ago in Rio Rancho, you're that poet...

I stay up late nights, sometimes

And wonder about people and places and things and what it means to be free;

I talk to the planets and the stars, and sometimes they answer me back..."

Al, who had been gazing back at him with a puzzled look and furrowed brow, suddenly broke his trance and picked up where the Indian had left off:

"...And speak to me of many things:

objectivity, for instance, and the nature of God."

With an elated smile, the Indian completed the recitation:

"And it was so soon I found myself

that I couldn't help but go looking yet again."

Al chuckled and clapped his hands together, "That was excellent. Now I recall you. How goes it? The road is treating you well, I hope."

The Indian answered him. He spoke very softly and pleasantly and told us many stories as we rode along; stories of the places from whence he had come and to where he was going. He and Al talked about poetry and recounted a night spent in harmony with nature, a night spent in requiem.

The hours passed quickly on the road that day, and before I knew it, we were passing through Paraje.

"This is it," Billy called from up front, "the town of Paraje."

It was indeed the town of Paraje—as the signs confirmed—but from the road, the land surrounding us looked little like a town. An enormous mass of rock loomed before us, and the cliffs kept their continuous perimeter all around us in the distance. Wooden and pueblo buildings were nestled out there amongst the rocks and the brush, but only a few with brightly colored roofs or siding stood apart from the ground, and even those were dwarfed by the landscape. It looked like a town for dolls.

"Ah, so it is," the Indian sighed, his gaze softening lovingly in response to the familiar territory.

"Where do you want me to take you to?" Billy asked. "I'll bring you right to your front door, hell, I'll bring you right into your living room if you don't mind a draft."

The Indian smiled, amused, "Well actually, if you don't mind stopping for the night, I would very much like to repay you for your kindness. You are all, as you say, *beautiful people*. Truly you are, and there is a very special place not far from here that I would like to take you to."

"Alright," Billy replied, "I can dig it. How about you, gang?"

We all offered our own enthusiastic replies, and so it was settled. The Indian became our navigator, and we traveled due south, away from our original destination and further and further into the Acoma desert. As we bumped along, he spoke no more of the place that lay ahead. Instead, he pulled out a small tin box from the inner pocket of his jacket and opened it up to show us the contents. Inside, wrapped in brown paper napkins were about two dozen or so round, green, fuzzy balls—peyote buttons.

"These are fresh," he explained. "A friend of mine picked them two nights ago in Chihuahua. It would please me greatly if some of you partook in this experience along with me tonight. Unfortunately, I only have enough for about five of us. Aladdin, I would like it if you were one of the five."

Al nodded in agreement, "Yes, I will take some."

Faye, who like the rest of us had been listening intently to him this

256

whole time, reached forward and gently tapped on the tin box and then pointed to her mouth.

Billy chuckled, he'd switched with Space at Paraje and was now sitting in the back with the rest of us, "I guess m'lady and I will be joining you tonight."

"I'd like to as well," Mary spoke up, and the Indian nodded.

"What about you, Bobby?" Space joked; I could see him grinning in the rearview mirror.

"Oh, hell no! You were there that one time we ate that stuff with those guys from El Paso. Shit's crazy, man, mad intense! Too heavy, much too heavy."

"For you, maybe," Mary replied. "The rest of us were just fine."

"You didn't see what I saw," Bobby insisted.

"You're bound to have a bad trip at least once," Al said. "That's just the nature of these things, especially when you over-do it," he added, alluding to something Bobby had failed to mention.

Bobby went back to smoking his cigarette and Mary turned to me, "Have you ever had peyote, Rhiannon?"

"No," I answered, "I haven't."

Mary's eyes widened, "You should take my share then. I've done it before, it's a life-changing experience."

"Are you sure?" I asked her.

"By all means."

I was able to guess the place the Indian was taking us to as soon as it came into view. Even from several miles out, I could see the flat-top mesa as it rose up out of the desert floor. From far off, it looked like the world's biggest tree stump. As we drew nearer and finally reached it, it appeared increasingly strange. It was a lone and solitary rocky outcrop, the only thing on the horizon in any direction and perfectly formed—as if some alien race or God himself had put it there right there in the center of the endless desert just for us. And not only that, the yellow sun—huge and bright in the cloudless sky—hung directly above it, like all forces had aligned for our arrival. Space pulled off to the side of the road and we all climbed out and just stood there and stared at it for a minute.

I was immediately overcome by reverence for this thing—for its ancientness, its natural beauty, and the supernatural energy that surrounded it and crackled in the air like electricity. The structure itself was only about five hundred feet from the road, and led by the Indian, we all walked toward it. He approached the red stone wall first, and once he reached it, he turned and asked Billy for a cigarette. He stood still for a moment and unwrapped the tobacco from the paper before scattering it around the base of the rock. We all watched him with piqued interest as he returned the paper to his pocket and then from the same pocket produced a very small bundle of green leaves tied with red string which he lit with a match and laid to smolder amongst the rocks. He stood before the smoke as it rose up from the ground and proceeded to lay his hands on the face of the huge rock and speak for a time in his native language. When the brief ritual had ended, he stepped away from the wall and turned back to us, a serene expression upon his face.

"What is this place?" I asked in wonder, gazing up at the top of this thing where several jagged pillars stood like sentries around the perimeter.

"We call this place Mesa Encantada, the land where my ancestors lived," he answered.

"Woah…"Mary breathed, subdued.

"Up on top there?" Billy asked, leaning back and pointing with his hand over his eyes to block the sun.

"That's right."

"Whew! Imagine that view? What the sunrise must've looked like in the morning? Like being on top of your own little world…"

The Indian smiled weakly, a look in his eyes I couldn't place.

"What did you say before?" I asked him. "When you were speaking in your language."

"I was praying to God for blessings upon this ground and asking the spirits of the mesa for the right of passage, that we may be welcomed peacefully and stay here tonight. I was asking them for guidance and truth in our visions," he answered.

"Is that why you burn the cedar?" Al supposed, identifying the herb by the pungent smell of its smoke.

The Indian nodded, "Cedar is to purify the ground. It wards off evil spirits and invites good ones nearer."

"Is that what the cigarette was for?" Billy asked.

The Indian nodded again, "Tobacco is an ancient peace offering to the spirits and a gift to the Creator. You can go now, explore."

We had already begun to drift and wander by the time he granted us this motion. The fragments of eroded rock that surrounded the structure crunched under my shoes as I advanced toward the wall and placed my outstretched hands upon it. I tried to clear my mind and concentrate instead on my breathing in order to bring myself to my center. It started gradually and faintly, but after a few moments, I could feel a deep vibration in my palms and my fingertips. It was the energy of something old and something pure—the Earth's vibration, amplified by the touch of my skin, a minor brush with infinity.

The sun had begun to set by the time we all gathered again. The Indian had seated himself upon a flat rock that poked up through the sand and was beginning to slice up and prepare the peyote for us to eat.

"If you three do not want to stay the night," he spoke to Mary, Bobby, and Space, "there's a motel back in Paraje. It's not the Holiday Inn, but it's clean and it's cheap."

Mary looked up expectantly at the two guys, "I'd like that," she admitted. "I dig a shower."

"We'll come back and pick you up in the morning," Space assured us.

Before they left, the rest of us followed them back to the Trips Mobile and gathered up a few things that we needed: the jug of water, a few joints and a pack of cigarettes, some blankets, the mandolin, and that little Indian water drum. Billy started stacking a couple cans of refried beans, but the Indian told him that it was better to take peyote on an empty stomach. With our arms full, we waved goodbye as they pulled away and started to drive off into the encroaching darkness. We watched their taillights recede into the distance, and then we were alone.

The five of us returned to the shadow of the mesa where we immediately began to consume the sacred cactus. The Indian had divided the pile of shredded green peyote buttons into portions—equal helpings for the four of us and a smaller section for himself. He ate his portion quickly and right away began crushing up handfuls of dried berries that he'd produced from another pocket in his jacket. Now, I was already aware that the peyote would taste bad—as the mushrooms had—but even so, I was not prepared for the rancid flavor that assaulted my tongue. I gagged even before I could get the first mouthful down. Their taste was not aided at all by their texture which was pulpy and rubbery, as if I was eating raw meat—some god's carcass, perhaps. It took me a long time, but I was finally able to get all of it down. Billy and Faye weren't having a much easier time than me, but Al and the Indian seemed entirely content just to munch on the cacti. Once we'd all finished eating, during that interim period before the nausea set in, the Indian passed around the jug of water into which he'd added the crushed berries—juniper, he'd said they were when we'd asked him—an old Acoma method to strengthen the

259

stomach. Once I drank the cold, fresh mixture, the more severe pangs of nausea subsided and I could relax more fully.

"What happened to this place?" Billy asked after the ritualistic eating and drinking had ended. "You said this was the home of your people, but there isn't anybody living here now."

"Eons ago, my people dwelled upon these rocks," the Indian answered him. "They'd go down to plant in the valleys in the summer months, harvest in the fall, and remain atop the mesa in the wintertime. The legend says that one day a summer rainstorm broke out when all the Acoma people were down in the valley. The rain from this storm fell so heavily that it caused a rockslide and the ramp by which my ancestors ascended and descended the mesa fell and crumbled, leaving them separated from their home and the three elder women who had remained behind in the village. Seeing that there was no way to reach the top of the mesa again, they moved north with the fruits of their harvest to another mesa and built their pueblos there. The three elder women lived alone in the village for some time more until the food ran out and they starved. In your language, this place is called the Enchanted Mesa—enchanted meaning haunted."

As he finished recounting the legend, a coyote howled in the distance, and a shiver passed through me. *Creepy,* I thought to myself, *but somehow, not quite.*

"Many spirits reside here even still," the Indian explained. "They watch over this place and protect it from occupants with ill intentions."

Mystified, Billy swiveled his head back around to look at the mesa again, as if he expected a spectral image to burst out from the rock.

"According to the Haak'u elders—Haak'u meaning Sky City, the place where I was born—when our people first came up to the Earth from underground—from Shipapu—they settled here, and afterward, in Haak'u. No one is quite sure where the city of Shipapu really is. Some say it is in the north, but I—like many others—believe that it is here, below this site."

We all looked down at the ground upon which we sat; it was old and sacred ground, without doubt—whether his story was true or not. It seemed as if time had been suspended here; the years had passed, but the lands had stayed the same. The rains had come along with the floods, the Spanish, the Gold Rush, and the railroad, but right then and there that young man was reciting the same story and espousing the same beliefs that his people had held to be true since the beginning of time. This land had not changed, and its people—these beautiful, peaceful, native people, as old as the Earth itself—had persevered.

260

This filled me with so much goodness and so much hope that gladness fluttered in the pit of my stomach.

"Is that the creation story of the Acoma?" I asked him. "That all humans came from underground?"

"Yes," he answered, "there were two sisters, Iatiku and Nautsiti, and they were born underground. Their father Uch'tsiti lived four skies above, and he sent a messenger, a spirit called Tsichtinako, to instruct them. Their father had given each of them a basket which contained images of all the life that would one day exist on Earth. The two sisters grew under the earth in darkness for a long time until one day they emerged out into the light. Once on Earth, Tsichtinako showed the two sisters how to give life to all the creatures and all the plants whose images Uch'tsiti had put in their baskets. They were happy, and life was peaceful and grand. One day while the two sisters were busy naming all the new creatures of the Earth, an image fell unnoticed from one of their baskets and upon striking the ground, became a serpent. After this day, the two sisters—caught up in the excitement of creating new life—began competing with one another, each of them trying to prove that they were better than the other. They began thinking selfish thoughts, and both girls became very sad and very lonely. One day, the serpent which had come to life of its own accord approached Nautsiti and told her that she would not be lonely if she had a child. She replied that Tsichtinako had told them that Uch'tsiti would one day allow them to have children, but not before then. The serpent told Nautsiti that Tsichtinako was evil and that he was trying to keep this happiness from them, and he instructed her to go to the rainbow. Nautsiti did this, and while she laid in the rain, life began inside her. Sometime after this, Nautsiti gave birth to twin sons and finding that she disliked one of the two, gave that one to Iatiku. At this time, Tsichtinako returned and finding the women with child, was very angry. He told them that they had committed a sin and that because of this, he could no longer return. The two sisters did not live happily together after this and one day decided to share what was in their baskets and part company. Iatiku left for the east with her child, and Nautsiti and the child she kept remained here on this land, and from them, all the children of the Earth were born."

While I listened to his story, I couldn't help but draw parallels to the Catholic beliefs that I knew so well—a guiding spirit, a tempestuous snake, a virgin birth—could it be that they were not in some way influenced by one another?

"Are these the things the Acoma have always believed?" I asked.

The Indian nodded, "Always. But ever since the white man came to this land, he has tried to force his religion upon us, so in many ways, the two have become indistinguishably intertwined. This story of origin, however, has always been told the same way throughout the generations."

"Has the peyote ritual evolved much since the Europeans came here?" Al asked him.

"Not substantially," he answered. "We take peyote ceremonially to come closer to God, to intercede for spiritual guidance from the saints, and commune with the spirits of our ancestors who have gone before us. That is the way it has always been. Taking peyote in this way teaches you many things because you can see far more with peyote than you can without peyote. But what we are doing now—rather, the way in which we are doing it—most of my people would not approve of."

"Why?" I asked.

"Well, if there's one thing the Acoma love, it's tradition. I'm sort of the black sheep of my family. I've been into the cities and the universities, I've visited other reservations, and I've seen a lot of things the others haven't. What I've learned is that you don't need rituals and traditions to find God. Back in the village, I take it for what it's worth. Some customs I continue to follow mainly out of respect, some are just in my blood, and others I've grown so used to by my upbringing, that I simply cannot imagine carrying out my daily life without them. Don't get me wrong, I don't see anything sinful in following tradition—it is in no way harmful, but it isn't *necessary*. Despite the complexity of our rituals, most of our beliefs are extremely simple."

"...the most simple of any religion I've ever encountered," Al added.

"Alright, shoot," Billy encouraged him.

"Well, we worship many gods—sun gods, rain gods, gods of harvest, gods of the seasons—but when you boil it down, it is simply nature that we worship, the forces that sustain our livelihood. The more connected you are to nature, the more connected you are to everyone and everything, mundanely, mentally, cosmically, and spiritually. Within us and all other things is what other tribes call the Great White Spirit. We are possessed by the same divine significance as the animals we kill for our food, the land on which we build our homes, and the stars that guide us. We exist in harmony with all of these things and must at all costs remain in that state of balance. This

262

world is but a mere stepping stone in the sea of spiritual transcendence, and you must reach enlightenment here before you can go on to the next world. If you do not, through holding on to too much pride or selfishness or anger or sadness, you are reborn into this world again and again until you learn."

"Do the Acoma believe that once you reach enlightenment, you go to a place like heaven as the Christians do?" I asked.

The Indian shook his head, "We believe that all the processes of life are cyclical and eternal. The cycles of life in the body, in nature, and out of body work in harmony. To stop the cycle and arrive at some pinnacle is contrary to every other experience of reality. We understand how nature works and how our bodies operate, so why should birth and death—existence apart from the body—be any different? After all, if you are in harmony with nature and with the cycles of life, it is not hard to find peace here on Earth. The Acoma lived peacefully for thousands of years before the white men came. They do not exist in harmony with their environment, and look what they did to ours."

Inside, I burned with shame for the unpardonable acts my ancestors had committed all those years ago. I wanted to weep for the richness that had been destroyed, for the peace that had been shattered.

"Man, these guys are like the original flower children," Billy said. "They had it going for them way before we ever had a clue. Hell, you guys may not wear britches, but at least you never went around slaughtering each other over minor religious discrepancies. How many people died in the first century, in the Crusades, in the Holocaust, in the fighting over Palestine...Christians killing Muslims, Jews killing Christians, Muslims killing Jews...and they all worship the same God! What a fucked up world it is."

"Don't we all worship the same God?" Al suggested. "Think about it. After all, what is religion other than man's futile attempt of explaining the world around him and less virtuously, his way of capitalizing on God?"

"God is God, no matter what you call him. The Truth is out there," the Indian agreed. "All religions have some parts right and some parts wrong—it's all a matter of discerning which is which."

Al spoke next, "We cannot correctly perceive what is true on this earthly plane, especially in the realm of religion and mortality," he affirmed. "The Christian states with certainty, *'My views are right.'* But how does he know he is correct? The Jew does not state, *'I am right, but you are more right.'* No, he believes that his views are exclusively correct in the same way that the Christian believes his are. A belief is not proven, it is precisely what it is: a belief. It is not something that can be stated as factually true or untrue; therefore, it cannot be forced or enforced in any manner, whether it be governmentally or socially. Throughout history, action taken to force or enforce beliefs has been nothing less than a game of power. No belief on this earthly plane can be truly known and regarded as doubtlessly correct. It is when people share their views and beliefs— instead of condemning each other for them—that the true virtues of religion are achieved."

That is just about all that I remember. The conversation continued, I'm sure, but it was at this point that I began to feel the effects of the drug and no longer attended to the exchange closely enough so that I am able to recount it accurately now. I cannot attempt to put into words the exact feeling that the onset of the drug produced, but it coincided with a feeling of increased restlessness and the amplification of all my senses. The sensation most demanding was that of my stomach and the activities therein. I could feel my gastric juices sloshing around in there, trying in vain to digest this foreign and most likely poisonous plant matter. I drank some more Indian tea and upon rising, became violently ill.

The sickness came on quickly. My body shook, my mind quaked, and the Indian was right there next to me as I purged. He spoke gently in a foreign tongue and tended to me until the awful feeling ended. It was all over shortly after it began, and once it was, a marked stillness came over me. No longer did I have the urge to wander, but I could see that Faye and Billy had gotten up and holding hands, had started off in the other direction. The Indian called to them saying, in effect, that they had all the room in the world to wander, but that it was far more productive to take their trip sitting down and to channel their inquisition within themselves.

"It isn't what's out there that's important, it's what's in here," he told them, tapping his chest. "Besides, you'll find all the same stuff anyhow."

They thanked him and continued on but returned in what couldn't have been more than a couple minutes after pondering his suggestion and finding the apparent validity in it.

Now, more than two hours into this experience—after taking the peyote, that is—I was still undergoing nothing that was characteristic of a psychedelic drug. Instead, the feeling that filled me came in waves; at first, it was very intense, and then it either tapered off or I adapted to it, because it lessened—but even this was not unlike a strong pot high. The effects of the peyote cactus may've been slow to arrive, but once they made themselves known, it was well worth the wait. In one sense, I guess it could've been perceived as dissociation, but I experienced it as a disintegration of boundaries. I stopped knowing quite for sure exactly where my body ended and the ground or the air or the body of another began. It was a very communal feeling.

I kept my eyes closed most of the time during the experience. There really wasn't much to see anyway. It was pitch black. The stars were out, but wisps of clouds darkened several swatches of the sky and the moon was new and bore no light. I couldn't see my hand in front of my face, but I could feel everything that was around me. And what was all around me was this world, a world I was normally blind to, a world I'd come into once or twice before and once I was back, I began to wonder why I'd ever left it for so long. My mind was totally present, my approach to reality unimpaired. I felt better than I ever had in my whole life.

My friends were beginning to embark as well. We could not see one another, but our energies were exuded with such clarity and strength it was as if we could. Across the circle, our Indian shaman had taken up the water drum and was beating upon it, letting fly these sounds that physically touched me and acted like a catalyst, inviting me further and further into the mystic allure of this novel, prehistoric world. His involvement was by far the driving force of my trip. I wasn't taking his trip, however—he was only a part of mine, gently directing my experience, guiding me along a road he'd already traversed and was now returning down to bring the rest of us through.

Along with his drumming, our shaman chanted loud and clear, calling out for blessings, protection, and enlightenment in a voice that washed out over the desert sand like a wave. Chills ran down my spine, and the hair on the back of my neck stood on end. I felt this unprecedented enchantment—in the Acoma sense of the word—as if the spirits of the ancient people of this land were rising up from the ground in every direction. I held my hands out before me and felt a strange tingling sensation, like light touches all the way up my arms.

Al leaned over next to me and whispered in my ear, "There's so much we can learn," he spoke excitedly, "they've done something we haven't yet!" Clearly, he was experiencing the same sensation as I.

The power in this moment had driven out the calm of before, and the wave of experience peaked again. Camped out below this ancient rock—this ancestral home—with native dope inside me and the spirits of the dead surrounding me, I felt like an Indian myself, connected with nature divine—a sensation that had both the solidarity of mushrooms and the visionary allure of acid. However, unlike acid, peyote isn't sugar-coated—even the sensations are raw.

I was aware of all my bodily processes from the beating of my heart echoing in my ears to the expansion and contraction of my lungs with every fresh breath and the kinesthetic sense of the soles of my feet on the ground. Each time I desired to make some kind of movement, it was a brand new adventure in motion. My limbs felt like they were attached to marionette strings, and every time I raised a limb, part of my consciousness lifted as well.

I was completely engrossed in these new sensations, and I took the time to explore them, waving my arms in the air and sending my mind up and down and around with them. Seated there upon the ground, I felt as if I was engulfed by hair, wrapped in my tresses like a shawl— like a kind of cutaneous grass that came out in tufts from the ground and continued to grow wherever it touched me.

Have you ever gotten the feeling that your body was melting? It's certainly not one of those sensations you seek to experience, but once it is upon you, it is curiously intriguing. The vast majority of my surroundings at that point were melting as well. All things of a spiritual quality began to glow, and all physical things began to turn to dust. Oneness is a condition of the soul, not the body, and to experience it expressed in that way is not something easily forgotten.

It was this sort of thinking that persisted during the peyote experience. I was aware of all measures of profundity that were abundant and appeared clearly in all things usually puzzling. The sheer intensity of the revelations was awesome. I felt like I was reaching toward something, coming closer to an infinite point. It was as if I was holding onto myself with one hand and grasping the banister of the stairway to heaven with the other. And little by little, the grip I had on myself began to loosen. My body continued to desolidify, melting down into itself and into the ground, but instead of collapsing into lifeless matter, which divides spirit and is eternally separate, all consciousness came into itself as one being. Spirit merged with substance, and everything within me and about me began to glow.

—And just then, at the very height of the wave, *BOOM*! Our shaman struck the drum one final time, and all and everything came crashing down.

Immediately, there was silence and…normalcy? As I opened my eyes and lifted my head, I no longer felt like I was tripping; that metaphysical link had been momentarily severed. I looked around…I couldn't see anything, nor could I feel if my friends were still near me. I supposed they were, but I couldn't hear a thing. Instead, as I listened, a strange silence greeted me; a silence that was mind-numbing. And although the desert night is soundless, as I listened intently, I began to hear things.

Whiny, far-off music that sounded almost like static for lack of sensitive enough perception hummed about my ears like flies and grew stronger and stronger, louder and louder. A blast of music randomly began playing as if from a source directly near me—but in reality, no such source existed, and the wave began to gather again in the great boiling cauldron of my mind. I heard instrumentation followed by a series of bells and the sound of a single jet plane overhead, the roar of which crashed and echoed off either end of the sky, its lights lost in the clouds. As all of this faded away, the Indian took up his drumming again after his silent intermission, and when I listened, it was as if the sound was passing right through me as effortlessly as through air. The tone the drum produced was different than before as well—it was warbled and distorted, as if I was holding my head next to a giant fan. The waves of sound hitting my eardrum changed and reverberated and were very pleasing.

When I closed my eyes, fluorescent hues colored the edges of the darkness like rainbow smog, and a captivating dance of twinkling lights and shapes I'd never seen before invaded my visual field. There were all sorts of things: prisms and patterns, figures and pictures that flashed slowly and repeated indefinitely. Jewels and precious metals studded the landscape behind my eyes and came alive, twinkling and communicating their ephemeral beauty to me in startling symmetry. Strange patterns spiraled down into the depths of my mind, dredging up those intrinsic, paradoxical revelations that you can only experience once you've moved far enough away from any possible source of prior knowledge and comforting familiarity. The visions I saw were not random but meaningful! A snake with a raised head and concentric body covered in diamonds welled up before my eyes. Its form and its motion rotated and spun into itself as it moved deeper toward truth—the truth that lies at the center of all things.

I planted my hands on the ground next to me to brace myself against the sudden influx of visions, and there I found the mandolin. I picked it up and having only rudimentary knowledge of how to make appealing sounds, began to pluck the strings between my fingers. Each motion created a new vibration in space, a transformation of energy that would persist forever. Strumming the mandolin and feeling those vibrations wash over me was a purely magical feeling that does not have any formidable analogy.

Meanwhile, the Indian had not rested. He was still drumming aloud, and by now, he had resumed chanting again. Billy and Al, having no instruments of their own, clapped their hands and slapped their thighs in time with the beat. Sometime before, Faye had risen from the desert floor and begun to dance. Don't forget—I couldn't see these things; instead, it was the muted impact of her bare feet on the ground and the tinkling of the temple bells she wore around her neck and ankles that alerted me to this fact. While she danced in the center of the circle, the rest of us laid back in the sand and made deep, visceral noises, grooving on the vibrations of our voices and trying out different shapes with our mouths: huffing, snorting, howling, and unleashing wild cries and primitive syllables into the still of the night.

At one point, a hand reached out and touched my own. I was unsure of whose it was at first, but their skin was soft and I could feel the rough, gauzy fabric of their sleeve, and through that, I determined that this hand was Faye's—but still the pounding of feet continued. My eyes blinked wide open as I tried to peer into the darkness unaided, but I was blind to my surroundings and the hallucinations did much to obscure my true vision as the dancer faded slowly away.

Overall, the darkness only enhanced my trip; for there was this persistence of vision whether I opened my eyes or kept them closed. The visions themselves were not of the same content, but on neither screen was there blackness, and before long, it became impossible to tell if my eyes were open or if they were closed. No matter how many times I blinked, a different set of pictures appeared. It was like an endless projection wheel—each time the shutter closed, a new negative was exposed.

In one such vision, the sky snarled like a wicked, growling beast, but yet I was not afraid. I was content just to observe. It was light in this vision; in my mind's eye, I could see the earth around me with darkness eradicated. The ground below me was vibrating because it was made up of millions of smaller particles—beads; little blue individual beads that everything in the world consisted of. The enchanted mesa loomed before me, and a woman steadily beat her back upon it, clapping in a different rhythm with her hands as she did. She threw herself against the rock with both force and composure and at the same time shook her head fast, so fast it almost looked like it was about to come apart from her neck. She was Indian, she was rhythmic, and the sky growled. She was small, an old woman, but yet she emanated great power and great strength. The immense rock she beat herself upon portrayed her strength; it rose one thousand feet in the air and was immovable, holy, and perfect.

As time passed, she grew tired and waved her hands in front of her instead, still maintaining that same rhythm—the perfect counter to the Earth's vibration. After all, when two opposites are in harmony with one another, their flow of energy creates infinity—and this is what she did with her hands. She was in tune with nature and in harmony with existence, with hers and with mine. Within my heart and permeating the whole of my being, I felt a profound love for all things—for this land and its people, all the creatures of the Earth, for the whole of the infinite universe, and all that exists therein. I approached the rock euphoric, ready to share with her my pleasure at her presence, my joy at her existence, when she disappeared—melting away into the rock like a mirage on a hot summer's day.

I blinked my eyes, and the scene changed again. First, to a broad and spacious landscape blossoming in a thousand colors beneath the azure skies and then to marvelous architecture: gothic churches, flying buttresses, and wrought iron fences sparkling with dew drops that glistened in the sunshine. Everything there was bright and shining, wrapped in the cotton wool of eternal daytime; a place where night kept outside the gates of dawn. From Paraje, New Mexico to the world inside my mind was a million miles. Within every superimposed vision, all things were suspended in a state of awe. These strange dreams of such wonder and perfection, of beauty so far removed from waking life, could not be found in a place other than the heavens—and with every blink of my eyes, they turned to the next world, each somehow more profound and momentous than the one former.

Visions of foreign lands, temples, and holy places predominated. Sometimes I saw them from far off at a distance, and other times they were right up in front of me. —And I can't exactly call them visions when these things I saw, heard, tasted, and felt had all the makings of a true perception…but all the while I knew it couldn't be because last I remembered and as far as I knew I was still in the middle of the New Mexico desert. Yet, there, looming up in front of me was not an ancient rock but a huge wall made entirely of cut stones. The thing was massive, and even looking straight up, it seemed to outdistance the sky. From it came strange vibrations, the same vibrations…

Unlike most other perceptions from that drug, this one wasn't entirely unfamiliar. I knew where I was, even though I'd never been there before. This place I visited briefly is located at one of the many energy vortexes that dot the Earth—holy, sacred, and revered places where the concentration of transformative energy is so dense that you can feel it working on you from all over. I wasn't alone there; many figures walked along the base of this structure, marveling at the sheer size of it as well as its sanctity—they too could feel the vibrations. They were dressed in religious garb with covered heads and hands holding scriptures outstretched toward the monument. They rocked on their feet, entranced and devout in prayer. With open, upturned mouths they wailed, and the sound they produced was the same as the Indian's, all the way back there in Acoma. With the crossing of these perceptions, this scene began to break apart. The wall came crumbling down, and I was swept away again.

When I found myself next, I was standing just inside of a jungle clearing, and I was alone. I could feel the damp air clinging to my face and my clothes as I bore onward toward yet another stone structure. I did not know where I was or how I'd gotten there, but I knew that I needed to get inside of the pyramid that towered over me now. It was made of old, gray rock, and its broad staircase had weathered and eroded after eons of years of sun and rain. The steps beneath my feet were rough and uneven, and as I climbed on my hands and knees, at times chips of rock broke off and tumbled down its steep sides. Sweat poured from my skin, dripped into my eyes, and made my hands clammy and my grip uncertain. Bizarre creatures were all around me, but they kept to themselves, soaring above me in the air or stalking below me in the dirt. They had strange forms that changed when I looked at them and colors that pulsated and shone. They stood out bright and unnatural against the forest green and even when I reached the very top of the pyramid I could still see them.

At the pyramid's highest point there were several stone doors. I wanted to enter through one of them—I *needed* to enter through one of them—but their shapes changed continuously. As soon as I reached forward to open one, its outline altered and blurred and together they oscillated, spinning away from me and recoiling from my touch. I couldn't enter as I was; it seemed I needed to shed something, some outer covering that isn't compatible with a state of purity such as that which existed behind those doors. I was ready, and I was willing; I wanted to know everything. I was eager to leave behind every known part of myself and venture out into the mysteries of existence, hoping to reemerge with some bounty. I wanted everything revealed to me, and in this state, I knew it was within my ken to know. I was so high, so close to *IT*, and yet, an eternity still separated us.

I'd climbed to such a place between all of my life's experiences, things learned and read in books, from others, and from this here state of mind that I realized right then and there that everything you accept to be true is wrong, and everything you believe yourself to be is only a seeming expression, a symbol far from communicating the truth. Perception of reality, amongst most other things, is learned. The only things that are not learned are the things that have always been, and for the first time in my life, I was approaching a level where I could truly *see*.

But my eyes were old. They had eighteen years of caked-on experience and they saw through the lens of history, tinted with preconception, assumption, and expectation. They were not pure, and what they saw was dependent upon my own understanding— subjectivity at its finest. To comprehend the world without relation to myself was unattainable without first abandoning my own ego. The seals of true enlightenment are closed to those who cannot cross the void of living without fear of the future or ties to the past: yesterday had no bearing on this place, nor did tomorrow. There was only here and now and being. There was a quality of stillness impending.

Now, the doors did not slow in their gyration; rather, it felt as if the energy within my own body sped up, and it was not so much my body as much as it was something deeper and more intrinsic—my inner self, my essence, my soul. I felt this updraft then, as if I was being lifted and carried away from my body. However, my ascent was not effortless; in fact, it took all of the strength that I had. I could feel the layers of myself, my identities—the very sheath of my humanity— peeling off of me and falling away like the shedding of snakeskin, and under each layer what was exposed was raw and tender. Repeatedly, I was confronted by memories—by true visions this time—by inklings that invoked such strong emotion: passion, shame, anger, resentment, desire—all those things that make us human. Despite the boiling up of these feelings, I kept on releasing each of them in suit, watching them go with an air of something like empathy for the ignorant creatures— I think Ram Dass once called it compassion. It was a battle of wills between my individuality and my personality, a showdown between my id and my ego. I was surrendering all control and welcoming any complacency-shattering, life-changing revelation I might encounter on the other side of that doorway while simultaneously hanging vainly on to the slightest thread of doubt, trying—although consciously I knew it was unnecessary—to maintain some sort of presence in my world. I felt like I was wrestling with an angel, grappling with some eternal truth. Like Achilles, I was all but fully submerged in the Styx, reaching further and further toward enlightenment until suddenly but gently, that thread snapped, and with great trust, I passed through the least of those transcendental doors.

On the other side of that doorway was a tunnel of light—no shadow, no substance, just light—shining brighter than the sun ever could, and I followed it. From the most glorious effusions of impending greatness came the enduring notion that once I'd surrendered all those things formerly known to me but now revealed as illusions, something intrinsically and irrefutably true would finally be understood.

—And I was right. The only thing I did wrong—the same folly as Lot's wife—was look back.

When I did, all I saw was a single, solid vision. There was no quality of illusion, no transience, and no discrepancy. I knew what I saw, and it yielded a sudden, striking fear—right to the very heart of all that is dear and holy. Behind me, suspended in the blackness, in the void of sub-enlightenment, was a large wooden cross bearing a bloodied human corpse. This was not the typical crucifix one sees upon the altar during Sunday mass, no sir, the body suspended upon this cross was *mine*.

You haven't known fear until you've seen yourself dead. It is one thing to leave your body, but to see it destroyed is something else entirely. It is like standing naked and exposed outside your home while a fire rages. The alarm drove me frantically back inside my sickeningly comfortable dwelling and set forth a whole array of dissonance; a fierce pounding inside my mind and a shaking of figure and ground that belied the whole of my experience up to that point. I was confronted by so many truths that I already knew, things I'd even experienced. I felt like Bobby at the edge of the river, afraid to peer inside—not for fear of what I'd see, but for fear of what would happen after. Last time we'd all been in it together, but this time it was just me and myself alone in the darkness. Everyone else had moved away, far, far away. I could sense that they were over there on the other side, but I couldn't see them, I couldn't feel them. I was so deeply disturbed by that vision that all I wanted was to come down. I was confused, afeared, debased. I was still here, still aware, but I couldn't get back inside my body—a body so cold and bloody and lifeless. I had to pray and plead for return—and in the midst of the dissonance, return had been granted.

Once I was back inside, my body began to twitch uncontrollably. I was high and sputtering and scrambling around in the dark with a mouthful of desert sand and eyes full of shocked bewilderment. Al and the Indian were upon me in an instant with Billy and Faye close behind, laying their hands upon me and cooing; it was the least they could do to keep me from booking out across the godforsaken desert. I was out of my head at this point, lashing out and trying to grab ahold of my own sane reality. I drew them close, felt their bodies and listened to their breathing and the beating of their hearts, but still, I shook with fear. It must have taken them quite a while to revive my sanity. Hell, just to understand their words seemed to take hours, but their love and their presence aided me immeasurably, for I could still reach out with those timid tendrils of the mind and feel that connection with that which is greater than I.

Clearly, I'd gone up far faster and more eagerly than any of them, seasoned mescaline users that they were. While I was out there teetering on the raggedy, raggedy edge of eternal revelation, they were just getting into the corporeal sensations. There was nothing about that vision that was overall stranger or even scarier than any other I'd experienced, but it was so much the opposite of what I'd expected and so sudden that it bummed my whole trip out in an instant. It is times such as these when you are reminded that psychedelics are like a dream you cannot escape from, bad or otherwise. There is no getting out of it, only altering the flow of energy.

I spent the last few hours in deep introspection. There was no hope in trying to go back up again and grab *IT* this time—even after the shakes and the fear had passed—because at that point the drug was beginning to wear off. I calmed myself with a smoke and some meditative exercises, after which I settled back down. If there was anything I believed in firmly by that point, it was that there is always something to be learned, and I just wanted to draw myself back into my own little alkaline space and analyze it for a moment. The trip was not over, nor was it bad—it was merely subdued. I could still pick and choose my own realities and open and close all the doors that I wanted entirely at will. All except for that last pair, that is, the ones made of platinum gold and lined with diamonds and precious jewels, the ones that settled the divide between mundane reality and cosmic consciousness. Outside those doors stands a box with a little slot, and beneath it there is scrawled a message, a quote from Hesse, the price of admission.

By the time the sun rose that next morning, my trip had begun to wane. I was mentally and physically exhausted, but I'd come away with some very profound stuff. I had this supreme afterglow, and I felt refreshed and joyful at having had the experience. None of us had slept, of course, and we were all still awake from the night before when the Trips Mobile came barreling down the road, throwing up clouds of orange dust in the bright and sparkling crystal-morning sky. Upon reaching the mesa, whoever was driving parked the van right in the center of the road, and all three of them jumped out to greet us.

"Howdy!" Billy cried.

Mary waved and made a beeline straight for me, "How was your trip?" she asked immediately. "How are you feeling now?"

I thought about it for a moment, reviewing all the ineffable glory and terror that had filled the last twelve hours. "Hungry," I answered, noting for the first time the uncomfortable emptiness of my stomach.

"Hungry?" Space asked. "Here." He dug into his fatigue jacket pocket and pulled out a handful of diner crackers wrapped in cellophane in one fist and a variety of different flavored jelly packets in the other.

I thanked him gratefully but refused. I had this powerful craving for nothing except fresh fruit and corn grits, so rather than spoil my taste, I settled instead for a cigarette and a couple hits off the joint that was circulating around. After we'd rapped to one another about each of our experiences, we gathered up the few things we'd brought with us and piled back into the Trips Mobile; all except for the Indian who stood outside and spoke to Al through the passenger-side window.

"So I guess this is it," Al said, shaking his hand. "You take care now, man."

"Are you sure you don't want us to give you a lift back to Paraje?" Billy asked.

The Indian shook his head, "No, I'll walk. There are many things I need to think about before I go back there."

Billy reached across Al from behind the seat to shake the Indian's hand, "You be well," he said, meeting his eyes with a look that expressed the deepest gratitude.

I'd hugged him myself before climbing into the van, and now I rolled down the window and flashed him the peace sign as we drove away. With a smile and a wave, he started off in the opposite direction.

"So how was it?" Space asked from behind the wheel.

"Beautiful, just beautiful," Al answered.

Next to me, Faye bobbed her head. Her eyes were still huge and unfocused, and something told me that she was still tripping.

"Except for one thing," Billy said.

"What?" Mary asked.

"We forgot the lantern, and there were no sticks to build a fire. We were out there in the middle of the desert all night and we couldn't see a thing."

I don't know what it was about his statement that made me remember, but suddenly I had my head out the window and I was calling out, "Wait!" after the Indian.

Space brought the van to a screeching halt.

"What is your name?" I cried to the blurry outline already half a mile behind us.

The Indian cupped his hands around his mouth and yelled back a string of words in his native language and then without my prompting, explained, "In English, it means *He Who Keeps His Eye On The Sky*!"

"Thank you!" I cried.

"What did he say?" Billy asked.

"He Who Keeps His Eye On The Sky."

"I wonder if any of us will ever see him again," Mary spoke, passing me the joint.

"If it is the will of the Universe," Al answered as the mesa sunk back into the ground behind us.

I slept most of the ride that day; a couple more hits of grass and I was down for the count. However, when I was awake, many thoughts filled my mind. I remember hearing Al recount a version of his trip to Mary and Bobby in vivid detail. Hearing him talk of the depth of meaning in the crystalline form and his realization that the whole outer appearance of our observable world is simply a reflection of its inner structure reminded me of the intensity of my own experience: the beauty, and the fear. I wasn't troubled in the wake of my experience; however, the vision of my own crucified body and its implications kept coming back to me. It was seared into my mind, and every time I thought of it, the same disconcerting emotions accompanied it.

In some ways, taking peyote is like a shotgun blast to the psyche; except it wasn't my body that had been wounded, it was my ego. My experience had evidenced the games of personality and the difficulties involved in escaping from them, and at the end of it all stood ego-loss, or rather, a glimpse of it. To remember it invoked a crisis of identity more than anything else. Back here, I was all those things I hadn't been up there; I was all those things I'd seen removed from me. I was still Rhiannon in terms of mind, body, and soul, but somehow that didn't match what I'd just experienced. All of a sudden, there was a stark disconnect between how I felt and how I was perceived; like a daughter of Zeus in the mask of a satyr. I was simply an accumulation of a series of perceptions, different for every person. I was not the one and only essence of Rhiannon, instead, there were twelve thousand of me and even my own name seemed hollow in comparison to the richness and glory of everything else that was out there, and as I now knew, a part of myself.

But I'll tell you one thing, I wasn't afraid of death anymore. I knew for certain that a lack of conscious awareness in this world does not signify cessation of being, it just means that you've moved onto the next space, the next level of existence. I'd learned that in leaving your body, you shed your earthly chains. Death is not an end, it is a new beginning, an exodus; and it is far more painful when you attempt to hold onto the things that this life has offered you. It was a very powerful, reassuring affirmation, and even this was not the full extent of the positivity that had been brought about by my experience.

I meditated on these things instead for the remainder of that day's drive, trying to put out of my mind the troubling fact that I could no longer come to terms with my own identity. Rather, I dwelled on the closeness that our shared experiences had brought us. Through half-closed eyelids between my rendezvous with sleep, I watched and listened to my friends talking and laughing, thinking all the while: *'All the world's a stage,' Shakespeare once said, and these, if any actors, know me best without my mask.*

It was almost sundown before I actually looked out the window. The land had changed drastically in the last few short hours. There were no more magnificent slabs of red rock bursting forth from the ground, rather, flat and barren tracks stretched far past the horizon with no mountains to catch them. The sky seemed much broader and endless, a pale baby blue ocean with wisps of white clouds drifting across its surface like boats. And, in that way, there were more boats than cars out on the vast, empty Texas highways.

I was still hungry. I'd always thought Jerry and the guys had been exaggerating when they said truckin' meant living off of reds, vitamin C, and cocaine, but we were almost at that point. If you substitute reds and cocaine with cigarettes, grass, and Chiclets, we were there already. Certainly, it had been a couple of days since we'd ingested anything of nutritional value, and I hadn't eaten anything since that awful peyote, so when we passed along the outskirts of what could've been a town out of any turn of the century mining novel and I saw a diner gleaming in all its metallic Pepsi-Cola Formica glory, I just about jumped out the window.

This diner experience was in many ways more enjoyable than our last back in Arizona. First of all, this time we were famished so the sub-par meals tasted twice as good, and secondly, the other patrons weren't looking at us crooked because we smelled so goddamn bad. Mostly this was due to the fact that there weren't any other patrons, but even if there were, they wouldn't have noticed anyhow because the whole place smelled like a horse trailer. This was partly because there was an overflowing dumpster just outside the open window and partly because everything in the whole goddamn state was roasting. That Texas heat is no joke, let me tell you; if we'd bought a carton of eggs and cracked them on the roof of the van, they would've been cooked through within five minutes.

There was probably no place less appetizing to eat, but we were all so hungry we hardly noticed. I finally got my fruit cup—actually three of them for that matter—and a bowl of grits, so there was not much more in the world that could've made me happier, especially after Bobby went over and put a nickel in the jukebox and I heard the resonant, crooning sounds of *The Weight* come pouring out through the speakers. For a moment—or possibly a little longer than that— there was nothing else in the world other than the seven of us in that diner along with one waitress and The Band, staring out a fly-covered window at a pink and purple sunset sinking beneath the land—a scene so striking that one might forget that they are not under the influence of a psychedelic chemical while they are witnessing it.

However, the most wonderful event of the evening had yet to occur at that point. Once we paid our check and walked outside into the liquid night—where the temperature had been reduced to a simmer— we all noticed something we'd completely ignored before. Right across the road, there was the most beautiful sight I could have ever hoped to see: a red and white neon sign flashing '*Vacancy*,' hanging just above the most inviting motel there ever was—at least in my book, anyway.

Even before Space had gone inside the office to score a room, I was already fantasizing about the shiny, white porcelain of the shower, and once we got inside, oh, it was even better than I could've imagined. I hadn't taken a good shower in months—since the day I'd arrived, to be exact. Unless I wanted to share with the pot plants, I had to go next door to the neighbors' house like everybody else, and in addition to being the owners of the world's smallest water heater, their shower was always a little too scuzzy for my liking.

Once I'd gotten in the tub that fateful evening, I just stood there under the stream of hot, clean water for a good ten minutes, rejoicing over all that is good and right in the universe. I used up two whole bottles of that complimentary shampoo that they give you and treated that bar of soap better than any lover I've ever had. I came out of there with a surface temperature of about 95 degrees and a cloud of steam behind me that filled the whole room.

They say cleanliness is next to godliness. I'd never quite bought that, but let me tell you, after a week out on the road in the back of a van, sleeping in the dust and sweating like a pig—all while wearing the same three pairs of clothes—I sure as hell did now, and you would most certainly believe it too.

A BRIEF AND BEAUTIFUL TRIP BACK

****

When we awoke the next morning, Bobby was adamant that he was going to be the one to do the driving that day.

"Alright, enough with this chauffeur bullshit, we've got a whole big state to cover, and I'm gonna be the one to do it!" he announced to us as we all said our parting goodbyes to the mattresses we'd so enjoyed.

None of us protested, so around noontime, we all piled back into the Trips Mobile and started off down the highway at a solid 95 miles an hour.

Texas is a bit of a freaky state to drive through. After a few hours of seeing the same vast expanse of flat, colorless desert extending out uninterrupted in all directions, you begin to think that you're stuck in the *Twilight Zone*. Half the problem was that we didn't know Fort Worth from Houston, and after a surprisingly short time, I was more than fairly sure that we were hopelessly lost and traveling in the complete opposite direction of the one that would actually bring us anywhere even remotely close to where we wanted to be. We'd long since left Route 66 behind, and the closest approximation of a location that I could venture was that we were still somewhere north of Mexico.

Some people don't like the desert, but to me, it feels like the safest place in the world. You could see a prairie dog poking its head out of its den five miles away, and when we stopped on the side of the road for the boys to take a whiz, it was so quiet you could hear a match lit from the nearest town. Forget about rapists and murderers on the lam from the law sneaking up on you, you were lucky if a snake could make a surprise appearance.

At first, it was fun and adventurous, but after a few hours had passed, it became monotonous and rather boring. We were all sprawled out in the back of the van, smoking a lot and eating whatever we could find, each in our own little corner as we tried to avoid bodily contact as much as possible. Even with all the windows open and the wind screaming, it was still entirely too hot. As the sun climbed higher and higher into the sky and the miles clicked by one by one, the temperature seemed to rise more and more.

"We must be heading south," I told Bobby as I wiped the sweat from my forehead and Mary helped me braid my hair back, but he insisted that we were still traveling east.

Nobody hassled him. We all figured he couldn't get us any more lost than we already were, and eventually we had to come across some major highway or another, so to occupy ourselves in the meantime, we played every driving game ever invented. A game of war would've been just sweet that day, but in our haste, we'd left our deck of cards back at the motel. Once we'd gotten tired of making a racket, we were creating funny sayings out of license plates, people watching whenever we drove through a town, seeing who could hold their breath the longest—hell, anything we could think of. But once we'd gotten deeper into Texas, where one car passed every hour, those games didn't really suffice. Somehow, we seemed to miss every town we saw signs for, and despite his earlier enthusiasm, even Bobby became uninterested in driving after a few hours. At that point, there was really nothing else to do other than tell stories.

"Forget about the Lone Star State," Space commented, "it's more like the Lone Car State. In the last fifty miles, I think I've counted three of 'em! There ain't even telephone poles out here!"

Al began to reminisce, "I remember my first trip to New York; on the way back, I hooked up with this one bum by the name of Sly. We started hopping freight cars all the way back in D.C, and man, do I remember riding through Texas! We'd go to sleep and wake up, go to sleep and wake up again, and the scenery outside would look exactly the same—like we'd gone nowhere, even though we'd been moving the whole time! It was downright spooky, and those freight trains roll along slow; it's nothing at all like driving."

I was intrigued, "What else do you remember from your trip?" I asked him.

Al just laughed, "What else indeed," he chuckled. "I've been off on the same trip for as long as I care to think back, that's a whole lot to remember."

"Well, where's the loneliest place you've ever been?"

"Oh Lord, the loneliest…that would have to be Highway 50, the road I took out of Frisco the second time. This was the summer of '65, I believe, and I found myself down and out in the Desatoya Mountains of Nevada. I can't tell you how I got there, and I can't tell you how I got out of there, but I'll tell you what—if there was ever one time I was scared, if there was ever one time I was blue, if there was ever one time I thought I might die, it was wandering out there alone on that road. All I had on me was a two-dollar bill and a pocket version of the Bhagavad Gita. I found God out there on that highway, because that's all there was for two whole days—just me and God."

"I remember Highway 50," Space said after Al had finished. "I was still fresh out of the city, only three or four months had passed by that time. I'd hitched a ride back in Eureka with a young couple and their son in a brand new Chevy station wagon. They were maybe about thirty and middle of the road, white, conservative folk, and I remember being surprised that they'd even stopped to pick me up. After all, I was just another misguided youth with nothing but a sack and a guitar case heading west that summer. I know I must've looked pretty wanting out there, and I guess they felt bad for me.

"I remember riding in the back with the boy; he was maybe about five or six with a stupendous imagination. We were playing with his superhero action figures most of the drive, and he talked just about the whole time. The parents were probably just relieved that he'd found something else to occupy his attention other than chewing their ears off—maybe that's why they picked me up. Anyway, the stretch of road we were traveling over looked as if it went on forever until somebody threw down a mountain range right on top of it in the west. Really, the country is beautiful out there, but desolate, let me tell you. I remember thinking to myself, *God, if we break down out here, we're finished*...and don't you know we did? The car started heaving and coughing a few times and then it just died...I couldn't believe it! I was like, *well, shit, man, this is how I'm going to go. This is it. This place is so isolated it'll take the vultures a week to find us*! I am totally convinced that we create our own realities, and this was one of those times that really proved me right."

The whole Trips Mobile had grown quiet while Space was talking, and now he too was silent and looking around, as if he expected someone else to speak.

"Well?!" Mary blurted out after a minute. "What happened?"

"Oh!" Space seemed startled, "What?"

"How did you get out of there?!"

"Oh! Oh, right, well, I'm fairly mechanically inclined, so I took a look under the hood and the fuel filter was jammed, the thing wasn't getting any gas. I fixed it, and we were on our way. They were really grateful, they even gave me some bread for the road—enough to last me all the way until I got to San Francisco. I never did know where they were headed, they left me at Reno..."

The rap that afternoon was a great deal of fun; we all took turns talking about everything from our favorite memories and chronicles of youth to Zen Buddhism and hypotheses about future technologies. The latter was particularly comic because they all regaled me and one another with tales of flying cars and space vacations, hypodermal

281

government trackers, test-tube babies and just about everything else Zager and Evans sang about. I enlightened them with the truth, telling them about personal computers, cellular phones, GPSes, the Internet, and everything else that would pop up by Y2K. In some cases, their guesses were all too accurate, such as surveillance cameras everywhere, genetic engineering, and robots that took the jobs of paying citizens. Considering that they got the bulk of these ideas from dystopian literature, their accuracy made me feel a little more uncomfortable than I would've liked to admit. When I thought about where these innovations hailed from, the time I was in now, it was hard to believe that despite our best efforts to avert it, we were still moving closer and closer to totalitarian dystopia. Ironically enough, this may have been the first time I really considered the future on a grand scale. Could *1984*, *2525*, and finally, *Brave New World* really unfold before us prior to our deaths in, say, seventy-five years? Was the future—my past—really as incredible and scary as they regarded it to be?

I tried to put these disquieting notions out of my mind, and eventually, the conversation moved away to another area of interest— probably something like polygamy or the legal statutes of nudity— and those startling convictions were forgotten almost as quickly as they'd arisen.

Just short of sundown, we came upon this bar. In all honesty, I'm not really sure why we stopped in the first place; it's not like we knew it was a bar when we pulled up to it. Although remote, outlying farmhouses had become common sights over the course of that day's journey, we hadn't laid eyes upon any kind of substantial establishment for miles, and even here we were still quite a ways from any sort of real town. The bar itself was just an old converted horse barn with a big metal spittoon outside the front door, which, may I add, was probably a good fifteen feet high—the door, that is, not the spittoon. The place was inordinately plain—there wasn't even a sign out front to let travelers know that there was booze inside. I guess they figured all those patrons they wanted inside would've been able to tell it was a bar from the clues provided, and we happened to be the unlucky few who were just that hungry and wanted a civilized restroom *that* bad that we decided to chance it. It was the redneck equivalent of a dive, their attempt at a club. It wasn't anything even remotely resembling our scene at all, but we figured the people couldn't be too bad. After all, if they were civilized enough to run a business, they probably weren't going to shoot us outright.

Faye, Mary, Space, and I were elected as recon, and as we approached the place, a bouncer opened the door for us. Once we got inside and saw that there were only a handful of people at the counter, that fact struck us as a bit strange—why in the world would they need a six-and-a-half foot, three hundred pound bouncer for seven people who looked like they'd have a reasonably difficult time trying to stand, let alone fight? That should've been our first hint at what we were getting ourselves into. However, initially indifferent to this, us girls hurried off to the bathroom and left Space alone with the rest of the inhabitants of this roadhouse, all of whom had turned to look at us as we entered, with the exception of the two who were passed out in puddles of whiskey and drool on the huge oaken bar.

When we came back into the room—which pretty much consisted of the entirety of the barn—we found that Space had started talking to one of the bartenders. He was standing in the middle of the room amid the dozen or so wooden tables that dotted the space. The floor was a mosaic of odd-fitting, cracked black tiles scuffed full of dirt and sawdust that most likely hadn't seen lacquer since the end of World War II. The few lights that hung up in the rafters had been dimmed, and the place was virtually soundless aside from the fluttering of birds in the empty hayloft and the clinking of bottles. And then there was Space, a blue and purple paisley wackjob strung out from the road, looking all around and rapping to everybody—who I could tell were hardly amused at his presence and less than interested in what he had to say.

"Man, there's a stage over there!" he announced, his voice echoing much louder than it should've, a byproduct of the vaulted ceilings. "Man, the acoustics in here have got to be sweet! Have you got a house band?"

By now, three men had gathered behind the bar and seemed to be conferring with one another. They deliberated for a good minute until one poked his head out and answered gruffly, "Yeah. They didn't show t'night. What's it to ya?"

"Well, we's got an outfit out there in the Trips Mobile, yessir—a rock n' roll outfit, you hear? You need some good tunes? —We'll play for free! Well, for comps, y'know? We'd really love to play, these acoustics are just groovy, yes?"

I wasn't sure whether he thought that if he tried to adopt their accent he'd have better luck scoring a gig or if due to the countless speed pills steaming in his synapses combined with the heat and the last god-knows-how-many hours out on the road he'd finally lost it, but either way I was sure his speech was making our situation worse. Let's just say I was more than a little surprised when the man behind the counter agreed, and I wasn't the only one.

"You're shitting me," Bobby gaped once we'd reemerged into the blazing heat and Mary let everyone else know how we'd be spending our night. "He did what?!"

The guys in the van peered out the windows with open-mouthed incredulity at Space who was literally cartwheeling through the dust in front of us.

"You know, we could just split now and keep riding," Billy suggested.

"Let him keep this up for another fifteen minutes and he'll forget all about it," Bobby agreed.

"Although, the acoustics in there were really groovy..." Mary added.

We all just kind of stared at her for a moment.

"Oh, come on guys! There's like half a dozen of them in there, how many more could really show up? Look at where we are! Besides, we're hungry, we're tired of driving, and it's going to be dark soon. There's no lights anywhere out there, we don't know where we're going, and we're almost out of gas. I'd feel better staying here."

We all listened respectfully and then dissented immediately. After that, there was a lull, during which I hesitantly replied, "Well, she does have a point..."

As we began unloading our equipment, this prickly, paranoid, hair-standing-up-on-the-back-of-your-neck-someone's-watching-you type of fear began to come over me. There was really no reason for it, and I blamed it on the hashish I'd been smoking since we'd run out of grass back there on the road. Regardless, this feeling wasn't helped any by Billy who was all up in my space the whole time whispering in my ear about how you only had to so much as look at a Texan wrong and they'd take you around back and carve out your liver with a bowie knife. I told him that I was sure they were nice people just as long as you didn't do anything too radical and went about setting up my kit in a dark corner at the back of the stage, never quite meeting any of their eyes and trying to ignore their not-so-subtle comments about our appearance and my playing the drums.

"A *woman?!*" I heard one of them say. "Have you ever seen anything so ridiculous? Next thing, they're going to have r'coons playing the g'itar and niggers running for president."

284

I knew they were ignorant, so I more or less let their quips roll off my back. I was more concerned with helping Space wire everything up. The only thing the roadhouse supplied was a stage and an outlet, and we'd brought along only minimal mics and amps—the extent of what we could strap to the van, which wasn't much. We had to get pretty progressive with the whole setup, but it worked, even though it took us a while to get it right.

Al stayed holed up in the Trips Mobile for the duration, and that seemed to be for the best. They could tolerate us, but he probably would have pushed them over the edge, especially since that day he was dressed in an Indian kaftan and had his long hair pulled back in a ponytail. It worked great for traveling in the heat, but if he'd gone inside, some poor, drunk hick might've tried to feel him up at the bar and gotten a nasty surprise.

All in all, it was a weird scene. After darkness fell, all these rednecks just started coming out of the woodwork, driving up in convoys of mud-splattered pickup trucks with steer horns wired to the grill and more of the bastids riding in the back. They all wore the same getup; I never saw so many flannel shirts and Levi's, cowboy boots and ten-gallon hats in one place. The chicks there were unlike any I was used to either. There weren't too many around, but the ones that were spoke loud and crass and wore plaid shirts tucked into short skirts. Most of them were heavy set and masculine, and not one of them wore flowers in their hair—it was more likely you'd find a revolver on any of them than a daisy.

And when it came time to play, man, that was a trip in and of itself; I mean, what do you play for hicks? We weren't about to launch into Sam Cooke's *A Change Is Gonna Come* or anything like that out of fear of being lynched, and I couldn't suggest we cover anything by Lynyrd Skynyrd because unfortunately, they wouldn't release anything until 1973. Instead, we tried to channel The Band. I wanted to play *The Night They Drove Old Dixie Down* and they probably would've dug it, but that too wouldn't be released for another month. It was times such as these when my extensive knowledge of future music became more of a burden than a help. Usually, we could do a pretty groovy rendition of *The Weight,* but there was just something off about that night. It was more than just the setting, it was the crowd. Oh, we were the center of attention, that was for sure. In fact, we were probably just about the biggest hit that old roadhouse had ever seen, but for all the wrong reasons. They were laughing and pointing, *haw-*

hawing in their thick southern accents, and occasionally one would throw an empty can or a balled-up napkin at us.

Throughout the night, more kept coming—and just to jeer! It was as if the circus had come to town and we were the freak show. The lack of respect and jive was foreign and appalling to us, especially since we were playing free of charge. We certainly weren't used to being treated in that way, but I guess that night we more or less deserved it.

In fact, we didn't sound too hot at all. By the time we got through the whole hassle of setting up and tuning, even the acoustics didn't sound that great—certainly not worth the drag that night turned out to be. Our makeshift PA system didn't carry the sound well at all, there was awful feedback if Space or Bobby moved anywhere out of a two-foot radius, and even Mary's singing sounded flat. I played decently, I guess, but I just couldn't get it together either. There were times when Billy and I were really able to sync in and Bobby and Space were able to harmonize and improv, but those times were terribly few and short-lived. Fittingly enough, if there was any one song we did do justice to that night, it was *Can't Find My Way Home*.

However, there were two things that made that night bearable. The first was Faye. She was either utterly indifferent or entirely oblivious to what everybody was saying about us and spent the duration of that night dancing on stage with her back to the crowd, making silly faces and swaying with the music. She gave us some sort of reassurance, someplace to anchor ourselves and our attention rather than having to stare out into the mocking expressions of what was probably half the population of southern Texas.

The other thing was the booze. We'd all loosened up after we got some drinks into us, but it certainly did nothing to improve our performance. In fact, it naturally made our playing even worse. I personally held off drinking until later in the night, but after a few hours I became so bummed out that I couldn't take it anymore—it was just such a bad scene. Bobby was taking the whole thing particularly bad and even left the stage at some point and went back out to the van—more than likely to shoot up—and when he came back, his playing was completely atrocious. Numerous times that night we'd stopped playing and started to unplug and disassemble, but each time the manager of this hick joint would come up to us with a shrewd smile on his face and remind us how much food and drink we'd consumed and how terrible he would feel if one of us, namely Bobby, were to trip and fall on the back steps and break his nose.

After hearing that, I didn't give a shit how awful we sounded; in fact, I even began to hope that if we kept drinking, eventually we'd sound so bad that they'd throw us out. Unfortunately, that was not the case, and instead, I just got really smashed. I hadn't been this drunk since Fresno. I'd drank a couple beers and taken a couple shots in the time that I'd been running with The Day Trippers, but they didn't really drink, and upon finding out that my party drug of choice was brew, they very quickly introduced me to the pleasures of a low-hop THC diet. During all the shows we'd played in all the bars and clubs we'd frequented in all the long nights we'd spent together, I'd never been more than tipsy, and suddenly, finding myself so grossly uncoordinated and in the grip of such dangerous excess, I felt extremely averse to it. I was entirely out of touch with the reality I preferred and within uncomfortable proximity to one I found to be far less desirable. There is no glory in drunkenness, and for me, no longer was there even enjoyment. I thought back to all the times we'd gotten 'fucked up' back in Fresno and realized the satisfaction we got out of it was simply because we knew no alternative. Now I did, and the farce was up.

The other problem that arose when The Day Trippers encountered alcohol was that we all reacted to it differently. We were all so awfully out of sync: Space was primed and on edge, every molecule in his body charged and excited, waiting intently to go, while Faye flowed, Bobby flopped, Mary staggered about promiscuously, and Billy stood last through it all. And in spite of the musical atrocities we were committing up there, out in front for everyone to hear, still, the night dragged endlessly on.

At some point late in the evening—or more likely, early the next morning—when I felt as if I'd played myself into a stupor and the last of the somewhat coherent patrons had stumbled out the door for the night, flinging their curses behind them as they left, complete and utter anarchy suddenly erupted in the crowd. It all started when—for reasons that escape me—somebody threw a chair, and following that, the whole floor beneath the stage became a writhing mass of warring bodies as drunken men turned blindly around and beat their neighbors into a pulp. That was when the bouncer came into practical use as an instrument other than a doorstop, but it would've taken half a dozen men even as formidable as him to restore order. We were utterly dumbfounded by what we were witnessing; it was like a zoo had suddenly been unleashed before our eyes. I couldn't even process what I was seeing. I just wanted to stop and stare and shrink out the back door, but Billy turned around and hissed with well-intentioned urgency, "Keep playing, maybe they'll forget we're here."

He was right. If they had turned on us at that moment, the result would have been devastating. To them, we were some kind of sick exhibit, some awful subclass of human brought about not by miscegenation but by what they considered to be a lack of moral instruction and a licentious lifestyle. Meanwhile, their sense of brotherhood was rooted in hatred and intolerance of the Other. In a situation such as this, it was easy to see that the careful aggregate of their community was not so firmly built. After a little too much brew, suddenly everyone became the Other and each man stood only for himself. In that moment, they were worse than savage dogs and so saturated in alcohol that if someone had lit a match in their midst, the whole building would've gone up in flames.

I awoke the next morning completely disoriented. I was in the back of the Trips Mobile—although I don't remember how I'd gotten there—and I had a killer headache. It couldn't have been ten o'clock yet, but I was already drenched in sweat, and between the Texas sun, the blankets and bodies that were packed up against me, and the fact that all the windows were closed, this wasn't surprising; it was like sleeping inside of a pressure cooker. I tried to yank open the door, but they'd all been locked. Upon peering outside, I saw that the parking lot had been abandoned—with the exception of Billy, Bobby, Space, and all of our equipment. They too were just waking up, with backs stiff from sleeping upright against their amps and guitar cases, each looking from one to the other, bewildered at the mass of instruments strewn everywhere and the fact that they were all inexplicably accosted, robbed, and hung over.

Space sat up and scratched his head, "Man…what a night… Does anybody remember how we got out here?"

Silence reigned. It seemed everybody's blackout had a cutoff time of about three a.m. Even Al admitted that he had been asleep when we'd come out.

Bobby dragged himself to his feet, and without even bothering to knock off the dust that had accumulated on his clothes, he crawled into the back of the Trips Mobile, muttering all sorts of profane iterations as he did so. Reaching across Faye, who was still asleep, he dug his hand into the trunk and pulled out his blue work shirt. From its pocket, he extracted the glasses case that contained his works, and upon opening it up, he unleashed a hoarse, *"Fuck!"* loud enough to wake

288

Faye.

"Oh, what a wonderful day we have in store," Mary exclaimed sarcastically.

"Aw, shut up, will you? Nobody needs to hear your mouth this early in the goddamn morning," Bobby countered, driving his head into a pillow.

"Hey, get a grip! That's Mary you're talking to like that!" Al retorted, his voice as stern as I'd ever heard it. "It's not her fault you ran out of dope."

Bobby just buried his head deeper into the pillow and his words came out sounding anxious and muffled, "Just get me to a city—any city—and out of this fucking queer redneck whorehouse."

"Fucking right on, man," Billy replied gruffly as he and Space hoisted our equipment back on top of the Trips Mobile. "Do you know what one of those motherfuckers said to me last night? He said, *'See ya later, Honey!'* Ooh, that really burned my ass, let me tell you! I wanted to spit right in his face, but that would've started a riot, so I just told him to go to hell."

"They should burn, all of 'em!" Bobby cried as he rose up out of the pillow, specks of spit flying from his mouth like a rabid animal as he continued to cuss them out to Billy's delight. It was really very ugly—and he'd been complaining about Mary's mouth….

"Alright, enough, both of you!" Al interjected, this time raising his voice and holding out his hands in an attempt to either stop or catch their fusillade of vulgarities. "Come on, get your heads! It's perfectly OK to defile institutions, but in wishing destruction toward individuals, you are no better than they are!"

"But look at how they live!" Billy urged him. "How morally corrupt, how *unnatural*, how evil!"

"Exactly how they look to us is how we look to them," Al explained, his voice returning to a normal level and tone once more. "The cultural sanctions they grow up with encourage them to behave that way."

"We don't allow ours to govern us," Billy protested, clearly playing the devil's advocate.

"Most people are deathly afraid of change. Xenophobia is rampant in this country—and most everywhere else for that matter. But what you've got to remember is that bigoted views such as racism are *learned*. These people are not innately bad, they've simply been brought up by ignorance. However, people do not like to change their views for the world, even after they've been proven wrong time and time again. In America, at least, this is the final frontier."

"All the more reason to make a stand!" Billy urged.

Al let out a long breath, "Listen, we love our cause, right?"

"Of course."

"—just like they love their cause. Even if it is evil, they don't see it that way. All will come to naught if we persist in showing them how much we hate their cause. What we have to do is show them how much we love ours and the ways in which our causes really are similar—that way, they will see how they can accept it and maybe even one day come to love it too."

Billy opened his mouth to say something, but then closed it again and remained silent, nodding to himself as he appraised what Al had said. Faye, who seemed to realize only that she'd been disturbed and that her lover was distraught, moved over to him and rubbed her eyes like a sleepy child before nuzzling into the crook of his neck.

However, even in the face of Billy's laying down of arms, Bobby persisted in his arrogant belittling. Despite Bobby's repeated provocations, Al refused to return fire and responded only by gazing unwaveringly at his brother with eyes full of disappointment and shame enough for the both of them.

I personally found Bobby's comments to be in extremely bad taste. To further mar this already wanting morning by interests stemming only from his own hurt feelings was exceedingly childish of him, but after all, what else did we expect from Bobby?

Having had enough of his brother's despicable attitude, Al climbed into the front seat without a word, started up the Trips Mobile, and steered us out of that derelict town. Bobby had ceased his ranting for the time being—more than likely with the presumption that he had won—but when it came right down to it, he didn't really care very much either way because before long, everything excepting his want of junk had been momentarily forgotten.

Behind my eyes, my skull was pounding, and I felt like a Crosby, Stills & Nash song. My freak flag was flying at about half-mast, and all I wanted in the world was a Lucky and a cup of joe, but there weren't really very many options for us. We were all terribly hungover with aching heads and an incessant need for coffee. However, in those parts, even if you did find a civilized-looking diner or convenience store, the best you could get was brown water, which wasn't worth the hassle or the stop. We'd already run entirely out of coffee and grass, as well as cigarettes and Bobby's dope, and besides the acid and speed, the only thing we had left was hash, and I was in no mood to be smoking that. Therefore, with as much space as possible between me and everybody else—purely in the interest of homeostasis—I spent a great deal of that day's drive staring blankly out the dust-covered window, starboard side, watching the dull, indeterminate landscape roll by. Nobody was in any kind of mood for jocularity, and Bobby's jonesing really put a damper on all of our recovering spirits.

There's nothing worse than riding with a dope-sick junkie in the 110 degree dry heat of the flat, morose, and nauseatingly endless Texas desert. There wasn't much more than cow skeletons out there; everything was dead—even the cacti were shriveled for lack of rain. We were the only seven living things for a hundred miles, I think. Despite our late start that day, time dragged on slow. The afternoon took its sweet time coming around, and even after several hours of nonstop traveling, we were still out in the middle of nowhere.

It was uncommonly quiet in the van the whole ride, spare a few ominous, painful moans or a cuss word here and there. This was the first time I saw Bobby in any kind of real despair for his drug, and I was not prepared for the intensity of the scene that I would witness. It was clear enough to see that this was a mode of the drug experience that everyone detested. Not only did we feel helpless in aiding his suffering, it affected all of us as well. Watching Bobby go through this reminded me of a wounded animal whimpering, thrashing, recoiling and moaning. It made me wonder why anyone would go back to a drug that caused such upset—but I also knew that there was no logic involved in the decision. I couldn't fathom the way Bobby was feeling, but I had smoked opium, so in some small way, I was at least aware of a hint of what he was missing. Surely, I could empathize with him, but no amount of sympathy or commiseration helped the situation, even upon making him aware of it. In fact, so uncomplimentary were his attitudes and actions that the rest of everybody else seemed to know better than to try and lessen his misery for him by sharing it.

As a respite from the woe, I took to watching the road rush by. I admired the unrelenting straightness and seamless continuity of that one white line and took particular note of the excrement that seemed to pile up beyond it. There were hubcaps and recaps and sometimes whole tires, tailpipes, crushed and broken lights—even a bumper! There was a continuous trail of cigarette butts interspersed by beer cans and those little bottles of liquor, and every so often you'd see candy wrappers and sheets of cardboard stopped up by rocks that prevented them from being blown away by the wind. Additionally, over the three-hundred miles or so that we traversed that day, we passed enough clothing to create a whole new wardrobe for ourselves. Sweatshirts, jackets, jeans, and crumpled up t-shirts littered the roadway along with one thing I could never understand—single shoes. Not a pair of shoes, just one shoe, and not one shoe altogether, but many different kinds of single shoes: women's pumps, sneakers, sandals—even a lone Birkenstock. I never could figure out how that happened, and although I spent far more time than I'd like to admit pondering this, I came to no logical conclusion and resolved that I needed to ask Al at a more opportune time.

Relief came by way of the city of Dallas. As Bobby had predicted, any city could offer the goods he desired, if only one were to look hard enough, and the stop also gave us the chance to stock up on those things we'd exhausted. Downtown, we unleashed Space, Mary, and Bobby, who was able to pull his shit together for long enough to go scrounge up a few more hits of smack, something Space refused to do, despite his skill in the trade. Once they returned, we were on our way again. Having seen *Easy Rider*, we decided that it was in our best interest not to cross into Louisiana and to get out of Texas as soon as possible. Even in a city like Dallas, the stares were harsher and more frequent than we were comfortable with, so we abandoned the southern route altogether, and instead Al drove us north into Oklahoma—not Bobby's 'east' this time, but due north—and by that time, our vibes were steadily improving. Bobby had gotten his fix and was sleeping comfortably, and the rest of us were toking on some grass and sipping hot coffee. The radio hummed quietly in the background, and we rapped casually to one another as the sun dipped below the tree line, which had reappeared for the first time in over five hundred miles. Inside the Trips Mobile, levity reigned once more.

"Hey Al," I called up to him in the driver's seat, "have you ever lost a shoe while you've been out on the road?"

He was slow to respond, "...no, why?"

"Well, why is it that there are so many single shoes all over the shoulder of the road? How in the world does that happen?"

"Yeahhh," Mary nodded, her eyes wide as if I'd just asked the most profound question ever, "how *does* that happen?"

Al was clearly bemused by my question, and I didn't have to look to know that he was cracking an enormous smile. "Well," he replied, "I'm not quite sure."

Where silence should have followed, Billy's voice did instead, "I know," he spoke, sounding completely serious.

292

"You do?"

"Yes. You know how when you put your clothes in the washing machine and you have both socks, but sometimes when the load of laundry comes out you're missing one of the pair? Well, that one sock gets transformed into a single shoe and deposited at random somewhere along the roadways of America for travelers like you and me to look at and wonder about."

Laughter ensued; however, we all had to admit that despite its ridiculous nature, his answer was as good as any. Just like the nature of consciousness and the constructs of reality, there are just some things in life that we don't have the means to understand.

By mid-afternoon the following day, the flatlands of Texas and yesterday's strife seemed far, far away. With distance, came relief. Those feelings of anger and discontent were all but bygone memories. There was no resentment still held by any one of us, and all of our grievances had been laid out in the open or since defused. Spats were almost entirely unheard of within this group of individuals, and as I now saw evidenced, forgiving and forgetting was a cornerstone of that harmony.

****

It took us two or three days to get across the Midwestern states, and in the time since these events have occurred, my memory of them has seemed to all meld together. Order and chronology are lacking in my recitation, but the feeling of the land and those rolling hills is as strong and clear in my mind as ever.

I remember waking up one morning to the sound of Mary's voice, rich with song. What a way to rise, in dawn's wake, as the baby blue sky extended its gentle reach out across the land. Upon blinking open my eyes, it was obvious that we'd reached America's heartland. The roads were open and desolate and bordered on all sides by fields and prairies and moors of lush, waving grass, rye, and hay. The towns we drove through were homely and lonely, with several miles or more of agrarian wonderland separating each homestead from the next. Most of the roads were flat and unpaved, and most of the houses were small cottages or one-room shacks with wooden siding. Nothing had changed in some of those towns since the Depression. Modest was a generous word, and in some cases, even humble was too kind.

However, their economic situation may very well have accounted for something because although we didn't interact with very many people, when we did, we certainly found that they were much kinder than those we'd run across in the Deep South. Their eyes were softer and less suspicious, and the sound of their voices was less accusatory. They seemed to shrug us off; we were just passing through, and I guess they figured that if they didn't hassle us, we'd most likely be gone within a couple of days. They seemed to focus their attention on more immediate concerns, such as the weather, the community, and the crop yield. They were slow, simple people living a meek, unhurried life, and there was something of a seeming autonomy about them—a kind of independence from any larger governmental body outside of their own town hall and greater interdependence between one another. They didn't seem to disregard or take advantage of the law, but they didn't seem to uphold it as God's decree either.

There was something about the atmosphere there that appealed to me most definitely. I could never live there—the silence and the monotony would drive me mad—but the vibrations were very beautiful. The locals weren't seekers by far; most likely they were

294

WASPs and dutiful church-goers, avid traditionalists unaware of the new age onslaught, but regardless, there was something about what they were doing and the way in which they were doing it that seemed inherently right.

Now despite their greater kindness, that isn't to say that they didn't think we were strange—because they most assuredly did, especially when we were together as a group. In fact, we got pulled over for the first and only time while we were passing through there. The patrolman who ran us down had been alarmed when our Trips Mobile came wheeling by him with Mary's laundry hung out the windows to dry, and as soon as we passed, his lights flashed on and he pursued us another quarter mile or so down the road. We slowed in a timely manner so as not to appear delinquent—we looked incriminating enough as it was—but surprisingly, none of us were apprehensive. With there being seven of us in the van, it was easy enough to hide the drugs. Bobby was asleep and Space and Al were the smooth talkers, so just as long as Billy didn't open his mouth and Bobby didn't wake up, we knew that we'd get off clean with no hassle.

—And as expected, we did. This particular officer of the law was round and green, and he clearly had no desire to get involved in whatever was going on inside our mobile motel room. With eyes wide once he realized what he'd encountered, he told Mary to reel in her dresses and undergarments and sent us on our way without a ticket, a search, or even a lecture. There were some uncomfortable stares and some noticeable shifting and fidgeting on his part, but that was all. We drove off triumphant; we'd played the cops and robbers game and won. I was reminded of the Merry Pranksters' psychedelic bus trip across America a few years prior and the rap they had for shirking the cops. The key to the whole thing, it seemed, was a display of copious humanity on both sides. A little bending and a little understanding on the part of the apprehender and the apprehended makes possible happier citizens and emptier jails. If only it were always that easy…

In town, arguably, we created a much greater controversy. The streets were neat and tidy, the lawns were well-kept, and the picket fences were newly painted and sparkling white. On Main Street—any Main Street, that is—there were barber shops, beauty parlors, markets, churches, hardware stores and ice cream parlors where we stopped to combat the heat—which was by no means as unbearable as Texas, but still unpleasant enough to warrant a fudge sundae every couple hundred miles or so. The main drag was the hub of activity, full of shops, businesses, and inevitably, a higher concentration of startled citizens. There were still the characteristic pointed fingers and gaping stares, and as we carried on down the sidewalk, groups of children poked their heads out of doorways and gathered in sweet shop windows as we passed, but there was far less whispering and far less vehemence. Their faces generally bore grins rather than scowls—and so much the better; we greatly preferred being considered humorous to being considered dangerous. After all, why should the rest of the world insist on taking us seriously when we didn't even take ourselves seriously most of the time?

I believe it was that first day after we left Texas that we decided to stop for the night. We were just a few miles shy of Tulsa when we pulled off the road on the side of a hill maybe an hour or so before sunset. We feasted on canned tuna and Ritz crackers and were laying back in the grass watching the clouds as they settled in wispy purple streaks across the sky. We were all gathered in this great big cluster on our backs with our heads close together, looking up and passing around joints and a family size bottle of Coca-Cola. At one point, Al reached up his hand and measured the sunset between his two fingers, barely an inch apart.

"Space and time, size and power...they're all relative," he marveled as he did so. "Right here we've got a nuclear fireball hanging in the sky, one million times the size of our puny little planet, which can scorch the Earth from over ninety million miles away, and yet..." Al closed his fingers, extinguishing the sun from our vantage point.

He was quiet for a time, then stood up and left our circle to journey back toward the van. I remained in the circle for some time more, picking out shapes in the clouds with the rest of them. However, I'd been meaning to talk to Al one-on-one for some time now, and upon realizing that I could easily catch him alone, I too left the circle and climbed the hill to where he had set up his canvas and palette and was standing in the grass, painting the scene his eyes beheld.

In the interest of elbow room and sanity, he'd only brought one canvas with him on this journey, which he worked on periodically throughout the trip. At each stop he'd paint a bit more, characteristic of what he was observing at that time. He painted in vertical strips, each another installment of the continuum that was the great American landscape, and this resulted in what was to be a comprehensive portrait by the time we reached the East coast. I stood behind him and watched for a while; he didn't know that I was there. In skill as well in as content, his masterpiece looked like a cross between something by

296

Bob Ross and Monet. He was so talented it was mind-boggling.

"To get kids like you two, what the hell were your parents like?" I asked him aloud, breaking my silence and making myself known.

"Average," was his curt answer. Al didn't turn around and remained fixated on his work, far less startled by my presence than I thought he would've been.

Even his answers bewildered me. What a true testament to endowment and personality that a foundling such as he—formally untrained in all but one of his arts—should emerge so strong, centered, and prodigious from so tumultuous a childhood.

"I can't imagine both my parents dying, having to take care of my little brother, and still being able to find time to be as creative and learned and well-traveled as you've been."

This time, Al did turn from his painting to face me, surprise and a glimmer of humor evident in his expression. "I can't imagine it either," he replied, "I am the little brother."

The implications of what he was saying didn't quite hit me at first, but when they did, I was just plain shocked. "You mean to tell me that you're *younger* than Bobby?!" I exclaimed in disbelief.

Al nodded, "Yes, by exactly two years."

"How old are you?"

"Twenty—I was born November 22, 1948."

"But, but, you're so precocious, so wise, so much more mature…"

Al shrugged, "To some degree, all that is born of my nature, and I've been able to watch my brother as I've grown up and learn from his mistakes, even if he never has."

We both turned now to look down the hill at where Bobby was staggering across the moor, waving his arms and heaving himself through the grass, dramatically telling one highly exaggerated story or another to the rest of our friends who were seated below him, rapt in close attention. He was like a drunken scop out of some old English poem, some sort of mad jester wrapped snug in a papaverous haze, an emblem of a world all his own.

"He moves through life as if he has no memory," Al had spoken to me after quite a lengthy silence. "True profundity proves to be too much for him at times. He's not a seeker; don't ever let him convince you that he is, he's only in it for the kicks."

"Well, what are you in it for?"

"The Truth."

"But how can you discern Truth from untruth?" I entreated him. "How do you know when you've really got it right? That you've experienced *IT?*"

His answer: "You just know."

Clearly, I didn't, because I continued to petition him for his understanding, and he regarded my questions calmly, without angst or the least annoyance.

"How do you even know where to look?" I asked.

Al drew in a large breath, "Nobody's really got it right in any discipline or walk of life: philosophy, esoterics, religion, or what have you, but I think that there is a great wealth of untapped power and sagacity inherent in this Movement. It may not be the only path or even the best path to enlightenment, but it seems, at this time, to be the right one for me. You've got to seek Truth in a manner that suits you. After all, Truth underlies all things—whichever way you go, you are going to find it, either in what you wind up pursuing or in its antithesis. Life is an upward journey toward self-actualization and onward to transcendence. If you're not headed somewhere, you maintain that it doesn't really matter where you go, and that can land you in some very bad places." He took another sideways glance toward Bobby, and in the silence that ensued, he turned back to his painting.

I watched him work for some time more until he finished up that day's vertical stripe.

"What do you consider yourself to be?" I asked him as he stood back to examine his creation. "A poet? A painter? A rock n' roll musician?"

"I may play rock music," he explained to me, a kind of grimace on his face, "but I'm not a rock musician. Rock n' roll is a manifestation of all the material world has to offer in hopes of discovering the infinite," Al replied. "I personally prefer jazz."

This was clearly one of his more eccentric days. "Alright, a jazz musician, then," I said, altering my former statement to his satisfaction.

What I found was that it didn't matter either way.

"I'm a writer," he answered, to my surprise, "but I don't quite know what I want to write about yet."

"Really?" I asked. "It seems like everybody knows you as everything but."

"That may be," he acknowledged, "but I *am* a writer. Everything I'm dabbling in now: music, poetry, painting, those are all supplementary—a prelude, you may be inclined to call them—to what I will do later on."

"What made you want to be a writer?"

"Well, the thing about being an artist is nobody appreciates you until you're dead, you know?" He had a smile on his face, but the tone of his voice showed no evidence of joking.

"Besides," he elaborated, "I've had many teachers throughout my life: Dickens and Alger, Steinbeck and Antione Galland…after all, my mother did name me after *One Thousand and One Arabian Nights*. She loved to read too, and she instilled that love in me. Bobby, not so much, but me for sure. Music and painting and poetry—those things have all come easily to me. It seems that what I really want to do is more of a challenge, something I really need to work at."

This speech, again, was followed by a momentary silence as I paused to digest what I'd just heard and Al paused to scrape his palette for the night. There was only one more question I wished to ask, only one more thing I desired to know at this time and in this place that really mattered. And so, after he was finished cleaning up and he turned to me and met my eyes, I asked him with the gravest of sentiments: "Who are you?" —But in asking him who he was, what I was really trying desperately to ascertain was *'Who am I?'*

His eyes widened at my probing, and the corners of his lips crept up his face in a smile, "I am who I am," he answered. "I am Aladdin Black. I am Al. I am all those things I create. I am a friend, a fellow traveler, a brother, a lover, a bandmate…"

He was right, but his answer wasn't what I was looking for, "Yes, yes, your self-concept may be influenced by your social identities, but when you remove society, when you take away those roles, when you take away the body even, then what is left?"

He could sense the growing anxiousness in my voice, and at that point seemed to understand the root of my question, "Ah, you mean *what am I?* I am my personality, my thoughts and my wishes, my dreams and my fears. I am a collection of past experiences, a body filled with mind—but what I really am is even deeper still and substantially harder to see. I am an inhabitant of a human body, a conglomeration of billions of atoms called Al, currently a living reflection of the energy pattern that existed on Earth at the moment of my birth. Am I a division of the collective consciousness? A soul? Or am I alone real and everything I think and perceive an illusion? —I do not know. What I do know is that I am everything and I am nothing. I am a vibrating wave. I am a reflection in the blazing sun, a part of and apart from everything else. I know that to know myself is enlightenment, and I know that I am God."

I listened, oh, how intently I listened to him—as if his words were the last thing that I would ever hear. Now I knew that Al didn't have all the answers—Christ, he was barely older than I was—but it was something in the way of how he phrased his points that made such clear and perfect sense. Everything he said to me was the most eloquent expression of all those jumbled near-inklings I'd been trying to work out in my mind since that night back in the New Mexico desert. I followed his train of thought as it progressed from the logical to the philosophical to the seemingly insane and hung on to every precious syllable because I knew that since his heart was pure and his search was true, even if his words weren't infallible and his knowledge had its limits, the intent itself—both his and mine—would be enough for me to at least get a feeling for that thing I so desperately needed to know. At that time, I still didn't understand what he vainly tried to explain because I hadn't experienced it myself; however, it was enough to make me breathe a sigh of relief, a sigh I didn't even know I'd been holding in those last three-hundred miles or so. Satisfied with his answer and at peace within myself, I laid back in the grass, dizzy with euphoria—entirely drugless, I might add.

"Was that closer to what you wanted to hear, maybe?"

I just nodded and gazed upward at where the stars—all 100 billion of them—had snuck into the sky while we were talking, blindsided by wonder at my own existence alongside something so magnificent. With my chin to the sky and my limbs spread-eagled beside me, I kept my eyes wide open and looked out into the infinite.

Several minutes after we'd ceased talking, Al tapped me lightly and extended his outstretched hand toward me, cupping something. "Want some?" he asked, holding the object out for me to see—it was a small, green peyote button.

I lifted my hand in decline, "I'm cool," I told him, then couldn't help but inquire, "You still have that from the other night?"

Al, who was sitting in the grass near my head, nodded and started chewing on a piece of it, "I've eaten a little bit every night for the last however many nights, and it's been really beautiful."

I remembered how quickly I'd eaten the peyote myself however many nights ago that'd been—I'd never even thought about saving any. "Why do you take psychedelics like vitamins?" I asked him. "Why do you always break the tab in half or nibble on the cactus?"

His answer was once again that of a prophet, "The only material thing you have any sort of responsibility for is your own physical body. If you are killing yourself in the process of looking for enlightenment, then you are defeating the purpose."

That final statement was followed by silence yet again, and this time for good. Al, having finished his psychedelic snack, picked up his canvas and palette and headed back toward the van to stow them. Rather than follow him down the hill to where the rest of our friends were still frolicking and prancing about, I looked up at the moon. It was the same moon I'd grown up looking at in decades yet to unfold. However, there at that moment, it seemed prehistoric, a giant eye—a peeping Tom that'd been looking in and watching humanity for eons. While the man in the moon was nothing but a childhood fairy tale— despite what Billy could very convincingly tell you about aliens—the moon itself had seen humanity at its conception. This celestial body had been around to witness the very birth of our species—and all other species, for that matter. It had watched the evolution of our planet and played a significant part itself. This heavenly sphere, if it could speak, could tell us everything we ever wanted to know about our history. It could answer all of our questions, even those questions asked by that very first human who turned his gaze to the skies and wondered about them and himself.

However, what the moon couldn't answer—even if it could speak—are all those questions that we ask about ourselves, though it could tell us when it was that man first became aware and turned his awe inward toward himself. *How long has humanity questioned its own origin?* I thought. *How long have we questioned our own purpose? Our own destiny?*

I wondered and I pondered and I philosophized, and beside me, my companion—upon his return—did the same. But when the night wind blew, it took with it those consuming thoughts that tax the brain and disturb the stillness and left me with a serene calm. Oh, it was beautiful—the cool August breeze rustling through my hair and blowing across my damp skin—and I remember laying out there under the stars in Oklahoma thinking, *Hey God, you're really cool*!

Now, although I wouldn't really call it a prayer, there was a certain sort of reverence and thankfulness and speechless, thoughtless wonder that I offered up to whatever supreme force had made possible my experiences of that night. The same awe that I felt then, I still feel right now, and that same gratitude for all those things and for being alive that I expressed that night, I still do in every waking moment—and I always will. For as long as there is breath in my body and light in my eyes, my life itself is a kind of prayer—a dedication, you may call it—a ceaseless offering to the cause of Truth.

A BRIEF AND BEAUTIFUL TRIP BACK

****

The next morning's drive took us out of Oklahoma and into Kansas. Now, Al had told us that the loneliest road he'd ever traversed was Route 50 and Space had agreed, but if you ask me, if you ever want highway hypnosis, double vision, and the like, take a day's spin through the American Midwest.

I remember one incident maybe about halfway through that day's journey:

Mary Jane had been singing and humming along just as I was nodding off for a time. Everything was calm and peaceful and groovy, and then suddenly, without any warning at all, she started screaming, "LOOK! LOOK!"

"What, what?!" we all responded alarmed as we looked around frantically for the deer we were about to hit, the cop speeding behind us with lights flashing, or the fire-breathing dragon that was swooping down from the sky to vaporize us—but the road ahead was just as empty as it had been for the last hour.

"A CURVE!" she cried as Space rounded the smallest possible bend in the road.

I just chuckled and shook my head, then closed my eyes and settled down again, pulling a bandana over my face to keep out the flickering yellow sunlight that streamed in over the dashboard and leather interior. Her enthusiasm had been valid, it was her approach that needed work. This sort of landscape didn't hold many thrills for a San Francisco native like Mary. After all, we'd been stuck in the flatlands for hours now, with not so much as a bump since Oklahoma. All there was out there was just corn, corn, and more corn; corn, and straight, flat, boring roads that just kept going on and on.

All in all, outside of a spattering of small towns and major cities, the Midwestern union is a pretty desolate place. In Kansas, the roads were red and endless, and they followed the telephone poles. There, even the major highways were unpaved and almost entirely empty— except for the occasional semi blasting past you at 120 miles an hour. In this way, it seemed to be even freer out there than in the desert. However, after several hours of this monotony, we needed to get out and stretch our legs.

Since we hadn't run across any diners or road stops yet that day, we were set on emptying our bladders, having some foot races, snacking on Triscuits, and seeing what we could find on FM—if we could even find FM—before the day was out. We'd pulled over to the side of the road, and everybody except Space had gotten out and was walking around, doing whatever it was that they needed to do in order to get their thing together. I had taken a stroll out into the cornfield, and on my way back, I could hear Space yelling out the window of the van for all of us to come over. He had found a news station and turned it up loud.

"What is it?" we all asked in unison.

"Is it the war?" Mary asked.

"The bomb?" Bobby supposed.

"It's Abbie Hoffman, somebody's shot him!" Billy spoke with conviction.

"Shhhh! And you'll hear it!" Space told us with angst in his voice.

We all quieted down. Space fiddled with the radio dial again as the station drifted, and a man's voice came over the air:

"...the latest murders were discovered during the night, the bodies of a man and his wife, found in their home. Leno LaBianca, supermarket owner, and his wife had both been stabbed to death...repeated stab wounds. On his body the word WAR *had been carved in his chest, then with blood, the killer had scrawled on the refrigerator door:* DEATH TO PIGS. *Hoods had been placed over the heads of the victims. With daylight, the police searched the premise; they found no evidence of robbery, no suggestion of motive. The bizarre circumstances of those two murders last night were strikingly similar to the five murders in a home in Bel-Air a few miles away two days before. This was at the home of movie director Roman Polanski. His wife Sharon Tate was one of the victims. She was eight and a half months pregnant..."*

We all stood around listening as the reporter went on to document the heinous details of the two ghastly crimes. Faye let out a mournful cry and turned from the open window, embracing Billy to sob on his shoulder. Across from me, Mary's face was tear-stained as droplets ran down her cheeks in silence. Even Bobby was wide-eyed and slack-jawed at what he was hearing.

"...one hundred and sixty-nine stab wounds..." the voice recounted through the speakers until Space—in a gesture representative of all of us—sharply turned off the dial.

We were all shocked. This degree of violence, this kind of careless disregard for and morbid waste of human life was inconceivable, despite the moral cesspool of society. It was disgusting, unprecedented—the complete opposite of the peaceful and loving community we'd left back there in California. It was heinous, unwarranted, and senseless—what kind of deranged, immoral monster could have perpetrated these horrid acts? Quite unfortunately, I knew.

This was one of those things you hated to learn about many years after the fact, let alone experience—yet, here it was unfolding gory detail by gory detail in 24-hour news broadcasts across the nation. It was an event that would go on to live in historical infamy; everybody knew about Charlie Manson, even into the next century.

"What kind of sick bastard would do that?" Space cried, looking ill.

I kept my mouth shut; there was no reason for them to know now. The truth would be out soon enough, they didn't need to hear it from me.

None of us knew what to say, so we remained there, gathered around the van, the only sound that of Faye's weeping—a moment of silence for those souls so wrongly burdened with pain and death.

And then, I'm not sure who started it, but one by one, we all started getting our instruments. Al picked up the flute, and Space and Bobby took out the acoustic guitars. I set up my snare and sat down on the bumper with Billy and his bass while Mary Jane and Faye scatted together, singing dirges while the rest of us played the blues, slow and grave. The music we made turned those awful emotions from that awful occasion into something meaningful and worthwhile and alleviated some of that terrible sadness by transfiguring those bad vibes that had arisen. In fact, we were so absorbed in our tribute that we were all startled by a man's voice calling out, "Fellas! Hey, fellas!"

All at once, we stopped playing and turned away from one another to stare ogle-eyed at the colored man who stood before us. Nobody had seen him walk up.

Bobby was arguably the most confused. Without even an attempt at a whisper, he asked aloud, "When did we pick up this guy?"

"We didn't," Mary told him, rolling her eyes.

The man himself went on to answer the question we hadn't yet asked: "I jus' come from a town a couple miles down the road. I've been at the mo'tuh inn there for three days now. I bin a-waitin' for somebody to come along and take me east to St. Louis—ain't nobody goin' that-a-way here, you know—and I walk out to git some fresh air, and by God, I can't believe my ears! I hear the blues a'playing, and I knows that anybody stark loony enough to be playin' the God-blessed blues out in the middle of a Missouri cornfield has got to be mad enough to drive little ol' Marvin Boyd fifty miles or so to St. Louis. So I's come a-runnin' and here you's all is, right in front of my very eyes! What in the name of the Lord are you people doin' out here?"

Now, I didn't know that we were a couple miles from anywhere, but here was this colored guy petitioning us for a ride, and none of us knew quite what to make of him. For starters, he was dressed very eccentric: he had on a plaid smoking jacket which he wore open over a blue button-up shirt and corduroys with round, thick-rimmed glasses balanced precariously on the bridge of his nose. Except for his goatee, he was clean-shaven, and on his head he wore a Brando-style biker cap cocked to one side, under which dark, nappy curls boiled up, pushing it a good two or three inches off his scalp. We could see that he was hip, but his voice was thick with a southern drawl—he certainly wasn't native to this area and looked like he'd never touched an unshucked ear of corn in his life. What he was doing out there was just as valid an inquiry as what we were doing—and in regard to that particular question, we weren't sure how to respond. What *were* we doing out there anyway?

"Brother, have you heard what has happened?" Al asked him.

Marvin Boyd looked around at each of us in turn, alarmed by our solemnity, "No, wha's happened?"

"There's been a murder in Hollywood!" Mary blurted out. "Of an actress and an heiress and—"

"—and the murderer, he came into their home and killed them all!" Billy cried.

"He shot one and stabbed the others," Bobby explained, "and wrote on the walls in their blood."

"Stabbed them?" Marvin Boyd echoed.

"Stabbed them," Billy repeated.

"One hundred and sixty-nine times," Bobby added.

"Killed them," Mary said, "and for no reason."

"Dead," Faye emphasized.

"Nobody knows why," Mary went on, "and it happened again two days later."

"—to an elderly couple with no connection to the first," Space added.

"It's odious, deplorable," Al shook his head remorsefully.

"Who did it?" Marvin Boyd asked.

"Nobody knows," Mary answered, "except the killer himself."

"Or themselves," Billy clarified.

Marvin Boyd took off his hat and rubbed his forehead and in a voice as appalled and somber as ours, he exclaimed, "Wuddah world we live in, *wuddah world...*"

All of us nodded or displayed our consensus in some way.

"Come on, let's go," Billy spoke up, throwing open the door to the Trips Mobile and hopping inside.

"Go? Go where?" Bobby asked.

"To St. Louis, didn't you hear the man?" Billy replied in a tone that suggested that the answer should have been glaringly obvious.

Marvin Boyd looked bewildered, "What? Fo' real? Alright!"

And with that, we peeled out of that Kansas-Missouri cornfield and headed east at top speed after stopping briefly at our hitchhiker's motel so that he could grab his rucksack and settle his debt. Once we were on the road again, we broke out the papers and the jar of grass and started passing around a couple of numbers. When one got passed to Marvin Boyd, he politely declined and pulled a curved, wooden pipe from his jacket pocket and started packing it with cherry blend tobacco.

"These crazed lunatics are products of the System," Billy—who still hadn't dropped this afternoon's scandal—told us grimly after his first hit that evening. "When you live in a society as sick and unnatural as ours, what you get are sick, unnatural people like this."

"That's how a lot of people look at us, you know," Al replied.

"Yeah? Well, fuck them," Bobby grunted over his shoulder from the front seat.

"Perhaps the killer is one of us then...no Movement is perfect, after all," Billy postulated.

Mary gasped, "It couldn't be!"

"Why not?" Billy continued unrelentingly. "A free radical is a free radical, no matter what body it comes out of."

I didn't say a word. Admittedly, I was quite astounded at the accuracy of his suppositions, and rather than confirm or deny his theories, I stayed quiet, wary that one of my friends might remember my perspective and ask me to expound on the truth. Secondly, the brutal subject had gotten more than enough air for one day, and we weren't doing those poor people any good—or harm, one could argue—by speculating on the identities of their killers, especially when we were so far removed from the crime. Therefore, rather than allow Billy to drag the issue out any further, I segued into the identity of our hitchhiker, Marvin Boyd.

"Hey, man...where are you from, anyhow?" I asked him.

"New Orleans," he replied. He said the phrase like a native, *New*

Orelins.

"Why'd you decide to come out to Missouri?"

"Well, they tend not to treat people like us too kindly down where I come from."

He said 'people like us,' but even though he was black, we were of the same kind after all: we were both different. It wasn't our differences from one another that mattered so much as the fact that we both deviated from what the Establishment said it was OK to be, and neither Negro nor shaggy was on that list.

"I wanna live someplace where I can look out over civilization, yet exist apart from it," he stated.

"And you're looking for that in St. Louis?" Al questioned him skeptically.

"Nah," he explained, "you see, I'm a writah…"

At this, Al's ears perked up like a sheepdog's.

"…Imma tryin' to get to St. Louis to publish a book o' mine," he continued, "I think I'll have bettuh luck there than down home."

"What is it that you write about, Brother?" Al asked him.

"Well," he explained, speaking slowly, "at its core, my book is a work o' fiction, but all of the characters are based off o' folks I've met throughout my life. It's a book about the human condition. Thas' what inspires me, the human condition."

"Yes, yes, I can dig that," Al replied, his eyebrows furrowed together as he listened intently. "Please, go on." I could tell from his expression that he'd zeroed in on Marvin and wasn't going to stop picking his brain until he'd learned all he could from the man.

"Well, I see myself less as an authah and more as a recordah, documentin' the trials and tribulations of everyday humanity: its joys and its pitfalls, its most endearin' moments which inspire hope, and its darkest evils which condemn our fate. Thas the one reason why I wanna publish this book—if I can earn bread by writin', I can live wherever I want. I won't be stuck in New Orelins my whole life, working down at the ports; I can travel, and I can learn. In never truly becomin' part of somethin', you will always see it objectively."

Al nodded his head in contemplative understanding. "Why do you write?" was his next question.

"Well, just like good art, good stories move y'all. I've-a heard many stories that have moved me, but very few people will evah hear those stories. I wanna be a megaphone for all those people with a quiet voice."

The two of them talked all the way to St. Louis. At city limits, we bought a map from a convenience store and continued onward. Marvin Boyd had an address scribbled on a piece of paper—Washington Avenue, I think it was—and that's where we let him off. He thanked us gratuitously, picked up his rucksack with his manuscript in it, and disappeared amid the throngs of people on the sidewalk. It was at this point that Space switched with Billy, and we drove on into the night. Al was insatiable the whole time—manic almost—and more animated than I'd ever seen him before.

"I've been inspired!" he declared as soon as Marvin had exited the Trips Mobile. "I know what I want to write about now!"

"What?" I asked him.

"The road!" he exclaimed. "There are no stories like the stories you hear on the road, and I've heard just about all of them."

I was puzzled, "How so?"

"There are only two reasons why people move: they are either trying to find something or they are trying to escape something. After all, in order to run to something, there is always something else that you are running from. Every story you hear on the road fits this model in one way or another. It is only in the minor details that they really differ from one to the next, and that is what makes these stories so inspiring, so universal, and so entertaining. A book of stories is what I will write!"

"What are you going to do about a plot?" Mary asked him.

Al looked disappointed by her lack of imagination, "Who decides that a story must have a plot? The stories they tell out there on the road don't have any plot; they're stories of raw living, and life doesn't have a plot, a goal—at least not in the objective sense of the word. The only goal of life is to live, and we sure as hell are doing that."

He was resolute and determined, and as soon as he was finished espousing his idea to us, he curled up with a notebook and began recounting the stories he'd heard. He stayed like this for hours, writing by moonlight, ensconced in his own little world of The Road.

The map that we'd picked up in St. Louis ceased to be of any use to us once we crossed into Illinois, but we must have been heading in the right direction because as we drove through most of the night and into the next day, I started seeing signs for Indiana, then Kentucky, and West Virginia beyond that. We hit Virginia on what I think must've been the third day after we left Texas, and by early evening, we'd made it all the way into Washington D.C.

Everything in that city was traffic and picket signs and old, dull gray buildings that looked like they might have at one time been white. That same drab coldness was reflected in the people as well, as men in suits with comb-overs and chiseled stone faces took to the sidewalks, all the pleasures of life lost in their expressions. We didn't stop there, but we did end up spending a fair amount of time in D.C. because we got lost, and between the seven of us—even with Al's savvy sense of direction—we couldn't find our way back to I-95 for anything.

By sunset, we were somewhere north of the city and about a mile or two from the airport when we came upon a man in green army fatigues plodding along the shoulder with his thumb out toward the highway. He trudged along with his head down and a worn, green duffel bag in his right hand. He looked more down-and-out than anyone else we'd seen along our journey so far, and Space slowed the van as we pulled up alongside him.

"What are you doing?" Bobby cried indignantly. "He's a fucking baby killer."

"Don't be an ass," Al told him, looking up from his notebook for the first time since Kentucky.

Bobby harrumphed and turned away from the window in disgust.

"Hey, you need a lift?!" Space called out to him.

The man stopped walking and turned slowly to survey the van before approaching us warily. When he got to the door, he leaned forward a little bit and glanced inside to the back where most of us sat.

"You ain't more of those Hare Krishna fuckers are you?" he asked suspiciously. He had a low, harsh voice and spoke in a tone that was dead serious.

"No, man, we're just a bunch of travelers trying to get to New York," Space replied in his usual airy voice, a stark contrast to that of the man.

He raised one eyebrow at Space, then yanked open the passenger-side door and eased himself inside. Mary slid over on the seat to give him some room. He dropped his duffel bag on the floor at his feet like a heavy burden amongst the empty packs of cigarettes and soda cans, then stared blankly ahead of him without a word.

"What's your name?" Space asked.

The man shifted his eyes to look at him, annoyed that we weren't moving yet, but he answered nonetheless, "Merrill. Steve Merrill."

"I'm Space," Space smiled, extending a hand toward him, "This is Mary. The rest of the gang is in the back," he said, pointing behind

310

him.

Mary leaned back on Space as he shifted into drive and playfully saluted our hitchhiker, "Gee, you look like you just walked out of Vietnam! Why such a hurry, soldier? Where's the war?"

He responded with an icy gaze that made it quite clear that he did not appreciate her jest.

Mary retracted her gaze and mumbled, "Gosh, I guess some people can't take a joke."

To my surprise, he answered her, "I flew into Oakland yesterday. I just got in at Friendship this afternoon. Some woman spilled her hot coffee on my class A's in the airport, and I missed the fucking bus."

"Yes, you most certainly did," I heard Bobby mutter under his breath.

Mary turned and shot him a dirty look.

"Where are you headed?" Billy asked him, placing a hand on his shoulder from behind.

To the shock and surprise of all of us, Steve Merrill whirled around and turned on Billy, lunging across the seat with his fist drawn back behind him, "Don't. Touch. Me." He let each syllable drop like a chunk of ice from between his clenched teeth and stared Billy down with a frightening gaze. His eyes were brown, but they were like steel—cold, lifeless, and unwavering. He had a square head and a square jaw which he kept clenched tight and a squared-off flat top crew cut which didn't very much help the condition of his head.

Billy was completely blindsided and held his hands out in front of him, palms open, "Woah, woah, man, stay cool! I'm sorry, I just wanted to know where you were headed, that's all."

Even Steve Merrill himself seemed a bit startled by the force of his reaction, "I'm good," he said, eyeing Billy and the rest of us one more time before turning back around. "Just don't touch me."

Mary climbed into the back with us, and we all shared an expression of fear and concern, both for Steve Merrill himself and for Space who was sitting next to him.

"I told you!" Bobby hissed.

Despite our misgivings, for the rest of the ride, everything was copasetic. Steve Merrill simmered down, and we all returned to our business as usual—albeit slightly subdued, so as not to rouse the volatile vet. We stopped in Baltimore for a few hours to score some cigarettes and chow, then kept trucking on toward New Jersey, but after we reached the Delaware River, Space pulled off the highway and into some sort of rest area with picnic tables and fire pits. It was dark, there were no streetlights, and no other cars were around. Save for the headlamps, all we had was dim moonlight to combat the misty night.

"Hey, what's going on here?" Steve Merrill asked. "How come we're stopping?"

"We've been traveling for over twenty-four hours now," Space replied matter-of-factly, "we're going to rest for a couple hours and get our thing together before going any further."

"I don't know about you people, but I want to get home!" he cried. "I live in Williamstown, it can't be more than two hours from here!"

"It's getting too foggy to drive, and I don't know this area," Space replied calmly, in a reasonable tone. "We could all use some rest. We'll leave as soon as day breaks again."

Steve Merrill continued to protest.

"Hey, you heard the man," Bobby—who couldn't resist adding his two cents—spoke above him, "we're staying until the morning."

Steve Merrill looked helplessly from Bobby to Space to the rest of us, and then, cussing under his breath, he exited the van and slammed the door behind him. While we all got busy dragging out the sleeping bags and gathering branches and twigs for kindling, he went and sat down on one of the logs surrounding the fire pit and started puffing away on a cigarette. My heart went out to the man, it really did, but there was nothing I could say to comfort him. Rather, I glanced around to see where Faye had gone.

"Faye!" I called to the girl poking around under the trees a few hundred feet from me, and she came trotting over.

"Go sit with him," I asked her, handing her a sleeping bag to give to the soldier, "please?"

Faye smiled, her two rows of tiny white teeth shining back at me in the dim light. She took the sleeping bag and padded with bare feet across the dirt to the log where Steve Merrill sat and handed it to him. He looked up at her, and I knew that she was smiling, all of her innocence and beauty radiating peace and good vibes. As she did so, his entire demeanor and body language changed ever so slightly. He stopped slumping, his shoulders shifted upward, and his chin moved away from his chest; his eyes softened. As I witnessed this, I too smiled; Faye could be a ray of sunshine to the ninth circle of hell.

As the night progressed, one by one, we all came to sit around the fire, which was built and lit without very much difficulty. Steve Merrill, though he seemed less disheartened than before, was still as guarded and unapproachable as ever. He was not nearly as

312

forthcoming as Marvin Boyd, and when he did speak, it was in short, curt sentences. However, once we'd gotten him smoked up and a little buzzed, he talked far more.

"Now tell me, man, what the fuck are we fighting for?" I remember Mary asking him at one point.

"You're asking me?" he replied with a snort of crude laughter. "How should I know? All I know is that three years ago I got a draft notice from the War Department, two weeks later I was down in Fort Hood, Texas doing basic training, and three weeks after that I was up to my ass in the foulest, dirtiest shit you can imagine, in a place I'd never heard of before, with people I'd never met firing live rounds over my head. That's all I know."

"How about a toast," Billy suggested in a booming voice, "a toast to *'Fuck Johnson!'*"

Steve Merrill unhitched a canteen full of whiskey from his belt loop, "Here, here!" he resounded.

"Violence is an American tradition," Billy spoke in a morose tone. I could tell that he was getting ready to launch into one of his long-winded anti-war rants, but Mary interrupted him.

"—and it's not only in America," she said sadly, "anywhere people are dying there is some kind of war. The whole world is an organism at war with itself."

"Right on," Billy added in the silence that followed her reply.

"What's up with him?" Steve Merrill asked reproachfully, gesturing toward Al who was sitting across from him and attempting to transcribe the ongoing dialogue in his notebook.

"Oh, don't mind Al, he's a writer," I told him.

"A writer, eh? Well, put this in your book," Steve Merrill said to Al.

Al looked up from his page, eyes wide and pen at the ready.

"In war, you are fighting against every natural human instinct a man has, and if your spirit ain't broken, you ain't gonna pull through. There have been nights when the sky wasn't dark from dusk till dawn because the jungle around us was exploding full of mortars and tracers and bombs. I know the smell of burning human flesh. I've heard the screams and the pleas and the prayers for mercy…not to mention the things I've seen. I've listened to the sound of chopper blades and monsoon rain on a steel helmet long enough to drive you mad. It got to be so that the only thing you knew anymore was the sound of rain pounding… relentless…and the fear of being in enemy territory where at any turn, at any moment—unexpected or through orders—you could be in a combat situation with countless ways to die. You became paranoid. The rain itself became other things—it embodied your every fear, all of your nightmares—you heard everything in the rain... And now, coming back to the World, I feel cold and dark and mean inside, like everything terrible in the jungle has come home with me."

Nobody knew quite what to say after that.

"How about another toast?" I suggested quietly, after a while of only the spitting and crackling of the fire to break the silence. "To peace."

Private Steve Merrill unscrewed the cap of his canteen a second time and held it up in the air, "To peace," he repeated before passing it to Billy beside him and on around the circle. Even Bobby managed to remain magnanimous.

That night, we slept beside the fire, and the chill and the dampness in the air was warded off by the dry flames and shots of Steve Merrill's whiskey. I awoke several times during the hours we were camped there, and each time I did, I got up and shook off the dew and the blankets to stoke the fire. And every time I got the chance, I snuck a glance over at Steve Merrill. He did not sleep a wink the entire night. Each time I checked, he lay just as motionless as before, on his back with his eyes wide open and aimed toward the sky—eyes deeply troubled with confusion and dread, eyes that searched for answers in the dark, starless abyss...eyes that sighed, unsurprised, when none returned.

The next morning, we left shortly after sunrise, just as Space had promised. Steve Merrill had barely spoken a word since the night before, and even when we let him off outside his house, he didn't say a thing to anybody except for Al, whom he'd told, "I better get a copy of that book." To my surprise, he gave the rest of us a salute, and we touched two fingers to our foreheads in turn and saluted him back. I peered out the window as we pulled away and watched him walk up the front steps toward his home and family and an attempt to return to a normal life which, as you and I know, would never be the same again. Sometimes even now I still think about Steve Merrill and wonder what became of him; if he ever warmed up to the World or if he, like so many others, had simply faded away into the night.

****

A BRIEF AND BEAUTIFUL TRIP BACK

****

Since the day before when we'd picked him up and the time of his stoic exit, Steve Merrill had left some pretty heavy vibes there in the Trips Mobile, but by the time we hit the Garden State Parkway, those feelings had evaporated just like the fog over the land. We were smoked up, of course, and feeling mighty good. We were talking and rapping, singing and jamming—there was a smile on every face and a joint in every hand. The end of our journey was nigh, and boy, we just couldn't wait to get out of that van! A couple hundred acres to roam on sounded like just as good a deal as any, and it filled us with excitement to know that we'd most likely be at the festival grounds by nightfall.

Now that we were in the Tri-State Area and close to New York City, the FM stations were groovy again—still not as groovy as the San Francisco stations, I might add, but groovy nonetheless. The station we were listening to was playing some songs off of CCR's *Green River*, which had been released earlier in the month. I told them that I had memories of playing *Lodi* with The Descendants back at the Joint in Fresno on New Years' Eve 1999—which was truly a strange thing indeed to remember—and they'd all remarked that that was pretty far out.

I've always loved the CCR; their music is the best soundtrack for anything novel and fun—hanging out with good company, getting high, cruising along the highway, high-speed road rage races... You see, Bobby was driving, and he'd had some beef with another driver in a yellow box truck, and before any of us knew what had happened, he'd power-shifted into high gear and the Trips Mobile lurched forward as he floored it and cut over two lanes while we were knocked around in the back like ragdolls. Recently, in lieu of his customary fix, Bobby had taken to rationing his junk and supplementing it with Space's cocaine—and for Bobby, cocaine was not a complementary drug, especially in situations like this when he seemed to zero in on something like a heat-seeking missile and not let up until he'd gotten his kicks. In this particular case, all that mattered was catching that damn box truck, even if we caused a twelve car pile-up or crashed into the retaining wall and died.

"Woahhh! Cool it, Steve McQueen!" Space cried, jumping into the front seat and wrestling the wheel away from Bobby. The Trips

Mobile swerved violently in and out of our lane for a couple seconds, and a few irritated drivers blew their horns at us, but the struggle was over swiftly, and then we were back in the slow lane doing forty with Space behind the wheel.

"Everybody alright back there, gang?" he asked, peering in the rearview mirror as he adjusted it to see.

We responded with a resonant groan, championed by Billy who'd had his head bashed into the guitar case he was leaning up against, "What gives, man?" he demanded, sounding genuinely annoyed.

"Di'ja see that fucker? Di'ja see 'im, di'ja see 'im cut me off?" Bobby pounded his fist on the dashboard, and then proceeded to roll down the window, stick his head out, and scream at the box truck—which was already far out of earshot and almost completely out of view—and his cries of "*Motherfu*—" were drowned out by the semi that passed us, protesting our speed with a lengthy baritone honk.

Mary was the only one of us who was entirely unfazed, and she just looked at him with this eternally calm expression on her face and said, "Oh, Bobby, you've got to mellow out, man! It's all good, it's all groovy—in fact, it's beautiful! He's rushing to get everywhere and do everything because he's afraid he'll up and die before he gets to do it all, and that's his trip; it's the whole East Coast mentality, they've all got that hang up."

It was no mystery that she had been dipping into our acid reserves as of late.

I waited to hear Bobby's reply, but by the time she'd finished expressing her sentiment, which she spoke in a very languid kind of sleepy tone, he'd already forgotten all about the box truck and was fixated on something else of acute interest to him outside.

"Hey man, would you mind closing that window? It really *stinks* in here!" Billy asked, and Bobby obliged.

Prior to Bobby's freakout, all the windows in the van had been closed in a somewhat vain attempt to keep out the noxious gases that blew in from the highway. In fact, much to our surprise and dismay, the whole state of New Jersey smelled like one giant, rotten egg. This was most likely a byproduct of the plumes and coils of smoke that were belched out of the nearby factory smokestacks at quite an alarming rate, filling the azure skies with vast clouds of thick, pale smog. It looked like a scene out of a certain Dickens novel, and this was pretty ironic considering the road upon which we were traveling was called the Garden State Parkway. In fact, we didn't see one garden, field, or farm until we reached New York, and after traveling

316

through New Jersey, it made New York seem all the more beautiful. After passing through Linden and Newark, we decided not to take the route through New York City, first and foremost because as far as human innovation is concerned, we'd already seen far more than we would've liked. Really, such squalid places made quite a mockery of our cause, and although it would've been groovy to visit the East Village, we didn't want to see even one skyscraper, yellow taxi, or flashing neon sign. Rather, we all had this insatiable desire for nature and its raw beauty. Besides, someone once told me that whole tracts of Manhattan are built on landfill, so if there were to be an earthquake, entire sections of the city would just drop off into the ocean, and to us, that sounded like quite the bummer.

It is not sufficient to say that hitting the New York State Thruway was a breath of fresh air, which it was, literally. It was almost as if we'd crossed into another whole country. Excitement levels were high—we were almost to Woodstock! But rather than be impatient, we were more at peace than we had been in a while. With that being said, it isn't to condemn our journey; after all, tensions rise and then they fall—thus is the natural course of human interaction. You try to get seven people to live together in a fourteen-foot van for two weeks or so and see if there isn't a tiff or two, especially when those seven people are a time traveler, a flower child, a conspiracy theorist, a heroin junkie, a gypsy, an eccentric writer, and an airheaded speed freak.

Improbability aside, those seven people were, at that moment, completely serene. We were out in the countryside now, so rather than bulldozers and smokestacks and retaining walls, there was a captivating abundance of natural wonders—deep, cool rivers and towering mountains, forests full of trees laden with glossy green leaves and vast empty fields of waving grass. Guitars and voices were ringing out again, this time alive with the sounds of *Blonde on Blonde* and *Song to a Seagull*. Mary, with her blond hair and cheery voice, did an imitation of Joni Mitchell with success and satisfaction while Space tried, quite comically at that, to capture the essence of Bob Dylan. Giggles, grins, and grass were plentiful in the Trips Mobile that day. Bobby had shot up and was beginning to simmer down—leaned up against *Connie* with his arm around me, as calm and non-confrontational as ever—while Billy and his lover took turns singing lyrics and strumming guitar and Al unceasingly recorded memory after memory in his now half-full notebook.

1969

The scenes that passed, clad in their bright summer colors, were singular in their beauty. All the windows were open now, and the scents of pine and forest blew into the van. I peered out the window closest to me and watched the hills roll by and the bright, fluffy, white clouds sink behind the mountains. Fields of tall grass and wildflowers dotted the shoulder and receded into the tree line, untouched by human hands and generally unaffected. To us, it seemed to be a road into the Garden of Eden.

And then, all of a sudden, there was this little child running in the fields. She was a fair girl of about eight or ten—or such was our closest approximation as we slowed and passed her. Barefoot, she gamboled about without a care in the world, without a vested interest in anything other than her own bliss, without any idea of how beautiful she looked to us. She was the freest spirit ever to live—liberty incarnate. There seemed to be no object which she pursued, nothing she was running after or looking to find, and the calm of her body, the lightness of her spins and her steps, were enough to confirm that there was nothing she was running from. However, up ahead—in a place she would reach shortly if she continued on her path—grew a beautiful peach tree, its branches heavy with fruit. It was the only one in sight; the only one we had seen our whole way upon this journey. To witness this sight brought tears to my eyes, and those tears were of the best kind—the sort that appear whenever joy and happiness are so great and so abundant that the only way they can be expressed is through the eyes. And I was not the only one; Faye and Al had also seen these things, and once again, without words—through nothing other than a momentary glance—what needed to be communicated was conveyed, what needed to be said, said.

The whole trip at this point seemed completely surreal. I couldn't believe where I was any more than I could believe where I was going. That strange feeling of unreality I'd felt when I first arrived there began to make itself known again once more. Logic attempted to structure my thoughts and explain my circumstance, but no good logic had been functioning in my mind for quite some time now. It had lost its validation and I my belief in the infallibility of human reason after it had been juxtaposed against the vast reality of creation at large. The universe is much grander than the confines of human reason make it out to be, trust me.

I have always regarded Woodstock with a sort of mystical awe. It was an event I considered to have been truly magical and deeply

318

spiritual in nature, a consequence of inimitable circumstance that stood alone in history. I was not alone in my opinions—not by a long shot—but having grown up without the firsthand experience of being there, all my views up to that point were purely objective.

There were two films of Jack's that George showed me as a kid that have influenced the person I am today unequivocally and beyond compare, one being *The Song Remains The Same* and the other being *Woodstock*, the 1970 movie. At six years old, when I watched Jimmy Page shred the guitar with that violin bow, I knew that I wanted nothing more out of life than to be a performer, and when I saw Michael Shrieve, Santana's drummer, play *Soul Sacrifice* at Woodstock, I knew that I wanted to be just like him. I'd watched both films enough times to be considered a fanatic, the latter probably slightly more than the former. I thought about that film now, and some really weird ideas started coming to me. After all, considering that I was about to be present for that very event, was it possible that I was in the film? Was it possible that on that very same VHS tape my father and I watched so often there was footage of me at this festival? Was it possible that he'd watch it again someday in the future and recognize me and know where I'd gone to? This train of conjecture was so intriguing that I remained upon it for quite a while until a bump in the road rocked me from my wild thoughts and brought me back to this somehow even more wild reality. However, this lasted only momentarily because by this time we were all out of grass again and were indulging instead in hash, a substance engineered for contemplation, and before long at all, I was off again on another thought-trip.

I don't quite know what any of us were expecting to see when we arrived—for me, it was probably fields of 500,000 like you see in all the pictures—but what we got when we finally turned off the Thruway onto the exit for Route 17B and rolled into White Lake was various different farms and road stands with tractors and barns and silos. You couldn't count a hundred people, let alone several hundred thousand.

"Hey, are you sure we're in the right place, man?" Billy asked.

"That's what all the posters said," Space replied.

"Rhiannon?" Billy consulted me for historical accuracy.

I nodded, "This is the place, or at least close to it."

He was almost incredulous, "You're putting me on! Come on now, where is it really?"

"I'm telling you," I insisted with a laugh, "we must just be early, that's all. It doesn't start until the 15th."

1969

"Well, what's today?" he asked.

We all kind of looked around at one another and shrugged our shoulders. In the midst of the subsequent silence, Bobby's voice rose up from next to me in the back, "You mean to tell me we drove all the way across the country to see a couple of cows and a cornfield?! What kind of bullshit is this? I thought this was going to be some kind of real happening, some heavy groups are supposed to be playing this gig!"

"Just you wait," I assured him, chuckling.

We drove for a couple minutes more on 17B and into Bethel itself—which was a squat little country town with one paved road—and there we began to see a disproportionate amount of cars to the number of few-and-far-between houses there were. They were parked all along the road on both sides, and we even began to hit traffic. This we regarded as unusual, but it wasn't until we started to see people like us, fellow freaks, that we knew we were definitely in the right place. At some point, we turned off of 17B where there was a huge red sign that told us the Aquarian Exposition was right around the corner. We drove until we couldn't drive anymore and parked behind a mass of cars that were already immobilized on the side of a hill. The sound of the Trips Mobile tires rolling over those last couple hundred yards of rock and earth were some of the most satisfying sounds I've ever heard. Almost immediately upon shifting into park, all of us were tumbling out the doors and into the soft, green, New York grass. We were finally at Woodstock!

The conclusion of our trip was a sound one, and even upon arrival alone we could all tell that the energy around this place was just positively unreal. There were people all over: walking down from where the cars were parked, or conversely, coming back up from what little town there was. There were heads everywhere, and there were more on the way. A line of cars showing no sign of stopping filed in behind us and more freaks emerged, chatting eagerly, waving hello, and flashing the peace sign to all their newfound comrades. The seven of us followed in suit. Space took the keys from the ignition and threw them in the glovebox, and then we started walking. In addition to all those who were traveling one way or the other, there were a fair amount of people just hunkering down in their cars, listening to the radio or playing guitar. There was this one young couple with Ohio plates playing chess in the bed of their pickup truck whom we asked where the music was going to be, and they pointed us in the direction we needed to go.

It wasn't too far of a walk straight down the hill to what was later coined 'the bowl,' but I don't think any of us would have minded even if it was. After being cooped up in the van for so long, the walk did us all a world of good. As we hoofed it along the road, getting acquainted with all the new sights, the conversation was light, yet filled with anticipation.

"Oh, man!" Mary cried, buzzing with excitement. "I cannot wait for this thing to start!"

"It looks to me as if it already has," Al mused, scanning the area.

"Just give it another couple of days," I predicted, paying heed to my futuristic roots.

"There's just one thing I don't understand," Bobby said, puffing away on a cigarette that was slowly making its way around to all of us, "if the concert's in Bethel and it was supposed to be in Wallkill, why do they call it Woodstock? This is nowhere near the real Woodstock! What kind of bonehead thought that was a good idea for a name?"

"I think they originally wanted to have it in Woodstock because that's where Bob Dylan lives, but there wasn't a big enough venue. The name of the group that put it together call themselves Woodstock Ventures," I explained.

Bobby shrugged, "Monterey was in Monterey, Newport was in Newport, Seattle was in Seattle—there's a trend here that begs to be followed."

"Well, this one is supposed to be unprecedented, right?" Mary added, somewhat sagaciously.

"Look!" Space cried, pointing down the road, "Hare Krishnas!"

Bobby's cynicism was averted by about twenty or thirty men and women dressed in orange robes with bare feet dancing toward us, throwing their arms in the air and beating on hand drums in succession. Some of the men had shaved heads, and some of the women had strings of beads and flowers hanging from around their necks; all of them seemed to be in a state of joyful reverence as they gleefully recited their Maha Mantra. They came upon us euphoric, surrounding us and absorbing us into their ranks, engaging us in their worship. They waved their arms around us and touched us lightly and repeatedly on our heads and shoulders, and for a few moments, we grooved with them in their ceremony. A few of the women removed their flower chains and beads and placed them around our necks, but they did not linger for long. Rather, they continued on, their devotion uninterrupted, and we watched them go from where we stood. Space,

321

who had the most leis out of all of us, laughed in an almost crazed sort of way after they had gone and started dancing himself, light on his feet.

"You know, I'm not sure what it is about those people," he told us, "but if there ever comes a time when I ain't playing music no more, man, I think I'm gonna run off with 'em and live in one of their ashrams—chant, meditate, bathe—be a religious freak, you know, man?"

We all chuckled a bit amongst ourselves just imagining it.

"You gonna cut your hair for it, man?" Bobby asked him doubtfully.

Space raised his eyes to look at the mess of ginger curls that had spilled over his bandana and onto his forehead, "Oh no, never," he replied, completely serious. "They'll have to make an exception for me."

By and by, we finally came upon the festival grounds, which at the moment were nothing more than fields of tall, green grass. There were already people all over, but nothing like you see in the pictures. Across the field from us, a bunch of people were busy putting up a long chain-link fence that encircled the entire area. Down at the bottom of the hill—which was enormous in and of itself—a structure, large even from our vantage point, was being erected. The legendary stage was still incomplete, and the huge yellow towers that stood beside it were currently in their infancy, surrounded by men up in cherry pickers with tool belts and welding guns. Beyond that, a bridge of sorts stretched across the road that ran along behind the stage, and off to the right, there was a field full of hundreds of cars. At first, all we could do was stand and grok at how magnificent it was. An energy like none other was already coming on, and despite all the moving around, the place itself evoked this unparalleled feeling of stillness and quiet—of complete peace.

As we scoped out the place, taking stock of our surroundings and making our way down to the stage, we became acquainted with some of the other pilgrims that had found their way there and swapped travel stories with them. At the very bottom of the hill, a whole bunch of men in blue t-shirts were mulling around the construction site. There were several dozen of them at least—maybe even a hundred—and many more new arrivals were standing around gawking and rapping with them. All in all, it was a relatively chill scene. It was hard to imagine how mad it would become in just a few days, as I knew it would.

We approached a couple of the builders who were sitting down and taking a smoke break in the grass, and they filled us in on all the goings-on. They told us that they were part of the Hog Farm Commune in New Mexico, the group that Michael Lang and the other festival organizers had contracted and flown in to do all the heavy lifting and general grunt-work, and they seemed very happy to be doing it, despite the mad rush. After all, the concert itself was due to start in only three days. They also told us that the infamous Wavy Gravy, formerly a Merry Prankster by the name of Hugh Romney and current Hog Farm Commune leader, could be seen roaming about in a white jumpsuit and broad-brimmed hat, playing the kazoo and directing traffic. Billy reacted to this with surprise and replied that he'd known the man well back in San Francisco during his Prankster days.

"You know Hugh too, huh?" the builder remarked. "You're the second one today who's said so. He's a gas!"

Billy agreed, "So why is it that they chose you guys to come in here and put this whole thing together?"

"Because there's a lot of us!" his partner replied. "And now I'm starting to wish that there were more!"

"Slow going, huh?" Space asked.

"Well, it's not only that; we only started to break ground a couple of weeks ago. They're expecting something like 150,000 people to come up here over the three days this festival's going to run. I don't know if we're going to be able to get everything done on time."

"Yeah," the other builder chimed in, "we ain't even got the whole stage built yet, let alone got the cameras or speakers in place. There's already a good ten thousand people here, I'd say, and they ain't got no way to collect tickets or anything. There ain't not one booth set up yet, and the food trucks and the porta-johns are still on their way."

"How long ago did people start coming around?" I inquired. "We just got here ourselves."

"Oh, maybe a week ago..." the somber builder replied, and the other picked up where he left off, a big grin spread across his face, "All kinds of heads and freaks from all over have been descending upon this little country hamlet. Anywhere you go you can see them: in the bars, in the motels, in the streets, in the fields. We outnumber the straights by far already, and the townspeople don't know what to make of us. After all, this is just a sleepy little farming community; drugs and revolution and rock music are for city folk. Apart from the occasional open smoking of marijuana, we aren't really breaking the law or disrupting their lives any. We aren't vandalizing, pillaging, robbing or fornicating in public like they expected us to—or at least the people in Wallkill expected us to. In fact, the buzz is that most of them seem pretty amazed at how well-mannered and peaceful we are. The Heat hasn't been around to bust anybody just yet, and I don't think they will as long as we don't make any trouble for them. I'm expecting it to be a real groovy scene."

His enthusiasm was contagious, "Right on, man," the formerly pessimistic builder said. "You know, even if we don't finish everything according to plan, this is still going to be one hell of a party. It's going to be something that none of us forgets for a long, long time."

"Where's the party now?" Bobby asked them. "Any bars around here with a good crowd?"

"Yeah, there's one just about a mile up the road," the cheery builder answered, "it's called Hector's Inn. You go straight back the way you came, then cross 17B and hang a left, it's right on the corner of the first cross street you come to."

"They got any live bands playing over there?"

"Not that I know of, yet. I was there last night—great beer, great people, great time."

Abreast of this new information, we thanked them and headed back up the hill, this time with a destination in mind. We stopped in at the Trips Mobile, took our instruments upon our backs, and hoofed it down to Hector's Inn. It was about sunset by the time we got there; the sky in the west had just begun to glow crimson, and many of our brothers and sisters had already gathered in and around the parking lot. It was then that we realized not driving was one of the best decisions we could've made. At first, we were all planning on packing back into the Trips Mobile and forgoing the twenty-minute walk, but it was Billy who pointed out that we had about a snowball's chance in hell of getting that same parking place overlooking the bowl once we came back that night. Additionally, parking once we got there would have been even more of an issue. It seemed like Hector's Inn was the place to be because there were more cars parked down the road, on the grass, and along that stretch of 17B than there were up near the bowl itself.

The establishment known as Hector's Inn was nothing more than a divey little one-room bar with whitewashed wooden siding and a slat roof, smelling strongly of chicken manure and grass. It was probably built to seat about ten to fifteen people around the bar and hold another fifteen more tops, but upon entering, we found that there were over forty heads crammed into that one little room—they'd even moved the

324

pool table and a bunch of chairs out onto the lawn to make room for the standing crowd. Dozens more people were gathered around outside, calling in their orders and passing cigarettes and joints through the open windows. It was a groovy scene; the only thing that was missing was the music, and that we'd come to provide. Somewhere amid the throes, a radio was playing, but it wasn't nearly enough to satisfy the insatiable need for live music that was present in that day. We asked the bartender if we could plug in and play, and since he had no qualms about it, that's what we did.

Unfortunately, in order to do so, we had to displace about five or six people, but the crowd was real good about sharing the venue, and throughout the night they rotated in and out through the open front door to see the show up close and order up a cold one or two. Luckily enough, Hector's Inn—like many other dives—already had a PA system as well as a few amps hanging around for traveling bands like ours. It didn't take us long to hook up and plug in, and once we did, boy, what a jam band we were! Mary's voice sounded as sweet as birdsong, the boys on guitar were locked in and all smiles, and Al's fingers looked like a row of little tiny dancers dipping and plunging and sweeping across the keys as he played. The dancing started up right away, and a young girl with a flute joined in and played with us for most of that night and the next. Considering the nature of the trek we'd taken, I'd only brought my snare, hi-hat, and one tom along with me, but to my surprise and delight, I found that the venue kept a bass drum—along with an accordion and—believe it or not—a stumpf fiddle—on hand. One of the regulars that was hanging around even rooted through the back room and supplied me with a pair of brushes.

That night was singular for a couple of reasons. Although we did play several covers, the best part of the night was when we started breaking out some of the new, original material that we'd never debuted before. The trip from California had been rich in the area of songwriting, and we'd come out on the other end of the country with a lot of first-rate material. Al, of course, was the driving force behind that, and although unintentional, the words he penned for Mary to sing and the riffs and melodies he conjured up for the rest of us jived completely with the energy we were all feeling that night. There was a certain sense of progression, of movement, of mystic, and of travel that was present in all of his songs. They—like his novel in progress— were meta-products of and about the road, a common denominator for all of us present. My personal favorite was one he'd written about hitchhiker's signs that he'd seen along the way entitled Riding My

Thumb—the best line of which was something like, '*I'm heading north to Boise, south to Anaheim, going nowhere in particular and running out of time.*'

Another factor that makes that night so memorable—or maybe less so—was the grass. I don't know whose hands Space had so graciously taken it off of and where the guy before him had gotten it, but let me tell you, the grass we smoked that week was some of the best I have ever smoked in my entire life—I think it was called meshmacon. Now, getting too high and trying to play music is no good, but on nights like that one when we were all on the same level it just *worked*, and everybody around us could dig it.

By the end of that first night, there were so many people inside that smoky little room it seemed like if any more were to enter at once, the walls would burst at their seams. At a certain point near to closing time when we were taking a smoke break, a short, thin-framed little beatnik-looking guy with a 35-millimeter Rangefinder camera slung around his neck, boat shoes on his feet, and a beret on his head emerged from the crowd and asked if he could take our picture. Naturally, we all agreed and posed there with our instruments as he snapped several with the 35-mil and then some with a Polaroid he had in a leather case strapped to his belt. The Polaroid prints he gave to us, and while we waited for them to develop, he asked for our names. We told him "The Day Trippers," to which he replied, "That's real groovy. What a charismatic group and what groovy music! The bunch of you are a great talent."

Bobby swelled with pride next to me, and the photographer went on to inquire about where we were from. We answered by telling him San Francisco and recounted some of the more memorable episodes of our pilgrimage. To this, he responded with great interest and told us that he was a music writer from *Rolling Stone Magazine* and that he went around to different happenings looking for fresh faces and groovy sounds. He explained that he wanted to do an article on the people he met at the Aquarian Exposition and that we were fantastic material.

Elated, we began volunteering information for his article, telling him about life in the City, the places we'd played, the musicians we'd shared the stage with that summer, et cetera. It wasn't very long before he produced a notepad from his pocket and a pen from behind his ear to jot all this stuff down and Bobby began filling him in on his life history and giving him the address of the Trips Center so that *Rolling Stone* could send him the first copy of the magazine when it came out.

326

The rest of us just shook our heads and let him ramble on—after all, it isn't every day you are personally interviewed for the top rock n' roll journal of all time.

Hector's Inn closed up for the night at around four a.m. I wasn't sure if it was because the crowd had finally thinned out or if they'd run out of beer; however, I was under the assumption of the latter because even long after nightfall, when we were trekking back to the van by starlight alone, those headlights just kept right on coming. Despite the lateness of the hour, there were still people everywhere. All the motels in the area were already full, so many people had returned to their cars and were camping out. Small bonfires were popping and crackling away, and 8-track tape players aired muffled midnight music amid the hush of waning chatter.

Our little beatnik journalist friend had disappeared into the throngs of beaded ladies dancing shortly after we'd struck up again, and that was the last we saw of him for the duration of our time there. Even though there had been no guarantee upon his word that we'd actually be featured in the article, we couldn't stop talking about what a stroke of luck it was. Bobby especially had gotten an ego boost out of the experience. However, it had been a long night, and eventually, our excitement ran out and we were enveloped in that warm and comfortable feeling of coming down. Our highs were tapering with the moonlight, our vision a little less blurry and our mouths a little less dry. The night itself had faded to a soft glow and the first hints of purple morning were beginning to creep into the sky as the crickets concluded their evening concert and were replaced by the first birds of dawn.

Billy was carrying Faye on his back, and Al was carrying *Connie* on his. Bobby had his guitar slung over his shoulder while Space held onto his own and Billy's. I had my sticks in my hand and my snare under my arm and Mary carried my tom, traps, and cymbals. We were all pretty beat and plodded back to the van exhausted, but we wore the widest of smiles on our faces. We trudged along, putting one foot in front of the other in a rhythm that quickly became so hypnotic that we all struggled to keep our eyes open, and pretty soon we were stumbling along in that wonderfully delirious kind of half-sleep that feels like you've been stoned silly. This went for all of us except for Bobby who had snorted some white stuff before we left in a vain attempt to keep the night from its imminent end. He was amped as all hell—darting around, talking nonsense to everyone we passed, and coming on to

327

me. I don't quite remember what became of him after we made it back to the van; we were all out cold within thirty seconds of hitting the blankets, and he was most likely off again in search of more thrills.

For the first few days after we arrived, there was no music. We passed the time by smoking grass, strumming guitar, roaming all around that wide open space, and greeting the newcomers as they came up the hill. From the time we awoke to the time we returned to our slumbers, we watched them flock to the fields. They came in droves; by the bus-load and car-load they rode in, seated atop vans and hanging out of RV windows in a ceaseless flow of traffic. Even by helicopter they arrived and in every other possible fashion—all kinds of people from everywhere, with license plates ranging from California to Maine. The cumulative total swelled by the thousands each hour, and by mid-afternoon of that very same day, the influx was restricted to foot traffic alone, for there was no more space to park. The two-lane dirt road that stretched in from the highway had become a one-way street, and people just started leaving their cars and walking.

Hundreds at a time they descended upon that half-finished stage, some of them with big huge rucksacks upon their backs, others with nothing at all. They came and spread blankets at the top of the hill, pitched tents in the woods, built stands, and carried in wares and artwork of all kinds to be set up, shown, and sold. That tiny little town had become a city, and just like any other city, it was alive all of the time. It was like being in San Francisco without the buildings or the fog; the air was fresh and clean, and there were no hassles of any kind. It was a beautiful exhibition, and nobody was prepared for what they were seeing. In fact, it was almost surreal to believe that it was actually happening. It was a coalition; a revival of everything we'd ever wanted or worked for or tried to achieve politically, socially, or otherwise. There were no fights, no violence—not even a frown, for when you walked up that hill and saw the bowl and all those thousands, you couldn't help but smile because you were within the growing borders of utopia, and you knew you had just entered into Eden.

I spent most of that day and the next listening to the boys play and Mary sing. They were smoothing out the rough edges in a couple of Al's new songs, and I was sunning myself atop the van with the transistor radio in my ear. Just about every New York station was buzzing with news of the festival, and all the announcers were talking in one of two ways about the impending concert: excitement or horror, to name them, and the version you heard was entirely dependent upon which station you tuned into. In general, the tone in which they voiced their opinions was unwavering and either positive and encouraging or majorly pejorative. In this way, it was real easy to tell the hip stations from those that were square. The majority condemned the festival and warned potential attendees about the dangers of embarking, citing a fear of anti-war riots, protests, and drug overdoses—none of which we were seeing, and we were right in the heart of it. But even so, interspersed amongst those more negative commentaries could be found stations with last-minute, stand-in hosts raving about the festival in excitement and envy, seeing as those normally contracted to do the show had split several hours earlier to catch the action first-hand.

The real gems, however, were those usually square news stations that gave Woodstock a fighting chance to prove itself before writing it off as just another ridiculous hippie gathering.

"What could make 200,000 kids leave their towns and cities and drive thousands of miles, some of 'em, all to go sit in an Upstate field for three days? —There's got to be something to it," a man on one of these such stations asked his co-host.

"God first planted a garden," Al chimed in, having overheard, "and paradise wears many façades."

"I don't understand it myself, Dan," the second man replied, "but it seems to be the music that draws them there. Music of any kind has never had a following like it does by today's young people."

"A lot of people think this thing is just going to end up being another demonstration, what do you think about it, Jim?"

"Well, when you get that many of those young people together, it can have quite the polarizing effect…I guess all we can do is wait and see what happens."

"The organizers have been promoting it as 'three days of peace and music,' what do you say to that?"

Jim, the more skeptical of the two, snorted in contempt, "Well, I'd say that's near impossible in today's world, wouldn't you?"

The voice of Dan, the initiator, seemed distant, "I don't know, Jim," he said, "they sure seem to think it is…"

"Man, they really can't dig it, can they?" Billy exclaimed, for he too had been listening in as well.

"They can't possibly understand us because we are so far removed from anything they have ever seen before," Al explained, "and besides, of late, there have been more problems in regard to the Movement. A lot of people have gotten more political, like in Chicago, in Berkeley, and they're afraid something like that is going to happen again—but they are right about one thing."

"And what is that?" Billy asked.

"The key factor, the reason why this isn't going to turn into a riot or a protest—music."

I looked around myself at all the people, all those beautiful people, and thought: *In this world of forever changes, there are only a few things that are eternal. Peace and love are amongst them; however, today they seem to be the hardest to find. But in this place, peace and love are all there is.*

Straights today have a hard time trying to imagine how peace and love can coexist with rebellion. What they don't seem to understand is that peace and love are the highest possible form of rebellion— rebellion against indoctrinated greed, racism, inequality, hatred, and fear. They can't imagine it because it can't be imagined, it must first be experienced; you've just got to do it. There was a lot of faith in what we did, a lot of trust placed in one another. While everyone else in the world was busy hating and warring and pursuing their own agendas, we wanted to be that shining light raining peace and love in the face of the established order. And in addition to the music, the reason it all worked was that we were all in it together. It was the lack of dissension and undermining that made up for our low credibility. We all believed it was going to work; therefore it would. After all, together we are all creators of the universe.

Now, this had not always been my conviction. In fact, until recently, my locus of control had widely been attributed to the universe at large, and I'd entirely disregarded the pivotal part I played in determining my own happiness, let alone the course of my life. However, as life went on and I underwent more and more experiences, this inherent truth became more and more apparent to me. Space was excellent proof of this; he could do just about anything, regardless of its absurdity and/or its impossibility. For example, it was that very same day when he told us that he was leaving.

After we'd all finished exclaiming our shock and disbelief, he explained to us that he was going to hitchhike the one hundred miles or so to Brooklyn and bring his sister back here.

"You'll never be able to do it," Bobby wasted no time in telling him. "The traffic out there is already real bad, and it's only going to get worse once this thing actually starts. You'll get hung up somewhere along the way and end up missing the whole thing! Why didn't you tell us back when we were passing the city? We could've picked her up then!"

"Yeah," Mary added. "C'mon, it's just not worth it to go now, please stay!"

I have to admit, at first, I had my own reservations as well, but after his eyes met mine, I changed my tune real fast. *He's going to do it*, I thought to myself. I'd seen a look of sheer determination in his face; not only was he going to experience Woodstock, but his sister was going to as well.

Shortly after he'd gotten our reactions and our blessings—or in Bobby's case, repeated misgivings—Space departed our company and went walking down the hill toward 17B where he'd attempt to bag a ride back to New York. I watched him go with a kind of admiration and awe. He'd left with nothing other than the clothes on his back, a pack of cigarettes and a few joints to boot, a handful of speed pills, and some chocolate bars in his pocket which were sure to melt before he reached the first traffic light. Billy had tried several times to offer him money, but Space held up his hands in decline after every attempt. More than any of us, he believed that money was the root of all evil and avoided using it as often as possible. I commended his efforts most assuredly, after all, for a group of people trying to move away from the System, our main source of sustainability continued to be the System's strongest instrument. By way of his selflessness and his ability to haggle and balance trade, he sure set a stunning example for the rest of us, and as he disappeared out of sight beyond the rise, I clasped my hands together and wished him all the luck in the world.

The six of us who remained behind played at Hector's Inn for the second time that night and returned back to the van following daybreak as the bright orange sun began to seep over the horizon and bathe the sky in its gentle hues. Believe it or not, it was already hot by that time too—and not only hot, but unbelievably humid. It hadn't rained yet and there wasn't a gray cloud in sight, but the air was laden with moisture and you could feel in the atmosphere and on your skin that the possibility of a shower or two was looming.

By that time, we were beginning to run out of clean clothes. We hadn't hit up a laundromat since Oklahoma, but we figured we could make it at least a couple more days because we weren't wearing very much to begin with. I'd traded in my jeans and t-shirt for a tank top and cutoffs, and in comparison to many of my companions, I'd still be considered overdressed. Most of everybody had their shirts off—both men and women alike—and in looking closely enough at those who kept them on, you could tell that they were damp. You could smell the rain in the air along with the salty, musky scent of the sweat of thousands. Thank God for the continual smoking all around, or else I'd imagine the odor probably would've been wholly unpleasant.

We all slept until sometime in the afternoon on that third day before the music started, and when we awoke, we could tell that in only a few hours, far more people had arrived. Surprisingly, I was one of the last awake—Faye and Billy had already split, and Al was sitting under the shade of one of the surrounding trees overlooking the bowl with his canvas, filling in what looked from where I sat on the bumper to be the final strip in his Spectrum of America. You couldn't even really make out the bowl anymore, only a dip in the population. The fields for as far as I could see—even with binoculars—contained a countless and ever-increasing number of heads and flower children patiently awaiting the start of the festival. The bowl was filled to the brim, but the atmosphere was free and easy. Everyone was sitting shoulder to shoulder with one another, sharing both the space and the things they'd brought with them. Even as thousands continued to stream past down the road to the festival grounds, that feeling did not falter; in fact, it intensified. To imagine it is mind-boggling; to witness it was tremendous. There are no words for such an experience. I was ecstatic, mystified, and yet, I still could not totally believe where I was. The energy that was around the whole area and exuded from every person there was completely indescribable. It was pure peace and love and good vibes—togetherness on a scale never before seen or recorded.

In such a setting, there was nothing to do but stare, and I looked all around me, groking at all the people and all the ongoing shenanigans. There was tree climbing and dancing, singing and shouting, and there were those obviously tripping. There was horseplay and there was serious philosophizing—those groups of heads just hanging around rapping with one another and smoking good bud, discussing politics and cosmic consciousness, telling stories and making music, all while wearing some of the weirdest things you could think to wear: chieftain's headdresses, feather boas, tie-dye vests, fringe, or nothing at all.

As I stood there and witnessed these things, I remembered a conversation I'd had what felt like a lifetime ago. It was a conversation I'd had back in Fresno with The Descendants—in Marty's living room, to be exact—about what the world would be like if that which was unusual ever became the norm; and this was it, exactly what we'd been talking about. How could any of us have ever guessed that the world we were imagining was thirty years removed from the time in which we imagined it—and in the past, no less! It was times such as these, triggered by memories, that made me wish more than anything that there was a way to communicate my experiences to the future.

These yearning moments—though intense—were fleeting, and as I continued to gawk in awe at the activity going on around me, the strangest of feelings passed over me—déjà vu, and with certainty! I'd been there before; not so much in that place, but rather in that state of being. And then another, stranger notion came upon me: this wasn't a gathering, a commencement—it was a reunion. But a reunion of what, I wasn't sure. Was it a reunion of souls? Of spirit? Of energy? Of life? The facts were uncertain, but the crux was clear—we had all been there before.

Journeying back to Hector's Inn on the third night, we were high. Not just on grass—although THC was present—we were high on the vibrations: the vibrations of Woodstock and the complete absurdity of the situation. It took twice as long to get down there that night than it did just two nights before. There was no road anymore, just cars parked bumper to bumper and every which way. A whole array of tents and stands had popped up all over the place within the last twenty-four hours as well. There were stands selling hats, stands selling hotdogs and hamburgers—even stands selling grass right out in the open, their shelves lined with dozens of Ball jars packed full of different strains of marijuana. There were guys and girls passing on horseback, riding like Indians without a saddle, and Led Zeppelin blaring from a radio somewhere above the whole menagerie. Everything about it screamed three-ring circus—it reminded me of photos I'd seen of the Moroccan bazaars in Tangiers, a description right out of the pages of *The Sheltering Sky*.

As we trekked down the hill toward the jam-packed 17B, I thought about Space somewhere out there along the road and wondered how far he'd gotten. I hoped that he had already made it to New York. If he hadn't, his return—despite his resolute determination—seemed doubtful at best. The downward slant of Mary's mouth and the concern in her eyes evidenced that she was thinking the same thing. The rest of our friends, however, were entirely spellbound. Faye was spinning and twirling, her rainbow skirts billowing out around her. Billy was shaking hands with everybody, and Al was jotting down notes as he walked. There was a big chestnut mare with a blaze on her muzzle tied to one of the fence posts along the road, and Bobby went over to her and began to stroke her face and neck and whisper softly to her. This unprecedented step out of character by Bobby was enough to turn all of our heads.

"He's got quite a soft spot for animals, you know," Al said to me, humored by our surprise, "especially horses. We were raised on a farm, remember? Growing up, he was a regular cowboy."

"Bobby? A cowboy?" I scoffed with a laugh. "Imagine that on Polaroid."

"Believe it or not, we probably have one someplace," Al replied before turning back to his notebook.

Down at Hector's Inn, there were far more people around than there had been in the last two days combined, and in response, there was a huge tractor trailer parked beside the building with rollers running from the back of it right through the window of the bar. Even in light of our surroundings, we considered this strange, and we went up to a group of guys reclined back in lawn chairs near the front steps and asked about it. A heavy-set hippie with a big brown mustache and a ponytail told us that the Heat had been hassling the owners about selling beer out of the trailer, so a couple of guys had started rolling them through the window.

"Dumb pigs!" he exclaimed with a laugh. "We've been watching those beers roll down all day long!"

By this time, we'd acquired quite a following at Hector's, and as we walked inside, a whole bunch of people we'd met came up to us and greeted us, asking us if the music had started yet down at the bowl and requesting coves. The first tune they wanted to hear was *Something's Coming On*—for obvious reasons—and we played it five more times that night. God, it was perfect. The camaraderie was fantastic, the music was sensational, and the beers were fresh and cold. I had a couple that night—but only a couple—and although I enjoyed them, by this time I was standing more and more frequently with the teetotalers.

We ended that last night at Hector's with an hour-long jam. We all must've soloed two or three times each and took turns breaking it down. At one point, I was so absorbed in the pure sound, in listening to what Bobby and Billy and Al were laying down, that everything else just went away. I saw nothing—no bar, no people, no dancers—not even Mary and Faye standing in front of me. All I could do was hear, hear every clear note of that rhythm, and before I knew any different, we'd completely run away with it. When we broke, clean of course, the next thing I heard was a loud cheer. Everybody in the bar was on their feet and clapping for us; they were whistling and shouting, and a couple of people even began chanting for more, but the owner was trying to clear the place out—it must've been near daybreak again.

As we walked back to the Trips Mobile long after sundown, everybody was friendly—even more so than on the Haight, which I would've considered to be impossible beforehand. We only had a mile to cover, and in that time, half a dozen people offered us water or cigarettes or something to eat, and half a dozen more asked us if we needed a place to crash for the night—a couple even asked if we needed help carrying our instruments. Everybody acted like old chums, and even more than the music to come, it was that evenhanded kindness that was the heart and soul of Woodstock.

When we got back to the van, the near-to-complete stage down there at the bottom of the hill was all aglow from the giant spotlights, and with binoculars, we could see all the goings-on. The builders were still at it, laying down plywood and running wires, and encapsulating all of it was this eerie blue glow from the welding guns that illuminated the planks in front of the stage and the field where sleeping bodies were scattered all about. It was truly a breathtaking sight, unimaginable in its beauty and unbelievable in its reality.

That next morning, August 15th, marked the first official day of the festival. I'd been counting the days since our arrival, and at that point, the true gravity of the situation had still yet to hit me. We'd been waiting for the music of Woodstock for so long that it seemed its advent would never be upon us. We were beginning to become comfortable with the conditions we were faced with. Mild hunger pangs from having to hunt down a meal every time we wanted to eat and uncontrollable munchies due to the marijuana haze in the air—in addition to having nowhere civilized to shit and nowhere to properly shower—were routine now. However, the sight of several hundred thousand people gathered together in the early morning awaiting something legendary never got old, and I never grew tired of watching them. To witness it, even time and time again, simply took my breath away. Naked and wrapped in a thin blanket, I was seated atop the van again that morning with the binoculars, and from that vantage point, I could see down to the stage where a shirtless man with a deep tan stood, himself visibly in awe of the scene he was witnessing. He stood before one of the many microphones that dotted the performance area, and his voice, a deep baritone, washed out over the vast audience from speakers mounted atop the two giant yellow towers on either side of the stage.

"To get back to that warning I've received," he said, *"you can take it with however many grains of salt that you wish, that the brown acid that is circulating around us is not specifically too good. It is suggested that you stay away from that. Of course, it's your own trip so be my guest, but please be advised that there is a warning out on that one."* As he spoke, I could hear the sounds of the men still hammering the last boards into place on the stage, amplified by the microphones and enormous speakers.

That day—for some odd reason—all of The Day Trippers had awoken before noon, Bobby being the last to rise, as usual. He stirred slowly as he emerged from his opioid-induced slumber and shook off the last vestiges of dream. While he pulled on his pants in his relatively sober state, as was typical of his disheveled, grumpy, early-morning self, he cupped his hands around his mouth and yelled back to the announcer, even though we were probably half a mile away, "Why don't you put some music up there already?!" before proceeding to chant, "We want music! We want music! We want—"

Billy cuffed him across the back of the head, "What the hell is wrong with you, man? Do you want to start a fucking riot? Shut up and be patient like the rest of us!"

Bobby shot him an irritated glare before crawling back into the Trips Mobile. The few heads around us that had turned in response to Bobby's commotion turned back to whatever had occupied them before, and Billy looked up at me, exasperated, "That kid..." he murmured.

Bobby emerged from the Trips Mobile sometime later with his guitar in hand, pinpoint pupils, and a substantially calmer air about him. He sat down on the bumper and began to play a ballad, entirely absorbed in his own world, alone on his island; we were only a mirage.

The most truth Bobby ever spoke wasn't with words, but rather with his guitar. Every chord that he played, every string that he caressed, rang out pure and true. There was no embellishment there; every note was as raw and real as it could get, and I could just lay there and listen to him play all day long as he took me inside his elusive little world for a time.

Mary shared my perch atop the van with me that day as we waited for the music to begin. Once Bobby put down his guitar and nodded off, we were left with only the radio to listen to, accompanied by the din of the thousands of voices surrounding us. No matter what station we tuned into, Woodstock was all we heard about, and unlike in days prior, some stations had dispatched reporters to the site. Somewhere down there in the bowl or in the fields surrounding it, there were little slack-jawed groups of radio personnel with their staticky, open-air microphones taking in the sounds of everything and trying vainly to describe to the folks back home just what they were witnessing. Many of the other stations, however, continued to issue dire warnings to all their listeners, frantically attempting at all costs to deter people from taking the trip to Woodstock. No matter which way you turned the dial, you'd get somebody else's perspective.

"All traffic is at a standstill," one newscaster declared. *"There is a ten-mile traffic jam on Route 17B, and the Thruway is backed up several miles behind that with delays up to eight hours. I heard this morning that the closest room you can get to the site is in Middletown, New York. Can you believe that? Middletown! And it's a slow ride from there on…"*

Another station had people on the ground conducting interviews with the festival organizers, one of which told the masses, *"Anybody who tries to come here is crazy! Sullivan County is one great big parking lot!"*

"The numbers I'm getting in now are showing that there's going to be somewhere in the area of a quarter of a million kids sleeping in Yasgur's fields tonight, and there's about a million more trying to get there," another radio host said. *"If you're out on the road now folks, take it from me, the best thing you can do is turn back around. Go home and watch it on television because you just ain't going to make it."*

Mary turned to me with concern in her eyes, "I hope Space can get back," she said in a worried voice.

"He'll make it," I told her reassuringly, but even as I said this, the tiniest hint of doubt had begun to creep inside my mind and make itself at home.

As morning progressed to afternoon and afternoon dragged on toward eventual nightfall, the sound of announcements from the stage filled the air. Announcements such as these were not unlike those we'd heard over the last couple of days, but they were more plentiful that day than any before. Most were personal announcements for people in the audience who were trying to find somebody or who needed something: their bags, their drugs, their medication—and there were announcements telling people to make their way down to the phone bank where there was a call waiting for them from anxious parents, angry parents, or just generally concerned parents who were hearing all about this seeming fiasco on the news. There were announcements telling specific individuals where to meet up with their friends or children that they'd been separated from and announcements providing the names of those who'd ended up in one of the medical tents because they'd cut their feet on one of the many glass bottles that were lying around or because they were having a bad trip. There were also announcements for the whole audience—whether it was another advisory about the brown acid, to reassure those folks who'd taken it that it wasn't poison, just poorly manufactured acid—or the most important announcement of the whole festival that reached us sometime in the mid-afternoon.

"It's a free concert," the voice of the announcer had declared with finality. *"That doesn't mean that anything goes, what that means is we're gonna put the music up here for free. What that means is that the people who put up the money for this thing are going to take a bit of a bath—a big bath. That's no hype, that's true, they're gonna get hurt. What that means is that these people have it in their heads that your welfare is a hell of a lot more important—and the music is—than a dollar."*

As he said this, applause rose up over all the land. Everybody clapped their hands and whistled and cheered. It was the first collective reaction I experienced at Woodstock, and god-damn was it powerful! Just thinking about it sends chills down my spine, and that was nothing compared with what was to come.

****

Later that afternoon, as the humidity inched toward one hundred percent, at the suggestion of Mary, we all left the van in search of the pond, which we'd heard was somewhere beyond the stage. Cold water sounded like nirvana to us at that point, and we were all long overdue for a bath. I was still wrapped in my blanket from before as we picked our way down toward the bottom of the hill, carrying bundles of clean clothes in our arms.

As we approached the stage, I could see where the chain link fence had been torn down and the places where it was still unfinished and would remain so for eternity. The area around the stage, however, had been surrounded by an even higher fence which remained standing despite the crowd. More organizers in blue shirts buzzed around inside, carrying crates and boxes and massive coils of wire. The bridge the construction crew had built across the road was currently in service as well as the Hog Farmers and roadies hauled sound equipment up to the stage from the landing pad where musicians were being flown in by helicopters since it was impossible to get them there any other way. The helicopters were touching down just beyond the road, and from our safe distance, we could see a whole bunch of hippies running all over the heliport, jumping up and down in the middle of this great big patch of grass while some guy with a bullhorn was yelling, "Get off the landing pad! Whaddya think that windsock is for?!" He shook his head in defeat, a look of pure bewilderment on his face. "You morons!" he cried above the sound of the chopper blades slicing through the damp air.

Bearing humored smiles ourselves, we continued on, and before long, we made it to that glorious pond. I'm not going to tell you that the waters were crystal clear and glistening like the waters of Elysium, but once we jumped in, boy did it feel like it! There were probably another dozen or so others in there with us, along with a lot of little kids who were diving and splashing and having a grand old time. *Little do they know*, I thought, *that they are at the forefront of one of the single most defining moments of the 20ᵗʰ century. They're making history right now, and all they're doing is playing in a pond.* But it wasn't just the kids; at that very moment, nobody was trying to change the world, but together, somehow we did, and really, it was by doing nothing extraordinary at all.

1969

By that time of day, the sun had already passed directly overhead and its rays reached us at an angle, refracting off the somewhat dark and murky water and making us squint from the glare. The pond was nestled in a little tree-lined cove where greenery of all kinds grew right to the bank. There were some roots and twigs and leaves floating merrily along as the ripples from the splashing kids and bathing adults sloshed up against the shore. It was a beautiful sight, and if you looked at it right, it appeared that the whole world was reflected in that pond: the baby blue of the eternal sky, the browns and greens of the earth, and all of its inhabitants living in complete harmony with nature and one another. To me, it seemed like a glimpse into an earlier time, or perhaps, a vision of the future. I admired this reflection for a moment as I stood waist deep in the water until a man dove in from the shoreline and a violent tide of ripples obscured my view. Peace—at least in today's world—is fleeting anyhow.

We hung around that pond for quite a while, goofing off and getting clean, and it was sometime while we were bathing that the first music of the festival was broadcast over the loudspeakers. As soon as we heard the announcer's voice replaced by the full, rich sound of an acoustic guitar, all of us stopped what we were doing and turned toward the stage, even though it was obscured from view by the trees—only the children kept on as they were.

Almost immediately, a cheer rose up from the pond and the forest and the fields, and it was so monstrous that it actually drowned out the sound from the speakers! And let me tell you, those suckers were *loud*!

"Well, here we go!" Billy remarked from where he stood beside me.

"Who'd they say is playing?" somebody else in the pond asked.

"Richie Havens," another man answered.

"Really? I thought Sweetwater was supposed to go on first..."

Their conversation continued, but I couldn't contain myself. As an impartial observer having previously peered through the looking glass of history, I was duly informed with prior knowledge of what this festival would encompass; however, no documentaries or novels or stories could have prepared me for what was—and will eternally remain—the singularly most incredible experience of my life. Tears began to well up in my eyes, and I was out of that pond like a fucking rocket. There were no thoughts going through my head, just prayers— prayers of thanks, invocations to God or the universe or whatever force there was out there that had arranged for everything I had ever wished for to come true.

I ran like hell to get down to the stage; I had been lusting after this moment my entire life, and I didn't want to miss a second! However, I couldn't run very far at all before I encountered a human traffic jam. Everybody who had been walking somewhere else before the music started had turned right around and was heading back toward the bowl, and due to this, it took me quite a while to get there myself. I've never been surrounded by so many people in my entire life, neither before nor since. I must've said "Excuse me!" ten thousand times.

By the time I made it to the stage—or rather to the twelve-foot planks that lined the front of it—Richie Havens had gone offstage, and the whole crowd was chanting for encores. I could feel my heart pounding like a jackhammer from anticipation and excitement. I felt dizzy, as if I was completely drunk on euphoria. Everybody around me was whistling and calling out for more. Some people were trying to climb up the fence to catch a glimpse of the action, and others were sitting on the shoulders of their neighbors. There were guys holding up their girlfriends, guys holding up other guys, and complete strangers holding up complete strangers. A tall man next to me bent down and asked if I wanted a lift, and I thankfully obliged and sat atop his broad shoulders while he held onto my legs. From this perch, I could see the whole stage, and as these sights filled my eyes, a feeling of pure bliss began to spread throughout my body.

I can't even venture a guess as to how long it was until Richie Havens reappeared—it could've been thirty seconds, or it could have been an hour—but when he finally did, an unrestrained cheer rose up all around me. Havens was a tall, African American man with dark, thoughtful eyes that looked out at the world from a kind face creased with laugh lines and filled with soul. He wore a long, sweat-stained tan kaftan and a pair of leather huaraches, and he walked back to the microphone carrying an acoustic guitar as a two-man band took their place on the stage behind him. He seated himself on the wooden stool that was set up in front of the mic and started tuning his guitar. As he did so, he began speaking to the crowd:

"A hundred million songs gonna be sung tonight. All of them are going to be singing about the same thing, which I hope everybody who came, came to hear. Really—and it's all about you, actually, and me and everybody around the stage and everybody who hasn't gotten here and the people who are gonna read about you tomorrow and how really groovy you were—all over the world. You can dig where that's at, that's where it's really at…"

And when he began to play, my God, I almost fell right off of the shoulders of the poor cat who was holding me—and he did let me down, after that. This was the performance I'd adored—no, worshipped—since I was old enough to appreciate what good music was and understand what kind of emotion and soul go into creating a performance like that, especially this particular song, which was completely improvised. It was an organic product of Woodstock, created purely from its vibrations—a little slice of the heaven that it was, preserved for the rest of those people who weren't lucky enough to experience it for themselves. It was just the congas and Richie fiercely strumming, riffing off the word freedom, but the vibrations…my God:

"Freedom, freedom, freedom, freedom…sometimes I feel like a motherless child, sometimes I feel like a motherless child, sometimes I feel like a motherless child a long way from my home, yeah, yeah Lord, singing freedom, freedom, freedom, freedom…"

As I listened to him sing those immortal words, I had my hands pressed up against the fence, feeling the vibrations of the music pumped out of those massive speakers wash over me and through me and through all those people around me who were dancing and stomping their feet. I can't tell you how I cried; it was an emotional purge, a release of epic proportions. I was overcome with such joy that all I could do was weep. And when he started singing, *"Clap your hands, clap your hands,"* the applause rose up, and it was just like a wave; an overarching wave. I was having a spiritual experience, and as I looked around me, I saw that everybody else was having a spiritual experience as well. Everybody understood and accepted and was hip to what everybody else was doing. It was freedom like you've never experienced, freedom like you wouldn't believe—freedom like you are unable to imagine. And in the midst of this, I began to experience a peculiar sensation. I started to feel as if the stage itself, as well as the audience and all the surrounding fields, had levitated—that is, become independent of the Earth—and hung suspended above the ground. It was a sensation of intense liberation, an expression of the purest kind of freedom—that which is both a philosophical concept and a physical liberty. We were unrestrained and unauthorized, completely free to do whatever we pleased, yet we were entirely united in both intent and action. It was the first time that the implications of my individuality—when in the midst of so many others—had felt so liberatingly meaningless. It was the paradox of that day.

Once the applause had faded and Richie Havens had gone offstage that final time, the loudspeakers fell silent once more. I just stood there with my hands against the fence, absorbing the last of those lingering vibrations until I felt a hand on my shoulder. I turned around and saw Mary standing there, a radiant smile on her face, her blonde hair still wet from our dip in the pond, my clothes in her arms. That's when I realized…God…I'd been buck naked that entire time and hadn't even noticed, or cared, for that matter—and neither did anybody else.

Once I'd finished dressing, Mary suggested I come with her on a walk.

"Walk where?" I asked her.

Mary Jane just smiled.

I don't remember talking much, we just walked back up the hill together as different performers took the stage. The audience was pretty tightly packed; people sat together anywhere and everywhere, and as we stepped around them, we listened to snippets of thousands of different conversations while Hindu invocations, folk songs, and more announcements were broadcast from the stage. Most of the time, Mary and I kept our heads down as we walked to caution against stepping on the limbs or bodies of those seated or sprawled in the grass. When I finally did look up, I saw that dusk and some clouds had begun to gather over the bowl. I asked Mary if she knew where we could score some chow, and she said our best bet would probably be to get back to the van, if we could find it—which, for all we knew, might take all night. However, when we reached the top of the hill, a very familiar voice called out, "Mary! Rhiannon! Over here!"

The voice was Bobby's, and lo and behold, we found that he along with Al, Billy, and Faye were sitting with a large group of others underneath one of the two trees at the top of the bowl. A few tents and blankets were encircling a small fire of twigs and kindling that everyone was gathered around as they rapped together and passed a couple joints between them. Mary and I sat down with the rest of them and partook in the merriments. However, as we soon discovered, grass wasn't the only thing being shared in this particular circle. Somebody had brought back a whole bunch of plates from the other side of the hill where there were stands distributing sandwiches and baked beans as well as granola, nuts, and sunflower seeds.

What a magnificent supper we had that night, gathered together as we got acquainted with all the others who were sitting around and sharing with us. There was this one kid who'd come up from North Carolina with a bus full of other heads, a few guys from Portland, this one Cherokee Indian chic who was a couple months pregnant, and her old man who was from New Jersey. There were many more of course—too many to remember—and what a time we had! This is one of those experiences which has set into the golden glow of memory full of a special kind of fondness and solidarity; the details have become increasingly hazy, but the feeling is as fresh and unforgettable as ever.

The first night of the festival was just beautiful. After the sun set into the trees behind us and darkness fell over the stage, the spotlights came on and the crickets came out. Thousands of singing little insect voices serenaded the night and made such sweet music for all to hear in-between sets.

That first night consisted primarily of folk artists, some of which I'd never heard of before, such as Bert Sommer and Tim Hardin, and to my surprise, I enjoyed them thoroughly. Their music was soft and acoustic, full of emotion and melancholy, blues and hope, and Bert Sommer did a rendition of Simon and Garfunkel's *America* that got the whole crowd—almost 400,000 people—on their feet. Can you imagine an entire hillside cheering for you? A whole city? It was positively unreal.

After the applause faded, the kid from North Carolina—I think he called himself Boots—started telling us all about how he and his buddies had been festival-hopping all summer. He said they'd been in Newport, Rhode Island, in Denver and in Atlanta, in Seattle and in Atlantic City, and in Bethel since the eighth of August. After Woodstock, he said they were headed to New Orleans, their last destination of the summer. And out of those half a dozen festivals, he told us this one was already his favorite by far.

"Music is an exposition of soul," he told us, "and when you attend concerts and festivals, you are sharing in that soul. I go to concerts like people go to church, man. To my family and me, music is spiritual; it is God in Its purest form."

"I'm not a musician," one of the guys from Portland remarked, "but to strike up like that in front of all those people takes some kind of balls, man."

"Balls of steel," somebody else agreed.

"I'd go up there right now!" Bobby piped up. "I'd love to be up there right now! I was backstage at Monterey, you know…"

All of us who knew him just looked at one another, rolled our eyes, and let him ramble on.

Although Space had split for New York, he'd left behind most of the good grass he'd scored the other night, and we were all still smoking it. There was at least one pipe and one joint circulating around at any given time, and understandably, we were all pretty high. There was no cap on the amount of grass we smoked, and there came a time when half the group was just completely stoned and absent from the conversation, grooving on the music silently, and the other half was engaged in what seemed like a very animated discussion about a variety of topics, the details of which I do not remember, more than likely because I was a part of the former category. Eventually, I began to opt out of my turn in the circle after I found myself unable to light the damn thing after it'd gone out. Stoner 101: you cannot light a doobie with a roach clip, no matter how hard you try. I got a good laugh out of that one.

The music only got better as the night went on, although nothing topped *Freedom*. That first night in particular was exceptionally dreamy; the vibrations were beautiful, and I could really dig the lyrics. Now, typically speaking, folk music isn't exactly my bag, but under these psychotropic conditions, in such an environment, I found I could really appreciate it. Aided, without doubt, by the grass, the music prompted imagination and envisioning, fantasizing and remembering. It was sad yet encouraging and spurred flashes of inspiration and enlightenment that passed in and out of my mind faster than I could fully comprehend them. I read some of Al's notes and was amazed to see so many things I had such trouble trying to explain in words transcribed so eloquently. It takes a hopeless romantic to be a writer, I guess.

On one of the pages, he'd recorded a conversation our little circle had had earlier, which was full of imagination and conjecture in regard to what we thought the crowded hill below us looked like.

"Wow, wow, wow!" Mary had gasped when she and I first reached the top of the hill and turned around to get a glimpse of all that we'd left behind. "Look at everybody down there! They look like, like, it looks like…well, what do you think it looks like?"

I was unsure how to answer her, "Ummm," I began, but Bobby beat me to it.

"It looks like an army, an army for peace," he said.

"I don't think it looks like an army at all," one of the guys from Portland replied. "To me, it looks like one great big family."

Another one of our more hungry friends suggested that it appeared to him as, "Half a million sardines all crammed into one tiny little can called Yasgur's farm."

Billy, translating for Faye, told us that she thought it looked like "A field of flowers all waving in the breeze."

Half a dozen more lines of conjecture continued on down the page to where I'd finally concluded, "It looks like heaven."

Beneath this dialogue Al had written, "YOU ARE YOUR PERCEPTION."

In-between sets, the clouds that had continued to gather after dark unleashed their burden, and rain began to fall over the crowd. Some of the people around us began to gather their things and high-tail it out of there before the drizzle became a torrent, but most, like us, stayed—either because they didn't mind the rain, or because they had nowhere else to go, since their cars were parked all the way back on 17B and they had no way to get there. Fortunately for us, the couple from New Jersey had brought a tent, and since we all couldn't fit inside it, we took the stakes out of the ground and opened it up over us like a huge poncho; it kept us dry for the most part.

When the rain seemed to be tapering off, another performer took the stage. Even from far away, his identity was easily distinguished, just by the sound of his voice alone. This man had a very thick Indian accent and greeted the crowd in-between plucks on the strings of his sitar. His name was Ravi Shankar, and his set was my favorite that night. The Indian ragas he played were soothing and meditative and not in contrast to the folk music of before, except with his music I found myself swaying to the beat a whole lot more and really grooving on his style.

"Ravi really gets me, man," I told everybody sitting around me.

"There's something really magical and fascinating about Middle Eastern music," our friend from North Carolina replied. "It's so lively and spiritual and yet so hypnotizing. Whenever I listen to this guy play, I feel like I'm a snake that's being charmed."

"There's much we can learn from the Eastern world," Al said. "The Western world likes to dismiss truths already known by the Eastern world and uphold the claims of their own culture. It is only recently that we've begun to discover just what we are missing. There is real richness and depth in Eastern schools of thought—ideas such as karma, reincarnation, Buddhism, Confucianism, the nonviolent teachings of Gandhi, yoga, the cycles of existence and meaninglessness of time, Taoism, *The Bhagavad Gita*, *The Upanishads*—and that's only scratching the surface. By far, the Eastern world has much more to offer us than what we are accustomed

346

to living in the West."

Most everybody in our circle-turned-huddle agreed with him. While we were rapping and carrying on about all of this, a clap of thunder and a bolt of lightning shook the night and the rain that had seemed to be trickling off poured down even heavier than before. The music onstage faded out and then stopped entirely. We all groaned and settled in to wait until the storm ended and the performers came back on again. However, we found that we didn't have to wait very long at all. Although the storm was far from over, music once more poured from the loudspeakers and flooded the soaked plains. Faye, in a burst of excitement, threw off the portion of the canvas tent that sheltered her and ran out into the rain. When she reached the rim where the hill ceased its ascent and began to slope downward toward the stage, she stopped and stood perfectly still, her arms outstretched on either side of her, staring blankly into nothing—straight into the void.

"Is she your lover, man?" one of the guys from Portland asked Billy.

"Yes, she is my lover," Billy replied, his voice full of pride and emotion. "She is the best lover, Faye. She is a gypsy queen, a mystic goddess. Look at how she stands right there on the brink of epiphany in her flowing robes and her golden headdress—she's like an allegory come to life. She's so intriguing in her sensuality and so alluring in her mysticism. I know hardly anything about her, and yet I've never loved another human person more. Her gaze causes you to suspend your imagination, and her kiss makes you doubt everything you've ever known…"

Billy and Faye were more perfect for one another than any other pair I've ever encountered. In fact, their personalities were such stark opposites that they actually completed each other. In their opposition, they created a flow of energy in-between poles that became infinity.

While Billy continued to rain praises upon his woman, she began to sway and dance to the rhythmic, carrying sounds of the sitar, tamboura, and tabla that washed out over the bowl and cleansed us of all our ills. There was not one troubled soul in all of Bethel that night; we were as beautiful as ever.

As I watched Faye dance with such carefree abandon, with such innocence and joy, she began to resemble another fair girl, the freest spirit ever to live—and she was not the only one. Her enthusiasm was contagious, and it set my soul on fire. It filled me full of inspiration and made me want to move and rejoice and send all of those good vibrations back out into the universe. Imbued by magic, I got up and ran over to Faye, and I stood beside her as I gazed down from the top of the hill. What I saw below me was a free-for-all, but it was the most wondrous free-for-all there ever was—who was making love, who was tripping out, who was dancing. There were so many people dancing, and nobody was paranoid or self-conscious, nobody was even aware of themselves at that moment; it was all about just *being*, being in the moment and grooving on whatever was in that moment with us. Even the rain was a blessing; by this time, most everybody was grooving on the rain.

When Ravi Shankar's set ended, so did the strength of the storm and the bulk of the dancing. Spent and breathless, I crawled back under the shelter of the canvas tent, but Faye continued to stand at the top of the hill and stare out into the infinite, and the eyes of the world stared back.

The next performer that evening was Melanie Safka, the most stereotypical flower child to take the stage at Woodstock. I had always thought that she was a bit overrated and silly and sounded like a precocious child, but there in that moment, she was perfect, utterly perfect. Her awe and her humor were infectious, and the dancing started up again right away. When the rain finally tapered off, we emerged from the canvas tent, lit up some more joints and listened to Melanie's set. I really paid attention to her lyrics, and for the first time I could really dig her—for the first time, she really made a hell of a lot of sense. One of the men from Portland was a Melanie freak, and together he and I were really grooving on her performance, especially that one song of hers, *Beautiful People*. In just one line, it all but summed up how most of us were feeling that night: *"beautiful people, you live in the same world as I do, but somehow I haven't noticed you before today..."*

"Melanie makes me trip a little, she makes me get some distance, you know?" the guy from Portland told me.

I knew that he meant objectivity, and that night we got some distance together.

When Melanie's set ended with the rain, our circle began to disband. Our friends from New Jersey re-staked their tent and crawled inside for the night, and everybody else went their separate ways in search of their cars or someplace vaguely dry to spend the night. The Day Trippers and I picked up our things and went walking along the rim of the bowl while several different voices poured out through the loudspeakers. The ground was soaked from the rain, and as we walked, mud leaked into our shoes. Billy and Faye had a blanket with them that had been spared the brunt of the deluge, so rather than search for the Trips Mobile in the dark and risk stepping on all those people who were sleeping right there in the fields, we decided to just sit ourselves down on the first empty patch of ground we came to and make camp for the night. When we finally found a suitable place—unoccupied ground was hard to come by, you know—it was right at the edge of the bowl, next to these two heads who were in the midst of a very deeply philosophical acid trip. They were clearly seekers; one was wrapped in a tapestry of Ganesh, and the other wore several dozen religious medallions around his neck. They introduced themselves to us about ten minutes after we'd sat down—which was about the time they noticed us—and offered us some of their stash. We all declined, except for Faye, who took half a tab, and other than that, they more or less kept to themselves. Every so often we'd hear them talking in riddles and parables and haikus, sometimes to one another, sometimes to themselves, and sometimes to nobody at all. They spoke in prose and in verse, some of which was original and some of which was recited—all of which was incredibly profound. They'd chosen a suitable spot to chase enlightenment. Below us, it looked like the whole world was made up of television snow, but in reality, those thousands of specks were people, strewn all along that rolling bulge of land, down to that golden dome of light that was the stage and beyond, where the glow was broken up into all those lights from the campfires and the performers' pavilion across the road. It was truly a beautiful thing to behold.

Arlo Guthrie, another one of my favorites, was the next performer to take the stage. We didn't have binoculars with us that evening, but the acidheads beside us did, and they lent them to us for the duration of his performance. We passed them around to one another in succession, each of us relishing in glimpses of the stage as he sang songs we knew and loved, such as *Coming Into Los Angeles* and *Wheel of Fortune* and launched into folk favorites like *Walking Down A Line*. However, I was lucky enough to have them in my hands when he greeted the crowd in that cheeky, charismatic way of his and said, *"Man, there's supposed to be a million and a half people here by tonight, can you dig that? The New York State Thruway is closed, man! Lotta Freaks!"*

It was another Woodstock moment that had been immortalized by film, one I'd grown up well-acquainted with and yet was somehow now bearing witness to as it unfolded before my eyes. I shook my head to dispel the unreality that had begun to creep in and turned toward the two guys tripping.

"What do you think about time travel?" I asked them.

"You've got to have time to travel," one of the two answered.

After Arlo had wished the half-asleep crowd a good night and left the stage, another acoustic performer was ushered on. Originally upon his exit, I was bummed that he'd omitted *Alice's Restaurant* from his setlist, but when I realized that the next performer was Joan Baez, all was suddenly copasetic again. Whenever I heard Joan Baez, I was always reminded of Shania, and I thought about her then, up on that hill, light-years away from the time in which I'd last seen her, an unfathomable position for any future thinker to approach. I wondered if I'd ever see her again and hoped that I somehow would.

Joan Baez ended her set with what I deemed to be a manifestation of all the emotion that poured out from all those thousands who called Yasgur's fields their home that night. In melodic orchestration, she expressed a collective, powerful love that I felt and that we all felt. In that moment, I was one with the music and with all those who were around me. I had rushes from my scalp all the way down to my toes! Her voice just pierced me, right through the heart. It had to do that to everybody because as I remember, a lot of people around me stopped talking and turned their heads toward the sound of an angel, and I drifted off to sleep that night to the sweet sound of her lyrics.

When I awoke the next morning, a different band was playing and all The Day Trippers were gone. I'd slept right there on the ground in the mud without a blanket or anything—a mud-soaked towel of unknown origin shoved under my head as a pillow. Waking up amidst the crowd rather than in the Trips Mobile added a much more authentic flavor to my experience of Woodstock. Now not only had I seen it and been there, but I'd also felt it in the cold rain on my neck and in the sweat on my back; I'd tasted the mud and inhaled its pungent odor and as if by second nature, entrusted my safety and well-being to a bunch of strangers. But they weren't strangers anymore...

We talk about collectiveness and we talk about unity, about working together and being as one—but to actually see it and be it, to give and take of it, is an experience like none other. We talk about festivals too, but this was by far the ultimate festival. If you've never been in a field full of half a million half-naked hippies and at the same time felt like not one of those 500,000 people was a stranger to you, then there's no possible way for me to describe it. Everybody in the world is just moving through life, doing their own thing and going their own way, but when a number of them start doing the same thing—as we were then—there's a whole lot of power in that. At Woodstock, there were 500,000 of us, and we were all in it together. It was a world I couldn't imagine, a time beyond my wildest dreams. It was complete freedom, as I've said before, but that's something I cannot reiterate enough because you have no idea what that's like, and don't you want to? In a world with complete freedom like this one, nobody told you what you could and could not do. You could go where you wanted, you could be what you wanted, and nobody hassled you—just as long as you didn't hassle anybody else. To see peace in action like that during such a turbulent time was truly unbelievable, and it filled all of us who were there with hope for the future. We all wanted so badly for this thing to work, and I think it was because of this that everybody did good for everybody else.

As soon as I woke up—after I finished reveling in awe of this place where I'd found myself—a small, tan Chinese girl wearing Granny glasses on the blanket next to me offered me some water to drink and a toke on the joint that was being passed around. She shared her blanket with two guys who were both Caucasian—one fair and the other dark. The one with dark hair had beautiful, piercing blue eyes and he offered me some granola that they'd been munching on. I didn't have much to offer them in return, but I gave them what I could, which was the rest of my pack of cigarettes and all of my matches. The group on the blanket next to them had cut into a watermelon and they gave half to us in exchange for a joint.

"Where are you from?" they asked me as we shared this simple breakfast.

"San Francisco," I answered.

"San Francisco is where it's at," the little Chinese girl replied. "I've always wanted to go to San Francisco."

The two guys she was with agreed with her.

"San Francisco is rad," I told them, "but our Movement is growing, it's getting bigger and moving away from its source. Like we're in New York right now, nothing like this is happening in San Francisco. Right now—this—right here, is where it's at."

She smiled when I said this, "I can dig that," she said.

"Did you see the UFOs fly over last night?" the brown-haired guy asked me.

"No, I was asleep," I told him. "Why do you think they were UFOs

351

that flew over?"

"I don't think they were UFOs," he corrected me, "I know they were. They looked just like the others we saw back in New Mexico."

"How do you know it wasn't just lights from the helicopters or an airplane?"

"They were soundless," he replied, "and their lights were flickering. Not like a plane, though, the flickers were irregular, like that of a flame, and they were moving faster than a plane moves. They came straight toward us out of the sky, and then when they got real close, they just darted off in the other direction and disappeared before they were far enough away to be out of sight."

I turned my gaze upward to the overcast sky. In this weather you couldn't see a plane at two-thousand feet, let alone some sort of crazed hovercraft; however, I'd experienced far too much in my life at that point to doubt them on the basis of my own understanding.

"You're real lucky then," I said. "Did a lot of other people see them too?"

"No," the girl answered excitedly, "mostly everybody was sleeping already!"

"That's pretty special," I told them, "you've seen aliens and met a time traveler all in one day."

The three of them looked around at one another and exchanged confused glances, "What time traveler?" the blonde kid asked me.

I thanked them gratefully for their generosity, then stood up and started off into the crowd.

****

I spent most of that day walking—which was not as easy a task as it may seem. Those that passed by me, people from all over the country, were people I would never see again in my life, and at every glance, a different face appeared. There were so many people wearing so many different clothes in so many different colors and patterns that it was like walking through a rainbow haze. I saw some incredible things as I walked that day and met some incredible people. There were gatherings of people all over: there were those outstretched in integral yoga poses following prompts from the group onstage, those swaying to their own inner rhythm, and those who were just talking or smoking. There were those who were horsing around and those who were still sleeping, and there were quite a few times when I had to cease walking and just stand still and take it all in.

I passed so many people that they went by me in a blur. I don't know how long it took for me to get close to the stage—several hours at least, I'm sure—and when I turned to look back at the two trees at the top of the bowl from whence I'd come, I was several hundred yards to the left, even though I had tried to walk in a straight line. It was almost like when you stand in the ocean and drift with the current—it was that same kind of passive motion that was walking at Woodstock.

Now, music had been playing since shortly after I'd awoken, and as I approached that spot on the hill where you were close enough to see the performers clearly but still far enough away so that the planks didn't obstruct your view, yet another folk musician with an acoustic guitar was at the mic. Since I was still clumsily navigating my way through this crowded Goldilocks Zone and most of everybody else was sitting and watching Country Joe McDonald, I decided to hunker down and stay right where I was.

From the very start, that day was chock full of synchronicity. Right as I settled down and greeted my neighbors, Country Joe began to play a song entitled *Seen A Rocket*, which is about a guy driving through the desert while pesky aliens dart all around his car. It made me wonder if those cats from New Mexico were still thinking about me and that time traveler trip I'd laid for them.

I'd caught Country Joe right at the end of his set, and the last song he played was by far his most well-known and beloved. If there was any single anti-war song that defined that generation, it was his *I-Feel-*

Like-I'm-Fixin-To-Die-Rag, and as soon as he started to strum the intro, everybody around me was already following along.

"Give me an F!"

"F!"

"Give me a U!"

"U!"

"Give me a C!"

"C!"

"Give me a K!"

"K!"

"What's that spell?!"

"FUCK!"

"What's that spell?!"

"FUCK!"

"Well, c'mon all you big strong men, Uncle Sam needs your help again. He's got himself in a terrible jam way down yonder in Vietnam, so put down your books and pick up a gun, you're gonna have a whole lotta fun!"

The song was like an anthem, one that everybody knew. It was almost as if the music itself was speaking to us and saying, 'strangers in the fields, children in the trees, children of the Earth, of the sun, of the sky, of the sea, come together, join hands and sing!' —And sing together we surely did:

"And it's one, two, three, what are we fighting for?! Don't ask me, I don't give a damn. Next stop is Viet-Nam. And it's five, six, seven, open up the pearly gates! Well, there ain't no time to wonder why. Whoopee! We're all gonna die!"

However, I guess it wasn't quite loud enough for Country Joe because in-between verses he chided us, saying, *"Listen, people, I don't know how you expect to ever stop the war if you can't sing any better than that! There's about 300,000 of you fuckers out there, and I want you to start singing, come on!"*

"And it's one, two, three, what are we fighting for!?"

When we all sang together, the sound was like a wave. All the hills, the trees, bloody hell, even the sky had voices joining in and repeating the words of this anthem. We were all there under one flag—the freak flag, that is—and for one cause—we were all there for peace.

Once he'd wrapped up that last tune and waved to us in parting, the announcer came back over the air and told us that Santana was up next, so I just stayed put and hung out with all the heads that were around me. Somebody a few yards in front of me was blowing bubbles, and we were all watching them float above us in the air, trying to catch or pop them. It was like being a little kid again; God knows we were just as carefree. All that was important to us at that moment was finding something to entertain ourselves with until the musicians were all set up and could do a proper job of it.

Already, today's vibrations were markedly different from those of the previous night; everybody was getting into the groove of the festival, and now the rock musicians were taking the stage. The longer I sat, the more anticipation and excitement built up inside me. However, nobody else around me seemed particularly elated about this next set. This was unbelievable to me at first, until I remembered that at that point in time, Santana was relatively unknown outside of San Francisco. This was especially mind-boggling considering that he was one of the only performers at Woodstock to continue their career into the next century—and successfully, at that. With a start, I remembered that it was this upcoming performance that would be his slingshot to fame and realized that I was the only one there who knew that. I was the only one out of all those thousands who knew what I was anticipating, and with that thought in mind, I could hardly contain myself.

Almost immediately after he emerged onstage, all of us in the audience could clearly tell that Santana was tripping hard. He was making all kinds of wild, ugly faces and strange and jerky motions as he played, and while these might be taken as eccentricities by some people, I knew better, and in light of that, it made his performance—earth-shattering as it was—even more incredible. To be able to keep your head while playing stoned in front of a whole sea of people for the first time and still sound better than any other performer who'd yet to grace the stage, you have to be one hell of a fantastic musician.

As soon as he struck up, everybody in the audience was captured by the sound. His frantic electric guitar, hypnotic congas, slightly syncopated keyboard, and the effortless constancy of the drummer backing him seized the attention of 500,000. Acidheads began popping up all over the place in the crowd as they threw their arms in the air with their eyes closed and danced. It was so spellbinding you couldn't help but nod your head and tap your feet at the very least. It was the kind of music that brought about a full-body experience in listening—electric music for the body and soul. That's what it was, really, and that's what it brought you to: it brought you to soul, what the soul really is, in its most intrinsic sense—God. It took you beyond any personifications tacked on by analysis and human logic and brought you right to its core where good vibes and divine truth were all that remained. You could hear, see, and feel the soul spilling out of those musicians right over the very edge of the stage and washing out over the crowd. For Santana, every ounce of his energy was spent through his fingertips, each lurch and lunge of his body serving to squeeze and drain every last drop of soul right through the instrument and out into the general populous.

This was especially true for the last song of his set, *Soul Sacrifice*. *Soul Sacrifice* was another one of those performances that I'd watched so many times on film that I could anticipate every note, but when I watched it in person that afternoon, it was like I'd never seen it before. There has never been a more accurate title for a song, either, for it was truly a soul sacrifice. It was like he'd bared every emotion he'd ever felt and laid them all out there on that stage for us. The power in that performance was enough to overwhelm even a deaf spectator, purely by its energy alone.

The rhythmic clapping of everybody in the congregation began even before the music did. Santana's guitar was better than ever, but from his face, you could tell that he was close to spent, somewhat strung out and wired, and that his trip was beginning to take him. That's when the drummer stole the show. No mass of people were ever more taken and impressed by a drummer than we were that afternoon at Woodstock. It was all anybody talked about afterward, even during the next few sets; all everybody wanted to know was that drummer's name, and it's plain to see, once you've heard his performance, exactly why that is.

The name of Santana's young drummer was Michael Shrieve, and not only is he the best drummer I've ever heard or seen play live, he was just my age at the time! It is acknowledged as a general rule that the faster and smoother the drum solo, the more skilled the drummer, and this drum solo was so damn smooth it was like butter, honey, molasses, silken lingerie—I was slack-jawed the whole time and didn't even notice until a bug flew in. I felt like time had been suspended, or otherwise, I wished that it had, for if that last song—full of all its screeching electric guitar and heavy bass and cymbal crashes, like thunder and lightning from Shrieve's flying sticks—could've sustained me, I'dve been sated for all eternity. I clapped so hard that my hands went numb.

I was so fired up after that. I couldn't bear the thought of sitting still while the stage was cleared and prepped for the next group, so I got up on my feet again and started to walk. I began heading away

356

from the stage in the opposite direction, toward the road and the woods beyond that. The crowd started to thin out as I traveled this way, but even so, I can't tell you how long it took me to get down to where all the tents were.

The first thing I came to after I made it out of the bowl was a long row of payphones with a burgeoning mass of people hanging around waiting to use them. Next to the phone bank was a tree, the bark of which was almost entirely covered by notes left by passersby in hopes that the friends they were looking for would read them and meet them in front of the stage or near the phones or in one of the nearby tents and so on and so forth—nobody here had pagers, after all. Fittingly enough, the tree also provided shade for those who were waiting; they'd be waiting a long time.

In addition to the handwritten notes, there were posters of all sorts, including ones donning the huge mustached face of Meher Baba with the words '*Don't worry, be happy*' printed below. One particular flyer I remember seeing a lot of was one that proclaimed, '*We have to begin to fend for ourselve*s'—a true testament to both the times and the general sentiment around there. To be frank, we couldn't have garnered the help of any outside organization even if it was imperative. Now that sounds pretty bleak, especially considering the lawlessness and the chaos that was plentiful and abounding, but the chaos was controlled chaos. There was never any fear or a thought in anyone's mind that the situation would or could blow out of control. We'd all signed ourselves up for three days of peace and music, and we were determined to get three days of peace and music no matter what we had to endure, and everything we endured, we endured together. It was truly a beautiful thing.

Truthfully, the only offensive thing about the whole scene was the toilets. I made one trip there and then resolved to find alternate arrangements for the next time. Five hundred thousand people—no matter how peaceful they are—are far from beautiful when they are all crapping in the same place. It goes without question that I moved away from that area soon after I'd arrived. Besides, by now the sun was alone in the cloudless sky, and the persistent beating of its rays upon my back was not only sweltering but exhausting as well. Sweaty and famished, I journeyed back across that wide open space, tangent to my initial direction, skirting sporadic gatherings of people and mingling with the rest who, like me, were on the move.

Before very long, I came to what used to be a road, but now was just a mass of cars parked helter-skelter and abandoned by their owners. Directly across from the road was the woods which were filled with makeshift stands and tents containing all sorts of whimsical and intriguing items. Under the trees, apart from those recruited by the festival organizers to pass out peanut butter and jelly sandwiches and sunflower seeds were those festival goers who had brought along their own wares to sell, trade, and give away. It was like the greatest hippie garage sale of all time.

There were people distributing pamphlets containing messages about VA benefits, animal rights, and passages from Ouspensky. There were those selling big, floppy hats and headbands which were suspended in the low-hanging branches of a nearby tree for easy view from potential buyers. There were stands selling hand-carved pipes, one-hitters, hookahs, and all sorts of other wild-looking pieces. There were those selling second-hand instruments, clothes, and shoes. There were those with stacks of albums and posters and 8-tracks, those who had a wealth of books filling the trunks of their cars, and those selling cups of orange sunshine mescaline for one dollar. There were even those who had their art on display. People were selling hand-blown glass, pottery of all shapes, sizes, and purposes, strings of beads beautifully made, and don't even get me started on the paintings! Some were fair, some were excellent, and some were just downright strange, but all in all, none seemed to compare to what I was used to seeing from Al. If he'd known, he could've been a main attraction; but then again, making that cross-country trek in a van full of paintings was a terribly uncomfortable thought indeed.

I spent many hours in the woods, following signs hung up on the trees that read Happy Avenue and Groovy Way, and on my way into a clearing, I passed by a whole bunch of kids playing on a jungle gym and hung around to watch for a while. They were absorbed in their own little fantasy world, a reality in which no pain or suffering existed—apart from the occasional skinned knee. They knew of no corporate or political games, and war was far from their minds. It was a beautiful, charming existence—one I'd left long ago. But as I'd recently learned, it was not at all impossible to return. Acid, for one, makes you feel like a child in that everything is perceived as new and full of awe, but it's not naivety that makes a youthful spirit, rather it is a way of thinking: an innocence of intent and a lack of malice, mellowness of character and compassion without vested interest, and most of all, a love for all things, including yourself. I knew that there were a lot of us around who could truly dig that philosophy—and if not purely for the fun of it, that would also explain why so many of the adult crowd were taking part in the playground activities as well.

As the woods thinned out, I could see a second field up ahead of me. It was akin in size to the one known as the bowl, but this one was full of tents. Upon further investigation, I found that it served as the temporary living arrangements for the Hog Farm Commune. After traversing this open space, I found myself in yet another stretch of woodland, this one full of campsites. Woodchips had been laid down all around, and tents and teepees had been erected every couple of yards. Under the canopy, the atmosphere around the campsites was free and easy. Everybody was sitting around their tents, cooking something delectable over the fire, and shooting the bull; you could smell the joints burning away. I continued to wander aimlessly without a destination, my feet gliding gently across the lay of the land steadily and instinctively—I'd been walking all day. Even from this far away, I could still hear the faint sounds of music and the crowd. I could still feel the vibrations flowing out over the landscape like a current moving just above the ground, affecting everybody and excluding no one—and throughout the day and into the night it just kept getting better and better.

When I exited that second stretch of woodland, I found myself in an open field dotted full of more tents and cars. There were semi-circles of vans and buses and a bunch of people filling in the spaces between them, camping together and sharing just about everything. One of these such gatherings consisted of about six or eight people seated on yoga mats beneath the retractable awning of a Winnebago. They had their legs folded in lotus position, but rather than motionlessly meditating, they had a big pile of red balloons between them, and they were blowing them up, tying them off, and letting them fly away. Curiosity got the best of me, so I walked over to the group.

"What are you doing?" I asked.

"Blowing up balloons," one of them answered. "Come and sit with us!"

I took a mat from where there were some hung over the trailer hitch and found myself a seat between the cheery young blonde girl who'd answered me and a tall, lanky, and dapper young fellow with a neatly groomed beard who sat beside her.

"You see," explained the thin colored man who sat across from me, "we are filling these balloons here with all our negativities and letting them go."

"We're expelling all of the hate, all of the gluttony, and all of the lust," another female member with widely-spaced front teeth declared.

"I want my soul to be a temple of pure love, I don't want no evil in me no more."

I stayed with them for quite a while and participated in this unusual ritual until all of the balloons had been filled and released. Afterward, we began a cleansing practice, meditating and breathing, clearing our consciousnesses and letting our minds steep in all the good vibes that were around us. At the conclusion of this practice, we were led in prayer by the senior yogi among us, a man in his early thirties with long blonde hair and a tan chest crisscrossed by many strings of beads. We chanted this mantra many times in Sanskrit: '*Lokah samastah sukhino bhavantu*'—the translation of which is roughly: may all the beings be happy and free.

And all the beings were happy and free. I felt like I had been doused in holy water and all those conscious and unconscious parasitic negativities and hang-ups that disturbed my inner peace had been washed away. My senses were open, my perception was clearer, and my soul was calm. Smiles prospered around the circle, gently adorning all faces but one. This rogue frown afflicted the man I sat beside; his lips were pursed slightly, and the skin of his forehead was pulled taut in serious consideration. He broke his own silence before any of us could ask what was bothering him.

"I don't think I can rid my soul of evil," he spoke. He had his arms outstretched before us, palms up. On one wrist he had tattooed the yin and yang, and on the other, the symbol for the sign of Capricorn. The wrist with the yin-yang he extended toward the middle of the circle for us to see. "Evil is a fact of life," he explained, "it is found in all of humanity. There is no escaping it; it is a side effect of incarnation."

"You are absolutely right," the senior yogi suggested, "but no part of the soul is evil. The evil we see around us and feel within us is learned, it is of the world. Our souls are not, they are otherworldly, and they are of God; therefore, they cannot contain any evil."

"In Genesis, it is written that we are born with original sin because Adam and Eve ate from the tree in the Garden of Eden and were banished from it," the colored man said. "Is there any way to free ourselves from that sin and evil while we are here in this world?"

"Be baptized," the girl with the gap teeth answered him.

He inhaled sharply through clenched teeth, "You see," he replied, "I have some qualms about a conclusion as simple as that. My next door neighbor is a Catholic; he goes to church every Sunday, yet he still hates me because I am black. He spits when he sees me on the sidewalk and lets his dog shit on my lawn. My landlord is an Elder,

360

yet he drinks and beats his wife. What gives?"

The yogi spoke up this time, "The tree you mentioned in the book of Genesis is called the tree of the knowledge of good and evil. What that implies is that before there was knowledge of something other than good, of something other than love, it did not exist; but it is that knowledge that makes us quintessentially human. By searching for the good in people and treating their sins with compassion, by forgiving and reacting positively to situations that befall us, we can evade that evil. By acting with divine intent, we can free ourselves from the bane of our humanity. An optimist once told me that there is no such thing as evil, there is only an absence of positivity. Just as there is no such thing as dark, only absence of light, there is no such thing as bad, only varying degrees of good."

We were all quiet for a moment as we contemplated the moral profundity of his speech.

The girl with the gap teeth was the next to speak, "What if that apple was a placebo? What if this whole world is an illusion: *Man's Big Trip*? What if we are all still in the Garden, and all this," she waved her arms to indicate everything that was manifest, "all this is a dream? What if it's all just a bad dream and all we need to do to get back is wake up?"

The yogi regarded her with a rather pleased smile, "And when you blink your eyes open for the first time, you will find that in the beginning, all creation came to be out of desire, out of desire for existence. Death comes from too much desire. In liberation, you are free from desire, free from beginning and free from ending because you are FULFILLED. At every moment you are fulfilled, truly present in the here and now simply because you are fulfilled by the moment."

Following the conclusion of his speech, most, if not all of us around the circle unleashed a spontaneous and passionate *"OM"* to confirm his words.

I would have loved to have stayed for longer, but it was at this time that the quick descent of the sun beneath the land became apparent to me, and I stood and told them all *"Namaste."* I turned on my heels, and with the yogi's words echoing in my mind, I started back in the direction from which I'd come.

The campfires burned bright in the encroaching darkness, and red and orange embers flickered and danced in the twilight sky. Children yelped and giggled, and somewhere close by, a dog barked. The voices of conversationalists abounded. Now that I was no longer a part of any formal discussion, I listened to those seated around me as I passed by, hearing only snippets of their conversations and leaving any further understanding to conjecture alone. There were those who were theorizing and discussing world news and politics and those who were gossiping and chewing the fat. There were those conversations that were cerebral in content and those that sounded like pure nonsense. The variety and profundity of people, their interests, and the wealth of knowledge they'd accumulated astounded me.

There was this one group that was busy philosophizing around a campfire, and as I passed, some dude spoke up and said that he was taking a psychology class in college which he'd been supplementing with psychedelics—a confession that incited laughter from the rest of the circle—and that he'd learned that perception is different for everybody in the world.

"What I see isn't what you see," he'd said, "and it's true that we can see anything we want if we convince ourselves it is so; our mental syntax can be very easily rewritten. We are creatures of perspective, perception, sensation, and emotion. We are continuously creating our own realities, and it is impossible to distinguish between a reality that is objective and one that we've created because we have no way of telling the difference..."

I dwelled on this exposition for a moment, and then not a dozen steps later, I heard a woman in another circle ask a question about karma and why it operates the way it does. The answer she received surprised me in its semblance to what I'd just heard.

"Reality is like a wave, that is why there is always a return," somebody else in the circle had explained. "The greater cosmic reality does not work under the principle of cause and effect as we perceive it, rather it operates on the principle of reflection. We merely see it as cause and effect because it is not our nature to perceive on an objective scale."

Reeling from this apparent synchronicity, I went on, only to encounter more. Just a couple hundred yards from the circle of dharma bums, I stumbled across a strange-looking man in a dark-colored burnoose who stood before a fire and proclaimed, "All the world is a manifestation of the struggle and opposition of the principle of truth, *Asha*, against the principle of untruth, *Druj*. The purpose of life is to strive toward and maintain truth."

Near the furthest edge of the official campgrounds, a large gathering had commenced around a fairly aged, fairly dark woman. She spoke to a much younger girl who was a part of the circle;

however, I felt that what she said was directed toward me.

"At the time of your birth, when the umbilical cord was cut from your mother and you took your first breath of air, the constellation of Leo was rising. Growing up, you were very close to your father, yes? And you are a performer; you love to be on stage, and you are very creative as well. You are very honest and loyal, but you have a bit of an ego, oh yes, that is what you struggle with. Always remember that you are never in a position to sit in judgment over others and that the best thing you can do in this life is provide those around you with not only love but compassion as well..."

The older woman continued her reading, but by this time I'd moved out of earshot and back into the Hog Farmers' field. Here, another group of aspiring yogis were seated around in the grass with their eyes closed, breathing heavily. One of them was speaking, but by now it was too dark to tell who. Nevertheless, this is what they said: "Breath is very important. Who you are is determined by your first breath. Who you shall remain is determined by your last. Never neglect your breath, for it is your very essence in and of itself."

After this, I stopped my peripatetic eavesdropping; it was all too much. 500,000 people and they were all talking about the same thing. I felt like I was moving closer and closer to some sort of revelation, but from where it would finally come and what it would contain, I was wholly unsure.

—And in the wake of nightfall, that wasn't the only thing I was unsure about. I was in search of the Trips Mobile and our stash of canned goodies, but I had no idea where to find it. One of my principle reasons for setting out earlier, hunger, had never been resolved, and now I was wandering aimlessly around the outskirts of the festival in the dark, quite misled. My landmarks of earlier had been people—people who had long since moved. Nothing there at Woodstock was stationary; everybody and everything was constantly in motion. In my philosophic mood, I took this as an allegory for life, but it didn't help me much in reaching my destination.

Once I passed the medical tents, I decided to stay due straight; the crowd had begun to thicken, and I assumed I was headed for the bowl. Shortly after, I hit the information tree as I had earlier that afternoon coming from the other direction, and I began to climb the hill in hopes that the grade would take me to the place where the van was parked. Overall, despite my hunger and general fatigue, the trek that night was in no way unpleasant. I still had a few cigarettes left out of a pack that had been given to me by someone earlier in the day, and the music playing over the air was just pure gold. A band called Canned Heat was on—they do that song called *Going Up To Country*—and as I started up the hill, they launched into a tune full of muted distortion and bass like crazy. It was all bass and reverb and some wonky guitar pedal that made everything sound like it was bubbling up from underwater. The drummer was just fantastic, so crisp and strong; he had chops like you wouldn't believe. I really enjoyed their set that night; the beat of their music helped me keep my step, and I continued up the hill without thinking of the ache in my legs or the pangs in my stomach.

When at once I stopped and turned, the song that had been playing ended, and Bob Hite, the singer for that group, spoke at the same time as the announcer, causing a feedback trip area-wide. I think every stoned hippie within audible range held their ears and moaned. However, their recovery was swift because the guitarist launched right into a thoughtful and twanging solo that brought just the right amount of electrical tension to the still, cloudy night. It sounded just the way heat lightning might if you plugged it into an amplifier and gave it some groove. After this went on for some time, the rest of the band struck up, and it was pure rhythm and blues—man, was it groovy.

Just as they finished up their set and I walked along, tired and content, I came upon a big green microbus parked by the edge of the tree line at the top of the hill. I rubbed my eyes for confirmation, incredulous at the occasion, but it was truly there—the Trips Mobile in all its glory. I rejoiced in seeing it and ran those last few yards over to it. At first, I thought I was the only one there, but as I was pulling open the door, I was momentarily startled when a hand reached down from the roof and tugged playfully on my hair. Bobby was up there with the binoculars, and Mary was inside, changing. We greeted one another excitedly, then began to talk over the day and exchange stories. I was so happy to have found them; I didn't think that timing any more perfect was possible, but it was only a couple minutes later when I was proved wrong yet again with the sight of Billy and Faye walking up the hill toward us. Surprisingly enough, when I asked, I learned that this was the first time that any of them had attempted to come back to the van, and somehow, we had all arrived there at the same time.

It didn't take us long to get our thing together, and with freshly rolled joints and our last clean blanket, we left the van together and sought out a groovy place to stay the night. We found a spot to sit relatively close to the top of the bowl, a lone patch of grass that had avoided being completely trampled, a respite from the mud. We settled in and lit up, and Bobby began to explain to the rest of us how he and Mary and Al had met up with some musician friends of theirs backstage.

"The producers are scared shitless," he explained, "and I would be too if I had that much bread invested and lost in a trip like this. They're estimating that there are over four hundred thousand people here."

"No shit," I replied, "I think I've stepped over that many alone."

"I rapped with the dude who came up with the whole idea for this festival, a cat named Michael Lang. It seems like he's one of four guys who put their heads together and conjured up a little investment opportunity called Woodstock Ventures. It's a pretty strange combination to pull off a trip like this—it seems like two of them are East Coast preppies, and the other two are heads. Anyhow, it's a complete financial disaster with no way to collect tickets and all, but they're not too hard up, there's a film crew here and all, and they're pretty smart cats—they'll make a movie out of it or something."

I smiled knowingly to myself, "I'm sure they will."

"Oh I just wish you came with us, Rhiannon," Mary said, wonder dancing in her eyes. "Everybody was backstage there. All the musicians have their own little area, and it's just like a great big VIP party. Grace Slick, Marty Balin and the rest of Jefferson Airplane are back there, Jerry Garcia, Bob Weir," she swooned, "Santana and the guys, Joan Baez, Janis," she swooned again, "Levon Helm, David Crosby, Neil Young, John Densmore, Joe Cocker, Roger Daltry…" she went on naming musicians.

"You didn't tell her the part where we got to go out on stage," Bobby interrupted.

"You got to do what?!" I asked in disbelief.

"Yes, yes," Bobby insisted, "not all the way out there while performances were going on, but we got to sit on the side of it and walk around while they were setting up. The thing is massive, and there's like this Lazy Susan in the middle of the stage that's supposed to rotate so one band can set up while the other is playing, but that didn't exactly work out as planned. Anyway, it's fantastic, really. You see those towers down there? I climbed up one of them, all the way to the top where they have the spotlights. The view is just…wow!"

"Far out," I spoke wistfully, my attention diverted from him for a moment by Mary who shook her head as Bobby started telling me about the towers.

"And look what I got…"

My attention was turned back to Bobby as he opened his outstretched hand to reveal several tabs of blotter acid, orange in color.

"From Grace and Marty; they had a sheet they split with Al. Al took a few tabs for himself and gave the rest to us."

"Let's take some tonight," Mary Jane entreated him. "Janis is supposed to perform tonight, and the Dead, and The Who!"

"Yeah, let's get loaded," Bobby replied, handing out the acid. The five of us took it, and then munched on a bit of food that we had brought with us. No new group had struck up yet, and while Bobby's chatter was momentarily quieted, I was left to look out over the crowd—out over the sheer mass in numbers for as far as my eye could see. I had never felt so slow in my life, so purposeful in my indolent motions, so aware of my lethargy. It was a calm, still night and a quiet, comfortable, and peaceful repose. I leaned back and watched the smoke from our cigarettes swirl and drift up into the sky above us and disperse amid the heavy air of that warm August night. As the flames from countless lighters shimmered and waltzed in the valley below us, the smoke from hundreds of cigarettes and joints left the mouths of thousands and wafted up into the sky to join that vast haze that hung over us all. It was a breathtaking sight, literally; we were one under the crumbling atmosphere and the shocked homeostasis of any air-breathing creature nearby.

The music that night—once it started up again—was positively unreal. Leslie West, the guitarist from the group Mountain, was an absolute genius. The sound his instrument made was so deep, heavy, and driving, that with only a few riffs and a half a dozen inversions he could touch all corners of a proper musical experience: suspense, exhilaration, hypnotism, and that feeling that no one can totally explain, the one that we musicians feel when we hear something so novel and inspired that it commands complete and utter respect.

After Mountain, the Dead came on, and their set felt like it lasted the entire night. We'd formed ourselves into a little semi-circle and were all laying down on our sides and laughing about something I don't quite remember. Admittedly, the four of us were all a little high. Faye and Billy—having been high even before they'd taken the acid—talked very little, but even so, they were still very much engaged in our conversation. Whenever Billy, in particular, would say anything it was oddly profound, such as this one gem he let out while we watched a man tiptoe through the surfeit of prostrate forms as he attempted to balance a heaping plate of food he'd gotten from somewhere on the other side of the hill:

366

"Don't walk along grooving on Kruetzmann's drum solo while carrying a dish of food through a crowd of 500,000, man, because if you spill it, somebody's gotta pick it up—it'll land on somebody else's plate."

Billy was speaking to us, not the man himself, but his statement contained a message suitable for everyone, and we rapped on that for a while.

Meanwhile, The Grateful Dead up on stage were terribly stoned. It wasn't great music by any conventional definition, but it was so radical and eccentric and even somewhat confused that everyone who was high themselves could really dig it. For me, just seeing them there on that stage was truly surreal.

To my surprise, Faye, who was typically animate enough for all of us, was unusually still and quiet. She was sitting off on the corner of the blanket by herself with her knees pulled into her chest and her arms wrapped around them, her eyes half-closed in a squint as if she was looking at something very intently and trying to decipher it, but there was nothing before her. Her trip was all inside her head. Alone in her mounting introspection, Faye was entirely composed. I daresay she never freaked out on a drug once in her life, she was too mad already. Every so often, she would stir and reach over to pat Billy on the head in order to reassure herself of his presence, but other than that simple action, she seemed entirely content and capable in her own estranged reality.

For me, the experience was only beginning. I didn't know how much I'd taken, so I didn't know what to expect. Apart from that paradoxical strange-yet-familiar feeling that always comes over you at the start of an acid experience and the stark improvement of the music, no visuals had arrived yet; nothing profound and nothing bizarre. There was simply a marked improvement over the usual, which as usual, previously felt as if no improvement could be made.

The first real indication that I'd taken LSD came as I watched Bobby smoke a cigarette. At first, the waves and spirals of smoke escaping his mouth seemed entirely normal, but after a couple more puffs, they appeared to wobble and jump in the air and change in color—only slightly at first, and then more sharply. Each time he exhaled it looked as if a whole slew of new, microscopic universes were being breathed into existence. When I looked toward the stage, I could see clear and fine and dandy, but on either side of me in my periphery, the flames from the lighters streaming down the hill became exaggerated in beautiful and intriguing bursts and spirals that looked like the kind of cosmic phenomenon you might see through a high-power telescope.

"Woah," I breathed, and Bobby held my hand.

I began to feel this incredible closeness with everybody around me; I just wanted to go out and hug everyone and let them know I loved them. The joy I felt bubbling up inside me was like nothing I'd ever experienced before, and a smile so wide it hurt spread across my face. I was looking down at the crowd below me—a single, massive living organism of which I was a part—an undulating gelatinous mass writhing and jumping; an amorphous form strangely streaming down the hill to a screaming stage alive with buzzing electricity, tickling the subconscious of all those sleeping people down there in the mud. Delightful and manic, controlled and chaotic, wild and peaceful, the music was the form and we were the imagination. It sustained our reality, and we merely existed inside it for a moment.

On and on into the night, the hallucinations continued to come. The Dead came and went, and the CCR took the stage. Billy, Faye, and Mary had gone off by themselves at that point, leaving Bobby and me alone. It was late in the evening, and as more and more people began to drift away into the gentle respite of sleep, we could see the stage more clearly—there were fewer heads in the way. However, I can't imagine that being much of a consolation for those who were to perform that night; I know I wouldn't much like playing to a field full of sleeping people. Seeming to sense this, some guy not too far from us shouted something encouraging to John Fogerty, and they struck up shortly after.

The music that night was awesome, just awesome. It might surprise some of you who don't know, but the CCR was originally from San Francisco, despite all that stuff they sing about bayous and bullfrogs and New Orleans. Frankly, their lyrics were oddly fitting for that late night in Yasgur's New England fields. With the humidity at the level it was and the mud we were all sitting in, it wouldn't have taken much to make me or anyone else believe we were in a Louisiana swamp. Additionally, there was this one song I really liked, *I Put A Spell on You*, the tone and chords of which sounded like they were taken directly out of a Creole voodoo ritual, and in my present state of mind, that kind of occult mysticism not only appealed to me but rapt me intensely. I remember listening to that tune with my eyes closed, my head bobbing back and forth like a pendulum as the colors and figures inside my mind traipsed about and wandered aimlessly along their own planes of shadow and substance. Whenever I did open my eyes,

I saw the stage in a strange new way, in some sort of fusion of real and unreal, such as that of a huge, rotating All-American apple pie with the CCR standing atop it, spinning just behind the shroud of the knoll. There was no sleep for me that night, oh no, and far from it.

My favorite of all the performers that night was Janis Joplin. I'd seen her band play before back on the Haight, and I'd even met her personally. She was a groovy woman and one hell of a performer. She was hard to describe—powerful and melancholy, yet full of so much love to give, broken and singing the blues, yet wholesome and proud. Janis wore a billion different people's expressions, and with each song, a different personality emerged; each of them reminiscent of a different experience, a different memory. Her voice was raspy and sensual as it wound its way around that space inside my mind—she was the harlot of my trip. Her hair, long and wild, shook loose around her shoulders and lined the robes she wore; it was like a mantilla of flowers cascading down from the temple atop her skull. Her words promoted self-examination and dancing, let me tell you! People you wouldn't have even known were awake because they had been so still before got up on their feet and began to clap and groove.

In the midst of this, I felt infected with a sort of crazed and blissful madness. We were free, the trip was life, and the music was *right now*. Everything in the universe was happening all at the exact same time, and her words fell like raindrops upon a florescent mantelpiece—that was the stage—and then split off into a million more droplets, each full of vibrations and passion like you wouldn't believe. The glow from the spotlights before me was bending and melting, becoming softer, number—oh, comfortably numb. Oh man, let me tell you, let me tell you about all those freaks there. You see, I knew nothing about them—only that they were me—and cast in the light, they looked more and more like candle wax dripping, as smooth as caramel glaze. Together they melted and fused, oozing past the juxtaposed logic strategically measured in my mind.

The music, you understand, the music is what drove our trips. Everything was "*Groove on this here, man*," and "*Dig this riff, man*," and as we listened, it pervaded us. That's what music does: it gets into your body and into your soul, and it makes you move. Music is energy, and it wants to be released back out into the universe. Whether you are the listener, performer, or dancer, you are just a conduit for the energy of your surroundings. Energy, electricity, vibrations or whathaveyou, they all pass through you:

1969

You are all the energy.

It is still somewhat of an understatement to say that my high peaked during the next set, that of Sly and the Family Stone, another San Francisco native. After Janis left the stage, I was still full of unexpressed energy, anxiously awaiting the debut of the next band so that I could unleash what I was holding inside. Luckily for me, the music of Sly and the Family Stone was a cross between a funky soul praise band and a psychedelic smorgasbord, a second wind for all those who presumed that moment was the right time to bed down for the night.

Their music struck you right in the center of your being and animated you from that point. I was one of those frantically gyrating bodies dotting the landscape, shaking my head back and forth to create equilibrium, my feet pounding the ground as mud splashed up around my ankles. The stage became an acid starburst composed of a collection of cylinders, a molten pigment at their center that shook and moved with the sound. The music took me higher and higher in a kind of euphoria that seemed to build forever, bringing me nearer and nearer to a climax that would never come. I felt like I could fly, like I wasn't confined to the ground anymore; like I was in two places at the very same time. I felt as if I was one with the glow of the stage, as far away as it was, and as my perception warbled before me and solo after solo delighted my senses, I had this wild feeling that I wasn't just a part of the crowd anymore, but that I was on stage, standing behind the performers. I could still see all of their movements, but now I was moving with them. Not only was I hearing the music, I was also making the music; it was coming from me. I was moving up and down the neck of Sly Stone's guitar, riding with the beat, and then I was soaring through the audience as they parted before me like viscid walls, somewhat akin to what I imagine the parting of the Red Sea may have been like. My spirit met my body with a burst of light and color that I felt rather than saw, and an orb of pure energy traveled up from my feet and erupted out through the top of my head.

I suddenly felt as light as air, like my body was entirely weightless, and all around me in some sort of wave-like expulsion, a lotus flower blossomed with me in its center. Strangely enough, rather than morphing into something else after a mere moment, this perception remained, and I could walk about and stand on the very edges of the petals of eternity. Fulfilled and calm, with all sensations of uncontrollable gyration ceased, a marked stillness ensued. I felt as if

I'd just been shaken out of a meditation of incalculable length, like I'd come upon something that might be mistaken for bliss, but even this, in all its glory, still was not the ultimate—not even this was nirvana. *IT* had evaded my grasp once more.

Once the music subsided and the delicate petals of the lotus had been blown away by the breeze, I sat down in the mud and watched Bobby trip beside me until the next band struck up. Sly and The Family Stone were followed by The Who, an act that most of us had been anticipating all day long, and as they took the stage, they immediately launched into the greatest rock opera of all time, *Tommy*. It was some obscene hour of the early morning when they struck up, and just about all of us who were still awake were completely gassed.

There's no better way to spend five a.m. in Vibrationland than with a purely perturbed musical number such as *Tommy*. The sensations induced by the music crawled across my skin, ran up my arms, and set all my hair standing on end. The sounds that came out from their mouths and their hands dazzled us in tantalizing wonder. There was a playful resonance in the sound and an assuredness in the beat. There was a continuation of theme, and yet a separateness, a specialization of every song. We all knew what was coming next, but even so, each note was a new surprise.

—And speaking of surprises, it wasn't Sally Simpson that got thrown off the stage this time, it was Abbie Hoffman—a somewhat ironic, forcible alteration of his trip that evening. Despite this interruption, they went on playing: Daltry's whining and chanting, Townshend's lyric, articulate guitar, Entwistle's driving bassline, and Moon's rumbling drums that sounded like he was summoning the thunder. At the very end, after the opera but before the encores, there was something else—another surprise—the best song of their set: *See Me, Feel Me*. Daltry came on neat and smooth in a pleading voice full of desperation as ribbons of blue silk flowed out from either side of him across the stage, enveloping the feet of the performers. And then came the encores, beginning with *Summertime Blues* which was like a roar—a physical, arching wave of sound that rushed toward us, washed over us, and baptized us in the new dawn soon to be on the horizon. After this, they left the stage and it was quiet, but they soon returned and did one more tune.

There was the characteristic squawking of instruments and a pause for the cheers, and then Townshend came over the mic again and said to the crowd, *"Thank you very much indeed, we're gonna play a song,"* and the quiet moment of before was obliterated by *My*

Generation.

Down at the bottom of the hill, the bodies of all those sleeping people ran together to engulf the landscape. It amazed me how they could still be asleep with the sounds of The Who blasting out over the fields, but they were dead to the world. I, however, could not sleep. The energized feeling I'd felt before was just beginning to fade. I would have loved to have closed my eyes and sunk into the receding waves of sound that had just finished pouring out from those awesome speakers and that now-darkened stage, but instead I remained awake for the rest of the night—or rather, what was left of the darkness—and stared up at the stars, contemplating existence in the light of this acid afterglow.

The empty stage loomed before me in the gray, hazy darkness. *At one time or another*, I thought, *all of us stand upon a stage.* We humans act out the whole of our brief lives in a dim theater in purgatory, where our karma is bared for all to see. This Earth is nothing more than a crowded stage where souls reenact the humor and tragedies of their past in an attempt to rectify their future. Moral law, universal Truth, and infinite awareness all sit in the very front row.

At dawn when the music stopped, people started leaving the fields, or finally exhausted, they fell to sleep where they sat. Shortly after the music ended, the lights from the stage went out, and complete darkness engulfed the land. The stars were bright again, and the moon had gone down. While it was still dark, the most incredible sound filled the air—birds. There must have been thousands of them, all singing their cheery songs of morning. They were so loud that I questioned whether or not the sound was coming from the speakers, but it wasn't—it was coming from the land. I've never heard anything quite like it before or since, and it was so beautiful that I could have easily wept for the misfortune of those sleeping people who in their slumbers had missed it. The birds sang, cooed, and let their presence be known to the world. They spoke in musical harmony, conversing in the sweetest tongue of all—but this only lasted a short while. For when the sky turned from gray to purple and the sun began to rise, bathing the horizon in the auburn hues of daybreak, they fell into stillness once again, their presence and their numbers once more a mystery. The sound of this silence was like a hollow echo, and peace and harmony resounded all around us—like all was one and one was all.

I was not alone in witnessing this spectacle. There were still a few dozen others sitting awake near me, not to mention those in transit. Once again, it became evident to me that it wasn't the music or even the circumstances that were the most incredible there—it was the people. As I leaned back, looking around at my vast family, a man walked past me leisurely and unhurried with his hands relaxed in the pockets of his shorts. When he saw that I was awake, he smiled as if he'd known me forever, "Peace, friend," he said, flashing me the peace sign. It is memories and experiences such as these that were the heart and soul of Woodstock and the ones I treasure the most tenderly.

1969

****

I was still wide awake after the sun came up when a new group took the stage. Now everybody was awake again, and Bobby was asleep beside me. The morning was bright, the sky, a pale blue, and a fine mist hung over the bowl. I began my day—or rather, ended my night—with a much-needed cigarette and the music of Jefferson Airplane. Grace Slick, a vocalist and front to whom there is no compare, greeted all of us out there in the audience: *"Alright friends, you've seen the heavy groups, now you'll hear morning maniac music. Believe me, yeah!"*

The guys in the band struck up, and morning maniac music it certainly was. The sound of all that warbling guitar sliced through the morning air like a knife, flanked by the voices of Grace and Marty, a psychedelic duet like none other.

Jefferson Airplane played a few songs that were new to everyone in the audience except for me, a sneak peek at their new album that would be released in November. One of these songs was *Eskimo Blue Day* and the other, I believe, was their cover of *Wooden Ships*. It was at the start of one of these songs that Grace addressed the crowd again, *"Sorry about those who got the green, we got a whole lot of orange, and it was fine—and it still is fine! Everybody's...vibrating..."*

Everybody's...vibrating...

I grooved on that, and when she said *we*, I felt as if she was speaking directly to me, and I was imbued by the strangest of feelings until I realized that she was! She knew that somebody out there in that vast sea of humanity was tripping on her stash, and that somebody was me. Grace Slick and I were tripping on the same batch of acid! Now if that's not far out, I don't know what is.

For those who were just starting to get their thing together, the music provided a whole new perspective for that day. They'd transported the vibrations of San Francisco and the Haight, of the nightclubs and the Park, all the way across the country to Upstate New York. It was the best morning of my life, the dawn of what was, by far, the best day. I didn't know it then, but I should have—the indications of such a realization were all around me. Everything was

374

finally falling into place. The energies told me that it was to be the greatest day in the history of man.

By the time they got to the last few songs of their set, the effects of the acid I'd dropped the night before had worn off completely, and I was finally beginning to feel tired. It started to come in waves, and no matter how loud the music or how noisy the crowd, I began to feel as if I needed to close my eyes, let the sounds fade to a whisper, and let the music and the voices I heard lull me to sleep. Somehow, I managed to stick it out until they finished their set, and as the rhythmic clapping of the crowd rose to a crest and broke out over the land, I sank into quiet oblivion.

When I awoke, it must have been sometime in the afternoon, but I couldn't tell; the sun was hidden behind the clouds. It looked, quite unfortunately, like it might rain again. I sat up and glanced around me. The blanket I'd been sleeping on had become one with the mud, and between my restless sleep, the events of last night, and the people walking, my hair, my clothes and every inch of my skin had become caked full of mud. I don't think I had ever been in such desperate need of a bath before in my life. I wasn't alone, either, for most of the crowd was full of mud, and the wild variety of colors that I'd been so awed by on the first day had faded to hues of dull brown all around.

When I turned to look beside me, I found that Bobby had disappeared while I'd slept. However, he'd left his bandana which was unusual for him, considering how convenient it was for tying up. Wherever he'd gone, it wasn't to score junk. Half-asleep and groggy, I just sat there for a while and reveled in the constant buzz that was going on all around me. Despite the numbers, nobody was unduly noisy. Instead, it sounded like one big conversation—and one big nonsense conversation at that. Once in a while, you could distinguish a sentence or a joke or a laugh, but for the most part, it was just static, like the kind of static you hear when you tune into an unoccupied radio frequency.

Once I'd gotten my bearings, I tied the bandana around my head and went out in search of the pond we'd swam in earlier in the week, hoping that on the way there I'd come across food of some sort; I couldn't remember the last time I'd eaten a square meal. As I walked along, I waved to those who looked my way, flashed them the peace sign, and smiled at them. I was having a grand old time, truly enjoying this moment of mine.

1969

As I made my way through the crowd, I could see that there was another group setting up onstage, and I watched them as I walked, trying to catch a fleeting glimpse of who it was. At one point, curiously, I decided to stop. I don't know why, really, and when I stopped, I looked down at my feet. When I did, I couldn't believe what I saw; there at my feet, half buried in the mud, was a page ripped out of a Bible, one of the verses circled in marker. I didn't pick it up or disturb it, instead I leaned down to read it, and this is what it said: *The Lord, your God, is in your midst, a mighty savior; he will rejoice over you with gladness and renew you in his love, he will sing joyfully because of you, as one sings at festivals.—Zephaniah 3:17*

I contemplated this for a little while, bearing in mind the likelihood that I should have seen the page at all—that out of all those hundreds of acres of ground and people, I had looked down just at that moment; as if someone had halted my feet and turned my head. And—trust me—I have thought about it many more times since, mostly because when I looked up again, a strange and wild-looking man stood before me.

"I am He and He is me, we are three—Exist!" he cried out, arching his back and throwing his hands in the air. This man was entirely naked, except for a tiny leather pouch he had strung around his neck and the long, straight brown hair that reached all the way down to the backs of his ankles. When I stood and met his eyes, I was overcome by a powerful reaction—I either wanted to turn and run away as fast as possible or stay and look into their depths for the rest of my life; that was the tremendous power inherent in this man's gaze. I had never seen eyes like that before, and I can say with certainty that I will never see eyes like that again unless I meet that man—and I know that I will not, because he is gone. He was a product of another place and another time, and it is quite possible that he only ever existed there, at Woodstock. And he changed my life.

At first, neither of us said a word to one another. There were no salutations, no pleasantries, and no explanation either, for as much as I can remember. When he looked at me, he gasped and pointed, "You!" Then he opened up his little pouch, extracted a pinch of something that looked like dust, and told me to open my mouth. I didn't right away, of course, and asked for some kind of reason.

"This is ayahuasca from the God-vine in Brazil. Don't worry, no danger—only enlightenment."

I have to admit that I did remember what Meredith had told me once about not thinking twice if somebody offered me something questionable to take, and in my own defense, I did think twice—and after I was finished thinking, I took twice the dose.

You see, everybody at Woodstock was looking for something. We are all spiritual people, after all, and in that time, people were finding spirituality in all sorts of different places: in the music, the drugs, in other people, the religious trip, even in the landscape—enlightenment was everywhere. At that point, I was already aware of a couple things: that God can be here and take any form, that I am not my body, that I am a spiritual being inhabiting a material plane, that reality is a very loosely-defined concept, et cetera. I was finding answers for sure—this whole time-travel thing had been the learning experience of a lifetime—but I was looking for more. I was searching for the ultimate reality. I wanted to see God, to bear witness to the birth of the universe; I wanted to know the Truth. I also knew that the answers I was seeking were all right there in my own mind, I just needed a little help getting to them, and I was aware that this was an experience that would never present itself to me again, and that the time was right; right here and right now.

I opened my mouth and let the man pour that mysterious powder under my tongue. It had an awful taste, but I was able to choke it down with the help of some water from a canteen that a witness handed me. After this curt exchange—which in all honesty probably lasted no more than thirty seconds—he staggered off into the crowd, throwing up his arms and proclaiming all sorts of mad-sounding spiritual assertions. If his spiel about the dust had been a sham, I might have forgotten the whole thing. However, it wasn't; and as far as forgetting goes, until my dying day, the subsequent events will never be erased from my mind.

It took quite a while for any feeling from the drug to come on at all. I kept walking down toward the stage as I had been prior to my encounter with the man, and at some point, the group that had been setting up onstage began their set. I was very pleased when I found out that it was Joe Cocker and the Grease Band, an act that I'd wanted to see for a long time. As they played, I continued to walk, enjoying the music and the show. However, before long, my legs grew tired and the crowd grew impenetrable, so I stopped to watch. Joe Cocker was a character for sure—he looked like he was playing guitar with his right hand and piano with his left as he sang, his form stiff and his motions jerky and somewhat uncoordinated. His music was a hybrid type—bluesy yet folky, heavy yet clean, and reminded me of Fresno in the

377

summertime: of late nights with The Descendants, gigs at two a.m, top-down rides on the freeway with the wind blowing through my hair—let's go get stoned! And as I listened and began digging it more and more, I was gradually overcome by a strange and unexpected sensation that I can only explain as insurmountable joy.

That is when the experience truly began, and from that point onward I can't explain exactly what happened to me, but I can explain what I've taken away from it. Overall, the very nature of the trip was totally different than any I'd ever taken before. It seemed like every time I tried something new there, the experience superseded the previous ones—with the exception of the DMT trip, which was unlike anything else I'd ever experienced before in my life. However, although the DMT trip definitely wins out in being stranger and more intense both in sensation and visual experience, the one that I took at Woodstock sneaks ahead in an area far more important: the entire experience, the drug itself and what I learned from it, was entirely organic; it was real in the truest sense of the word.

Now, just one more piece of clarification before I go on: there is a stark difference between knowing and understanding, and while this particular trip did not provide me with anything I hadn't already *known,* it gave me the experience I needed to truly *understand.* The whole thing was my birth, my death, and my beatific vision altogether. This is how it began:

It was the middle of the afternoon, and as Joe Cocker finished up his historic set with *A Little Help From My Friends*, big, dark storm clouds heavy with rain hung ominously over the fields of Bethel, New York. Once the music stopped, the rain just came right on down. The musicians left the stage in a hurry, and the festival coordinators and Hog Farmers began running around trying to secure all of the electrical equipment. The announcer got back up on the mic again and said, *"Alright everybody, just sit down, wrap yourselves up—we're gonna have to ride it out. Hold on to your neighbor, man!"* In the background, you could hear the frantic voices of the musicians whose instruments had gotten caught in the downpour.

It was all sort of chaotic for a short while; just try to imagine half a million muddy hippies standing out in the middle of a field with no shelter and no music to listen to, trying to light soggy joints. To me, the silence that ensued sounded like the people who'd put this thing together holding their breaths. This was especially true when the announcer came back to the mic again and began telling those people who'd climbed up the towers near the stage to get down. I had watched

378

those towers go up—hastily is one way to describe the process—and the last thing they needed was a few dozen people hanging on them, especially in the middle of an electrical storm. With my eyes, I traced the trajectory of those towers if they were to fall, and the result was catastrophic. For a few moments, it seemed like we were all about to be fried or crushed—but the panic I felt was fleeting. Luckily for us, a different man came to the mic, this one wholly sanguine and optimistic, and he called out to the crowd, *"Hey! If we think really hard, maybe we can stop this rain, yeah!"*

All together, the whole crowd began to chant, "No rain! No rain! No rain! No rain!" But it was to no avail; if anything, the rain came down even harder. However, we'd been distracted, reminded that we were all in this together and that it was up to us to keep this whole thing riding.

As the rain came down with no sign of stopping, people started leaving the fields or covering up the best they could to shield themselves from the brunt of the deluge. Where there was once grass, mud bubbled up out of the ground. I was not afraid, nor was I bummed; the rain felt magnificent! I watched as the dried mud turned aqueous yet again and ran from my skin. I groked at this, and upon looking up, watched as millions of raindrops descended from the sky and all at once, turned into a hundred different spectrums of light. Stoned, euphoric, and whathaveyou, I worshipped the rain. As the sky cracked open, I felt every last vestige of hatred, restriction, ignorance and naivety wash away from me. I was full of love, free from the games, imbued by wisdom, and approaching enlightenment. Just as the rain cleansed my body, it also purified my soul. This was what I'd been praying for back in Fresno what felt like a lifetime ago, and now it had finally come.

Before I knew any different, I was lined up with about a hundred others waiting to run and slide down the hill in the mud. A long strip of ground had been vacated, and everybody who wasn't afraid to get dirty was standing around watching. A bunch of people were clanking empty beer cans together and chanting *"Whoaaohaohohoh!"* to the beat kept by a couple of guys who'd brought their bongos along. It might have been the single most humorous spectacle I've ever witnessed—grown men and women playing and splashing in the mud like children. When it was my turn, I wound myself up, and with my arms spread, ran down the hill feeling like I could fly.

—But just like everyone else who tried it, at a certain point I slipped and fell and went hydroplaning down the hill, and the warm mud sloshed all over me as the rain continued to fall from above. Somewhat disoriented, I laid on the ground at the bottom of the hill in a fit of laughter, surrounded by walls of people. There was no way out, but there was no sense of claustrophobia; instead, there was a feeling of complete and utter union. What I was witnessing once again became an allegory for life, and what I saw affirmed for me was that this is a world of bonding and separating. Some people split apart from the group and ran down the hill, but when they reached the bottom, they melted back into the faceless crowd. *We are all one, and we are beautiful,* I thought, *We are all a part of one another, both the same and the opposite. We are all part of the same great circle; everything in the world is. We are fully a part of and apart from everything at all times.* Experiencing that connection and that shared energy so fully was one of the most powerful feelings I've ever felt. It was a vibration I'd experienced before, but that time it was with an intensity that was unparalleled. Getting there, to that level, was like tuning in on a wavelength, exactly as Tim Leary had put it.

That was only the first of many, many realizations that day, each one more powerful and telling than the last. As my trip progressed, all sense of time ceased. It just—*poof*—vanished, as if it had never existed. Now the feeling wasn't just that of not knowing whether or not any time was passing, that was far too ordinary. Rather, it was a feeling that encompassed the realization that time is actively constructed by our feeble minds and that really the only existence is Here, the only reality is Now—and it was like being on the other side of that illusion, with the understanding that the instant I was experiencing wasn't in time, but rather that time is in the instant.

I got up out of the mud and stood right there in the center of the crowd, looking up at the sky like I was in a trance, and I could see all different levels to it like it was unraveling. And as I was witnessing these things, a feeling was growing inside me; but it was more than just a feeling, it was an experience. I *was* those things that I was witnessing. It felt like there was an orgasm building in every fiber of my being. There was no way I could fight it, I had to let it take me—I was no longer afraid. As I looked up, I saw that the sky was rising, rising, rising…higher, higher, higher. The clouds were lifting, lifting, lifting…to a reverberating point that shook the whole world.

I remember seeing a flag whipping and churning in the wind. It flowed outward in an undulate, completely covering my field of vision in an expanse of red, and I was entirely immersed in its essence. It became the whole of my environment, and I could sense it with every part of my being: the smell, the taste, the sound, the color, the feeling of red. It washed over me and consumed me, and I was baptized in vermillion synesthesia.

When this passed, all around me, the rosy, vibrating people began to come apart at their seams, and everything I saw broke apart into molecules that started to drift away from one another like a pointillism painting. Multicolored atoms hung in a space that was all their own, ascending toward the zenith, the Godhead—a vast, white expanse with colors of great receptive, acoustic multitudes surrounding it. It wasn't exactly white, but that is the only word I know of that I can use to describe it, and that being said, it was the purest, brightest white that has ever existed—so white it was almost colorless.

Visions of all kinds abounded as I grew closer and closer to the Godhead, as the earth rose up beneath me to kiss the sky and I and everybody else—one and the same—moved with it. The ascent was tremendous; it surpassed any sensation I have felt before or since and was at the same time both ephemeral and eternal. Ensconced in bliss, rapt in that sensation of insurmountable joy, I fearlessly approached the Godhead and consciously allowed everything else to fall away.

And then, there I was again, at that same doorway. I looked down and my body was gone. All form and substance were gone. All the visions were gone. I'd gone beyond the visions to the Void and passed through the Void into objective reality, where all is One. This was ego loss. This was the Godhead.

The Godhead is the first step into the universe of form. It is God manifested as well as God manifesting the world. You are not only God, you are the entirety of the universe, the start and the end, all in all. It is pure energy; it is energy becoming form. Wherever there was energy, matter began to appear where none had previously existed. It was then that the ultimate revelation surged upon me: God is energy—that force that cannot be created nor destroyed—and since everything is composed of energy, everything is God; and because we are all one, we are, in that sense, all God...

It was then that I experienced *IT*. It was as if God winked at me. It only lasted a millisecond, a fraction of a moment, but the reverberations lasted a lifetime. Eternity springs from a point unseen and so does human experience.

With a shocking realization I remembered what Avi had once spoken to me:

"You've got to be one with the universe, man, because you ARE *one with the universe. Everything else is a game, and games*

separate."

"*IT*'s all part of itself, man!" I cried out in utter fulfillment, "*IT* is one with I, and I am one with *IT*. I am within *IT,* and *IT* is within me. I am *IT,* and *IT* is me!"

I was one with the universe, the true and gameless universe, not only in dimension but in *meaning*. I wasn't anything specific, but everything! I was part of the continuum that stretches infinitely across space and time and pervades everything in the universe so deeply that its very essence cannot be experienced fully except within the passing of a single moment...

I felt as if I was seeing the world for the first time. I *was* seeing the world for the first time. I was seeing things as they truly were, as they were truly meant to be seen, as I'd never seen them before. And this sense of a certain continuity, a certain connectivity, revealed to me that I was inhabiting the Center of the Universe in as much as I *was* the Center of the Universe; we all are. We are all microcosmic universes experiencing the macrocosm of which we are all a part. We are the universe giving birth to itself. And as I bore witness to this, somewhere inside my mind, I could hear Faye whispering *"Ouroboros."*

This was bliss; this was *IT*, finally. I felt like it had taken me lifetimes to discover this, and yet, I had actually known it all along. However, *IT* isn't something that you can just know, *IT* is something that you must experience. And all I'd experienced, really, was the difference between Is-ness and *IT*-ness. Is-ness is the ego, the quality of being defined and of having an identity. *IT*-ness is the quality of being universal. I existed there in that oneness for only a moment, but it's okay because a moment is eternal. Within a moment there is nothing: no sight, no sound, no thought, no sense—but all those moments make up everything. Within nothingness, there is all, and within all there is nothingness.

From that point onward, the trip was like a lucid dream. That moment of revelation had opened me up to a brand new experience of the world. I could see and experience the fusing of opposites, and all the while I had total control. There was complete understanding, cerebral peace—peace of mind and body and soul. I and *IT* were still and calm.

I did not feel as if I was living my life through conscious decision, but rather it was if I was watching it unfold before me. I existed in a state of pure objectivity, but rather than a paralyzing, fearful response to this realization of total separateness, it was an experience of identification with all other things. I was not apart but *of*, I was not alone but *in*.

And for the record, I was not I. Once I let go of that which was I, I could be a part of anything I wanted because *IT* is truly all the same. I could merge with anything that was around me or anything that was inside my own mind. I could leave that setting completely and travel—astral project, as it were—to all other places and all other times and I could see everything—everything in relation to everything else.

And just as time and space are, for all intents and purposes, limitless, so are you. Even as a mere form in an infinite universe, you yourself are just as limitless. From a body to a collection of tissues to a conglomeration of cells and a spattering of atoms, what defines you becomes smaller and smaller yet. Every part of ourselves is at all times divine, infinite, and ubiquitous, and the most fundamental part of us is a force; a force that can be measured by its strength but not quantitatively, a force that exists, yet does not exist—that is *IT*: Energy.

In the midst of all of this spiritual transcendence and revelation, I roared with laughter because, frankly, it was the funniest thing. I'd run into the city, into music, into drugs, and into the desert to find myself, but what I realized now was that the whole time I had really been trying to lose myself. It's true that when you are on the inside, you are too close to see *IT* clearly because *IT* is found inside, and the deeper you get, the more Truth you find.

At some point in the experience—for it was more than just a trip, therefore it cannot be called that—I had another one of those inspired moments. As I was squatting there in the pouring rain with my head between my knees, laughing in the mud, something told me to stand up and turn around. When I did, I saw none other than Al picking his way through the crowd. I ran to catch up with him, and while I was still quite a ways off, I called out his name.

"Hey, Al!"

He turned immediately, and when he saw me, a huge smile spread across his face. "Rhiannon!" he cried and doubled back to meet me.

Even from a distance, he knew that I was really far out there; he could tell from the look on my face, and I could tell from the look on his. I was exploring nirvana, and Al was right there with me.

"Al, what is God to you?" I asked him as soon as he got within earshot.

"What is God to me?" he repeated. "God is perfection. What is God to you?"

383

"God is Truth," I replied, and we began to rap off of this.

"God is positive pursuit."

"God is endless, forever, infinite."

"God is non-personified."

"God is omnipresent."

"God is all energy and all matter."

"We are all God because God is all; God is in all, God is in us," I told him.

"God is *IT*," he told me.

"Amen," I said.

There is but a single Truth so profound yet so self-evident that it evades the minds of most men; however, once it is realized, all come away bearing the same expression. It may be described as a kind of awe, a kind of celestial glow; an air about them that transcends all measures of time and space. Once you've experienced *IT* for yourself, you gain the unique ability to discern between those who have and those who haven't through only a glance; Al had.

As he and I walked together in relative silence, I was so high that I was straight. I was so filled with enlightenment, an experience no drug alone can create. Something bigger than me and bigger than all of us was working. I was still inside my bliss, although the intensity had waned and the visions had returned, appearing slow and silent—an indiscernible synthesis between psychedelic and perception. Faces passed before my eyes along with shapes and substances with no explanation; there were forms and words, things that morphed and things that stayed the same, and vines that grew out from everybody and everything and connected us all to one another.

Late in the afternoon after the rain stopped, choppers flew in and dropped dry clothes and flowers to the couple hundred thousand waterlogged people still stranded in the fields as the announcer shouted over and over, "They're with us, not against us!"

This whole time I had been following Al, for I knew not where we were headed. As we trekked through the mud and the crowd, music began to play again, and by the time I realized where we were, the Trips Mobile was already within view and I could see Mary and Bobby chasing one another around it, laughing and shrieking.

I smiled, "They really love one another, don't they," I asked Al.

"There are some souls that seem to find one another in every lifetime," he replied. "They have been together for several."

As we drew nearer to the van, more and more familiar faces came

384

into view. Billy and Faye were there and—as I noticed with both shock and glee—Space and his sister, whom I later learned was named Laura. Almost everybody was in their underwear, and Space was crouched down behind the van drying out all their clothes with the heat from the muffler, which he'd needed to dig out of the mud to reach.

"Space! You made it!" I cried, running up to him and gathering him in an embrace. "When did you get here?"

"I'm not real sure how long it's been," he replied, "but we heard Joan Baez."

I gaped at him in both admiration and disbelief, "Jesus, that was the first night! How did you do it, man? Every radio station in the state is saying that it's like one big parking lot all the way from here to New York City!"

"They're not wrong; it wasn't easy, that's for sure," he replied. "I had to pull out all the stops." Having finished drying everyone's clothes, he shut off the van, handed them back out, and then sat down to tell his story. The rest of us lit up and settled down to listen.

"You can't imagine what this thing looks like from far away," he spoke with inconcealable wonder in his voice. "Man, this thing is really something, it's something really big!"

He went on to tell us all about the kinds of things they'd seen on their journey, the places they'd gone, and the people they'd met who had helped them along the way, while his sister sat calmly beside him and smiled.

Laura was a sweetheart. She wasn't a hippie or a flower child or a head, but she was a musician—a flutist in her high school band, to be exact—one who knelt down to pray nightly for a scholarship to Julliard. She was a ginger like Space, but her hair was cut neatly just past her shoulders, and despite being somewhat unkempt after an incredible three-day journey on the state highways and back roads of New York, she still managed to appear clean and conventionally pretty. She wore a patterned Twiggy-style dress, mod boots that had mud caked on the toes, and her make-up—despite the rain—was flawless. All in all, she was the perfect straight sister. She was not afraid of or angry with what she saw, and she was certainly not a square. She did not pass judgment on her brother or the Movement, she laughed at the strange people and things that she saw, and she asked clarification of those words and customs she felt she did not understand. She wanted no part of what we were, but she had no qualms about association. She loved her brother, the freak that he was, and therefore, she loved it all. She was the quiet type and let Space go on with his story, as peppered with hip lingo as it was, which she seemed to have a bit of a hard time following and we found endearing.

"You'll never guess what we saw down near the stage," Space spoke excitedly.

"Frank Zappa?" Bobby guessed.

"No."

"Two pigs burning a number?" Billy supposed.

"Close."

"Aw, come on, man, we don't know!" Mary entreated him.

"Nuns!"

"Nuts?" Billy asked.

"No, nuns!" Space repeated. "You know, the ones that wear those long dresses and the habits and hit your knuckles in school."

"Nuns?!" Billy echoed. "What are they doing here?"

"They're here to play in the mud," Bobby suggested.

"I don't have a clue," Space replied, "but they seemed to be having a real groovy time."

"I really like it here a lot," Laura spoke up in a gentle voice, "The people are really very nice, and the music is lovely. Even the mud and the rain aren't that bad."

"Not that bad, eh?" Billy replied. "Space, your sister is our kind of woman. Can you imagine Melinda being out here in this mud?"

Space laughed, "Oh shit! Melinda would freak out, man."

"Ah, it's just dirt! Hell, we're made outta dirt!" Bobby exclaimed.

I do not remember some of the finer points of that conversation because I was still tripping the whole time, fading in and out of that reality. The effects mainly came in waves. When I did see visuals, they were extremely intense and overtook my vision entirely, transporting me into what felt like other dimensions. However, I had complete control over what I was experiencing; the drug itself had no power over me. I could deny myself the experience, but I knew that I was safe and I recognized the profundity inherent in my state of mind; therefore, I allowed it to flow without rebuttal, and it lasted on and on into the night. Some of the places I traveled to during those endless hours were strange, and others were highly enlightening. There were places that were beautiful, and there were places that were tremendous, and on all levels, cosmic thoughts abounded.

One of the many places in which I found myself that night was a city, a strange city, and I remember feeling so short, so insignificant and small against the cruel, lifeless skyscrapers and the twisted metal buildings that lined the streets. My legs felt like little baseball bats, and I was trying to run on these ridiculous little baseball bat legs all around that city as I searched for someone—a specific someone—somewhere in that city.

—And then that was it; the scene changed. Something like a premonition it was and something like a memory. All through the night, several different scenes erupted in my mind, all of them both similar and dissimilar to the one I just described.

However, as night spread out over the land, my restless mind seemed to settle down contentedly into the here and now. The music that final night was just phenomenal, and whether or not it was enhanced by my psychedelic lunch is insignificant. The vibrations out there in Yasgur's fields were even more amazing than they had been earlier in the week and even earlier in the day. We'd made it through the heat and the mud, through the rain and the absence of necessities, through the bad acid and the technical problems, and through all the other minor upsets that had kept this thing from running smoothly and as planned. We were triumphant, and we were triumphant together. As for me, I was living, working, and existing inside of a whole new perception of reality. Not only did I feel like I was connected with all those who were there, I felt like I was connected with everyone in the world. I was full of vigor, refreshed, and revitalized. I felt like I never needed to rest again; like I had enough pent-up energy to last me the rest of my life. I was acutely aware of my own existence, but not self-conscious. I was continually in awe, but not hysterical. I was spaced out, but in no way was I out of it.

At a certain point in the night, a few of The Day Trippers and I took a short trip from the van to the top of the hill so that we could look out over the bowl. In the clear darkness, all the thousands and thousands of people below were illuminated in the light from the waxing moon. All together they glowed as heat and energy left their bodies. From above, it looked like a sea of light, a mirage, but this time it was not; not psychedelic or misperception—it was real. I fell down on my knees and cried. There was no sobbing or convulsing, just rivers of tears that flowed from my wide open eyes. Here I was, in the Garden. I'd made it to the other side of that cosmic doorway and entered into eternity. If I had died at that moment, I would have been glad; in fact, I prayed that God would take me. There was nothing more I wanted out of life except to remember this forever, exactly as I experienced it. I decided right then and there in the middle of my trip that I'd never take psychedelics again to further my enlightenment. I'd hit it, the higher octave. I'd been roused from my waking sleep, I'd been enlightened, and I was aware.

—Oh yeah, and I'd never smoke cigarettes again, either. At some point, Bobby had gone and offered me one, and as I went to take it, a bug crawled out of the pack followed by a second and then a third, and when I dropped it in disgust, it disintegrated into a writhing mass of worms that crawled away on the ground. I would never touch that shit again.

The last thing we heard that night was Crosby, Stills & Nash. Through the binoculars, I could see them playing down there at the bottom of the hill, and as the surreal and evocative sounds of *Wooden Ships* filled the night, I was once more reminded about my chronologically displaced condition. I didn't know whether or not I was actually in some kind of psychedelic coma back in Fresno, but for all those who might doubt me, my soul and my life force were there at Woodstock at that moment. The means will always be a mystery, but the fact of the matter is clear, and because of my experiences therein, I will eternally be indebted to that force—*IT*, by name—that made possible my step into another time and the enlightenment that followed.

A BRIEF AND BEAUTIFUL TRIP BACK

****

I awoke that final morning of the festival to a riff by Jimi Hendrix. I had been sleeping inside the van alongside the other Day Trippers, although I haven't the foggiest recollection of how I'd gotten there. The last memory I had of the night before was of standing at the top of the bowl, and upon merely thinking about it, all those emotions I'd felt came pouring back to me. Despite the intense, somewhat otherworldly joy I was feeling, I was completely sober. The last of the ayahuasca had left my system sometime during the night, and what followed was the most glorious morning of my life. I was experiencing an afterglow like none other. The world had gone from looking flat and granulated to looking like a three-dimensional photograph of heaven, as if I'd been looking out a window with a screen on it for my whole life and now my landlord had finally removed it.

Just like what followed any other psychedelic experience, that morning's afterglow was kind of like a temporary extension of the trip; an altered state of mind without the drug, a constant reminder of the peace and sync and beauty that had existed mere hours ago. However, unlike any other experience I'd had, this afterglow ceased to fade as the world crept back in. The feeling that possessed me was entirely different from any I'd felt before and utterly powerful in how strongly it gripped me. The sheer magnificence and joy to be alive that I felt was so intense that it threatened to be permanent. Having undergone the experience of fleetingly brushing up against *IT*, I held it as my own, and I will possess it for the rest of eternity. All those superficial pretenses former versions of reality had offered me were entirely absent now. I was joyous, happy, and most of all, fulfilled. There'd been a transferal of needs from myself alone to the entire universe of which I was a part, and due to that fact, love proceeded to guide my actions in everything I did because I had a brand new understanding of the universe now, and I could see the importance of love's place in all things. I felt just like a little kid again, with all these childish emotions rolling over me, and I felt this captivating sense of wonder, wonder at the most ordinary things; things we experience every day yet completely take for granted, like waking up, eating, breathing—if everyone understood how important breath was, this would be an entirely different world.

As I spent that morning basking in my afterglow, I came to figure

389

that maybe that was why I was there and experiencing those things—so that I could tell other people about them and impart that wisdom that had been imparted to me. Overall, the most important thing that I've taken away from the experience is that the Truth in its essence is to know that you will never really know and to just be in complete wonder at existence at all times. *IT* isn't about knowing everything, it's about doing the best you can with what you do and finding comfort in uncertainty and in those enlightened principles that substantiate existence.

Enlightenment is a strange subject; it is so simple that it cannot help but become paradoxical. For although I'd undergone an experience of enlightenment, by no means would I ever dare deem myself 'enlightened,' because I knew that there were men and women who had experienced the same thing as me through entire lives dedicated to meditation, reflection, yoga, and service. However, there was no mistaking *IT* when I experienced it, even though what I'd done to get into *IT*'s realm was something to the effect of a shortcut.

I spent a good deal of time reflecting upon these things, although the duration is something of a mystery, for time still did not have and would never again regain its meaning. However, there was a certain point when the wailing electric crescendo that was Jimi Hendrix mesmerized me completely and drew me out into the light of day. The midmorning sunlight was blinding in its brightness, but once my eyes adjusted, I could see that there were far fewer people around. Many had started clearing out of the fields during the rain and throughout the night. The bowl was half-empty now, and I could finally see the ground where everyone had been standing for the last three days. Down there on the stage, Jimi's drummer, Mitch Mitchell, just laid into that cymbal, and Jimi stood up there with his band of gypsies waving to the crowd like a prophet in burning incandescent light.

It wasn't long before the wall of sound pouring out from the speakers enticed all the others to emerge from the depths of sleep into the joy of wakefulness. Some of my friends were already awake: Space of course and Faye and Billy who were up on the roof of the van smoking a joint. When Bobby woke up, he crawled out of the Trips Mobile and came to sit down next to me. He shot up first thing, then kissed me good morning and began snacking on Chips Ahoy. Mary, Laura, and Al followed in the last wave, and together we all bore witness to the incredible events of that last hour of music and the iconic, legendary performance that is today known all around the world.

It was right about then that Jimi came to the mic and said, *"Before we go any further, I just wanna say that you've all had a lot of patience—three days' worth. You proved to the world what can happen with a little love and understanding and sounddddd..."* and with that, he broke right into *Voodoo Child,* rapping on the words, *"Peace and happiness! Yes, happiness!"*

It was truly unbelievable. Jimi was yet another musician I'd previously said I'd never be able to see live, and yet, here I was—despite all odds—at the concert of a lifetime, watching the performance that would define the whole festival.

The last tune he played, an improvisation of the *Star Spangled Banner*, was so great it was purely maddening. You didn't even have to hear it to know; you could tell plainly from the faces of any one of the onlookers that something brand new and monumental was being created and witnessed at that very moment. Bobby, in particular, was having one hell of an experience; the pleasure he was feeling from his high in conjunction with the music must have been insane. He was listening so intently that he looked almost as if he was in pain, and as the electric screams and whistles from Jimi's guitar climaxed, Bobby's eyes rolled back in his head as if he had fainted, as if his ears were being electrocuted. And he was not the only one; as Jimi struck the final chord, an unrestrained cheer rose up. All the people around us and all those down there in the fields held up their hands formed in peace signs as every guitarist in the audience bowed their heads to their god as he alighted the stage.

And then it was quiet. When the music stopped, everybody left. We were ready to pack up and leave after the encores—by that time it was an old scene. The only problem was that the Trips Mobile was sunk up to the bumper in mud on both ends, and there was no hope of getting out without a tow. As the crowd dispersed, I could see that the fields were a mess. All the crops in the area had been completely destroyed, and where there had been lush green grass at the beginning of the festival, mud and garbage were all that remained. People with trash bags and pokers had already begun the mother clean up, and being stuck there like we were, we grabbed trash bags ourselves and helped out.

We passed the next couple of days that way, cleaning while the sun was up and rapping with the Hog Farmers and our fellow stranded festival-goers at night. A common thread of conversation for just about everyone I talked to seemed to be the mention of how they had been changed somehow and the ways in which they were now altering how they went about their daily lives. There were those who said they were never going back home, never going back to work, never drinking again, never tripping again, leaving the army, leaving the country, becoming musicians, becoming roadies, becoming spiritual, or becoming better people by nurturing their souls. There were even those who said they never wanted to leave that place and planned on settling down there permanently. No matter what path they had personally chosen, the gist remained constant throughout; Woodstock had been a transforming experience and no one who was there would ever be the same again.

The change was even reflected in the landscape. As the mud dried in the hot sun after a few days, it began to claim evidence of the festival that we then needed to dig out in order to throw away. There were thousands upon thousands of soda cans, beer bottles, chip bags, paper plates and blankets mired in the mud. Occasionally, we'd find real gems amid the debris: beads, rings, necklaces—even clothes that had been left behind; however, a great deal of those things had been lost to the mud. You wouldn't believe how much mud there was if I told you; even I had no idea myself until I made my way down to the stage. There, the streams of mud from the storms had been stopped up against the twelve foot planks and was now packed up against them in such vast quantities that when I stood atop the bulge, the tops of the planks only came up to my chin, and I could peer right over the top at the empty stage. I remember Bobby standing back behind me as I did, his eyes wide, "There's got to be bodies in there," he murmured.

However, his morbid assertion was wrong, thankfully. For as far as anyone knew, only two people had died; one as a result of a heroin overdose and one when he was run over by a tractor in his sleep. And while any death is sad, the universe seemed to be working at its full capacity because we also received word that two babies had been born; one on-premise and one in a car en-route. Frankly, with the conditions the way they were and the sheer volume of people, it is a complete and utter miracle that no more deaths occurred from any variety of factors—in fact, it was a statistical anomaly. Additionally, over that week—and it was a week, really, that such a mass of people had gathered in Bethel—there was no violence. Everybody had stayed true to their promise of peace and love, all set against a backdrop of the best music ever to be performed in the same place at the same time.

On the third day after the concert ended, we were finally getting dredged out of the mud. The guy who pulled us out was a local, about fifty-something, and dressed in proper farm attire: plaid shirt, suspenders, and work boots. We were one of the last vehicles he had to tow, since we were at the top of the hill and all, and although he'd been working like this for three days, it had still taken him this long to get to us. Once he'd freed the Trips Mobile, the man got down off his tractor and stood back between the trees with his hand across his brow to block the sun so that he could see the stage down at the bottom of the hill.

"Something really incredible happened here this last week," he spoke, "the likes of which have never before been known. Really, I shouldn't be surprised."

"Why's that?" Billy asked.

"This is the town of Bethel, after all," he answered.

"So?"

"In Hebrew, Bethel means '*House of God.*'"

Chills ran up and down my spine, and all the hair on my arms stood on end.

"I think all of us felt Him walking around down there at some point, I know I did," he said. "This thing was really something else; I never thought I'd live to see it. I'd like to think that it's going to be a different world from now on…"

He stood perfectly still for a moment as he admired the site, and then he bid us goodbye, climbed back on his tractor, and continued up the hill to the aid of the next marooned vehicle.

As we left the site and drove out through the town, it felt completely and utterly surreal. There were still a whole bunch of heads hanging around, and a large group of them lined the shoulder of route 17B headed east, all of them holding out their thumbs with their left hand and flashing us the peace sign with their right. That's all we saw for about half a mile, the peace sign; that iconic V for Victory—but victory over what? The Establishment? War? Inequality? Hatred? Ignorance? It symbolized the banishment of evil and the triumph of love, and in that place, it was near enough to taste.

Once we'd gathered up a hitchhiker out of the throng, the van was full to bursting. Now we were really like a can of sardines; however, close proximity was nothing new to us, and after that last week, none of us could have minded. A kind of melancholy was spread throughout the whole Trips Mobile; we were all coming down. It was like a massive hangover, and we were all painfully sunburned. For the most part, we were all quiet and kept inside our own minds where we sorted out our own thoughts. We were headed back to the real world again, back to responsibility and picking up our lives where they'd left off when we'd headed out to Woodstock, and it was plain to see that none of us were very excited about it.

From my pocket, I pulled the Polaroid photo that journalist had taken of us playing at Hector's Inn, and immediately, I was back there again. As soon as I looked at it, the good vibes and euphoric energy of that night coursed through me once more. This was a feeling that would never leave me, and that picture was a beautiful, heart-warming tribute to the best week of my life. It was a fantastic photograph, one that completely captured the essence of The Day Trippers.

I was in the center of the picture, off toward the back behind my drums, seated on a little wooden stool with my sticks crossed in front of me. Off to the far left, Al stood behind *Connie* with his head bowed and his fingers spread across the keys, an eccentric, contemplative smile on his face; his thousand-year-old eyes shone. Space was off to the far right, his eyes and hair huge. His guitar was slung across his chest, he had both arms outstretched, and his hands were formed into peace signs. He had a funny look on his face as if he had been in the midst of talking or laughing when the picture was taken.

In the foreground, directly in front of me, Mary Jane stood holding the mic and posing cheekily. Her smile was bright, and her eyes were full of love. Beside her, Billy stood with his bass, his fingers at the ready. His cheeks were raised in a smile that was concealed almost entirely by his beard, and his eyes were averted slightly from the camera, directed instead toward his muse and the object of his affection, Faye, whose chin rested upon his shoulder. Her short, light hair bunched up around her shoulders, and her eyes stared off into the distance past the cameraman, past the bar, through the wall, out to the fields and into the future.

Last but not least, Bobby stood on the other side of Mary, his head dipped down slightly—he may have even been playing at the time. A couple pieces of hair fell into his face, and through narrowed eyes, he looked into the camera, as if he was daring any viewer to examine him closer. His charismatic allure was exuded even through the photograph; his chiseled features and mysterious little half-smile serving to capture the attention of anyone who was to glance at it.

After I'd examined it thoroughly and took careful note of every little detail, I held that photograph tight to my chest as I remembered

394

that night and the days that followed it with an exuberance and fondness unlike any other. This was my most prized possession. It was a testament to my presence; I'd been there.

As we headed toward the Thruway and left Woodstock behind, a kind of panic coursed through me. How could we go back to the City after experiencing this? It was like that part in *The Dharma Bums* when Ray had to climb down the mountain and go back to his previous life after living alone atop Desolation Peak all summer where he'd witnessed the miracle of existence—complete solidarity—and upon his return, realized that most of everybody else was unaware of those things that he had learned. Here we were in the most contrary of situations and experiencing the same thing. It was that same inexplicable essence, that feeling of being let back into the world with the knowledge that what I was leaving behind wouldn't be there to greet me when I got home. In fact, I felt like I was leaving my home. I never wanted to return to the world that I had known before, a world with war and hatred and ugliness. I wanted to stay right there and settle down, start a commune and live in peace for the rest of forever—but that reality was unfortunately too good to be true.

As we embarked upon our trip back across America, I went through a thorough evaluation of what had just occurred in my life. There was one thing I knew for sure: Woodstock was Eden—or the closest that human beings of this age could come to it. For a very brief space in time, a couple hundred thousand of us had gotten back to the Garden— a place of peace and simplicity, nature and love—and it would never happen again.

As we began seeing signs for New York City, for the first time in a long time, I remembered the future, and I was left with a gripping feeling of hollow sadness. It was then that everyone began slowly drifting apart. Everyone was off to their own respective corners of America. Everyone was off to the next thing already. The sea of humanity had dried to a riverbed. Woodstock was dead and gone.

And the thing was, everybody who left there, left wanting to change the world—but we already had. In and of itself, Woodstock was eschatological—there was an end in there somewhere, an end of something bigger than itself; a fin de siècle. And we all knew it, we all felt it, but none of us knew exactly what it was.

PART III

The trip back to San Francisco was swift. This time we made far fewer stops, and if I remember correctly, we made it back to the City by the first week of September. After we dropped off Laura and our hitchhiker from Woodstock in New York City, we lit out across the country, this time through all of the northern states on Route 80—which is literally a straight line from New York to downtown San Francisco. We drove through Pennsylvania, Ohio, Indiana, Illinois, Iowa, Nebraska, Wyoming, Nevada, and eastern California all within a few days. Our journey was expedited by the fact that we made no stops to play and only a few to eat or sleep. For the most part, there were only piss-stops the whole journey back, and due to this, our return trip was far less eventful.

This directness was mainly due to a sense of urgency to get back to San Francisco imparted mostly by Bobby and later taken up more or less as a cause by Mary Jane and Space. They were convinced that our band would have far more popularity and notice in the days directly following the release of that month's *Rolling Stone Magazine* with the Woodstock article in it. They figured that while the news and success of Woodstock was still fresh in everybody's minds and The Day Trippers' name was in print all across America, we would have a breeze of a time getting gigs, and maybe even something more, like a contract. Bobby had even shown the foresight to make a long-distance call to San Francisco in order to assure that everybody at the Trips Center knew that when the mail came, anything addressed to him should be set aside in a safe place until he got back.

A BRIEF AND BEAUTIFUL TRIP BACK

Since we weren't stopping to play, most of our equipment was packed up on the roof, and since there was more room in the Trips Mobile, we picked up far more hitchhikers. For Al, it was a blast, a perfectly-timed opportunity to conclude his book. For me, hailing from a time when hitching a ride was widely frowned upon, the variety of faces and stories to be found in contemporary thumb-travelers was both amusing and intriguing. All sorts of people could be found on the roads of America, not just heads.

One of these such nomads appeared on our radar just outside of a filling station someplace in the Midwest, in the area of Nebraska or Iowa or one of those other states therein. We were pulling away from the pump, just about to hit the pavement and get rolling again, when this funny-looking little bum materialized on the side of the road where clouds of dust were just beginning to settle after being roused by a passing semi. He had his thumb out toward the highway and a bulging rucksack at his feet; he and all his belongings frying in the noonday sun. We couldn't pass up a traveler in need, not when we had the room, so Billy swung over to the shoulder, and we picked him up. Once he climbed into the back with us, we noticed something that hadn't been so startlingly apparent from a distance; this was an old man. He was short and skinny, no more than 5'5" and maybe 130 pounds. His muscles were taut and sinewy, his body sunbaked and tan. The skin of his face was creased and leathery; around his eyes, crow's feet were prominent, and around his mouth, laugh lines abounded. His hair was pure white, and what was left of it was pulled back into a short ponytail. A long, white goatee grew from his chin and caught droplets of water as he drank from the canteen we handed him. He was most assuredly one of those types that Al called Chronic Drifters. He looked to be about sixty years old, and he'd been out on the road a long time.

"Where are you headed?" Billy called back to him above the roar of the wind that rushed through the open windows as we accelerated down the highway.

"West," the Old Man called back in a cracked, dry, unused voice.

"Anywhere in particular?" Billy asked.

"No," he answered.

"Do you know if there's a truck stop or a diner around here where we can score some decent chow?" Bobby asked him.

"I suppose so. About 20 miles up the road there's a malt shop and a Motel 6."

"Are you from around here?" Mary asked.

397

"I'm from everywhere," he replied.

Al lifted his head out of his notebook and for once, put down his pen, "How long have you been out on the road for?" he asked the man, sizing up his rucksack.

The Old Man just chuckled. He had a very plain, very deliberate manner of speaking, and he answered something like this, "I hit the road in 1920 when I was fifteen years old. I grew up in Colorado on the family homestead just outside of Five Points—that's the Negro district in Denver. My Pa was a logger and a moonshiner, and my Ma was the kindest woman I've ever met. I'm the youngest of eight boys; four of 'em went off to war, and the other three, well, they just went off. I've never been one for working much, ain't never been one for standing still, neither, so when my Ma died and my Pa went back to the mountains, I left home in a boxcar. I've been travelin' ever since."

His story had captured our attention; even Bobby was rapt in his tale.

"That's close to fifty years, man, what are you still doing out on the road?" Space spoke, bewildered.

"I could give you a whole crock of shit about how livin' this way is cheaper—that I've spent my whole life travelin' cause I ain't gotta pay taxes, that the jobs were plentiful and the money was good—but the long and short of it is simply that I enjoy it. I've got no demands on me. I've got no wife, no kids, no house, no land, no car. I don't got to live in fear of the weather, of disease, of the tax collector. I'm not tied down to a job that I hate, I'm not a slave to routine. I roll into a town and stay a few weeks—drink a little, gamble some, maybe do an odd job or two—and then I move on. Right now I'm headed for Bailey Yard to work on train cars. If I make it, I'm guaranteed a job. If I don't, I'll just find something else. This way I'm free."

I looked over at Al, for this was a man after his own heart, but his eyes were averted, buried deep in his notebook once more.

"How come you never settled down?" Bobby asked. "You never had a woman?"

The Old Man chuckled again, "Oh, sure, I've loved many a woman, but never enough to convince me to stay put. Love and commitment are two entirely different things."

"Right on," Bobby replied with a laugh.

For miles, the land was flat and featureless, and at twilight, the sun spread out over the horizon. We drove west in near darkness as we watched the road rush by and the low hills roll back behind us. With intent to salvage the last of the daylight, we pulled off to the side of the road near a cluster of small trees and bedded down for the night. Al and the Old Man chatted as they built us a fire, conversing as only two wanderers can, and the rest of us lit up a few joints and sat around to listen. They recalled days of counting mile markers, months spent winding along rivers of concrete and asphalt with no destination in mind, winters walking the tracks down around El Paso, and summers schlepping through the mountains of Oregon and Nevada. The Old Man had fifty years' worth of stories to tell, and Al's respectful deference made it obvious to the rest of us that meeting him was quite the humbling experience indeed.

He was an extraordinary character, a man who had survived many unfortunate circumstances. He was a weathered, seasoned traveler with an antidote for everything and an anecdote to match. He was a soft-spoken bachelor, none too philosophic. He was a simple, uneducated handyman, a rough-and-tumble itinerant whose whole world was the road. His mind and body were products of the road, his every memory handcrafted by highways and automobiles. His life was an odometer, his eyes the steel gray of worn pavement, and his hair the same color as marking paint. Each word he uttered was unmistakably real and with a flash, illuminated the night like those eastbound headlights.

"Do you think you'll ever give up traveling?" Mary asked him during a lull between stories.

"Never," he answered with finality.

"But you're an old man," Bobby interjected with his usual tactlessness. "What about when you can't anymore?"

The Old Man laughed, "I'll tell you what, Youngin', when these ol' legs don't go no more and these ol' hands can't work, then I guess it's time for me to up and die, right?" He laughed again, "And that's exactly what I'll do. There ain't nothin' holding me back. On to the next thing, right?"

"You're not afraid to die?" Mary asked.

"No. Should I be?"

"Well, it's just that it's impossible to know what's after this…"

The Old Man just shook his head and chuckled, "Oh you young kids with your speculation and searchin' and all that nonsense. Don't bother your head. I ain't looking for nothin' in this life. Never have. Don't believe in anythin' either. Simpler that way. And I'm happy. Nothin' I do in this life means anything at all. I ain't makin' this world no better, but I ain't makin' it no worse, neither. I'm just passin' through, so I do what makes me happy. Travelin' makes me happy, so

I travel. Sunsets make me happy, so I watch the sunsets. Soda pop makes me happy, so I drink soda pop. Anythin' more makes you worry, and why worry?"

I caught a glimpse of Al's face while the Old Man was saying this, and he looked more conflicted than I'd ever seen him before. Al, the super seeker and Dharma bum extraordinaire who strove to unlock the secrets of *IT* and enlighten all others along the way was having his every philosophy negated by a man he may very well have respected more than any other sentient being. The Old Man was an utter nihilist and yet a hedonist at the same time, one who derived the most luxurious pleasures of life out of the simplest of things—sunsets, soda pop, and the road. I thought back to my experience of *IT*—of *IT*'s simplicity, of *IT*'s cohesion, of *IT*'s universality—and saw that this here old man was just another example of *IT* in *IT*'s purest form.

"So you aren't afraid of what might happen to you after you die?" Billy asked him. "Of possible judgment? Of heaven and hell? Of ceasing to exist?"

The Old Man shook his head, "To be perfectly honest, I haven't thought much on the subject. Don't intend to, neither. If there ain't nothin' more after this life, then that's perfectly OK by me, I've suffered enough, and if there is an afterlife, well, I hope that there's a road to travel there."

We were all bowled over by his answers, and I wondered how many other men there were like him. Was this what fifty years out on the road does to a man? Or had his listless existence only strengthened his preexisting philosophy? We'd never know.

Al was flustered, and I could see his mind frantically turning as he attempted to stay cool, "I believe that when we die, our souls leave what we perceive as a material world and, if enlightened, eventually reach the zenith, nirvana, an inconceivable station of absolute peace which there is nothing beyond," he blurted out.

The Old Man smiled gently at him and patted him on the back like a protégé, "Just so long as it makes you happy."

A contemplative silence ensued until Faye reached out and swatted a moth away from the fire, crushing it between her hands, *"Gott ist tot,"* she declared.

The next day after the sun had risen over the plains and we'd cooked up breakfast over the fire, we set out on the road again. We left the Old Man near North Platte, out on the shoulder of Route 80 as he had been 200 miles back. We were still several miles from the rail yard, but inexplicably, he'd told us to pull over and let him off there. He thanked us for the lift, as he must've done thousands of times before, eased on his rucksack, and stepped out into the dust. He started walking before we pulled away, his steps slow and unhurried. He was completely comfortable and totally content, happy just to be, or not to be—to him it made no difference.

"Hey Al, I think we just met your future self," Bobby called to his brother from up front.

I turned around and looked at Al to see his response, but he hadn't heard him. For the first time in weeks, his notebook was closed and his pen was capped—which could only mean one thing, that he had finished, finally—and he stared out the rearview mirror at the Old Man as he journeyed away.

I spent a good deal of time thinking about the Old Man as we drove that day, and as I did, I realized that being a hobo in thirty years wouldn't be such a glorious existence; that it might even be quite terrible, actually, with all the laws, restrictions, and the cost of living. His reality was whole realms away from mine, and I still can't wrap my head around how the world could've changed so much, so fast. As a society, we've become so phenomenally detached, so out of sync with the basic principles of life. And the most depressing part of it is the assurance that as we continue to make strides in material advancement, we will just continue on along that same path of self-destruction and keep on spinning further and faster out of the way. There might even come a day when there are no more travelers, no more wandering folk who call the open road their home—and what a sad day that will be.

Between Nebraska and San Francisco, we picked up two more hitchhikers. They were a pair of Mexican farm workers traveling to find jobs in California and brothers, as far as we could tell. We crossed paths with them along a stretch of Route 80 in Wyoming—a beautiful yet barren wilderness. For Mexicans in America, they spoke English quite well, but even so, they were far more reserved than the Old Man from before. They talked to one another sparingly in Spanish, and Al asked them a bit about their travels, but other than that, they kept to themselves. When Al asked them what they missed most about their homeland, Oaxaca, they both replied, "The food."

"Really?" Space asked.

"Yes," one of them answered, "tamales, empanadas and Mamacita's cooking. There are no Mamacitas in America—no siestas either."

When they spoke, they were friendly and jovial, and the little bit that they told us about Mexico made it seem like the golden destination. It was a place where everything was affordable, even if you didn't make more than a couple dollars a day. It was a place where the food in the marketplace was fresh from the fields, where the drugs were clean, and the mezcal, pure. Luxury in Mexico, they said, cost very little, and there were American expatriates in every major city exploiting that. The expats were relatively few and isolated, and these two, in particular, did not resent their presence; in fact, they seemed to boost the local economy.

To me, Mexico sounded pretty rad. Music and good food were the cornerstones of a deep and ancient culture. Volatile societal turmoil—at least at that time—was largely far off, and the tight fist of the law closed somewhat looser around those who habitually sampled the local vegetation. It was easy living; the fiestas there lasted eight days, and there were siestas every afternoon—even Bobby could get behind that.

After we let them off in Sacramento, there was talk circulating around the Trips Mobile that we might abandon our route to San Francisco all together and rather head due south to Oaxaca and Acapulco and Mazatlán on the coast in search of Jules and the circles of American expats who'd boasted the likes of Bill Burroughs and Malcolm Lowry. However, Bobby was adamant in his staunch opposition to such a suggestion, and our dreams of foreign stardom faded as quickly as they'd arisen as we continued on our overnight express to San Francisco.

To me, the majority of our trip back to the Haight was an absolute blur. Between the monotony of the road, the absence of stops, and the last of that good Woodstock weed, I'm lucky that I can remember anything at all. However, there is one episode that is quite unforgettable, even to this day.

Home must have been close at hand because there was this edgy feeling of anticipation that permeated the van that I just couldn't shake. At least one of us felt it; therefore, we all felt it. And between that and all the bouncing around for four or five straight days on the road, I was a bit unsettled, physically and mentally. Because of the rush to get back, there hadn't been time in the mornings for me to meditate and do my yoga exercises. I didn't complain—it was only a few days after all—and I knew that before long we'd be back home again, but I couldn't deny feeling a remarkable difference within myself after failing to return to my practice. All The Day Trippers were laughing and joking and carrying on, and I was too, in part, but what I really wanted was to get back to my center and clear my mind for a bit to prepare myself for our return home. I remember turning away from the jocularity and focusing my attention on Al instead. He was seated with his back against the rear hatch, and his eyes were closed. He wasn't asleep, but he was unaware of his surroundings, his body moving with the bumping and rocking of the Trips Mobile, his mind and focus turned inward. I wondered at his ability to shut out all the noise and stimulation and find that kind of peace in this hectic setting. For a man capable of so much motion, he possessed an unparalleled stillness, and I wanted to be where he was at.

This attempt of mine to meditate on the move began with something quite the contrary—complex thought. My meditation began as a reflection, a reflection of all those things I'd learned since I'd arrived in the past. I thought about how vastly different the Rhiannon of now was in comparison to the Rhiannon of then; in and of itself, my current endeavor was a true testament to my growth. All of my worries, spite, hatred, anxiety, and despair had been lost in time. I was at peace with myself, in love with my life, and living in harmony with the rest of existence in the very place I'd always wanted to be. I thought about Woodstock, once a distant affair, unreachable in the past, and now, while my perceptions were changed forever, the experience had come and gone and it was just a memory; a part of the past yet again, more and more distant with every passing minute.

I thought about how I'd felt there: the connectedness, the fluidity, the revelation, the indescribable experience of *IT*. I thought about how momentous *IT* was, how supersensory, how *IT*'s experience had redefined my reality; how *IT* had entirely dwarfed the importance of the mundane world and heightened immeasurably that of the here and now. And I thought about how even so, there would always be more to learn. After all, all language, all supernatural theories and speculation, all myth, and all religion have come into existence as an attempt to explain what *IT* is. They are all intellectual products of those people who've experienced *IT*, as well as those who have merely basked in conjecture. Until you've actually experienced *IT* yourself and caught a fleeting glimpse of the infinite up close and personally, these things serve only to communicate a partial message—somebody else's vain attempt to convey what *IT* might be.

In fact, *IT* is something that is purely extrasensory; it simply cannot be perceived. This is because there are flaws in perception; from within the vessel, nothing about the perfect and infinite universe can be understood in its full capacity. You see, we *are* the universe, and in order for the universe to become aware of itself, sensation must become the middleman. In theory, if you did not have your senses, it would be impossible to become aware of anything outside of yourself. However, there are faculties that evade the senses, telepathy, for one, and intuition—that sixth sense—that *inner knowing* that we all possess. In most places in today's world, our extrasensory perceptions are silenced in preference to our physical ones, and over time they lose their acuity as *IT* fades slowly away.

However, when those senseless perceptions are embraced and exercised, the deceits of the flesh become more and more apparent, with time as the most heinous offender. In fact, the passing of time is nothing but a charming illusion to us Earthlings. The prevailing concept of time is that it is relative, measured, predictable, and passing—or so we make it. The true definition of time is that it is elusive, irrational, inexplicable, unending, and merciless. Time is an invention that cloaks the incomprehensible. The concept of time is that of eternal progression locked in an eternal stalemate in the unending quest for NOW. Believe it or not, the feat of escaping time is possible for anybody at any moment. For, in essence, each moment is inherently the same; therefore, it is possible to be anywhere, anytime you want simply by being in the moment. While the form may change, the essence remains the same. Today's paradox is that eternity is contained within an instant. In the ultimate reality, every moment is NOW. At every moment we exist, and at every moment we are eternally present. NOW can be found in the absence of both reflection and speculation and in the presence of observation. NOW escapes all of our various senses, but can be found and experienced in its purest form through silence.

At the heart of every moment is total and abiding silence. And that silence—that eternal stillness—is inherent within all manifestation and always the same. Silence is when life is the most real—and as for all the noise and distraction, there isn't as much merit in tuning it out as there is in accepting it and finding the silence hidden deep within it. Silence is a virtue long forgotten and in some ways, still yet to be learned. In a world filled with so much sense and sensation, silence is hard to find, and inner silence—cerebral stillness, a state beyond all thoughts and all words—is nearly impossible to approach. We overcompensate for our fear of silence by making more noise; useless noise, depthless noise. There is profundity and sanctity in silence that is absent in sound. There is something old and something primitive, something intrinsic and something elusive contained within an instant—the pause between heartbeats, the hush of bated breath. We avoid seeking silence in today's world because in the silent world there is no reassurance that we do indeed exist. Within silence there is nothing, and a certain degree of enlightenment and trust must first be present before venturing into the silent world. There must first be a loss of ego, fulfillment within oneself, and a resolute search for absolute stillness—the very essence of peace. In the van that afternoon, my search for stillness commenced. The acute distaste I'd felt for silence had left me. It cannot be seen, heard, smelled, tasted, or felt, but within silence there is awareness, and within awareness I sought to be.

In and of itself, commencement is a very paradoxical word. It is a word that, as defined, means beginning; however, within every new beginning there is something ending, and within every ending there is, subsequently, something beginning. This is the essence of the ouroboros, something that all of us seem to have forgotten on the day of our return to the Haight.

✳✳✳✳

We arrived back in San Francisco on a gloomy, thunderstorm-pending afternoon. It had recently rained, and the entire city was cold and damp with a chill that penetrated your clothes and pierced you to the bone. Thick fog and dark clouds ensconced the city, and thunder rumbled high in the atmosphere; it would soon be raining again. Those that dared to brave the cold, brisk streets did so wrapped in winter coats with their heads bowed against the wind and fog that buffeted their faces. These were conditions I was surprised by and ill-prepared for. Even with the windows closed, it was chilly in the van, and whoever was driving had kicked on the heat. As far as I was aware, it was only the first week of September, and the first week of September in Fresno usually arrived along with steady temperatures of ninety plus and clear, sunny skies. This was not the case in the City. In fact, according to Mary, this sort of weather was more or less here to stay.

As I peered out the window at the sluggish city streets and the dreary sidewalks, there was something about the scene that struck me as changed; there was something different and something unsettling about it. Everything looked the same, rather it was a familiar feeling that was somehow absent, a kind of carefree joy that had left with the warmth and the sunshine. There was something of a rosy hue to the place that had been displaced by gray. In a way, the rain made everything seem more real.

Surely, it was a product of the weather, that all these people who'd taken to the streets looked so dismal. In their faces, they all bore a hint of a pained expression. The panhandlers were frowning, and the squatters were soaked. There were a lot of different people that I hadn't seen around before that I began noticing—bums camped in the mouths of alleyways, junkies huddled together in phone booths, burnouts wandering aimlessly, confused and astray. They must've always been there—after all, we'd only been gone a month—but somehow I'd never noticed them, they'd managed to evade my view. Or maybe, I hadn't really been looking.

I think we were all relieved when we pulled into the driveway of the Trips Center; however, what we got when we finally arrived wasn't at all what we'd been expecting. I remember Mary tumbling out of the van the moment after we stopped moving and kissing the ground where she landed. Billy was equally excited and swore up and down that the previous night was the last time he'd sleep crammed in a van with six other people and within any sort of proximity to another man's rear end. Faye was babbling earnestly about something, but none of us could understand her. Al was the last one out and the only one of us who exited the Trips Mobile with any sort of poise or dignity. After all, he was content no matter where he was, just as long as he didn't stay there for very long.

With the threat of rain looming, we didn't attempt to empty the van right then and there, but most of us took an armful of blankets or clothes or instruments or anything else we could carry and lugged it up the steps to the front door. Bobby was the first one inside. He hadn't brought anything along with him, and rather than help us organize, he made a beeline straight to the study to check for any mail that had been set aside for him. However, he had left the door wide open for the rest of us, and bearing our burdens, we followed him in.

Once we'd emptied our arms, Billy called out in a booming voice: "Honey, I'm home!" But much to our surprise, nobody came to greet us. A couple of extremely stoned heads who were sprawled out on the couch smoking a hookah turned their heads and waved, but Melinda and all of our friends were nowhere to be seen. In fact, most of the people occupying the Trips Center were strangers. As we all stood there looking around, Bobby returned from the study holding a stack of mail and noticed this for the first time.

"Hey," he called to the heads on the couch, "is Melinda here?"

"Who?" one of them answered.

"You know, Melinda," Billy replied, holding his hand to the height of his shoulder. "Short, dark, Indian chick. She's always here."

The head shrugged, "Don't know 'er."

In fact, the only person there who *did* know Melinda was a tall, blonde, mod-looking girl named Delilah who shed some light on her unexplained absence. "After you guys split for Woodstock, a whole bunch of new cats moved in—friends of friends, you know how it is. Anyway, some new guy got all handsy with her every chance he got, and after a while, she just got fed up with it and told me she was going to buy a bus ticket and go back home to her folks up in Oregon. She didn't say when she'd be back. The guy left too, a few days after she did. He was a bit of a creep, I'm glad he's gone."

We all looked around at one another and frowned. It was a bummer to come home and find that discordant vibrations had been alive and well at the Trips Center during our absence. And that wasn't the only thing that was disheartening; Melinda was long gone, and all those familiar faces that usually hung around the Trips Center were nowhere to be found—even God had split the scene. Some of the people there we vaguely knew from around the Haight, but others were just freeloaders. Worst of all, the Trips Center was a complete disaster. When Melinda had been there, it was what she called an organized mess. Now it was just a mess. Whatever had happened there in the time that we'd been gone must've been one hell of a party. All the cabinets in the kitchen had been left open, and all of them were empty. The sink was filled with dirty dishes, and flies buzzed around the overflowing trash can. Empty beer bottles and clogged ashtrays were strewn everywhere around the house, and in the living room, dirty clothes and empty takeout containers littered the floor and the coffee tables. Somebody had spilled something sticky on the carpet, and the china cabinet in the corner had been knocked over and its contents smashed. No candles or incense burned, and the wall speakers had been blown out. The bowl of bread beside the front door had been emptied, and in the corner, a stain on the rug smelled suspiciously of urine.

—And that's not to mention my car. It was such a shame— somebody had been living in it during our absence, or so it seemed. There was what looked like a nest of blankets in the back, and the upholstery had been ripped. There were soft drink stains on the red leather interior and on the carpet, empty packs of cigarettes and cans shoved under the seats, and the cup holders were crammed full of old candy wrappers and stale granola. It took me the rest of the day to clean it, and as if that wasn't bad enough, I discovered that the mechanism that rolled the top up and down had been busted and that the canvas cover only came up halfway. Until I scraped together enough bread to get it fixed, I'd have to leave it parked inside, which meant that our usual practice spot would be temporarily out of service.

As I was grumbling to myself about these things, Bobby appeared in the doorway, elated.

"Rhiannon, Rhiannon, look, look! He came through! That little beatnik bastard actually came through, damn it! Look!"

He was frantically waving a copy of this month's *Rolling Stone* in front of my face, more excited than I'd ever seen him before. I tried to steady his oscillating hand in order to read it, but he pulled it away and read it to me himself.

"It's right here on page sixteen, an article all about The Day Trippers! You gotta hear what he said about you! Listen!"

He opened the magazine to the page containing our article and began to read:

"*Day Trip: Woodstock; Peace, Love, and the Music Before the Music*

"*I was there, and so were they. There is a group currently drifting along the roads of this great nation, temporarily surfacing in dives and truck stop bars, then disappearing back out into the indeterminable mass of towns and highways in-between the coasts. They call themselves The Day Trippers, and in my opinion, they have the potential to change the face of today's music scene.*

"*While exploring the convention-shattering peaceful demonstration and cultural exposition that will be known forever to posterity as the Woodstock Music and Art Festival, I found myself in the audience of a shining achievement, three days before the music onstage began. Crammed into the back corner of a little Upstate New York dive called Hector's Inn—the only bar for miles—this curious ensemble put on a show that got all the beautiful people on their feet, both inside the building and out.*

"*They are an unusual and uncompromising band, a six-piece in all with an accompanying dancer/tambourine player. Their sound is an interesting fusion of traditional rock n' roll and bluesy psychedelia paired with a spattering of jazz-inspired improvisation and topped off with original folk lyrics. The luscious and lovely Mary Jane Greene— homegrown vocalist and band front—is both seductive and contagiously bubbly. The lyrics she sings—penned with help from keyboardist Al Black—are full of beautiful imagery, both real and fantastical. Like most fledgling bands, their material is a blend of popular favorites and ingenious originals. Lines like 'You can find me at the bottom of a teacup or floating on the edge of a breeze, but wherever it is you may find me, don't look down, if you please,' are sung in an alluring contralto robust enough to endure the test of a strong bassline and two dynamic guitarists. Backing such a powerful and illustrious force is a striking group of musicians.*

"*The first one to catch my attention is a heavy, blues-infused lead who later introduces himself to me as Bobby Black. He tells me how he and his band have come out here from San Francisco—the place of The Day Trippers' inception—to catch the show. He explains to me how his band is something of a hip thing on the scene back home and tells me stories of wild nights spent playing in dives and ballrooms alike. As he reclines against his amp, coolly smoking a cigarette that he's extracted from his leather jacket, he is quite the rebellious figure.*

1969

In image and essence, he is the perfect front man for this band—a compelling counter to the beautiful Mary Jane—at the same time both a revival of the bad boys of early rock and something new and equally intriguing. He plays a black 1965 Ibanez Goldentone and even with Mary Jane standing right there before me, I find myself unable to retract my gaze from this man. His style is inspired, casual, and somewhat unrehearsed. He's clearly a natural, both as a musician and a performer, and he exudes a cool confidence in his craft that is entirely warranted. There is nothing complex or even dangerously challenging about his playing, but there exists a daring simplicity that when backed by the rest of the band creates an extremely irresistible combination.

"Bobby Black has a brother playing in his band, a keyboardist who handles a Vox Continental like a professional, producing sounds that can only be described as psychedelic rhythm and blues. His sound is contemplative and his style sleek, hailing strongly from modal jazz, although his structure suggests that somewhere in the distant past he was trained in classical piano. His name is Aladdin, and he is something of an eccentric; a real eloquent oddball with licks comparable to a nascent Manzarek or Charles.

"Alongside him is a second guitarist, a real personable kid called Space who plays a red 1967 Domino Dawson and is a uniquely versatile member of the band. His exact role within The Day Trippers varies from song to song, as he plays strictly rhythm on many of their covers and spends much of his time otherwise harmonizing with either the bassist or the lead. His sound is incredibly lofty, not quite unfocused, but certainly unpredictable—the sweet and melodic result of never using a pick.

"Supporting all this rhythmic wandering and exploration is a stout bassist with arms like shipyard rope and a chick wrapped around his neck in-between every song. She has a tambourine in her hand, and he has a Fender Jazz Bass in his. His name is Billy Smith, and he is adept at balancing this band. His is the distinct bottom to The Day Trippers' sound, but even so, he plays with a suggestive, lyrical flair. His influence is the tipping point between too much and not enough, and he effortlessly guides his bandmates along their cerebral meanderings.

"Backing this groovy harmony is the most incredible piece yet. What kind of colossal force does it take to tame this electric symphony? The answer seems to come in only one form. Sitting behind a single snare, bass, cymbal, and tom is a free-spirited drummer; one

410

who is aware, calm, smooth, and perfectly timed. She plays equally well with both sticks and brushes and can play both hard rock and cocktail music. She's highly capable at soloing; in fact, she is so proficient that The Day Trippers call her solos 'easy rides,' and they are featured in almost every number. Her breaks are as sharp as a razor's edge, and her transitions are consistently clean—a musician in professional standing, no doubt. And yes, there is no typo, this fantastic drummer is indeed a tall, beautiful, blue-eyed woman! What a victory for the women's libbers! I highly doubt that very many in the music industry have ever seen anything like her before, and I give her my highest compliments. Any drummer who can hold this renegade band together with only three drums and a cymbal must have serious chops, and she is no exception. She shyly introduces herself as Rhiannon and smiles at me.

"In the beginning, when I was first given this assignment, I thought that I was going to write an article about the music of Woodstock, but after seeing this band play that first night—hidden away in a little farmhouse dive with chickens running around outside, no less—I changed my mind. A hundred articles are going to be written about the Woodstock Festival, but only a few will tell of those experiences that haven't already been witnessed by half a million others, and I feel that these are of equal, if not greater importance. The Day Trippers and their counterparts are the new wave. These bands are what we will hear at the next festival like Woodstock and all the great many that will follow. With such a harmonious sound and an easygoing air, I was all but shocked to find that the current members of this band have only been playing together for three months. I wish them the best of luck in their endeavors and envy the success of the first label to nail them down."

My eyes and mouth had grown progressively wider with every line, and by the time he was finished reading, I was standing there slack-jawed and almost as euphoric as he.

"Holy shit!" I cried. "That's amazing! He didn't say one bad thing about us! He really liked us, a critic!"

"What's not to like?" Bobby replied in earnest. "Do you know what this means?!"

"We have a chance to make it big and play all the hip clubs in L.A. and the Village! We could be signed and record an album! That's far out, man!"

"More than that, baby, this is our big break, you're looking right at it!" he cried, thrusting the magazine in my face. "As soon as this article hits the stands and a couple big club owners and producers read it and get us in their ear, we'll have to start changing our names and getting ready to move, man! We'll be on the radio and on TV! We'll air with Ed Sullivan, and then we'll really be on the scene! We'll sign an international record deal and be millionaires! We'll have a private plane and tour all around the country, in England, France, and Australia! We'll have to beat the groupies off with sticks! Our faces will be all over the media, Rhiannon! We'll be as big as The Beatles or the Stones, just give it a couple of years!"

As complimentary as it was, the article didn't exactly lead me to jump to the same conclusions as him, but I won't deny that I was excited as hell! *Could it really be true?* I thought, *Could The Day Trippers really be famous? Could we really be the next rock sensation with audiences that follow our music and love our sound? Could we really play gigs at places like Winterland and the Whisky, in New York City and Chicago?* At that moment, nothing seemed impossible; the realm of reality seemed to encapsulate everything I'd ever dreamed of and more!

Bobby split before we could rap about it any further, probably to go flash the magazine around the clubs and proclaim our fame from the rooftops. I figured that with him in charge of publicity, we'd get a call in no time. I was positively buzzing; I couldn't believe what I'd just heard, and I couldn't stop imagining all the opportunities the future might bring. After all, if this really was our big break, the possibilities were endless!

Needless to say, this news drastically improved what had before been quite a dismal day, and I finished cleaning in no time. When I emerged from the garage, I expected to find a group of ecstatic Day Trippers hanging around the Trips Center living room like in earlier days, lighting up and rapping about this most recent development, but instead what I discovered was curiously divided. Space had left with Bobby, and Al had disappeared into the study. Mary had attempted to tackle the pile of dishes in the sink, but she hadn't made very much progress before giving up and taking a nap instead. Billy and Faye were toking with the stoners on the couch, and they greeted me when I entered the room.

"Rhiannon, did Bobby read you that article?" Billy asked me.

"Yeah! How fucking cool is that?!" I replied.

"Sweet, right? I wonder if it will take us anywhere."

"Bobby sure thinks so!"

"Well, don't let him get your hopes up too far yet," he cautioned.

"You know how Bobby is. Even if it comes to naught, it's still groovy. Not everybody gets their picture in *Rolling Stone*."

I sat down with them for a while with the intention of rising at some point and shaping up the living room, but it had been a long trip, a long time since we'd been home, and I decided that at least for this first night, a good long rest was in order—one in a bed all to myself without the company of others and the bumping and jostling of a speeding van that I was all too familiar with. I'd begin the cleanup in the morning.

—Or so I'd envisioned. Uncharacteristically though blissfully, I'd slept through the night and all the way into the early part of the afternoon. I was just making my way downstairs, hoping to score one of the last apples or figs from the garden before the frost in the coming days sent them into dormancy, when Mary came bursting through the front door and let out a terrible, mournful wail. Alarmed, I ran over to her, and in-between bursts of tearful blubbering, I was able to discover the source of her hysterics.

That morning, Mary had taken the Trips Mobile over to Richmond in an attempt to see her mother, but when she arrived at her old home, she found that Sophia had recently passed away. A mourning wreath had been placed upon the door, and many of Sophia's things had been put out by the curb. The only thing she had salvaged was Sophia's favorite blue dress.

I sat with her on the couch for hours, comforting her as she cried. As terrible as it sounds, I'd almost entirely forgotten about Sophia's terminal illness. There was something about her condition that seemed to deny the inevitable, or maybe it was the way that Mary had presented it to me. Mary had to have been aware that Sophia was going to die at some point, but somehow I don't think she ever really considered that a reality for her. There seemed to have been something endearing about Sophia's illness, something Mary felt she could help; a condition that hadn't been entirely real, until it was. As I listened to her lament, I suddenly remembered something I thought might help and went digging through a shoebox I kept in the mandala room where I'd saved ticket stubs and photographs throughout the summer. Toward the bottom, I found the photo of Mary's family that I'd rescued from her father's wrath that fateful day of the Apollo launch; I'd been unable to replace the frame which had been destroyed, but Mary didn't seem to care and was grateful anyway.

At one point or another, the boys came home, and Billy and Faye reemerged from outside, where they'd been entirely unaware of the

413

goings-on inside the Trips Center. Once they'd learned of that morning's events, they were an even more powerful force in consoling her. Bobby put her favorite album, *Surrealistic Pillow*, on the turntable, Billy gave her a backrub, and Space announced that he'd scored three nights of shows for us at The Matrix for the following weekend alongside three other local bands: Mendelbaum, Womb, and Shag.

Space's input was by far the most crucial because there was a kicker: not only would we be playing at our favorite club for three nights, we were going to be the main attraction—headliners for the first time! This news was enough to improve even Mary's mood, and according to Space, no special requests had been necessary to secure such a gig. In fact, from what he told us, it seemed like our San Francisco club circuit following had missed us during our month-long hiatus and that there had been much talk in our absence about whether or not we'd already been signed and if a looming record deal was what was responsible for delaying our return. Pete Abram, the talent booker for that club, had come right out and suggested the lineup, Space explained to us. He'd even told him that the turnout would be well above average if we played a double set.

Needless to say, for good or for bad, Mary's mind was immediately occupied with matters demanding her attention in the wake of Sophia's death. Once she had somewhere to anchor herself and business to distract herself with, Mary seemed to cope incredibly well with the circumstances. In fact, to a great extent, even her mourning was confined to the two days directly following the news and our return. Even the pain of bereavement wasn't enough to keep the ebullient Mary Jane down for very long.

Between our fantastic reviews in *Rolling Stone* and the sudden opportunity to make a name for ourselves as headliners, we were restored, revitalized, and ready to please. We'd rehearse for hours in the garage on the days the weather was nice enough for me to pull my car out, and those sessions were some of the most enjoyable we had together since before we'd left on our trip. We were incredibly in sync—all of us wanted to see just where this chance might take us. Al's songwriting had improved drastically while we were out on the road, and a lot of our new material was extremely groovy. Sometimes we'd spend whole days just working on one song. We'd all sit around and listen to Mary sing the lyrics and Al try different chord changes and melodies, and in-between tokes, the rest of us would call out suggestions or play along in harmony. We weren't the type of band that took the time to write out our songs longhand while we were putting them together, and a lot of the time much of what we adopted into our prevailing repertoire was entirely spontaneous. We'd work for a while on one line or verse, and then more often than not, the rest would materialize out of an extended jam session in that key. Whatever we liked, we tried to remember for the next time, but seeing as the reliability of our memories was fairly arbitrary, many of our original numbers went through several different versions before they evolved into their final form. Most times, this process would even take place while we were performing, but following the *Rolling Stone* article and Pete's move to bill us as headliners, Bobby warned us that our days as a jam band were limited, and as the time went on, our rehearsals became more structured and industrious, with less goofing off and more serious composition.

The vast majority of our time before our first gig as headliners that Thursday night was spent working out the licks for our newest tune, the one that had been quoted in *Rolling Stone* and was still unnamed. We wanted the song to have its West Coast debut at that first gig, but it was still in its infancy, and we were trying to cram a whole lot of sophisticated changes and harmonies into that one number. I was still working on the drum fills the night before.

On the day of the gig and to the surprise of us all, Bobby was awake bright and early and was instructing one of the burnouts who'd taken up residence in the attic which of the mounds of equipment to load into the Trips Mobile. It was quite a humorous spectacle to behold. We had almost twelve hours before we were scheduled to be onstage, and Bobby was having his lackey haul ass at a breakneck pace. Additionally, this poor cat was either mighty stupid or incredibly fried because he couldn't even seem to remember—let alone comprehend— whatever Bobby told him, especially if he spoke more than one sentence at a time. Once we discovered this scene in the garage, we relieved the lackey of his duty, and he scurried back into the attic while we assumed the position of instant roadies.

To be honest, by and large, I was quite impressed. I'd never before seen Bobby so outwardly focused, possessed, and dedicated to something that didn't concern his immediate benefit. He was actually working toward a goal, and he did so with conviction—albeit with an attitude. Believe it or not, under Bobby's direction, we actually got to The Matrix so early that we made it there even before our opening band. Bobby's assumed authority was extremely entertaining and at times, even gratifying. Of course, we all knew that his already monstrous ego was getting one hell of a workout, but somebody needed to be in charge and none of us were chomping at the bit, so at one point or another we all acquiesced and let him run with it. If there was one thing besides playing guitar that Bobby was terribly efficient at, it was running the show. Sure, Space was personable, crafty, and could sell you your own shoes, but his approach was gentle, and as we'd later learn, occasional forcefulness is required when dealing with bigwigs and businessmen. Bobby, on the other hand, could talk and no matter how falsified, always managed to make everything that came out of his mouth sound like it was as true as gospel. Not only was he persuasive, he was intense and dramatic. He had the look and the charisma and a distinct air about him that clearly indicated to others that it would be best for them to let him get what he wanted. A band itself may be comprised of an interplay of equals, but a gigging outfit needs somebody in the driver's seat, and as long as he didn't run us into any brick walls and let us crash and burn, we figured it was worth our while to let him have his kicks. When he was good, he was very good, and when he was bad, well...

Our first gig as headliners at The Matrix had a pretty good turnout. I think Pete Abram was impressed, and to be perfectly honest, so were we. The place was packed, and most of the crowd started filtering in as our openers finished up their set, which meant that they'd come to see us. Marty Balin was there, and his drummer, Spence Dryden, had tagged along as well. The two of them talked with Al the whole time we were setting up and during our intermission when Womb got up on stage and played a set. It had taken months, but I was finally getting used to interacting with these rock icons on a daily basis and didn't go into a cold sweat every time somebody from Jefferson Airplane or The Grateful Dead greeted me or one of my friends on the street or in the clubs. It was this aspect of historical living that had taken me the longest to adjust to, by far.

All in all, that show was a smashing hit. We brought it big time, and both sets we played were full of energy and excitement. We were in sync with one another from the time we stepped out on stage until we finished packing up our instruments for the night. All the rehearsed material we played was nearly flawless, and the jam session that night was riveting perfection. Bobby especially was a powerhouse; he soloed in almost every song, and the audience applauded so loudly that we had to turn up our amps. Needless to say, the dance floor was full from the time we struck up until the place closed for the night.

In the middle of Intuit—which was the name we'd eventually given to that tune *Rolling Stone* had quoted—everything felt so right on; our flow unbroken, our telepathy ceaseless, and I was overcome by a feeling of pure exhilaration unlike any I'd ever felt as a result of music alone. Inspiration filled me with such a force that it just poured out from my hands and I broke out into a ride that rivals anything I've ever played before or since. Bobby followed me immediately—he lit out on those strings like a bat out of hell, screaming. I felt a strong and undeniable flood of euphoria hit the stage and spread throughout the band as one by one, everybody fell back in behind Bobby and me. All seven of us were standing on tiptoe, as if a rush had shot up our spines, moving us to the very brink of an improvisational chasm—*Edge City*.

Fuck, it was awesome! If you've ever listened to *Are You Happy* by Iron Butterfly, I can tell you that it sounded a little like that. That night at The Matrix was the best gig we'd played since Woodstock, and now that I think about it, it may very well have been the best gig we ever had. In hindsight, it is plain to see that it was the last time the muse took the stage with The Day Trippers.

At the end of the night, as we were closing up our cases, comfortably gassed and satisfied by our performance, Bobby reappeared from where he'd been rapping with a group of girls near the back door, and he held a poster in his hand.

"Look at this!" he proclaimed proudly, unrolling the slightly psychedelic poster like a scroll and presenting it to us, "we're headliners, baby!"

As he did this, two men emerged from behind him. One was tall and thin and wore a dress shirt and a sport coat; the other was short and stout and wore dark sunglasses and a beard. They materialized out of the smoky darkness like a mirage and came wielding business cards. What they spoke of amazed us all.

The first man introduced himself as Kent Stephens and told us that he was what they call an A&R executive from Reprise Records, an offshoot of Warner Brothers, the same label that had produced Jimi Hendrix, Van Morrison, and Joni Mitchell. His partner then chimed in and added that one of their affiliates had signed the Dead, and with them had produced three albums, their self-titled first, *Anthem of the Sun*, and most recently, *Aoxomoxoa*. They provided that the reason for their impromptu visit to this gig of ours was to hear how we sounded live. They'd read the article our little beatnik friend had written and in

417

turn, hunted us down with an offer. They told us they'd felt compelled to act fast due to that last sentence there at the end that congratulated the first record label to successfully approach and sign us. Apparently, talk of our having advanced with a record contract was not confined to San Francisco.

"So you are the famed Day Trippers, the ones who played before the music started at Woodstock," the first man said as he approached us. "The group with a chick who plays the drums. You know percussion is traditionally a man's gig, right?"

Much to my surprise, Bobby jumped up to defend me right away, "All those men drummers wish they could play like Rhiannon—never mind that she's a girl!"

Kent Stephens, the record man, held up his hands, "We aren't saying anything bad about her playing, it's just remarkable, that's all. Nobody's ever heard of a female drummer before in a hot, big-time rock band."

"Aw, well, we ain't no hot, big-time rock band, we just jam around the Bay Area. I'll bet nobody outside of San Francisco even knows who we are," Billy replied.

"Ah, you see, that very well may have been the case in the past, but you have something now that you've never had before: publicity—and publicity can go a long way. You see, we're both from L.A, but we read that article *Rolling Stone* did on you, and it made us curious. Everybody's curious. America wants to know just who these Day Trippers are. That is the power of publicity, and do you know the best way to capitalize on publicity?"

We all looked at him expectantly and waited for him to continue. What he spoke of sounded alright to me, but his demeanor made me feel a tad uneasy. He wasn't quite a suit, but one could easily be misled. I assumed that was why he'd enlisted the presence of the guy with the beard, whose name was Larry.

"You sign a deal and cut a record," Larry announced. "We can get you out on vinyl and in the hands of the general public in less than six months, while that *Rolling Stone* article is still fresh in everybody's minds."

"How, uh, groovy would that be? Can you, uh, dig that?" Kent Stephens prodded.

The seven of us turned our gazes toward one another with eyes wide. This was it, the offer we'd all been waiting for.

"We can dig it," Bobby responded, assuming his position of resident authority within The Day Trippers. "Now you two aren't the

418

first to come to us with a proposal. Tell us your offer, and we'll think about it."

The two men exchanged a glance, "Reprise Records is prepared to offer you $10,000 in advance..." the quasi-suit began.

Considering his bullshit move of before, designed to make these men scramble, I assumed that Bobby had intended to appear composed and only marginally interested, but before the words had even fully left the man's mouth, Bobby replied in earnest, "We'll take it!"

The record men, apparently fooled by Bobby's casual approach earlier, were caught off-guard by his sudden agreement.

"Um, uh, well, do you have a manager we can speak to? Somebody we can work the business end of this deal with while you all focus on making the music?"

"You've got him right here," Bobby said, pointing to himself. "I self-manage The Day Trippers."

The record men shared a look I couldn't quite place, something along the lines of a gentle scoff meant to imply a sentiment to the effect of, "*Could he be serious?*"

"Now look here," Kent Stephens explained, "I don't think you understand just how much *business* is involved in getting something like this off the ground. To be as effective as you want it to be, this deal has got to go down quickly, and you know you don't want to be bothered with all the official *business* necessary while you're busy creating, am I right?"

To me, having a manager didn't sound like such a bad idea. All we'd need to do was play music while somebody else would be in charge of booking gigs, managing money, negotiating contracts, and all the rest of that corporate bullshit; the only thing we'd have to do was give him a piece of the action—but Bobby had it all figured out already.

"I'm capable," Bobby replied, "don't you worry about that."

The two of them shared another glance. "Well, alright then, it's settled," the man named Larry concluded. "You take our cards, and we'll be in touch with you sometime within the next couple of days with more information. Is there a phone number we can reach you at?"

Space gave them the number to the payphone outside the Trips Center, and then they went away as suddenly as they had come, and we were left standing there in an empty, darkened room with instruments scattered around us, shocked smiles on all our faces and butterflies in all our stomachs.

After that, there was no backing Bobby down. He had shifted into high gear and was roaring full speed ahead. Add a little coke, as he did that night, and one might mistake him for a narcissistic Space.

"I told you, I told you, I told you," he reminded us repeatedly as we lugged our equipment back out to the Trips Mobile. "Isn't this exactly what I told you would happen if we got back to the City fast? Aren't you guys glad you listened to me now instead of wasting time down in fucking Mexico?!"

His seriousness was lost on the rest of us. We were all relishing in this newfound excitement, cutting up, and poking fun at Kent Stephens' attempts to be hip. At one point, Al, who had been trailing behind us, somewhat unsettled, spoke up.

"Hey, Bobby…"

Bobby sniffed, rubbed his nose, and turned around, "What?" he asked.

"Bobby, if you include me in this, just know that no matter how far we go, I'm only here to make music. I'm not in it for the money or the fame or the drugs or the girls, and I will walk if it becomes too much, I just want you to know that."

Bobby was eight miles high. I'd be surprised if he'd even heard a word of what his brother had said, "Yeah, yeah, yeah," he replied. "OK. Fine. Whatever."

A BRIEF AND BEAUTIFUL TRIP BACK

****

Things changed very quickly after that. Kent Stephens called us back the following day and made arrangements with Bobby for us to come down to L.A, negotiate a contract, and start recording. When we asked him the reason why we couldn't record at one of the studios in San Francisco, his answer was that they simply weren't as good. At that time, the studios of choice were all in Hollywood. Branching out of our usual club circuit and trying out a new scene—especially one as star-studded and happening as Los Angeles—sounded like a good idea to me. We'd been successful in San Francisco, but we decided that this might very well be an auspicious opportunity to broaden our horizons. It was time to see whether or not fame and its accompanying good press would follow us south.

By the time we finished up our stint as headliners at The Matrix, it was common knowledge that The Day Trippers were moving up and out. At first, we weren't quite sure if we'd be able to score any gigs down there right away, but Space got on the horn and less than an hour later we were booked as week-long openers at a club on the Strip called Thee Experience.

We left for Los Angeles on a Monday morning and arrived there sometime in the afternoon. It was hot in L.A. when we got there, and the long pants and jackets we were wearing to combat the weather in San Francisco didn't help any. The first establishment we visited in L.A. was a thrift shop. We weren't planning on stopping, but prompted by several complaints from Bobby, of all people, that his leather pants were becoming more and more constricting the further south we drove, a trip to one of L.A.'s plentiful and infamous boutiques eventually became unavoidable. This proved to be a rewarding move. I think a great majority of the good, clean fun we had in L.A. was in that thrift shop on our first day there. They had everything from floor-length silken evening gowns to feather hats, tie-dye nylons, paisley bloomers, and what looked suspiciously like bondage gear. As you can probably envision, any combination of these things was unimaginably hysterical. For a while, all of us, including Bobby, forgot about the urgency and importance of our pending appointment, and instead, we dove headfirst into the excrement of Hollywood costume directors and hippies alike and emerged looking like a cross between Phyllis Diller and Jimi Hendrix in drag.

Therefore, it's no surprise that we showed up to the studio three hours late with Mary wearing a Japanese kimono, Space in a blue pilot's uniform, Billy decked out in psychedelic miscellany, Faye in a duck costume, Bobby shirtless and wearing spaghetti western fringe chaps and a matching brimmed hat, me in a neon purple jumpsuit, and Al in a velvet smoking jacket, complete with a pocket watch and ten cent tobacco pipe. If there was any day we were fit for an album cover photo shoot, it was that one. The look on Kent Stephens' face when he had to introduce us to the resident producer and sound engineer at that particular studio was worth every cent we'd paid.

The studio we'd chosen—or rather, that had more or less been chosen for us—was located right on Sunset Strip, only a few blocks down from the thrift shop that had waylaid us. It was called Sunset Sound, and it had hosted the likes of many famous groups including The Doors and The Beach Boys, respectively. The sound engineer we ended up working with was an incredibly groovy guy named Paul Stryker whose musical prowess was at least as impressive as ours. He had perfect pitch and could tune just about any instrument by ear. He played guitar, bass, drums, piano, and saxophone, and despite the fact that he was a stocky, six-foot tall hipster with long hair and a braided beard, he could sing soprano.

Our producer was another hip-looking fellow, far more so than Kent Stephens could ever hope to be. His name was Jerry Greco, and he was born and bred Southern Californian—as evidenced by his appearance but not at all by his demeanor. He was tall and had a surfer's body, curly blonde hair, and striking blue eyes. His voice was low and soft, but when he spoke, more often than not, the words that tumbled out contained some form of biting sarcasm, and he carried about him a startlingly staunch air. He may have looked the part, but there was something about his character that lacked some intrinsic quality I tended to expect from hippies. Was it empathy, or was it depth? —I never could put a bead on it. In any case, his ego entered the room about a dozen steps before the rest of him, and from the very start, he and Bobby seemed to be gearing up for what would be an unending battle of wills every step of the way. Maybe it was because he couldn't take Bobby seriously as our manager in his cowboy getup, or perhaps it was because he perceived Bobby's exaggerated persona as underlying insecurity. Maybe he felt that Bobby threatened his authority. It was impossible to know, but whatever the problem was, it was a match made in hell. The only thing that was entirely certain was that the two of them were far too similar to get along.

On that first day, as Bobby and Jerry Greco continued to sniff warily around at one another like two unfamiliar alpha dogs, we began to get acquainted with the people and the workspace that we'd be seeing a lot of during the next few weeks. We'd never set foot in a studio before—we hadn't even recorded a demo—therefore, we knew nothing of what to expect. We had wanted to rush right in and start laying down tracks, but that first day was just talk. In addition to having limited knowledge of what putting together a record consisted of, we were even less educated in regard to the process, even though Bobby tried to sound as though he was up on the times.

Together with Stryker and Jerry, we tried to put together a rudimentary list of the songs we wanted to include. They talked to us about the importance of having songs that were fit for radio play, and we discussed the image that we wanted to project. They told us that we needed to look at the album as if it were a story, with comprehension and continuity. Singles, Jerry said, were overrated and useless in today's music industry. They talked about target audience, estimated profit, commerciality, and a whole lot of other boring-sounding business terminology that I regrettably tuned out—I was lusting after the drum kit in the corner.

Once all the talk of corporate standards and other assorted noise had ended, there was some shuffling and signing of papers, and then Kent Stephens hit the road and Stryker finally got to show us what all of his fancy-looking equipment could do. He used a lot of complicated terms that I was unfamiliar with, like audio compression and dynamic range. I tried to pay attention, but anything more advanced than bass, treble and balance was lost on me. I figured that it would all make sense when I could actually hear those techniques applied, and therefore, rather than burn out my brain trying to listen, I spent most of that time looking around.

The studio itself was relatively small, granted, it contained quite a bit. There was a control panel with well over a hundred switches that took up almost one whole side of the room we were in, and a desk and a bookshelf were nestled together on the other side. There was a clock on the wall situated above a filing cabinet and a reel-to-reel player, and a couch was pressed up against the front of the desk. There were rolled-up wires and a pile of instrument cases in one corner and a tower of speakers in the opposite corner. The wall running along the front of the control panel was actually made of glass, and upon peering through it, apart from that sensuous drum kit, I could see several mics and amps and a few high-backed chairs designed for rumination scattered around the much larger performance area. Behind the main performance area was what they called an isolation booth and used mainly for vocals, and beside it was an echo chamber, complete with state-of-the-art equipment that was in high demand due to the affinity for psychedelic audio effects that was present in those days. Of all the bells and whistles the studio had to offer, the echo chamber excited us the most. I was already imagining all of the wild experimentation that would take place within its walls before I ever set foot inside.

The next day when we came into the studio, we found that all of the amps and speakers had been set up to simulate a live gig. We'd told Stryker that we wanted to emulate a live sound, and to our surprise and delight, when we showed up that morning, all we needed to do was plug in and jam. Despite all that stuff they tell you about how precious studio time is, that first day of recording Stryker and Jerry basically just let us mess around and explore all the new possibilities available to us. The tape was rolling only half the time, and really, it was quite a blast. Jerry Greco was in and out all day, so together with Stryker, we screwed around with the different levels and effects on the console. It was really sweet to see all the cool shit we could do to the sound, especially when we got into the echo chamber. We stuck Bobby and Space in there for a while, and they laid down the guitar track for Dawn Train—the song we'd postulated to be the first on our album—and then Mary went in there after them to do the vocals. The end result was by no means good enough to keep, but it was mad interesting for sure.

For me, the highlight of the day was when I finally got behind that drum kit. The thing was freaking ridiculous: it had the biggest kick drum I'd ever seen surrounded by four toms—two floor, two rack—a couple of snares, a hi-hat, two rides, and Zildjian crash cymbals that hung from all over. There were probably about eight, all of them different sizes, and the whole thing was miked up. The kit was within its own little nook behind this glass partition in the corner, and they could've left me in there for hours or days and I wouldn't have known the difference. Hell, I would've even played with the next band to come in if they had let me.

I think that first day was a lot of fun for everybody. Bobby was amped up to the max, and for once, his playing improved with his agitation. Space was drooling over all the new gadgets he got to play with, Mary got the chance to hear herself sing, and everybody else was just relishing in the experience—even Al was intellectually engaged. He found the technology behind recording to be fascinating, and they had a harpsichord hanging around, so if nothing else, that made him very happy.

With the exception of Jerry Greco's hovering, it was a carefree day. The hours passed without concern, and in some ways, it was just like being back in the Trips Center garage when I'd first arrived on the Haight with the addition of a lot of expensive sound tech and a big, hairy guy at the helm. I really dug Stryker; he had a true passion for music—playing it, listening to it, and using all his equipment to make it sound as groovy as possible. As much as Jerry Greco was serious and critical, Stryker was light-hearted and fun. He knew how to pose suggestions without being overbearing and could sense the right time to step back and let us work amongst ourselves. He was able to capitalize on and display our strengths as well as downplay our weaknesses—although if you asked Bobby, we didn't have any of those.

One of the few things I'd gathered from Stryker's lecture the night before was that all their equipment was state-of-the-art and that they used a four-track recorder. What that meant was instead of recording all our parts on one track, our parts would be divided, and the tracks could be recorded and edited separately. Initially, Stryker had Billy, Faye, and me on one track, Bobby, Space, and Al on another, and Mary on the third. The last track, he told us, would be saved for overdub. A whole track free really opened up the door for imagination, and immediately, we began spitballing over all the possibilities it would allow us. We could have Mary record on two tracks and harmonize with herself, Faye ad-lib in the background, or splice in all kinds of extras—real train whistles on Dawn Train, or psychedelic sound effects like in that Airplane tune, *Chushingura*. I even suggested recording on two tracks myself to make it sound like there were two drummers. However, just as we were starting to get really creative, Bobby interjected and told Stryker that he wanted a whole track to himself. Stryker tried to explain to him how much that would limit our potential, but Bobby insisted, and rather than put up a fight, Stryker had us record like that for a bit so that Bobby could hear the difference for himself. But even in the face of it, Bobby was adamant, and all of our fledgling ideas evaporated.

However, Stryker possessed his own reserves of ingenuity, and despite our limitations, he was able to leave room for additions and effects. He and Al and I worked out an organ/harpsichord/drum part to be played on three separate tracks that would mimic the train sounds and still allowed Bobby to have the fourth track all to himself.

At around six o'clock that night, Bobby hustled us out of the studio with our instruments in tow and drove us down to Thee Experience for our first gig at that venue. Now, we'd all heard of Thee Experience before, and according to the prevailing word of mouth, it was quite a happening joint—*the* place to be that summer. Once we got there, it wasn't hard at all to understand why; I mean, the place had just about everything going for it. It was a corner outfit right on the Strip, and it was decked out with psychedelic regalia to the max, both inside and out. Moreover, they served food and ice cream, which certainly upped its appeal over a traditional dance club. If there's one sure way to attract hippies to your business, it's by serving munchie-friendly meals. It was a small club, but it was by no means hard to find; this was because the whole outside of the joint was covered by a giant mural of Jimi Hendrix, and the front door was his mouth. You walked in through Jimi Hendrix's mouth, man! How much more trippy can you get?

Another thing that made Thee Experience so great was that it catered to jam bands. There was always somebody billed for the evening, but after their set was over, the stage was open to anyone who wanted to get a jam session going, and there were quite a few musicians in the audience ready to jam at any time. There was even one night when Jimi Hendrix himself was in town and showed up at Thee Experience to jam.

We ended up spending a lot of time there, even when we weren't gigging. I mean, the place was practically made for us; it was a club for jam bands after all, and that was our natural habitat. A lot of the time we'd play earlier in the night at one of the other local clubs—be it the Troubador, Gazzari's, It's Boss, or any number of other smaller establishments along the Strip—and then, at one time or another, we'd find ourselves back at Thee Experience either listening to local talent or jamming ourselves. By far, the best music we played in L.A, we played at Thee Experience. By and large, this was because we played best when we weren't performing, per se, but rather when we were purely jamming—when we needed to be entirely absorbed and synched in to make it work and nothing at all was rehearsed. For me, Thee Experience was a diamond in the rough; a real, cool scene in the midst of a plastic, neon wasteland. Needless to say, it was my favorite club outside of those in San Francisco and by far my favorite place in L.A.

The whole dynamic of The Day Trippers and a lot of what we did changed entirely once we made it to L.A. The question of the evening used to be, "Can we jam?" After which—in the case of an affirmative—we'd set up and play for the next few hours at any one of the various dives that would have us and get paid depending on how well they did that night. Did we ever get cheated out of payment? Sure. Did we have to play three to five sets a night for a salary that amounted to the cost of a lid of grass? Sure. Were most of the stages smaller than the garage back at the Trips Center? Yup. Did most of the places we played at smell like stale beer crossed with a skunk orgy? Of course. Was it all that bad?

Bobby may have been the first to say yes, but he knew he had one hell of a wicked run at those dives. Those managers knew us so well that Space only had to walk through the door to score a gig, and more often than not, we would make tips from the audience. There was something about the atmosphere of those underground rock clubs and the people that frequented them that exists nowhere else in the world. The roots and foundations of everything the Counterculture Movement ever grew into can be found under a layer of smoke and a coating of grime in the dives of London, New York, San Francisco, L.A, and everywhere in-between. The seeds of what eventually became cornerstone ideals were first spoken from the bandstands there and first heard at the bars. There was a closeness, an intimacy, a sense of security and like-mindedness there. There was anarchy and ill-repute interwoven with immunity, awareness, more drugs than you can imagine, and fantastic fucking music night after night.

However, after we started to get big, all of that went away. The way we dealt with club owners changed altogether—they spoke to us differently, payment became something that was agreed upon ahead of time, and there was a lot of signing papers—we started approaching them on entirely different pretenses. I began to recognize the all too familiar elements of game reality inherent in these practices, but I figured that to a certain extent it couldn't be helped, that it was just part of the corporate bullshit that was unavoidable in this way of life. And if that weren't enough, the venues got bigger, which forwent the intimacy of dives in exchange for diversity, and the type of people we played for changed. In and of itself that was in no way a bad thing, but in L.A, a startling inconsistency could be found that was by far unthinkable back in San Francisco.

Everybody in the audience may have looked like they were heads, but it wasn't anywhere beyond the realm of possibility to get talking to the cat sitting next to you at the bar who was dressed in tie-dye and paisley with long hair and tooled boots and hear him talking about political garbage or his place in the rat race, along with a whole slew of other topics widely considered to be entirely un-hip. These low-lying straights weren't hard to spot. Usually around the time they started in with the partisan bullshit, they'd take a pass on the joint that was making its way around the bar, typically accompanied by a quip about how they were already 'too far-out.' These were people for whom hip living was a weekend affair—either because they couldn't find enough appeal in it or because they feared the ramifications of splitting entirely with straight life and the security it offered. To them, roughing it was a few too many, and a heavy trip was a contact high. On Monday morning, they would return to their midtown flats and commute to their forty-hour-a-week grind where they would sit around with fellow squares in the breakrooms flapping their lips about the decadence and immorality of their peers.

In L.A, it was more of an image thing than anything else. That isn't to say L.A. is full of phonies—that's another issue altogether—but there was most definitely a sector of people with little or no convictions of their own who were continually on the make for the newest fad. Billy called them trend whores, and their presence really messed with his head. He'd always considered anyone in a club who didn't start their sentences with the words 'man,' 'dig,' or 'fuck' to be a narc, and a good half of the L.A. club circuit patronage fit that description. Between that and how often the Man prowled the Strip, Billy's inherent paranoia eventually shot through the roof. Only in L.A. could you find straights impersonating hipsters for some reason other than to get them busted. Needless to say, Billy was quite unhappy about our choice of locale.

In the closet-squares' defense, I say they were really just lost. It was a confusing time, and I can understand wanting to try on the Movement before making a final purchase, but I really have no sympathy for the trend whores. How can you profess to stand for something utterly and irrevocably when you don't have a clue in the world what it is that you're standing for and then change your mind a month or two later when a new viewpoint is 'in?'

Maybe part of it was the age range. In L.A, the kids we played for were truly kids—sometimes as young as fourteen. In San Francisco, the age of the crowd was generally evenly dispersed amongst the twenty-odd set with a few minors thrown in, but in L.A, rock clubs were all the rage with the teenyboppers. Bobby couldn't get enough of them, and I'll admit that they were young and pretty and more than occasionally promiscuous, but playing for a crowd of high-schoolers just made me feel weird. Curious teenagers are often closely followed by suspicious parents—as was the case in my own past—and as I knew all too well, that was a bad scene.

All things considered, that first month we were in L.A. was in no way wholly unpleasant, although the differences to our previous way of life were startlingly apparent. There was definitely a degree of uncertainty regarding the nature of those changes and whether they were for good or bad, but there was never really any serious discussion about it. We seemed to take them more or less in stride, each of us rationalizing them as we saw fit. To me, they were aspects of fame we'd just been unfamiliar with before. To Billy, they were byproducts of L.A. To Space, they were necessary games. Bobby saw them as us finally getting somewhere, Mary was by far oblivious, and Faye was stoic. Only Al took to openly brooding. I, on the other hand, failed to see the use in mulling over the possibility of some impending bummer. It was easy enough for me to avoid being directly connected with any corporate business games, and Al had even more wiggle room than I did. As a whole, we basically left all of the official stuff to be handled by Bobby and Space. For me, it was more or less out of necessity; diligence in business affairs is a skill I most assuredly lack, even to this day.

For the sake of self-preservation, I tried as hard as I could to keep my real name off of paper as much as possible. First of all, I had no way of officially identifying myself, and secondly, Bobby was in the habit of cautioning all of us that before very long we'd be getting interviewed by all the big radio and television stations and that we all had to get our stories straight because they'd more than likely be verifying them. I couldn't go around telling those kinds of sources my history in Fresno because if on the off chance they did go digging into my past, they would discover that I didn't have one. I wanted to be one of those entertainers known only by their stage name, and on our first album I planned on being credited as Rhiannon Ryder. For all intents and purposes, at least for the time being, my past was nonexistent. The entirety of my acknowledgeable life had begun only a few months ago on a side street in San Francisco. All the rest—for the moment—might as well have been forgotten.

1969

To be honest, most of my memories of that first month are a total blur. Some incidents stand out more clearly than others, but for the most part, I remember it as a constant shuffle between the studio, gigs, and late night parties. To be clear, my hazy memory is in no way due to the volume of drugs I consumed during that period. In fact, I think I spent more hours sober during that month in L.A. than I did the entirety of the time I spent in San Francisco. I chalk it up to the fact that we spent most of that month in continuous motion. There wasn't much time for taking breaks or just hanging out like there used to be. The mornings we used to spend smoking or sleeping or walking the streets of San Francisco together, we spent working in the studio. Taken on its own merit, without all the other variables necessary to describe the big picture, it really was a great deal of fun. However, when you consider the pressure of our time-sensitive contract, Bobby's eternal conflict with Jerry Greco, and the frustration of having to produce normally spontaneous creative material on command, we had more off days than on.

The act of performing itself incurred its own changes. The clubs we played at were bigger, which meant that we needed to adjust our setup. Space went into a musical surplus store one day and emerged with two half-stacks of 100-watt Marshall Amplifiers. They were so big that they couldn't be safely strapped to the roof and had to ride inside the van with us. If we'd thought that it had been cramped before, it only got worse over time. It even got to the point where at least three of us would usually opt to walk or bag a separate ride to our gigs. Although, as inconvenient as they were, they sounded crazy good, and that made all the extra hassles worth it. With the addition of those Marshalls and a schedule that sometimes involved us playing two separate venues a night, we started playing longer and louder. In the back, I was sandwiched between those two big ass amps—pumping at full volume, may I add—for four or five hours a night, and sometimes my ears would ring from the time the show was over until the time I went to bed.

Outside the studio and off the stage, the world of our everyday lives was different as well. Our local fame had prevailed to such a point that former audience members would recognize us in all different corners of the city, and more often than not, they'd make some sort of a scene. We'd be walking down the road and people would come up to us and ask for our autographs and girls would scream and point, usually at Bobby. It certainly was strange getting used to. That kind of stuff would never happen in San Francisco; Jesus could be walking down

430

Haight Street and the most he'd get was a peace sign flashed at him. Of course Bobby loved it. I definitely thought it was cool that they liked and listened to our music and that we could put something up there that so many people enjoyed, but to be treated as if we were superior to them in some way never failed to make me uncomfortable.

I've always seen myself first and foremost as a musician; I never got all wrapped up in that 'messenger of the gods and voice of a generation' trip. It used to be about music and music alone, but after The Day Trippers got involved with Reprise Records, everybody started veering off after their own interests, and that was the strangest of feelings, the starkest contrast to what had existed before when we'd all been in it together. Our trajectory may very well have been regarded as progress, but as much as we were progressing in the context of success and acclaim, there was something about the way we were going that felt more and more like we were losing our grip on something we'd previously held firmly. Now hindsight is 20/20, of course, and I'm sure these sentiments weren't what I'd felt from the beginning, but always in the back of my mind, I knew that The Day Trippers were straying from the tight, intimate group of musicians we'd been before, and the likelihood of our being able to return to that level of sync seemed less likely every day. After all, things were different now.

We began splitting up after shows. Bobby would generally take off with a group of girls or to a party, sometimes Mary or Space would accompany him, and only occasionally would we all go together. We began staying in different motel rooms or different motels altogether. There was more bread around now, which lent itself to the opportunity, although sometimes, inadvertently, we'd end up adjacent to one another. There's nothing like falling asleep to an orchestra of grunting and giggling and creaking bed frames next door, especially when you know who the musicians are.

That's another thing that drove a wedge between us—the girls. Well, to be fair, it wasn't just the girls, because there were men too, and they all arrived ready and willing to meet the needs of us musicians. When we began to embark upon going pro, everybody got romantic attention, not just Bobby. Even I received a new level of notice from the audience. The *Rolling Stone* article, our precursor to fame, had hyped up the fact that I was a female drummer, and now at every show there seemed to be a whole lineup of guys interested in finding out if I could dance the horizontal tango as well as I could play the drums—a great many of them with consistently kinky suggestions.

431

Sometimes I took their offers, but most times I left our shows alone. I wasn't used to the attention—romantic or otherwise—stemming from my role as a drummer, and I wasn't so sure that I liked being a focal point in the band. Bobby, on the other hand, reveled in it; he had a different girl every night and sometimes two at the same time.

In response to this I felt, well, I hesitate to call it jealousy—because it wasn't; rather, I guess I just felt used and a bit easier than I would've liked to admit. It's not really that I minded him being with other women, but once we got to L.A, he dropped me almost entirely as a sexual partner, and the frequency of our interludes diminished almost to the point of being nonexistent. Sometimes that old spark would ignite on the road or in the studio, and when it did it was very good, but change had even weaseled its way into the depths of our passion—even our intimacy wasn't the same. In some ways, I was glad that he found sexual gratification elsewhere; the thought of all the other people he was sleeping with in such a small window of time and how little he bathed skived me out entirely.

Occasionally after shows we'd rent adjoining hotel rooms, open all the doors, and have one great big party. There was something about this practice that rekindled elements of Trips Center gatherings, but again, just like everything else in the world of L.A. notoriety, there was more than just a thread of difference. The nice thing was that more often than not, all of The Day Trippers would be there. There'd be laughing and jocularity and fraternizing, new music on vinyl or local musicians come to jam, and a sampling of the local underground dope. There were a few times when it got way out of hand and turned into bacchanalia galore—at which time Al and I would cut out and head down to Thee Experience—but for the most part, those parties were fairly tame. However, tame or not, those were long nights, and the carousing usually didn't end until after daybreak. Sometimes, we would have to be in the studio by noon of the next day, and damn, would we be beat! That's when the cocaine started popping up more and more.

There was something else I noticed after we started gigging as headliners: as the shows got longer, the crowds got bigger, and the adrenaline got more potent, Bobby started using more. As the rush of performing grew stronger, the contrast of coming down when the night was over became much more apparent. Bobby was an up-and-coming guitar god, and he wanted to be worshipped as such both on and off the stage. When he didn't have the votive attention of a captive audience, the rush of junk filled the void and provided for him what must have felt like artificial veneration. Before very long, it was evident that his ego had at least doubled in size and was quickly overtaking his sense of rationale and moderation. He'd do a line of coke right before he went out onstage and fix almost as soon as he walked off. He was shooting at least two or three times daily, without taking into consideration the speed and other assorted uppers, downers and around-the-benders that he was sending down his gullet throughout the day. In some ways, when taken to its foul extremes, fame itself is worse than the drugs; it is up and down, up and down, night after night. It is oscillation and confusion. To Bobby, it was constant disappointment.

As far as the cocaine is concerned, Bobby wasn't the only one indulging. You can only run on three or four hours of sleep a night for so long before you start feeling like you're dead on your feet. There were quite a few times that I went out on stage when all I wanted to do was sleep. Usually, I was able to power through anyway with the help of a little coffee and a little smoke, but there was this one night I was so worn out that I was off the beat for a whole song—and in my book, that is entirely unacceptable.

Bobby and I raided Space's stash that night, and in the back of a strange car on the way to some party out in West Hollywood, the two of us snorted what was probably a gram of cocaine. I was wired—I mean *way* wired—I felt like I'd just taken about twenty-five shots of espresso. I felt dizzy and jittery, the way watching Space clean a room made you feel. It wasn't a bad feeling, but it wasn't a slap in the face of euphoria either. Moreover, the party itself wasn't that great. Alcohol was the vice of choice at this particular bash, and by the time we got there, it was already winding down. I—on the other hand—was on sensory overload: colors, lights, music, voices, smells, and everything else sprocketed around the inside of my skull like a ricocheting bullet. It wasn't synesthesia—it was dissonance. After about a half hour, when I got over the initial rush and came down a little bit, it was better; I could actually focus my attention on one conversation at a time, comprehend what others were saying, listen to the music, and enjoy the sensation.

I learned quickly that with cocaine, once you go up and over, it kind of platforms; there's a wide grace period between feeling it and feeling it *too* much. Once you get to that point, that's all you really need—the rest is pure ambiance, and past that is a spiraling cacophony of paranoid palpitations and grinding teeth. If one thing is for sure;

however, there was no question of my wakefulness—the only way I could've slept that night was if somebody had whacked me up the side of my head with a Louisville Slugger.

If I remember correctly, there were only three of us at the party that night, and when it came time to leave, I remember looking outside for the Trips Mobile. Finding that it was absent from the scene, I freaked out, "Somebody stole the Trips Mobile! Somebody stole the fucking Trips Mobile!" I remember screaming.

Bobby came over to me, laughing, "Chill out, baby, the Trips Mobile is back at the Tropicana."

"What? Then how'd we get here?" I cried.

"Austin, don't you remember?" he said, pointing to a man sleeping on the couch who, along with everybody else in the room, was entirely comatose.

Flashes of that remembrance came back to me, and I felt awfully silly, as well as needlessly paranoid. "Well, then how are we going to get back?" I asked, casting doubtful glances around the room at the rest of those sleeping people.

"I hope you got your boots on," Space said, "cause it looks like we're hoofing it."

Usually we were lucky enough to bag a ride back to the Tropicana no matter the time of night, but we had to be in the studio in a few hours, so we did indeed hoof it—all the way from someplace in West Hollywood, down streets we barely knew, traveling in the general direction of Sunset Boulevard. Unfortunately though predictably, we took a couple of wrong turns and wandered aimlessly until we came to the intersection of Santa Monica Boulevard and some street Bobby recognized, at which point we knew we were going right. Before we left, we'd smoked ourselves up and psyched ourselves out, and we'd snorted the little bit of blow that remained. The cocaine had made us giddy like children at first, but by the time we hit Sunset, it was morning. The nine-to-fivers were already up and about, my feet felt ground into the pavement, and the high had dissipated along with my enthusiasm. I was tired again and now irritable on top of it—I either wanted to stop walking or more cocaine. But there was no more cocaine to be had, and by the time we finally got back to the Tropicana—our Trips Center substitute during most of the time we were in L.A.—it was past eight o'clock.

When we walked through the door, we found that Mary had already fired up the hot plate and was cooking eggs for everybody, and Al was flinging paint Jackson Pollock-style onto a canvas he'd fixed to the

434

ceiling. He'd covered the floor with a drop cloth, and Faye was laying spread-eagled upon it, catching the splatters of falling paint with her body. Billy was seated in a nearby armchair smoking a cigarette, drinking coffee, and watching humorously.

"Good morning!" he called.

Mary turned away from her eggs, "Hey guys, hey Rhiannon—Jesus your eyes are red! You look exhausted! Long night?"

I forced a nod.

Bobby followed me inside, "Anybody got any cocaine?" he asked.

I groaned and made a beeline for the bed.

I tried cocaine again a couple times after that, but I found the appeal to be generally lacking in several regards. I'd rather smoke a joint than snort a line, and I'd rather feel cozy, secure, and a little stoned than anxious and all amped up. I'd rather be deliriously tired than have all of my marbles scattered around the room, only to blow them apart again just as they started to come back together. Additionally, I really didn't like the way it did my body—cocaine has the tendency to bind you up in a most unpleasant way. After all, unless you're seriously hooked, you really only crave coke when it's in your system. Once it's out, you couldn't care less one way or the other whether you have it or not. The problem for those who find fancy in it is allowing enough time to pass for it to leave their system. I think I did it a couple times a day for a week. I'd always figured that if I spent enough of my life as a musician, I'd eventually become nocturnal, but at that point, between the daybreak encores, parties, and cocaine, I was afraid that I already had. Take Space, for example, the only way he could go to sleep at night with the exception of cutting off his speed intake sometime around sundown and suffering through eight hours of withdrawals was to pop a goof ball or two and wait twenty minutes.

Somewhere in the middle of that week was a thirty-six-hour period when I didn't sleep at all, and that's when I decided to drop it all together. I prefer a couple of desperate cat naps throughout the day to nervousness, hard comedowns, and sinus pressure. However, for my bandmates, the rush continued. Space and Bobby were the habitual users, but Mary also began using for herself once we got to L.A. The three of them went to some happening down in Beverly Hills one night when Al and I stayed behind to catch Jimi Hendrix at Thee Experience, and Space returned packing an ounce of coke, a block of hash, and ten sheets of high-grade blotter acid. Nobody knew how he'd gotten it and he wouldn't tell, although in the following days we found that his state-of-the-art Fender guitar amp had mysteriously disappeared, and Bobby had one hell of a time trying to find the stash of heroin he'd squirreled away in the Trips Mobile.

Needless to say, with Monday soon approaching and no gigs scheduled, they went on what we in the nineties called a bender. I don't think they did anything but cocaine for three days, and man, were they hyped up! Not one of them could sit still for anything, and they laughed like there was no tomorrow. It was positively contagious; either Billy, Al, Faye, or I would usually get them started, and once one of them got going, the rest would soon follow, and before long, the whole group of us would be immobilized wherever we were for about twenty minutes. We could hardly help it; the four of us had been testing out that hash he'd scored, and it was some of the strongest shit I'd ever smoked in my life.

I didn't so much mind them getting high, just as long as I was off the stuff. After all, I'd much rather see Bobby alert and pumped up— even bordering on overbearing—than to see him slouched down in some corner getting his nod on. The only problem was *everything* became a competition—who could do more faster. It became nauseating to watch after a while, and there was no sense in trying to talk them down. Although, in the end, they were productive; they could set up all of our equipment and have it plugged in and everything in about fifteen minutes. In the studio, the three of them were on their own wavelength, and admittedly, what they were coming up with was pretty good, though fractured. They weren't easy to work with in that condition, that was for sure, and the rest of us were tempted to take some ourselves just to be able to keep up. Jerry Greco—analytical and compartmentalized as he was—was just about at the end of his rope, and Bobby was as quarrelsome as ever. There was one day Jerry got so fed up with us that he kicked us out of the studio about a half hour after we got there and told us to come back the next day—without the cocaine. I don't blame the guy; as much of a royal pain in the ass as he was, it was fair to say that we hadn't recorded anything of much value since the whole cocaine bender started.

After that, the three of them seemed to realize the seriousness of it all and took it easy for a few days. Bobby returned to the heroin as usual, and Space and Mary cut back. In addition to hoping to ease Jerry Greco's growing frustrations by doing so, the talent booker for a new club had approached Space and scheduled three nights of shows for us. When he told us where, I was even more excited than I had been when I first found out that we were coming to L.A. Believe it or not,

436

we were going to be playing as headliners at the venue of my dreams: the Whisky a Go Go!

Initially, I could hardly believe it. Could it really be true that the experience I'd always considered to be the first major stop on the best possible course for my life was finally within my grasp? Could it really be true that I'd play at the Whisky a Go Go—the *real* Whisky a Go Go—before it was remodeled and its history became just that? Could it really be true that I would perform on the very same stage as The Doors, Love, and Frank Zappa? Could it really be true that the experience I'd spent countless hours dreaming of was about to unfold before my eyes? The determinable answer was an overwhelming *YES*! There was nothing standing in the way of my dream this time: no overprotective mother, no deficient fan base, no lack of funds—I was ecstatic.

Our first gig at the Whisky was on a Friday night. We rolled up after dark in the Trips Mobile with all of our equipment crammed in the back and Al at the wheel. Given our lack of space, Mary and Bobby were on their way separately. Driving down Sunset Strip at night was like being in the midst of an exploding carnival—in L.A, even the churches had neon lights. Even with a good deal of hash in my system to mellow me out, I was still boiling over with excitement.

The Whisky was a big red building on the corner of Clark and Sunset with quaint little striped awnings over all the windows and a huge marquee just to the right of the door that declared: *The San Francisco Day Trippers—Tonight, Tomorrow, Sunday!* I just about screamed when I saw that. All I could think was, *The Whisky—we've made it!*

We arrived there about an hour before we were scheduled to go on, which meant that we got to catch the end of our openers' set before we had to go out there ourselves and set up. We came in through the back as usual, and I surveyed the scene. So much of what I saw resonated with me and echoed what I had daydreamed about so many thousands of times before. From the stage, I could see that much of the scene was cloaked by a smoky haze that all but totally obscured the second-floor balcony as the foggy mass drifted up toward the spotlights. The cloud caused the spotlights to spread out and thicken so that the lighting in the place resembled that of a sunrise through the fog on an early San Francisco morning. Many tables dotted the floor, and booths lined the walls around the perimeter. Up on the balcony, a glass booth boasted two beautiful and heavily made-up dancers in go-go boots and matching skimpy attire, and the smoke from below swirled around their enclosure as they grooved and swayed to the music. The wide bar in the center of the room served a continual line of thirsty customers, and I could see several familiar faces in the crowd—fans of ours who'd taken to following us around L.A. One girl whom I'd rapped with at Thee Experience noticed me and waved. My heart swelled with emotion to witness these things; the greatest, and in some ways, the most plausible of my dreams was finally coming true.

Our openers' set ended around eight-thirty, and Mary and Bobby arrived shortly after. When they did, they were noticeably gassed— more interested in grooving on the building's aesthetics than gearing up for the show. According to Mary, they'd sampled the acid that Space had scored a few hours ago, and it hadn't quite worn off yet. The rest of us weren't exactly thrilled to hear that. Usually, we didn't care much at all about what the rest of our bandmates were dropping, smoking, or snorting just as long as it didn't get in the way of their own or anybody else's well-being, but now there was another consideration we had to take into account: the music.

Here's the thing about acid: when taken together by all of us at the same time, it either improved our performance dramatically by increasing our psychic awareness of one another, or it hindered us equally. Regardless of the effect, we always rose or fell collectively. When a few of us took it and the rest of us didn't, it was like trying to play music over the telephone—there was a sensory lag on our part and a miscommunication on theirs.

Now the fact that we weren't all peaking together wasn't necessarily a death sentence for the gig. The two of them were chummy and all smiles, rapt in a world of their own and totally harmless at that. After all, partial hallucinogenic dosing of a band has been known to add flavor and zest to their playing. However, according to Bobby—who, no matter how high he got, couldn't seem to lose that ego-trip of his— what we needed wasn't zest but structure. Of late, he'd decided that three sets a night of no-holds-barred jamming was no longer going to cut it and that from now on, we needed to make setlists and stick to them every show. And even while he was tripping, he still saw the need to enforce his logic, even though he was entirely incapable of following it.

The saving grace for us was that even when we were playing from opposite ends of consciousness, we were still tight enough and adaptable enough to sound good—at least most of the time. Throughout the night, Bobby and Mary were rapping off of one another, and the rest of us played behind them and filled in the cracks. For the most part, as long as it sounded decent, we let the two of them break it down and overrode only when it became too gnarly or experimental for the stage.

As per Bobby's setlist, we opened with *Born to Be Wild* followed by Dawn Train and Intuit, which lasted most of our first set. During Al's solo, they'd turned on this big, bright spotlight from the second floor, and Mary—who'd been dancing to the music—stopped dead and became fixated upon it. Billy dropped a few bass chords to add to the moment, and Mary, who stood at the very edge of the stage and looked out past the audience seeking visions of the whirring mechanical parts deep inside that spotlight, began to sing, "*Twinkle twinkle little star, how I wonder what you are…*"

Christ, was it fantastic! At that time, the audience approval of a psychedelically-inspired, on the spot rendition of a classic nursery rhyme was unparalleled, and they cheered like mad! For all of those heads right then and there, that was their freak—The Mary Jane Greene Trip—and man, did they dig it! All seven of us jumped on that train fast—to hell with the setlist! I added a few fills, and Space came in with a few riffs in C. I had hoped that Mary would ad-lib some additional lyrics, but she just repeated that same line a couple times when the tempo changed. From a bluesy ballad, the ending of Intuit turned into a heavy rock n' roll exposition, and we finished out that set at full throttle. That jam may very well have been the best damn version of *Twinkle Twinkle Little Star* ever played, and embarrassingly enough, it was probably our best tune of the night—at least by my standards. Even Bobby begrudgingly agreed that the whole *Twinkle Twinkle Little Star* jam had been pretty groovy. However, during our ten-minute backstage breather in-between sets when the audience could call in requests and all attention was turned to the dancers, he told us that he wanted to return to the setlist for the rest of our show.

When it was all said and done, *Twinkle Twinkle Little Star* remained the crowning moment of that performance. Besides that ten-minute improv, there was nothing the least bit new or interesting created at that show. Everything was played exactly as we rehearsed it, and as a whole, the show was overwhelmingly ordinary. It was the most mediocre, unfulfilling performance we'd yet to give. Okay, maybe that's a bit of an exaggeration, but compared to the starry-eyed expectations I'd built up for years, it was average as hell. The audience loved it, but I was displeased. What I'd always expected to be a final drumbeat followed by surging euphoria was actually a trickle of doubt.

439

We'd be back tomorrow with a chance to outperform, but that was inconsequential—my first taste of the Whisky had been overwhelmingly disappointing.

That striking feeling of realization made my stomach feel like it was sinking into oblivion, yet Bobby went on parading around like he had just played center stage at the Rose Bowl. After the show, while we were packing up, a bunch of girls crowded around the stage and Bobby was flirting with them, showing them his guitar, and playing each of them a couple of licks. As I was walking by, one of them pointed to his wah-wah pedal and asked what it was. In all of his hubristic glory, he replied, "The wah-wah pedal is like a gas pedal, and I handle it much like a woman—you have to treat it gently and respect its integrity. I got this one from Eric Clapton himself." The whole group of them swooned simultaneously. I felt sick and headed over to Al who was perched on the other side of the stage, watching.

"Can you believe that?" I asked him, pointing at his brother. "All that shit he's feeding to them? And they're eating it right up…"

Al looked as drained as I felt, "Truth is just a five letter word to him, and they're only an illusion…" he said somberly as he shook his head. "Sometimes I wonder if even we are real to him…" he paused, *"Fame is just the most delicious morsel of our self-love."*

I turned away from Bobby and faced Al, "That's Nietzsche," I replied.

Al nodded, "It's easy to love the whole world when you are the only one in it."

That sinking feeling in my stomach was making its way up the back of my throat.

"I need some air," I told him and slipped outside.

As I was sitting outside atop a tower of crates beside the back door—not literally fuming as one might suppose, but rather contemplative—I became aware of a shift in perception. This was not all it was cracked up to be, and playing the Whisky was just another gig. In an instant, all my childhood dreams of achievement and grandeur evaporated like fog over the land on a hot day. I felt terribly jaded. What more did I have to look forward to as a performer? What greater honor was there than to play at the Whisky, the place where my idols—rock's predecessors—not only played but started out? I never wanted to be famous, and although record deals, cash cow gigs, and magazine articles were nice, they all amounted to nothing if we weren't enjoying ourselves; if *I* wasn't enjoying *myself.* Now that we had all of those things, all I wanted was for it to be the way it had been back when fame was far off and we were all after the same thing: to make good music. It used to be that we would just jam and let the audience call out requests, but now in addition to compromising in the studio, disagreeing amongst one another, and all the drugs, even our pursuit of the groove had taken a backseat to setlists.

It was then that I truly put my finger on it. It was a togetherness that had been sacrificed, a unity of purpose that had been severed in the pursuit of commercial success. There was no question about it now, even in the world of counterculture psychedelic rock, fame was still a game in the third degree.

Now that I'd played the Whisky, I was perfectly content to play coffeehouses for the rest of my life—just as long as the experience was as real and pure and full of good vibes as it had been during those first few months in San Francisco. During my time in L.A, I'd gotten a glimpse of fame, and for what it's worth, I found it to be incredibly ugly. Underground San Francisco had won my heart, and I could give no love to the trend whores or the teenyboppers or the groupies of L.A. The intimate connection between the people and the music that could be found everywhere in San Francisco was almost absent in L.A. Maybe it had been there in earlier years when Pandora's Box, the Trip, and the London Fog were still hopping, or maybe it still was, maybe the people of Los Angeles were just harder to reach. Regardless, if enlightenment itself existed at all in L.A, it was hidden somewhere deep underground, and on the surface, imitation is all there was. Everything was meant to catch the eye and assuage you, but nothing had any kind of real depth to it—and it hasn't changed a bit. Most of everything is fake there; even the people slip into difference façades depending on the occasion.

I thought about *IT* and my ayahuasca experience at Woodstock and the Truth it had contained. That was the thing that was fundamentally lacking in L.A: Truth. *IT* was surely there somewhere, but where, no one—at least no one that I'd met—could tell. Rather, what flourished there was a playground of conjecture, a confused mass of misled people trying vainly to convey in many different forms the essence of Truth as they saw it, and many of them failed miserably. What emerged was senseless vanity, impunity, arrogance, and sloth—the pretexts of fame—an excuse to flaunt the human ego and glorify our imperfections. It was the cradle of ignorance, the antithesis of enlightenment, and the bane of Truth—all carefully hidden under a blanket of neon and a thorough dusting of cocaine.

And there is another thing that I'd recently learned, much to my

441

own discredit. Acid is everything that is, except it isn't. It allows you to see for a time into a very real, utopian world that exists right beneath our feet and can be seen most clearly through the dusty lens of prehistory, a time when we lived in harmony with nature and each other and existed as *one*. It shows you what is really real in this world of illusion and debases all else. However, the reality in which we are forced to live does not operate on those principles. As a result of society, the System, Big Brother, the human condition, original sin, or whatever it is you may call it, our existence is far closer to dystopia than utopia, and this sad fact makes the day to day life of the frequent user of psychedelic drugs very painful because we know something that most of the world is ignorant of. We've gotten a glimpse of *IT* and can see how this world needs to change, but the most realistic among us know that it never will. True utopia cannot be achieved until all the world has known *IT*.

By the time I'd gathered myself and my revelations and made it back inside, the Whisky had emptied out completely. Most of the lights were off except for the ones above the stage, and a few busboys were hustling around, sweeping the floors, polishing tables, and dumping empty beer and liquor bottles into the trash.

"Are you with the band?" one of these men asked me.

"Yes," I replied, although by looking around I could see that everybody else had left already.

"Clear out already, would ya? We wanna get out of here too you know. These lights are going off in five minutes; if you're not outta here by then, you're gonna have to find your way in the dark."

"Alright, alright," I replied.

This is nothing like S.F, I thought to myself as I headed toward the front door, *The Fillmore West would stay open until four in the morning, sometimes later if the music was groovy enough.*

I peered over at the clock that hung on the rear wall. It was already past four. I was shocked; our set had ended at two…had I really been out there for two whole hours?

As I pondered this, flabbergasted, to my great surprise, I saw Al coming toward me from around the other side of the stage.

"Rhiannon."

"Hey Al," I greeted him. "I didn't know you were still here. Where is everybody?"

"They left to go to some party or another, to—in Bobby's words—*'continue the high of the evening.'"*

442

I knew as well as he did that for Bobby that meant speed-balling till dawn, then taking a final dose of either coke or heroin at daybreak which would effectively set the course of his mood, emotions, and productivity for the rest of the day. Neither was particularly desirable, and the drug he took depended entirely upon which end of the manic-depressive seesaw he was riding at the moment. I liked him far more when he was off the stuff. In fact, the point at which I had experienced Bobby at his most approachable, at his most empathetic, at his most human, was when he had been smoking opium alone. But those days were far gone, and he was slipping further and further into the clutches of refined narcotics, engineered for maximum destruction.

"Thank you for waiting," I told Al.

"Of course," he replied, "I want to go back to the motel anyway and get a few hours of rest, Jerry Greco wants us in the studio in the morning."

We called a cab from inside and hung around in front of the darkened Whisky a Go Go until it showed up. Al was quiet, and so was I. The sky was cloudless, but the stars were impossible to make out. Instead, airport traffic took their place, masquerading as heavenly beauty as they stayed their course over the city, flashing red and green.

That night was the first time since I'd arrived in 1969 that I was aware of the time passing, and it felt like it was passing me by. More and more it felt like the time was there and that it was ample, but that it was being wasted. I felt like we had the opportunity to be doing so many more meaningful things than we were, like all this hanging around—always waiting on somebody or something, perpetually aware of the tick of the clock and always afraid of someone not showing up on time or not being on time for our next appointment.

When we got back to the Tropicana, we were the only ones there; everyone else had found alternative lodging for the night. I had a killer headache. My forehead was pounding, and I could barely open my eyes. Al suggested that I take some aspirin, but I was wary. I knew that Bobby and Space hid their speed inside bottles of legal pharmaceuticals, and the last thing I wanted at that moment was to fuck up and take the wrong pill. Instead, I took a few hits off the hash pipe that was lying about and promptly split the scene.

The dream world I arrived in was hardly more pleasant, and though I do not remember what they were about, I was fully aware of the strangeness and confusion of my dreams when I awoke the next morning. However, to my relief, my headache was gone. Al was up already examining a canvas, and he'd brought back breakfast from the concierge downstairs.

I sat up in bed, "Do you really feel like going down to the studio today?" I asked him.

Al looked up from his painting and shook his head.

As of late, we'd been having a hard time reconnecting as a group in the studio. Our daily separation and disparity of interest were beginning to manifest in our music. Even on the days when all of us showed up, the odds were that mentally, at least one of us—usually Bobby—would be someplace else entirely. But it wasn't just Bobby either, most times it was a spectrum of ails that kept our recording sessions from running smoothly: who was tired, who was late, who couldn't get it together, who was still zonked from the night before— and sometimes on that now rare occasion when we were all in sync and working together, Jerry Greco would come in and find fault with something and put the hold on our flow, and that inspired moment would slip away in silence. Getting everybody to be mentally, physically, and emotionally present in the studio was by far the biggest challenge, but even after we got past that obstacle, there were more hassles awaiting us.

As we might have expected, the first real challenge in production that we encountered in the studio was regarding song length. When we were gigging, we never played any songs that were less than ten minutes long. Additionally, since we'd been out on the road with no place to rehearse, most of the new material that we wanted to showcase still required a lot of work—at the very least in shortening those numbers to a duration that would even be remotely considered for an album. Several of our songs—with the exception of Dawn Train and Riding My Thumb—had no unanimously agreed upon ending. They were—as we called them—open-ended, while Jerry Greco said they were 'unfinished' and 'lacking structure.'

Moreover, we wanted to record two long numbers—one on each side—in order to really convey the way we sounded when we played live, but Jerry Greco insisted we settle on one. Even I opposed him on that ruling. As Al had told him from the beginning, we weren't really looking for something commercial; rather, we wanted to present ourselves to wider audiences as we really were—we didn't want there to be a gaping contrast between the way we sounded in the studio and the way we sounded live. Bobby, on the other hand, would do just about anything for commercial success—just as long as he wasn't the one whose creativity was being compromised. Therefore, ironically,

444

on many of the most pressing issues, he and Jerry Greco were in agreement.

Another point of contention revolved around the covers we wanted to record. Initially, the seven of us had decided that we wanted to include three, but Jerry Greco docked it to two. For the sake of avoiding an argument, we decided to settle, but then it was choosing the songs that became a problem. Our unequivocal best at the time were *Sunshine of Your Love* and *Something's Coming On*—our Woodstock patronage that we played at almost every show. Additionally, we wanted to include our rendition of *Wooden Ships* which we'd been working on for quite a while and had since become our most requested cover. When forced to choose, most of us wanted *Something's Coming On* and *Wooden Ships*, but Bobby insisted we swap one with *Born To Be Wild*, the Steppenwolf song that contained his nickname. It wasn't our best cover for sure—it wasn't even his best—and we rarely, if ever, played it live, but as always he was obstinate, and in time, his decision prevailed. Mary wanted to be cheeky and have *Day Tripper* be our first song. I thought it was clever, but unless we really worked with it, a line by line cover in no way exhibited our musical abilities. That early Beatles stuff really is bland, after all.

As the weeks passed, our studio dates ticked down, and our $10,000 advance began to dwindle. We were fast approaching crunch time. Our initial contract hadn't anticipated it taking us this long to record. Our hopes that our first album would be a magnificent standing testament to our abilities were starting to become compromised. The milk and honey of our dreams was beginning to sour and curdle. In the studio, we began to hear a lot of technical talk about subtle changes: what to cut out and where to alter. I felt like our group creativity—at one time spontaneous and magical—was being dissected. In some ways it was being improved, no doubt, but in others, it was being sacrificed. I knew that all of this was part of the process of cutting a record, but to me, it was incredibly boring—especially on the days when we spent more time in the studio deliberating than we did actually playing.

Jerry Greco was becoming more and more stifling. The catch was, Jerry was extremely good at his job—he was too good, actually. As far as coming up with a finished product after Stryker had finished manipulating the recordings is concerned, he was first-rate, and he could pen lyrics where Al left off, which made use of a lot of instrumental improvisation that we had left languishing in a corner for lack of words. By himself he wasn't impossible to reason with, it just took time and convincing. However, with Bobby thrown into the mix, any progression became tedious and exhausting. Despite Jerry's impenetrable cask of self-absorption, the only real problem was that Bobby didn't like him. I wasn't overly keen or running out the door to see him every morning, but he did his job and made ours a hell of a lot easier, and if that isn't the definition of an effective producer, than I don't know what is.

There was no way to anticipate what each day's studio time would bring, and both unintrigued and wary, Al and I took our grand old time getting moving that morning. We were only just leaving the hotel at noon, but even still, it was extremely likely that we'd be the first ones there. We spoke sparingly as we trekked the two miles down to Sunset Sound, and I clearly remember the things that he told me.

"Al, what do you think about fame?" I asked him.

Al put his hands into his coat pockets and exhaled a heavy breath, "Well, I think it's a lot of responsibility."

"Why is that?"

"There's a lot of people watching you."

"So it's an image thing?" I asked him in surprise.

"No, not exactly, but it is up to us to share what we know with the rest of the world, not to be arrogant and materialistic, but to be humble and didactic."

"And if we're not?"

"Then what's the point of being famous if you're not bringing something good to the world? This world doesn't need any more drama, any more games. What this world needs is healing. Even in entertainment, this world needs teaching," he replied.

"Even now with the way things are going, there's still a lot of riffraff in the public's eye," I agreed.

"All the greats are great because we made them that. Fame is pure democracy. That which the people want to see, they make famous, and they hang on your every word. They talk like you, dress like you, and idolize you. The strength of the Movement is most effectively gauged through publicity, but fame is a double-edged sword. It's not something I desire, but if through the course of my life it becomes inevitable through good circumstances, I might as well make the best of it."

I thought about Bobby, "Those the gods wish to destroy, they first make famous," I spoke.

When we walked into the studio, to our great surprise, we found that we were the last to arrive. However, everything was in a terrible state of disarray. Usually, no matter how bad the day there'd be somebody tuning up or practicing, but when we arrived, there was no music playing at all. Bobby was slouched down in one of the armchairs, comatose. Of late, he'd started taking drugs in the studio, in addition to every other time of day. Space was sitting on the floor in the center of the performance area disassembling some major piece of equipment with fervor. Billy, whose sleep deprivation and hashish intake were beginning to catch up with him, was more paranoid than I'd ever seen him before. He was barricading the doors to the echo chamber and isolation booths with guitar cases and unplugging all the mics. He had on a pair of noise-canceling headphones which he at once took off and flung across the room, his eyes wild, "Shhh! Shhh!" he insisted. "Lay low, lay low! I hear the pigs talking in my headphones, man! They hear everything we say! This whole room must be bugged! Big Brother is everywhere!"

Faye sat listlessly in another one of the armchairs smoking a cigarette and refusing to play. A tambourine lay motionless on the table beside her. After all, you can't have music without the muse.

"Is he high?" I asked her, pointing at Billy.

Faye turned to me and shook her head, there was sadness pooling in her big blue eyes.

Billy continued on with his rant, which was directed toward no one in particular, "...microwave ovens are killing us with radiation! There's poison in the tap and in the ice you buy in stores—peanut butter too!"

In the corner, I could see the very top of Stryker's head above the console. He had headphones on as well, probably in an attempt to drown out the sounds of the nuthouse that had erupted in the midst of the studio. In the other corner, Mary Jane and Jerry Greco were engaged in an escalating argument. Al and I looked at one another in disbelief. This was getting way out of control.

Together, we went over to Mary and Jerry to see if we could help them to chill out, but it seemed that our sudden appearance only further compounded the issue.

Mary's voice was shrill and taut, I had never seen her so angry before, "Al! Rhiannon! Thank God you're here! You're not going to believe this! Tell them, Jerry, tell them what you just told me!"

Jerry sighed and rolled his eyes, "The Day Trippers' contract with Reprise Records and Sunset Sound Recording Studios has within it a minimum commitment clause. Because of the limited time in your contract with me as your producer, you are required to deliver ten commercially acceptable tracks at a releasable standard within two months of signing. That's two weeks from now, and the chart potential on your record is way low. What I was *attempting* to explain to Mary here is that we have two options to make that date. A—you all get your shit together and give me something worthwhile within those two weeks, or B—I will have to go ahead and put together the best possible product out of the recordings that I already have."

Mary shrieked, "I can't take it! Al, Rhiannon, what he's saying is that he's bound by his contract not to work with us, but to pervert our recordings into something that *he* thinks will sell! And he didn't tell you this part—we won't even have access to our own master tapes, the studio *owns* them! They own *our* material! And this is the real kicker, ain't this a slap in the face, listen! Once our sub-par, unsatisfactory record hits the shelves, we have to pay back our advances, recording costs, and this son of a bitch out of our royalties!"

Al and I shared a glance. "Well, Mary," he began, "you know we have to pay our dues, we—"

Mary cut him off, "Twelve percent," she said.

"What?" I asked.

"That's the percentage of royalties we get after it's all over. Twelve lousy percent! And you know what? —It's not about the money, I don't give a shit about the money—it's about the principle! How could you do this to honest musicians?! What kind of scam are you running here?! You didn't tell us any of this!"

It was right about then that Bobby woke up, and unlike Mary, he did care about the money. He was livid. As he fought his way out of his stupor, he pushed us aside and got right in Jerry Greco's face. Enraged, his voice shook, and profanities flew from his mouth like ballistic missiles; he just about bit Jerry's head right off. Everybody stopped what they were doing and gathered around.

As unprepared as he was for the force of Bobby's reaction, Jerry didn't back down in the slightest. As smug and pompous as ever, he just continued to beat on the same retort: "You signed the papers! You signed the papers—you all did!"

"Fuck the papers!" Bobby yelled back. "The content of our album is not yours to decide!"

"It is now, you signed the papers! A record contract is a legally binding agreement. Everything you're fighting me on is laid out in the contract, and you signed it! You did read it, didn't you, manager?"

448

For the briefest of moments, Bobby faltered. The rest of us looked at one another doubtfully.

"That contract is full of encrypted corporate jargon; any good lawyer could see right through you! You come and dangle a get-rich-quick scheme in front of the noses of green musicians like it's their big break and then ensnare them in all your fancy words and business games and rob them of their rights!"

Jerry Greco smirked, "So you admit that you're green?"

"I'll admit that we were unsuspecting of such a racket!"

"You're just upset because you all don't have the talent and ability you thought you did! You cracked under pressure! You can't make it big time!"

"You'd like that, wouldn't you? You'd like to see us flop so that you can make this album the way *you* want it!" Bobby accused him, and then, out of nowhere, he declared, "That's why we're taking a vacation. That's right, Monday morning we're leaving L.A. and going back home for a week. That means that you're on vacation too because until we get back, you won't touch a thing without our consent."

"I already have your consent, you signed the papers."

Now it was Bobby's turn to smirk, "I assure you, you won't, because if you do, I'll sue. I'll sue you, your mother, the company, the studio—hell, I'll sue him!" Bobby cried, pointing to Stryker who was still sitting behind the console.

"Bullshit!" Jerry Greco laughed. "An international corporation versus one dissatisfied customer? —And a long-haired, narcotics-using customer at that! Get real!"

Bobby became very serious for a moment and then unleashed this outrageous claim. How he invented this one, I'm not entirely sure. "Our father is the sole proprietor of Turnstile Mutual Investments," he spoke, shooting a glance at Al who was completely aghast. "It's a multi-million-dollar corporation. I'll take my chances. See you next week, Dick."

After that, it was all over; he just grabbed his guitar and walked right out. The rest of us weren't exactly going to stand there with our mouths gaping, so we all did the same. Nobody said a word until we were all in the Trips Mobile and probably about a half mile down Sunset Boulevard.

Billy was the first to speak, "Now what?" he asked.

Immediately, everybody started talking at once. My emotions were all jumbled up inside. I wanted to congratulate Bobby and tell him off all in the same breath. He definitely hadn't read those papers before he

signed them—presumptuous bastard—but then again, I hadn't either.
And that whole Turnstile Investments trip he'd laid for Jerry hadn't
exactly been kosher, but when it comes right down to it, what better
way is there to combat a con man other than to beat him at his own
game. Besides, a vacation! The word itself was blissful to speak.
Finally, he'd come to his senses, and for once, his arrogant,
confrontational temper proved to be useful.

But, *'now what?...'*

Billy's question was certainly evocative, and we decided to greet
this breath of fresh air with a mighty gasp. We may have all had our
own particular beef with Bobby, but rather than allowing our
aggravation to get the best of us and letting the insults fly, Al took us
down to the seaside. A romp around Venice Beach gave us all a chance
to cool off and get our heads, and a few hours later, we were unloading
our equipment at the Whisky, smoked up and calm. Agitation and
catharsis were distant regions in the mind.

The show that night was another average reproduction of the night
before, although, despite our adherence to the setlist and lack of
whimsical improvisation, it was still better than our first performance.
At least this time we all had a common bond between us again, even
if it was raging disappointment.

That night was one of the few times all seven of us went down to
Thee Experience together. We didn't all leave together afterward, but
the time we spent in one another's company was in many ways more
enjoyable than it had been in the preceding weeks. The pressure was
off for the time being, but it was bittersweet. The sting of the record
contract fiasco was still all too fresh.

Sunday, the next night, marked the last of our gigs at the Whisky.
As we were going over the setlist backstage about a half hour before
we went on, I pulled out all the stops and threw myself on the better
of Bobby's sympathies and what I hoped were some leftover feelings
for me.

"Let's scrap the setlist," I pleaded. "Let's just jam instead like we
used to, like old times. Please Bobby, just this once? I've wanted to
play here for almost as long as I've been a musician, so let's just play
tonight. Let's play for us, for the crowd—reel in the energies like we
used to…remember?"

To my surprise and delight, Bobby acquiesced, and we jammed the
night away—but it was all wrong. The audience was just as
unreachable as ever. Of course, there were dancers out on the floor

450

and those who were cheering, but there were also those people who didn't look entertained at all, not the slightest bit moved by our display—and we were jamming! These were our souls bared for them to see, and they were uninterested—I even saw one yawn! During our second set, I just wanted to jump up and grab the microphone and scream, "Don't you understand what we're doing up here?!"

—And then I had a thought, and it chilled me right through to my soul: *What if it was us*?

The show went on, as they always seemed to, but that thought stayed with me. I wanted to believe that it stayed with me because it was a horrifying notion, a terrible impossibility, but I knew—although I could hardly bear to admit—that it was true.

1969

*****

The next day was better. In fact, everything seemed to be better after we left L.A. We checked out of the Tropicana that morning and were on the road by mid-afternoon. The shock of the last few days could be felt clinging to the edges of our awareness, but more than anything, we were all happy to be going home. Living the way we had been was becoming taxing. A body can only withstand that sort of forced proximity for so long. Don't get me wrong, we all got along and loved one another dearly, but that much time spent as a group with expectations to be productive will drive anybody stir crazy after a while. The whole ride there we were talking about how excited we were to be getting back to San Francisco and splitting up for some much-needed alone time, but as soon as we arrived back at the Trips Center, that decisiveness faltered.

Now that we were back, the circumstances and the way we interacted with one another felt for once to be almost normal. Being crammed together in the Trips Mobile like that for the last two hours had actually proved to be therapeutic. Suddenly, everything was copasetic. We were laughing, joking—really getting on well together for the first time in months. Everybody was all there—present, in every sense of the word. We left all our gear in the van and spent the first few minutes getting reacquainted with the Trips Center which during our leave of absence had once again changed faces, and in no way for the better. To be honest, the place was in need of some real work. Nothing had ever gotten cleaned up from the first time we left, and by the second time we returned, it was really in shambles.

As we were reorienting ourselves, picking a few things up off the floor and relaxing, Jon from next door dropped in for a visit.

"Hey, hey, you're back! I thought I saw you come in!" he went around and hugged all of us in turn. "How was L.A? Totally rad?"

We nodded, there was no need to go into the whole nine yards with him now.

"Groovy, groovy," he replied. "Hey, well, there's a man on the phone line outside. He's asking for you, Space, and it sounds important."

"Thanks, man," Space said, and he headed out the door while Jon took a seat on one of the overturned couches.

452

"It's probably fucking Jerry Greco," Bobby said. "Space, if it's Jerry, tell him to fuck off, will you?"

Space turned back around in the doorway and grinned, "Don't worry, Bobby, that's just what I had in mind to tell him myself."

Not two minutes later, Space came back in and told us that the man on the line was in charge of booking performers for the 'Second Woodstock,' a truly free concert being held at the Altamont Speedway in early December. We had been chosen for a spot on the bill, and he asked us if we wanted to take the offer. We all jumped at the chance, literally.

Bobby leaped off the couch, "What did you tell him?" he demanded.

"I didn't tell him anything yet; I wanted to see what you all had to say first, he's still on the line," Space explained.

"Well go tell him yes, already! Jesus Christ, don't keep him waiting!" Bobby cried.

Space hurried back out the door to the payphone, and we all shared in jubilation.

"Jefferson Airplane is going to play at Altamont!" I cried. "And the Stones! We're going to play on the same bill as The Rolling Stones!"

Jon was just as pumped as we were, "Well, I guess I'll get to say I knew you when! Far out!"

Excitement doesn't quite encompass the feeling that was coursing through all of us. Bobby was truly elated. When Space came back in from outside, we were all drawn into a fantastic group hug, and that was all it took; suddenly we were all in it together again. For a moment, I felt a familiar flicker—could it be the muse, back again for round two?

"You should all go out and celebrate!" Jon declared.

"Yeah," Bobby replied. "Yeah, we should!"

"Let's go to The Matrix tonight," Mary suggested.

"Mingle a bit with some of the old crowd," Billy added with approval.

A chorus of agreement abounded, and my own voice was among them.

"Ah, good choice," Jon complimented us. "The New Riders of the Purple Sage are playing there tonight. Do you mind if I tag along?"

We shook our heads, and as soon as we emptied the Trips Mobile of those giant Marshall stacks and all the other assorted equipment, we were off in style.

1969

We got to The Matrix just after the sun had set. Daylight Savings Time had ended since the last time we'd been in the City, and along with the early onset of darkness, the chill of winter had arrived. The flower children who'd pranced about in flowing dresses and shirtless in cutoffs a few months ago were now bundled up under layers of coats and scarves and boots. Groovy pins and patches were now the new in-thing.

As we were walking in the door, some of the locals recognized us and waved. Two girls and a leather-clad man who was well-acquainted with Bobby and wielded a pocketful of cocaine beckoned us over to come and sit with them. We were rolling, they were rolling, and the music was, well, let's just say I wish we could've played like the New Riders when we were down in Texas.

Most of the conversation that night was on the subject of Altamont. Just about everybody on the music scene in San Francisco had already gotten wind of it. In addition to us and Jefferson Airplane, Santana, Crosby, Stills & Nash, and The Flying Burrito Brothers had also gotten the call. With the ever-burgeoning selection of hip musicians on the scene as of late, we were feeling mighty special to have been selected alongside such well-worn names. We all might have even let it go to our heads, just a little bit—such as when the two girls accompanying us started flirting with Space.

"Are you Space?" the dark-haired girl sitting next to him asked.

"The very same," he replied.

"I heard you can give me anything I want," her companion said.

"No matter the size," the other alleged suggestively.

"Look at those eyes…"

"I want him in my space."

They both giggled.

Space blushed the same color as his hair.

"You ain't kidding," Bobby replied, "ol' Space can get you just about anything."

"And he can do it without spending a cent," Mary bragged.

The dark-haired girl's eyes widened, "Is that true? Can you really?" She had her delicate little hand on the back of his neck.

Space sucked in an anxious breath, "Yup."

"Can you get me some grass?" the second girl asked. "My old man left me, and he took his stash with him."

Space nodded, "Sure, I can do that."

"I want some too!" the other girl insisted.

Across the table from me, Jon shrugged, "Hell, I never turn down

454

a guy who can score me real good shit, get me some too!"

"Why don't you just go pick up a pound and bring it back for us?" Bobby suggested. "Then we can split it between us—an ounce each—and Space, you can keep the extra. You can do that, can't you?"

"You betcha'," Space replied as he got up from the table and pushed in his chair, "I'll be back in a jiffy."

"I want to know what it's going to cost us," the dark-haired girl asked.

"Yeah, Space, what do we gotta do for you?"

"Well, my sources get me the best of the best, and their costs aren't cheap…" he replied.

"How much is it? We can afford it," the dark-haired girl said, reaching for her bag.

"Yeah, tell us!"

"Your price will be…" he thought about it for a moment, "…one kiss each. And none of that puckered-up closed-lip bullshit, I mean real kisses!"

The girls both giggled. The one seated beside him reached up from her chair and laid one on him. After her, the dark-haired girl stood up to give him a proper embrace, and he leaned her way back and kissed her for a full minute. The rest of us at the table laughed and cheered.

"Alright, I'm leaving now," Space told us after the commotion had died down. "Bye!"

The girls giggled again, "Bye-bye!" they called in unison.

"I want to see him bring back a kilo," Bobby's friend spoke up as Space was heading out. "Now that would really be something."

Space stopped and turned around. He was hesitant, "I-I guess I could," he stammered. "I mean, I know a few cats who are usually holding a hell of a lot more than that…"

Mary's eyes widened, "Do you really think you can do it?" she asked.

"Yeah…" Space replied. "Yeah, I don't see why not…I'll see you all later."

"Bye!" the girls called again.

Space left, and the night progressed on toward morning. As the joints continued to circulate and the glasses on the table numbered more and more, the stories began to flow. Al and I talked about Thee Experience to our four acquaintances who had never been, and Bobby told wild and lavish tales of the parties he'd attended in L.A.

Late in the night, during a break between New Riders sets, a local cover band whose name I forget started in with a Beatles tune, *Your*

Mother Should Know, the one with the line, '*Let's all get up and dance to a song that was a hit before your mother was born.*'

When Bobby heard that, he paused right in the middle of whatever he'd been saying and started rapping on it, "Man, that's where it's at, man! That's real, man! After Altamont, people will listen to my music forever, man. Once we get our record out there, man, kids thirty years from now will know my name!"

He was in all his glory: red-nosed, red-eyed, crass and hysterical. If left to run its full course, in about an hour or so he'd become at first irritating and then downright bothersome, but at the moment, he was harmless and thoroughly enjoying himself.

However, the annoyance for some began earlier than for others, and Al was usually the first to become cross with him. Typically, once Al stepped out for the evening, the rest of us would follow in suit shortly after, and it triggered the conclusion of our night. More often than not, this exodus began with Bobby pestering everybody about the condition of his or her high.

"Are you stoned? Are you really bombed? Or are you just coasting?" he would ask, as he did that night.

"It doesn't matter what I am. It's only how I feel that is of any consequence, and I feel just fine sober right now," Al replied.

The laughing faded out. Al's serious tone had a way of breaking up the hilarity around the table.

"Ah, don't let my brother bother you," he told his other friends, "he's a square. Now how about some coke?"

Al slipped away after that. I went to visit him outside at one point, but he'd gone back to the Trips Center. The rest of us hung around The Matrix until it closed, but even as daybreak neared, there was no sign of Space. After last call, we all went our separate ways—The Day Trippers back to the Trips Center, Jon back to the head shop, and our three acquaintances back to wherever they'd come from.

Now, it didn't really cross our minds that there might be something wrong when Space didn't come back to the club that night. We just figured that he'd finally bit off more than he could chew and couldn't deliver. Besides, picking up a kilo of grass on a Monday night in San Francisco can prove to be a challenge for a guy every once in a while, no matter how many connections he may have. It was either that, or he'd gotten caught up doing something else; it'd been known to happen. You'd go out to somebody else's pad to score, and it'd go something like this:

'*Hey, here's that grass you wanted, but, uh, we were going to go*

456

down to the Fillmore West and see what's happening over there. You wanna come with us?'

'Uh, yeah, sure, groovy! I really need to get this back, but I can come along for a few hours.'

Then, while you're there you start dancing, you get involved with somebody you like, you end up going home with them, and you don't come back to the Trips Center until about noon of the next day.

Some variation of that same series of events had happened more than once to all of us in some way, shape, or form, so we didn't think anything of it until we heard Jon and a bunch of hippies from up the street banging on our door the next morning so hard that it sounded like they were going to take the door right off its hinges—which induced a feeling of stark paranoia in and of itself. We yanked open the door still bleary-eyed and half asleep and saw them standing there with that morning's paper in their hands. The front page read: *San Francisco Rocker Arrested In Possession of Copious Quantities of Marijuana.*

From that point onward, the rest of that day was carried out under a haze of disbelief and the looming threat of reality. Fear, paranoia, uncertainty, and panic were never more real to me than they were that morning. Up until then, we'd all laid low. The Man was a constant concern, but in San Francisco, on the Haight, he was hardly a worry of ours. Now, that cocoon of security had ruptured. How could this have happened? What had he told them? How much had they known already, and which one of us was going to be next?

These questions and many like them swarmed relentlessly around my mind like hornets as we involved ourselves in a flood of activity. I felt absolutely terrible for Space. He would've never attempted to score so foolishly and haphazardly if Bobby's friend hadn't put him up to it—but then again, there was no telling what had happened.

Compounded by our rude awakening, confusion and dread pulsated throughout the Trips Center. Bad vibes were all around. News of Space's arrest had spread like wildfire both throughout the music community and the City alike. A reporter from the Oracle even came down to the Trips Center to get The Day Trippers' take on the situation, but Al sent him away. We might have hoped that our names would be in that day's paper, but in regard to our future appearance at Altamont, not a major drug scandal. The golden era of The Day Trippers and our newfound second wind had lasted a whopping twelve hours. We were crestfallen—not to mention scared. Luckily, the article had included

457

the address of the police station where he was being held in addition to his real name. It would've been pretty embarrassing to have gone down to the station not knowing our best friend's actual name, especially for Bobby and Mary and them who'd been living with him for over two years now. Like I've told you before, many of those traditional values that straights tended to keep failed to be of much value to heads. After all, Space was a much better-fitting name for him than Eric Cantor Jr.

We got to the station around noon after stripping ourselves of any incriminating drugs or paraphernalia in case of a pat down. Once we arrived, they made us wait half an hour before they let us in to see him. The hands on a clock had never turned so slowly before, and Bobby paced back and forth across the room the entire time, the cleats on his boots click-clacking on the tile floor, the sound mingling with the tapping of typewriter keys in the otherwise silent room. After a while, the strain of waiting and the tense atmosphere combined was simply maddening, and just when I wanted to stand up and shout to relieve the pressure in my skull, a member of the Heat—dressed in blue from head to toe—ushered us into a little room. They only allowed three of us to go in at once and for five minutes only. It ended up that Bobby, Mary and I were the ones who got to see him while Al waited outside with Faye. Billy had refused to even come down to the station with us.

"It's a trap, I'm warning you," he'd told us. "Don't say anything about knowing he was going to do it, don't say anything about putting him up to it, don't even mention grass. In fact, don't say anything at all. Just find out what his bail is and when we can get him back. Act as straight as you can, play dumb. I'll stay here and bury all our shit in the yard for when the fucking narcs come and raid this place once and for all!"

"Bury my dope and you'll have another thing coming to you when we get back," Bobby told him.

"You wanna get us all fucking thrown in the can? Fine. I'll hide it in the…in the…" he looked both ways then whispered the rest in Bobby's ear.

Bobby rolled his eyes and nodded, "Alright, fine."

While Billy took great pains to defend against the Fuzz on the home front, the rest of us were deep inside their lair. The room they took us into contained a desk at its center, which was divided down the middle by a great Plexiglas sheet. On the other side of the Plexiglas sat Space. He was still wearing the same clothes as he had been the

458

night before, except they'd taken his coat, his beads, his wallet, and his belt. He appeared small and frail under the fluorescent lights and the guard's cruel gaze. He was shaking slightly as if in one continuous shiver, and his eyes were darting all around the room. He looked like he was ready to climb up the wall.

"Space! Are you OK? They didn't hurt you, did they?" Mary asked, she was crying a little.

Space shook his head, "No," his voice was hollow and dry.

"What happened? Are they doing a sweep, or were they only after you?"

Space pointed to himself, "Only me…God, I can't believe they busted me! How could I be so stupid…"

"Yeah, man, we were just getting on the scene! Why'd you have to go and get us all that bad press for?" Bobby spat accusingly.

Space's eyes widened, and his voice rose, "Hey man, don't you lay that on me! I didn't mean for to get *arrested*, get put in the slammer! It wasn't up to me!"

"Bobby, Bobby, cool it!" Mary cried in an attempt to talk him down. "That's not what's important right now. What's important is getting Space out of here! Besides, press is press."

"Hey," Space asked us, his voice lowered in an anxious whisper, his eyes dancing in fear, "what did they say about getting me outta here?"

"Your bail hasn't been posted yet," I replied, repeating what the officer behind the desk had told us, "we don't know."

He put his hands up against the Plexiglas, "You've got to get me out of here," he entreated us.

"We're working on it, man, get a grip on yourself," Bobby replied.

Space's shaking intensified, "You know what's a tad harder to get in the slammer?" he asked us, leaning up real close to the glass. "Speed."

While we were talking, two cops entered on his side of the room and took him away to the adjacent courtroom for his bail hearing. His bail was set at $30,000. When I heard that, my jaw just about hit the floor and my heart began to race. Even if we sold everything we owned, we still couldn't come close to that much money. If only Reprise Records had paid us a greater advance—we were just a stone's throw away from flat broke as it was. Hell, we couldn't even hire him a good lawyer; he was at the mercy of the public defender. Forget about Bobby's phony Turnstile Investments suing everybody and their mother, poor Space was stuck in jail until his trial—which, for better or worse, was coming up in three weeks.

Two officers escorted us through the front door of the station and out onto the street. Nobody spoke; for once, all of us were at a loss for words. We were still reeling—the implications of this new development were still being processed. After we'd walked about two blocks and were out of direct view of the police station, Bobby started jumping up and down screaming, "Fuck! Fuck! Fuck! Fuck!" He even kicked a parked car, "FUCK!" he howled.

"Alright Bobby, chill out," Al said. "That's not going to help."

"We just lost half of our rhythm section! What do you mean, chill out! How can I?!"

"There's nothing we can do," Al responded morosely. "There's nothing we can do…"

"The hell there ain't!" Bobby snapped. "Space, that motherfucker! He would have never gotten popped if he hadn't been showing off for those broads! Fuck!" He marched off in the direction of the Trips Mobile, cursing Space all the way.

The rest of us stared at one another in shock; we couldn't believe our ears. All of us wanted to confront him, but none of us thought it was worth the ramifications of trying to explain to him that *he* had been the one to pose that suggestion to Space in the first place. I'd never felt so incredibly helpless before in my life, and it only got worse from then on.

The days following Space's arrest passed painfully slow. Between looking over our shoulders every few minutes to check for narcs, the daily media pot-shots, and Bobby's relentless vulgar lamentations, those first few days were by far the most excruciating. Adjusting to daily life without having Space around was no better. We were in terrible need of his levity and humor, and his sudden remand left us missing his companionship something awful.

In addition, none of us had the skill or the connections to the underground trade the way Space did, which meant that we needed to spend far more dough than usual on things we were previously unaware we even needed. None of us ever really thought about the cost of gas, food, and most of all, drugs—those were all things Space usually acquired for us through crafty bartering, and without him, expenses really started to add up. To make matters worse, we didn't play even one gig that first week without him, which by itself was a serious drop in income. For the first time ever, I regretted having a profession that relied so heavily on emotional and mental focus. We were all so bummed out that it took a few days before any of us picked up our instruments at all, and when we did, the only music we played was melancholy—although that's not to say halfhearted. Some of the best musical numbers ever written came flowing out of the wake of broken hearts and distraught minds; however, we were all so scattered emotionally that hardly anything we played together sounded good at all. It required a lot of discipline and focus that not all of us were willing to put forward in order to make it through a gig. It was the first time in my life that being a working musician actually felt like work, and I'll tell you right now that I didn't like it, not one bit. Some vacation this turned out to be.

In fact, we got a call from Sunset Sound a few days after the news of Space's arrest began to spread. To our surprise, it was Stryker that called, and it was Mary who answered the phone. He told her that due to the bad press and the impending trial, Jerry was in no position to go ahead with the final reworking and release of any material, and therefore was actually halting the recording process until the trial was complete and the media criticisms had blown over. Bobby, as usual, took this to mean the worst possible thing—that our chance at stardom was gone and our record would never be released—that we blew it, essentially. No matter how often the rest of us tried to convince him otherwise, he truly believed it and, it seemed, was uninterested in searching for the silver lining, which the rest of us saw as much-needed extra time.

There was this terrible feeling of desperation that cloaked the Trips Center during that interim period between Space's arrest and his sentencing, and no matter where we went, it seemed to follow us. With the exception of Bobby, who seemed inexplicably resolved to continue on along his downward spiral, the rest of us tried as hard and as often as possible to remain positive. Although, with all the confusion and uncertainty around, even to keep on keeping on became a challenge. As much as we all felt bad for Space, in the back—and sometimes the front—of our minds, we were all very much afraid of a similar fate. Al was the only one of us who seemed consistently able to keep a good head about him. Mary Jane was maudlin, Billy was in rare form, and Bobby was downright insufferable.

He was born equipped for fame, but not for its perils. Bobby was a histrionic nightmare—erratic, unpredictable, and dreadful. We had our own small-scale Jim Morrison on our hands. After all, this was the summer when stories like the Miami incident were all over the news, and more and more fans seemed to be intrigued by dramatic and

461

scandalous performances. After Space got thrown in the clink, Bobby started showing up late or high to gigs and playing really poorly. Twice, he went on the nod right as we were supposed to go onstage and perform. That was bad, but when he was manic, he was arguably even worse. He was a terrible taskmaster, completely illogical, and even delusional at times. It was hard to tell to what degree it was drug-induced and how much of it was the result of his ever-loosening grip on sanity. He'd swing from one personality to another so quickly and extremely that it became almost impossible to communicate with him, even on the most mundane topics.

I remember going out to the mailbox one time and coming back with a handful of envelopes all with the word *'OVERDUE'* stamped in big, red letters across the front. I took them to Al, and he looked grave.

"I never remember seeing bills at the Trips Center," I said.

"We used to give Melinda a cut of our pay, and she always used to take care of them for us. Our utility bills are all three months overdue," he told me regretfully. "Our electric bill alone is $189. I don't even think we have that much. Everything we make goes toward food, and Bobby buys more dope with every dollar he can get his hands on."

From across the kitchen, Bobby, having heard his name, raised his head from where he was shuffling around in a drawer, looking for his works, "Eh?" he grunted dazedly.

"Bobby, you gotta clean up," Al pleaded. "If we don't start to go right soon, we are going to go very wrong."

With no warning at all, Bobby exploded and threw his works on the floor, "Fuck you, Al! I'm the manager of The Day Trippers, you listen to what *I* say! I've been talking to Steve Winwood you know, and if he wants in, you're out! I know what you want, Al, you wish I was in the car too! That's what you wish! You want what I have, and I can tell you right now that you're not going to get it!"

"Bobby, you're completely entrenched in fallacy! You don't even know what's genuine anymore, you believe your own fabrications! Put the needle down for just a second and look around you!" Al implored him. "The rest of us aren't living in your chimera world!"

In a millisecond, his temperament changed again, this time from rage to contempt, "Al, can you please for once in your fucking life say something normal—something real people can actually understand?" he retorted before storming past us out the front door.

Taken aback, we followed him to the window and watched as he lit up a cigarette and marched into the phone booth, leaving the door wide open behind him.

"He's crazy," I murmured.

"Worse," Al replied, "he's so crazy he can actually make you believe that you're the one who's insane."

We were both silent as we watched Bobby gesturing madly inside the phone booth as he chewed out some poor bastard on the other end of the line.

"There is no reason why every individual cannot be enlightened," Al said as we watched him, "no reason he cannot be aware; no reason he cannot be happy in all the ways that we in today's society define the word. We all have the power within us to pursue enlightenment: to learn about ourselves, to love one another, and to be at peace with our existence. But we have been so conditioned by our society that many of us believe that happiness only can and only should follow individual success gauged by such frivolous concepts such as rank, position, and power. My brother is a slave to that system. Bobby is never satisfied, he's never happy."

Bobby was yelling now, and we could hear him from inside. "Couldn't get it?!" he cried, incensed. "Whaddya mean you couldn't get it?! That's horse shit! You can't swing a dead cat around here without hitting somebody who sells smack!" He then let out a series of profanities that made me cringe and made those on the street who'd been passing by without a glance before turn and look toward him. He slammed the phone back into the cradle and glared menacingly at those who were staring in his direction. His shoulders were hunched up around his ears, and his jaw was set. He stalked back across the sidewalk without a word, but his angry eyes swiveled from side to side like an injured animal threatening all other creatures not to come too close.

"What's wrong with him?" I whispered to Al as Bobby reentered the Trips Center and made a beeline toward the stairs without even a passing glance in our direction.

"He's sick," Al replied, his voice heavy. "If something is not done in excess, there will never be a need to give it up. In keeping moderation, you maintain control over your desires. The problem with human nature is that when we come across something we like, we just can't let it be. Instead, we feel the need to recreate it and try vainly to experience that same feeling over and over again. We are addicted to the rush and moreover to reliving it, as often and as intensely as possible. In the process, our sense of reason deteriorates. We become the sole masters of our own destiny, and in that station, no matter the circumstance, we find the potential for power. In time, power never fails to destroy—either the man himself or the things he rules and oftentimes both together."

"How did he get to be this way?" I asked. "I mean…what makes a man become like this?"

"For Bobby, being dropped out into society at seventeen took its toll mentally. He may very well think that it hasn't affected him, but it has. When you lose your structure like that, everything in the world lays down upon you at once. You are spinning free in entropy, and it is so much of everything that it becomes nothing, meaningless. For Bobby, it has been a typical case of anomic self-destruction."

"You're not like him though, why is that?"

"The circumstances that cause one man to die will cause another man to thrive; it all depends on the condition of the man."

"Are you saying that Bobby is weak?"

"I am saying that he is a victim of his own desires. As a wise man once wrote, '*Neither the world's broadest oceans nor its highest mountains can serve as a defense against those drugs which enslave the human brain, enervate the mind, and force the body to follow vices which are fatal to its very existence.*'"

"Some burn like a match burns," I spoke as he alighted the stairs.

A BRIEF AND BEAUTIFUL TRIP BACK

****

Three excruciating weeks after Space's arrest, Monday, November the 10th marked the day of his trial. It was a pretty big deal on the Haight; just about everybody knew Space one way or another, and the courtroom was packed from wall to wall. Additionally, because of our recent spike in publicity both before and after Space's fall from grace, there was all sorts of news media there as well—a couple different newspapers, at least one radio station, and one cameraman from the local television channel. As for the rest of us Day Trippers, we were holding our breaths. It wasn't a question of whether or not he was going to get off—there wasn't even a chance of that happening. He'd been caught red-handed, and the evidence stacked against him was overwhelming. For his sake, what we all wanted to know was the severity of his punishment. Somber, pensive, and clad in the nicest clothes we owned in fear of being thrown out of the courtroom otherwise, we arrived at the Hall of Justice on 7th Street early that morning.

The courtroom was abuzz in the moments before Space and the judge entered. From the time we got there, all eyes were on us. It was an awful sensation that made my skin crawl—everywhere I looked there was somebody staring. We'd made sure that we were clean before we left the Trips Center—even the van had been wiped down—but in spite of my better knowing, I still felt the need to check my pockets every few minutes. After about a dozen glances at the clock, I decided to quit looking—either the batteries needed to be changed, or only thirty seconds had passed. I just couldn't wait to leave that place and return to the Trips Center, and the more I thought about it, the more I couldn't bear the fact that Space wouldn't be coming with us.

Once the endless wait was over and two armed, blue men walked Space out to the bench, I immediately wished that I'd stayed home. He was dressed in a prison-issue jumpsuit and hardly recognizable—they'd shaved his head. When he got up on the stand, it was even more apparent how terrible he looked. In just three weeks, his appearance had changed dramatically. He'd lost at least ten pounds, and without his familiar shock of red hair he looked pale and weak, with sallow cheeks and eyes full of pain. Between three weeks of cold turkey kicking and thousands of self-recriminations running through his skull

465

at every moment, his body had been at war with an all but invisible enemy—withdrawal—and I'm sure not once had he been offered the slightest bit of sympathy.

My heart was breaking as I listened to him up there on the stand—he'd entered into a plea bargain and cut a deal with the D.A. in which he plead guilty to possession but escaped the treacherous and looming trafficking charge. When I learned of this, I couldn't help but smile a bit to myself. Even trapped on his back between a rock and a hard place in the midst of a shit storm, Space still retained his savvy. After all, he'd never sold anything to anybody, and because he didn't have baggies or foil or cash on his person at the time of his arrest, he found himself at the mouth of a gaping inconsistency, and luckily for him, a loop hole.

However, luck and good karma can only get you so far when you're at odds with a system of corruption, and the judge still sentenced him to thirty years in state prison. It wasn't life, but it was pretty damn close. When that gavel came down, it wasn't Space alone who was met with a sentence—for me, it felt like all those hassles and troubles I'd been free from in my time there all came back on me at once. A heaviness now afflicted me. The immunity was gone, and the farce was up—looking at Space up there was chilling because it just as easily could have been any one of the rest of us. He just happened to draw the shortest straw. We all felt now that it was only a matter of time.

At the conclusion of the trial, we tried to get close to Space in order to speak to him just for a minute and edge in a few encouraging words, but they whisked him away before any of us got the chance. They marched him off toward the paddy wagon in chains, handcuffed like some dangerous criminal, and for the life of me, I couldn't understand why. He was guilty as charged, there was no doubt about that, but when considered from a strictly moral standpoint, without regard to the faulty code of a unjust Establishment selfishly serving its own ends, what had he done that was so wrong? Two pounds of heroin or speed is one thing, but two pounds of grass is something entirely different. Unless you fix it to the end of a stick and club somebody over the head with it, two pounds of grass can't kill you. He hadn't hurt, endangered, or killed anyone or even jeopardized his own well-being—he hadn't even been creating a nuisance. The only reason he'd been searched in the first place was because of his appearance. At that time, in the eyes of many cops, probable cause was merely skin deep. And now, Space, an honest, true, and peaceful man—a man with such a beautiful mind and beautiful soul—an ethical, moral man who took daily pains to avoid the societal games the rest of us are forced into playing, was marked as a felon. Space, for whom peace and freedom were everything would now be forced to live the better part of the rest of his life in state prison alongside rapists and murderers.

I'm not going to lie, I was angry—both at the Establishment and at us, in regard to the way in which we had been acting as of late—and moreover, I was disappointed. In light of the charges levied against him, Space did not deserve his fate—not in the slightest—and his case was poignantly representative of the thousands of injustices served up to hippies at that time, many of whom wanted nothing to do with the Establishment and were simply minding their own business, a bother to no one. I would never profess to say that heads and flower children were always victims of injustice—after all, true criminals can be found in any walk of life—we were just terminally misunderstood.

We walked out of the courtroom that day defeated and dejected, and we made our way to the Trips Mobile in a hurry, hoping to avoid the prying eyes and ears of the media. Billy was on fire the whole way home, "The System is nothing but blind control of the masses! They take away our rights under the guise of public safety, trade us peace and happiness for fear and dependency, and give us license under the false name of freedom! It's a crock of shit! Where does it end?!" He went on and on. Faye held him tightly as he shook with rage and looked up at his face with concern in her eyes, but he was inconsolable. We expected that he wouldn't be the only one. Bobby had been so mad at Space—blaming him for the bad press and for fucking up our stint of good luck—that he hadn't even gone to his sentencing. However, we figured that once we told him about how Space had been royally screwed by the System, Bobby would rally around him once more. Although, what we got when we returned to the Trips Center was something else entirely.

Outside, it was dark already. The fog had blown in, the winds were picking up, and everybody out on the streets was rushing to get home. Inside the Trips Center, it was dark as well; it looked as if nobody was home. All the lights were off both upstairs and down, and when we flipped the switch upon walking in the door, nothing happened.

"Must've blown a fuse somehow," Billy muttered, breaking his reproachful monologue for the first time in over half an hour.

He headed into the garage to check the fusebox while Mary searched for candles to light. As Al and I stood there, we began to hear low murmuring coming from elsewhere in the room along with the smell of cigarette smoke.

Al's eyes narrowed, "Something's not right," he murmered before calling aloud, "Bobby!? Bobby, are you here?"

Within the still darkness of the room, a shape emerged from amongst the rubble, but it didn't answer him.

"It's not a fuse," Billy said, coming back into the room with Mary quick behind and two flashlights in hand.

Al took one and shined it into the room, illuminating a hunched-over figure dressed in rags who squinted against the light, "Hey now, man, don't shine that in my eyes, will ya?" He had a cracked smile, yellow teeth, and a swollen abscess on one arm.

"Who the hell are you?" Billy demanded.

"Gary," he answered.

"What are you doing here?" Al asked.

The junkie Gary didn't answer, instead he pointed to another shape, this one nestled between a speaker and the shattered china cabinet. It was Bobby, and he was on the nod.

Al stiffened, and as he began to pick his way through the mess and make his way over to his brother, more bodies began to rouse out of their opioid slumber and blink, yawn, look around, and reach for the needle again. As Al looked from face to face around the room and realized the number of waking junkies in his midst, the expression on his face began to change, first from confusion to concern, and then to a look I'd never seen on him before, one I couldn't quite place until he opened his mouth.

"GET OUT!" he bellowed. "GET OUT OF THIS HOUSE! NOW!" He began flipping over coffee tables and chairs—it was the most out of control I'd ever seen him. I'd never even heard Al raise his voice before, and now, infuriated, he hollered at the itinerant junkies who, alarmed, gathered their junk and their works and ran out. There must have been half a dozen of them, but for Al, it wasn't enough. Flashlight in hand, he went from room to room chasing out all those freeloaders who'd made their home there in our absence and hollering at the top of his lungs—I could feel chills running down my back.

However, when he was finished, no one else remained. All our friends who at one point had been staying there had since moved on, and we were alone. As Al came back into the living room, still enraged, Bobby shuddered and slowly awoke. He blinked his eyes open and scanned the room. His emotion—if he even had one—was something like suspicion.

468

"Bobby, what the fuck is going on here?" Al implored him. "This morning I handed you money and asked if you would go down to the electric company and pay that bill while we were at court. You said yes, and now we come home to find our power shut off and you on the nod with six other junkies! You didn't pay that bill, did you? You used that money to buy more smack!"

"Aw c'mon Al, why are you getting all bent out of shape, man? It's no big deal, we have a gig tomorrow night, we'll get paid again. My dealer just came back into town with some real good shit—China white, you see, none of that black tar crap. I got it before he stepped on it, but I had to pay double—you understand…"

"Oh fuck," I heard Billy exclaim and watched as he threw his hands in the air and headed upstairs with Faye in tow, "he's fucking impossible…"

Al hung his head, "Bobby, that money was for us, here. Jesus, this place is a complete wreck! Don't you think electricity is a little more important than getting high? We can't even practice now because we have nowhere to plug in…"

"Hey, that was my money too, man, I've got a right to it!"

Al sighed and hung his head, "Space got thirty years…" he told him morosely, "we're not even thirty years old…"

Bobby was indifferent, "He was careless," was the only reply he offered.

Al shook his head, "Bobby, I'm leaving," he said.

My mouth dropped open in shock, and beside me, Mary's did as well. My heart sank as I realized the implications of what he was saying. It was something I hadn't expected in the least, but all the while its imminence should have been obvious. In all honesty, it was a miracle he'd hung around for as long as he had, and now the time had come for him to go forth and move on.

After hearing this, Bobby responded with unexpected force, "You can't leave!" he cried.

"Bobby, I told you, I warned you right from the very beginning that I was going to leave the band if this whole fame thing got out of control. I wanted to wait until the album was finished, but with you in this deplorable condition, I doubt that it ever will be."

"No you didn't!" Bobby shouted back. "You never warned me! You're lying!"

"Bobby, I'm telling the truth. Have you ever known me to lie to you? You just don't remember because you're always high all the time!"

469

"You're fucking over The Day Trippers by leaving! We were just hitting the big time, about to go up and over! You must want to see us fail!"

Al's eyes narrowed, "I'm fucking over The Day Trippers? Bobby, look at yourself! You're dirty and living in squalor! You'd rather stay here and shoot junk than go see your best friend one last time before he goes to jail! You'd rather shoot yourself full of that rotten shit than have electricity in your own home! And you're telling me that I'm the one fucking us over? Listen Bobby, Space is put away, he's not coming back. The guys from Sunset Sound called, they don't want us in there. Every club is wary about hiring us. You tell me if you think we're going up and over or down and out!"

"Oh so everything is my fault now, isn't it? You just blame me so you don't have to take the responsibility, so you can get off scot free and go paint your stupid little pictures out in the wilderness! You never could commit to anything. I never should have included you in my band!"

"Bobby, I'm leaving because I refuse to hang around here just to sit back and watch you kill yourself! I'm not going to enable you, you need to wake up! We're supposed to be fighting ignorance, not perpetuating it!"

"You don't care about me at all!" Bobby yelled at Al. "You probably came back just so you could pull the rug out from under me now! Go, good! We'll be even better without you, you'll see!"

Suddenly, Al reached out and touched Bobby's arm, all his anger changed at once to sorrow. "Bobby, please," he begged, there was emotion in his words, his voice was thick with it, "we don't want to see you like this anymore. Let us get you help. That's the only way you'll get me to stay."

Bobby wrenched his arm away like a furious child, "Fuck off, Al! Thanks for the memories!" He snorted sarcastically and then took off toward the stairs.

Al, Billy, Faye, Mary and I stayed awake most of the night, talking. Bobby had holed himself up in the attic and refused to see or talk to any of us, despite our repeated attempts throughout the evening to reach out to him. We sat up in the mandala room long into the wee hours of the morning, huddled around a transistor radio discussing Bobby and the future. What used to be lighthearted late-night philosophizing had turned into angst-filled discourse that made life seem terribly grim. I kept mostly to myself, listening closely but contributing very little to the conversation. The things they talked about were very hard to hear, but I stayed because I knew that it was the last chance we would all get to be together for a long time.

The next morning after everybody else had headed off to sleep, I went into the yoga room and brushed the cobwebs off the Buddha statue in the corner. I did a few sun salutations as the new day broke over the horizon, but it was very hard for me to concentrate; I had Al on my mind. While I had my legs crossed in lotus, trying to clear my thoughts, I heard the muffled creaking of footsteps down the stairs and the sound of the front door opening and closing. I knew that it was Al, leaving.

I abandoned my meditation and went to see him off. Before I followed him outside, I went into the garage and dug through my glovebox until I found the two photos of us at Woodstock. One I left in its place, and the other I took with me to give to him.

I met him out by the corner on the other side of the road where he stood holding out his thumb and watching the cars roll by in silence. He had a rucksack on his back and a few choice paintings beside him. The sun was nearly up, but the streets were still and quiet. The cars passed slowly, and one lonely songbird in the large tree above us offered up its early morning melody. Al saw me approach, but he didn't greet me. I didn't say a word for quite a while either. I just stood there with him, watching the wheels.

"Where are you going to go?" I asked him finally.

"I'm going to look for that little girl running through the field," he replied.

We were silent again for a spell. I handed him the photo. He looked at it, and a small, fleeting smile crept onto his somber face. He thanked me.

"Al, I miss playing music," I said, "and the way things used to be."

Al nodded, "So do I. It's funny how we only desire the things we cannot have and only miss the things we took for granted."

A car pulled up alongside the shoulder and stopped in front of us. He pulled me into a hug.

"I love you, Al," I told him. He knew how I meant it.

"I love you too, Rhiannon. In the future, somewhere, someday, we will see one another again."

All I could do was nod. I wanted to say more, but I was getting all choked up. For one insane moment I seriously considered getting in the car with him, but I refrained. Instead, I waved as he pulled away and continued to do so even after he was long gone. It was then that it dawned on me, something I should have known all along, but was too close to see: the real Übermensch was the other brother.

Once the daytime bustle hit the streets, I returned inside. To my surprise, Bobby was standing by the window.

"Al left?" he asked me.

I nodded, wary of what his reaction might be.

"He's never satisfied," Bobby replied as he shook his head in dismay and walked off.

****

A BRIEF AND BEAUTIFUL TRIP BACK

****

A few days after Al's sudden departure, things on the music scene began picking back up again. Our bad press didn't seem to have made any kind of terrible, lasting impression. The heat following Space's arrest had dissipated and been replaced by other equally scandalous news. Now the reaction we seemed to evoke was sympathy and in some places, pity. To our great surprise, Jerry Greco called from L.A. and told us that he wanted us back. Now, I highly doubt that Jerry really bought Bobby's Turnstile Investments put-on, especially after the whole ordeal with Space, but he was definitely approaching us with more of a human flair as of late. Maybe he'd finally stumbled across his potential for empathy, or maybe he was just waiting on the pharmacy to refill the script for his daily dose of ego. In any case, he seemed to have realized how much of an ass he had been and was trying to set things right—that or some higher-up was on him to produce some sort of marketable material in good time.

When he called, he'd offered us a deal, "If you get back in the studio and show me something substantial, we can talk about renegotiating your contract," he'd told us.

It was the kind of thing that would've been best to jump on, but in our current state, in the midst of several hang-ups, we needed to put it off. Bobby was just too unreliable, and with the absence of Space and Al, we needed to seriously rework much of our material. In the studio, we'd be able to collaborate with Stryker who would provide us with alternatives, no doubt, but every hour of studio time cost money, money we didn't have—money we wouldn't have until the release of our album. We were fast approaching a vicious cycle. Disenchantment was setting in. The muse had skipped the country, and our inspiration had fled the Trips Center along with our means.

However, we didn't stop playing gigs—oh no, not by a long shot. In fact, I think we may have been working more than ever. Directly following Al's departure, we played a weekend stint at The Matrix and a five-day, five-sets-a-night gig at a local bar downtown. During this time, we received a call from a club owner out in Oakland who was looking for us to play four days at his club as their main attraction, and we signed on. We figured that if we were ever going to get back down to L.A, we might as well practice cooperating first.

Before we set out, getting back on the road sounded like a great idea—lighting out of San Francisco for a spell, hitting a new scene, seeing some new faces—what could go wrong? I thought that maybe it would be like when we were trucking east to Woodstock, and that if this first gig came off good we could hit a new town each night all the way down to L.A. and finally finish our album. However, once we tried it, it was even worse than it had been before we left, which was really saying something. Bobby was as hot-headed and arrogant as ever, and with Al and Space gone, we were in serious need of gentle diplomacy. He wouldn't listen to any of us about anything. One night he played a whole set completely out of tune because he refused to grant any of us the satisfaction of his full attention. Wherever his head was at, it must've been mighty far away from that Oakland stage.

Additionally, Bobby and Billy weren't getting along at all. They were barely talking, and when they did, most of it was done in raised voices accompanied by blistering red faces. Mary and I tried to be mediators, but neither of them were very interested in using our services. The biggest and most pervasive problem was Bobby's playing. He thought that he was phenomenal and getting better every night, but the awful truth was that most of the time he sounded at best, decent and at worst, downright horrendous. The setlists that I'd so strongly disapproved of before turned out to be our saving grace. Frankly, with Bobby high the way he was, our capacity for straight jamming wasn't just limited, it was gone entirely. We fell back on those songs we knew well out of necessity, not just because we wanted to sound good and give the audience a fair show, but because we needed to come back the next night in order to get paid. It was a painfully true fact that I wished I could avoid entirely, but I cared so deeply for these people I'd befriended that it was unfathomable that I should leave them now, especially in the broken-down state they were in.

Discontent was universal among us, and every day laid the foundation for another conflict. Most of them went something like this:

More often than not, Bobby would show up for our gig in an awful state: wearing the same clothes as the day before, usually smelling terrible, his eyes cold and emotionless, and his stories more extreme than ever. I remember this one occasion when it was probably about fifty degrees outside and Bobby showed up in a t-shirt, the track marks and welts on the insides of his arms clearly visible.

"Jesus, Bobby!" Mary had exclaimed. "If you're going to shoot that shit, at least wear a jacket, will you?"

"Why should he?" Billy had interjected. "If he wants to look like the burnt-out manic-depressive junkie he's becoming, then by all means let him! Maybe when people see that and hear the shit his playing has become and start turning off to his music he'll get his fucking act together...what the hell, with how fucking phony the music industry has become, he's such a goddamned spectacle it may draw more, vampires that they are!"

"You're always fucking hassling me, man!" Bobby had replied. "Shove off!"

Billy had always been Bobby's right-hand man, and they'd been friends a long time, but Billy was red-hot angry with him now, and he went off on him, "I've been living with you for almost three years, man, and I've never hassled you a bit! That was because we could all hold our own shit together, but you can't now! You're completely out of control! I can't imagine how you don't see that! Look at yourself, Bobby, look at your fucking arms! You look like shit! You've got to stop living for yourself, man, you have too much to lose—*we* have too much to lose!"

Needless to say, after our four shows in Oakland were over, we drove right back across the bridge into San Francisco.

"We should've kept on heading further after Woodstock," I remember Billy murmuring to himself in the van that day, "we shouldn't have tried to come back to the City."

"Why?" I'd asked him.

"You know what they say, *'you can't go home again,'*" had been his only reply.

We laid off the gigs for a little while once we got back that time, but not exactly of our own volition. There used to be a couple clubs around the Haight that would always hire us regardless, but now it seemed like no one wanted us, and we didn't pressure them. According to the papers, The Day Trippers had gone underground.

What our involuntary hiatus did give us was some time to reflect and get our heads, and it provided us a break from all the conflict. Bobby took off not long after we returned and didn't come back to the Trips Center for several days. We tried calling around, but we couldn't raise him anywhere. On one hand we wanted to make sure he wasn't in any kind of trouble, but on the other, it was a welcome relief to have him out of the house for a while.

On one of those days when Bobby was gone, Avi, Vishnu and those guys dropped by the Trips Center. I really dug seeing them; we hadn't hung out since before we'd left for L.A, and being around them made me think of earlier times—happier times. We were just hanging out, smoking some grass and jamming a bit the best we could. Avi couldn't play guitar, but he had a strong sense of melody on the accordion. We were all gathered around in a portion of the living room that we'd shaped up for the occasion and were really having a blast when Bobby walked in with a couple of girls, one of whom was stoned out of her mind. Our little impromptu jam session broke down at the sight of them, and I watched Avi do a stunned double-take as if he couldn't believe that it was really Bobby he was seeing.

He looked different from the last time I'd seen him, therefore he certainly looked a hell of a lot different from the last time Avi had seen him. For me, his appearance was surprising not because of the unfortunate metamorphosis of his physical body, which I knew Avi was reacting to, but the look in his eyes. Rather than empty black sockets drilled out of his skull, his eyes contained a spark reminiscent of the one they used to possess, but upon closer examination, it was clear to see that this spark was artificial, a side effect of something he'd ingested earlier. It wasn't heroin, but it was no less sinister. The handful of little white pills he held provided the first clue to what it might be.

Upon swaggering through the front door, Bobby clumsily chucked a few of the pills to Billy. Billy caught them in one fist and examined them with disdain, "You know, man…what is this shit?"

"Ah don't worry about it, man, its good shit," Bobby replied. "It'll help you out with that chip on your shoulder."

Billy looked utterly disgusted. He shook his head and threw the two pills back at Bobby, then stood up and left the circle, muttering disbelievingly as he went, "That chip on *my* shoulder!?"

"Aw, man, don't be like that!" Bobby called after him. "Alright, alright, they're bennies!"

Billy just kept walking, and Faye followed him. The circle disbanded shortly after.

That night, Billy and Faye gathered Bobby, Mary, and me in the living room and dropped a bombshell on us.

"We're leaving," Billy announced.

The rest of us gasped.

"What! Why?" Mary cried.

Faye pointed to her belly. Despite the grave nature of our gathering, she wore a beautiful smile on her face; she was positively glowing.

Billy put a gentle hand on her stomach, "Faye and I are going to have a baby," he replied.

For a moment, the somber news of their leaving was all but forgotten, and Mary and I offered our congratulations to the parents-to-be. Bobby, however, was not having it.

"What do you mean you're leaving?!" Bobby interrogated them. "Why can't you have your kid right here?"

"Come on, Bobby, get real! The City's not like it used to be, man. Where are we going to stay? Here at the Trips Center? This is no place to raise a child!"

"But, but the record deal! The band!" Bobby was incredulous.

"Listen, Bobby, face it: there's no such thing as The Day Trippers anymore. As soon as Space got popped, that was the beginning of the end. We'll never make it big this way; not now, not with things the way they are...not with you the way you are."

Bobby just stared back at him with his arms crossed in a combination of what looked like shock and disdain. There was something noticeably pained about his expression, as if this was a true moment of realization for him—as if what Billy said had just confirmed the very thing he'd secretly feared all along.

"Bobby, I'm sorry things didn't work out for us the way you wanted them to, I truly am." There was not a trace of animosity in his voice, not a thread of frustration—he was completely sincere and calm at that. He knew that it was over, and he'd made peace with that fact. Bobby, however, was far from calm. He was still composed, but his eyes were wild. We all knew that he wanted to respond, but it was as if he was at a sudden loss for words. I believe that for once, he truly didn't know what to say.

Before he could collect himself and render some searing remark to fling back at Billy, Billy tried to hug him goodbye; but Bobby just turned his back on him and walked away, more than likely to fix.

"I'm sure he'll come around," Mary said, but despite her assurances, the rest of us knew that any chance of that happening was highly unlikely.

"Where are you two going to go?" I asked them.

"We haven't decided yet," Billy replied, looking at Faye, "whether we're going to head south toward New Mexico and carve a new life for ourselves or head back down to La Honda and stay with my folks."

"Here," Mary said, pulling a large bag of grass from the pocket of her coat that hung near the door, "take this with you."

"Thanks," Billy said, graciously accepting her offer.

Faye kissed her on the cheek.

"There's just one other thing…" he mentioned, trailing off.

"What is it?"

"Is it at all possible…I mean…would it be OK if…"

Mary cocked her head to the side, her eyebrows knit together, "Yes?"

"…if we took the Trips Mobile…?"

Mary's eyes widened, and she looked at me. Bobby was going to have a cow when he found out.

"Yes," I answered quickly—to hell with what Bobby thought, "it's the right thing to do."

"You're sure now, right?" Billy said, looking for confirmation.

Mary Jane nodded this time, "Yes," she replied, echoing me, "it is the right thing to do. Take it, but it'd probably be best if you left before morning."

When we awoke the following day, they were gone. Billy and Faye slid out quietly and under the wire, the exact moment of their exodus known to none except for the watchful eye of God. In the wake of their departure, everything commenced to falling apart, and it was hardly merciful. The death rattle of The Day Trippers had come suddenly, and the end came swiftly after that.

****

****

It couldn't have been more than a few days after Billy and Faye lit out for a better scene that Jerry Greco called again, this time with a message that afforded us little choice and even less leniency.

"Reprise Records is terminating your contract," he told us over the phone. "I once saw teeming potential in The Day Trippers, but whatever talent I once saw is gone now, gone without a fucking trace."

Mary and I canceled our appearance at Altamont too, and we did so reluctantly and with heavy hearts. There was no use at all consulting Bobby about it because in lieu of him kicking heroin on the spot—a truly impossible feat—there was no way in hell we were going to be able to make it there and make a good name for ourselves at the same time. After all, we weren't even The Day Trippers anymore, just a hollow shell of what once was.

When the three of us did play gigs—and we only played a few— we marketed ourselves as The Day Trippers: Stripped Down; a happy euphemism for dismantled and left for dead. It was Mary Jane and Bobby on acoustic guitar and me with a bass drum, snare, and cymbal doing Ringo-style licks on covers of Crosby, Stills & Nash and Buffalo Springfield. One gig we played at that same downtown bar where we'd done a week-long stint two weeks earlier was so bad that we were booed offstage by a bunch of inebriates and had to go back later for our instruments. It was positively mortifying.

That was the last gig any semblance of The Day Trippers would play together. If I'd known that at the time, I probably wouldn't have been able to bear it. I kept holding out for that one slim chance that we might get up on stage one evening and everything would be like it used to—that Bobby would snap out of it, Al would return, and a bassist would approach us with visions of grandeur—but that would never happen. It was impossible, even as a dream.

I sat in a couple of times for another local group who needed a drummer. It was a welcome change, and at times, they even came out with some pretty groovy stuff, but when it came right down to it, they were strictly average—just another aspiring band whose tireless efforts would amount to nothing—one of countless groups whose local prevalence would be swallowed up by the gaping maw of history and lost to posterity.

1969

As for myself, I turned my considerations inward and spent the great majority of my time in careful introspection. I was nearing the brink of a mounting existential crisis, and worries surrounding Bobby crowded my mind. Night after night, countless memories passed before my eyes. I kept thinking back to the way things used to be, and it seemed almost inconceivable that this would be the end result of what once was. At the very beginning when I'd first arrived there, a deeper meaning seemed obvious: that I was being awarded a chance to seek enlightenment in the era of my dreams, but now, what could be the significance of bearing witness to *this*?

I passed a great deal of my time in the Trips Center, the condition of which didn't do very much at all to improve my mental state. After Al had thrown all the junkies out and asked all the other undesirables to leave, the Trips Center was totally empty except for the three of us. Nobody came around anymore; sometimes the neighbors would drop by with food, but that was the extent of it. There always used to be some kind of music and activity going on inside the Trips Center, that's what made it so much more than just a building, what filled it with life, but after Faye and Billy left, it was silent, empty, cold, and dead. And now, along with the power, the city had shut off the gas, so we had no heat and no stove, and it was beginning to get very cold in San Francisco.

Bobby was beyond all hope. He wasn't even Bobby anymore; he was somebody else entirely. He wasn't in control of his guitar; therefore, he could hardly profess to be in control of anything else. When he was sober, he was angry, pissed off that he'd been robbed of his claim to fame, and when he was high, he was indifferent. It seems like a strange contradiction, but when he had his dope, that's all he cared about. For him, it filled the void, utterly and entirely. Heroin was his safe place—when he was high, he was happy; he could dream again. At a certain point, he just gave up. Henceforth, all he cared about was getting high, and all the time he was either looking to score or fixing. Heroin, of course, was his main vice, but he'd traded in his coke habit for bennies and whatever other downers he could get his hands on. It was hard to be around him, partially because of the great displeasure it caused me to see him in that state, but moreover because of how strongly I pitied him. In both nature and nurture he'd come up short. My childhood may not have been perfect by any stretch of the imagination, but it wasn't marred by tragedy as his was—I wouldn't trade my life for his no matter what the reward.

Meanwhile, Mary was blindly optimistic and sanguine to an excessive degree. Despite the bad press, our skeleton band, and Bobby's all-consuming heroin addiction, she continued to go out and look for gigs. More often than not, her search would turn up empty—which came as no surprise to me. Club owners have this great underground network; they know which bands to take a chance on hiring and which to tell to walk, and it seemed like every club owner as far out as Sausalito knew of Bobby's recent track record.

However, there was this one day in early December that Mary came bursting through the front door of the Trips Center elated, calling my name throughout the house. I met her down in the living room where Bobby was on the nod.

"Listen up guys, I got us a gig!"

"Where?" I asked, somewhat skeptical of the reputation of any place insane enough to hire us in our current state.

"At that bar down on Mission Street," she replied cheerfully. "I practically had to beg the guy, but it's no matter."

I glanced at Bobby. He was sitting amid the twisted wreckage of the living room, looking utterly bored and spaced out as he watched a drop of blood roll down his arm, tracing the valleys where his veins were sunken in, down to his fingertips like a tear. He turned his head toward her slowly, and she began pulling on his arm.

"Come on Bobby, you big fiend, we have a gig tonight! You got to get showered, get cleaned up, and get your guitar!" She let go of his arm and he stumbled backward, sliding back down the wall to the floor.

"Come on, Bobby!" she entreated him. "Don't you want to *play*? I got us a *job*!"

He just stared at her blankly, uninterested. I looked at her and shook my head, then I pulled her aside and confessed my worries about Bobby, but she was impervious to my concern.

"I've seen him like this before," she said. "In fact, he's been far worse. You should've seen him a few years ago, even I was afraid for him then, but he just gets like this sometimes. It's just a phase of his, he'll be fine. He's just upset about Space and Billy and Al leaving. Just give him some time, everything will be back to normal again."

I tried reasoning with her, "But Mary, we need money! The city is going to evict us if we don't pay the taxes for this place…"

She thought about it for a moment, "Well, I have a friend who works at a topless place up in North Beach. They tip pretty good over there, or so I've heard. I could ask her if I could work there a couple of days during the week, maybe cover her shift—you know, just until Bobby feels like playing again."

The thought of dirty, crusty old beatniks up in North Beach rubbernecking at Mary's scantily clad body made my skin crawl, and I tried like hell to think of alternatives, "How about we sell the pot plant in the tub or Bobby's chopper?"

She looked at me like I was crazy, "Rhiannon, don't you know? Bobby took that bike to auction weeks ago, and the pot plant disappeared while we were at Woodstock."

"Damn…"

Mary put her hand on my shoulder, "Oh Rhiannon, don't worry, everything will turn out OK."

She gathered me in an embrace and then went out again to go and cancel. I turned back to Bobby, but he'd gone on the nod again and was dead to the world.

I sat near him until he woke up. Once he began to stir, he was slow to regain consciousness and realize where he was. It was several minutes before he even noticed that I was beside him.

"What time is it?" he asked me in a sleepy, raspy voice.

"Beats me," I told him, "but it's night."

He turned away from me nodding, his eyelids fluttering and never opening past half way. He reached into his pocket and pulled out a cigarette.

"Have a light?" he asked me.

I lit it for him. A few moments passed.

"What time is it?" he asked me again.

I paused for a moment, "Nighttime," I replied.

He reached down beside him for his works. He opened up the eyeglass case and finding it empty of junk, stood up shakily on weary legs and stalked through the ruins of the Trips Center to a hole in the wall. He put his arm inside, felt around for a bit, and then pulled out a foil-wrapped package before coming back to sit beside me. Junk is the greatest motivator in the world, but only to get more junk.

He pulled out his spoon and his rig and began preparing the wicked solution, "Got a light?" he asked me.

If I hadn't given it to him before, I would have told him that I didn't have one, but now it seemed like I had no choice, and I handed it to him reluctantly.

Wincing, I watched as he indulged himself in the ritual of junk—that unholy ceremony—the most intimate involvement one can have with the slime that coats the bottom of the barrel. And despite what many care to believe or admit, we're all inside that barrel. Heroin isn't just a San Francisco problem, or a West Coast problem, or an American problem—it lies unnoticed in the tall grass of every country in the world, waiting for those above to fall, and when they do, it wraps them in its warm embrace and swallows them whole.

As Bobby filled his syringe with the drug, I laid my hand upon his arm. "Bobby," I said, "realizing and admitting that you need help is the first step to healing."

My words rolled off him as if they had never been spoken, and he did not even so much as pause before burying the needle deep in his arm. And as he did, I watched with my very own eyes as the devil climbed back into his body. As soon as he shot up he changed—not into some evil demon, but into a small and helpless man.

"Rhiannon," he addressed me, his voice flat and cold, "there's a risk in everything, and the greater the risk, the greater the reward."

I wanted to reply to him. I wanted so badly to find the words I needed to convince him that he was wrong, that it wasn't worth it, but words that yield that sort of power cannot be found in any dictionary in the world. Instead, I sat alongside him in pained silence, listening to each of his shallow breaths rattle inside his bony chest, wondering all the while what he could possibly be feeling that would excuse a life such as this.

I thought of this one time when he'd told me about how he'd reached nirvana and experienced *IT* through the use of heroin—the very first time he'd shot up—but I remember looking in his eyes and knowing that he hadn't. What he had seen was simply a besetting illusion. Evil, after all, is fatally beautiful.

Toward the end, rock n' roll for Bobby wasn't about the music at all. He got caught up in the desire and the decadence of it, and it became for him like lust. It was all about the fame and the glory and the girls. It was about the notoriety, the immunity—about becoming a god like his idols. It was about power; control over the thoughts and feelings of the masses. He was obsessed with excess, and when he found those things were out of his reach, his ambition took a sinister turn inward—to annihilation. He'd been lured and scuttled by his own siren song.

I remembered a time that felt to me like long ago—back when the sun warmed the shores of San Francisco and The Day Trippers played as one—when Bobby and I had talked about heroin. At that time, he had no qualms admitting to me that he used to be an addict because in saying so he projected a sense of authority over the drug—it made him more powerful than one of the worst physical dependencies known to man. However, now, as he lay disheveled, dirty, and under the spell of junk on the Trips Center floor with a blood-filled dropper in his hand, there was no getting him to admit that he needed it. But he did need it. He needed it with every cell in his body. Junk was his fig leaf—it made him untouchable, and without it, he was naked and vulnerable.

To me, junk sickness had always appeared more like any other sickness than it did an addiction. After all, the daily ritual of sticking a needle into your own body seems adverse to every logical process of human behavior, and for many there's even an innate fear that seems to accompany the act. Have *you* ever seen a child eager—or even unafraid—to receive their yearly immunization?

—Only if they know they'll be getting a lollypop afterward.

Apply the same principle, and you get what an addict looked like in my eyes. Initially, my attraction to Bobby had hailed from his intense ambiguity—his dark eyes, his calm stoicism, and his mysterious past. However, what I now knew—in not so much a gradual sense as much as in a crashing realization—was that all of that had been misinterpreted apathy; a superficial interest in sex and rock n' roll doctrine and a much deeper concern for power and junk—a pair for which greater antonyms do not exist. This was something that no longer eluded my jaded perception, something I was now painfully aware of—something I was ashamed I had been misled by for so long. And now there was nothing, nothing at all that I could do about it.

I awoke the next day and—gone again—Bobby was nowhere to be found. It wasn't unusual for Bobby to disappear like this—in fact, it was almost routine—but for some reason that day I was highly aware of his absence. I had a gnawing itch in the pit of my stomach when I first got up, and it remained with me the entire day as I wandered absentmindedly around the Trips Center and attempted to shape up the place. By twelve noon it was unbearable, so I went out to look for him. With my coat pulled up around my ears, I combed the Panhandle and canvassed the Haight. Considering Bobby's recent infamy, even the bums would have been able to tell me if he'd passed by—but I had no luck at all. I walked up and down Oak and Masonic and all through the Park and could find not a trace. I looked down all the alleyways, behind dumpsters and garbage cans—I wanted to find him…I *needed* to find him. I could feel the heroin in the City—it was a heavy, suffocating presence. There were junkies on every corner, and the alleys were full of them. They crowded around public ashtrays waiting for butts with downturned mouths and solemn expressions. They squatted in storefronts, panhandling, all of them with long, straggly hair and shrunken frames; gaunt, with sullen, dirty faces.

In a panic, I turned onto Page, and as I hurried down the sidewalk—practically in a full sprint—I passed a familiar alleyway and turned back around. About halfway down the alley, I came upon a street peddler wrapped in coats and blankets to keep out the cold. His face was turned away to ward against the wind, but when he heard my approach he spun around and the corners of his lips raised in a smile.

"Rhiannon, right?" he asked me.

"Y-yes," I replied, shuddering fiercely as a gust of wind came tearing down the alleyway. "Have you seen Bobby? I'm looking for him…it's really important."

"Heavy?" he replied. "Yeah, he was here. I didn't sell him anything, of course, all he wants is junk."

A rush of relief spread all the way down to my toes, "Which way did he go?" I asked.

He pointed behind me, "Around the corner, 1451 Page. The pusher who lives there is a fucking snake."

I thanked him hurriedly and rushed off in the direction he'd sent me. Adrenaline pumped through my veins with a brand new intensity. I wasn't about to just walk through the front door, so I hopped a couple of fences and came around through the back. I could hear the house before I saw it. I figured that there must have been one mother of a party going on inside because they were blaring Led Zeppelin so loudly that I could hear it all the way down the street. Once I'd shimmied through a gate that was propped halfway open and into the backyard of house 1451, I turned around and found myself face to face with Bobby.

Really, it was more like navel to face because he was slouched down next to a back porch with a bloody syringe beside him, his head craned forward. There were two people—a man and a woman—standing on the porch talking like nothing at all was out of the ordinary. The man was drinking coffee, and the woman was laughing—all with Bobby unconscious on the cold concrete not ten feet from them. A violent surge of fear and dread coursed through my body, and I dove down next to him.

"Bobby! Bobby!" I urged, grabbing him by the shoulders and shaking him slightly in order to rouse him. There was no response.

"Bobby! Bobby!" I spoke, louder this time as I cupped his face in my hands and slapped his cheeks lightly. Nothing. For a paralyzing

485

moment I wasn't even sure if he was breathing; even when I held my hand beneath his nose I could hardly tell. When I felt his neck for a pulse, I found that it was faint, but present.

I'm not going to lie, I freaked out.

"Didn't anybody see him!?" I screamed, running up to the porch. "Isn't anybody going to help him?! Give me that!"

I grabbed the hot cup of coffee out of the startled man's hand and ran back to Bobby, holding it under his nose while calling his name all the while. It was no help. So I threw it on his face.

Gasping and sputtering, he partially regained consciousness, but only for a moment. Terror filled me; I could feel my heartbeat in my feet. I ran back past the two astonished bystanders and wrenched open the back door to the house. There were people all over, but no matter how loud I yelled, nobody heard me over the music. I approached a few people closest to the door and tugged on their sleeves in an attempt to get their attention, but they brushed me off. Desperate, I tunneled through the crowd in the center of the room and unplugged the stereo. The room fell silent immediately, and everybody stopped what they were doing and turned to look.

"Somebody's got to help me!" I cried. "Bobby Black is overdosing on heroin outside, and I don't know what to do! Please!"

Everybody just gawked at me for a moment and exchanged various glances amongst themselves, but before I had a chance to say anything further, a woman came rushing toward me with a syringe in her hand.

"Here," she said, handing me the syringe. It was filled with a clear liquid, "this is Narcan, it's an anti-overdose shot."

I thanked her profusely. I thought she was following me back outside, but once I got there, she was nowhere to be seen. I wasn't about to wait around. Now, I didn't have a clue what I was doing, but I was running on pure adrenaline at this point, and since I'd seen Bobby shoot up numerous times, I figured I'd just duplicate the process. I knelt down beside him again and rolled up his sleeve. His arm was limp, bruised, and full of bright red sores that budded out of thin, blue veins. I took the syringe in my hand, placed my finger on the plunger, and hesitated. Reality surged upon me at once. What the hell was I doing? I'd never even given an EpiPen injection before, let alone an intravenous one! Besides, that syringe could have been filled with anything—how did I know it was really Narcan?

However, after a few seconds, all traces of rationale were obscured by panic, and I aimed for the center of one of those sores; then I sat back and prayed. It worked. The wave of relief I felt when his eyes fluttered open was so dizzying that I almost felt like passing out myself. I searched his face for the expression of gratitude I expected to see, but once he focused his gaze and saw me kneeling before him, he looked at me with pure hatred in his eyes. The intensity of his anger was so strong that it proved physical, and although he never laid a finger on me, the force of his gaze alone left me breathless, as if he had really struck me. To him, I'd done the unthinkable, betrayed him in the most unholy way—I'd stolen his fix, taken his high away.

Without a word, he dragged himself to his feet and sulked away. His wet, dirty jacket hung loosely from his skeletal body, and his jeans were muddied, bloodied, and torn at the ankles. There was this terrible smell wafting off of him. When it hit me, bile immediately rushed up the back of my throat, and I turned my head and retched. By the time I recovered from this wave of sickness, the party inside the house had started up again, and Bobby was gone, off to score his next fix.

As I walked back to the Trips Center in the mounting darkness, I felt small and helpless. Worry rallied in my mind with a fearsome new intensity. I was so cold that my face and hands were numb, and freezing rain had begun to drizzle from the clouds that cloaked the city. The fog had started to blow in again, and it threatened to snuff out the streetlamps. To me, San Francisco was all but entirely unrecognizable, and the soft orange glow of bygone summer nights had been permanently replaced by the cold, blue December moon.

When I reached the Trips Center, I found that it was empty. Mary was gone, and Bobby hadn't returned. Suddenly, I was overcome by a shudder of fear. For the first time since I'd arrived in the past, I truly felt unsafe. I even considered locking the door, but if my friends came home, they wouldn't be able to get inside. Instead, I went into the attic, pulled up the ladder, and slept in the bunk where Bobby and I had once made love.

****

****

The next morning, he was back. I came down from the attic shortly after daybreak to scrounge up some breakfast and saw that Bobby was hunkered down amongst the debris, cooking up a shot. After yesterday, I was apprehensive about how my presence would be received, but when I sat down next to him, he barely even acknowledged me. My stomach churned as I watched him handle his drug with care, and my eyes followed his hands as he measured it out in the spoon, melted it down, and drew it back into the syringe all so calmly, so perfectly accepting of his fate. This time I just couldn't let him do it.

As he went to shoot up, I held onto his arm, "Why do you do it?" I asked him.

He met my eyes with steely resolve, "Why do you breathe?" he responded before turning away and continuing to prod for a vein.

I held onto his arm even tighter, "Stop it, Bobby, you don't need this shot. Come on, let's go for a ride around the City, let's go up to Twin Peaks, let's jam for Christssake! It'll be fun, a hell of a lot more fun than sitting here and staring at your shoe for the next four hours!"

After that, everything just escalated so quickly. He took my arm and shoved me aside, then went to shoot up. I lunged back, grabbed the needle from him, and chucked it across the room.

"Fuck you, Rhiannon!" he screamed. "Fuck you!"

"No, Bobby, you did fuck me!" I yelled back, my voice thick with emotion. "And you told me you loved me! You don't love me now! You don't love anyone, only yourself! If you loved any of us, you'd stop! You're destroying us and killing yourself! Just look at yourself! You think you're invincible, Bobby, but you're not!"

In one swift motion he grabbed me and put me up against the wall, his fingers tight around my throat, "You know, you fucking time-traveler or whatever you are, tell me, where are The Day Trippers in the future? Huh? If I ever became anything big you would've known about it! You would've swooned over me the first time you saw me! You would've done anything to play with me! Tell me, Rhiannon, do I ever become anything in history?"

Tears were streaming down my face now, "No!" I choked out. "But Bobby, you're so good—or at least you used to be! Maybe if you weren't a fucking junkie you would've done something with your life! It doesn't need to be like this!"

I heard the crack before I felt the sting, and it was deafening. Once, twice, and a dozen times more, he slapped me across the face as I flailed under his grip. He only stopped once I gave up and went limp beneath his hands. He released me, and I dropped to the floor choking on air and gasping for breath. I curled up into a ball and held my head tightly as he stood over me and emptied my pockets of money. Through tearstained eyes, I watched as his boots crossed the wreckage on the floor and disappeared out the door that slammed behind him. I covered my stinging face and sobbed.

What felt like moments later—but in actuality was probably more like hours—I heard footsteps coming up the walk and the doorknob jiggling. I braced myself in case it was Bobby coming back; after that shocking display, god knows what he might have done. I tried to duck down behind the china cabinet and hide, but the big blue eyes that went along with the shock of blonde hair that came in through the door saw me.

"Rhiannon?" Mary asked, rushing to my side. "What happened to you?"

Deeply shaken by the events of the last two days, I told her everything.

She was so shocked at first that she barely believed me, "He's dramatic, self-inflating, and mad, but he's not dangerous!" she'd replied after I'd explained what had happened, but nonetheless, we both went out looking for him.

We went back to the house I'd been at yesterday, consulted Doobie and talked to everybody on the street, but nobody had seen him, so we drove through every neighborhood from Haight to Soma. Finally, and as the result of nothing other than dumb luck, we found him in an alleyway off of Harriet Street—a place that wouldn't be inappropriately coined the skid row of San Francisco. He wasn't the only junkie there either; in fact, there was a whole line of them down on the other end of the alley. He was on the nod, as usual, his head bowed so far down it was almost in his lap, the needle still in his arm. I ran over to him and tried to rouse him to no avail. As I slid my fingers onto his wrist to check his pulse, Mary began interrogating the other junkies, "How long as he been here?" I heard her ask them.

"Mary…" I called back to her; my heart was in my throat, and my voice was shaking. "Mary…I can't get a pulse."

She ran back over to me, and I wrenched his head up. Immediately, we both staggered backward.

There was this chill that passed through my heart, a feeling that no cold or touch or fear could ever recreate. His eyes…they were still open, and upon his lips was a smile so faint that you'd never see it if you hadn't known to expect it. I felt numb. A realization like that doesn't hit you like a thud, in fact, it's more like a whisper, like a pause…there are those couple of seconds when your eyes aren't sure if they're actually seeing what they're seeing and your brain doesn't exactly comprehend. Then there's this feeling, this sort of looking around; one last breath of denial before understanding and emotion come rushing back in.

"Oh My God!" I heard somebody scream. It took several moments before I realized it was me.

Mary fell to her knees in front of him and grabbed his cold, lifeless shoulders. "Bobby…" she whispered. "Bobby…"

There was no answer, of course.

Enraged and beside herself, Mary began shrieking, "*BOBBY!!!* This was NOT how it was supposed to end! Remember?! All those things we used to say about being great and people knowing our faces!? About being hip news!? It was not supposed to end like THIS!" She leaned forward and slapped him across the face, and his body crumpled limply beside her.

Mary was visibly disturbed by this. I could see her slipping. She backed up, her eyes wide with panic as she shook her head and murmured, "No…no…no… no…no…" And then—just like that— she fled.

I was crying, I felt frozen. I wanted to run after Mary, but I couldn't leave Bobby there like that. I turned back and knelt beside him and hugged his limp body close. I couldn't believe it. Just five minutes ago we were out in the desert dancing under the stars, and now his skin was colorless and dappled, his lips were blue, and his cold, bony hands were still bloody from where a cut had opened on my face. He reeked of that same terrible smell from yesterday—it was the smell of death. It's impossible even for you to try and imagine how I felt—you can't.

I left our final embrace sobbing uncontrollably and ran full bore to the nearest payphone. I tried like hell to contain myself.

"Hello, 9-1-1, what is your emergency?" the woman on the other end of the line asked.

"I'm on Harriet Street, on the corner of Harriet and Brannan. There's a man in the alley, he's dead!"

"OK, ma'am. I'm sending an ambulance there right now. Are you sure that he's deceased?"

"Yes."

"Did you move the body or attempt to revive him?"

"No, he's dead! He's dead! I know he's dead! His name is Bobby Black, he's a famous musician!"—the tears had returned full force with no chance of stopping.

"Do you know him, ma'am?"

"No," I lied.

"OK, ma'am," she said, "I'm going to need you to stay there until a squad car gets to you, OK? What is your name?"

I fell silent. A burst of fear arrived to join the tears.

"Hello? Ma'am? What is your name?"

I hung up the phone and ran to my car to chase after Mary.

For the second time in two days, I sped through the City, frantically searching for my friend; a friend I was afraid I'd never see alive again if I didn't find them soon enough. And for the second time in two days, darkness fell as I did so. The onset of night deemed my search impossible, so I returned to the Trips Center praying that Mary had as well.

When I threw open the door to the Trips Center, it was dark and empty inside. It looked as if it had been ransacked and abandoned. However, imperceptible at first, I noticed that there was one dim light shining into the upstairs hallway.

"Mary?" I cried, my voice echoing throughout the empty house.

There was no answer, and I was filled with dread when I thought of what awaited me at the top of the stairs.

I found Mary in the bathtub. Her clothes were strewn across the floor, and several candles had been lit and haphazardly placed around the room. The mirror had been broken, and several hundred shards of glass, some of them bloody, covered the floor and glinted in the candlelight. The faucet was still running, and the water was up to her chin and beginning to pour out over the sides of the tub into the room. In her trembling hand, she held one of the larger shards of glass from the mirror, upon which were several small piles of indistinct white powder.

She hadn't heard my approach. Her eyes were bloodshot and encircled by black where her mascara had run down to her cheekbones. Her nose was full of blood and white powder. She had rolled up one of The Day Trippers' calling cards and was using it to snort that shit—or so I'd thought—until I looked closer and realized that it was the photograph of her family. In horror, I watched as she raised the glass to her face and snorted another line of god knows what. I stood directly in front of her in the doorway, yet she did not see me. I moved closer to her, and when she finally noticed my presence, she cracked some kind of crazed smile, "Rhiannon…"

Panic shot through me like a bolt of lightning.

"Come on, get up," I instructed her, trying to hide the fear in my voice. I shut off the faucet and grabbed her arm, yanking her up out of the tub. The glass fell from her hand and all the powder dissolved as soon as it hit the water.

"No, Rhiannon," she protested languidly, but she didn't put up much of a fight. She could hardly bear the weight of her own body. "I'm so warm in here," she moaned, "don't make me go out into the cold. It's so cold out there. And I'm so, so warm…"

I wrapped her in a towel and shoved her out the door. Somehow, I managed to get her down the stairs and to my car. Outside, it had begun to rain.

"Not you too," I told her through clenched teeth as I eased her into the front seat as gently as I possibly could. "Not you."

Before we'd even left the driveway, she started shaking—trembling so fiercely that I was afraid she'd die of hypothermia before she died of an overdose. I threw the car in neutral, took off my jacket and put it on her. Of course, the top to my car wouldn't work no matter how hard I yanked on it, and the further I drove, the harder the rain came down. The whole way to the hospital, Mary was mumbling incoherently about seeing Bobby and her mother, a notion that struck an unimaginable degree of fear into my heart. I blew every stop sign from Haight-Asbury to Mission.

As I sped toward the glowing red cross in the distance, in spite of all the raging panic and boiling grief, a twinge of surprise is what arrested my mind. This was the first time Mary had so much as mentioned her mother since the discovery of her death, and in the wake of this most recent tragedy, Sophia's name was the last thing I expected to hear. Suddenly, I became aware of a very real, very upsetting fact that I and everyone else had unintentionally ignored: Mary's sanguine optimism hadn't been optimism at all—it had been staunch denial in the face of a painful depression. Of course, at that moment, the grave extent of her condition was glaringly obvious, and it was unfathomable to me how we could have allowed Mary to become a casualty of our ignorance. I reviled those games we had not only permitted but invited to rule over us since our return—those

492

games that had nullified our good sense and prompted a resurgence of ignorance; the very same ignorance we had vowed to expel. Inside myself, old anger bubbled up out of the throes, and recriminations against all of us abounded.

However, a good dozen blocks from the hospital, that anger took a quick turn back into even deeper realms of fear when Mary stopped talking. I looked over and saw that she was slumped down in the seat, her eyes closed and perfectly still—she wasn't Mary anymore, she was broken; no more than an empty shell. My heart broke. I wanted more than anything in the world at that moment to pull over and check her pulse, to reassure myself that she was still alive, but I knew that it was futile. Even if she was, she wasn't long for this world. At every second her body was struggling against its own collapse. One wasted moment could mean the difference between life and death, and if I stopped now, her blood would be on my hands. I pressed the pedal to the floor and urged my car on faster, but the slick roads were unmerciful and I skidded and fishtailed—just barely in control—all the way to the hospital.

When I was finally able to bring that speeding hunk of metal to a shuddering stop, it was on the sidewalk outside of the emergency room, underneath an overhang designated *'Ambulance Entrance Only.'* When I opened the driver's side door, the rain that had pooled to my ankles poured out onto the pavement. I ran around to the other side of the car, wrapped Mary's limp arms around my neck and struggled to keep her upright as I lurched toward the glass doors. Luckily, the nurses stationed at the triage desk spotted us and came running outside with a wheelchair. Immediately, they whisked her away through several sets of swinging double doors, and I ran after them, frantically. They brought her into a large room filled with rows of beds separated by partitions, lifted her up onto one of them, and began to strip her of her soggy coat and wet towel. They dressed her in a dry gown and started hooking her up to several machines so that all manner of tubes and IVs protruded from her arms. Her face was full of blood and pain.

"She's overdosing," I cried to the nurses who worked over her.

One of them stopped what she was doing and called for a replacement, then came to consult me with a clipboard in hand. It seemed like they hadn't even known that I was there.

"Are you related to this girl?" she asked me.

"No," I replied, talking fast in a trembling voice, "she's my friend."

"What is her name?"

"Her name is Mary, Mary Jane Greene, that's Greene with an E."

The nurse wrote all of this down quickly, "Uh-huh, and what did she take?"

"I don't know," I replied as I stole another helpless glance at Mary, "cocaine, maybe heroin, all I know is that there was all this white powder and she was putting it in her nose and—"

Suddenly one of the machines began squawking, and one of the nurses hovering over Mary yelled, "She's coding!"

Another nurse rushed in followed by two doctors pulling a cart with a defibrillator. The nurse I'd been speaking to led me by my arm out of the room and then pulled the curtain. It was almost impossible to make out the directives of the imperative voices inside over the sound of the machine's alarm. "What's happening?" I cried. Tears were streaming down my face as I tugged on her sleeve, "Please tell me what's happening!"

"Don't worry, the staff here is very good. They are doing all they can for her," her voice was terse. "Now if you could just answer a few more questions for me…"

However, she never quite got around to asking. In an instant, it seemed like everything happened at once. From outside, ear-splitting sirens drowned out the already intensely morbid sounds of the hospital, and then there were voices shouting and the pounding of running feet on the tile floor. Two men with a gurney came bursting through the double doors before me, and the nurse with the clipboard was swept away with them.

"Out of the way! Coming through!" they shouted. I pressed myself up against the wall. From behind the curtain, the mechanical screeching grew even more urgent, and someone called for a clergyman.

Despite the nurse's prior reassurances, I was downright terrified. I'd watched enough television dramas in my day to know that coding was just another clever restatement for dying. Suddenly, my hands and knees collided with the blue tile floor, and my vision became obscured by tears. Unreality began to set in. I felt as if an eternity separated me from the curtain that hid Mary's dying body. I was frozen there; stock-still in shock, in fear. I couldn't move; I'd forgotten how. The world around me was foggy and faded. Everything, it seemed, was very far away.

I don't know how long I stayed there, staring unmoving at the blurry, undulating curtain, waiting for some sort of certainty; a statement of either hope or dreadful imminence—a fated decree. The ball was in God's court now. Would she be spared and live? Or was she doomed to die?

As if sent to jar me from that place, that horrible suspension, the pith of mortal contemplation—a rhetoric reserved only for the most heinous of criminals and the unluckiest of sentient men—was a voice, one that grew consistently nearer with fearsome, mounting intensity.

"WHOSE CAR IS THAT?!" it screamed. "THE WHITE ONE BLOCKING THE EMERGENCY ENTRANCE! SOMEBODY'S GOT TO MOVE THAT CAR!"

At that moment, reality made a startling reemergence. I picked myself up off the floor and dragged myself along the wall for support as I made it for the doors. Through a blinding curtain of hot tears that swam in my eyes, I sought refuge from that place—that perpetual battleground where angels in white revoked the reviled agents of death. This was humanity at its most raw. This was Armageddon. I tore through the lobby like a bat out of hell as behind me all the while voices entreated me: "Weren't you the one who brought in that overdose case?" "I need some information from you!" "Miss, what is your name? Miss!" I jumped in my car and lit out of there altogether.

As freezing rain dropped out of the sky like a deluge and swirled around me in torrents, I swerved and skidded through the tangled web of parking lots and landscape islands until I reached a physical ultimatum. I'd found myself in some stranded outcrop of overflow parking where the white lines had faded and weeds had burst up through the cracks in the pavement. There was no further ahead I could drive unless I wanted to uproot the landscaping, and there was no way in hell I was going to turn around and go back the way I had come. Trembling and overcome by shock, I shut off the engine and sat for a moment in enveloping silence.

I tried in vain to rouse myself, in hopes that I was dreaming—that all this was nothing but a terrible nightmare—but it was to no avail. All around me, that crumbling utopia was just as real as any other part of my experience. Once again, the pain of reality itself had become my arch nemesis.

Out of the distance, the sirens' dreadful screams grew nearer, and flashes of lightning crept closer still as a long dormant thread of reality began to weave its way into my mind. It was only then that I realized the true desperation of my situation. I was the only Day Tripper left on the Haight. Bobby was dead, and it seemed like Mary would be following him shortly. Al was unreachable somewhere along the two million miles of road between San Francisco and New York, Space was in the slammer, and Billy and Faye were departed to reaches unknown. I was flat broke, and the only home I knew was in shambles: without power, without heat, and soon to be reclaimed by the city— not to mention filled with copious quantities of various illicit drugs. I had no legal documentation, no birth certificate, and a driver's license that had been issued in 1999. I was sitting in a car registered under my father's name, and in that time he didn't know me from Adam. From across the parking lot, I watched as a hippie my own age came running out of the fog with a transistor radio in his hand, wailing aloud his most terrible lament, "It's over! It's over!" he cried. "We blew it! It's over, and we blew it! They beat him, they killed him, and they've buried us all! It's finished, it's all finished!"

His words struck me with unparalleled ferocity. I felt like I'd just walked backwards off the edge of a cliff. It was then that I realized what he was talking about, and not only did it resonate with me, the implications of his words washed over me in a suffocating wave; it felt like a soft, cold blow to the heart. Just like that, I remembered everything.

It was December 6th, the day of The Altamont Free Concert, and the death he spoke of was that of Meredith Hunter who had been beaten to death by Hells Angels in an attempt to keep the peace. Every semblance of a shelter for humanity had been torn away, and the rain came pouring down. This was it: the end.

The events that were soon to follow, those most regrettable of truths, those things I had hoped to change by ignoring their imminence, boiled up from the depths of my mind with a brand new, painful significance. This was the death of the Movement, the shattering of the peace. The expectations of victory would begin to falter now, and the interests of those spearheading it would become more divided than ever. There would be a resurgence of violence, a definite loss of moral principle, and a lack of interest in the pursuit of Truth. Acid, grass, and psychedelics of all kinds would remain criminal, those that indulged would continue to suffer trips tainted with paranoia, and many would suffer a fate similar to Space's, served under the amoral hand of the law. Narcotics would become more dangerous and widespread and the System ever more corrupt. Those whose only wish was to live peacefully would become more and more oppressed. The war overseas would escalate, and thousands more would die. All over the world, conflict would continue to rise. World peace would once more elude the hands of men and fade further and further away until it was merely an idyllic principle, as inconceivable

496

as it was impossible. Women would continue to be objectified, and blacks would continue to be discriminated against. Capitalism would spike with a sinister and lasting intensity. The truth about the Manson Family and the wicked acts of the Weather Underground would soon dominate the airways. The tragedy at Kent State was on the horizon with Watergate soon to follow. The talent we idolized would soon pass away—Jimi, Janis, Jim, Keith, Bonzo—all of them in the pain-tempered footsteps of Bobby. In just about ten years, some crazy miscreant would shoot John Lennon.

The future rolled over me like a freight train and closed in around me like a bad trip. At that moment, the loneliness and despair that I should've felt upon my arrival came crashing over me. This was not my time; it never was. I needed to get out of there; I had no place in that world. If I stayed, sooner or later, I'd be discovered. They'd be looking for me, after all. They'd seen me bring Mary in, they knew what I looked like, and they'd seen me run. Somebody would find that bloody scene in the Trips Center, and the news of Bobby's death would be in the papers tomorrow. I'd have to spend the rest of my life running away, and when they did eventually find me, I'd become a prisoner of the state. Hell, maybe they'd even think I was a Soviet spy, as undocumented as I was. I didn't even have a goddamned social security number. Suddenly, I was struck by an unprecedented thought: *Maybe Jules had left for good reason. Maybe when I arrived, everything had gotten fucked up. Maybe none of this would have happened if I'd never come here.*

I was resolute; I needed to leave. I needed to put things back to the way they used to be. I needed to go back to my own time somehow, no matter the ramifications, and there was only one way I knew of that such a feat could possibly be achieved. As thunder rumbled deafeningly across the sky, I reached into my glovebox and held in my hand Dave's mysterious pipe and the second crystal of DMT.

To be honest, there was no thought of *what if I never come back?* What was there for me to come back to? The vast spectacle of beauty and wonder and peace and love that I'd discovered there had all collapsed into a smoldering wasteland within a couple of months. When you are eradicated from circumstance and preconception, that is when you are truly alone. Physically, mentally, and emotionally, when you have nothing left, you cannot lose a thing. For me, there was no fear at all. The only real fear I knew was in that place. The worst thing that could've happened to me was to be left there, for that was like being on the other side of death. Even if I died, it would simply be the end of the story. I was not afraid of death. Death, after all, is only transformation, and it is only painful for those outside of the experience. I needed to go home to set things right again, and if that meant dying, then so be it.

With a new staunch determination, I surrendered myself to my fate—whatever it was. My nerves were calm as I packed the pipe and lit it. I breathed in several successive lungfuls of the thick smoke and held my hand above the bowl as I did so to shield it from the pouring rain. Almost instantaneously, the world around me began to wobble as if it was nothing more than a reflection in a pool of water. My senses began to fail as the limits of my perception were surpassed. My eyes darted to the rearview mirror, and there I saw the reflection of Mary's face; there was so much fear in her expression I could taste it—but it wasn't really Mary's face at all. As I looked closer, I saw that it was my own face, and as I raised my hand to touch it, to reassure myself of my own existence, the reflection began to split up and drift apart in the weightless space around me.

No feeling is as complete or intense as one you cannot anticipate, and as I shifted my gaze once more—perhaps to gaze out at my surroundings, to take one last long look at this sentimental reality of mine—it was like someone turned off the electric force, and the entire world fell apart. Suddenly, there was no more world—no more physical reality, no more body, no more mind. It felt like I'd pressed the eject button for my soul; it was intrinsic separation on a grand scale. It was a portal to the infinite, and I was well on my way.

The space around me began to break apart into dim points of light that oscillated before me. Living, breathing patterns were formed out of the fray and reached down out of the shimmering abyss to touch me. Geometric shapes and mandala-like archetypes filled my field of vision and the void around me and transported me…Elsewhere—to the other world; a world far, far beyond the one in which we carry out our daily lives. To go there is to step outside of the marginalized reality in which we live, not into some parallel universe, but rather into an experience of reality on a grand scale. It is reality before the brain constricts it to a rendering we can easily perceive.

Freed from the bounds of fear that had seized me so tightly the first time I embarked upon this experience, I was able to see so much clearer. However, I was still caught up in a crystalline flood of cognitive dissonance, apprehended by a volume of information. There were facts, figures and revelations—clues pointing to the very nature of existence, but they were impossible to comprehend all at once. It

498

was like trying to read every book ever written, watch every television program ever produced, and listen to every radio show ever aired all at the same time. It was positively overwhelming; however, as velocity ensued, much of that information was left behind, and I sped past it at a rate fast approaching the inconceivable as those facts and figures split into fractal images that rained about me. There were visions and fragments of visions, beautiful imagery that exceeded any possible explanation, and profundity on a scale unprecedented.

I sped further and faster into the very heart of deep space, toward the point from which all numinous lore hails—the faded, hidden Truth that lies at the center of all things. Around me, invisible, immaterial objects sailed by, suspended in negative space. I was headed back to the inner world, a world that is, by and large, much more vast than our physical reality could ever profess to be. After all, matter is only a casual byproduct of consciousness, the brain—merely a channel, the body—a vessel.

I shed my humanity like an old cloak, eager to be welcomed once more into the ranks of the infinite where I was no longer bound by illusion and uncertainty. As I did so, I became aware of a cosmic pattern. All that was around me traveled in waves, and although spirit and manifestation sprung from every angle and morphed out of every corner, everything vibrated at once on the same frequency. Everything existed with the same undertones of cadence and climax and disintegration, followed by restoration once more. All of time, creation, and the universe aren't linear; they are cyclical—*infinite!*

Imbued with this lasting notion of infinity—another fleeting glimpse of *IT*—out of the chaos, cosmos befell me in perfect order. I had reached a divine realm; broke on through into a world free of perception where I was light, I was love, I was cause, I was effect, I was the source, *and* I was the reflection. Peace unlike anything I had ever felt before enveloped me. It was so pure, so true, so beautiful, and so powerful that it resonated throughout the entire universe. Here was stillness, silence, emptiness—here was the crux of the unmanifest. It wasn't nothingness as I had experienced it before, it was *all of being*—the soul in its pure state. I went back to that place willingly and without fear because I knew that it was the place from which I had come, a place I had been many times before, and a place I would return to infinitely more.

My merging with the infinite was again only a momentary experience. A resurgence of sensation and visualization once more came upon me, and I felt myself to be inside a massive structure, one constructed entirely of rosy, diaphanous glass, glass that rose and fell with the tenor of the universe—glass that breathed. Its beauty compelled me, but only for a moment. For along with sensation came that inevitable motion—driving, forceful, propulsive—and the glass that towered above me in a vast expanse shattered—and so did I along with it. I was no longer I; that which was formerly I was now cast across the universe in a gentle dusting. However, instead of fear, a mounting sense of anticipation marked me. As the rapid motion accelerated and the vacuum of space stretched and condensed and transformed, I bore witness to a resurrection.

If only I had looked for longer at my crucified flesh back in the desert. If I had, I might have seen—as I did now—the reclothing of my scattered form by the miraculous. This was my rebirth. As the molecules of my being began to coalesce once more—in an order that was familiar but a feeling that was brand new—the culmination of my experience appeared imminent. A tunnel appeared before me—one that was concentric like a spiral—and I traveled along it, down into its depths, slowing as I approached its terminal end.

Coming down, I was enveloped by an intense, gripping sensation that at one time I might have perceived as fear. However, rather than fear, what I experienced this time was a feeling of parting; like I was losing something, something I couldn't quite define, yet was central to my very existence. Instead of reaching back for it, I opened my hand and let it go, and I did so with the certainty that in time I'd be aware of its presence once more. After all, it wasn't the peace that was leaving me—that I had the luxury of holding onto. As I approached the end of the tunnel, where a bright white light had appeared to greet me, I felt this enormous back pressure in my head, as if I was shutting off an immensely powerful faucet. I blinked my eyes open, and as I did so, I experienced the whole trip all over again. Every detail was as fresh and raw as I'd experienced it the first time, every vision just as vivid, every feeling just as pure. The pressure that I'd felt in my head continued to build all around me, and when it reached its limit, it forced me back out into the world. Following this was my reemergence into reality, and just like a butterfly cracking open a cocoon, I was met with an old world that I was experiencing for the first time.

PART IV

The moment I first regained consciousness after that experience is still unknown to me. It took a while for all those necessary parts of my brain to be revived and begin working together again and for me to discern waking life from the element of my dreams—not unlike the first time. I still had my eyes closed in an attempt to suspend for a moment my disbelief. Remember, at that moment I was still entirely uncertain of my whereabouts. I could still be in San Francisco just as easily as I could be on another planet for all I knew—or in the year 3000. I had faith that Fresno would be on the other side of my eyelids, but there was no way of being sure, and I was savoring the last of my blissful ignorance if it wasn't. Suddenly, an ear-splitting car alarm began to sound, and my eyes shot open. Immediately, the advent of sight—a glaring, vibrant dissonance—was upon me. The sun shone directly into my eyes, illuminating a brightly colored world full of green grass, baking asphalt, cars painted in shimmering high gloss, and The Joint, vacant in the daylight. I was back.

If I'd had more time to think about it previously, I would have imagined that I'd react in any one of several ways upon my return. Earth-shattering relief, tears of leftover shock, or even an upsurgence of melancholy were all likely contenders; however, what I experienced was none of those. Every sight, sound, motion, and sensation was extremely raw, and I looked around at this once-familiar scene with a feeling inside me that closely resembled incredulity, but was probably more like a combination of astonishment and unreality combined. One would not be entirely wrong to call it numbness, but they would certainly be in err of capturing the big picture. Every sound was crisp, every vision clear and breathtakingly bright—even my sense of smell had been immeasurably heightened. My perception of this place that had hosted my former life had never been richer.

Looking around me, I could see that not only was I back in the parking lot of The Joint, I was in the exact same parking spot. Could it be that I had never left? Could all of it have just been a psychedelic trip, a temporary manifestation resulting from my consumption of the drug? Could the whole thing have been in my mind after all? The thought was compelling, but there was one factor that negated those otherwise pragmatic theories: my memories. Those standing testaments to rational and scientific impossibility—proof of a miracle, one might say—remained just as clear as my perception. The shock and devastation that had concluded my brief stay in that other time was no dream, and the beauty, love, and enlightenment of my experiences were no manifestation of the mind.

I looked down at my body, and immediately my suspicions were confirmed. The bottom of my hair was blonde. I was wearing the jeans I'd bought in L.A. and one of the peasant blouses I'd bought on the Haight. My floor mats were soggy, my upholstery was ruined, and I still had on Mary's green boots. A chill passed through my body.

Mary...

The horror of that night returned to me in striking detail. It had been real, yes, it must have been real—and those things were real now, alive inside my mind. However, reality—as it existed for me—had been permanently redefined, and the force of my emotional reactions to those memories had been lessened quite severely. This may very well have been a side effect of my most recent experience. It comes as no surprise to me that the intensity of those memories was dwarfed when set against a slingshot across eternity.

Every one of my actions was preceded by a succinct and deliberate pause as I turned and moved about my car as if I was in a trance. I tugged on my car top, but it would not budge. On the passenger's seat, I found the little pink baggie that Dave had handed me...yesterday. It was empty. In the cup holder laid my lighter. In a frenzy, I tore apart the car in search of the pipe. I checked every nook, every cranny, every possible and impossible place where that little pipe might have fallen when it left my hand—but it was gone. Either I'd dropped it out the window in transit, or it had been taken from me—intentionally removed from my charge. Was this the universe atoning for its most grievous of fuck-ups—allowing me to enter into another time?

I opened up the glove box and in some sort of massively subdued shock, picked up the photograph of The Day Trippers that fell out when I did so. In some ways, I couldn't believe that it was still there. Maybe I expected it to have disappeared with the pipe, but it remained, and I held it with conviction. It was my only link to that place, the only material proof of my experience; a reassuring testament to the last of my enduring sanity. My eyes scoured their faces and my own, looking for the first clues to what had gone wrong, but none could be found. There in that moment, Woodstock and the heyday of The Day Trippers felt like two lifetimes ago. A tinge of melancholy seeped into my heart, but it did so accompanied by the gentlest reminiscence. Tenderly, I traced the faces of Mary and Bobby with my finger, and a single tear fell into my lap.

Oh, I must have stayed there for hours just thinking, lost in the timeless regions of memory. The sun was nearing the zenith by the time I stirred, and when I did, a startling revelation came upon me. My return was now paired with circumstance. Consequence rained about me as I thought of and remembered the intrinsic and current facts of the reality I was stepping back into. All those situations—sticky or otherwise—that I'd left unfinished would now be resumed. All those events that seemed like distant memories had occurred only yesterday, and those people that I felt like I hadn't seen in years were expecting my return. I wondered how long I had been gone and what had transpired in my absence.

Still dazed, I slipped the photograph into my shirt pocket, turned the key in the ignition, and my car drove itself home. My mind was someplace else entirely. I might have expected all those thoughts and emotions that accompanied this place and time to come rushing back to me, but none did. Instead, I was still so shaken by the events of…yesterday…that I wasn't sure if I'd ever recover. My mind continued to return to thoughts of Mary and Bobby—I could hardly help it—but that hadn't been yesterday, not for this world. All of those events so painfully new to me had occurred thirty years ago. Hell, Space was probably out of jail by now!

I'd spent yesterday in this reality at Marty's house after a fight with my mother. I'd met and talked with Dave the dealer, and he'd given me that DMT, after which I'd gone home and fought with my mother again. God, how ignorant and temperamental I'd been—it didn't even feel like me in my memory. I'd stormed out in anger and driven to The Joint in tears. It was there that I'd smoked that drug, and the rest was history.

And, you see, there's the rub. If it hadn't been the drug, then what had it been? For me to go to San Francisco in 1969 of all places, to meet The Day Trippers of all people—The Day Trippers who'd just lost their prized drummer—to have had the experiences I'd had, and to have returned to the exact same place of my departure—as if I'd never moved—there had to be something to it; something that ran long and deep and strong and was meant to be. It was all so perfect, so exact. There was an order, a method, a reason for it, and I knew that no matter how much I knew, I would never really know how and maybe not even why...

There seems to have been a rip in the fabric of space-time, one that I fell through, and as I turned into my driveway, a deep sense of surreal came over me. I felt as if I had been away for years—thirty at least. This life felt much too foreign to be real, and the ways in which it differed from the time I'd just left outnumbered the stars. I pulled up next to my mother's tan Buick still in a trance. I shifted into park, shut off the car, and stared at it. It was in the same place as it had been when I'd left; it hadn't moved an inch. And that wasn't the only thing—everything was the same. The door probably hadn't even been opened since I'd slammed it behind me as I stormed out in vehemence. I shook my head in bewilderment. This place had eighteen years of familiarity going for it, but it in no way even began to compare to the peace and welcome that I knew had once existed on the Haight. That was the atmosphere in which I had truly, and for once, felt at home. However, that was the atmosphere I had watched flicker and die out, and it had been dead thirty years. Its realm had been invaded and trampled and aged, never to be again as it was, and the only truth of existence that still remained was what I carried with me in the six inches of Haight between my ears.

My state of mind, as measured by any system, would not in any way be regarded as sane. However, I felt insane, and that in and of itself was reassuring. To me, that was the surest test of sanity imaginable because I've known my fair share of insane people and they all thought themselves to be perfectly rational.

I remember getting out of my car thinking that my life could not get any stranger. As I walked toward my front door, I made peace with whatever might greet me on the other side. After the last twenty-four hours I'd had, there was no room for apprehension or fear. I didn't even waste my time imagining how my mother might react to my return; after all, to her, it might seem like I'd only been gone a few hours. There was no point in rehearsing an argument or rebuttal to a hypothetical charge. I couldn't even resurrect the charred ashes of my animosity toward Meredith. I wasn't about to run in there and hug her, but all traces of conflict had left my heart. I would deal with the scene that befell me respectfully and in whatever manner would allow me to peacefully arrive in my bedroom where I could maybe lay down and iron out a few things in my mind. God knows I needed all the ironing out I could get.

I approached the door, and after a few deep breaths, I opened it. It was unlocked. I saw Meredith before she saw me. She was standing at the counter with her back to the door—she hadn't heard me pull in. It was only after I'd stepped into the house that she became aware of my presence, and she started in with her lecture before she even turned around.

"Finally, Rhiannon! Where were you?! You—"

I just blinked and stared. How in the world was I to answer that question? I'd already prepared myself for the worst, so I just stood there, ready to endure her wrath. Every charge she levied would probably be true, after all. However, as it turns out, I didn't have to answer her at all. Meredith never finished her sentence. Instead, what began as a double take had turned into…I don't know what. When she saw me, her whole body stiffened, and she clutched the edge of the counter so tightly I could see her knuckles turn white. In fact, her whole body turned pale, as if she'd seen a ghost. She staggered backward toward the kitchen table, and there she lowered herself shakily into one of the chairs and began to weep. She looked me over from head to toe in a motion I was familiar with, but this time something was different and terribly, terribly wrong. The look on her face was one I'd never seen on anyone else's ever. Her eyes bulged, and her lips parted in…what? Not anger. Awe? Shock? Fear?

I began to get that uncomfortable, skin-crawling feeling you get when you have one of those dreams where you are standing naked in front of your freshman English class. I looked down to make sure that I did indeed have clothes on, and I did, the very same ones I'd been wearing in the car—the same ones I'd been wearing the night before in San Francisco. There was my hair, but that wasn't it either. I even took a few quick glances around me to make sure that a wormhole hadn't opened above my head and that there wasn't a monster stepping through the door behind me—after all, that's what it would've taken to get a reaction like that out of my mother. Could I have been gone longer than I initially thought? Was this her display of relief to my return? Or was she was having a heart attack or something of the sort? The truth, I learned, was even more outrageous.

Shocked, confused, and stunned, I crossed the kitchen to console my mother; after all, for a moment I even thought that she might be dying! I knelt down next to her, and as I did, the photograph of myself and The Day Trippers fell out of my pocket and landed between her shoes. With her head hung between her knees, there was no chance of me snatching it up before she saw it. She picked it up, and upon focusing her gaze, began sobbing even harder.

Oh shit, I thought to myself, *I know I prepared for the worst, but how in the world am I going to explain this?*

As my mind raced, Meredith regained enough of her composure to choke out a few coherent words in a shaking, raspy voice, "You don't know who I am," she whispered.

I was taken aback by the shock and strangeness of it all, and as calmly as I could I asked her, "Who are you?"

In response, Meredith raised a single trembling finger and pointed it at the figure of Mary in the photograph.

Remember that old adage: '*A picture is worth a thousand words?*' Well, I've come to the conclusion that they are worth a hell of a lot more than that. A photograph is a frozen moment, and a moment is a priceless thing; it is condensed eternity. A photograph can embody a lifetime, even a generation. It can solve a mystery, change relationships, mend or break hearts—and as for a thousand words, for me at that moment, that picture was worth every word I could have ever spoken and was more indispensable in aiding communication than a dictionary could ever be.

That worm of suspicion started weaving its way through my mind, and before very long, I realized that worm wasn't a worm of suspicion at all, but a worm of truth! It made no logical sense whatsoever, and yet couldn't be more plausible. Suddenly, everything in my life made sense and as if in one of those eternal moments I'd experienced so many times before, we were both drawn into an embrace that never seemed to begin nor end though we broke.

Once the two of us were able to regain our sense of reason and composure, she filled me in, and I will never forget the things that she told me for as long as I live. She told me all those stories I'd never heard, some of which I'd already lived along with her, and others that hailed from her childhood and the years that followed the breakup of The Day Trippers and my departure. I was floored the whole time—I defy wordmakers to invent a phrase that describes the feeling that engulfs you when you learn that your best friend, who you thought

506

was dead, has, in fact, gone and given birth to you.

Meredith—for whom I now learned Mary had been a childhood nickname—went on to tell me about how she'd been released from the hospital in San Francisco after two weeks of painful withdrawals and psychiatric observation and found herself utterly alone. She'd attempted to go back to the Trips Center but found that it had burned down. She'd looked for me and couldn't find me—not in San Francisco or anywhere else. She had nothing left and nothing left to lose, so she set out across the country hitchhiking and scoring dough by singing in bars when she could. With nowhere to go, she'd gotten caught up in a whole lot of things as she drifted along from town to town, using whatever drugs she could find to supplement her growing alcohol dependency. She'd had a very turbulent and listless existence for quite a while, and just when she thought she was nearing the end of her rope, when she felt like she couldn't bear drawing the short stick one more time and there was nothing else good left for her in the world, she received a long-overdue letter from a legal practice that informed her that her father had passed away and that there was an inheritance coming to her.

It was only after she knew of the actual sum of the inheritance that she learned how she came to acquire it. As it turns out, Sophia had bequeathed to Mary a hefty chunk of her possessions; priceless heirlooms and expensive jewelry that Mary had never seen. But after Sophia's death, her father Job had kept them for himself. In addition, Sophia had owned property in her own name that she'd left to Mary and her brother, but her brother had died in an accident two years after Sophia, so Job acquired the rights to the property and sold it for a pretty penny. Since he'd retained the provisions from Sophia's death and saved the money from the sale of the property, he was worth a generous sum when he died, and since he hadn't written a will, Mary, being next of kin, had been awarded all of it. The total sum, she told me, had been something like $500,000.

"After I had all that money in the bank," she explained to me, "I felt like I could do anything. However, I knew that if I stayed where I was at the time, I would have blown it all, so with nothing more than a suitcase and a checkbook, I set out again. I remember getting on a bus in Bakersfield and heading north without a clue in the world of where I'd end up, and don't you know one of the stops was here, in Fresno? I got off at the bus station and just started walking. I'd been in Fresno once before when I went looking for you after you...left...and I got down to 7th Street and saw that the house you'd told me had been yours—this house here, Rhiannon—had been for sale. Don't you know I bought it? I paid for it outright, entirely on a whim.

"Now, even that kind of inheritance can only take you so far, especially when you're hooked on alcohol, so I started working. My voice wasn't nearly as good as it used to be, so I began waitressing and bartending, and it was at a bar I'd been working at downtown where I met George. That was in 1980, and I fell in love. I can't tell you the reasons why—after all, is love ever something you can explain? We began living together, and shortly after that, I found out I was pregnant. I was still drinking heavily at the time, and I told him that I didn't want a baby. I felt that I was entirely incapable of caring for another human life, considering how royally I'd screwed up my own. And with George..." she shook her head, "...George being the sober and level-headed one, he told me that I'd forever regret well...terminating...my pregnancy and that he wanted to have a child with me, so I hung in there. We got married, I quit drinking—and let me tell you, that was no easy feat. Oh, I struggled with it for years; I can't say that even now I don't from time to time. When you were born, I named you after the girl who had saved my life, Rhiannon.

"At first, it was wonderful, more wonderful than I could have ever imagined, but when you were only a few months old, I had a nervous breakdown. That's no exaggeration, Rhiannon; it was a real bona fide nervous breakdown with all the bells and whistles. George was visiting me over in the wiggie ward for months. And you know," she laughed somewhat incredulously, "he'd come in with you and talk to all the nurses and receptionists and tell them all about the time he saw the Dead at Winterland in '73 or the Hollywood Palladium in '71, and even after hearing about all of *that* they never even attempted to hold him for observation. Maybe it was because I was the one screaming my repressed memories of heroin overdose, inoperable brain tumors, and mysteriously vanishing girls in white convertibles over in the next room. The doctors attributed it to postpartum depression and a troubled past and treated me accordingly with enough tranquilizers to kill a horse and enough psychoanalysis to send Freud screaming into the night. It was October by the time they released me.

"What happened after that...well, at the time I felt like I had no other choice. After dealing with all those old, painful memories of my mother and Bobby and the breakup of the band, the literal disintegration of my lifestyle, and years and years of substance abuse and depression, I decided that I'd had enough. I felt like the only thing I could do to move on and get better from it all was to cut myself off from anything and everything that reminded me of my past, of that lifestyle. I divorced George, quit my bartending job, and started going to church. I wanted to get full custody of you, but George wouldn't allow it, and with my history, he had the upper hand anyway, if we ever went to court. He'd never blackmail me, but I felt guilty all on my own. He was a good father, so we split custody. It was a hard thing for me to do—divorcing George. After all, I still loved him, but for the sake of my own welfare and sanity, I couldn't stay with him.

"It took a few years for me to recover, but once I began to feel like I was stable, like I was moving on from the trauma of my past, like I had a handle on my life, you started to grow up. You started playing the drums, you started listening to all that old music, your personality started to emerge, and from the time you hit puberty, even your voice began to remind me of someone else; someone I'd known once before. I started to believe that there was something terribly wrong with me, that I was going insane, that I was delusional, because every time I looked at you—my own child that I gave birth to—I saw instead the Rhiannon that I had been friends with, the Rhiannon I'd played music with, the Rhiannon I'd traveled the country and gone to Woodstock with, the Rhiannon I'd done so many drugs with, the Rhiannon that had saved my life...

"On one hand, I knew it was impossible, it was too far out of the realm of reality, but on the other, I couldn't deny it. To live in that kind of fear of lucidity for that long is agonizing. I couldn't tell my therapist, I couldn't tell George, and I sure as hell couldn't tell you—and as time went on, it just got worse and worse. I started to realize that if anybody ever found out how insane I really was, they'd take you away from me, and if they found out how insane George was, they'd take you away from him too, so I kept my mouth shut. Really, I've been lonely for a very long time. George—as sad as it is to say it—is my best friend. Sure, I have acquaintances with whom I am close, but they and I share no similar experiences. I am in a much healthier environment both physically and mentally, but there are certainly times when I ache for the days of my youth when I was living in the Trips Center in the late sixties with The Day Trippers. Nobody that I've known in years have I been able to call a friend in the same way that I called Bobby and Jules, Al and Space, Billy and Faye, and...and...*you*...friends. With the friends I have today, I lack that closeness, those common bonds, that unconditional love—that comfort to be able to say and do and feel anything I want and not be judged for it. It's hard to find empathy in this town—and in this world—nowadays.

509

"And all the while, compounded by the loneliness and the fear, I watched you become increasingly enchanted with the lifestyle I'd tried so hard to spare you from. I didn't know what to do. All I could think was that I couldn't let you go down the same sad road that I'd gone down because I didn't want you to get hurt the way I did. I love you very much, Rhiannon, and I projected all my fears onto you. Protecting you is the only thing I could focus on that kept me sane, that kept my mind busy, that made me feel like I was worth anything in this life, but now I realize that it caused us to grow apart and that in trying to protect you, maybe I hurt you after all..."

Somehow, I'd been able to hold myself together during the whole time she'd been telling me this, and when she finished and sat back in her chair looking tired and old, I just burst out into tears—which on the whole is probably a hell of a lot better than the maniacal laughter I'd felt boiling up inside me earlier. I wept for the absurdity of it all; for the beauty and for the pain, for desire—that primal urge that both drives man's greatest feats and nullifies all his accomplishments. Tears flowed from my eyes and ran down my face and neck and over my breasts as so many memories flashed through my mind; memories of the past that we shared—the past that had made us—and the future that would be so much richer for it.

In-between ragged gasps for air, I uttered the words I never thought I'd hear myself say, "I understand you, Mom."

Now, as you can imagine, we were both a mess, but it was the most beautiful mess I had ever witnessed. It was the kind of scene that makes the gods smile, the kind of endearing moment found occasionally amongst the throes of humanity that incites the possibility of forgiveness for all our wretched shortcomings and inspires maybe even the slightest bit of hope. After all, I was only crying because there was no room for tears in my swelling heart.

"I'm sorry," she blubbered.

"No," I replied as I dried my face on my sleeve, "I'm sorry. You've never hurt me, but I've hurt you. There was no way I could have understood...I can't blame you for anything."

A shudder of release passed through her, and a cry escaped from between her lips. There was no way to hold back the tears.

Once we'd finally emptied our tear ducts and our consciences alike, we just gazed across the table at one another through exhausted, tearstained eyes and sighed. Looking at her in the eyes, she wasn't my mother anymore—the woman I'd resented most of my childhood—she was Mary, the tender, innocent friend whom I'd shared the best times

510

of my life with. Her face was unrecognizable, and her ebullience and optimism had been worn down by years of hardship, but when I looked into her eyes, somewhere deep inside, the Mary I'd once known was still there, and even if no one else could see her, I could.

"You know," she spoke hoarsely with the faintest of smiles on her face—an expression so foreign I was surprised her muscles remembered how it was done—"even though I searched for you all those years, I always knew that I wasn't going to find you. I remembered what you'd told us about being from the future, and when you disappeared from the hospital and I couldn't find you in San Francisco, I knew then that I wasn't going to find you at all. I knew that somehow, someway, you'd gone back. And even though I searched for you and knew I wasn't going to find you, I still had this inexplicable sense that I was going to see you again. No matter how much time passed, I always felt that way, and now, here we are at last—seeing each other again. It's been a long time."

By the end of this exchange, my head was spinning. In fact, the whole room was spinning. It was all just too much for me to take in at once. I couldn't cope with all these stunning vicissitudes without allowing my brain a chance to reboot. I left the kitchen and I laid down on my bed in a room I was shocked wasn't covered in dust and cobwebs upon entering. I tried to sleep, but those poor neural turbines of mine had been firing like a machine gun for so long that stillness was just too far outside the realm of reality. Even with all my practice in meditation, there were some nagging thoughts, revelations, and questions that couldn't resist making a curtain call.

I was in complete standing awe of how much my life had changed since the last time I had lain in this bed. I was a completely different person when I walked in that door than I had been the last time I'd walked out. I almost felt as if I was revisiting a past life. I began to experience a tinge of that feeling I'd felt when I first woke up in San Francisco—that all this was just a dream; that I was going to wake up soon and find myself back where I'd been before, trembling in horror. But just like last time, reality persisted. Was it absurd, absolutely unbelievable? Yes; but it was also real. Science might call it a relative illusion, theologians might call me possessed, skeptics might discount the whole thing as a coincidence, but what was undeniable here was that there were forces at work we couldn't pretend to explain or even begin to understand.

All I knew was that I wasn't the only one anymore. Mary, Meredith, my mother—she knew too, she understood, but she had paid a heavy price for her empathy. She had wandered thirty years in a tangled forest of uncertainty and was only just now emerging back out into the light of truth on the other side—I was the lucky one by far.

I felt like I'd stepped into so many different worlds over the last couple of months, and now I had so many questions, the most imperative of those being: *what had happened to everybody else?* As much as I tried to hold back these inquiries, it was like trying to stop up a river without a dam, and my thoughts continued to steamroll me again and again.

I hadn't been alone for more than ten minutes when the phone rang, and a feeling like cracked glass spread throughout my body. The first time, I just let it ring—there was no way I could answer it—but it rang again, and then a third time. I'd just come down from the psychedelic trip of a lifetime, traveled thirty years in one night, the dynamics of the most important relationship in my life had just been entirely altered, and I couldn't even get a cat nap. Finally, just to silence the damn thing, I got up and answered it. It was Marty on the line, and as soon as he heard my voice, he began talking a mile a minute.

"Goddamn, Rhiannon! Finally! I've been calling all morning, where were you? We're getting everything together to leave now. You won't believe who showed up this morning—my fucking father! Come over, will ya?"

"I'll be right over," I said and hung up the phone.

I swayed on my feet. I was experiencing cultural whiplash, and I really needed a hit of something to at least slow down my mind before I blew a fuse or something. I sat back down on my bed for what was supposed to be only a minute, but this time I must have fallen asleep—probably just out of sheer exhaustion—and woke up about an hour later. Boy, was Marty going to have some questions for me. Although, the sleep—however brief—had been entirely worth it. I no longer felt like my head was cracking open, but I was still extremely withdrawn. I hadn't even had time to reevaluate the events of this once-removed reality before being thrown back into it. I felt like I was stepping back onto a treadmill that was already moving, and the transition was clumsy at best.

****

****

In the garage, I broke down my drum kit and heaved the cases out to the back door before setting off across the street to Marty's. I felt like I was walking around inside of a dream, treading inside of my own mind—is it any wonder at all everybody thought of me as distant that day?

When I walked in the door, I saw that everybody was gathered in the living room. Several duffle bags, backpacks, and Shania's matching three-piece luggage set dotted the all-but-empty room. To my surprise, the living room was almost clean; all the garbage had been picked up—although Marty's room looked like a bomb had hit it.

"My father complained about the mess," he explained as soon as I appeared in the doorway.

"It's nice of you to show up now that we're all done cleaning," Jeff chided me playfully.

"Where the hell were you all morning?" Marty demanded. "Seriously!"

I grappled with how to answer him. Luckily for me, Shania intervened.

"Woah, Rhiannon! You didn't tell me you were going to dye your hair like that!" she came bounding over to me and examined it. "This is really pretty! You look like a little hippie! Did you do this for tonight?"

"I hadn't exactly planned on it…" were the only words I could manage.

"You should've been here last night," Jeff interrupted. "What a blast! Ecstasy is a great drug, Rhiannon, you've got to try it! It's like weed without the munchies—full on sativa! We were blasting *The Soft Parade* at like three in the morning and dancing, and you should've seen the TV! The graphics in *Final Fantasy* looked like they were coming right out of it! It was so fucking cool!"

Deep down inside myself, I was shaking my head. I can't say that I was prepared for their ignorance, and I had to remind myself that they were just stepping out. To them, the experience had truly been a wild night, even though when compared to mine, it was like a single toke…on a cigarette. The role reversal was quite shocking, to say the least—only twelve hours ago I had been the amateur. I didn't want to be a buzzkill, so I went along with him for the time being.

"Far out!" I replied. "I can dig it. That sounds really groovy!"

I was substantially taken aback when they laughed, and the look on my face must have evidenced my surprise.

"Aww, Rhiannon, I didn't mean to laugh at you! I thought you were saying that to be funny," Shania apologized.

"Oh...well...I-I was. I mean, yeah—that's, um, really cool, Jeff, really cool..."

"Dave told us that he gave you some really serious shit," Marty said, "DMT or something like that. He told us that it's the most powerful psychedelic ever discovered."

I nodded.

"Are you really going to take that shit? Are you really going to try it, Rhiannon?" Jeff badgered me.

"As a matter of fact," I replied in a shaking voice, "I did."

Jeff's feet almost left the ground, "Holy shit, Rhiannon! Really?"

I nodded again.

"Is that why you're so out of it today?" Marty asked.

"I suppose so..."

"Well, what was it like?! Tell us!"

I shook my head to try and dispel the awe and disbelief that enveloped me whenever I thought about it, "It was...life-changing."

"Well fucking A, Rhiannon! Come on, tell us! Don't leave us hanging!"

"Believe me, Marty," I replied, "I wish I could...I really, really wish I could."

He held up his hands, "Alright, alright, we won't bug you. It's your trip after all."

"Thanks," I said.

"—But if you ever decide you want to tell us about it, we're all ears," Jeff couldn't resist adding.

"We're about to go get a bite to eat before we pack up the truck and head on out of here, you coming?" Leanne asked.

"Oh...no, I think I'll pass. I'm not hungry," I answered.

"You sure? It's a long drive," Shania said.

"Yeah."

"Alright, suit yourself," Leanne shrugged.

"Let's go, gang, vamos!" Jeff cried. "To Taco Bell!"

At once, everyone turned and walked single file out the door, but just a couple seconds later, Marty poked his head back inside and said to me, "Hey Rhiannon, Jeff broke the toilet last night, so if you need to use the bathroom, you're going to have to use the one in my *father's* room." He screwed up his face when he said the word. "The door's unlocked."

"Thanks," I replied, and he disappeared out the door once more.

To my surprise, it felt like his suggestion had invigorated my bodily processes because, for the first time in thirty years, I felt an overwhelming urge to relieve myself. I headed down the hallway and turned into the last room on the left. As soon as I walked in, the first thing that I saw was none other than Al's Spectrum of America painting which hung in full view above the bed. My mouth fell open, and my eyes just about tumbled right out of their sockets. Marty's father—of all people—had bought that painting. Of the six billion people in the world and the two hundred million or so that lived in America alone, Marty's father had bought Al's freaking painting.

As I gaped at it, all those memories began to flood my mind: the bliss, the wonder, the excitement, the fun, the joy, the peace, the love, and the beauty that had abounded during our journey across America and that month we'd spent living together in the Trips Mobile all came back to me at once. How fantastic it had been…unequivocally the best time of my life. I didn't suppose that painting had any contact information on the back of it; my heart still ached for Al. God, how I missed the way things used to be.

Once I'd gotten over the initial shock and my eyes began to drift around the room, I noticed with surprise that it was decorated thoroughly. It looked like a miniature art gallery, and all the paintings were of a similar style. It seemed like Marty's father was some sort of a connoisseur. As I examined the numerous canvases, my gaze came to rest upon a series of framed photographs sitting atop a dresser. There was a picture of Marty's mother as a young woman and a few photos of Marty as a child, and as I looked closer, all the way in the corner, poking out from behind the others, I recognized a photograph that was all too startlingly familiar—way, way too familiar. I moved the others aside and just about toppled over in shock—no, shock is not a strong enough word to describe how I felt—for the photograph I held in my hand was the very same one I'd left with my mother back at the house…the very same one I'd given to Al the last time I'd seen him before he'd departed from the Trips Center on that fateful day. I could hardly believe my eyes, and as I racked my brain to try and arrive at even a remote semblance of an explanation, I heard a voice from behind me speak my name, "Rhiannon?"

I spun around and was met with a man who was all but a virtual stranger to me. I was surprised that he even knew my name; after all,

I'd only met Marty's father once or twice. His presence was unremarkable, and his voice was unfamiliar; however, when I looked into his eyes, I found that they were two thousand years old. He'd lived many lifetimes since I'd seen him last, and now the rest of him had aged to match. His head which had once boasted hair as long and as beautiful as mine was now bald and shaven, and his goatee was rapidly fading to gray. He was still as thin as he had been the last time I'd seen him and maybe even thinner now. His body was worn down from the road, and although his eyes still retained that familiar spark that they'd had in his youth, they had dimmed somewhat.

"Al..." I whispered, dumbstruck.

"I knew it!" he spoke in an excited whisper. "The others suspected but I knew! Oh Rhiannon, Rhiannon!"

I lunged into his arms, and tears of consummate relief streamed down my face.

"Rhiannon, Rhiannon..." he repeated my name again and again, the tone of his voice wavering between shock and disbelief. "I knew I'd see you again someday! I knew you were really from the future! Do you know how I knew, Rhiannon?" He took my hands in his and met my eyes, "I have a confession to make," he said. "Do you remember the first night The Day Trippers played the Fillmore West?"

I nodded.

"Well, I drove your car back to the Trips Center after that show. I'd been speaking with Mary earlier that day, and she'd told me all about you and how you'd said that you were from the future. I've never been one to pry, but I couldn't resist a look, a glimpse into the future, if you will, and I found it in your glovebox—along with the half gram of DMT that confirmed your story—in the form of a CD. It was the first of its kind that I'd ever seen and the last I laid my eyes upon for a good twenty years. It was a copy of Ten Years After's *A Space In Time*. I listened to that CD, Rhiannon, I just couldn't help myself. I slipped it into the curious-looking slot beneath the radio, and I listened to the whole damn thing, then I put it back in its case in the glovebox and never spoke a word to anyone. In and of itself, that wasn't the most astounding moment of my life—that is, until now, of course—that came in 1972 when Ten Years After released that album, and again, when CDs came out.

"Throughout my life, Rhiannon, all those things you spoke of— those glimpses into the future—I watched manifest all around me. I've thought of you often, Rhiannon, and I've carried you with me—that photo of us with me—throughout all corners of the world. And now—

516

" he shook his head in awe, "here you are again in the flesh, exactly as I saw you last. You haven't aged, you haven't changed—not at all! You remain young while I have grown old, and yet we share the same memories from so long ago. How it could be true..." he stepped back from our embrace and caressed my face, "I will never know."

I touched his hand to reassure myself that he was really there, that he was really real, "Tell me, Al, what happened after I left? With The Day Trippers, I mean. Have you stayed in contact with anyone?"

Al smiled, "I have," he said. "I made it my mission for a while to reconnect. Billy and Faye, surprisingly, were the easiest to locate. They settled out in New Mexico, a few miles from a town called Taos. They've got all this acreage down there, and they've got a bunch of other people living with them, kind of like a little commune. Their kids and grandkids live with them there, and they've got a barn and a guesthouse and a bunch of trailers parked all around. They've got a garden and a well and some horses and chickens too. I was out there maybe about six months ago, and I did a few paintings.

"I found Space too, and he proved to be more of a challenge. They let him out of the clink after twenty-five years because of good behavior—and some sweet-talking I'm sure—and then he fell off the radar. I got back in touch with him about two years ago. He still lives in California, but way north, on the border of Oregon. He did go and live in an ashram for a while, and now he teaches yoga five times a week. He got married not too long after he got out to a nutritionist named Alexa, and they have a daughter now who's probably about four. For a man who's done that kind of hard time, he's very much at peace with his life, very much the same man he was before he went away. He still plays music too, he's in a little pick-up jam band that gathers once or twice a week and does some shows in town. I played with him a couple times just last month, he's still got it.

"Eventually, I found Jules too. When I last saw him about six or seven years ago, he was living down in Panama, high on the hog. I spent close to a year in South America before I located him, and since then, we haven't kept in touch. He's still a bit fried from when he lit out of San Francisco. It's sad to say, but he burned out; his mind never really came back together the way it should've..." he trailed off. "But you know who I never found and I think of often? Mary Jane. In all my years of traveling and searching, I never did find Mary Jane."

Out came the maniacal laughter. The irony was almost too much to bear—that the only one who had evaded Al's tireless search for so long was the one who had lived across the street from him for almost twenty years. Now it was Al's turn to reel in utter astonishment as I explained to him the events of the last couple hours. He was so overwhelmed that he had to sit down on the bed, and I joined him.

"There's something else I must ask you," Al implored me, "about Bobby. I didn't return to San Francisco after I left until the following April. By that time, it was common knowledge that he'd moved on— gone west on the back of a pale stallion, as Avi broke it to me. I can't say I was surprised, but I took the news of his death harder than I'd expected. Maybe it sounds callous, but I knew long before his demise that Bobby wouldn't make it to thirty. He was terminal; he had a fatal attraction to his own reflection—like a moth drawn into a flame—but little did he know that flame was the flashbang of his own ego. To see his image mortally wounded the way it had been, he couldn't cope. I saw it in his eyes the day that I left, and I'd seen it numerous times before—defeatism, bitterness, and self-loathing—the suicidal trifecta. Every other time; however, he'd bounced back, and it wasn't the result of anything that I or anyone else said or did, it was simply because he found some worthwhile reason to keep on keeping on.

"As his brother, I almost had to deaden myself to that fact—maybe I even found solace in it—but when that awful nightmare finally came true, it didn't make it any easier. Part of it was because no one seemed to know exactly what had happened. According to everyone I'd talked to, he'd shirked all public notice in the weeks leading up to his death and resurfaced in an alleyway on the day of that Altamont debacle. Somebody had found him and tipped off the authorities, but nobody knew who. I always presumed it to have been you or Mary," he inhaled sharply. "Was it?"

I proceeded to tell him all about those last few days of Bobby's tragic and tumultuous life. It was somewhat therapeutic to speak of it, to let it all out, and when my account was finished, although he was assuaged, I was the one sighing in relief.

"So you don't think that it was me who sent him over the edge?" I asked.

"No," Al reassured me without a shred of doubt, "he was dead set on his fate."

I gazed up at the framed photograph of us, "Do you think that he was afraid?" I wondered out loud.

"No, I don't think so," Al replied after a moment. "All Bobby was concerned with was getting out; I highly doubt that he thought much about what might greet him on the other side. And as far as dying is concerned, he knew exactly what he was doing. I know my brother.

He kept going back to that stuff because it was the only way he knew that he had control over his life. It was the power he spent the whole latter half of his life looking for. When he was high, he could be his own god; he had the power to end that which he hadn't begun. Whenever he measured his dope in a spoon or a dropper, he knew he was taking his life into his own hands."

I cast my weary eyes down to my boots and nodded.

"You know," Al spoke after a lengthy silence, "there's something—an energy, a thought, or an idea—that pervaded that space in time and didn't climb out of there with us. It got left behind, just like those people who did, like Bobby. You can't find it around here anymore; it's almost like it couldn't stand the light of day, as if it were a delicate dew that evaporated in the new dawn, a substantiating principle that shifted under the weight of so many expectant gazes—each one expecting something different. Once everybody turned to look, it was gone. Or, maybe it wasn't gone at all, but rather changed; just like anything good and pure, once it's on Earth for too long, it gets crucified or corrupted. We stumbled across something that couldn't be named, and we all knew it…and yet, before we knew it, it was all over in the blink of an eye. You know what I mean, Rhiannon?"

I nodded slowly, "I can dig that."

"Nothing quite like it could ever exist again. What we witnessed, what we were, and what we became was all the result of a combination of factors that no one could ever hope to replicate. You're lucky in a way, Rhiannon," he told me, "you weren't there to see it fade away, corrode over the years, turn inside out, and start lapping up the mud. You didn't have to watch it die before your eyes, become mundane, cliché…"

"I wondered then and I wonder now, how is this what we've become?" I implored him. "Girls were boys and boys were girls, we lived in the moment and meditated on forever. We sat down for freedom, and we got in bed for peace. We played music to change the world and took drugs to change ourselves. We made love like there was no tomorrow, but we believed we'd prevail forever. Where'd we go wrong?"

"We treated rock n' roll like a religion and straight life like suicide, and to this day I can't quite decide which was more heinous."

"Do you think it was us who screwed up?" I entreated him. "Was it the System that caused us to fail? Was it just the wrong time, the wrong place?"

He met my eyes, "I think it was fate."

We were silent for a moment. "You know," I spoke in melancholic awe, "back then, everybody had the same look in their eye…you still do."

"So do you," he replied.

"Well," I whispered, "that was just yesterday."

As we studied one another's stunned countenances in silence in an attempt to reconcile our mutual, persistent disbelief, I heard the sound of everybody returning from lunch. Immediately, it seemed, the depth of our shared connection was strained as reality walked back in through the door. My brief stopover in timeless limbo was over all too soon.

"That's my cue," I told Al. "I have to go now—I don't want to have to explain this."

Al nodded his shared sentiment, and I made a beeline for the bathroom. As I came back down the hallway, everybody else met me by the door with arms full of equipment. I'm not exactly sure what expression I wore at that moment or how it was perceived, but it was most certainly different from everybody else's grand smiles, and I must've stuck out like a cynic at a revival. I knew because Marty's face fell when he saw me.

"Are you excited at all about going to San Francisco?" he accused me. "You show up late, you flake out on lunch, and you look like you just watched your dog get hit by a car! What gives?! I always thought you'd be the first one to the door if it meant getting out of here!"

"Oh, Marty," I replied, "of course I'm excited! It's just that everything is so sudden, you know? Everything is different now."

"Of course it is!" he replied, exasperated. "That's kind of the point, isn't it? I'll tell you what, Rhiannon, don't be a wet blanket just because your asswipe mother has been breathing down your neck for so long. Once we get to San Francisco, you'll be free of her! You won't even think about her, that bitch!"

I didn't answer him. I felt this uncanny urge boiling up inside me— the urge to defend her—and it was so unprecedented that I had to allot time to analyze it.

"She's not so bad," I murmured.

"Not so bad?!" Marty cried indignantly. "Ha! Rhiannon, she reported you as a missing person because you were two hours past your curfew!" He spun around and started walking out the door, "Come on, Rhiannon, let's go meet our big break before she gets any deeper into your head."

I set my expression and collected myself, then followed him

outside.

"Let's take two cars," Shania suggested, "so we have more mobility when we're there. How about you boys and Leanne take the truck, and I'll go with Rhiannon in her car?"

Everybody agreed, and while Leanne and the boys piled into Marty's truck, Shania followed me back across the street and helped me load my drums into the back seat.

She gasped when she saw my car, "Rhiannon! What happened to your interior? It's all torn up!"

"Oh, that..." I trailed off. Despite the fact that it was true, burrowing hippies was not going to be a suitable explanation. "I'm not real sure," I replied, "maybe it happened when we were moving equipment. I left the top down last night, maybe a raccoon got in here."

Shania was dismayed, "But, Rhiannon, you love this car! Aren't you upset?"

I shrugged, "It can be fixed. I'm surprised it's stayed as nice as it has for this long, considering how much it's been through." I tossed her the keys, "You drive."

"Are you feeling OK, Rhiannon?" she asked me, I could sense the concern in her voice.

"I'll be fine," I answered, "I'm just tired. I need some time to sleep and get my head."

"Long night last night?" she assumed.

I climbed into the back and cleared a space for myself in-between the drum cases, "You wouldn't believe how long if I told you."

The fact that I was withholding something major was blatantly obvious, but I was afraid that if I spoke too much, all of those things that I'd recently heard and had just barely been able to swallow would all come back up out of my mouth.

"I'll tell you what," Shania said, "here's the map. You nap in the back there, and I'll wake you when we get closer to the City and I need directions. I'm not all that great at driving stick, I just hope I don't fry your transmission between here and San Francisco; you'll have bigger problems than just the upholstery."

"Everything will be copasetic," I assured her as she turned the key in the ignition.

As Shania shifted into reverse, I began to settle in for the ride. However, we weren't even all the way out of the driveway yet when I yelled, "Wait! Stop!"

Poor, startled Shania brought my car to a bucking halt and spun around to face me.

"I'll just be a second," I explained and disappeared into the house.

Meredith was still sitting at the kitchen table with the photograph in her hand; she hadn't moved.

I stood in the doorway, "Mom?" I called. "Mary?"

She lifted her head, and her gaze softened when her eyes met mine. Her cheeks were still tearstained, her blue eyes still bloodshot, but the faintest trace of a smile had replaced the scowl that she'd worn for so long. When her eyebrows weren't knit together in a grimace, she looked to be about ten years younger. The Mary I used to know was still in there, flitting about somewhere deep inside and only appearing on the surface in momentary glimpses, but those glimpses gave me hope. Her transformation had already begun. That characteristic heaviness that I'd always felt when I was in her presence had lifted. She'd finally let down the burden that she'd carried for so many years. Fear and disapproval were absent from her eyes and instead what radiated from them was gratitude and love. I ran to her.

Our embrace was liberating in every sense of the word. I was leaving and she knew it, but she also knew that I had it in my mind to come back. She'd made peace with it. She wasn't afraid, and I wasn't desperate. She trusted me, and I trusted her.

"Take lots of pictures," she whispered as she held me.

"I love you, Mom," I replied.

"I love you too, Rhiannon," she spoke in earnest. "Thank you."

"For what?" I asked.

"For saving my life."

"There's something else you'll be thanking me for," I said coyly, trying to stifle the grin that struggled to overtake my expression.

"What's that?"

"When I leave, I want you to go across the street to the house where my friend Marty lives and knock on the door until his father answers."

"Why?"

My smile was incorrigible, "You'll see." I kissed her on the cheek and fled to the door, "I'll call you when I get there."

Shania was still idling halfway out of the driveway when I returned to the car.

"What did you forget?" she asked me.

"To hug my mom," I answered.

She didn't reply, but the shuddering and bucking of the car was enough to give me a clue as to what it might have been.

The fact was, this reality was far stranger than the one I'd recently returned from. The connection I'd always shared with my friends had been stopped up with differences in opinion and untranslatable experience. Communication was becoming increasingly difficult between us, and the person I had the most in common with was Meredith. Now I was sure that I must've stepped into a parallel universe.

Curled up on the seat as the dry summer air flowed over my body and rippled through my clothes, I looked down at my feet, still clad in Mary's green boots. There's an old idiom floating around out there, something about walking a mile in somebody else's moccasins—well, I'd done that, literally, and it hadn't been just one mile, it had been several thousand. There was an unbreakable bond hewn between us now, one unlike any other. Understanding abounded on a level I would've previously thought inconceivable. Those boots had seen me through the fantastic, and the wear on the treads alone served as evidence to the impossible.

Despite the dizzying pace of my mind, respite in the form of sleep arrived promptly upon our departure and lasted until Shania's screaming woke me as we crossed over the Bay Bridge. Her exact words were largely incoherent, but her horror was clear. After all, driving an unfamiliar car through Oakland rush hour traffic, unsure about which of the ten lanes you're supposed to be in as a toll approaches and the map flies out the window is enough to rattle even the most serene motorist.

"I don't know where to go! I don't know where to go!" she shrieked over the roar of passing semis and those honking as they attempted to merge. She was almost in tears.

I shook off the last lingering vestiges of sleep and leaned forward on the console, "Just stay straight," I instructed her as we left the bridge and exits and cross-streets began to appear on all sides of us. "We're going to the Fillmore, right, the old one that they remodeled?"

"I don't know!" she cried. "All I know is the Fillmore!"

"Alright, take it easy, Shania. I'll get us there."

"How!?" she wailed.

Luckily, I'd paid close attention to the stories The Day Trippers had told me about all the old clubs, and I knew that Bill Graham's original Fillmore Auditorium stood on the corner of Geary Boulevard and Fillmore Street—piece of cake. However, my confidence did nothing to calm Shania's nerves—I think it was all the hills that sealed the deal.

"I'm never driving your car again!" she cried as she struggled to shift into gear on a sixty-degree slope.

However, she changed her tune immediately as we pulled into the parking lot of the Fillmore unscathed and without need of a detour.

"Christ, Rhiannon! What did you do, study the damn map? How could you possibly know how to get here? I thought you'd never been to San Francisco before!"

All I could do was shrug and smile.

It was a while before Marty and the others arrived, and during that interim period while Shania remembered how to breathe again, I took the opportunity to make some calls from the payphone outside the Fillmore. Instinctively, I pulled a dime from my pocket, but I needed to insert one more and a nickel before I could place my call. I dialed Meredith first, but there was no answer. I smiled to myself when I got the answering machine—I figured that meant she was still with Al. The second person I called was George, but Jack answered instead.

"Hey Jack, it's Rhiannon. Is my dad there?"

"Hey, Kiddo! Naw, I hate to break it to you, but he's off on another trip. Jerry and the guys played the Beacon Theatre this week in '76. He's gone to pay homage to the man."

"I know where that's at," I told him. "When you hear from him, can you let him know I made it to San Francisco? Can you tell him I—no, never mind, I'll tell him myself."

"You got it, Kiddo," Jack replied. "Have a blast in San Francisco! Peace!"

I hung up the phone and glanced up at the marquee. None of the acts listed were familiar to me. An insane surreal feeling came upon me then, along with a thought that was equally as strange: Bill Graham's original Fillmore ballroom—which had been decommissioned before I'd even set foot in this city—had been revitalized, but all those rock gods San Francisco was known for were either dead or long departed. Jefferson Airplane, Janis, Big Brother, the Dead, Quicksilver, New Riders—hell, even The Day Trippers— were merely names for the books, seen now in these parts only on the backs of t-shirts and scrawled on hand-drawn posters that sold at auction for ten bucks a pop. History had staked its claim here too, and that wasn't the only evidence of change—differences abounded at every glance.

However, just like before, I didn't get the chance to reel in this hardly believable absurdity before reality barged back in, each time with unprecedented force. This time it took the form of Marty's car horn. He pulled into the parking lot and just blasted it, making everybody in the vicinity jump. Jeff was hanging out the window yelling, "We're here! We made it!" He had a beer bottle in his hand, and as Marty jerked the truck to a stop, foam bubbled out of the neck.

Marty rolled down the window and shouted to Shania and me, "Hey! We're mad early! He said eight, and it's only six-thirty. Let's see if we can find a motel where we can dump all this equipment."

Everybody voiced their agreement, but nobody moved. After all, where was there a cheap motel to be had in this unfamiliar city?

"I know a place," I spoke up finally.

"I'm NOT driving," Shania declared.

I sucked it up and got behind the wheel. Despite my spinning head and that persistent feeling of unreality, I was still more fit to drive than Shania or Jeff. At least Marty had the luxury of an automatic transmission. Shania rode shotgun, and Marty followed us down to the Travelodge on Market Street. The name had changed and the motel had been built up, but it was still as cut-rate as it had been back in the day, although the terms and conditions of what was considered 'cheap' had been radically altered. A cheap motel in 2000 cost us fifty dollars, while a room in this place thirty years ago probably would've gone for twelve bucks, and Space could've secured it for two weeks with an 8-ball.

After hauling all our equipment up to a second-floor room via the stairwell, we set off again in the direction we'd come, this time all together in my car. I wouldn't have minded driving the fifteen minutes back to the Fillmore, but Marty decided that it would be a worthy challenge to brush up on his stick shift skills, and the rest of us climbed in warily and braced ourselves for disaster.

"You knew how to get to the club and to the motel, did that map you were looking at happen to show which streets were the flattest?!" Shania implored me as Marty took the wheel.

"Let's drive down Haight Street," I suggested.

"Where's that?" Marty asked.

I pointed up the road.

"Does that take you out of the way?"

"Sort of."

He checked the clock on the dash, "It's seven-forty, we only have twenty minutes to get back."

"Come on, please, please, please!" I pleaded.

"Oh, alright," Marty acquiesced and swung the car around.

Innumerable memories flooded my mind as we sped along.

"Wow, here we are…in San Francisco!" Jeff marveled as more and more Victorians popped up along the road.

I was floored. Yes, we were there in San Francisco, but in my mind, I was a million miles away. I was in San Francisco too, but in another time. Visions of dancers and beatniks abounded, and memories of traveling heads, smoking yogis, painted ladies, and existentialists just hanging out lined the streets. Reality, however, was much duller. No marijuana haze cloaked the avenues, and no music played to give it its characteristic ambiance. There was a marked absence of VW vans, although there was a strange preponderance of Toyota trucks. The sidewalks were busy as usual, but of those that passed by, many were dressed in straight clothes—no face paint or picket signs were to be seen until you hit the Castro. As we approached Buena Vista Park and the main drag, my eyes widened and my breath caught in my throat. "Slow down! Slow down!" I begged Marty.

"Why?" he asked, surprised at my insistence. "There's nothing to see here, it's just old houses." But he slowed down anyway.

We passed 1216 Haight Street—the address of the Trips Center—but there was no Trips Center to be seen. That big, white historic Victorian had undergone a massive overhaul after the fire. The garage had been rebuilt under the living room, they'd opted for vinyl siding rather than clapboard, and the bay windows had been changed for regular ones. They'd painted it yellow instead of white, and there were certainly no cherubs on the roof. In front of it stood a large tree covered in ivy—it too was a new addition. With my mouth agape, I watched it pass in disbelief as we crawled up the street.

When we got into the heart of Haight-Ashbury, where shops and apartments took the place of the Victorians, I begged Marty to pull over so that we could get out and walk.

"Rhiannon, don't you understand that we're going to be late to the most important appointment of our lives? We can come back another time and sightsee!"

"Come on guys, this is important! This is the Haight for Christssake! As far as rock n' roll and counterculture are concerned, this is *IT*! This is the place where it all began! We need to pay heed to the dues of history..." I went on, but Marty ignored me and just kept driving. I'll admit that at that moment I was being unreasonable, and I stopped hassling him once I caught sight of the intersection: Haight/Ashbury.

There was a Ben and Jerry's on the corner, Holcomb Jewelers was now Haight Ashbury T-Shirts, and a bunch of mad expensive boutiques stood all around. I incurred a row with one shop owner later on in our stay when she tried to convince me that selling forty dollar tie-dye wasn't their stake in ripping off the culture. So much had changed, and yet it was still the same place. The Haight's modern-day proprietors had ensured that all tourists would be aware of its cultural significance by painting the place with murals and mandalas, psychedelic lettering and Day-Glo, but the intrinsic air of this place— my old home—had been eradicated. Their intent was commendable, but their execution was lacking. The Diggers free store was nothing but a bygone fantasy, and iron bars came down over the shop windows at night. This idyllic paradise was no longer even a peaceful place.

Needless to say, the energy around was markedly different. There were many tourists, as usual, but they'd come for something that'd since passed and had been gone a long time. The Haight itself had died with the Movement. The fire of revolution and experimentation, of spiritual seeking and universal brotherhood had burned out long ago. Now it was just a relic, preserved for those who wanted to get a sense of what it once had been—but that was impossible in this place, this terribly unfamiliar place. For those like me who were returning, it was haunting and incredibly sad. In some corners, you could catch a fleeting glimpse of *IT*, but what you saw was only a remnant, a distant echo. The streets were once more filled with strangers: many homeless, many junkies, many burnouts, and some unhinged and disillusioned folk mixed in for good measure. I felt sorry for them; they were here in search of something that'd since departed and taken with it all its glory, leaving behind nothing but rust.

There were still a lot of young people around, along with a fair amount of old men and women with graying beards and fading tie-dye—diehard hippies who'd never moved on. It was them I identified with far more. It was them I wanted to rap to. They, like I, had seen the Haight at the peak of its summum bonum. I really felt bad for all the young people dressed in all the colors of a revolution they'd only ever see in photographs—they'd never truly know what they'd missed.

We arrived back at the Fillmore on time; doors were at eight, and the show started at nine. We weren't really sure what we were in for. Our friendly Track Records A&R guy Dev Marshall had instructed us to meet him at the San Francisco Fillmore at eight o'clock, but he hadn't told us anything about Fear, Smogtown, The Stitches, and Incredibly Strange Wrestling—as the marquee declared we would be seeing that night—and he hadn't mentioned the sixteen-bucks-a-head cover charge either. The first official sign that we were patronizing a scene that wasn't for us came when we saw the line of pink-and-green-haired, Mohawk-and-leather-wearing pierced punk rockers crowding around the will call. The second came when I noticed the large wrestling ring set up in the center of the dance floor which, by the way, was designated standing room only. Actual dancing was frowned upon in this establishment. It might have been Bill Graham's Fillmore Auditorium, but the vibes were all wrong. There were posters for shows both recent and historical that lined the walls of the in-house restaurant, and the architecture was retrofitted and beautiful, but that was just about all there was that resembled the hip San Francisco dance halls of my memory. They even checked our bags and IDs at the door.

The characteristic haze that hung over every hip music venue from San Francisco to London back in the day was absent as well—indoor smoking had been banned. Therefore, there was no scent of grass or patchouli about the place; instead it smelled of cheap perfume and spilt whiskey. When the show actually began later on in the night, I was appalled. Our sixteen-bucks-a-head show consisted of three hardcore punk bands and their head-banging, brain-scrambling noise blasted at an inhumane volume as half-naked tattooed wrestlers pounded one another into a sweaty pulp in the ring. I would've paid sixteen bucks for earplugs. The patrons were different as well, that was for damn sure. They were angry, brassy and crude and their harsh vibrations seeped into the walls where peaceful heads had once gathered. There was no sense of peace or love for one another, and the only form of collectivity that abounded was their incessant rooting for violence and destruction as the wrestlers were flung from the ring into the audience. And yet, a barrel of apples still stood by the door. If Bill Graham could see this, he would've re-decommissioned the club on the spot. These flowers weren't just wilted, they were dead.

When Dev Marshall and his companion—our future manager, Tommy Grilis—finally did arrive—sometime after eight, mind you—they were in high spirits. They apologized for the wait and encouraged us to order anything we wanted from the menu as conciliation, in addition to a round of drinks entirely on them. The boys both ordered a steak dinner with all the trimmings, the girls split an order of lobster, and Jeff guzzled two beers before the food even came. I opted for a tall glass of water and my reveries.

Between my frequent escapes to the lobby bathrooms for some peace and quiet—you could still hear the mayhem from the ballroom in the restaurant—and my periodic retreats into my memories to call up happier times in this city with a better soundtrack, I was left with an abridged version of that night's meeting. They talked about all the routine topics typically covered in an A&R interview: skill set, aspirations, experience, and material—as well as Dev's intent to sign and Tommy's intent to manage—but there were conditions. Dev told us that we needed to record a demo before his label would approve an advance, and Tommy told us that he needed to hear us play live and watch our interaction before he'd take us on. For the most part, I let everybody else do the talking for me, but I wasn't entirely absent from the conversation. After all, I was the one who spoke up when the two of them first arrived and sat down with us at the table.

"You know, what's going on there in the other room…that's not what we're about at all," was the way I'd prefaced our meeting.

"Oh, yes, yes," Dev had assured me, "we're well aware that you play classic rock—covers by request, to be exact. But wouldn't you like to play at a venue like this?"

We all nodded.

"That one band, The Stitches, plays seventies-style punk rock. Tonight, they're playing with Fear, their forefathers, who have been around since the seventies themselves. With us, you can be like them, playing in a beautiful—not to mention sold-out—auditorium, opening for your own idols. You'd like to play with Jefferson Starship or Santana, right? I asked you here to show you that anything's possible."

That was one way to bag a couple of signatures. Their approach was unorthodox, but it sealed the deal, literally. Dev left us with his deal memo in hand and the promise that he'd call us once he received our demo. Tommy hung out with us for a while longer and on a much more informal basis, but followed Dev shortly after.

For the remainder of the evening, everybody was just ecstatic. They were joking and laughing and talking about this most recent development—along with last night—amongst themselves. They were most certainly no longer high on ecstasy, but they'd been drinking and were euphoric and giggly. I'd never tried E, so I didn't know what it had been like, but even though their experience hadn't been as powerful as those I'd undergone myself, they'd still been through it together which, incidentally, made me an outsider—as if I didn't feel that way enough already. They didn't mean to exclude me, in fact, they weren't even aware that they were doing so, it was just a side effect of the experience.

I spent most of that night off by myself. I needed a chance to recoup my hold on reality, and thus far, I hadn't been able to secure it. I was melancholic, disoriented, and suffering from the worst case of jetlag known to man, and the abysmal scene in the room over did nothing to exalt my spirits. When I did interact with everybody else, I tried to do so in good taste so as not to sour the evening or betray my inner turmoil, but once again, I felt like I was stepping back onto a speeding treadmill, and this time I fell flat on my face.

I was seated at the bar drinking a Coke and dreaming of a fat joint when Marty swaggered over to me, lightly toasted.

"Hey-y-y Rhiannon! Want a beer?" he asked, clapping me on the back.

Unfortunately for my reputation, I'd made unthinking honesty a habit of mine during my romp in the past, and now the words just rolled off my tongue without a censor. Strangely enough, I felt as if I was dealing with relative strangers, "Uh—no, I don't drink," I replied.

Marty was substantially taken aback, and I don't blame him, "Rhiannon, what the fuck are you talking about, you don't drink? The last time we played at The Joint, we carried you out!"

"Yeah, well, that was a long time ago," I answered.

"Rhiannon, that was last week! What do you mean that was a long time ago? Man…you've been acting fucking weird all day. What the hell is up with you?"

"Nothing," I replied, shifting uncomfortably. "I'm just—I'm just tired, that's all. I've been thinking a lot."

"Ah, that's what your problem is, you think too much," he declared.

"I've got some heavy things on my mind," I attempted to explain.

"Don't we all?" he replied dismissively. "Say, you got a cigarette? You want to go out for a smoke?"

"No, I-I don't smoke."

"Rhiannon, what the fuck are you talking about, you don't smoke? I bought you a pack of cigarettes yesterday, where are they?"

I paused, "They're gone," I murmured, "I smoked them. I don't have any cigarettes."

He jumped up from the barstool, "See!? That's exactly what I'm fuckin' talking about! You smoked a fucking pack of cigarettes yesterday and you're telling me you don't smoke?!"

"I quit," I replied sullenly, realizing for the first time how I must sound to him.

"Pfft! Quit! Ha!" he exclaimed, unable to contain his incredulity. "Rhi, you better get your head screwed on straight or people around here are gonna start thinking you're fucking crazy or something!" He spun around and walked back to where everybody else was gathered and started gesturing and pointing at me.

I turned back to my Coca-Cola and stared at the posters on the wall. I wasn't too concerned with them thinking I was crazy, after all, they hadn't been entirely sure of my mental stability from the start. It was their disbelief and jest that I couldn't bear. For them to believe that the things I told them were merely figments of my atrophied imagination was something I just couldn't take, and any one of my accounts would lead them to that same conclusion.

Jeff came up to me and tapped me on the shoulder shortly after Marty had gone away.

"What's this I hear about my drinking buddy voluntarily demoting herself to designated driver? We're just about to hit the big time and party for real! We're finally out of Fresno and you've suddenly gone square on me?"

I wasn't really sure how to answer him, "I decided that I don't like the way it makes me feel," I said. "Getting shitfaced is no longer high up on my list of priorities."

The surprise in his expression made it obvious to me that he had a hard time understanding how anyone could possess such sentiments, "Well, will you at least come and hang out with us then? We don't like it when you're sitting all alone."

His concern was noted, but all I wanted to do was leave. When I posed that as a suggestion after I returned back to the group, Marty whined that he didn't want to waste sixteen bucks, but we decided to leave anyway—after all, the entertainment was definitely not for us, nor was it worth the money.

That first night we found ourselves crammed into two twin beds in that crummy little downtown motel in an attempt to ration our funds. One thing we'd evidently forgot, however, was that Jeff snored loud enough to wake the dead. All of us had trouble sleeping that night. Normally, I could sleep through just about anything, especially after all I'd had to put up with in the Trips Mobile, but I couldn't sleep that night. Although, it wasn't so much Jeff's fault as much as it was the result of all those things that were on my mind.

I remember laying there for hours just trying to comprehend the notion that I was truly back. It was just so incredibly surreal and far too much to process all at once. For everybody else, only twenty-four hours had passed since nine o'clock on June 8th, 2000, and while those twenty-four hours for them might have contained more than what the average person experiences in that length of time, without question, mine had still contained much, much more. I wanted more than anything to explain this to them and dispel their confusion and suspicion, but I didn't know where to begin. I wanted to tell them everything, but what was I supposed to say?

✽✽✽✽

****

The next day we played our first gig out of Fresno at a little downtown bar five or six blocks from the Fillmore. It was just one step above a dive and one of those post-hippie establishments that had popped up during the time I'd been gone. It was a small place with a bar and a few booths in one room and a pool table and high-tops in another. Fifty people would've strained the capacity, and we filled the place out to a whopping thirty-five. It wasn't a sold-out auditorium, but for us, it was still a step in the right direction. First of all, it wasn't The Joint, and just having different faces in the audience for once was a welcome change.

To be honest, I was pretty nervous about that first gig; I didn't want to let everybody down. I knew that I was fit to jam with no problem at all, but as far as our rehearsed material was concerned, I was out of practice. We hadn't played together in what for me was months and felt like years. We spent most of the morning going over our setlist, and I spent most of the afternoon trying to remember fills and solos. Mainly because the motel would've kicked us out, a last-minute refresher was out of the question, and I drove to that gig praying that the audience wouldn't request anything outrageous.

Tommy had already arrived when we got there and rapped with us while we set up. I would've loved to just jam; after all, it felt like forever since I'd had a real good jam session even with The Day Trippers, but we had a packed setlist for that night and no room for improv. Because we were in the City, in order to appeal to the local sentiment, we decided that all the songs we covered would be from San Francisco artists. The first tune we played was *Volunteers* off of the Airplane album of the same name, and the last was *We Can Be Together*. *Volunteers* had been the hottest new thing on the scene when I'd split. It had been released only a week or so before Altamont, and it was one of the last things I'd heard before the shit hit the fan. It was an oddly fitting album for such a moment in time. It was as if the Airplane too had sensed the change that was underway, and when I heard Shania and Marty sing the lyrics, emotion welled in my eyes, *"One generation got old, one generation got soul, this generation got no destination to hold..."*

By the time we played *We Can Be Together*, I couldn't hold back the tears. My flagrant display of emotion had no bearing on the quality

533

of our performance. It turned out to be a good show, nothing more and nothing less, but when I played that music—that powerful, beautiful, evocative music—I just couldn't contain myself.

Once Tommy left, we packed up, and the bar was set to close, everyone confronted me.

"You played really good tonight, Rhiannon," Leanne approached me saying.

"Yeah, like really good," Marty added, a hint of suspicion in his voice. "You've been holding out on us."

"I've never heard you play like that," Jeff confessed. "You always play tight, but that was just plain dirty! And that solo you banged out in *The Other One*? —You just killed it! You kept that up for like five whole minutes!"

"You've just been full of surprises lately," Shania said.

"I wonder what else she's got up her sleeve," Jeff marveled.

"Whatever it is, I say save it for our demo," Marty declared.

Everybody else voiced their agreement.

I just whispered my thanks and started carting my drums back out to the truck.

Back at the motel that night, even with the help of Leanne's hash, sleep eluded me once more. Now that I'd begun to make peace with the fact that I was indeed back, the notion that everything I once knew was gone tugged at my heartstrings. The transition back into this old reality was a difficult one, and this wasn't the first or the last night that I'd spend torn in this way.

In fact, I laid awake many nights upon my return. I thought about Billy and Faye, and I thought about Space, and even more so I thought about Bobby. I thought about Al and Mary—old—and I felt old. The more I thought, the more foreign I felt. I felt out of place in my own world, and when I heard that old music it was so bittersweet, and I was overcome by a kind of haunting melancholy. I couldn't listen to it without becoming nostalgic, and I couldn't play it without weeping. I felt myself to be a proponent of a bygone generation, an actor in a suit of benign intent, a portrayal of the past that exists solely in memory— a waking legacy of what once was.

Many nights I'd get up and go walking around so that I could lose myself in the City once more. I'd feel the air on my face, smell the flowers and the trees in the Park, close my eyes, and pretend for a moment that everything was again as it once had been; that I'd gone for a stroll down along the Panhandle in the early morning and that when I decided to return, the Trips Center in all its former glory would be standing there on Haight Street. Inside, Mary, Bobby, Billy, Faye, Al, and Space would be waiting for me so that we could jam. Melinda would be cooking pancakes. God would be swinging from the light fixtures and schooling us on doors of perception. The pot plants would be standing tall in the tub, and the Trips Mobile would be parked at the corner. Doobie would be selling enlightenment out of the back alley, and the Fuzz would be eating doughnuts back at the station. Music would be playing from every house and store along the street, and all the doors would be wide open. The heads would be laughing again, and the community would be whole. In this, the world of my memories, there was no such thing as overdose, no such thing as a record contract, Altamont, Kent Stephens, Jerry Greco, overdue bills or heroin. There was no such thing as melancholy, no such thing as loneliness—no such thing as pain.

Now, it was reassuring to know that Space was out of jail, that he'd gotten married and had a daughter—that even though he'd spent the best years of his life incarcerated that he was still making good with his freedom. It was reassuring to know that Billy and Faye were still together, still living the dream and making it work—proving that in some corners of the world, with a little persistence and a little vision, it could still be done. It was reassuring to know that Al was still around to listen and share his wisdom with me. It was reassuring to know that Mary, whom I'd known my whole life, would be there for me no matter what—that she understood even if no one else did.

The place where the buck stopped, where my neatly woven blanket of reassurances donned a hole, was with Bobby. The only one who I didn't and couldn't know about was Bobby. Was his soul still wandering around a gray and shadowy wasteland awaiting rebirth? Was he working out his karma in another life? Or was he still here, hanging around? The possibility alone made me shiver. Could it be that he was trapped here in the city where he'd seen his dreams destroyed, where his humanity had finally caught up to him?

That was the rub—to be here in this city that served as such an integral part of so many memories and experience it so differently was surreal. To see it changed in this way was almost painful.

One time, as I was crawling back into bed after a pre-dawn walk along the Haight, my midnight ruminations still ceaselessly ruminating, I heard Leanne's voice speak my name. I rolled over and saw that she was wide awake beside me.

"Tell me, Rhiannon, where is it that you go at night?" she asked me.

"Oh, I just walk around the City…" I answered her.

"Why? What's out there now that isn't there during the day? What is it that you're hoping to find?"

"Memories."

"Whose?"

"The world's."

"Are you meeting someone?"

"Only ghosts."

Leanne chuckled, "Rhiannon, when did you become so philosophical?"

"A lot can happen overnight…" I replied.

"You've become a lot of things overnight," she said.

"Yeah, like a pain in the ass!" Marty's voice sounded from across the room. "Some of us are trying to sleep! Can it, will you?"

Leanne rolled her eyes, "What a grump!" she exclaimed. But she obliged, and in-between Jeff's snores, silence reigned once more.

Now, after about the first week, I seemed to come to grips with myself and what I was facing. My motivating factor was largely sleep deprivation. I was new to the ugly world of insomnia, and I wasn't planning on getting cozy with its inhabitants. After we got paid for our stint at the bar, we let Jeff have his own room, and that change was instrumental in and of itself. Additionally, that's when things really started happening in regard to Track Records and our professional aspirations. Tommy decided that he was going to work with us and moved into the room next door, Dev got us three days at Hyde Street— formerly Wally Heider studios—to lay down some tracks for our demo, and I was forced to turn my attention from the past to the present.

When I first got back, all those truths I'd learned about living in the here and now, being fulfilled by the moment, the transient nature of reality, and inner peace, et al. sort of lost their merit. *Here and now?* I'd thought, *More like here and how?!* It required a grace period, but once I'd settled back in, I experienced a resurgence of those truths, escorted by an invaluable new perspective.

I decided that it hadn't all been for naught. The height of the Movement may have passed, but the world is still reeling in its wake. The war in Vietnam has finally come to an end—dozens more have started since and millions have died, but hey, at least the Far East is free of commies! The Cold War too has ended and not in a nuclear fireball—although weapons of mass destruction continue to be manufactured all around the world. Uncle Sam has decided that he's killed enough reds and has now turned his ceaseless tirade toward the oil tycoons. Civil Rights has certainly strived forward in leaps and bounds, but discrimination still persists in countless forms around the globe. Women don't have to burn their bras anymore to be taken seriously, but they still get paid less in the workplace. The current revolution seems to be on the side of the queers, and the outcome of that particular Movement remains to be seen. People themselves are no less ignorant than they were thirty years ago—and maybe more so, if you consider our generation—but the opportunity for enlightenment is still there. It always has been, and it always will be, just as long as there are souls willing to fearlessly journey on toward Edge City and go furthur: turn on to *IT*, tune into the vibrations, and drop out of the status quo. As long as there are leaders there will be followers, and if the conditions are right, those followers will be free-thinking, radically-living beautiful people with hearts set on utopia and minds enveloped by the here and now.

It took me a few days to readjust and reset my perceptual gauges for the here and now, but once I did, I emerged back into this reality as a force full of conviction. At first, my old tendencies of woolgathering and dreamland escapism began to reemerge, but I fended them off. I was resolute this time. I was here, and I was going to stay here because I was meant to be here. There'd been a good reason for my experience, and likewise, there was a good reason why I was back; therefore, I was determined to make the best of it. I decided that I would bring those things I'd learned in the past into my experience of the future and use them in a way that might provide inspiration to others and make this a better reality for everyone. I felt that maybe my experience could bring The Descendants success where The Day Trippers had found failure.

Now, I just kind of tried to let on like normal now that I was back, but their normal and mine differed, and there were still times when everybody would look at me kind of funny. This was the way it was the first time we all smoked grass together in the City. First of all, everybody found it endearing that I called it grass instead of weed, and when the joint got passed around to me and I took my hit—just a regular old hit mind you, the same kind I'd been taking for the last six months—everybody just stopped and stared at me. That wasn't the only time, either. Their reactions were largely the same when they discovered that I'd 'suddenly' taken up yoga, my strange changes in vocabulary and dress, and the newfound philosophies I now embraced. Additionally, following a unanimous vote, I'd been appointed chauffeur while we were in the City, partly because I was dry, but mainly because I seemed to know where everything was. They chalked it up to years of preparation and George's accounts—after all, that's the only realistic explanation they could come up with for why I could get them all the way from the motel to the Presidio without needing directions.

However, when it came to the places themselves—like the cool coffeehouses and groovy boutiques that I used to frequent—half the time I was right on the money, but in many places, everything had changed. Whole neighborhoods were gone, and new suburbs, business districts, and super-chains had emerged in their place. The ferocity and speed at which the City had grown was a bit unnerving, and now the hippies of yore were slowly being traded in for the new millennial hipster—a hybrid breed. The only way I can describe them is a cross between yippies, yuppies, and beatniks, and while they lack many of the tragic flaws had by their counterparts thirty years ago, it is difficult for me to imagine them as a compelling force of good. The experience was interesting and unprecedented, to say the least. I still ached for that which I used to know, but I didn't want it back. I knew that if I appealed to any point in my memory, no matter how beautiful, that it would eventually come to end just the way that it did. I was finally at peace with this reality, but ironically, that which had all but entirely sustained my lucidity before—playing music—was what unsettled me now.

Upon arriving in San Francisco that first time, jamming with The Day Trippers opened up a whole new world to me, and the last thing I wanted was to return to structured, tedious, and mundane rehearsals. Of course, in the case of a cover band like The Descendants, it was necessary, but there was an element of spontaneity and creativity that was definitely lacking. The creative license entrenched in the very fibers of The Day Trippers made jamming a part of what made them, and without it, they were just another fully-loaded sideshow. Now that we were embarking upon what seemed to be our own big break, spicing up our setlist didn't sound like such a bad idea to me. We'd always prided ourselves on the accuracy of our covers and held ourselves to a very high standard when it came to reproducing the original material, but now that sort of repetitive imitation seemed useless to me. I wanted to be a part of creating something new while resurrecting the old; however, when I brought this up, nobody seemed to share my sentiments.

"Let's jam a little bit today," I'd suggested to everybody as we tuned up in the studio on the third day.

"Why?" Marty asked bewildered as if I'd just suggested we go jump in the bay with all our clothes on.

"It'll be fun," I answered.

"But we're here to work," Shania replied. "We have to pay for this studio time."

"I'm not saying that we should jam all day," I clarified. "What if we just gave it a shot, just for a little while? We never just jam."

"That's because there's no reason to," Marty said. "If we want to be serious about this, we can't waste time. Just jamming isn't going to get this demo finished!"

"Anybody, anywhere in the world can turn on the radio and hear Jimi Hendrix or the Stones or Led Zeppelin," I tried to explain. "What they can't hear is what it feels like to play final call at The Joint at two a.m. They can't hear what it feels like to watch a writhing mass of people take to the dance floor at The Matrix. They can't hear the yells of euphoria, the shouts of joy, and the calls for revolution. You can buy *Physical Graffiti, Bold as Love,* or *Let It Bleed* at any self-respecting record store across the globe, and those songs that we play, anybody can play if they practice enough. If they really work at it, anybody can play the notes, anybody can reproduce the sound, but what they can't reproduce is the soul—you can't manufacture a moment that's already passed. That's what people hear when they turn on the radio or a record—they're remembering. When we play, it's evocative and entertaining, but it's empty. Our covers may sound the same and stand as a tribute to what once was, but they're missing the most intrinsic part. Those songs that we play night after night are old, they're tired, they're worn out. Why don't we just let them lie for a while and create something instead that's representative of us, of now, of our revolution?"

I'd gotten all worked up trying to persuade everyone, and although I received some looks that would've been more appropriate if I'd grown three heads, they consented.

However, when we did jam, I found myself wishing that I hadn't even suggested it. The appalling nature of the whole ordeal could have partially resulted from half-heartedness, but even when I laid down a beat, Leanne was the only one who could really lock in with me and at the same time explore her own creative domain. Marty gave it a shot, but he always ended up working off of riffs and chord progressions that he already knew. Shania didn't have any clue at all what to do with herself when there were no set lyrics to sing, and Jeff just couldn't keep up.

When our impromptu jam session culminated in a horrid squawking of guitars out of time, Marty turned toward me in exasperation and contempt.

"Is *that* what you were looking for?!" he asked sarcastically.

It perturbed me greatly to find that The Descendants weren't really the expert musicians I'd always considered them to be. In no way did they approach the level of comfort and mastery The Day Trippers had exhibited, nor were they interested in trying. In comparison, we were just first-rate plagiarizers!

I knew then that I couldn't keep on like this—that I had to find a new scene; one that met the needs of my augmented skill and expanded consciousness. However, for the friendship and support they all had provided me with throughout my angsty teenage years, I felt like I owed them at least the satisfaction of the success they earned. For that reason alone I kept on, even though I felt like Ringo at the conclusion of *Sgt. Pepper's*. I told myself I'd stay until our album was finished or until they found somebody to replace me, but each day the thought of leaving both exhilarated and crippled me.

I didn't have much time to seriously consider my exodus because success continued to find us. After a few weeks of playing at every seedy bar off of Highway 1 from Daly City to San Jose with Tommy at our side, Dev gave us a call back and informed us that our demo had been approved, that we had a $50,000 bonus coming our way, and that our recording dates were set for early July. In the meantime, Tommy booked us a ten-night stay at the Whisky.

When I first heard this, I was incredibly put-off, painfully nostalgic, and a glimmer hopeful all at the same time. My first experience there had been undesirable for any musician; however, playing at the Whisky was of much greater importance to us than it had been to The Day Trippers, for whom it was just another venue. The Whisky had been our main objective, our be-all-end-all since we'd formed as a group, and the day we finally got to play there had been a long time coming. I felt like maybe our stint there could redeem my attempt thirty years ago to achieve my dreams, but I already knew that it wasn't satisfaction we would be finding—that is found only in the moment and in every moment equally.

Our spin down Sunset Strip prior to our arrival at the Whisky was not quite what I'd expected. Of all the places I'd revisited of late, L.A. was by far the most unchanged. To my surprise, although Thee Experience and many places like it had gone with the times, the overwhelming air, the neon lights, and the phonies were just as prominent as they were the first time. As easy as it might have been to do so, I didn't jump to conclusions right away. For that, I waited some and gave the city and our long-awaited performance at its prize venue the benefit of the doubt.

We arrived there early as any professional band should, and together with Tommy, we met with the manager. He was an older man with a name that escapes me, but his face was familiar and invoked in me that strange feeling that I'd seen him before.

"The Descendants—another cover band, eh?" he greeted us. "What's so special about your show that I ought to give you ten days running?"

We all sort of looked around at one another. We weren't real sure what Tommy had told him.

"Do you destroy your instruments like The Who?" he asked.

We shook our heads.

"Do you light your guitars on fire like Jimi Hendrix?"

"No," we replied.

"Crawl around the stage like Jim Morrison?"

Again, our answer was no.

"Is there a light show?"

"No."

"Color projection?"

"No."

"Dancers on stage?"

"No."

"No?" he echoed. "Then what *is* so good about your show, huh?"

"We make good music, convincing music," Shania insisted.

"And the performance?" he asked. "You five *are* performers, correct?"

I spoke up this time, "We don't need all of that peripheral stimulation. We propose that our music, in and of itself, is enough to hold the captive attention of your audience for one night or for ten."

"Why is your music better than that of any other cover band then?"

I opted for honesty, "Ours is a vain attempt to convey the experience to those out there who are vainly trying to relive it."

The manager—who was clearly expecting a load of ass-kissing and hogwash from me at that moment—was appeased by my candor, although my bandmates were less so.

"Vain, Rhiannon!?" everyone berated me once he'd gone, but they got over it pretty fast once they saw the inside of the venue. It was as much of a surprise to me as it was to them.

For as much as the rest of L.A. had stayed the same, the Whisky had undergone some significant changes. From the outside, it looked quite similar to how I remembered it, but inside, it was nothing like that which I used to dream about. Just like at the Fillmore, they inspected your bags at the door to make sure you weren't carrying in any drugs, and the bouncer dutifully checked IDs. The whole place had been painted and remodeled, and there were no go-go cages for sure. A few languishing booths remained around the perimeter, but besides the seats at the bar, this venue too was now standing-room only. The haze that hung over the audience had dissipated over the years and so had the heads along with their hair. It was a different world now.

As always, our show began with a drumbeat: slow, concise—like a heartbeat manifesting those things I used to imagine into the realm of reality. At first, that was the only sound in the place—my drumbeat and the silent anticipation of the audience—and then quickly, quietly, the rest of the band started to fade in. It began with Marty and Jeff on their guitars—heavy and dynamic—and Leanne on bass—melodic and contemplative. Finally, Shania's voice emerged out of the brew— strong and powerful in her best Robert Plant imitation—as the sounds of *Rock and Roll* shook the walls of the Whisky a Go Go. After that song, we played another, and then another—all in near perfect likeness to the originals; first-rate plagiarizers we most certainly were! Two hours and fifteen minutes later, with aching arms and an insane smile on my face, I struck the final beat, and the scene in front of me was transformed as the crowd erupted into wild applause.

From behind my drum kit, I could see Jeff, Marty, and Shania standing in front of me, the three of them facing out into a sprawling audience. This was nothing like the abject handful of leftover hippies that came to watch us perform at The Joint on Friday and Saturday nights. From the elevated stage, I could see that the club was packed from wall to wall and they were cheering, loudly chanting, "Encore! Encore!" Jeff arched his back and pumped his fist in the air, and Marty shouted, "ROCK ON!" before throwing both his arms up, palms out, and backing away from the mic. Shania placed the microphone back in the stand, took a corner of her dress in each hand, and curtsied for the insatiable crowd. I turned to my right and shot Leanne a grin, but she was looking out into the audience, her eyes glazed over with satisfaction—she did not look at me at all. From my parallel perch, I could see that along with the satisfaction which raged intensely, there was a faint glimmer of desire there, like it wasn't quite enough, like something was missing now that it was all over. The Whisky was supposed to be our be-all-end-all, but instead, it left them as it had left me—wanting more. Amid all that joy and euphoria, I could plainly see that their first taste of the Whisky had gotten them hooked.

As far as venues The Descendants played at are concerned, The Whisky was our crown jewel, and every night we played better and better. There were far fewer liberties, a setlist that persisted night after night, and little outside creativity, but for those ten shows, the music sustained itself and captivated me purely on its own merit. Those were by far our best performances.

Afterward, as the excitement and grandeur of those shows quickly faded, it was back to San Francisco and back to the grind. June rolled into July, and the recording sessions started, which—to my surprise—were in every way far superior to that ordeal I'd encountered with The Day Trippers. It was in this niche of the musical profession that I finally found an area in which The Descendants out-performed—organization and efficiency. The Descendants may be inferior musicians, but they're far better professionals, and that, despite all the controversy it sparks, is what is necessary for commercial success.

As July rolled into August, the recording sessions at Hyde Street continued to go off without a hitch in two-week stints at my insistence, and in our time off, Tommy booked us gigs in nearly every town along the California coast. I can't say that I wasn't having a good time; I was, but not nearly as good of a time as I'd had with The Day Trippers. The Descendants are fun companions with a high capacity for jocularity and low tolerance for boredom, but as in every aspect of this second go-round of touring, recording, and trying to make it, there is a certain level of intellectualism that The Descendants lack severely in comparison. They certainly aren't dumb by any stretch of the imagination, but to them, suggesting a rummage through a collection of old books is about as off-putting as a romp through a dumpster, and a conversation about synchronicity is about as interesting to them as a high school lecture on family living. I may have shared their bad marks in school, but contempt for the educational system does not excuse ignorance—not in academia or esoterica. I've always espoused this belief, but my trip through time has only served to enhance its prominence in my mind. I demanded more from my everyday existence now. Playing two sets a night and drinking and fucking around in the meantime just wasn't going to cut it anymore. I was sick and tired of competing to see who could get more gassed—now all I wanted to see was who could get more enlightened.

The Day Trippers and many like them in that time made it a point to discuss the terms and conditions of their rebellion; they weren't ones simply to rebel for rebellion's sake. I'd made profound and unforgettable memories with a group of people for whom philosophizing was a way of life and had now returned to spend my time with a group who were perfectly content in being spoon-fed the reality they observed on a daily basis. I didn't blame them. I couldn't. They were unaware of the superior order of things, the divine significance of every moment, timelessness, ego-loss, that the whole world is comprised of energy, and that they and God are one.

I found comfort away from these differences in long talks with Mary—who spent much of her time now with Al—and solace in meditation. I found that I could return to that place I'd been at Woodstock whenever I wanted and stay for as long as I wanted because that place resided within me. That isn't to say finding time or a place to meditate effectively wasn't a challenge. Jeff and Marty always poked fun at me when I attempted to do so in their presence. They didn't mean to hurt me; they just didn't understand.

As the days rolled on, the dates brought with them bountiful memories which I wanted more than anything to share but could not— all on account of words. Words can be powerful, words can be moving, they can be vicious, and they can be enlightening. Words can be rehearsed, spontaneous, and even inspired; but there are no words to adequately describe experience—or at least *this* experience. At times I even felt as if I had taken a vow of silence, and this was especially apparent around the middle of the month.

On August 15th, I returned to our hotel with Leanne and Marty after scoring some takeout down the street, and when I walked in, I saw that the tape playing in the complimentary VCR was none other than the Woodstock movie. I stopped dead in the doorway. The music that played through the tinny Panasonic speakers was enough to bring me to my knees, and the images that flashed across the screen did nothing but intensify that feeling. It was the part when Joe Cocker took the stage just before the rain and played *A Little Help From My Friends*.

Seeing him up close on the screen and watching the emotion play across his face and the soul in the words leave his lips, I did fall to my knees, right in front of the TV which I sat facing for the rest of that performance so that they might not see my tears.

"Imagine being there for that?" Shania whispered. "Feeling that air, that rain...that's got to be the richest memory."

"That's where Rhiannon wishes she was," Marty replied. "Right, Rhiannon?"

Outwardly I nodded, but inside, my mind was screaming, *"I was! I was!"*

After several repeated views, I can't tell you how happy I was when Shania took the movie back to the Blockbuster and Tommy told us that we were bugging out of San Francisco now that our completed recordings had been turned over to the studio for editing. Our tour of California continued, and August rolled into September, bringing with it a new degree of notice and many changes. A mention in the entertainment section of the local newspaper isn't quite an article in Rolling Stone, but for us, it was the near equivalent, and when we got a call from the talent booker at the Whisky asking if we'd be interested in another go-round, it sealed the deal. For all intents and purposes, The Descendants had 'made it'—at least that was the case according to The Descendants.

Track Records had been our ticket out of Fresno, but now that we were out, Marty, Leanne, Shania, and Jeff seemed to be in a mad rush to expel every trace of ultra-conservative Fresno from themselves as well. We would, as Marty said, return to L.A. as a hot ticket band, and that being the case, we needed to look like a hot ticket band. After we checked into our new motel in L.A.—the Tropicana, where else—the four of them went out for the day and came back with new wardrobes and new countenances to match.

Shania walked back in through the door sporting a new blonde hairdo and dragging several bulging bags of clothes behind her. Upon closer inspection, I saw that her normally dark eyes were a striking sapphire blue—the result of the colored contacts she wore in her eyes. Jeff, who'd let his iconic Mohawk grow out, had cut his hair as well—this time evenly all the way around his head—and he arrived wearing leather pants and a faux Hells Angels' vest from a local thrift store. Marty too had on leather pants, but he matched his with a leather jacket, motorcycle boots, and a wallet chain that hung from his pocket. He'd had his ear pierced, and from it hung a silver peace sign.

However, it was Leanne who looked the most startlingly different. She'd had her long hair cut and dyed, changed from a fiery red to a pastel blue to match her guitar. It seemed like she had also visited the tattoo parlor because now her lip was pierced in addition to her nose, and she had gotten a spray tan—I could tell because she was wearing a lacy, sleeveless dress. For this, I needed to sit down.

Excuse me for being blunt, but it was all just too sudden for me to exert the time and tact it would've taken to be eloquent. I think the first thing I said was something along the lines of, "Leanne, are those your arms?!"

"They sure are, and look at mine!" Marty announced, rolling up his sleeve to uncover The Rolling Stones' Hot Lips logo he had freshly tattooed on his bicep. "How rad is this?! Our fans are going to see this beauty talking while I play!"

In all honesty, they felt as changed to me as I did to them. The difference was, I knew that underneath their new personas, they were still the same; whereas I'd changed more than they could ever know. I knew that the things I'd learned would surely be of use to them, but there was no way even to approach the issue.

To me, it felt like even though I was the one who had gone, they were the ones who had really left, or rather, that I had returned to a place that had been changed—not in form, but in essence. After all, reality is open to interpretation and ultimately forged in the mind. If the mind itself has been changed, the continuity of reality too must falter.

For me, this current reality was a strange product of all the worlds I'd dabbled in as of late; whereas for them, they were static, unchanged in all the ways that really mattered, paddling around in a closed pool of ignorance that only after I'd dried off did I realize I'd escaped from. They were still engulfed by the illusion that this ephemeral world substantiates all and everything. I saw in them a part of myself that I'd happily surrendered. I saw in them naivety typical of their age and station in life as platitudinous products of a system engineered to shape and carve the bodies and minds of youth into forms desired by society, excluding and alienating all those who fail to meet the bar and those precocious enough to detect it. I saw in them a distinct cynicism, nurtured by some absurd notion that you either need to fit inside a box or exceed some unrealistic level of sensationalism in order to succeed. It is so incredibly superficial, all these things we are led to believe— evident even in the ignorance of my own past—it is so painful to see others led wrong.

546

I wasn't sure what to say. I wanted to be encouraging, but inside myself, I harbored this sinking feeling that just wouldn't allow it.

"Why?" I asked them.

"Why what?" Shania asked, crestfallen at my lack of enthusiasm.

"Why do you guys feel the need to change like this all of a sudden? People liked us just fine as we were, as ourselves. You don't need to go for looks and prey upon that morbid human infatuation with all that is strange and different to find fans. Don't get caught up in the game. Success, not fame, was what we wanted, remember?"

"You've changed, why can't we?" Marty replied defensively.

"Superficial and fundamental change are two entirely different things," I answered.

Marty turned on me in an instant, "Rhiannon, I feel like I don't even know you anymore!" he cried. "Ever since we left Fresno, you've been acting like a completely different person! You used to live just for gigs, to go out and play music and party, oh, besides, of course, for daydreaming."

"Well, what if one of those daydreams became real?" I asked him, shrinking.

"Oh, come on, Rhiannon!"

"No, Marty, I'm serious," I replied.

"That's only because you're delusional, Rhiannon, you're like schizoid or something."

"I'm not Marty, you don't understand!" I insisted.

"Well, then make me understand."

"I can't make you understand."

"Explain it to me."

"You won't believe me!" I cried.

"You can either explain it to me or you can't," he declared.

"Well, then I can't," I decided.

"Then I say you're delusional!" he shouted, exasperated.

"Marty, that's not fair," I replied. "You're not justified in making that assumption!"

"Then try me, tell me a little bit about this *fundamental change* of yours that's too big for our brains!"

I was tired of keeping silent. After a few more confrontations like this ending in nothing but frustration and reticence, not only would they see me as insane, but as the world's biggest pushover. A softer touch was definitely warranted there, but at that moment, I had neither the patience or the ability, so I just began to blurt things out, "Oh, the things I have seen," I cried, my voice shaking. "The things I have seen though I was only gone a night. I've seen fluorescent villi flagellating from the red face of an Indian. I've seen shadow faces rush past in refracted rays of tubular nebulas. I've seen heaven spread out before me like an endless garden of lights, and I've seen it all collapse into a vast spectacle, an explosive cloud of crystalline particles and rainbow rayon dust...oh the things I have seen..." I trailed off.

As I might have expected if I'd thought the whole thing through, my gentle lament was met by faces red with stifled laughter and broad grins that hid behind the hands that covered their mouths.

I cast my eyes down to the floor, "It just so happens that the best feelings in the world are the ones you can't describe, and the best experiences are the ones that have no words," I murmured, subdued.

All of Marty's earlier animosity had dissipated, and now he just patted me on the shoulder and walked away, teasing me lightly, "Right on, man, right on."

Is it any surprise to you that I spent the vast majority of my time out of Fresno speechless and silent? After all, what was there to say? What succinct words were there that would do my experience justice, that wouldn't make a mockery of myself and my cause? I'd always been reserved, but as of late, I'd been even quieter than Leanne—which was not only a great feat, it was downright unnatural—and Leanne was the only one who noticed that I was genuinely agitated and upset, an old form of myself that had been almost entirely absent since my return. After my humiliating attempt at an explanation, her eyes met mine—not with the understanding gaze I was used to receiving from The Day Trippers, but rather with eyes full of pity. All of them—Leanne included—must have thought that I was bat-shit crazy, that I had finally and effectually fried my marbles. I'm sure that's what it sounded like, but then again, the Truth always sounds insane to those who have never experienced it, to those who do not know what it feels like to come face to face with the infinite, to those for whom *IT* is a foreign concept to which they pay little attention and even less regard.

I turned away from them then and went out to sit on the balcony, but I left the door open behind me. I could still hear everyone talking from outside, even though they were trying hard to whisper.

"What the hell was that?" Marty exclaimed.

"Whatever Dave gave her must have scrambled her brains," Jeff said.

"She sounds like her father," Shania added.

"Should we call someone?" Leanne asked, concerned.

548

"Who?" Marty replied with a laugh. "The people offering motels with padded rooms?"

"I was thinking about a therapist," she replied.

"Oh, she'll be fine," Marty answered dismissively. "She's not hurting herself. If it comes down to that, we'll just nail the mattresses to the walls."

I got up and shut the door.

It took a couple of days, but everyone soon forgot about my blundering faux pas; a few more hit gigs and blackout nights and we were all chums again. There was another factor to be considered also: while we were in L.A, we became acquainted with a four-piece Doors tribute band, The End, who opened for us at the Whisky. They partied as hard as they played, and night after night, we were invited to a general admission carousal at their pad. Marty fell hard for the guitarist taking the place of Robbie Krieger, and Shania began a fast and furious fling with their imitation Jim Morrison. After that, they started hanging around a whole lot. My quick descent into madness was no longer as much of a concern to them, which both relieved and troubled me.

My initial impression of The End was that they were prodigious musicians worthy of respect and a few good jam sessions to trade skills, but they lacked a certain humanity. They dressed right and talked right, but something about them reminded me of the punk rockers back at the Fillmore—a heaviness seemed to surround them. The culprit, I found, was their vice of choice—heroin. Drugs of all kinds had surrounded us since our big city debut, but opportunities to indulge were often passed up in favor of brew for them and grass for me; however, The End seemed to possess an unlimited supply of anything and everything we could have wanted.

****

September rolled on, and local fame followed. Changes in demeanor now accompanied The Descendants' changes in appearance. Marty began refusing rehearsal time in exchange for cheap thrills, Shania regained her socialite status as the focus of a vast following of admirers, Jeff was perpetually inebriated, and Leanne just seemed incredibly taken at every stage by the experience. Day by day, I watched the divide between us grow. I still loved them, of course—in fact, I felt like I loved them even more now. However, it used to be them who looked out for me, but now I felt like it was I who was constantly looking out for them. I felt like a mother figure saddled with the responsibility of corralling these renegades—a chaperone more than an equal. Splitting the scene became an ever more serious consideration for me, but I still felt leaving to be terribly unfair. This had been our dream together, after all, and even if I left, where would I go?

This last romp around L.A. was rounded with a phone call from Dev back in San Francisco who let us know that our album in its current state was ready for perusal at our convenience. Of course, we left immediately, and The End came with us. We docked ourselves at a suite at the Hilton in Union Square, and The End found themselves a dig a few streets down in a cheaper hotel better representative of the Tenderloin District in which we were staying. There was much talk of touring together, especially between our manager and theirs. In San Francisco, the gigs continued, but for me, they'd lost their allure—worry dominated instead. We began splitting up after shows. '*Divide and conquer*,' Caesar once said, but few know that he was quoting the devil. Late nights with strange people in strange places, lust for fame, and cocaine all reemerged. History had begun to repeat itself and laid out before me none other than my worst nightmare in the form of Marty's return to the suite after spending the night over at The End's place with a couple of local girls.

"Hey guys!" he announced after he'd come back into the room around noontime, "I've got to tell you about the night I had last night!"

We all paused in our respective activities and listened to him as he wove for us a tale taken directly from the pages of the book of my deepest horrors. It was a tale that began with a night out on the town, sustained by excessive flirtation, and capped with an offering of a drug he'd never tried, that is, before last night. I just about held my hands over my ears to drown out the sound of those three sinister syllables always followed by death and destruction on all sides—evil in the form of an angel—heroin. At first, I hoped that he might be lying, but the look in his eyes—that faraway gaze of remembrance—spoke volumes.

Inside I was freaking out, but I waited until I could take him aside to unleash my fury, "What are you doing to yourself, Marty?! You've got to stop this! Never take that drug again, do you hear me? Heroin is bad, Marty, really bad! This is getting dangerous now. You're not just jeopardizing our band, you're jeopardizing your life! You can't do this!"

Marty was blindsided by my rage as I'd hoped he'd be. Shock value was everything here. I wanted to scare him, he needed to be scared—he'd learn no other way. His reply, however, defied my every word.

"Who do you think you are, Rhiannon, telling me what I can and cannot do?! Why are you being such a bitch? Why are you flipping out on me like this? I had a great fucking night last night, I wasn't in danger! Everybody makes heroin out to be such a bad drug, but it's not! You wouldn't know, you've never done it! Besides, it was just one time, Rhiannon, you're treating me like I'm a fucking junkie or something!"

"Just one time, Marty?" I countered, my voice shaking with blinding rage and paralyzing fear. "Just one time? That's what they all say, it's always 'just one time!' Every junkie and addict that's ever lived started out with their 'just one time,' and it wasn't a big deal to them either! How many times has it been 'just one time' for you, Marty? Just one time you smoked a cigarette, just one time you got wasted, just one time you smoked grass, just one time you tried ecstasy, just one time you used speed? Why is this time any different? You're dealing with something you think you can control but you can't! You think you're invincible, Bobby, but you're not!"

I heard the words that came out of my mouth after I said them, and I shut down immediately.

Marty snorted and shook his head, completely unfazed, "Un-fucking-believable..." he got up and tried to leave, but I beat him to it.

"Where the hell are you going now?" he yelled after me. "Rhiannon, we have to be in the studio in an hour!"

I sped past Leanne, Jeff, and Shania and ran out the door in haste.

I couldn't look him in the eyes anymore—when I did, all I saw was Bobby. The comparisons between the two were innumerable; however, for Marty, it wasn't egotism that was going to punch his ticket, but errant, careless, misguided youth. I took to the stairs as his angry words faded into silence behind me. In fact, the whole world faded out around me. All that shone before me was my objective—the lobby payphone.

I picked up the receiver and dialed Mary, but I hung up after just two rings. I'd hid the incredible truth behind the pretense of eccentricity for too long, in turn, making myself seem unreliable just when I needed their faith the most. What I needed now wasn't consolation or sympathy, what I needed was direction—and what better place was there for me to find it than in the Übermensch himself?

I dialed Marty's home number, and to my dizzying relief, Al picked up the phone. "Al, I…" I looked around at all the other people in the lobby and then decided, "I'm coming over. Don't leave. I'll be right there." I hung up before he could ask me any questions.

I could see my car in the parking lot outside and I was about to make a beeline for it, but instead, I dialed one more number. This one rang five times then went straight to voicemail. Jack's cheerful voice told me that I was welcome to leave a message if I felt like it.

"Hey Dad," I spoke to the answering machine, "I don't know if you're back yet, but I just wanted to tell you—I don't know how to tell you—I'll explain it all to you one day, somehow…but I met Jerry. I met him at the Fillmore West in 1969. I played there with a band called The Day Trippers. I had an apple. I'll tell you all about it someday. I'll find a way. I promise." I hung up, then jumped in my car and hit the freeway.

I made that three and a quarter hour drive in about two and a half. Pavement, desert, mountains—they all passed by me in a blur, all looking very much the same. My heart hammered away in my chest, slowly making its way higher and higher into my throat. The car was wide open, but I felt like the world was closing in around me. I needed release. Somehow.

Finally, I just couldn't take it anymore; the wind rushing past my ears for hours on end was maddening, the road began splitting in two before my eyes, and the sunset crept ever nearer. I felt as if I was in a race against time. I felt like I held Marty's life, our future, and my own sanity all in the palm of my hands. I turned on the radio, and Pink Floyd rushed out through the speakers, *"So you think you can tell heaven from hell? Blue skies from pain? Can you tell a green field from a cold steel rail? A smile from a veil? Do you think you can tell?"*

The synch was overwhelming. I wondered if he could. I wondered if Bobby could; if any of us could.

"—we're just two lost souls swimming in a fishbowl year after year, running over the same old ground. What have we found? —The same old fears."

I drove faster.

When I finally stopped, it was in Marty's driveway. I brought my car to a shuddering halt and practically jumped out while it was still moving. I burst through the door and called Al's name. I was frantic, and he appeared in the doorway looking equally as startled. It took a couple minutes longer than usual, but his peaceful spirit calmed me promptly.

"Take it easy. What's going on, Rhiannon?" he asked me once I'd gotten a grip on myself and stopped trembling from the road.

"It's happening all over again, Al," I whispered, "everything that happened to us—The Day Trippers, I mean. It's not Bobby, it's Marty this time. He's using heroin."

On the outside, Al remained composed, but I could only imagine the inner turmoil my statement awoke within him. I watched him exhale heavily, as if I'd kicked him in the stomach and all the air escaped at once. He sat down, "Before you go on, Rhiannon, there's something I must get off my chest. I know you've come for my advice; therefore, you must know this first."

I nodded and allowed him to continue.

"There are tendencies inherent in my nature that have allowed me to see very far but at the same time blinded me up close. I've made my fair share of mistakes. From everything in life, I've tried to gain wisdom, but wisdom is not free; it comes at a price. It's not something you can barter for, it's something you toil long and hard to achieve, and it's something you pay dearly for. For me, wisdom has come at the price of my family—Marty's mother, my wife, she was a beautiful woman..." he looked up at the photograph on the dresser, "she was tender and loving, strong and intelligent...she was perfect—too good for this world. She was a schoolteacher. I met her in a coffeehouse in 1973 while I was passing through here. She was reading my book, and I couldn't resist hearing a candid opinion. We spoke for hours. She was a profound woman, her mind was as sexy as her body—and that's really saying a lot. She offered me a room, a place to clean up. She asked me to stay the night. I declined, but I came back. I found her again in the same coffeehouse. We talked again, and I left again. This went on for years. I'd pass through here purposely just to see her. I knew from the first time that I loved her, and she did too. She waited for me. After five years she decided enough was enough and she asked me to marry her, to settle down. I went up to Mount Shasta, consulted the gods, took a romp around my subconscious, and tripped for three days. I came back down and told her yes. We got married, just like that.

"In the beginning, it was incredible. She let me have all the space I needed. I'd leave for the week alone and spend weekends and summers with her. We'd travel together all over—Europe, India, Asia—she loved to travel and loved to learn. In 1981, Marty came along, and we continued on the same way, our love only grew. Then she got pregnant again about six years later. We were both ecstatic. For the first seven months, everything was fine, then one day…I don't know what happened, she was in so much pain… I took her to the hospital and…waited. The doctors told me something had gone tragically wrong…that she was gone. The baby followed her a few hours later. It was some kind of infection…" Al trailed off. There were tears in his ancient eyes.

"I was lost. The only structure I'd ever had—the only structure I'd ever wanted—was gone. Marty was inconsolable. He was so young, he couldn't understand. I didn't know what to tell him. I know what it feels like to grow up without a mother, and that is the last thing I wanted for my son. I told myself I'd stay put, no more wandering, but I hadn't banked on how hard that would be. It was torturous, Rhiannon, staying in this house with all those memories…I just couldn't do it. I put Marty in school when he was old enough and had him stay part time with my wife's sister and part-time with me. He needed a woman in his life, and I knew I'd never marry again.

"At first, I only took day trips on the weekends—out to the desert or up into the redwoods—but then as Marty re-adjusted and school took precedence, I'd go more often and stay away for longer. I took Marty with me during the summer and on breaks, but he didn't like it. I tried to teach him as much as I could, but he wouldn't have it. He wanted to stay home."

Al shook his head, "We just grew apart. Maybe I'm a terrible father, maybe that's just the way he is, or maybe it's a combination of both. Marty hates me, he's told me that to my face from the time he was just a child. He hates me because I'm not his mother; he loved her so much, they were so close. It hurts to be told that, but what hurts more is the fact that I can't bring her back. I kept coming back here to do what was right by him, but every time I did it only got worse and worse. I let him have everything that was mine: the house, all my savings…the only thing I didn't allow him to touch was my work. I always hoped that every time I went away I'd be inspired, that I'd discover a new way to deal with him, that when I came back it would be different, that he'd be excited to see me, that I could get through to him—but every time I was wrong."

Al stood up and lifted the photo of Marty as a child off of the dresser, "When I go away, all I can think about is Marty and how I've failed him. I've painted so many pictures of my boy that in Chicago they have a whole gallery full of just paintings of him…" he trailed off again, "and now you tell me he's on the stuff…that seems to be a Black family weakness, heroin. I'm not surprised. My son reminds me an awful lot of my brother. He's strong-willed, hotheaded, and incredibly stubborn—he too is easily hurt. Unfortunately, Marty and I do not have the luxury to compensate for our differences in opinion. We can't level the playing field with music or drugs. I will always be his father, and he will always be my son."

His story humbled me greatly, but in hearing it, the angst inside me only grew. If Al himself in his infinite wisdom couldn't get through to Marty, I might be the only one who could. "So what am I going to do, Al? How can I get him to listen to me, get him to stop before it's too late again…"

Al shook his head, "I don't know. There comes a time in every seeker's life when he feels he has discovered the answer to it all—to every question he has ever carried on his breast, to every inquiry he has ever pondered and explored—if only he were always right. I felt that way once. I wasn't wrong, but I was only half right—I've only ever been, and somehow, that hurts even more. I've looked for Truth in every corner of the world and found it only in pieces. I try and communicate it to others through my work and tell myself that one day it will all come together, but my search is in vain. Maybe *IT* isn't here at all, only parts of it are—scattered across the universe like stars—maybe I always knew that, maybe that's all I ever wanted to find. Maybe it isn't the muse that leads me on after all—maybe it's just a whiff of her hair, a brush of her skin, a fleeting glimpse of her face… I know full well that I'm looking for something that cannot be seen and searching for something that cannot be found, I know full well that I will not find Truth as I seek it in this world, and yet, I cannot seem to give it up. I know nothing else." He sighed resignedly and was silent.

My lips trembled and faltered as I searched for the right words, "Al...I've tried. I've tried so many times to tell them, to explain to them those things that I've learned, to share with them, to teach them, to impart to them the wisdom I've paid for, to spare them the time and energy and pain of having to learn it for themselves. They don't believe me, *I* wouldn't even believe me if I hadn't been the one to experience it. You've got to give me something I can take back to them. I have nowhere else to turn."

Al met my eyes, "Just tell them your story," he suggested simply.

The ease with which he said it was infuriating, "But *what* am I going to tell them?" I was almost shouting. "That I fell down a rabbit hole like *Alice in Wonderland?* Because that's what it feels like, and that's the truth, but they'll never believe me! If I go back to them and tell them I know what I know and am how I am because I smoked DMT and went back in time and played with The Day Trippers—who actually turned out to be you and my mother—met Jerry Garcia, saw Led Zeppelin, went to Woodstock, and experienced *IT,* do you know what they'll say? They'll say *'now you've done it, Rhiannon, you've really done it now! You've fried your marbles! You're crazy!'* They'll laugh at me, Al. You know what that does to me..."

"You've got to tell it to them just the way you experienced it..." he began again.

I cut him off, "Al, you don't know what it's like. You may have experienced the same things as me and more, but you grew and changed and experienced along with everyone else. You have the passing of time as an excuse for why and how you are the way you are. You may be precocious, but linearly, you and everyone else your age has experienced 1969, 2000, and everything that was in-between. For me, it's different, I can't say that. I left them, and twelve hours later I came back a different person. It's been nine months since I smoked that DMT, but for them, it's been only three. I can't pretend I haven't changed, and I don't want to. I want to be out-front with them, but they don't take me seriously. What I have to say is too far out for them, too far removed from what they know..."

"There's a reason you've been given a voice, Rhiannon," he replied, "and they are your captive audience. You must tell your story, it's the only way. They must listen first before they can understand. Start at the beginning, from a place that is familiar to them, and gain their trust that way. There is a reason you've experienced all the things you have, so tell them everything."

"But what about all of those things we used to say about the imperfections of words and how it's impossible to even begin to describe existence and—"

Al cut me off this time, "Of course words aren't perfect, but they'll have to do. Just like how music is more than just the notes that are played, a story is more than just the words it is built from. In both cases, the whole contains more than the sum of its parts. They both express something. The words themselves are meaningless, just as notes alone are—both are merely sounds—but when they are strung together, they create something far more powerful than they are capable of alone. A story is eternal; like a photograph, it is a frozen moment."

"But I'd need every word ever spoken to explain *IT*, and that still isn't enough," I insisted.

"Yes, but you and I both know that it is impossible to explain *IT*. That isn't what's important, is it? It is how you came to discover *IT* for yourself that you want to share with them. If you put your heart, your soul, and the experience itself into telling your story, then they will understand you.

"We all have a story, and it is a pity that so few of us tell it. We are left to infer from passing glances as to the struggles and hopes, thoughts and dreams, joys and tragedies of another. People themselves, like words over time, become meaningless because we've shut them off, we haven't listened to them—because to us, they are absent from the human story. We may feel like they are only props, part of the everyday scenery that makes up our world—disposable, almost—and many feel that way about you and I. That is where compassion and empathy come in and why they are needed now more desperately than ever. You know that old golden rule—*'Do unto others as you would have them do unto you.'* You may not know another person's story, they may not speak it loud enough for you to hear, they to you may be only a word, but behind that word is a story, and a story demands respect and attention from all. Words themselves may be meaningless, they may be dross, rot and insufficient—but within each word is a story, and a story is sacred. Life itself is the untellable story. That is the paradox here tonight, and that is the paradox I give to you." He reached into the top drawer of his dresser and pulled out a paperback book which he handed to me.

"What is this?" I asked as I examined it.

"My own vain attempt," he chuckled, "and proof of your existence

557

from the mind and hand of a madman."

It was entitled 'The Road' and it was the very same account I had watched him write in a little spiral-bound notebook that he carried with him to and from Woodstock. The copyright inside was stamped 1971. The first line read, *'You cannot get hurt when you are constantly on the move. This is a maxim I now believe because I've gotten hurt every time I've settled down.'*

Mine would not be the only story told tonight. Inspiration, in large and potent doses, filled me instantly and continued to flow forth in waves. I hugged him tightly, and then fled to the door. When I reached the end of the hall, I met his eyes. Words, at least for us at that moment, were unnecessary.

Outside, a storm was brewing. Towering thunderclouds gathered on the darkened horizon, and heat lightning flashed across the sky. I jumped into my car and took off back the way I'd come so many times before.

As I sped back toward San Francisco, alone and quiet in the darkness except for the periodic crashing of thunder and passing of cars, I was given much time to think. I assembled my arsenal, my words. I smiled at those memories I'd soon recount—the good and the bad alike; after all, together, they'd made me. I thought of Al—a mere mortal—he too was only human. He was always driven to find something and ran after Truth with such unbridled passion—he was so brilliant, and yet failed to see, even after so long, that you can be the smartest, most talented and experienced man in the world, but if you do not have inner peace and contentment, you have nothing. This is happiness. This is satisfaction. After a while, even seeking becomes about nothing more than the thrill of the search, and before long, there arises a fear and hesitation in actually discovering anything. Even for an Übermensch to enter into the magic theater, there is a price of admission. As for me, I'd already paid my dues.

I was on fire, and even as I drew nearer and nearer to the City and the storm clouds that met me there unloaded their burden upon me, my flame could not be extinguished. After all, the fire of *IT* does not light with any earthly match, and not even a deluge can wash away the Truth.

I washed up in the hotel parking lot soaked to the skin and raving. Lightning crashed and I laughed. Thunder cracked and I rejoiced. I took the stairs up to our suite two at a time. I stuck my key in the lock, ran to the balcony, and threw open the doors. A deafening thunderclap woke everyone in the room with a start.

"Rhiannon!" Shania cried, holding her heart. "What in God's name are you doing? It's the middle of the night! Where were you?"

"Just get up, get up!" I threw on the lights, and everybody cringed.

"What's happening, what's wrong?!"

"Nothing's wrong, but boy have I got a story to tell you!" I exclaimed.

I ran down the hall to wake up Jeff and Tommy and brought them back into the room.

"Can somebody please tell me what's going on?" Tommy implored us as he struggled to close the balcony doors against the raging wind that blew into the room.

"Ask Rhiannon," Marty answered him. I could tell that he was still miffed at me from before on top of being woken up in the middle of the night, but it was of no consequence. All that would change soon— I knew it. I could feel it in my bones.

I sat everybody down in a circle, got a few joints circulating for conciliation and effect, and began to speak. For once, everyone wanted to hear what I had to say.

"You see," I began, "I seem to have one of those very strange lives that feels like it is folding in on itself."

"I don't understand," Marty said.

"Neither do I," Shania agreed.

"Of course not, you have to listen before you can understand," I smiled, quoting Al.

My hands were shaking, but it was with exhilaration in its purest form, not anxiety or fear. I was finally at peace. I took a deep breath, calm and assured, and began my tale as it all came back to me:

"It was hot in Fresno…